Pyramids Road

Pyramids Road

An Egyptian Homecoming

≈

Midhat Gazalé

The American University in Cairo Press
Cairo ≈ New York

To my parents, in memoriam

≈

Dar el Kutub No. 16141/03
ISBN 977 424 832 5

Designed by Andrea El-Akshar/AUC Press Design Center
Printed in Egypt

❧ Contents ❧

～ Illustrations ～

My mother and sister Marlène, Virginia, 1984
Muhammad in Luxor, 1985
With Sister Emmanuelle, Cairo, April 1993
My son Stéphane, 1986
My daughters Valérie and Olivia, 1987
My grandson Fabio, 2000
My granddaughter Clara, 2003
My granddaughter Helena, 2003
With my brother and my childhood friend Robert, 2002

~ Acknowledgments ~

I wish to express my appreciation and gratitude to Moataz Al-Alfi for his unflinching support over the years; to Cuban poet Juana Rosa Pita, who translated this book into Spanish, providing me with invaluable suggestions and encouragement; to Kismet el Sawi, who has, from very early on, been an avid reader of my vignettes as they came to life; to my children, Stéphane, Valérie, and Olivia, who have provided me with their love and support; and last but not least to Neil Hewison of the American University in Cairo Press and Mina Abdel Malek of the American University in Cairo, without whom this book would not have been possible.

~ Preface ~

My mother never failed to remind me that my very first breath was charged with Mediterranean mist, boasting that July 19, my birthday, was the ancient Egyptian New Year, when Sirius, the brightest star in the sky, rose with the sun on the horizon, announcing the bountiful flood season. Otherwise, we lived in the center of Cairo, amidst a cosmopolitan French-speaking community of French, Jews, Greeks, Italians, White Russians, etc.

When asked what culture I belong to, I invariably reply "the Mediterranean," for I belong not to a country, but to a sea. What is uniquely peculiar about Mediterraneans is the countless traits they share, transcending geography, language, and national differences: the hospitality, the food, the indolence, the sense of time (or lack thereof), the giving, the warmth, the love of children, the need to touch one another, the interminable palavers, the sense of humor, the art of the metaphor and that of the paradox, the capacity to gaze in contemplation at the sea, and, most of all, that superb aloofness which makes noblemen out of the most destitute amongst them. "The Mediterranean is the only liquid continent," wrote André Siegfried. With that elegant metaphor, he captured the history of a mosaic of peoples, each of whom, at one time or another, appropriated and enriched the multitude of other cultures bordering the Mediterranean, that melting pot the Romans proudly called Mare Nostrum, and Plato referred to as "the Frog Pond."

But if I belong to a sea, I also belong to a river—the Nile—without which Egypt would be only an immense forlorn desert, Libya to the west and Arabia to the east, that could never have become the cradle of civilization. Herodotus was right when he wrote, "Egypt is the gift of the Nile."

In the midst of a protracted and cruel war, with the Germans practically knocking on Egypt's door, my carefree childhood and adolescence were spent in the Lycée Français, to which I am indebted for kindling in my heart and mind "a certain idea of France," as de Gaulle would say.

My university years in Cairo, however, were not a long, tranquil river, for opposing British occupation became the absolute center of our lives. Beginning in 1948, Egypt's defeats at the hands of the Israelis unsettled the Middle Eastern landscape forever, and ushered in the revolution that eventually overthrew the Egyptian monarchy.

After graduating from the Faculty of Engineering, I sailed for France and enrolled in one of its celebrated engineering schools. As a consequence, most of my adult life was spent in that country, where I married a young political science student from Marseilles. My son Stéphane was born in that city, whereas his sisters Valérie and Olivia were born in New York and Tokyo, respectively.

Egypt became a very different country under Nasser, who instituted a disastrous economic policy inspired by the Soviet model, within a climate of suspicion and terror. Everyday, I would hear that this or that schoolmate had migrated to the United States, or France, or England. I had difficulty corresponding with my family. The mail and phone services were in disarray, censored letters took forever to reach their destination, and telephone connections were hardly possible, if at all. I came from a country to which I no longer belonged, and lived in a country where I barely belonged. Sadat's historic visit to Israel in 1977 and his memorable speech at the Knesset changed all that, marking a turning point in my life. How can I forget that magical moment when the heroic statesman emerged from his airplane onto an Israeli tarmac, to be greeted by his fiercest enemies of yesterday? In 1981, I returned to Egypt for the first time after exactly thirty years of absence, only to witness Sadat's assassination.

When I retired in 1993, I decided to devote what is commonly referred to as my active life to Egypt and its kind people. My good fortune had it that I befriend a group of individuals—university professors, architects, scientists, businessmen, and ministers—who shared my ambition and were quick to accept me within their dedicated cenacle. Whereas they were immersed in the economic, political, and social mainstream, I decided to remain in France, close to my children and grandchildren, where I could keep abreast of the latest scientific and industrial developments in the world and share them with my friends. Over the years, I have taught, lectured, conducted studies, advised, and debated, contributing my modest stone to their undertaking. Without exception, my friends have since risen to positions of leadership from which they continue to dedicate their energy and intelligence to the country's well being, in the face of sometimes severe adverse circumstances.

As a child, I wanted to become a scientist, and, following in my erudite grandfather's footsteps, favor culture over knowledge. Never having adhered to the so-called 'values' flaunted by multinational companies to conceal the universal underlying value of greed, I jealously attempted to preserve my intellectual integrity by cultivating a secret garden, science. When I retired, it was like emerging from a chrysalis. I decided to return to my frustrated passion, and jot down some of the mathematical ideas I had come across over the years. They eventually constituted the substance of two books that were published in America, the first in 1999 and the second the following year.[1]

In this book, I have assembled a collection of short stories or *vignettes*, inspired by events that actually took place during my blissful childhood and tormented adolescence, against the backdrop of Egypt's contemporary history. Other stories recount later episodes within Corporate America and elsewhere.

Whereas several hundred books are published every year on the subject of ancient Egypt, it seems that the public's interest subsides with the burning of the Alexandria Library and Cleopatra's tragic death. And yet, Egypt's subsequent history is rich with events of considerable magnitude—Christianity and Islam, the Arab and Ottoman conquests, the Napoleonic expedition and the digging of the Suez Canal, British occupation and the fight for independence, World Wars I and II and war against Israel, the downfall of monarchy and revolution.

Throughout the book, I have therefore included short historical footnotes, in the hope that the reader's curiosity about post-pharaonic Egypt might be kindled, whether or not he or she finds my personal story relevant.

∽ Years of Bliss ∾

∽ Roots ∾

A man's glory does not ascend. It descends.
The Nile at its source is only known to a few Ethiopians.
At its mouth, who can ignore it?

François René de Chateaubriand (1768–1848)[2]

Every Sunday, my grandmother hosted the traditional family lunch with everyone in attendance. En route, my brother, my sister, and I were jubilant with anticipation at the prospect of spending the day with our cousins picking grapes, mangos, and guavas, and stuffing ourselves with the unripe fruits. By the time lunch was served, our bellies were full, and the mere sight of stuffed grape leaves, stuffed eggplant and zucchini, stuffed cabbage and tomato, roasted chicken and duckling, not to mention the sempiternal *molokhia* (a leafy green vegetable), made us feel nauseous. It was impossible, however, to turn down my grandmother's injunctions to taste this and that morsel and we politely complied, so eager were we to please her in deference to what she regarded as her most gratifying accomplishment, that of feeding the family.

My grandfather's villa, known as El Beit el Kebir, the Mansion, was located on Selim I Street in the Cairo suburb of Zeitoun, named after the olive orchards that grew in the area centuries earlier. The street itself was named after the Ottoman sultan who defeated the Mamluks in 1517, putting an end to six centuries of Arab rule and two and a half centuries of Mamluk rule.

My favorite room was the huge library that was literally crumbling under hundreds upon hundred of books, some new and some very old. Samir, the oldest and most ignorant of my cousins, was not allowed in that cave of Ali Baba, and, with special permission from my grandfather, my brother Waguih and I were authorized to carefully unfold the papyrus scrolls or play with the ancient amulets that filled one of the drawers. The shelves were cluttered with polychrome wooden sculptures and pink granite figurines, as well as an impressive collection of rocks and fossil shells. A large glass case contained three illuminated manuscripts, one of which was a very ancient Qur'an and another a medieval Gospel. I do not recall what the third book was, other than that it consisted of a number of little booklets *(karras)*, loosely piled on top of one another inside a leather jacket. The unassembled manuscripts were intended to be read by several persons at the same time, each borrowing the *karras* of interest to him.

One Sunday, as we were admiring these treasures, my grandfather, whom we fondly called *Gueddou*, entered the room, sat in his worn-out armchair, and silently observed us. He then awkwardly climbed the sliding ladder without uttering a word, and pulled out a leather-bound book which he handed me, saying "Take this book. It is yours." He then walked to the other end of the room where he picked up an ancient Egyptian statuette representing a female figure, blew away the dust two or three times and gave it to my brother.

The book he gave me, I realized much later, was an original illuminated manuscript of the *Maqamat* of al-Hariri, whose fifty "Sessions" remain the unequalled model of Arabic poetic prose. My grandfather added, "These are the adventures of Abu Zayd the vagrant. You will be able to read and enjoy them when you grow up. I have always wanted to translate these magnificent pieces, but I am getting old, and I do not believe I'll be able to go beyond half a dozen or so."

My brother's statuette looked very much like the beautiful Dame Touy, whose tightly adjusted robe and opulent hairpiece may be admired at the Louvre. The last time I visited him in Virginia, the statuette was sitting in the center of his mantelpiece.

When, at the age of nine, I obtained the Certificat d'Études Primaires, my grandfather rewarded me with Amédée Guillemin's *Les Phénomènes de la physique*, a science book for the layman printed in 1869. I spent hours struggling to understand the text, and gazing at representations of austere scientists wearing pointed beards and well adjusted frock-coats, surrounded by intricate assemblages of glass pipes, concave lenses or convex mirrors, turned brass pedestals, and other magical objects I dreamed of possessing. (Our subconscious mind is astonishingly consistent, for later on in life I patiently assembled a large collection of nineteenth-century instruments). With the scarce resources available in Egypt at the time, finding a glass tube or even a copper wire was a veritable *tour de force*. I nonetheless managed to repeat some of the experiments in the book. They seldom worked, but when they did, my excitement had no limits, and I was encouraged to further pursue my scientific adventures.

Waguih was always attracted by anatomy. For Christmas, he had once requested a dissection kit consisting of a pair of lancets, scissors, and strange-looking tweezers. He dissected every animal he could lay his hands on, from chickens to rabbits, and frequently went frog hunting at the Sporting Club, whose immense golf course was a haven for the little batrachians. After making sure they were dead, he would pin them down on a wooden board, cut their bellies open, and foray into their entrails. He would then put down his instruments, lay his drawing pad flat on his desk, and draw the hapless animal's innards with incredible precision. I envied his talent despite my natural aversion to the objects of his passion. He was barely thirteen and I eleven. The next memorable present he received was *Gray's Anatomy*, the standard reference work on the subject. Having expeditiously polished off his homework, he would sit down and carefully copy the book's multicolored drawings upon his precious pad. He later specialized in orthopedic surgery at the Cleveland Clinic, faithful to the pledge made to our sister Marlène when she came down with polio at the age of nine.

My grandfather, Habib Bey Gazalé, was born in 1861, the year following Abraham Lincoln's election and eight short years before the Suez Canal inauguration. He was a dedicated government official, whose life spanned the reign of no fewer than seven monarchs, from Viceroy Said to King Fuad. Family legend has it that the dignity of bey was bestowed upon him by Viceroy Abbas Hilmi II in recognition of the role he had played in curtailing the cholera epidemic of 1902.[3] He was also awarded the Order of the Nile, a large five-pointed medal that he proudly sported on special occasions.

He had just turned twenty-one when the British bombarded Alexandria and began the occupation of Egypt. Following the invasion, Egypt became a *de facto* British colony, with a tame khedive sitting on the throne and a semblance of allegiance being paid to the Ottoman sultan.[4] The first British consul general to be appointed after the attack was the autocratic Lord Cromer, alias Evelyn Baring, who ruled Egypt with an iron fist. He is remembered for his contemptuous treatment of Egyptians, his ignorance of their history, and his disregard for education, and for impeding the growth of local industry, leaving no choice to the Egyptians but to buy imported British goods, while he amassed a considerable fortune for himself from cotton speculation. In Cromer's own words,

It may be doubted whether any instance can be quoted of a sudden transfer of power in any civilized or semi-civilized community to a class so ignorant as the pure Egyptians, such as they were in the year 1882. These latter have, for centuries past, been a subject race. Persians, Greeks, Romans, Arabs from Arabia and Baghdad, Circassians, and finally, Ottoman Turks, have successively ruled over Egypt, but we have to go back to the doubtful and obscure precedents of pharaonic times to find an epoch when, possibly, Egypt was ruled by Egyptians. Neither, for the present, do they appear to possess the qualities which would render it desirable, either in their own interests, or in those of the civilized world in general, to raise them at a bound to the category of autonomous rulers with full rights of internal sovereignty.[5]

Cromer's social and educational programs were deliberately inadequate. He demanded that the level of instruction Egyptians received only allow them to execute commands given by British supervisors. Rural instruction was rudimentary, barely allowing the pupils to pursue their education beyond the primary levels. When they could afford the expense, lower middle-class students attended mediocre colleges that cruelly suffered from Lord Cromer's deliberate decision to curtail education and oppose the creation of a university.

After ruling the country for twenty-four years with profound disdain for the Egyptians, Lord Cromer resigned in 1907 following the mass execution of a number of villagers in retaliation for a British officer's death. The tragic event took place in the village of Dinshiway in the Nile Delta, where a group of British soldiers were shooting pigeons. A grain silo accidentally caught fire, causing the peasants to run after the hunting party in anger. One soldier panicked, and shot and wounded the wife of a local official. The crowd caught up with him and, amidst threats of more shooting, the British soldier and several Egyptians were killed or wounded. Peasants were arrested at random and summarily tried at Shibin el Kom by a servile Egyptian court martial. Legend has it that scaffolds were being erected before the sentences were even pronounced. There is no exact record of the number of people who were hanged on that memorable day, nor of those who received life sentences or were flogged in public. One man, Zahran, stands out as a popular hero celebrated to this day in countryside palavers. He gallantly walked to his death, setting an example of pride and courage for generations to come. In his memoirs, Anwar el-Sadat confessed that his role model in childhood had been the heroic Zahran.

To get a flavor of the times, it is enough to read the November 22, 1884 issue of *The Graphic*, where a candid news correspondent reports that "the camel under British tuition is developing unlooked for intelligence, has learned the words of command, and pulls up sharply at the cry of Halt."

Even the camel had to wait for the British to become emancipated!

When my grandfather retired in 1921 from the Ministry of Public Hygiene, his director, W. Hastings, was an Englishman! Seven years earlier, on December 8, 1914, Egypt had become a British protectorate after the Turks sided with the Germans during World War I. The following day, the 'protectors' brutally deposed Abbas Hilmi II and replaced him by his uncle Hussein Kamel.

My father's family originated in a predominantly Christian region of Upper Egypt, where today's Copts pride themselves on being the aboriginal descendents of ancient Egyptians. While it is true that Egypt became Christian as early as A.D. 40 and did not fall under Muslim rule until six centuries later, it is also true that the Islamic combatants, who were not in excess of a few thousand males, upon coming across a Coptic population of more than five million, married Coptic women in large numbers.[6] The women were allowed to remain Christian, but their children, male or female, were automatically Muslim. Copts and Muslims are therefore blood brothers. Having said that, it must be remembered that the country gave way to so many different occupiers over the centuries — Greeks, Romans, Byzantine, Persians, Arabs, Crusaders, Mamluks, Ottomans, French, and even British — that it would be presumptuous to assert that any one of its inhabitants, including its rulers, descended from this or that single origin.

Like most Copts at the time, my grandfather nurtured strong sympathies toward Saad Zaghlul, a national hero who relentlessly fought for Egypt's independence, and is regarded as the father of Egypt's awakening. Following his crushing victory in the 1924 elections, Zaghlul submitted his cabinet list to King Fuad, who took his pen and tallied the ministers, then exclaimed, "There must be a mistake . . . I count eight Muslims and two Copts when tradition has it that only one Copt should be included." Zaghlul's historic reply was "This is a revolutionary Cabinet, not a traditional one. When the British exiled the revolutionary leaders to the Seychelles, they exiled four Muslims and two Copts. When they sentenced the leaders to death, they sentenced four Copts and three Muslims, and when they shoot at us in demonstrations, they do not make any difference between Muslims and Copts." Thereupon Fuad signed the royal decree.[7]

That episode took place five and a half years before I was born, but I heard it recounted by my grandfather on innumerable occasions.

Another family legend had it that my grandfather was fluent in five or six languages, including Coptic and ancient Greek, and could also decipher hieroglyphics. Be that as it may, he translated, among other works, the celebrated *Poem of the Nile* authored by his friend Ahmad Shawqi Bey, the Prince of Poets. The poet al-Manfaluti regularly convened his inner circle of disciples at the Mansion, where they spent endless afternoons sipping tea or Turkish coffee and smoking waterpipes as they listened to each other's latest works. These sessions inspired al-Manfaluti to translate Edmond Rostand's *Cyrano de Bergerac* into *al-Sha'ir* (the Poet), [8] where the rendering of the Gascon swaggerer in Arabic is truly admirable! I have the good fortune of owning an original edition of that book, along with some of my grandfather's eclectic works, such as *The Coptic Alphabet*, *A Compendium of Pharaonic Idioms in Egyptian Dialect*, *The Napoleonic Heritage in Egypt*, etc. And yet, the very Napoleon that my grandfather admired so much had instructed his officers to discourage the emancipation of Copts, arguing, "no matter how we treat them, they will always remain our friends." Hundreds of naive Copts had enrolled in the Yacoub Legion and fought on Bonaparte's side.

Between his retirement in 1921 and his death in 1942, my grandfather never allowed a single day to go by without sitting several hours over his books. Following the family lunch, over which he absentmindedly presided, he extracted his ancient watch from his vest pocket and wound it endlessly as he dragged his slippers to the library, reciting Turkish or ancient Greek verses along the way, or perhaps uttering curses that only he could understand, then locked himself up until my grandmother, whom we lovingly called *Teta*, woke up from her nap. His pince-nez was so murky that I often wondered how he could see anything at all, let alone decipher esoteric manuscripts. If my brother or I teased him about it, he retorted that he could see well enough to kick our behinds.

Ever since their wedding day on June 6, 1884, a Sunday, my grandfather had made an immutable habit of personally fetching my grandmother's tea and bringing it to her in bed. He would then sit in the armchair at the foot of the bed and engage Teta in their daily ritual chat.

June 7, 1942 was also a Sunday. School was just out, and we jubilantly went to the Mansion to partake of the very special banquet that followed my cousin Wafik's first communion. My cousins and I were playing in the garden when we heard a strident shriek the likes of which I had never heard, and which seemed to tear the sky apart. We dashed inside the Mansion and found everyone in disarray. My mother was desperately trying to keep us away from my grandmother's bedroom, where everyone was flocking.

There, I saw Teta sitting up in her bed, holding a rosary between her joined hands as she silently stared at my grandfather with tears running down her cheeks. His eyes were shut, his head gently leaning on the headrest, and his arms limply hanging on either side of the armchair.

My aunts were moaning and crying. One of the maids stood by the window, pulling her stretched out headcover back and forth against the back of her neck as she intoned a Qur'anic verse and implored God's mercy upon the soul of the kind departed man.

As I stood in the doorway, my whole body irrepressibly shaking, I heard my elder brother murmur, "Gueddou is dead." My sister Marlène, who had not yet turned eight, was not allowed in the room and remained blissfully unaware of the unfolding tragedy. Because of the June heat, the window had been left open and a gentle breeze filled the bedroom with the light scent of the tamarisk tree that my grandfather had planted outside their balcony thirty years earlier.

Never before in my short life had I seen a dead person. I could not believe that my beloved grandfather, my own Gueddou, was not just dozing and that he would not soon rise from his armchair, rub his spectacles between his thumb and forefinger, and drag his slippers to his den.

Following an unbearably long silence, my grandmother, looking at my grandfather with a faint smile on her face, finally whispered, "Be patient, *ya Habibi*,[9] for I shall join you in Heaven before the month runs out of days." She closed her eyes on June 29, twenty-two days after Gueddou.

Between December 12, 1887 and May 27, 1910, Teta gave birth to no less than eighteen children, only six of whom lived. My father, one of the six survivors, was born on October 9, 1903. Faithful to family tradition, he joined the civil service, confirming Naguib Mahfouz's observation that "the ideal citizen of other nations might be a warrior, a politician, a merchant, a craftsman, or a sailor, but in Egypt it was a government official. . . . Even the Pharaohs themselves, he thought, were but officials appointed by the gods of heaven to rule the Nile Valley by means of religious rituals and administrative, economic, and organizational regulations."[10]

He also inherited his father's passion for the Arabic language, which he taught to generations of European students, all of whom remember him fondly. He died at an early age without having had a chance to express his talents fully. The profoundly Catholic Charles Péguy may find it natural that the parent should die before the child, but the pain is great when he dies so young and so far away. To this day, I loathe the Egyptian consul general of the time, who would not allow me to travel to Egypt for my father's funeral unless I committed myself not to return to France, where my young wife was still studying at the Institut des Sciences Politiques, and my son Stéphane was only a few months old. These were the days of Gamal Abdel Nasser's dictatorship, and I had no desire to be forcibly enrolled under the authority of some despicable Soviet advisor, whose cohort of fifteen thousand would be curtly kicked out of Egypt by Anwar el-Sadat in 1972.

The morning after Gueddou's passing, Edgard Gallad, founder of the *Journal d'Égypte* and a close friend of my grandfather's, wrote in his obituary: "Habib Bey Gazalé, érudit, homme de lettres, grandement apprecié pour ses oeuvres de bien . . . ." I asked my father what the word *érudit* meant. He replied that it referred to someone whose knowledge was vast and encompassed every field of human knowledge.

At that moment, I vowed to be an *érudit* when I grew up.

⤙ Discovering the Nile ⤚

He who drinks from the Nile
Shall return to the Nile.

Egyptian proverb

The Franciscan Sisters were strict and unforgiving. I was the youngest of my class and found the daily recitation of the alphabet extremely boring. As a consequence, I became inattentive and very talkative, two major sins which caused me to be severely reprimanded, sometimes with a rap on the knuckles.

My brother did not fare any better and his grades were appalling. Though my mother had little patience with our conduct, she was not particularly pleased with the daily punishments that my brother and I had to endure.

One day, we were playing in the schoolyard during the mid-morning recess when I noticed something unusual. For some mysterious reason, the school gate had been left wide open. I ran toward my brother, who was playing with our cousin Samir, and pulled him by the sleeve, drawing his attention to that godsent opportunity. We sneaked past the janitor's door, which was always ajar, while Samir, already a total maverick, was only too pleased to stand in the doorway and block the janitor's view. No sooner did we feel the street's pavement under our feet than we dashed home without looking behind. That is probably the fastest sprint we ever ran.

When we committed a misdeed of that magnitude, our angry mother would usually threaten to denounce us to the "man with the green turban." We had never seen that fearful character, but the vision of an old bearded beggar with a green turban filled us with unreasoning fear. Sometimes she would exclaim, pressing her palms against her temples, "Some day I will end up in Nuristan." We imagined some faraway land like Pakistan or Afghanistan, whose foreboding names evoked multitudes of bearded characters with green turbans lurking in dark, insalubrious alleys, looking for little boys. Several years later, we discovered that *Nuristan*, a distortion of the word *neurasthenia*, was the name given to the Cairo insane asylum.

My brother and I were inseparable accomplices and often nagged my mother in unison until she gave in to our whims, declaring that we were worse than Munkar and Nekir, two frightening angels who were believed to harass the deceased in their sepulcher, endlessly questioning them on the genuineness of their faith.

We were catching our breath in the hallway when we suddenly realized the extent of the crime we had just committed, conjecturing what our mother would say, and what explanation we might come up with. We never lied to our parents, one of the most heinous sins in Middle Eastern cultures. Thereupon, my elder brother had a stroke of genius. "Cry!" he commanded. I was taken aback for a few seconds, then heeded his order and started crying. I felt like crying anyway.

We hit two birds with one stone. First, my mother did not punish me since I was already crying. Second, Waguih, his little brother's keeper, was not only innocent; he was brave.

It worked like a charm. Mother took me on her lap, wiped my eyes dry, and kissed my cheeks as she squeezed my brother's little hand between her palm and long delicate fingers. Amazingly, she did not send us back to school, and I think I never enjoyed staying home and playing with my brother as much as I did on that day.

At the time, we were not aware of my father's plans to move from the suburb of Zeitoun to Cairo, where he had been offered a teaching assignment. When he informed us of his plans, we felt extremely proud and exhilarated at the thought of establishing ourselves in the mythical city. Cairo . . . can you imagine? We soon left our provincial suburb, never to return to the Franciscan Sisters School. On December 1, 1935, we moved into our Cairo apartment at Number 5 (later renumbered 13), Mariette Pasha Street.

No sooner had we moved in than my father decided to take us on an exploratory tour of the great city, where neither my brother nor I had ever set foot. My sister Marlène was barely a year and a half old. We begged my father to let us ride in one of those magical horse-drawn carriages called a *hantur*, for we loved its slow pace, the clank of the horse's hooves, the crack of the long whip, and the coachman's crude cursing whenever the horse showed signs of recalcitrance. At regular intervals, he mercilessly lashed the little vagrant stowaways who took free rides on the back of the carriage by deftly cracking the whip over the canopy that shielded us from the Cairo sun. Thus perched, the fearless boys would travel to one end of the street, then hop on the back of another *hantur* traveling in the opposite direction, until some idle passer-by would shout "Whip behind!" in the coachman's direction, and enjoy the ensuing scramble.

We reached a roundabout called Midan Ismailiya, which would soon become the pivot of our daily lives, halfway between our house and the Lycée. My father explained that the *midan* owed its name to the khedive who presided over the Suez Canal opening celebrations sixty-seven years earlier. Our *hantur* then took us across Qasr el Nil Bridge, at the ends of whose iron structure sat two pairs of frightening lions, eternally standing guard. We emerged from the bridge in front of the Moorish gardens, whose fountains, benches, and vases were adorned with splendid white and blue mosaics. The garden overlooked the Nile, which I discovered for the first time in my life, unaware that I would be bonded to it as if by blood ties as long as I lived. Slowly drifting with the current, a dozen white triangular sails slid by without haste, as if they had been granted all eternity to reach their mythical destinations. My father made us pause in front of the statue of the poet Ahmad Shawqi, pensively gazing at the river whose odyssey he sang so well. "It was Gueddou who translated his famous poem about the Nile," proudly declared my father.

Suddenly, the horse reared up, whinnying and stirring the air with his forelegs. The coachman cried "Demonstration!" as he backed up and turned around. In the distance, a violent street fight opposed two large groups of men. At first, I thought it was a kind of game they played in the streets of Cairo, for one group was clad in green shirts and the other in blue. I soon realized that a bloody clash was under way between people who seemed to be at each other's throats. Years later, I understood that what I had witnessed on that singular day was a confrontation between two paramilitary formations, the liberal Wafd in blue shirts and the fascist Young Egypt in green shirts.

Thus began my first encounter with Cairo. Little did I understand that Egypt was in the midst of an unrelenting struggle against the British occupant, with its consequent confrontations among the people of Egypt themselves. Little did I understand that Italy's invasion of Ethiopia was imminent and that three years thence the greatest of all wars would engulf humanity in endless suffering, changing the world forever.

⤚ En Route to Alexandria ⤛

Alexandria, Bride of the Sea

Egyptian saying

Summers were extremely hot in Cairo. No sooner was school out than my mother packed our suitcases and off we drove to Bab el Hadid station, a truly beautiful example of Islamic design, with its blue and ochre arabesque windows and graceful arched doors. Facing the station stood a gigantic statue entitled *Egypt's Awakening*, whose sheer size never ceased to fill our hearts with awe.

There, we boarded a slow train that seemed to take forever to reach Alexandria. Leaning out of the window, Waguih, Marlène, and I enjoyed every minute of the utter chaos that preceded our departure. My mother, who was very superstitious, always forced us to look back before boarding the train, for fear that we might not return safely. That ritual became a second nature of mine, and to this day it would never occur to me to board a train or even an airplane without casting a fleeting look over my shoulder.

We were brimming with impatience as we waited for the strident whistle and the first slow strokes of the steam engine to signal our departure.

My mother would finally lean back in her comfortable seat and heave a sigh of relief, exclaiming "Enfin!" in French. Though we spoke Arabic at home, my father, a true dandy out of the thirties, sometimes spoke to my mother in French when he wanted to impress our neighbors as he helped us get settled in the compartment. That set us apart from the common people, because of the insuperable social chasm between our communities that had always been and would always remain one of the givens in our lives. He never traveled with us on the train, but usually joined us later for a few days. I shall forever remember him waving his white silk handkerchief as he vanished in a cloud of black smoke and white steam, having made his perennial recommendation to my mother in Italian, "Appena arrivi, scrivi!" ('The minute you arrive, write!').

En route, we stopped in Benha, then Tanta in the Delta's center, then Kafr el Zayyat, and finally Damanhur, four rural towns where hundreds of fellaheen, the Egyptian peasants, scrambled to get on or off, loudly greeting each other and shouting "May you go and come back in peace."

They traveled with geese, ducks, or chickens cooped up in crates made of palm stalks, as well as sheep or goats with a hemp rope tied around their necks. The noise they made was deafening, added to the huffing and puffing of the heavy black locomotive.

My brother and I would wait until my mother fell sound asleep, with the breeze blowing on her gentle face, then sneak out of the compartment and squeeze our way back to third class, where our faithful servant 'Abdu escorted us amidst the peasants, ten or twelve coaches behind. We had to walk through a string of second-class coaches jammed with civil servants whose dignity did not allow them to travel in third but whose finances could barely afford second.

I loved the dizzying smell of the cumin and coriander the peasants carried in their jute bundles, mixed with the rich fragrance of the black tea or aniseed they brewed on board. They also carried *foul* sandwiches that consisted of boiled fava beans seasoned with oil and salt, stuffed between the two halves of a loaf of home-baked bread, together with a few slices of raw onion and pickled turnips.

After carefully wiping their mouths with the palms of their hands, they took turns drinking out of clay jars that dangled in the window frame at the end of a short rope. The porous clay let the jar sweat, as they would say metaphorically, referring to their own perspiration in the sizzling heat. That kept the water surprisingly cool. I never confessed to my parents how often I drank from similar jars placed by Cairenes on the ledge of their windows for the anonymous passerby to quench his thirst. Because of the heat and dry weather that plague the area in summer, offering water has been a tradition in the Middle East since the days of the pharaohs.

The travelers also carried sugar canes that they broke at the knuckles by vigorously bending them over the knee. They then peeled off the skin with their front teeth, and chewed the pulp dry. The way we dressed and spoke made us look as though we had descended from another planet, but the peasants generously shared their mouth-watering sandwiches and cool water with us.

My brother's hair and eyes were pitch black, and were it not for his soft manners and natural elegance, he could have easily passed for one of the little peasant adolescents. Their toil and misery had tanned their faces and roughened their hands as well as their manners, but he mingled with them with great ease, as I watched them play at knucklebones on the dusty floor.

I was a shy little boy, and my blue eyes did not help, for the blue eye was believed to portend bad luck. To provide against its maleficence, the women sewed little blue beads onto their children's clothes or simply attached them with a safety pin, or even threaded them into a lock of their hair. Most children also wore a charm against the evil eye—the *higab*, a little triangular cloth bag containing Qur'anic verses, or the ninety-nine epithets of God scribbled on little pieces of paper.

I had to be very careful never to compliment a mother on her baby's beauty lest she spread her open palm against his chest, as the number five was believed to be an effective shield against the evil blue eye. She would chant, "I seek God's protection from the eye of the envious," and sometimes mimic the act of spitting. If a child was presented to an adult, he would have to exclaim *Ma sha' Allah*, meaning 'Whatever God wills,' but never voice his admiration.

(It is said that in the days of Muhammad Ali, the women feared for their boys more than for their girls, and a beautiful boy's features had to be concealed from the passerby with a handkerchief that his mother held before his mouth. During the procession that preceded a circumcision, the boy usually rode a richly caparisoned horse through the neighborhood streets, preceded by the barber who was also the officiant, as well as a group of musicians, whose number depended on the family's fortune. The aspirant was usually dressed as a girl, his elaborate female ornaments being intended to divert the onlooker's eye from his features.)[11]

When the incantations were over, the spell was exorcised and the women could now marvel at my blue eyes and fair complexion, two uncommon traits in their villages. They would gently stroke my hair or squeeze my chin between their thumb and forefinger, exclaiming, "Ya nunu y-abu einein zurq" ('Cute little blue-eyes!').

I have never seen a nation whose people love children as much as the Egyptians, and that love miraculously transcends social barriers. I was pulled by my little head into the light of this world by an illiterate midwife, and was breast-fed by one of those third-class peasants. That probably accounts for the immoderate love that I shall harbor for the Egyptian common people as long as I live.

Upon reaching Benha, we returned to our compartment and quietly opened our school bags, where we had stuffed our comic books along with the material for our mandatory and very boring summer assignments. The minute we left Benha, my mother invariably asked my brother, the tallest of the three children, to climb onto the seat and reach for the lunch basket. She always wondered why neither my brother nor I were ever hungry on the train. The ice-cold Spathis lemon soda, however, was a welcome change from the acrid taste of the clay jar.

Tanta was a much larger town, where the train stopped for several minutes. We were authorized to get off and dash to the pancake man, who was forever stationed in the same spot. My favorite was the chickpea and white-sugar pancake, and my mother's the sesame, two renowned specialties of El Sayyed Badawi, the famous Tanta confectioner. Reaching the stall was no easy matter, for we had to elbow our way through the dense human cluster. Having bought a copious assortment, we hurried back to our seats with my mother and 'Abdu posted on the steps of their respective coaches, ready for an emergency, though nothing ever happened to us and we never missed the train. En route, we would give 'Abdu four pancakes of each kind to share with his fellow travelers.

"I hope you didn't catch any fleas," my mother used to say, for fleas we invariably caught, and secretly itched until we jumped in the bathtub the minute we got home. One of us also inevitably caught a cinder in the eye, a very painful experience, but my mother was an expert at delicately removing it with the tip of her tongue.

How many times, upon crossing the drawbridge at Kafr el Zayyat, did we hear my mother's account of Prince Ahmad's drowning in the Nile. There were many versions to the story, all of which agreed on one point. Eighty years earlier, on May 15, 1858, an impressive assembly of princes and other members of the royal family were on their way back to Cairo from a reception hosted by Viceroy Said in Alexandria. The train was traveling down the recently inaugurated Cairo–Alexandria line when their carriage fell into the Nile's murky waters upon reaching Kafr el Zayyat. All of the passengers drowned, with the exception of Prince Muhammad Abdel Halim, who miraculously jumped out of the carriage and swam ashore. One version has it that the drawbridge had accidentally remained open, another that the carriage was being transported across the Nile by barge so that the indolent occupants might comfortably remain in their seats when, for some reason, perhaps excessive enthusiasm on the part of the cheering peasants, the overloaded barge toppled, sending the royal party to their death. It was Ahmad, not his younger half-brother Ismail, who would have inherited the throne, had it not been for that terrible tragedy. By some dubious turn of destiny, Ismail had remained in Cairo, not feeling well.

How many times had we heard of barges toppling, and of the horrible fate of those who got sucked into the Nile's myriad treacherous whorls? That terrifying story always filled us with awe, and kept us begging for more gory details until we breathed a sigh of cowardly relief upon emerging from the iron structure onto the Nile's western bank.

Upon reaching Damanhur, we became very agitated, because Alexandria was drawing near. Damanhur, my mother never failed to remind us, derived its name from the pharaonic *demi n Hur* 'town of Horus,' the falcon god. Another hour, and perhaps a short stop in Sidi Gabir, a suburb of Alexandria, and we were almost there. 'Abdu had fought his way to our compartment, balancing his bundle on top of his head, ready to unload our luggage.

Finally, finally, Alexandria! Marlène was four years younger than I, and I two years younger than Waguih. The three of us jumped up and down chanting the magical name. Outside Misr Station, as it was called, dozens of horse drawn carriages were stationed in their nauseating puddles, with the horses' ears barely emerging from the oat-filled jute sacks hanging from the backs of their necks. We needed two carriages to take us home, and chose to sit in the cleaner of the two, while 'Abdu followed with our luggage. We took it in turns to sit next to the coachman, high above the others, and nag him until he let us crack his long whip. When your turn came to occupy that privileged observation post, you became the lookout man, and were entrusted with the responsibility of shouting "Sea, sea! " the second you caught sight of its thin blue line on the horizon. It was like Christopher Columbus's epic, only in reverse, and we imagined the sailor perched atop the mast of the Santa Maria, praying for the moment he would shout "Land, land!" We soon recognized the Mediterranean's smell, like an infant its mother's.

A few years ago, I was traveling by car to the seaside resort of Borg el Arab, about one hundred kilometers west of Alexandria on the Mediterranean shore. A very dear friend of mine, a minister in the Egyptian government (who was later appointed prime minister by President Mubarak), had invited me to attend a conference that he was to address, under his chairmanship, the urgent need to protect Egypt's northern seashore against further deterioration. The sudden and chaotic proliferation of hundreds of holiday resorts was devastating the landscape and gravely polluting the water. I was the minister's advisor on a number of science and technology issues, and he had asked me to accompany him in that capacity.

En route, we had long chats, some having to do with serious issues, some in a lighter vein. At some point, I told the minister of our childhood expeditions to Alexandria, which were no doubt akin to some of his own. Half an hour later, I was intently listening to something he was saying when he suddenly stopped and stared out of the window, shouting "Sea, sea!"

It is one of the characteristic traits of Egyptians never to part with their wonderful sense of humor, regardless of the seriousness of the subject at hand. That characteristic, together with an unshakeable faith in God, perhaps lightens the burden of poverty on that brave kind people, and gives those in charge of their destiny the will and courage to persevere.

⤚ Petit Lycée ⤚

A few days after moving from Zeitoun to Cairo, we found ourselves sitting on the benches of the Lycée Français. Having turned six in July, I was admitted to tenth grade. In the French system, you started in twelfth grade and counted backwards. My brother, who was two years older, didn't rate any better than ninth, which put him one year behind the norm throughout his high school years. He was the tallest of his class, a cause of constant harassment by his teachers and mockery by his classmates. That, I believe, gave him an unusual drive to outdo his peers. He became a brilliant and successful orthopedic surgeon later in life.

With the exception of the Arabic-language teachers and the redoubtable janitor who mercilessly shut the entrance gate at eight o'clock sharp, everyone in the Lycée spoke only French. Madame Escalère, our principal teacher, had been assigned to the Lycée by the Mission Laïque Française, a body established in 1902 to promote the French cultural presence in the Middle East and perhaps fend off British influence. Not speaking a word of Arabic, she had to rely on the other pupils to translate our exchanges, which they deliberately distorted, laughing at my helplessness. My first few months were a nightmare. Had it not been for my mother's infinite patience, her two Egyptian boys would have never bridged the cultural gap that set them apart from the French-speaking cosmopolitan microcosm. Children can be very cruel at times.

As for my sister Marlène, she went to another Franciscan Sisters school nearby, where they spoke mostly Italian, and was quick to catch on.

My brother and I were *demi-pensionnaires*, which meant that we had our daily lunches at school but did not partake of the meals offered by the Lycée. My mother would never entrust anyone with feeding her children other than herself or our cook, whom she had personally trained. Furthermore, the Lycée catered to an essentially foreign population whose cooking she instinctively distrusted. To her mind, only oriental cuisine was real food. She insisted, moreover, that our meals be served warm. Our servant Ahmad thus brought us our daily home-cooked meals at twelve o'clock, and I do not recall that he was ever late. He carried the food in a four-tier aluminum lunch box and a straw basket. The bottom pan contained the stew, usually veal or lamb and sundry vegetables immersed in tomato sauce, or sometimes the traditional *molokhia*. The next pan contained the inevitable white rice, the third a salad, and the fourth an ever-changing variety of oriental pastry or fresh fruit. The little basket contained the Syrian bread together with the plates and silver, as well as two zinc drinking glasses with our names engraved in Arabic. Our napkins had our initials embroidered in such large characters that no one would have ever dared pinch them.

During the first two years of lycée, Ahmad picked us up at the end of the day, and the three of us merrily walked home. En route, he would give us daily object lessons on the things of the street, so foreign to our sheltered universe. He would also train us in the art of kicking an empty can, an exercise that kept us busy until we reached home.

One afternoon, he decided to give us a taste of a very sweet decoction of *helba*, a strong-smelling herb of which the habitués of oriental cafés were very fond, but which was never served at our house, or any other house we frequented. No sooner had we crossed the threshold of our apartment than my mother flew into a rage "My God, Ahmad, how dare you let the children drink that disgusting beverage?" It took several baths in the days that followed to get rid of the foul smell that our skin exuded from every pore. Madame Escalère never alluded to the stench, convinced, as it were, that even the best Egyptian families indulged in that nauseating beverage.

We would often stop at the sugar-cane shop that was full to bursting on hot summer days. The man would pick up two or three canes and, with a swift swing of his machete, decapitate them and stuff the beheaded sticks between two metallic cylinders connected to a large crank that his little helper turned, huffing and puffing, biting his *gallabiya*, which was stuck between his clenched teeth. The juice flowed into a sticky tin funnel, then into a summarily rinsed glass, foaming like a head of beer. Having absorbed the nectar, we would bravely fend off the flies and emerge into the blaring sun. Needless to say, we never confessed that sin to our parents.

Whenever my mother, because of some urgent errant, could not greet us upon our return from the Lycée, she charged our older maid with preparing our *goûter* and instructed Ahmad not to linger on the way home. He seized that opportunity to introduce us to the game of backgammon at the far end of his favorite coffee shop, and initiate us into the science of choosing between the alternatives offered by a fortunate cast of the dice, amidst the brouhaha raised by the other players. Half the pleasure consisted in announcing your moves in Turkish and Persian—*shish-bish* for six-and-five, *habyak* for double one, etc.[12] (It is said of someone who is cross-eyed that he is *shish-bish*, for one of his eyes sees five where the other sees six.) He who was not capable of announcing his moves in the foreign numerals was deemed amateurish, and not desirable as a rival. A particularly lucky throw of the dice led the players to slam their ebony or ivory checkers onto the worn-out inlaid mother of pearl triangles, as if to say, "Take this!" and further exacerbate their opponent's rage.

We also learned an easy game of cards called *basra*, along with one or two others that did not require you to rack your brains unduly. My father never allowed a pack of cards to cross the threshold of our house, arguing that indulging in that vice was the road to perdition, having led uncountable victims to their downfall. Jojo, one of our schoolmates, once transgressed that rule, and smuggled into our apartment a pack borrowed from his mother, an inveterate addict. "Go back to your gambling den," shouted my father, as he vigorously threw the *corpus delicti* out of the window. I can still see the fifty-two cards delicately spinning round and round, displaying one face then the other, before landing at the far end of the museum garden nearby, pushed by the gentle sunset breeze.

When my brother and I were old enough to bring home the aluminum lunch box and the straw basket, I was too short to avoid the clank of the aluminum against every bump on the asphalt, and the bottom pan was soon severely battered.

One day, Madame Escalère instructed us to bring an empty shoebox the next morning. The idea was to assemble a wheelbarrow using the rectangular box, with the wheel and arms cut out of the lid. I only understood that we had to bring a shoebox, but failed to comprehend what the intended object was. My schoolmates volunteered all kinds of interpretations, none of which I believed, so wary was I of their treachery. Upon asking my mother if she could spare an empty shoebox, she haughtily replied that we were not in the habit of saving that sort of rubbish. Furthermore, our shoes were seldom purchased from stores, but handmade by Abbas Abul Ela in his little workshop on 15, Madabegh Street, across the street from the *al-Ahram* daily newspaper. He would make us sit on a worn out piano stool and press our bare foot flat on an old newspaper, then carefully draw its contour with an old pencil stump and facetiously tickle us in the process. One thing my mother did keep, however, was hatboxes, because she did not want her hats crushed by some clumsy porter. She offered me a truly elegant round hatbox, hand made by her Romanian *modiste*, and adorned all around with Parisian *élégantes* clad in turn-of-the-century crinolines and wearing elaborate floppy hats. I had the strange feeling that something was not exactly right, but did not wish to counter my mother's choice.

When I showed up at school the next morning, sheepishly holding on to the pink satin ribbon, the children surrounded me from every direction, pointing their fingers at my cumbersome burden, giggling and laughing as they chanted, "La fille, la fille."

Needless to say, cutting a rectangular wheelbarrow out of a round hatbox constituted an insurmountable challenge. Madame Escalère charitably declared that it would be a pity to turn such a pretty box into a vulgar wheelbarrow, and suggested that I take it home intact. Instead of winning a prize for the most perfect wheelbarrow, I was awarded that for the most beautiful box.

(Around 380 B.C., Plato posed the problem of squaring the circle to the students of the Athens Academy, a riddle that several generations of ancient Greeks grappled with, to no avail. Given a circle, the idea was to draw a square equal in area to the circle, using only compass and straight edge. Every time that problem crosses my mind, I recall the shoebox and the hatbox, and remember my mother with infinite tenderness.)

Another time, Madame Escalère asked us to bring a hard-boiled egg, a saucer, and a knife. Here again, the object was not totally clear, but I chose not to solicit my schoolmate's intercession. The word she used for saucer was *soucoupe*, a somewhat unfamiliar word among French-speaking Egyptians, who say *plat* instead. Having decided that nothing was too good for her little boy, my mother gave me a hand-painted Royal Worcester eggcup that my grandfather had brought back from one of his London trips. She told me to be careful with the sterling-silver knife, and also gave me a matching fork, just in case.

The object was obviously not to eat a hard-boiled egg in class, but to draw its cross section. Madame Escalère instructed us to peel the egg, then cut it through the middle and lay the two halves side by side in the saucer. I don't know which was the greater challenge, that of squaring a hatbox or flattening an oval porcelain cup, but my classmates were quick to draw the teacher's attention to my unorthodox utensils. As tears ran down my cheeks, Madame Escalère expressed admiration for the cup, knife, and fork, and asked me to convey her congratulations to my mother for possessing such refined objects.

When I think of my teachers, the first name that comes to my mind is Madame Escalère's. I can still hear her gentle voice patiently teaching me to articulate my first words of French. How fortunate I was to be able to speak two languages, I thought, my mother's and Madame Escalère's!

➤ Grand Lycée ➤

To Said el Zayyat
In memoriam

The Lycée Français was a melting pot where dozens of different nationalities rubbed shoulders, whether they were pupils or teachers, amidst a rambling community of refugees from all over Europe—Jews, antifascists, White Russians, etc.[13] The Lycée nonetheless abided by the demanding curricula of the French Ministry of Education, requiring my little Egyptian schoolmates to recite parrot-fashion the famous opening paragraph of Ernest Lavisse's classic French history book intended for France's Third Republic schools:

> Our ancestors, the Gauls, were intelligent and brave. They were not able to defend themselves against the Romans. Gaul was conquered by the Romans fifty years before Jesus Christ despite the beautiful defense put up by Vercingetorix. Gaul remained under Roman rule for more than four hundred years. It became educated and rich. It became Christian.

Our Lycée, in a building designed by the French architect Victor Erlanger, was located in a section of town called Bab el Luq, nicknamed "Babel look" for it housed an unusually large number of private schools of different nationalities. The American University in Cairo, known as the

AUC, was immediately adjacent to the Lycée Français, within a stone's throw of the Collège des Frères, the Italian and German schools, and others.

Strangely, we never mingled much with our AUC neighbors. Our basketball teams had been rivals since time immemorial, taking turns at winning the annual college championship. The Lycée students were outwardly discreet, with the girls wearing natural-colored cotton uniforms that barely revealed the hem of their skirts. The kids next door wore extravagant colors, taking for role models American movie stars of the day. The boys were Mickey Rooneys, and the girls Judy Garlands. They involved themselves in numerous extra-curricular activities, a luxury we could not afford, given the amount of reading that was required of us daily.[14]

The large majority of students came from well to do "European" families who lived in the center of town or its immediate vicinity, within walking distance of one another and of their respective schools.

My closest friend Robert Farhi and I were barely eleven when we discovered that we were both in love with Madame Moulin, our history teacher. Her Christian name was Germaine, a slightly old-fashioned choice by today's standards. When I told that story to the beautiful and talented French actress Fanny Ardant, she confessed, amidst one of her legendary laughs, that Germaine Moulin sounded like a name out of the French Resistance. Not so much because it reminded her of the mythical and heroic Jean Moulin, but because Germaine called to mind an adolescent messenger wearing a long ample skirt and rolled down socks, riding a rusty bicycle on a rural pathway with the Germans lurking behind the bushes in their drab green uniforms.

Considering that we were "inseparable," Robert and I decided to share Madame Moulin. The secret name of our brotherhood would be GRV, our initials joined to hers (throughout my Lycée years, my first name was Victor). We carved the secret logo on our school benches and on the bark of trees, we drew it in the courtyard sand and on our copybooks, and we sealed our conspiracy by uttering the magical word every time we shook hands, in the manner of knights out of our fair teacher's history book mixing their blood.

It was Madame Moulin who taught us the first rudiments of ancient Egyptian history, the object of her passion and soon of ours. La Phalène bookstore carried a seemingly endless collection of pharaonic postcards, and I never failed, upon receiving my pocket money, to buy one or two, and neatly paste them down in chronological order in a little copybook: the Old Empire with the pyramids of Giza, the Middle Empire with Sesostris (one of my grand uncles was named Sesostris), and above all, the New Empire with the emblematic figures of Thutmose, Hatshepsut, Akhenaton—said to be the precursor of monotheism—his beautiful wife Nefertiti, the mythical Tutankhamen and the greatest of all, Ramesses II. Having reached Cleopatra, my copybook ran out of pages, but the history of ancient Egypt had come to an end anyway.

Thereupon, I mustered all my courage and decided to show my album to Madame Moulin. She tucked it under her arm, and invited me for tea at five o'clock at her apartment, promising to diligently examine my magnum opus and return it to me that afternoon.

"What about Robert," I asked myself? "How will he react when he learns of the invitation?" After much soul searching, I decided that the time had come to behave like men, for we could not carry on loving the same person forever. After all, Madame Moulin had made her choice, hadn't she?

I bolted down my lunch and dashed to the bathroom, washed my hands and face, wet my hair, and carefully combed it with my father's Yardley lavender brilliantine, making sure that it was impeccably parted. Having checked that my knees were clean—I wore short pants at the time—I put on my best outfit and off I went. It was nearly three o'clock when I reached her apartment house near the Brazilian Coffee Stores on Qasr el Nil street, where I ordered a milkshake and drank it down very slowly. After an hour and a half of pacing the sidewalk, the fateful moment came at last. My heart was furiously throbbing when her Nubian servant opened the door.

Her apartment, which was heavy with the fragrance of bitter-almond floor wax, was very different from ours. Whereas my parents insisted on having nothing but French-looking furniture, hers was furnished with oriental antiques, probably gleaned from the Khan el Khalili souk. I had visions of Sheherazade emerging from behind an arabesque screen when Madame Moulin appeared, wearing a straight gray skirt and a white cotton blouse with a tiny silk scarf tightly wrapped around her neck. She sat next to me on a soft Turkish *diwan* and slowly flipped the pages of my copybook, sometimes pausing to offer this or that comment. But I only remember the way she puckered her lips every time she uttered the word *pschent*,[15] her light perfume, the warmth radiating from her body close by, and the thin blue vein that ran under the translucent skin of her cheek. When the time came to take leave, I shyly asked her if she would care to keep the copybook. She gave me a soft kiss on the cheek, promising always to cherish that memento of her dearest-ever Egyptian pupil.

Monsieur Marie, our math teacher, was redoubtable. His oral interrogations invariably began by chalking up a problem on the blackboard then proceeding with the roll call in alphabetical order. Upon being called, we sheepishly went to the blackboard and embarked upon our own flight of fancy, praying that it would contain enough substance to escape the ultimate sanction, the zero mark. Such a performance entailed a two-hour *consigne* (detention) in the *permanence*, a sinister classroom where the habitual inmates went straight to their perennial seats, and the zero achievers sat in silence under the watchful eye of Monsieur David or Monsieur Neemetallah, a true sadist. Another sadist was Monsieur Bradke, a supervisor of nondescript origin whose specialty was tugging ears or pulling the short hairs of the temples while vigorously shaking his hand to exacerbate the pain.

I was relatively immune to that form of punishment, having collected an impressive number of *satisfécits*. These were little cardboard certificates that you earned if you scored among the top three students in any given subject. First place allowed you to erase three hours of *consigne*, second place two hours, and third place one hour. Wary of breaking into my capital of certificates, I used the red three-hour *satisfécits* to erase shorter sentences. Monsieur David would then write across the certificate "Valid only for one hour," or "two" with the precision of an accountant, unless the *consigne* bulletin bore the fatidic "irredeemable."

It was not uncommon for the entire class to be called to the blackboard without anyone coming anywhere near the solution, affording Monsieur Marie the pleasure of inking on the register an uninterrupted garland of zeros, from Alphandary to Zalzal. Not having quenched his sadistic thirst, he would sometimes be in the mood for another round of torture. When called, we would merely rise, despondently shake our heads, and sit down. The garland would soon become a string of double zeros, with Monsieur Marie announcing every new birth with a laconic "Bicyclette." Thus equipped, we had no recourse but to go to the Lycée on Thursday and serve our sentence.

The dapper Chalem, perpetually clad in expensive custom-made Prince of Wales check suits, shamelessly lacked mathematical ambition. When his name was called, he collected his things and silently slipped out of the classroom, saving Monsieur Marie the effort of dismissing him according to an unvarying ritual that filled us with joy and admiration for Chalem's spirit and independence.

Monsieur David was short, heavy, and bald. Most of all, he was a moralist. Never having qualified as teacher, he was only appointed supervisor. In the *permanence*, he gave free rein to his frustrated pedagogical inclination by dispensing his unchanging parables to a captive audience: one rotten apple is enough to rot a basketful, etc.

Our beloved Arabic teacher El Etr—meaning fragrance—forced me to read aloud my grandfather's translations, for I was, in his grandiloquent words, the grandson of the "illustrious Habib Bey."

We called our non-Egyptian teachers *Monsieur* or *Madame*, whereas the Egyptians were addressed as *Ostaz*. Ostaz El Etr was so nearsighted that he could barely decipher a text unless he pressed it against his thick spectacles. He forced us to memorize difficult Arabic poems, a grueling task for non-Egyptians, to whom even colloquial Egyptian was foreign. During the recess preceding Ostaz El Etr's class, one of us always sneaked into the classroom and wrote out the day's poem on the blackboard. All we had to do when our turn came was rise and read it off the blackboard.

One day, the Ostaz, nearsighted as he was, realized that something fishy was going on, for Chalem's recitation was too good to be true, amidst the giggles that accompanied his masterful performance. Upon discovering our ploy, the Ostaz ordered Chalem to erase the blackboard and again recite the poem. That episode augmented Chalem's already abundant harvest of zeros. Necessity being the mother of invention, we imagined a still more devious ploy that consisted in writing out the Arabic poem using the letters of the Latin alphabet, thus:

Yukhatibuni-l safihu bi kulli qubhin
Wa akrahu an akuna lahu mugiban.
Yazidu safahatan wa azidu hilman
Ka-'udin zaadahu-l ihraqu tiban.

Which translates as:

When the fool addresses me without deference
I refrain from gratifying him with a retort.
The more impertinent he becomes, the more clement I remain
In the manner of an incense twig
That exhales its fragrance when touched by fire.

Hundreds of White Russian immigrants, many of whom belonged to the defunct aristocracy, had found refuge in Egypt when the revolution broke out in their country thirty years earlier. Princess Wolkonski, our English teacher, belonged to the Czar's family. She looked fearful with her flame-red wig tightly tucked under the black turban she never parted with. The word was unkindly passed down from generation to generation that the poor woman had lost her hair overnight when the revolutionaries massacred her family. She was one of a handful of survivors, a very young one at the time. I was one of her favorite pupils whereas my unruly brother was her *bête noire*, whom she regularly expelled from the classroom with the unvarying "Oy oy oy, quelle horreur de garçon!" Otherwise, she inflicted upon him *le piquet*, forcing him to stand at attention facing one of the corners of the classroom, head bowed and hands joined behind his back. The punishment usually lasted until the recess, unless she took pity on him and authorized him to return to his bench if he showed, or usually feigned, signs of fatigue. The princess taught me my first words of English, and patiently helped me shed my Egyptian accent, at least partly, for I believe I have kept indelible Russian traces to this day.

Counts Preobrajenski and Andreevski, both of whom once belonged to the Imperial guard, were employed as supervisors. They treated us with the brutality of Cossack officers, but we never dared complain to our parents. When their paths crossed Madame Wolkonski's, they bowed very low, clicked their heels, and kissed the tip of her haughtily outstretched hand.

Another Russian immigrant was our art teacher, Professeur Stoloff, who insisted on being addressed as *Maître*. He was short and heavy, wore his long hair artistically unsubmissive, and never parted with his floppy black bow tie. Despite his frightening facial expressions and thundering voice, we never really feared him, and his art class was deliciously chaotic. Our undisputed mischief leader Chalem never ran out of imagination when it came to putting the plaster models to unorthodox use, such as having Apollo's statue mount that of Venus. Art grades did not weigh heavily in the overall annual score, which caused his class to be consistently half-deserted without the master noticing, or perhaps even caring. I was fairly good at drawing and enjoyed his comments on my work, which were always enlightening though never charitable. He would rub his chin and declare loudly enough for the entire class to hear, "Le dessin s'adresse à l'intelligence," ('Drawing rests on intelligence'), adding that given that premise, not one of us would ever make the grade.

The White Russian community organized weekly musical evenings, usually in Andreewski's apartment, whose walls were covered with sabers, medals, brightly adorned tunics, fur hats, capes, etc. The apartment was crumbling under an odd assortment of gilded icons, orthodox crosses, and other Russian memorabilia. They drank vodka, played the balalaika, and sang nostalgic songs in chorus. They also cried a lot. I remember Suzette —I believe her mother was Russian—once telling me that they had a lot to cry about, but that in general Russians loved to cry.

During the ten o'clock recess, which lasted twenty minutes, we played at cops and robbers. No sooner had the bell rung than we scrambled downstairs, trying to beat the other boys to the center of the courtyard, where the players were being picked out by our undisputed leaders Farhi and Abul Ela (in those days, we went by family names unless we became really intimate).

First, they tossed a coin to determine who would lead the robber's gang and who would lead the police squad. That in itself took some time because we first had to find a coin, not an easy matter. The two leaders seldom carried any money at all and we, the rank and file, did not fare any better. We had to wait for the triumphant arrival of Chalem, whose father was a wealthy merchant, and whose pockets were bulging with coins. Chalem made it to the scene in a nonchalant pace, jiggling the coins in his pocket, perfectly aware of the decisive role that we expected him to play. Despite his fattish build, which made him a rather slow runner, he was always first to be picked amongst the lot, as the leaders took turns at selecting the players. We thus gained a keen awareness, early in life, of the privileges that money can buy.

As the selection progressed, the players who remained unpicked were less and less athletic, hence less and less desirable. The leftover kids would shout "Me, me!" for fear of being forsaken altogether. They were picked anyway, because since time immemorial each team had to consist of ten players. That process was not a peaceful one. The leaders usually became involved in noisy haggling because the rules of the game authorized them to acquire a coveted star player in exchange for this or that strategic advantage. Remember that we were being raised in Cairo where bargaining is an art form and an integral part of the surrounding culture.

Finally, the ritual was over and we were ready to start playing. No sooner had we decided on a strategy and taken our respective posts than the bell would ring, signaling the end of the recess. The next morning, we had to reorganize all over again. In retrospect, we perhaps enjoyed the preliminaries more than the game itself.

The school was divided through the middle into the Lycée des

Garçons and Lycée des Filles on either side of the physics and chemistry labs, the only shared premises. The labs afforded us an observation post from which we could glance at the girls on the other side while holding a test tube against the light, pretending to be looking for the mythical white precipitate, a ploy that was surely responsible for my brother's scientific vocation. A small enclave in the Lycée des Filles sheltered the Petit Lycée, a little cocoon that comprised the Kindergarten as well as the eleventh, tenth, and ninth grades. Graduating from ninth to eighth was a major event in a boy's life, for it marked the separation of the boys from the girls and their admission into the *Grand Lycée*.

Shortly after the end of the war, former prime minister Edouard Herriot visited our Lycée amidst unprecedented festivities. Classrooms smelled of chlorine, benches and blackboards received a new coat of black paint, and the little porcelain inkpots sunk in the benches were filled to the brim with violet ink. The map of France was hung on our classroom wall side by side with a large framed board entitled *Faune et flore de France* that displayed a variety of animals and flowers we had never come across in the Egyptian countryside. The courtyard was thoroughly sprayed and adorned with uncountable red, white, and blue streamers. When Herriot appeared on the balcony, flanked by Monsieur Gossart, our headmaster, and the Egyptian minister of education, a brass band played the *Salam el Malek,* the Egyptian royal anthem, followed by a dissonant *Marseillaise*. We stood at attention, each class neatly lined up in two rows behind a little tricolor shield bearing the number of our grade and the initials RF, for République Francaise.

I had just turned eight when I made the big jump from ninth grade to eighth, one year earlier than the norm, which caused me to be the shortest pupil in my class, and probably in the entire Grand Lycée. I was therefore placed in the forefront of my class and entrusted with holding the shield. Edouard Herriot stopped squarely in front of our class and patted me on the top of my head saying "Bravo, mon petit bonhomme."

From one year to the next, we would reunite with our comrades as if we had never parted. I befriended Said, who enrolled in the course of the academic year, took him under my wing, and introduced him to the tribal manners of my peers, who usually welcomed newcomers with circumspection and distrust. His build was frail and his emaciated face resembled that of Egyptian aristocrats of Turkish or Circassian origin. We soon discovered that we were both attracted by science. One morning, he introduced me to the mysteries of photography and the magic of sensitive paper, of which he carried a few sheets wrapped in a black envelope. Having taken refuge in a dark corner of the courtyard, he extracted from his pocket with infinite precautions a small white sheet, explaining that it was *virgin* and would turn black if exposed to the sun. He then pressed a little flame-tree twig against the paper, presented the lot to the rays of the sun as if it were a ritual offering, counted till five, then stuffed it in his pocket. Back in our dark corner, we marveled at the thousand ramifications of the twig, delicately printed in white against the paper's black backdrop. Alas! The evanescent pattern gradually and inexorably melted under our eyes until it vanished completely, filling us with wonder as well as sadness. "That is our common lot," said Said, "for it is written that each one of us shall sooner or later founder in the dark."

At the end of a three-month furlough spent in Alexandria, I was brimming with anticipation at the thought of reuniting with my comrades, Said in particular.

My mother bought us brand new clothes at Cicurel, and Abbas Abul Ela's little errand boy—he must have been eight or nine—delivered to our doorstep two pairs of thick-soled brown shoes that strongly smelled of leather.

The courtyard resounded with greetings and laughter. Our skin tanned by the Alexandrian sun, we frantically looked for familiar faces, exchanging impressions and stories of summer adventures. I scanned the effervescent crowd, looking for a glimpse of Said. In vain . . . .

Back in class, our teacher gravely declared, "Children, I have sad news to share with you on this first day of class. Said will not return amongst us. He died this past summer of typhoid. Bow your heads and think of him for a few moments. You may now take your seats."

I kept silent until I reached home. Back in my room, I let my school bag fall to the floor and fell on my bed in tears.

∽ What's in a Name? ∽

My first name as given at birth was Midhat, my brother's Waguih, and my sister's Ragaa. For some mysterious reason, the fancy took my father to give us French first names upon enrolling us in the Lycée Français. Until I reached fourth grade, my first name was thus Victor, my brother's Raymond, and my sister's Marlène . . . out of the blue! When I later applied for the Egyptian baccalaureate, my first name was restored, but my application was turned down unless I changed my last name from Gazalé to Ghazala, for that was the strict transliteration of our Arabic name according to a grumpy employee in the Ministry of Education. As a consequence, I went from Midhat Gazalé to Victor Gazalé to Midhat Ghazala. With our wedding imminent, my father-in-law was able to. extract from the City of Marseilles a document entitled *Acte d'individualité*, establishing that Midhat Gazalé and Midhat Ghazala were one and the same. I am grateful to him for allowing me finally to recover my original name after twenty years of schizophrenia.

My brother enrolled in the Faculty of Medicine in Montpellier under his real name, Waguih Gazalé. When he later applied for American citizenship, he changed his first name to William, preserving the initial W, but dropping the *accent aigu* on the *é* of Gazalé. That made him a true blue American, whom his associates call Bill, something he had not anticipated and which did not immeasurably please him.

My sister's first name has remained Marlene to this day, but without the accent, for she also has become an American citizen.

Faithful to an old Egyptian tradition whereby, upon the birth of the first male child, his mother is referred to as "mother of so-and-so" forever after, my mother was addressed as "Mother of Waguih" as far back as I can recall. Never mind me! My uncle Antoine, art teacher at the Heliopolis Lycée Français, is remembered by generations of students. His wife, Tante Ratiba, bore four children, all of whose first names begin with the letter W: Wafik, Wafaa, Wessam, and Walaa. God knows why! Wafaa married Wasfy (coincidence or destiny?) and in turn gave birth to four children, all of whose names also begin with W. Whether because Christian names beginning with W are rare, or because of another tradition I may not be aware of, the children were named Walaa, Weam, Wessal, and Wessam—three girls and a boy twelve years younger than his elder sister, upon whose birth Wafaa became "Mother of Wessam."

My mother's maiden name was Georgette Debs. When my father suffered a stroke while visiting me in 1955, she attempted to have her Egyptian passport renewed in order to join us in Paris. These were the days when the lowliest Nasserite civil servant could decide on a whim whether to let you travel or not. As it turned out, it was easier to have a new passport issued than an old passport renewed, for that required the husband's authorization, and my father was in no condition to fill in a myriad forms. Had she applied for a new passport under her real name, she feared some zealous civil servant would discover her ploy, despite the legendary bureaucratic chaos that pervaded the administration. Someone suggested that she borrow the name of her sister, who had died at birth and was christened Adèle. My mother was torn between the anguish of not being able to join my ailing father, and that of committing that sacrilegious imposture. However, she received the blessing of the church where she was baptized, and which kept exact records of its flock. Her passport was issued in no time and she was able to fly to Paris within days.

Several years later, whenever my children teased her about her age, asking her what year she was born, she would simply reply, "Adèle was born in 1910," and refuse to belabor the matter further. The only thing we ever knew with certainty was that she was born on a Fourteenth of July, the French national holiday.

~ Ismailiya and Soliman Pasha Squares ~

We lived on Mariette Pasha Street, which owed its name to a French Egyptologist born in 1821 of modest parents in Boulogne-sur-Mer. He discovered the fabulous treasures of Saqqara, west of the Giza pyramids, which my brother and I never failed to admire from our balcony against the setting sun's ball of fire.

Mariette pillaged Egyptian antiques, shipping thousands of pieces to France, among them *The Scribe*, one of the Louvre's most valuable possessions. Upon being elevated to the dignity of bey, then pasha, by Viceroy Said, he went from looter to staunch defender of Egypt's millenary heritage. The museum he created in 1863 received so many new pieces over the years that it had to be moved to its present location in 1902, across the street from our apartment.

Following his death in 1881, he was succeeded by Maspero, another Frenchman, who interred his illustrious predecessor in a sarcophagus underneath a small pharaonic mausoleum facing the museum's entrance. On hot summer evenings, my brother and I often sat on the balcony to do our homework. Two or three stories below, one of our neighbors, obviously very fond of oriental music, turned on his radio every night with his windows wide open, affording our studious pair a delightfully mellow musical background. It was as though the music rose from within the museum, and we loved to fantasize that the palace musicians and dancers were performing for the pharaoh.

"We live in the heart of French archaeology!" proudly exclaimed my father, for Mariette Pasha Street was perpendicular to Maspero, Champollion, and Antikkhana streets, the latter word meaning 'antiquities museum' in Turkish.

Midan Soliman Pasha, the focus of Cairo's cosmopolitan life, was only five minutes away. Built in 1924, the celebrated Groppi's tearoom adorned one of its corners with its beautiful arched entrance and art deco mosaics. Every afternoon, having emerged from their naps and abundantly dabbed their faces with lavender cologne, idle French-speaking Cairenes met for tea and pastry to the music of a skimpy European chamber orchestra, unless they crossed the street to Café Riche, the rendezvous of intellectuals, political activists, and artists. Soliman Pasha's statue stood in the middle of the square, facing the street that bore his name. Converging on the roundabout, Soliman Pasha and Qasr el Nil streets were the most Parisian of all.

Soliman Pasha was none other than Colonel Sève, a French officer who contributed to three of Napoleon's most disastrous defeats, then converted to Islam and changed his name. He was placed by Muhammad Ali at the head of the new Egyptian regiments in 1819, eight years after Bonaparte's defeat at the hands of the British, and later elevated to pasha. We only vaguely knew that his great-grand-daughter Nazli had married King Fuad and given birth to King Farouk in 1920. Soliman was buried in Cairo under a charming cast-iron pavilion, not far from his wife Maryam.[16]

I remember Cinema Miami, Cinema La Potinière with its open-air theater, and the festive opening of Cinema Metro, the only place in town with air-conditioning and wall to wall carpeting, where *Gone with the Wind* was premiered as World War II raged.[17] All three cinemas stood within walking distance of one another on either side of Soliman Pasha Street. Little did we know that La Potinière, named after the Parisian Théatre de la Potinière, meant 'gossip corner' in French, and that Miami was a faraway American summer resort. The Italian owner of Cinema Miami, Mr. Bianco, who lived on the fourth floor of our building, offered my parents a permanent pass that entitled us to sit in the first-tier box every Saturday afternoon, a major contribution to our vast cinematic culture. I owe my command of English and my hatred of the Nazis to Hollywood's MGM, RKO, 20th Century Fox, Universal Studios, United Artists, etc. We did not discover French films until after the war, without much enthusiasm I must confess, as we felt little kinship with Jean Gabin's scabrous adventures or Maurice Chevalier's Parisian pranks, despite our fluency in French. One of the few exceptions was Jacques Tati's *Jour de fête*.

The luxurious stores bordering Soliman Pasha Street bore foreign names, written in French. They closed on Sunday, and remained open on Friday, the Muslim holiday.

En route to the Lycée, we crossed Ismailiya Square, facing the infamous British barracks, a daily reminder of their colonial presence on our soil. The square owed its name to Khedive Ismail, who was remembered for the lavish festivities that accompanied the Suez Canal opening, eventually dragging Egypt into bankruptcy. At the request of the French and British, Ismail was exiled to Turkey. En route to Emitgan, he paid a visit to King Umberto of Italy at the Favorita Palace. He died in exile in 1879, three years before the bombardment of Alexandria by the British.

From our balconies, we could see 'Tommies' from all over the British Commonwealth parading on Empire Day and other similar occasions — Scotsmen in tartan kilts, bearded Sikhs, Aussies wearing Indiana Jones hats. We became familiar with their marches and their nostalgic songs. To this day, I cannot help being stirred by the sound of a bagpipe, poignant, proud, and heroic.

Upon reaching Ismailiya Square, we passed the famous Issaievitch restaurant which served the most legendary *foul* and *falafel*[18] sandwiches in town. The place was owned by two brothers, probably Yugoslavian, and had become the rendezvous of the city's patrician *jeunesse dorée*, who relished that poor man's delicacy. One of the brothers sat at the cash register, perched atop a platform near the entrance, from which he kept a suspicious eye on the comings and goings in his establishment. The server ladled the steaming beans out of a large spherical copper kettle into the warm freshly baked Syrian bread and seasoned them with oil, adding a dab of salt that he scooped out of a tin bowl with a scruffy teaspoon. Issaievitch was particularly vigilant when our group of Lycée students was being catered to, because we often slipped the server a minuscule bakshish in exchange for a surreptitiously generous serving, causing the owner to grumble in the server's direction "Lighter, your hand, lighter!" probably the only Arabic words he knew.

Upon leaving the square, we would pass the barbershop where we had our once-a-month haircuts, then the Astra milk bar,[19] where a mixed crowd of Lycée and American University students daily flocked. The milk bar also attracted a group of handsome young Egyptian army officers who idly palavered over a milkshake, and sometimes merrily chatted up the girls in English.

Little did we suspect that the Astra milk bar was precisely the place where a group of young officers, perhaps the very ones we knew, plotted to assassinate finance minister Amin Osman Pasha on January 6, 1946. They were led by an obscure lieutenant named Anwar el-Sadat.

The Miracle

Abraham lived in Egypt for a time; Joseph was Pharaoh's minister there; Moses "was trained in all the wisdom of the Egyptians" (Acts 7:22) . . . . Jesus found refuge on the banks of the Nile.

Christian Cannuyer[20]

At school, my brother and I discovered strange new names that were foreign to our ears, such as Chalem, Levy, or Bensoussan. My father explained that these names belonged to the Jewish people, a community we had never before come across. They all spoke French, though Matzner and Falk spoke German when they played together. The mystery became thicker when Maurice Bensoussan asked me to his birthday party. His grandmother spoke Spanish and served little strange-tasting biscuits called *rosquettes*. My confusion reached its peak upon learning from Falk that his grandparents spoke something called Yiddish.

Most of my classmates went neither to church nor mosque, but to the synagogue, a word that sounded mysterious and somewhat foreboding. On Friday evenings, I often bumped into them in the center of Cairo, where most of us lived. They were on their way to the synagogue with their parents and wore little caps on the back of their heads that were secured with little metallic pins. More than once, I had hoped that Bensoussan would ask me to accompany him, but he peremptorily replied that, not speaking Hebrew, I would not understand what was going on.

Upon learning that a rabbi gave him private Hebrew lessons, I became very frustrated at the thought that he was learning something that I was not. Having decided to emulate him, I asked my mother to arrange for the rabbi to come to our house and teach me Hebrew. Needless to say, I never learned Hebrew, and it was not until one of my close friends married several years later that I finally discovered what the inside of a synagogue looked like.

Our nextdoor neighbors were Jewish, and their children also went to the Lycée. Both were particularly brilliant, and Molly, the younger of the two, always made it to the top of her class. No sooner had she finished her homework than she came knocking on our door, asking my mother if I had also finished mine and if she could come in and play. We spent hours in my room, busily playing at all sorts of games. I would show her my latest inventions and sometimes make them up as I spoke. She would show me her drawings and let me read her poems.

Their religious holidays were different from ours, though they sometimes coincided, Passover with Easter, and Hanukkah with Christmas. During Passover, they ate unleavened bread that looked slightly burnt and tasted vaguely like the eucharistic host. I remember my mother cautioning us never to get close to their apartment if we carried bread, for fear of infecting them with something called yeast. That word elicited in our minds the pungent smell of milk that had curdled in the heat of summer. For some reason, we were immune to that sort of predicament and the Jews were not. We therefore took great care not to contaminate them.

Molly had just learned the Seder, a kind of question and answer game they played during Passover, where the smallest child in the family asked his parents why the bread was baked without yeast, why food had to be soaked, why they had to drink lying down and eat bitter herbs. Molly resolved to teach me the game, and we took turns at questioning and answering each other.

The Seder stories had to do with the suffering their people had endured upon being forced by Pharaoh to leave Egypt. I could not quite fathom what terrible crime they had committed. Except for their strange habits and their lack of fluency in Arabic, they were very much like the rest of us. I was troubled, though, by her account of the plagues that befell my country in response to their prophet's imprecations. I had learned in catechism that God was love and forgiveness, and knew no vengeance.

Be that as it may, I was relieved at the thought that these events were a thing of the distant past, since Molly's people had safely returned to Egypt by now, and the little Jewish girl could freely play with her Egyptian neighbor.

During Hanukkah, the Jewish Festival of Lights, our neighbors lit one candle of a nine branch candelabra on the first day, two on the second day, and so on, during eight days in a row. The ninth candle served to light the other eight. Once, due to grave family circumstances in Alexandria—one of the grandmothers was dying—they had to leave unexpectedly. They were in the midst of Hanukkah, and had only lit four candles. As my mother offered her sympathy on our doorstep, Molly's mother asked her if she wouldn't mind lighting the remaining four candles as she handed her the silver candelabra. My mother of course accepted and promised to light the candles diligently. She was extremely superstitious though, and I have a sneaking suspicion that once entrusted with that mission, she feared some terrible misfortune would befall our family should she not fulfill her promise. She placed the candelabra atop a console in one of the rooms, remarking that it looked rather nice after all. The following day, as I walked into the room to bid my Mother good morning, I found her kneeling on a pillow in front of the candelabra. I did not interrupt her, for she was praying. She repeated that ritual every morning. No sooner had the eighth candle burned out than the doorbell rang. The neighbors were back, and the grandmother had miraculously recovered. "You are a saint, Madame Gazalé," exclaimed Molly's mother as she kissed mine.

Bensoussan invited me to his Bar Mitzvah, which he described as the equivalent of our First Communion. I was dismayed not to attend the ceremony at the synagogue, for I was only invited to the party that took place in his apartment. Bensoussan was very excited as he opened several envelopes that contained monetary gifts, and lined up an impressive collection of wallets and Parker fountain pens, as well as four or five wristwatches.

For my First Communion, I received mostly books, with the exception of a single fountain pen, a gift of my mother's closest friend Carolina, a Romanian Jew. My mother had told her that the First Communion was a kind of Bar Mitzvah. I used to call her Tante Nina, for we always called our parents' closest friends Uncle or Aunt. It was several years before I realized that Tante Isis, Tante Angèle and Tante Emilie were my father's sisters in actuality, whereas Tante Nina, Tante Becky, Tante Waheeda, and Tante Rose were not related to our family. The thought that Tante Nina and Tante Becky were Jewish and Tante Waheeda Muslim never crossed my mind.

In the course of the coaching that we received before the big day, Father Augustin Buisson, a Canadian priest, told us the story of Napoleon who, upon being asked whether his coronation or the Austerlitz victory was the most beautiful day of his life, simply replied, "My First Communion." I therefore woke up that morning repeating to myself that I was about to experience the most beautiful day of my life. The Grand Mass at St Joseph's was awesome, and I shivered irrepressibly as the big bells rang. The girls sat on the left side of the aisle in their virginal wedding-like dresses and white gloves, with the mother of pearl rosaries wrapped around their missals. We sat on the opposite side, proudly sporting our white silk armbands wrapped around the left arm, on the heart's side.

It was a beautiful day indeed, for my grandfather, who seldom left the big house, attended the service and gave me ten gold pounds. A fortune! Also on that day, I met Yvette, a frail and sensitive young girl whose family had just moved into our building. She taught me the Lambeth Walk and I offered her a huge serving of chestnut filled *mont-blanc* that Molly's mother had baked for the occasion, and an equally large portion of cream-filled *kunafa* that my own mother had baked. I believe she kissed me on the cheek.

By some accident of history, my family is Coptic Catholic, whereas most Egyptian Copts are Orthodox.[21] As a child, I attended High Mass at the Armenian church, which was Catholic as well as close to home.[22] What really inspired me to choose that particular venue was the prospect of sitting next to Huguette, the youngest of three exceptionally beautiful sisters, as we awaited our turn to enter the confessional. Huguette, who could have been fifteen or perhaps less, wore a navy blue skirt, a white blouse, long white socks, and patent-leather shoes buttoned on one side. The sisters also wore little berets, probably imported from Belgium, their family's homeland.

The redoubtable bearded priest asked all sorts of indiscreet questions regarding not only our deeds but also our innermost thoughts. We were going through adolescence, and our imagination was inhabited by a multitude of romantic fantasies inspired by the American films of the day, where the lovers at last exchanged the long awaited kiss near the end of the picture, sealing their imminent marriage. These thoughts were nonetheless deemed sinful by the unforgiving priest, and the penance inflicted upon us was sometimes so tedious that mass would be said before we could partake of Holy Communion. In those days, we could only receive the host on an empty stomach, and my brother's penance was usually so interminable that he actually fainted one Sunday in a church charged with the heady smell of flowers, incense, and burnt-out candles.

Huguette and I never spoke, but spent several years innocently exchanging sidelong glances during mass.

Decades later, I find it quite extraordinary that the photograph chosen to accompany Arthur Rimbaud's biography in my French encyclopedia shows a charmingly shy young boy clad in first communion attire. And yet the sensuous revolutionary poet, in his short thirty-seven years, had laid the foundations of symbolism and even surrealism, obviously a lesser claim to fame than his First Communion.

⟋ First Cigarette ⟍

From atop this pyramid
forty centuries are watching you.

Bonaparte to his troops

It was our last year in the Lycée Français, and we were looking forward to the *Baccalauréat* with apprehension as well as anticipation. The Baccalauréat was a quasi- magical event that marked the end of our college years, a time of our lives filled with bliss and insouciance.

After much anguish and many sleepless nights, the Baccalauréat results were finally out. With few exceptions, our entire class had made the grade, and we decided to celebrate our success by riding our bicycles to the pyramids, climbing atop Cheops, and smoking our first cigarette. Our group of six boys convened at Soliman Pasha Square under the big clock. That initiation rite was not meant for fragile young girls from good families, and the unavowed object of our expedition was precisely to impress them with our daring and endurance, not to mention defying our parents.

At nine o'clock sharp, we started pedaling in the direction of the pyramids. Our first stop took us to a dingy cigarette shop where we each purchased a ten-pack of Hollywood cigarettes, the cheapest brand available, that we stuffed into our pockets with the detached air of true connoisseurs. We also bought one matchbox for six, then resumed our journey in the shade of the eucalyptus trees.

When we reached our destination, Nessim, who had never been that close to the pyramid, was so impressed by its majesty and the size of its massive stones, that he decided to forego the climb and sit in the shade, where he volunteered to keep an eye on our bicycles. He was actually rather fat, and sheepishly confessed that he was afraid of heights. Having someone guard our machines was a welcome initiative anyway, and we expressed our gratitude by offering him one cigarette each after reassuring him that we would not say a word to the girls. "Had I known," he said, "I would have bought a chocolate éclair instead of cigarettes!"

The authorized path to the top was carefully marked out and it was required that you be accompanied by a dragoman[23] in exchange for the inescapable bakshish. We defiantly resolved to climb the monument on our own, on the opposite side of the pyramid. We soon realized how reckless that initiative was when the dust that blanketed the better part of the stones started crumbling under our feet with each block we climbed, sometimes causing us to fall dangerously backwards.

I do not remember how long it took to reach the wide, square area where the pyramidion once stood, twenty-six hundred years before the birth of Christ. The platform was covered with graffiti, some dating back to the ancient Greeks, the Romans, the French, etc. I imagined my ancestors laying the ultimate stone at that awesome height thirty years after their fathers laid the ground stones.

I also imagined Napoleon Bonaparte haranguing his harrowed soldiers at the foot of the monument, boasting that forty centuries were contemplating them from atop the pyramids.

The view of Cairo beyond the Nile's glittering thin line was breathtakingly crisp beneath the deep blue sky. Slightly to the left, the Mena House hotel and the village of Nazlat el Samman, a dense patch of bluish-gray palm trees, contrasted with the surrounding sand. I could distinctly hear the peasants' palaver and the roar of a camel rising from below, amidst the desert's millennial silence. Nessim looked minuscule as an ant, sitting in the pyramid's shade next to the pile of bicycles.

My friends were joyously horsing around, trying to catch their breath, oblivious to the beauty that surrounded them. We finally sat down and conscientiously lit our cigarettes, protecting them from the wind with our cupped hands. I fantasized that we were celebrating some kind of pharaonic rite, though it vaguely seemed to me that ancient Egyptians did not smoke. We had been told that once you drew your first puff, you had to take a deep breath before exhaling. The ensuing exhibition of coughing and choking was a sight to behold. My head madly twisting and twirling, I lost my cigarette and firmly pressed both palms against the stone beneath me, hoping to remain upright.

A minute or so later, I opened my eyes and saw Cairo dancing on the horizon. I was no longer nauseous, but experienced a strange feeling of exhilaration. I was happy to be alive. I was happy to be sitting on top of the Great Pyramid with the desert wind blowing on my face. My parents were alive and well. So were my brother and sister as well as every person I loved. I had just obtained the coveted Baccalauréat, and my future was unfolding in front of my eyes like a white sail on my beloved Nile, pregnant with great achievements to come.

We gave the remaining cigarettes to the dragoman, who had been furiously swearing and cursing at the foot of the pyramid, and that miraculously appeased him.

I never climbed the pyramid again. Every time I visit the Giza plateau, I fall pray to an indescribable ecstasy.

～ First Love ～

History is what happened;
Poetry is what could have happened.

Aristotle

Cairo seemed destined to last forever. The perennial smell of freshly cut grass filled the Sporting Club's evening air as we danced on the edge of the pool to the wartime tunes of Glenn Miller or Tommy Dorsey. The girls wore necklaces of threaded buds of *foll*, an Egyptian variety of jasmine, which encircled their frail necks and exhaled a heady perfume. We were always careful not to betray the mad pace of our heartbeat as we gently pressed their breasts against ours.

Nicette's skin was fair and her hair as black as her eyes. As we were once dancing a slow, I asked her what perfume she wore, and she confessed it was Soir de Paris or some other Parisian fragrance she had borrowed from her beautiful and elegant mother. I went to bed that night breathing the palm of my left hand until I fell asleep.

I could never muster enough courage to declare my feelings but fiercely carved her name on bench after bench as the years went by and we graduated from one class to the next. How enraged I became upon discovering that her name had already been engraved by some older bloke and could still be deciphered in spite of the heavy coat of black paint that was applied every summer over the previous year's.

We referred to those carvings as our hieroglyphs. Our history teacher had once recounted the legend of Senenmut, Queen Hatshepsut's architect and lover, who, upon finishing the terraces leading to her magnificent temple in Deir el Bahari, had secretly carved his name in a hidden corner of the monumental structure.

When morning classes were out, I dashed from the boy's side of the massive building to the opposite side, where the girls would be trickling out of the large gate, slowly dragging their feet to afford the boys a chance to catch up and walk them home. I would offer to carry Nicette's heavy school bag, but she seldom accepted, reluctant as she was to reveal any particular preference, and stubbornly pressed it against her chest until we reached her house. I was relatively good at math, and she often asked me to help her understand this or that problem. We would stop around the corner, where I supplied her with protracted explanations, hoping that she would ask more questions and that the sessions would never end. Upon reaching home, I would rush to my room where a large calendar hung above my desk, consisting of large glossy sheets adorned with Egyptian landscapes. If I had caught sight of Nicette on a given day, I would draw a Horus eye next to the day's number, and if I had had the good fortune of walking her home, I would draw an *ankh*, the symbol of life. My brother always quizzed me about the significance of these hieroglyphs, but I never revealed my secret to anyone, least of all Nicette.

How many times, having finished my homework, would I dash back to Bustan Street and just stand there, across the street from number 13, hoping that she would perchance show up and trot along with her thick black hair bouncing up and down.

I remember the annual Russian charity ball at the Auberge des Pyramides to which Nicette and her best friend Suzette were invited. My brother and I had the privilege of escorting the young demoiselles.

The Auberge, as it was fondly called by the habitués, was a European-style night club on the Pyramids Road that attracted idle noctambulant Europeans and wealthy Egyptians. Though Egypt jealously guarded its Muslim traditions, alcohol freely flowed at the Auberge while scantily clad showgirls from the Folies Bergère and other similar European venues performed on stage. The Auberge was looked upon by most Egyptians as the rendezvous of Cairene debauchery, at the center of which floppily sat Farouk, almost nightly—though he never indulged in alcohol.

Like a child, the insouciant king was throwing paper streamers at the ladies. I was petrified at the thought that he might invite Nicette or Suzette to his table, an offer that could cost them dear if they turned it down. The monarch was in the habit of dispatching his aide-de-camp to the tables of the most beautiful ladies and inviting them to the royal table, then to the palace. My mother's best friend, whom I fondly called Tante Rose, was exceptionally beautiful, and her fiancé, a Greek ship owner, often took her to the Auberge where she loved to dance to the tunes of the day. That night, Farouk noticed her and dispatched his pimp to their table as usual. The couple conveyed their apologies to the king, arguing that they had to leave urgently. Tante Rose's fiancé was given exactly twenty-four hours to leave the country. Had it not been for my mother's presence of mind, Tante Rose would not have survived her suicide attempt, having ingested her entire supply of sleeping pills.

I wore a tuxedo for the first time in my life, and Nicette's lipstick, which never went beyond light pink at our parties, was surprisingly red that night. As I am trying to recollect her features, which are now blurred by the years, I remember the pure line of her upper lip. I danced with her till dawn, but never told her of the fire that burned inside my adolescent heart, and never returned to the Auberge des Pyramides.

One Sunday morning—we were in early March 1946 and I was not yet seventeen—Nicette, Suzette, my brother, and I had thoroughly prepared ourselves for a bicycle ride to the pyramids. The previous day, we had taken our machines to the bicycle shop in Bab el Luq, where the mechanic had inflated the tires, tightened the loose spokes with his special tool, aligned the front wheel by firmly holding it between his knees as he twisted and untwisted the handlebar, greased the chain, and finally adjusted the saddle's height in case we had grown taller in the course of the year. Suzette was wearing a long ample skirt, and Nicette a pair of white shorts that she usually wore when playing tennis at the Sporting Club.

We pedaled in the direction of the pyramids in the shade of the eucalyptus trees until we came to a field that exhaled the fragrance of orange blossoms. We stopped our bicycles and asked a peasant if we could rest under one of his trees. "Alf marhaba," ('A thousand welcomes') was his reply. He then ran to the far corner of his field and came back with a traditional earthen jar filled with cold water. My brother and I drank wholeheartedly, for we had developed the appropriate antibodies over years of secretly drinking from similar jars on hot summer days. The girls politely thanked him, patting their chest with their hand, signifying that they were not thirsty. My brother made to give him a little coin, but the peasant turned it down, saying, "Not for water, my son. Not for water." He waited until we were finished, took the jar, and disappeared amidst the orange trees.

We sat in the grass, the girls having delicately folded their legs to one side with their round knees neatly joined. We joyously chatted, making more or less charitable comments on this or that student in our class.

I planted two sticks of different lengths in the ground and attempted to explain how the Greek mathematician Thales, as early as the sixth century B.C., calculated the pyramids' height by measuring the length of its shadow as well as his own, then applying the rule of proportionality learned in class. How exhilarating, I thought, to be able to talk about that historic achievement at the very foot of the pyramid.[24] How privileged we were to be living in Egypt.

At that point, Nicette's knee caught my eye, and I noticed her thighs for the first time. From the knees down, her skin was tan from being exposed to the Cairo sun. The inside of her thighs, however, was extraordinarily white. As I gazed at the gentle transition between dark and light, I felt a fiery urge to kiss her exactly there. I had a vision of the Nile flowing between her thighs into a warm fertile delta. My heart was pounding so violently that I decided to look away. I jumped to my feet and walked around, pretending to be contemplating the pyramids. I said, "Do you also get the impression, seen from here, that Chephren is taller than Cheops?" My brother, who I am sure had been absorbed by the girls' legs as well as every other attribute, and shamelessly enjoying every minute of it, idly replied that it was only the perspective.

Thereupon, we decided to ride back to town. I felt a bitter taste in my mouth. How silly of me, I thought, to be boring the girls with Thales and the pyramid's height instead of letting them savor the fragrance of orange blossoms.

The last time I saw Nicette was in the fall of 1946. The Lycée years were over and our adolescence gone. I enrolled in the Faculty of Engineering and embarked upon a different voyage.

⤳ The War Years ⤵

⤳ El Alamein ⤵

Your enemy's enemy is not your friend;
he is twice your enemy.

I was a small child when the war broke out, but I remember those black days as if it were yesterday—the air raids, the deafening sound of bombs and anti-aircraft guns, the powerful beams of bluish light feverishly scanning the night sky, and the unmistakable sound of German and Italian bombers above our heads.

We would be awakened in the middle of the night by the intermittent blare of sirens, and scramble in the dark to the second floor of our building where the Hamaoui family's apartment served as a makeshift air raid shelter. We had been told by the authorities that the second floor of a five-story building was the safest, and we lived on the top floor, the worst of all. The terrace above our apartment was blanketed with sandbags, a derisory shield against incendiary bombs. Long after the war was over, the sandbags had not been removed, and we played at bursting them open and spreading the sand on the terrace, transforming it into a makeshift beach, albeit without a sea. Such was the fate of countless endeavors whose vestiges outlived their original purpose, in the manner of those ancient tombs whose long-gone dwellers had fallen into oblivion. Our windows were painted blue and crisscrossed with bands of paper-tape intended to prevent shattered glass from flying all over the place. The paper-tape pattern resembled the Union Jack, which caused our maid to be torn between the dread that the British flag might attract enemy bombers, and the no less superstitious belief that it could repel them and protect our household. Our apartment was dangerously close to the British Qasr el Nil barracks, and hundreds of neighboring civilian apartments had been forcibly requisitioned to house allied soldiers.

Despite my parent's admonitions, my brother loved to watch the fireworks and would always be last to leave his room. Once, as he stood squarely in front of the window, he shouted "Bombers, fighters!" I rushed to his side, and against the backdrop of a full moon in the cloudless Cairo sky, whether we actually witnessed an aerial battle or simply wished we had, the sight of exploding anti-aircraft shells filled us with awe and exhilarating trepidation. My father swiftly put an end to that grandiose show as he tugged my brother by the ear away from the window. We never saw the outcome of that battle.

The previous summer in Alexandria, having heard that an Italian plane had crashed nearby, my brother and I had rushed to Cleopatra beach where we sometimes went swimming with our cousins. There we saw the partly immersed wreckage of an Italian bomber, probably a Savoia Marchetti. On the sand nearby lay the pilot's intact body, flat on his back, with the brown leather helmet crowning his peaceful boyish face. A large silent crowd had gathered around him and stood stricken with stupor. An old Egyptian woman emerged from the crowd, quietly crouched down in the sand, and lifted the pilot's head before gently putting it to rest on her lap. As she rocked her body back and forth, I could hear muted prayers in Arabic, French, Greek, and Italian all around me.

The previous night, we had rushed one more time to the shelter where, amidst the chaos and deafening noise, someone said, "Questo è un aereo Italiano, lo sento!" ('This is an Italian airplane, I can hear it!').

I cannot erase from my mind the vision of that young man putting on his flying-suit one summer evening, then climbing aboard his airplane never again to see his beloved homeland.

Many Egyptians loathed the British occupier and regarded Hitler's National Socialism as the emerging paradigm of national independence and social progress. Hitler, who was aware of Farouk's penchant for German cars, offered the king a superb red and black coupe and dispatched the infamous Dr. Goebbels to Egypt on April 6, 1939. Rudolf Hess later visited Alexandria, his birthplace, in defiance of that city's large Jewish population.

As Samir Raafat describes it, "A month later, in May 1939, it would be the turn of the Italian Governor-General of Libya, Air Marshal Italo Balbo, to visit Cairo. Count Mazolini, the cocky Italian Minister in Egypt, was already ruffling his feathers." [25] That tragi-comic unyielding determination by the Germans and Italians to upstage one another was masterfully illustrated by Charles Chaplin's *The Great Dictator* in 1940. The film's showing in Cairo was a major social event, and everyone flocked to the cinema to hear Chaplin's voice for the first time. We had seen all of his silent movies, without exception.

In November of that year, as we listened to the BBC one morning, the speaker announced that the town of Coventry had been all but wiped out. More than five hundred Luftwaffe bombers had pounded the city all night, killing thousands of civilians. My anguished mother asked my father if that meant that the British would soon give in to Hitler. France had capitulated in June, and the German advance seemed irresistible.

It was rumored that a pact between Hitler and Mussolini would leave Egypt to Italy by virtue of the latter's presence in Libya and Ethiopia. It was also rumored that Mussolini, who was devoured by the ambition to build an African empire, intended to parade in the streets of Alexandria mounted on a white horse, following in the footsteps of Julius Caesar. I remember the girls rehearsing the Fascist youth anthem *Giovinezza* every morning in the courtyard of the Italian Franciscan Sisters School that bordered our apartment house.

The Muslim Brotherhood and Young Egypt were gaining momentum in the country as Rommel's troops dangerously advanced along the North African seashore, getting closer and closer to Egypt's borders.[26]

In February 1942, King Farouk refused to break diplomatic relations with Vichy, causing Prime Minister Hussein Sirry to tender his resignation indignantly, and British ambassador Lord Killearn, alias Sir Miles Lampson, to order the French embassy closed.

To the British, the hour was obviously grave. On the fourth of February, Lampson stationed his tanks outside Farouk's palace and, having been asked by Hassanein Pasha to leave his two armed escorts in the anteroom, he stormed the king's study and threatened to depose him unless he appointed Nahas Pasha—a popular figure at the time—prime minister. Adding insult to injury, the abdication papers were drafted on British Embassy stationery.

Because he had sided with the allies, Nahas came to be viewed as pro-British and lost much of his luster. At one fell swoop, Lampson was able to discredit the king and the leading pro-independence party as well.[27]

In the summer of 1942, following a series of defeats inflicted upon the Allies between the Mediterranean shore and the Qattara Depression, Rommel's troops crossed Egypt's western border and reached the town of El Alamein, 65 miles west of Alexandria. The newspapers even reported that a German scout had lost his way and entered Alexandria on his motorcycle. Egyptian throngs freely demonstrated in the streets chanting "Forward, Rommel!" The Alexandrian beaches of Stanley and Sidi Bishr looked eerily empty, most Jews having refrained from vacationing dangerously close to El Alamein. Italian males were parked in concentration camps, and the Greek and Italian populations were pitted against one another. It was not uncommon to witness street fights between adolescents of the two nationalities.

In those days, it was not unusual to read in the press that a group of German travelers had lost their way in the Western Desert. As it turned out, their expeditions were intended to plot every inch of the uncharted terrain. That summer, a German spy named Eppler was arrested in Cairo, leading to the demotion of Anwar el-Sadat and his detention in the Zeitoun prison, together with a number of Syrian and Lebanese citizens who had offered their services to the Vichy government.[28]

In his autobiography,[29] Sadat later wrote:

It was agreed that one of us would be sent to El Alamein to tell Rommel we were honest Egyptians who had an organization within the army; that, 'like you,' we were fighting the British; that we were prepared to recruit an entire army to fight 'on your side,' and to provide him with photographs showing the lines and positions of the British forces in Egypt; and we would take it upon us not to let one British soldier leave Cairo, in return for granting Egypt complete independence so that we would not be given to Italy or fall under German domination, and so no one whatsoever would interfere in her affairs internal or external . . . . At last, I thought, we should be able to communicate with Rommel and to present our terms for cooperation . . . . Rommel might be in Cairo any minute now, I reckoned; if that happened without prior agreement, that is, if Rommel didn't know of our resistance to the British and the assistance our organisation was willing to give him in return for Egypt's independence, the British occupation of our country might be replaced by another—whether German or Italian. The only way out of that impasse was to contact Rommel directly.

In retrospect, I can imagine what Molly felt with the Germans standing at the doors of Alexandria. She told me what little she had overheard of her parent's conversations, and most of her poems had to do with the Germans and their cruelty to Jewish children.

One morning, I asked Falk and Matzner why their countrymen were so cruel. It turned out that their own families had fled Germany and sought refuge in Egypt, where the British were standing guard. I had not realized that they too were Jewish, and promised not to reveal that terrible secret to anyone.

I do not recall that our neighbors had made any plans to flee the country. What were they waiting for? Were they resigned? Were they hoping, against all odds, that the irresistible German advance would miraculously stop? Remaining in their apartment was suicidal.

I remembered Molly's Seder stories, and was overwhelmed with sadness at the thought that, following in her forebears steps, her own turn had come to leave Egypt.

In July of that year, Winston Churchill paid a secret visit to Egypt. In September, he relieved General Auchinleck and placed the Eighth Army under the command of Marshal (then General) Bernard Law Montgomery, who had served in France and Belgium when the war broke out. On October 24, in the course of the historic battle of El Alamein, he crushed the German front, changing the course of World War II. He was later raised to the peerage as First Viscount of Alamein, and died in 1976.

As the fierce battle of El Alamein was raging, the Cairo barracks became the scene of incessant comings and goings. For my part, I was bedridden with recurrent fever, an infectious disease that entails repeated episodes of fever, sometimes accompanied by attacks of delirium. The epidemic had entered Egypt from Libya, the scene of violent battles between the axis powers and the allies, causing uninterrupted troop movements across the country's western border.

As I lay in bed with my eyes wide open, I had visions of interminable convoys of army trucks roaring at the foot of my bed, and begged my mother to stop the procession. She told me to calm down, reassuring me that the trucks were not in my room but on the street outside. "Come and see for yourself," she said as she helped me to the balcony. I leaned over the railing and was petrified by what I saw. Hundreds upon hundreds of open military trucks were rolling in one direction within inches of one another, packed with clean-cut soldiers in full battledress, while hundreds upon hundreds of ramshackle trucks rolled in the opposite direction, packed with harassed, worn out soldiers, many of them wearing bloodstained bandages. The two contingents were within yards of one another, with the harrowed bunch flashing the V-for-Victory sign to the relieving guard.

The barracks were eventually torn down under Gamal Abdel Nasser, along with several other symbols of British occupation. In 1955, the Nile Hilton was erected exactly where the barracks once stood, and the immense courtyard became el Tahrir ('Liberation') Square.

Fourteen years after El Alamein, Molly and her parents were forced to leave Egypt anyway. Their exodus was a consequence of the 1956 attack on Port Fuad and Port Said by a coalition of Israeli, English, and French armed forces.

The attack also dealt a deadly blow to French interests in Egypt and led to the demise of our cherished Lycée, where we had spent so many happy carefree years.

~ The Chocolate Cake ~

Toward the end of World War II, we came across American GIs for the first time. They all looked tall and lanky in their impeccable uniforms, with their neckties tucked between the second and third buttons of their neatly ironed shirts, in contrast to the British Tommies whose attire was generally shabby and tired. It seemed like an army of the rich and an army of the poor fighting side by side. We had been eagerly looking forward to seeing and touching those mythical characters, most of whom, we fantasized, came from Atlanta where they grew up with Clark Gable and Vivien Leigh, or like Mickey Rooney and Spencer Tracy, alias Thomas Edison, had stopped a runaway train in their childhood and invented the gramophone in their later years.

Their pockets were filled with Mars bars, Hershey's chocolate, or Spearmint chewing gum, and they joyously shared their goodies with the children on the street. They once gave my brother an Eversharp fountain pen whose streamlined shape I remember to this day. Another time, they gave me a large khaki flashlight whose sheer weight was impressive. I used it parsimoniously, for Eveready batteries of that size were very hard to come by. They never stopped giving us all sorts of things, for we lacked everything. We were emerging from a protracted war and suffered many hardships amidst the chronic underdevelopment brought about by centuries of occupation by foreign powers.

One day, my father came home very excited, telling my mother she wouldn't believe what he was about to tell her:

"I ran into a bunch of young American GIs who had lost their way. After expressing surprise at my command of English, they asked me if I knew what chocolate cake was, and whether they could find any in Cairo. They hadn't had chocolate cake since leaving home, and were dying to sink their teeth in one. I replied that I very well knew what a chocolate cake was, and that the best I ever tasted was baked by my own good wife, God keep her hands. I went on to deplore that there was neither flour nor cocoa to be found anywhere in the stores, and that sugar was rationed. Had these ingredients been available, God is my witness, said I, my wife would have baked the best chocolate cake you ever tasted. They jubilantly replied that there was plenty of all that at the PX, and that they would have no problem supplying us with as much of each ingredient as we wanted. Thereupon, I invited them to come to our house on Sunday around four, but insisted that the goods be delivered in the morning. When one of them asked how many could come, I replied as many as you like." That was typical of my father.

Sunday morning, the bell rang and our Nubian maid opened the door. She found herself face to face with a huge American soldier who carried three enormous brown paper bags, and whose skin color was about the same as hers. She ran away shrieking, "Mistress, mistress, there's a djinn at the door!" When my mother assessed the size of the loot, I am sure she panicked at the thought of the number of cakes that would have to be baked. She thanked the GI and offered him a cup of Turkish coffee the likes of which he had evidently never tasted. He politely drank it down, thanked my mother, and said with a huge grin on his face "Bye, ma'am. See you at four. There will be twelve of us, okay?"

At four o'clock, the bell rang. My father opened the door himself and greeted the guests one by one, as they trickled in, all twelve of them. "Welcome to our house. God bless you all and keep you out of harm's way." Four large round chocolate cakes sat in the middle of the dining room table with a smaller one in the center, bearing the inscription "Well-Come!" awkwardly traced by my mother with home-made Chantilly cream. I don't recall how many servings they each had, but when we retired for coffee in the living room, the cakes had all but vanished.

They asked my brother and me how old we were, and we shyly replied, exercising the rudimentary English we had learned in school. They marveled at the command of English two little boys could possess in faraway Egypt, then extracted from their pockets an unbelievable number of trinkets—chewing gum, a Zippo lighter, a harmonica, pens, pencils, even an ocarina, a musical instrument I had never seen before. One of them took my little sister Marlène on his lap and kept stroking her long curly hair, saying that he had one just like her back home. They pulled dozens of photographs out of their large shirt pockets—mothers and fathers, brothers and sisters, wives and fiancées, children and friends, houses and farms. Everyone looked beautiful and kind, and every landscape green and peaceful. They came from states we had never heard of, such as Ohio, Wisconsin, or Minnesota, and other more familiar states such as Texas, Arizona, and Wyoming, for our cinematic culture was vast, and these were the places where Gary Cooper and John Wayne invariably defeated the fearful Indians.

Upon taking leave, they insisted on kissing my mother, something that is not done in Egypt, where only men kiss. My mother and father laughed to their heart's content, and I was overwhelmed with a feeling of immense happiness.

As he was about to shut the door, my father said, "May God protect you all, my sons, and allow you to safely return to your loved ones."

I wonder how many returned to their loved ones, and how many quietly sleep beneath the thousands upon thousands of crosses in Normandy's green pastures.

∼ Armistice ∼

It's a long way to Tipperary . . . .

English wartime song

We were in November 1944, exactly two years after the historic battle of El Alamein, and the German threat was now a bad memory. The Americans had landed in Normandy in June, and the heroic battles where thousands of GIs lost their lives had brought the Allies to within months of winning the war.

We had mixed feelings about the British presence on our soil. On the one hand, they were occupying our land with immeasurable arrogance, and on the other, those poor soldiers were sweating it out in Cairo, waiting for their turn to be called to the front and perhaps lose their life in the sizzling desert heat, far from their green pastures and their loved ones.

Cairo still overflowed with British soldiers from every corner of the empire: Englishmen, Irishmen, Australians, Indian Sikhs, etc. They were not allowed to stray into the more populous sections of town, which were barred by large "OUT OF BOUNDS" billboards. All over town, you would come across other billboards bearing such messages as "SAVE PETROL," "SAVE YOUR TIRES," "WALLS HAVE EARS." Civilian apartments were forcibly requisitioned by the British to accommodate their troops, especially in the immediate neighborhood of the Qasr el Nil Barracks, a stone's throw from where we lived.

Our apartment came very close to being requisitioned, but was spared by the landlord's able maneuvering and powerful connections. The building next door was occupied by a shifting mix of soldiers, men and women, who never stayed more than a few weeks at a time. With its terrace on a level with our apartment, it afforded us a unique vantage point from which my brother and I could unabashedly gaze at the women of the WAAC[30] as they sunbathed in the Cairo sun, scantily clad if at all, right under our adolescent eyes. Our autumn sun was obviously much hotter than at Brighton beach, causing them to turn into steamed lobsters in one afternoon, much to our delight.

We befriended two soldiers who had just returned from the front and were convalescing from wounds received during one of the furious battles their regiment had taken part in. Ginger had received a bullet in the shoulder, and Cowey in the thigh. They installed a net across the terrace, and spent their afternoons playing volleyball or badminton. These were not exactly world-class championships, and they laughed at each other more often than they played, Ginger struggling with one arm strapped against his chest, and Cowey hopping on one leg. We engaged in daily

conversation on either side of the narrow passage between the two buildings, and they had a million war stories to tell. They belonged with pride
to the Royal Northumberland Fusiliers, and did not look charitably upon
other regiments. They flooded us with an unbelievable hodge-podge of
war memorabilia gleaned in the battlefield—British and German military
badges, an Italian bayonet—probably one of Mussolini's celebrated
eight million[31]—a Wehrmacht helmet and God knows what else. I guess
they were not allowed to carry home more than a specified amount of
war trophies, and were only too happy to give away their crop to two
Egyptian boys they would probably never see again.

My father had given my brother for Christmas a Daisy air rifle that
shot little round copper buckshot with great precision, and he had turned
into a surprisingly good sharpshooter. Ginger would hold a cigarette
butt between his thumb and forefinger, daring my brother to hit it from
a distance of no less than ten or fifteen meters, and my brother never
missed. I guess a little buckshot did not really scare Ginger after all he
had been through.

I remember our parents cautioning us not to get too close to the troops,
particularly the Australians, who were allegedly drunk all the time, and
the Maoris, who had the reputation of being fearful rapists. They did not
need to caution us against the Sikhs, for they brought back fearful memories of the man with the green turban. Ginger and Cowey were the exception, and my mother had them for tea once or twice. In return, they offered
my parents a carton of Craven A cigarettes and another of John Player's
Navy Cut procured from the NAAFI.[32] My mother blessed them, praying
for their safe return home, now that peace was finally in sight.

As I came home one night and was about to turn on the light in the hallway, I stumbled upon a human form that I immediately recognized to be
that of a British soldier, because of the characteristic smell he exhaled—
a strong mixture of beer and sweat. He was huffing and puffing with his
khaki pants down on his knees, revealing his nauseating skin. I believe
he was a sergeant or something as fearful as that. Flat against the wall
stood another soldier who looked much younger and was irrepressibly

shivering. I could not fully understand what was going on, and started shaking violently myself as I muttered, "Excuse me, sir," and rushed toward the elevator. At that moment, the older man, who was tall and massive, turned around, and kicked me so violently that it was several days before I could again sit on the wooden bench of the Lycée. As he kicked me, he shouted, "Fuck off, Gippy." That is what we were often called. The word derived from "Egypt," and was not meant to be kind. Sometimes they would also call us Gippo or Gipsy, a word that sounded odd to our ears, for we were vaguely aware that it referred to homeless tribes from faraway lands.

My brother Waguih was two years older. When he heard my story, he flew into a rage, cursing and swearing, "The filthy dogs, doing that in our hallway, and kicking my brother in our own house. I'll show them, I swear I'll show them!" He climbed on his desk chair and reached for the rifle, which was stashed away atop a cupboard, loaded it, then stepped out on the large balcony. A group of British soldiers were standing exactly beneath, chatting and laughing. I begged him not to use his rifle, for perhaps one of them was Ginger or Cowey. He told me not to worry because they were all officers. He aimed, and fired.

Less than fifteen minutes later, the doorbell rang, accompanied by a raucous command to open up. On our doorstep stood no fewer than five Egyptian policemen in black uniforms and an equal number of civilians clad in gray *gallabiyas* with checkered scarves wrapped around their necks. The officer solemnly asked, "Who shot the Englishman?" Having confessed to the crime, my brother was ordered to fetch the rifle and bring it to the officer. He sheepishly went to his room and reappeared with the puny weapon. The officer examined it with contrived seriousness as he exchanged knowing glances with his companions, then asked my brother what had prompted him to do such a thing. I was dumbfounded by the boldness of his reply: "Because two Englishmen were doing dirty things in our hallway, then hit my little brother." To our amazement and relief, the officer, without once crossing our threshold, returned the rifle to my brother saying, "Consider yourself lucky the man suffered no harm. Don't do it again, champion."

When my parents came home from an afternoon spent at Groppi sipping tea and listening to light music, they were horrified upon hearing our confession. My father asked my brother if he had gone mad. Had he forgotten that one short week earlier Lord Moyne had been murdered in Zamalek by two Jewish terrorists?[33] Cairo was in a virtual state of siege, and British constables crisscrossed the city day and night on their motorcycles.

My father ordered my brother to rush next door and apologize to whomever was in charge. Two soldiers were standing guard on the threshold of the building. We told them we had come to apologize, and were led into an apartment turned into a shabby makeshift office. A crimson-faced officer with a bushy red moustache sat behind a wooden desk under a large portrait of King George VI and a smaller portrait of Winston Churchill. "Why do you shoot British soldiers?" he solemnly asked before we could open our mouths. Unflinchingly, my brother replied, using Madame Wolkonski's favorite vocabulary, "Because they misbehaved in our house!" "You speak English well, boy. Now get out of here, both of you." My brother was steaming. The man had added insult to injury by not acknowledging our noble gesture. He vowed to get even some day, but as it turned out, it was I who settled the account thirty years later.

In February 1945, the BBC announced that the city of Dresden had been wiped out by Anglo-American bombers, killing 250,000 civilians and destroying the city's invaluable baroque heritage. I remembered Coventry, and the fears that my mother harbored regarding England's possible surrender in the wake of that immense disaster. Little did I suspect then the indomitable character of the British people, the genius of Winston Churchill, and the unflinching courage of the royal family.

On May 8, my brother and I were coming home from the Lycée when we sensed that something out of the ordinary was in the air. The oriental cafés along our familiar route were jammed as we had never before seen them, their radios blaring from one café to the next in one uninterrupted deafening stream. Civil servants were huddled up against one another in dense swarms on the tramway's running boards. Automobiles were blowing their horns and *hanturs* madly galloping. Seized by the overwhelming sense of urgency that surrounded us, we started running home as fast as we could. As usual, the lift was out of order. Upon reaching the fifth floor anguished and breathless, we found our apartment door wide open, as well as our neighbors'. In our entrance hall, Molly's mother was hugging mine, repeating over and over "L'armistice! Madame Gazalé, l'armistice!" We suddenly understood what was causing the commotion, but could not believe our ears. We rushed to the balcony, so strong was our desire to again immerse ourselves in the surrounding pandemonium. On the terrace next door, two dozen Tommies and WAACS were frantically dancing, hugging and chanting every wartime song they knew: It's a long way to Tipperary . . . , Pack up your troubles in your old kit bag . . . , etc., etc. When Ginger saw us, he came to the edge of the terrace and shouted amidst the maddening chaos, "Come with us tonight to the Anglican cathedral on Maspero Street. A special thanksgiving service is being held."

Though Maspero Street was within walking distance from where we lived, we had never gone that far and never entered the Anglican cathedral. The church was packed with soldiers in uniform, shoulder to shoulder, men, women, officers, and rank-and-file alike. It was as though military ranks had been abruptly erased by the armistice, giving way to a kind of universal brotherhood. Within a matter of days, I thought, they would all be civilians and return to their loved ones. Suddenly, the loudspeaker announced that His Majesty King George was about to address the world on the BBC. I remember his ill-assured voice and, amidst a painful stutter, the words "triumph," "unconditional surrender," "armistice," "gallant," "peace," and "God."

The cathedral resounded with the words "God save our Gracious King . . . ."

~ Years of Wrath ~

~ February 21, 1946 ~

The streets had become rivers, rivers of people flowing from the outskirts of the city to its center. Rivers of life that had welled out from their subterranean sources in the factories, the colleges, the schools, from every place in which men and women toiled to live. The rivers carried white sails inscribed with the hope of a nation. Thousands of fists were raised to the sky. Voices cried out their slogans and were answered by a roar from the crowd.

Sharif Hatata, *The Eyes with an Iron Lid* [34]

In those days, the Ministry of Education organized yearly nationwide contests in a number of fields beyond the school curriculum. Enrolment was optional, and applicants chose whatever subject they preferred. I decided to take physics, having fallen in love with that discipline ever since my grandfather had offered me the 1869 edition of Amédée Guillemin's *Les Phénomènes de la physique*.

The written exam took place on February 21, 1946 in an Egyptian public school near our house, a stone's throw from Qasr el Nil barracks, the archetypal symbol of British presence since the bombardment of Alexandria and the occupation of Egypt by their troops.

My mother and father saw me to the apartment door with the traditional "May God be with you, may God bring you success," etc. Faithful to my Mother's superstitious prescription always to look back upon embarking on some adventurous journey, I saw her leaning out of the window, waving goodbye and throwing kisses.

Upon reaching the school, I was confronted with a whole host of students the likes of whom I had never mingled with before. Many were poorly dressed and wore the tarbush, a traditional crimson headdress that looked like a truncated cone, with a tassel of black silk dangling from its crown. It reminded me of an engraving entitled "Men of the Middle and Higher Classes" and another entitled "Women and Children of the Lower Classes" in Edward William Lane's fascinating *Manners and Customs of Modern Egyptians*.[35] There was no notable difference between the second illustration and the way lower-class women still dressed one hundred years later, whereas higher-class men's clothing was totally europeanized, with the exception of the tarbush and the knee-length frockcoat worn by dignitaries.

The students glanced over their notes one last time, wondering which applicants would emerge on top. The rule of the game had it that only the top ten students won a full scholarship for the duration of their university years. I was feeling somewhat uneasy, for I did not personally need the scholarship, whereas most of the others probably depended on it to pursue their studies. I had applied *pour la gloire*, hoping to see my name posted on the Lycée bulletin boards.

The exam was not really difficult, and I finished long before the time limit. I was hindered only by the extreme paleness of the ink that was supplied in identical glass inkpots. Using government ink was mandatory, so that no particular clue might be given by a student to a corrector he knew or that his father could have bribed.

Be that as it may, I picked up my pen, pencil, and ruler, the only authorized instruments, turned my paper in to the invigilator, and left the room, to the amazement of my peers.[36]

On the way home, relieved and light-hearted, I heard a strange muffled clamor that grew louder and louder as I approached the barracks. Ismailiya Square, which bordered the barracks, was jammed with thousands upon thousands of demonstrators chanting, "Down with British imperialism! Evacuation in blood! Long live independence!" The demonstrators were banging on a British armored car with their bare fists, when a panicked British soldier opened fire. The demonstrators lay in puddles of blood, some dead, some moaning. One man took off his *gallabiya*, smeared it with blood, and raised it atop his cane in the manner of a flag. I was standing petrified amidst the compact crowd when I suddenly found myself within yards of the car, and caught sight of the young Englishman's blue eyes staring at mine. That brief encounter probably saved my life. My soles gluey with blood, I turned around and made my way out of the crowd as the stampeding protestors shattered the windows of every foreign-owned shop in sight.

What sparked that day's events was an appeal from the National Committee of Workers and Students, created one short week earlier. King Farouk had been implicated in numerous scandals, and his prime minister Nuqrashi's false show of negotiations with the occupier, compounded by the rampant corruption and lack of social reforms, had shattered every hope of getting rid of the British, whose interests were closely tied to those of the ruling class.

A few days earlier, on February 9, thousands of students were marching from Cairo University to King Farouk's 'Abdin Palace when a violent clash opposed them to the Egyptian police as they were crossing the Abbas bridge. Nuqrashi ordered the bridge opened, causing more than twenty young men to fall to their death, some drowning in the Nile, others crushing their bones on the iron structure. More than one hundred were seriously injured. That event, which forever lives in Egyptian memory as one of the most dastardly, triggered more demonstrations in Cairo, Alexandria, and a multitude of smaller townships.[37]

The February 21 massacre began as a peaceful demonstration until the armored cars provocatively charged the crowd. Students from Cairo University, the Islamic University of el Azhar, and a host of secondary schools had initially converged on Opera Square, then marched on to Ismailiya Square. Hundreds of workers had also flocked in from the Dickensian textile factories of Shubra el Kheima, which belonged to a handful of wealthy Egyptian families close to the Palace and the ruling party. They also came from Helwan, Ghamra, Abbasiya, and the railway workshops.

More than fifty people were wounded or killed on that day of infamy. Nuqrashi, who had been replaced by Ismail Sidqi following the events, was reinstated by a whimsical Farouk in December, only to be assassinated the following year.

My father was feverishly looking for me at the risk of his own life, for he was an effendi who never parted with his red tarbush, making him one of those literate middle- and upper-class Egyptians that the British had loathed since the early days of Orabi's and Saad Zaghlul's independence movements. He pressed me against his chest saying, "Thank God you're safe. Your mother is mad with anguish. Thank God you're safe."

March 4 was declared a day of mourning. We stayed home all day, and Cairo became a dead city. We heard on the radio that similar clashes had taken place in Alexandria, leaving large numbers of dead and wounded.

It dawned on me that I had been living in an ivory tower populated with foreign minorities, and moving around in a privileged microcosm between the Lycée Français and our friends' elegant apartments in the center of town or the posh villas of Giza, Garden City, Ma'adi, and Zamalek, unaware of the heart that throbbed one bridge away, in Bulaq and other similarly squalid quarters of Cairo.

And yet we were Egyptians, and it was our own history in the making.

Surely the voices of all those martyrs would be heard somewhere, I thought, and something would be done. Where was Farouk, so handsome and cherished when he sat on the throne nine short years earlier?

It was hard to believe that an Egyptian prime minister had deliberately ordered the police to massacre hundreds of students like ourselves, and that another had allowed the British to open fire on the miserable crowds that toiled in hell. Prime Minister Ismail Sidqi's swift response came in July in the form of a brutal crackdown on political opponents, cramming Egyptian jails with hundreds of respected intellectuals, renowned independent journalists, vocal labor leaders, and student leaders. The charges invoked were pitifully classic; they were all communists plotting to overthrow the corrupt regime. Where was Egypt's allegedly liberal government? Where was the Constitution of 1923?

Sidqi flew to London in October and concluded with British prime minister Ernest Bevin a mock agreement whose sole purpose was to appease the crowds: the British were to leave Egypt within three years.

When classes finally resumed, we decided to get even with the only Englishman within our reach, Mr. Inglott, our English-language teacher. Just before his course began, Abul Ela sneaked into the classroom and chalked on the blackboard

EVACUATION WITH BLOOD

awkwardly translated from a slogan painted on every wall in town. When Mr. Inglott entered the classroom, expecting the blackboard to be wiped clean as school tradition required, he looked at the inscription and, without departing from his habit of chewing on a tea leaf with his clenched front teeth, phlegmatically wrote, as if he were solving Abul Ela's mathematical equation,

EVACUATION WITH BLOOD = DYSENTRY!

With the exception of one or two Europeans of nondescript origin, nobody laughed at the teacher's contemptuous English sense of humor. The insensitive teacher was deriding a condition that plagued millions of Egyptian peasants who daily fed themselves on what little they could afford, ignorant as they were of what caused the disease. I suddenly recalled the painful kick in our hallway, and felt profoundly humiliated.

I realized at that moment that dignity and national pride were more powerful movers than the loss of independence.

~ First Day of University ~

A healthy nation is as unconscious of its nationality as a healthy
man of his bones. But if you break a nation's nationality it will think
of nothing else but getting it set again. It will listen to no reformer,
to no philosopher, to no preacher, until the demand of the Nationalist
is granted. It will attend to no business, however vital, except the
business of unification and liberation.

George Bernard Shaw [38]

As the summer of 1946 drew near its end, I was ready to embark upon
my five-year voyage at the Faculty of Engineering at King Fuad
University.[39] The summary physical examination consisted in determin-
ing whether or not we were infected with bilharzia, a deadly disease
caused by a microscopic mollusk that thrived in Egypt's stagnant backwaters. The parasite entered the patient's veins through the skin of his
feet, then, following a protracted itinerary, ended its journey in the liver
or bladder, causing the latter to bleed profusely. The ensuing hematuria,
or presence of blood in the urine, was so common in the countryside that
it was believed by the poor ignorant peasants to be a natural condition,
akin to menstruation.

We were asked to fill a test tube with urine then hand it to a medic
who, judging from the color of the sample, decided whether or not we
were infected. We fell in line behind makeshift wooden screens, waiting
for our turn to fill the tube. I had just filled mine, which contained no
trace of blood, when an emaciated young man handed me his empty
tube, begging me to fill it in his stead. I was bewildered by that request:
here stood a very sick young man whose disease had probably reached
an incurable stage, and who was bent on concealing it from the medical
authorities, whose aim was in reality to cure rather than punish him. I
was overwhelmed with compassion as I took the tube and filled it.

Thereupon another young man came with the same request, then another and another, until I could no longer comply and was forced to apologize to the next applicant. He implored me not to leave, and came back minutes later with a bottle of Coca-Cola and a big smile on his sad gray face. I imagined the magnitude of his financial sacrifice and forced myself to swallow the beverage despite the lump in my throat. He kissed me on both cheeks as I handed him the precious liquid. That is how I brutally emerged from my sheltered world, and discovered that my heart was Egyptian.

My very first day of university was a memorable one. I had risen early and prepared myself with great anticipation for my first encounter with Egypt's public education system. I adjusted the silk necktie that my father let me pick out of his considerable collection, put on my new double-breasted jacket, and dashed downstairs, accompanied by my mother's profuse blessings.

The Faculty of Engineering's first year premises were not located in Giza with the rest of the university, but in Abbasiya, a remote and rather poor district of Greater Cairo, verging on the desert.

We sat in the large auditorium, anxiously waiting for the inaugural course to begin, restless with anticipation and chatting for the first time with a bunch of boys in whose company we would spend the next five years of our lives. Suddenly, the amphitheater door burst wide open, letting in a dense cluster of visibly agitated youth chanting "Down with British imperialism! Long live independence!" One of them, who appeared to be the leader, jumped atop the large lectern and delivered an impassioned patriotic speech. With remarkable eloquence and a perfect command of literary Arabic—Egyptians normally speak a dialect derived from Arabic—he lectured us on the infamy of British occupation. He gave us a spellbinding account the slaughter of February 21 which I had personally witnessed, as well as a graphic narration of the Abbas Bridge episode where he and his peers desperately clung to the railings while their fellow students were mercilessly thrust over the edge. We could no longer depend, he said, on heroic figures such as the late Orabi or Zaghlul. The governments of Sidqi and Nuqrashi were corrupt. Only the courage and determination of students like ourselves would boot the hateful occupier out of the country. *In the name of our martyrs*, he exhorted us to join the demonstration that was gradually swelling outside.

I followed the crowd, my heart pounding furiously at the thought of embarking upon some gallant episode of our country's liberation. My baptism of fire was about to begin, setting me apart from my European Lycée schoolmates, many of whom had already sailed overseas to attend foreign universities, or joined their father's businesses, getting ready to contribute to their respectable family fortunes.

We first stopped under the shed where the students parked their bicycles. There, we were instructed to smash the wooden comb-like structure and arm ourselves with the makeshift bludgeons. I sensed that our demonstration was not intended to be a peaceful one, and began having qualms about using my weapon. Never before in my life had I hurt anyone, and I did not have the faintest inkling about who my adversary would soon be. Would it be an Egyptian policeman of the kind that opens bridges and pushes fellow Egyptians to their deaths, or an Englishman of the kind that shoots unarmed crowds with a machine gun? As we crossed the faculty gate, I wondered where that adventure was taking us—the Opera Square under the equestrian statue of Farouk's great grandfather, or the infamous Ismailiya Square, a stone's throw from where I lived?

Before long, I found myself on the edge of the pavement at the forefront of the combatants, brandishing my derisory club and chanting slogans. It dawned on me that we were standing face to face with a dense black cluster of Egyptian policemen whose rifles were squarely aimed at us. A fraction of a second later, I felt a violent jab on the left side of my face and body as a burst of fire emerged from the rifles' barrels amidst a deafening noise. My face and neck were bleeding profusely. One of our leaders grabbed my arm and pulled me away. "Go to the infirmary, comrade. It's in the main building. Just follow the others." As he released my arm, he added "Bravo 'alek ya shabab!" ('Congratulations, young one!')

On my way to the infirmary, I recognized Tewfik parading side by side with Gamal, ten or twenty rows behind the front line. Both had been active communist recruiters in the Lycée, endlessly lecturing us on the necessity of overthrowing the system and praising the courage of the Soviet Union's proletarian revolutionaries. With their jackets negligently thrown upon their shoulders, they looked like a pair of Napoleonic officers witnessing a battle unfold from the rear. Tewfik patted me on the shoulder saying, "Well done!" but I briskly walked away without replying. He was the haughty theoretician, I the soldier.

The infirmary was brimming with bleeding young men, its floor strewn with a hodgepodge of bloodied garments. The policemen had used buckshot, and those who were hit at pointblank range lay on the floor, twisting and turning.

One of the male nurses shouted, "The prime minister has just authorized the police to violate the hallowed university grounds. The students in this room will be arrested before anyone else. Run, run!"

I noticed that the left side of my trousers was also soaked with blood, and suddenly felt a thousand pinpricks all the way down to my ankle.

An older man, obviously a professor, commanded me to follow him and not say a word. He led me to the courtyard's rear rampart and gave me a leg up over the wall into the desert. The far end of the narrow perpendicular street was blocked by police trucks. If I went in their direction, I was sure to be arrested and beaten up. The building across the street was a maternity hospital in front of which stood a taxi with its engine running. I begged the driver to help me out of my predicament, but he replied that he was hired by a woman who had just given birth and would soon emerge from the hospital. When she saw me, she hugged her little bundle, exclaiming, "By the Prophet's prayer, is all that blood for my son to see on his first day?" I implored her to let me ride along, saying, "God will reward your son for your charitable deed." The cab driver contributed his own unsolicited piece: "Yes, Madam, God will reward you. May your son be blessed with health and long life!" He then turned in my direction and added, "God bless Egypt's youth!" The face of the young mother, who was about my age, was full of fright and compassion. She suggested that I take my jacket off, turn it inside out, and drop it on the floor, as she tucked my shirt collar under my pullover. She then pulled a handkerchief out of her purse, wet it several times with her own saliva, and wiped the blood on my face. Upon crossing the police line, the officer summarily glanced inside the cab and signaled the driver to go, having wished the newborn *mabruk* ('blessings') and long life.

I reached inside my jacket and pulled out the fountain pen that I had received several years earlier for my First Communion and never used, saving it for my first day of university. I offered it to the young mother saying, "Please accept this small gift on behalf of your son. May it accompany him throughout his life and help him become a respected educated man."

"May God protect you," she replied as she got out of the cab.

Where would I go from here with my face and leg riddled with buck-shot? Nicette's father was a doctor, whose office on Bustan Street was close to where I lived. That gave me every reason to seek treatment in his clinic rather than some public hospital where the secret police, which infested literally every corner of town, would be prompt to ask all sorts of questions and perhaps arrest me.

En route, I imagined a Hollywood-like scenario where Lauren Baccall opens her door to a bleeding Humphrey Bogart and throws her arms around him crying, "My God, what happened to you, darling?" My heart was pounding as I rang the doorbell, praying that Nicette herself would open and see her hero dripping with blood.

The scenario did not exactly unfold as I had wished, for Nicette did not throw her arms around me. Still, she cried "My god, Midhat, what happened to you?" I replied "Nothing much. We were demonstrating against the British and the police opened fire. Is your father home?" She ran to the back of the apartment and reappeared, shivering and looking very pale, with her father. He briskly ushered me into his office, then asked me to roll up my trousers and lie down on the white metallic table.

As he twiddled his instrument inside my flesh, searching for the buckshot that were lodged under my chin, he asked me if I wanted an injection. I stoically replied "Ça ira," and felt Nicette's warm hand reaching for mine. Every time I clenched my teeth, she pressed my hand a little tighter. I don't remember how long the operation lasted, but it was one of the most passionate moments of my life, and the closest I ever got to Nicette.

I often wonder what became of the little boy whose mother tended to my wounds on that memorable day. Might he still be using my fountain pen?

Post Scriptum
The summer of 2003 was exceptionally hot in Paris, with temperatures in excess of 40 degrees Celsius and unheard of levels of ozone pollution. As a consequence, I came down with one of those dreadful sinus episodes that had plagued my student years in Cairo. The doctor prescribed a scan of the skull. Lo and behold, he discovered that three pieces of buckshot were still lodged in my face: one in the earlobe, one under the lobe, and the third in my left jaw. . . . As if I needed that belated reminder of my wild student years.

⌐ Aftermath ⌐

On my way home from the clinic, I was feeling elated and rather proud of my involvement in the day's demonstrations. Having heard of the events that unfolded at the Faculty of Engineering, my parents were anxiously awaiting my return. I had blood on my clothes and bandages all over my face. This time, I had not been caught unawares in the midst of a bloody demonstration, but had deliberately involved myself in the action. My father was beside himself, and a deluge of imprecations befell my ears. What was I trying to achieve by joining that unruly mob? What future did I have in mind for myself? Had he toiled all his life only to see his son forsake his ambitions and turn into a revolutionary? He stormed into my room and in a matter of seconds, tore to pieces two posters that I had pinned up against the wall. They were black-and-white reproductions of paintings dating back to Picasso's Blue Period. One of them represented a one-eyed woman, probably a beggar, and the other a destitute

Spanish woman holding a baby in her arms. My mother, who was holding my chin as she assessed the damage by turning my face to one side then the other, told my father,

"Calm your nerves, ya Youssef! How many times did you recount your own demonstrations when Saad Zaghlul was exiled? You were barely seventeen at the time. That is your son's age. The apple falls at the foot of the tree."

"And what have we achieved? Please tell me. Wasn't Zaghlul forced to resign after winning landslide elections, then die a despondent and disillusioned man. What have we achieved? Look out the window and tell me how many Englishmen you see parading in our streets and despising our people."

"Yes, ya Youssef, you are right. Things haven't changed much. But isn't that why your son is angry? Didn't you tell me of your own anger when you were his age?"

My father flopped into an armchair and never uttered another word. My mother put her forefinger to her lips and said under her breath, "Change your clothes and don't come out for a while. Give your father a chance to calm down."

Lunch was served by our servant Ahmad amidst a deafening silence. He gave me a sidelong knowing glance with an imperceptible grin on his face, and I could sense a warm wave of affection radiating toward me as he bent to serve me. I often joined him in the kitchen after lunch, where we chatted about the events of the day as he cleaned the dishes or swept the kitchen floor. He was eager to get a first-hand account of the demonstrations, for he was neither a student nor a factory worker nor a civil servant, and his loyalty to his employers forbade him from taking to the streets.

Ahmad, whom I regarded as a kind of elder brother, often took me to the mosque on Friday for the noontime prayer. I was overwhelmed with a sense of peace every time I crouched down on the worn out carpet, listening to the muezzin's chant.

From him, I learned the *Fatiha*, the opening verse of the Qur'an, one of the cornerstones of Islam. Beyond attesting that there is no god but

God and Muhammad is His prophet, prayer is one of the important duties enjoined by the laws of Islam, others being alms-giving, fasting, and pilgrimage. His working hours did not allow him to pray five times a day as required, but he managed to acquit himself of that duty at least twice, at sunrise and sunset, his head turned toward the *qibla*, the direction of holy Mecca, after having duly performed his ablutions. He unflinchingly fasted during the month of Ramadan, during which he was released from work and usually went back to his village of Mit Abul Kom,[40] not to return until the joyous Eid el Fitr, celebrating the end of Ramadan, his bundle full of delicious home-cooked pastries. Ahmad never failed to bring back from his village, on behalf of his mother, several sheets of sun-dried apricot paste, known as *amar el din*, meaning literally 'moon of the religion,' perhaps because the delicacy was traditionally eaten during the month of Ramadan, a time of worship, contemplation, and reading of the Qur'an, which teaches that fasting disciplines the soul and prayer quiets the spirit. On the 27th of Ramadan, the Muslims celebrate the revelation of the Qur'an to Muhammad. My parents cautioned us never to eat or drink in public places during Ramadan for fear of offending the Muslims.

His condition did not allow him to give any alms to the countless beggars and crippled who lived on charity, but he regularly shared his meals with some of his more destitute friends. Sharing is another cornerstone of Islam, without which millions would probably suffer from deprivation and hunger. It was one of our family traditions to daily prepare an inordinate amount of food, enough to feed our family as well as the multitude that depended on us for subsistence.

One of Ahmad's most cherished ambitions was to visit Mecca before retiring to his village and be called 'Hagg Ahmad' by family and friends.

My father, who was usually buoyant and had a million stories to tell at the dinner table, was silent and looked very pale. He barely touched the food that was presented to him and kept stroking the veins of his left wrist. My anguished mother asked him if he was in pain, for he had been through an extremely trying experience the previous year, when he suffered his first heart attack. "It is nothing," the doctor had said. "It is all in the mind, Professor Gazalé!" Another doctor had diagnosed some mysterious nerve inflammation that accounted for his episodes of severe chest pains. Yet another declared that one of the arteries, which had been blocked for a while, was now miraculously clear, and that his heart was in perfect condition.

My father rose from his chair and slowly walked to his bedroom. He was now stroking the center of his chest, slightly bending forward and leaning on every piece of furniture along the way. My mother rushed to the phone and asked Dr. Talaat to come right away. It crossed my mind that our family doctor was perhaps incompetent. Hadn't he misdiagnosed my sister's polio three years earlier, and let my young and beautiful Aunt Gladys choke to death with diphtheria? My sister and I were anxiously waiting for Dr. Talaat to emerge from my parents' bedroom, when he finally appeared, paler than death itself. Strangely enough, my father was not taken to the hospital, and resumed his treatment at home.

I was overwhelmed with guilt, and felt responsible for his relapse. Didn't the sight of his son's swollen face cause his anger? Weren't heart diseases caused by violent shocks such as this?

I asked my mother's permission to see my father. She acquiesced, recommending that my visit be brief, for he was under sedation. I sat on the little *chauffeuse* by his bedside where he often sat on weekends, clad in his striped robe, with his feet resting on top of his slippers as he read a book or the day's papers.

"Come close," he said, with a faint smile on his face. "You think it is all your fault, but it isn't. You know, I had been through a lot before you were even born, and my father before me. He was barely twenty when he demonstrated in support of Orabi Pasha, and I had just turned seventeen when the British deported Zaghlul for the second time. Many of my friends were killed in the demonstrations that followed. One and a half years later, Egypt's independence was proclaimed, and the English are still here. I understand your anger but I want you to be careful and stay out of harm's way, for your mother's sake. I now want you to promise me that you will not marry before your sister's turn has come."

I nodded and kept my head bowed. "Now go to your room and concentrate on your homework. Don't worry about me. I shall be all right in a day or two."

The next morning, hundreds of students were gathered outside the Faculty, which had been ordered closed by our despicable prime minister. I returned home and headed straight for my parents' bedroom. My father was sitting up in bed looking better, with the morning papers piled up by his side—*al-Ahram, The Egyptian Gazette, Le Journal d'Égypte, Le Progrès Égyptien*, and more. He urged me to return to the Lycée and enroll in Mathématiques supérieures, a class that prepared students for the demanding entrance contests required by France's "Grandes Écoles." He had made up his mind, I realized, that I was to pursue my education in France. My elder brother, who had decided to study medicine in the southern French town of Montpellier, was already enrolled in another class called PCB, for physics, chemistry, and biology. He sailed to France the following summer.

In January 1947, the British began pulling back their troops to the Canal Zone. Not content with that half measure, a left-leaning organization called the National Popular Front was pasted together, involving Wafdists and an underground Marxist organization known as the Democratic Movement for National Liberation, demanding total evacuation of the Nile valley, Sudan as well as Egypt.

Many of my childhood companions had enrolled in the Democratic Movement for National Liberation and actively supported the Wafd, whose ranks were riddled with communist sympathizers. I was often invited to their *hafla*s, informal parties that took place in their parents' comfortable apartments around *foul* sandwiches. They debated all sorts of issues ranging from class struggle to sexual liberation, in light of dialectical and historical materialism. There, I learned that I was laced with petty-bourgeois prejudice, inferiority and superiority complexes, and a whole host of sins that befell people like myself who did not have the good fortune to be born to the working class, that mythical social body none of them had ever come close to. Because of my fluency in Arabic, a talent few of them possessed, I was once or twice pressured into selling *al-Gamahir* ('The Masses'), a short-lived weekly pamphlet that distilled leftist doctrine under the innocuous guise of a liberal student magazine. The nearest section of town within my reach where working-class candidates could be found, was a backstreet named Ma'ruf, where dozens of auto-repair shops were crammed side by side. The destitute mechanics toiled in the street and on the curb outside their shops, filling the air with the clang of metal and the smell of Duco body paint. That day, I sold fifty copies of *al-Gamahir* to a bunch of bewildered workmen who couldn't fathom why a well-dressed youth like myself would want to tread their insalubrious quarters and care for their well-being. Selling newspapers was the lot of barefoot children of the most miserable kind. Meanwhile, haughty theoreticians debated the Movement's strategy in light of the latest position of the USSR on this or that issue. With the exception of Muhammad, perhaps the brightest young man I have ever met, whose aristocratic upbringing and natural elegance contrasted with the avowed goals of the Movement, I felt little kinship with the other militants, and could not bring myself to adhere to a doctrine so totally devoid of spirituality. To my mind, history and religion could not be explained by the dogmatic recourse to historical materialism, and science would never be able to encompass every phenomenon, observable or not, for I believed in Providence, Grace, and the divine essence of Man.

I stopped going to the *hafla*s altogether, never having taken advantage of the sexually liberated, promiscuous, and otherwise beautiful adolescent girls. Many of my childhood companions were thrown in jail, from which they emerged only to be later jailed by Nasser's police.

Fortunately or unfortunately, I shall never know, the university reopened its doors and I returned to Abbasiya. Never before had I been so totally immersed in a genuinely Egyptian atmosphere, for our tranquil life had unfolded in the upscale sections of town amongst people who spoke French at home and frequented the Lycée or other foreign establishments. University students, on the other hand, seemed to emerge from some nondescript layer of Egyptian society. Their parents, who might have been civil servants, teachers, small landowners, shopkeepers, merchants, even lawyers or doctors, were neither rich nor poor, and inhabited the rambling less favored sections of Cairo.

My first year of university was totally chaotic. Classes were constantly disrupted by demonstrations and clashes with the police. The leaders belonged to two competing student groups, the liberal Wafdists and the virulent Muslim Brothers to whom the fight for independence was a holy Jihad where Copts did not belong.

I remember being torn between my love for science and my frequent involvement in student demonstrations. I was also torn between our comfortable family life and the prospect of being arrested and dumped into one of those filthy prisons whose horrifying reputation was laced with flogging and sodomy. During the day, I was caught in a whirlwind of shouting, pushing, and shoving. At night, I returned to my hospitable quarters, showered, had a hearty dinner, and stayed up late over my books, brimming with scientific aspirations.

Cinema Metro had opened in 1939 on Soliman Pasha Street, a stone's throw from where we lived. The cinema, whose architecture was somewhat reminiscent of Radio City in New York, was built by Metro Goldwyn Mayer, the mythical studio whose stars populated our fantasy world. Who can forget the first private showing of *Gone with the Wind*, with the theater's balconies filled to the brim with royalty? To the tenement dwellers and radical political groups, that cinema was a constant provocation, with its upholstered armchairs, air-conditioning, heavy carpeting, and the indescribable gracefulness that filled the air.

On a hot day of May 1947, moviegoers had flocked to the early afternoon show, hoping to escape the suffocating heat, when a bomb went off, killing several people.[41] The terrorist act, attributed to the Muslim Brotherhood, caused a panic wave to ripple across the land. We lived in a climate of terror we had never before experienced, for that cowardly act was directed at the civilian population. It was several weeks before the aficionados resumed their weekly movie-going ritual.

That year, I failed the physics exam, my favorite subject. Perhaps I was "unconsciously ashamed of my self-centered petty-bourgeois scientific aspirations," as I was led to believe by one ardent communist I had met at the Lycée. He was curiously jubilant upon hearing of my failure and derided my scientific aspirations with unusual cruelty.

I decided to spend the month of July in Alexandria with my mother and sister, then return to Cairo for the rest of summer, and study for the September make-up exam.

Around the middle of August, I ran into Essam, a fellow student whom I liked and admired for his intelligence and moral rectitude. He also harbored scientific ambitions that unfortunately were stymied by the historic upheavals that took place in the fifties, shortly after my departure from Egypt. God knows how many vocations were thus thwarted.

He had heard that the Front was organizing a massive demonstration a week thence, on August 22, following the Friday prayers at el Azhar Mosque. Not being inclined to support the Muslim Brothers, though their fight for independence coincided with ours, I elected not to get involved and decided instead to go to the morning showing of an American film near the Opera House. I had barely emerged from the dark theater into the glaring August light when one of the largest demonstrations I had ever witnessed almost literally hit me in the face. It had already gained considerable momentum and the uproar was deafening, with people converging on Opera Square from every direction. A student seized my arm and dragged me into the dizzying crowd. Minutes later, my head twirling, I found myself straddling the shoulders of two demonstrators, shouting "Down with British imperialism" and *al-Gala' bi-l-dima'* ('Evacuation with blood'). From my vantage point, I noticed a large group of demonstrators engaging the police in an exceptionally brutal and bloody confrontation. I jumped to the ground and took refuge in the cinema's entrance, my back hunched under the ruthless blows dealt by the police with their blackjack (to this day, I suffer from a recurrent pain in the cervical area). I was soon joined by other demonstrators, many of whose skulls were dripping with blood. Those most severely wounded were brutally whisked away by the bloodthirsty police. The radio announced that afternoon that close to fifty policemen and an equal number of demonstrators had been killed.

My father died on October 28, 1959, two weeks after his fifty-sixth birthday.

~ Cholera ~

*The Egyptian workers live in unhealthy and overcrowded dwellings—
they are so overcrowded in many areas that the workers occupy the
dwellings in shifts as in a factory; they sleep in the streets and in any
old corner; servants and their families sleep under staircases, in sheds
and in gardens or in quarters of the more modern buildings which are
often not sanitary. Their nutrition is usually inadequate and lacking in
food values. Their health conditions are appalling and the provisions
for dealing with diseases are totally inadequate.*

A British labor counselor, 1882

The world has known a long history of cholera epidemics, one of the earliest on record having originated in India in 1817 as the British troops were getting ready to crush the last pocket of resistance. The epidemic reached Great Britain in 1831, claiming 50,000 victims.

Following the 1882 British bombardment of Alexandria and the landing of their troops in the city, a devastating epidemic struck Egypt, originating precisely in Alexandria. That year, the famous German microbiologist Robert Koch,[42] while studying the causes of the Alexandrian epidemic, brought to light the microbe that caused the disease, and observed two years later that it belonged to the Indian strain.

Sixty-five years and several epidemics later, in January 1947, the British pulled back their troops to the Canal Zone. On September 22, the population was stunned upon hearing that cholera had struck again. It was later claimed by the Egyptian health authorities that the British troops were responsible for introducing the deadly microbe into Egypt, albeit unintentionally.[43] In August 1946, the Arab League suggested quarantining travelers from India and Pakistan, where the epidemic had originated, but France and Great Britain refused to comply. British planes landing in the Canal Zone were never quarantined, including those flying in from the infected confines of the British Empire. Cases that were detected amongst the British garrison were not revealed, and it was not until one hapless Egyptian worker employed by the British in the town of Qarinayn came down with the disease, that the microbe's presence was recognized on Egyptian soil.

In those days, one out of every four children died during infancy, nine tenths of the population suffered from bilharzia, and three out of four from a multitude of eye diseases disseminated by the voracious flies, compounded by the sun's blaring light and Cairo's perennial dust. My brother and I caught trachoma, and my sister suffered from a particularly virulent form of ophthalmia. Had it not been for the loving patience of my mother, who spent twenty-four hours by her bedside swabbing out her eyes with rose water, my sister would have probably lost her sight. In 1942, I came down with recurrent fever as the battle of El Alamein was raging, causing massive movement of troops across the Libyan border. In the forties, malaria had entered from Sudan, recurrent fever from Libya, and cholera through the Canal Zone. Being constantly exposed to a variety of ailments, we had to take infinite precautions everywhere we went and whatever we did. In all my years in Egypt, I never went as far as even dipping the tip of a finger in the Nile for fear of being infected by some deadly parasite. That precaution was derisory as well as useless, because parasites only proliferated in the stagnant backwaters of irrigation canals. As if to punish me for my excessive distrust, the fragile skiff aboard which I sat with my three fellow oarsmen under the watchful eye of our redoubtable helmsman as we competed for the annual university trophy, capsized following some awkward maneuver, plunging our crew into the murky waters, of which I swallowed a hefty swig. The only ailment I suffered in the days that followed was a bad cold. "He who drinks from the Nile shall return to the Nile," says the wise old proverb.

Every summer, we were administered the vaccine against typhoid, a perennial disease that took a toll of thousands. The vaccine was made available by the Ministry of Public Hygiene in public dispensaries, and only there. The doctor used the same needle over and over to deliver the vaccine, injecting a tiny dose at a time, until he ran out of the precious liquid and switched to another perfunctorily boiled needle. When the fateful day came, my mother made sure we stood at the forefront of the long line of postulants. Obviously, a fat bakshish helped a lot, and we miraculously escaped such horrors as hepatitis and God knows what else. We also lived in constant fear of catching tuberculosis, my poor Uncle Edouard having succumbed to that debilitating disease at the age of twenty.

And yet, we belonged to the happy few who had means and lived in the more salubrious sections of Cairo, shielded from the filth that filled the streets, the sewage puddles stagnating in the simmering heat, and the myriad flies swarming in and around the mouths and eyes of sleeping infants. We also belonged to the one million Egyptians who could read and write, out of a population of sixteen million.[44]

No wonder, then, that cholera would spread like wild fire in the cities and villages, where the occurrence of cases reached 150 per 100,000 inhabitants. It was not uncommon to come across someone sick with cholera wallowing in his fluids in the middle of the street, a sight which caused the passers-by to flee the scene frantically, knocking over everything and everyone on their way.

When the university reopened its doors, student leaders were quick to organize voluntary squads whose mission consisted in visiting the most destitute quarters of Cairo and reporting every case of cholera they uncovered in the miserable dwellings. Each squad was led by a student in the final years of medicine, who trained his fellow members in identifying the dreadful symptoms and providing elementary first aid measures whenever possible, in addition to educating family and neighbors, one of the most urgent and demanding tasks.

We learned that the disease spread through water or food contaminated by human feces, either directly or when carried by flies. The age-old habit of drinking out of irrigation canals and washing vegetables in the very water were the fellaheen defecated, was one of the main factors favoring propagation of the disease among peasants as well as city dwellers.[45] We also learned to identify the symptoms: strong colorless and painless diarrhea, vomiting, and lowered body temperature, sometimes causing the sick to shiver irrepressibly. In the most severe cases, the resulting dehydration led to kidney failure and arrhythmia, then death.

The tragedy lay in the concealment by the families of the infected members for fear of seeing them whisked away to the hospital, a place where, in their not altogether unjustified belief, one went to die. Our problem was compounded by the asymptomatic five-day incubation period, which required us to visit suspected locations over and over again, an impossible task. And yet, treatment was relatively easy in the first stages of the disease. We learned to administer bicarbonate, potassium, and sodium salts, sometimes mixing them with glucose. We also explained to the families that raising stomach acidity prevented the onset of the disease, and we recommended absorbing large quantities of lemon or diluted vinegar. Our pockets were always heavy with lemons that we freely distributed to the poorest among the poor. We taught them to wash their hands and food with diluted permanganate and refrain from drinking unboiled water. If the patient looked very ill, we informed the Red Crescent, whose squads swiftly carried him or her to the nearest hospital where massive perfusions were administered intravenously. We pleaded with the health authorities to let us administer the vaccine ourselves, to no avail. People had to walk or travel by tram to the nearest dispensary, perhaps contaminating others on the way. And yet, when small pox claimed the lives of thousands of newborns in the days of Muhammad Ali, the Frenchman Antoine Clot had trained the barbers to administer the vaccine, resulting in a spectacular drop in infant mortality. One of the major obstacles however, lay in the fact that the peasants themselves were reluctant to receive the vaccine, convinced as they were that it was a government ploy aimed at preventing them from ducking the draft!

Coming home from these expeditions felt like returning to a salubrious island amidst an ocean of squalor. I first scrubbed my shoes against a mat soaked with Lysol, then thoroughly showered with antibacterial soap before touching anyone or anything. For weeks on end, our apartment smelled of disinfectant and Fly-Tox that our adolescent maid Rawhiya sprayed several times a day with a contraption consisting of a tin cylin-

der where a piston was thrust to and fro until the air became unbreath-
able. My mother also rubbed our hands and face with Extra-Vieille
cologne imported from France, that was supposed to keep the infection
at bay. That belief probably dated back to the medieval plague epidemics, when people placed little cotton swabs soaked in strong smelling
herb concoctions inside their fearful cone-shaped masks.

To this very day, the slightest whiff of Extra-Vieille carries me back
fifty years into the Cairo of my adolescence, with my mother pinching
her lips as she soaked my hands with the cologne, and Rawhiya turning
her pretty face away and shutting her big black eyes with every stroke of
the Fly-Tox machine.

The cholera epidemic of 1947, which affected 25,000 people, took
the life of 15,000 hapless victims.

≈ Out of Egypt ≈

≈ The French Landlady ≈

Liberté, Égalité, Fraternité

During the better part of my student years in France, I stayed at the Cité Universitaire, a miniature town on the southern edge of Paris where, for a token rent, we enjoyed the amenities any student would have dreamt of in the fifties: clean single rooms, twice-weekly showers (can you imagine?), subsidized restaurants, sports grounds, concert hall, etc.[46]

Until I was admitted, I rented a scruffy furnished room from Madame Moralène, an old widow whose husband was shot by the Resistance in 1945, the very week Paris was liberated. He had apparently collaborated with the Germans and was responsible for denouncing his Jewish neighbors to the French militia, whose zeal sometimes surprised the Germans themselves. Following the denunciation, a family of five—the parents and three children—were arrested in the middle of the night on July 16, 1942, then taken by bus to the Vélodrome d'Hiver, and from there to an unknown destination from which they never returned. The collaborator's summary execution took place in front of his apartment building under his own wife's eyes.

I was sternly instructed to utilize water and electricity parsimoniously, and the landlord's son, who lived upstairs, closely scrutinized the bill every month. The only bathroom in the apartment was strictly out of bounds, and I was only allowed to use the tiny washbasin and bidet at the foot of my bed. As for Madame Moralène, she never used the bathtub, which was packed with a nondescript bric-a-brac of old chairs and other junk. I doubt if the bathroom even remembered what its purpose in life had once been. I had no recourse but to go to the nearby Bains-Douches, where five francs bought me a shower that lasted exactly fifteen minutes, at the end of which the hot water supply was shut off and the grumpy female attendant knocked on the cabin door shouting "Terminé, terminé." On Saturdays, the Bains-Douches were particularly busy, and we sometimes sat for an hour or so in the damp waiting room that smelled of chlorine and perspiration. That afforded us some interesting and fruitful encounters with young working-class girls who were easily impressed by our social status. To their minds, our presence on these premises could only be transient for we would soon move on to the bourgeoisie, becoming doctors or lawyers. They never turned down an invitation to attend the dances that were held every Saturday night at the Cité Universitaire.

Every day at 6 p.m., my landlord's son would knock on his mother's door, tucking under his armpit a *baguette* that was neatly cut through the middle. What a pious son, I said to myself, as he gave his mother her daily bread. That thought redeemed his mother's pettiness and his father's cowardice, a delusion that was soon shattered when I discovered that the poor bastard actually charged his mother for the *demi-baguette* and kept a precise account of how much petty change his mother owed him from one day to the next.

For someone out of Egypt, these people were from Planet Mars.

I was on the verge of packing up and sailing home, when I received a letter from the Pavillon des Provinces de France notifying me of my admission. Deliverance at last! I called on Madame Moralène to settle my bill without waiting for the month's end. She was sitting in her rocking chair facing the window, absentmindedly gazing at the drab gray building across the narrow street. When I told her of my intentions, she sprang out of her chair like the devil out of his box, snatched the bills from my hand, and stared at me with piercing blue eyes, shouting "Allez au diable!" She was foaming at the mouth as she nervously pulled on the tips of the black crochet shawl that was eternally wrapped around her shoulders. I picked up the suitcase that my mother had lovingly packed, insisting that I also take along this sweater and that scarf for fear that I should catch cold in that forlorn country.

As I walked downstairs, Madame Moralène was bent over the railing, swearing and cursing. Her raucous imprecations drew the concierge out of her hovel. She was Madame Moralène's only ally in the building, given the paltry annual bonus she received from her. She dwelt in a dingy little room on the ground floor, adjacent to the main entrance, where she disposed by her bedside of the traditional *cordon*, a kind of bell-pull that allowed her to open the door without getting out of bed. If I came home after ten, I had to shout my name as I rang the doorbell, and if I ever failed to shout "Merci," she would utter all sorts of curses having to do with my foreign origins. The cordon, which she never pulled without grumbling, no doubt symbolized the authority she wielded in that loathesome universe of hers. As I crossed the hallway, I held my breath as usual, so strong was the stench escaping from her rat hole. The concierge accompanied Madame Moralène's vociferation with her own variations on the recurrent theme of the *sale étranger*, whose sole purpose was to eat the bread out of their mouths.

French concierges were usually the first to be questioned regarding the presence in their buildings of "undesirable" foreigners, and they zealously provided the police with self-serving denouncements. The Third Republic,[47] while boasting *Liberté, Égalité, Fraternité*, had allowed several overtly racist directives to be issued by left-wing ministers, directing the prefects to curtail immigration, particularly that of Poles, Czechs, Russians, and Jews expelled from Germany.

Recently uncovered police archives reveal no fewer than 685,000 names of foreigners and French citizens whose behavior was deemed unorthodox. The Third Republic collapsed with France's capitulation in

1940 and the proclamation of "L'État Français" by Maréchal Pétain, who obligingly communicated the secret archives to the Gestapo.[48] Someone once wrote that the Third Republic had been Vichy before Vichy. Could it be that the post-war Fourth Republic was Vichy after Vichy?

The French Revolution, notwithstanding its humanitarian proclamations, had been notoriously ambiguous in its treatment of foreigners, wavering between exclusion and hospitality, suspicion and universalistic ideals. Hadn't the Revolutionary Assembly issued a decree requiring foreigners to wear a cockade indicating their origin? [49]

With the exception of my Jewish lab director, who had endured the suffering and humiliation of German concentration camps, most Frenchmen never made the slightest effort to make me feel at home in their country. I was only tolerated by the do-gooders, and a *sale étranger* to the others. When people tolerate you, they tell you that you are not as good as they are, but that they accept you nonetheless.

Not once during my student years was I invited to cross the threshold of a French home. Some of my schoolmates, who lived with their families in comfortable Paris apartments, often called on me in my little room only to pick my brain, for I was among the top students of our class. I would help them with their assignments and share with them the oriental pastries that my mother lovingly sent me from Cairo at the cost of unbelievable harassment at the hands of the Egyptian police and customs authorities.

⌁ Café Babel ⌁

Lapland begins north of Lyon,
and Egypt just south of Rome . . . .

Arghyris (celebrated Babel philosopher)

On the opposite side of Boulevard Jourdan, the Chalet du Parc and the Café Babel were full to the brim with students from all over the world. I don't recall how many hours of my life were wasted in one or the other café undoing and redoing the world, or chatting up the female half of the Cité's population.

I belonged to a little group of five or six friends whose daily ritual consisted in having coffee at the Babel, which well deserved its name, after having had lunch at the International Restaurant. I cannot tell whether it was sheer coincidence or cultural affinity but, as it turned out, our group consisted mainly of Mediterraneans. Our leader was the unmistakably Greek Arghyris, the only student who could afford, day in day out, to pick up the bill for the whole bunch of courtiers that we were. No one knew exactly how old he was or what he studied. We only knew that he had a rich brother in Athens who mailed him a fat check every month. We would gather around him as if he were some ancient Greek master and we his disciples, and listen to his preferred philosophical dissertation, how to seduce women. I am ashamed to admit that we only listened to his prescriptions in consideration of his prodigality. You first have to make them laugh, he would say, slapping his thigh as he burst out laughing.

Alain was a murky, bleary-eyed character who did not belong to our group. After spending several years in Indochina, he was repatriated in the wake of the 1954 cease-fire agreement. No sooner did that bloody war come to an end with the disastrous French defeat of Dien Bien Phu than the Algerian rebellion broke out. The National Liberation Front was established in Cairo under the auspices of Nasser, who supported and armed the rebels.

French citizens of European origin living in Algeria were referred to as *Pieds-Noirs* ('Black Feet')—nobody knows exactly why—perhaps because they wore shoes whereas native Algerians went barefoot. Be that as it may, Café Babel was the scene of daily verbal confrontations between the Pieds-Noirs and our group of friends. My sympathies instinctively went to the Algerians, who were fighting for their independence as we had, and were daily exposed to the most inhumane tortures at the hands of the French, some of whom were students like myself who had been shipped to the Aurès Mountains against their will.

Alain's humiliating experience in Indochina had made him irredeemably xenophobic, and he naturally sided with the Pieds-Noirs, holding me personally responsible for Nasser's bias.

"Yes, I am *facho* ('a Fascist')," he would proudly bark when addressing us "and you are only a bunch of *métèques*." Little did he know how right he was, at least etymologically, for *métèques* we were indeed. So were Aristotle and Alexander the Great![50]

That afternoon, we were having coffee as usual on the terrace of the Babel when Alain made his daily appearance, gratifying us with his habitual litany of racist abuse. Arghyris was in good spirits and in the mood for open conflict. He threw some uncharitable epithets in Alain's direction, mostly having to do with the size of his male attributes and their competence—or lack thereof. The debate heated up as they fired more and more virulent shots at each other. In a moment of despair, Alain haughtily told Arghyris: "Anyway, I have no intention of wasting my time with a Greek. Go home to your uncivilized country."

We were flabbergasted and bewildered. Uncivilized, the Greeks? "Did he actually utter that enormity?" we asked each other in disbelief. How was Arghyris going to respond to that ignoramus? It was High Noon. The protagonists were standing face to face in the saloon, their hands frozen beside their holsters. We were petrified in our chairs, waiting for the retaliation to come. Arghyris finally broke the unbearable suspense. He looked his foe squarely in the eye, clenched his right fist except for the middle finger, which he pointed at Alain's nose, and calmly declared:

"I, not civilized? . . . Well, let me tell you, you ignorant blighter . . . When the grandfather of your grandfather's grandfather dragged his woman by her filthy hair into his cave, the grandfather of my grandfather's grandfather was . . . homosexual!"

Alain stood dumbfounded and speechless. The Babel, whose indolent onlookers had witnessed the duel in silence, resounded with applause.

Arghyris saluted the cheering crowd, took a few bows, then sat down with the grin of a victorious Alexander-back-from-Persia. In order to let out the leftover steam, he went on mumbling insults in Greek, some of which I could clearly understand, having spent my childhood vacations in Alexandria, where the Greek population was abundant, especially around the suburbs of Ibrahimiya and Cleopatra. American films shown at the Ibrahimiya Palace were subtitled in French, with the Arabic and Greek translations projected on a little auxiliary screen to the right of the main screen. When you learn a foreign language from your playmates, the first words they teach you are usually scurrilous, to say the least. I had also come to learn some very gratifying Italian compliments that were surprisingly akin to those favored by the Egyptians.

In a more serious vein, I thought to myself that the Greek language had enjoyed exceptional permanence since the dawn of their great civilization. I remembered our family trips to Greece, where the islands, the mountains and the tiniest places were still called by the very names we had studied in our history books, taking us back to the fifth century B.C.

Following the summer holidays, we were on the outlook for newly landed innocents who were eager to discover Paris and usually found us curiously obliging. I met the beautiful Marielle at the Pavillon Néerlandais, where a whole host of bright young Polytechnique graduates were on the lookout for a bride. She had enrolled in the Institut des Sciences Politiques after obtaining her bachelor of laws in her hometown of Marseilles. Shortly before Easter, as she devoured a peach pie with shameless gluttony at the Babel, I asked her to marry me. She had just turned twenty-one and marriage was the last thing on her mind. She replied that it was too early, that she had other plans for the immediate future, that we did not really know each other, etc., etc. As I walked her back to the Néerlandais under a light spring drizzle, I was only able to mumble, "Il bruine," ('It's drizzling'), something she loved to hear because my Egyptian accent made me roll the r's, a shortcoming she affectionately derided.

When she returned from an Easter furlough spent with her family in Marseilles, she asked if I could offer her a peach pie at the Babel. There, she told me that on second thoughts, she had changed her mind.

~ The Croix de Guerre ~

Morts pour la France

During the summer of 1951, my parents and I sailed to France to visit my brother, who was studying medicine in the southern town of Montpellier. I had just graduated from the Faculty of Engineering and did not exactly know what to do with myself. Professor Hammam Mahmoud had offered me the coveted position of lecturer, followed by a scholarship in the United States. The catch was that when you returned to Egypt with your Ph.D., you were committed to spend a number of years working for the government.

In the course of our stay in Paris, my father introduced me to one of his good friends, a Sorbonne professor who offered to allow me to join his laboratory and apply for a Science Doctorate. After much soul searching, I opted for the French solution and decided to remain in France.

It was early October 1951; the skies were black and it rained incessantly. The Metro washed down a miserable underground crowd that sucked on yellow Gauloise butts smelling of horse manure. Going back and forth to the Sorbonne became increasingly depressing. Located in the historic building, rue Victor Cousin, the laboratory was shabby and ill equipped. The pre-war instruments at my disposal were not only obsolete, they didn't even work, and I had to spend the first three months repairing them.

I kept repeating to myself that Pierre and Marie Curie had discovered radium in worse conditions a few hundred yards away, but couldn't find any solace in that thought.

That afternoon, I hung up my white gown on a rusty nail that someone had planted generations earlier behind the lab door, and went out for a walk. As I turned the corner of Boulevard Saint Michel, I came to Café Capoulade, always full to brim with idle students sipping cafe-crèmes and smoking Gauloises. I sat down and lit a cigarette. Thereupon, a miracle happened. Standing in front of me was César, a Lycée student who lived one block away from our Cairo apartment. "What on earth are you doing here?" "And you?" As it turned out, César had just graduated from the École Supérieure d'Électricité, nicknamed Sup'Élec, one of a handful of Grandes Écoles whose reputation was impressive.

"Don't waste your time at the Sorbonne. You are a graduate engineer, and that automatically entitles you to enroll in Sup'Élec without having to sit the dreadful admission contest. That is exactly what I did, as well as a few others before me."

Following his directions, I took the Metro and emerged at Porte de Vanves in the middle of an immense barren space reminiscent of Vittorio de Sica's post-war neo-realist films. A few dozen Gypsies were aimlessly wandering about in their shabby horse-drawn caravans. In those days, Paris was surrounded by a green belt so trashy that people referred to it as *La zone*, and its inhabitants *les zonards*, an expression which to this day applies to the most destitute suburban dwellers. I would have turned around and plunged into the Metro's abyss had I not caught sight of Sup'Élec's stately building, which starkly contrasted with the surrounding tenements.

I pushed open the entrance door and found myself in the midst of a large group of students, mostly male, criss-crossing the entrance hall in every direction. When I told the young lady in the administration department of my intention to enroll, her reply was "But, *mon pauvre monsieur*, enrolment is closed for this academic year. You may apply for next year if you wish. Here are the forms."

I suddenly felt relieved and elated. I now had every excuse to go back to Egypt and spend the rest of my days in a land whose sky was eternally blue, whose people were kind, and whose children honored their parents. I would ride my bicycle to the pyramids and, who knows, fall in love again.

As I walked toward the gate, oblivious of the students who had suddenly become total strangers, a large marble plaque caught my eye. Dozens of names were carved on either side of a bronze palm branch under the sober inscription *Morts pour la France* ('Died for France'). I stopped to browse among the names of those unfortunate young men who, after spending so many years over their books, had fallen for nothing. How old were they? Where was I when they fell? Did their brains liquefy in the blink of an eye, dissolving the science with which they were charged?

As I mulled over these somber thoughts, the young lady came running toward me. She said, out of breath, "Am I glad you are still here! The director just came in. He wants to see you right away."

The director's office smelled of old books and leather upholstery, and reminded me of my grandfather's library. He told me that Cairo University honor students usually made it to the top of their class at Sup'Élec, adding, "You should understand, however, that compared to what you will be learning here, you haven't learned anything yet. You will soon discover that younger men who are not graduate engineers like yourself know a lot more than you have ever learned so far. The first few months will be difficult, for you will need to catch up with those kids and learn to think for yourself. Forget you are a graduate engineer and go back to basics. After that, if you are still with us, I have no doubt that you will rank among the best. Now don't waste any time; run downstairs. before Louis de Broglie's inaugural class begins."[51]

Had I not stopped to read the marble plaque, my life would have taken a completely different course. Who knows which?

No sooner had I joined Sup'Élec than Prime Minister Nahas Pasha, who no doubt aspired to regain his lost political virginity, unilaterally abrogated the 1936 Anglo-Egyptian treaty,[52] declaring Farouk king of Egypt and Sudan, and demanding total evacuation of British troops.[53] Violent student demonstrations broke out in Cairo and elsewhere. 'Liberation battalions' were formed, Egyptian workers withdrew from the British base, food supplies to the Suez Canal Zone were cut, and guerrilla groups began harassing the British, calling for the immediate evacuation of the Canal Zone.

Having abandoned its mandate for Palestine and evacuated Abadan in Iran, [54] Britain was not about to also relinquish its Middle Eastern stronghold on the Canal. Extremely violent clashes ensued, turning the region into a veritable battlefield. Students and workers demanded that Egypt declare war on Great Britain and supply them with weapons. The

Lancashire Fusiliers charged the crowds, killing several demonstrators, and in December, British bulldozers and Centurion tanks demolished fifty Egyptian mud houses in an attempt to open a road leading to a water supply. On January 25, 1952, British forces surrounded a police station in Ismailiya whose Egyptian officers were suspected of connivance with the rebels, demanding their surrender. The ensuing battle left forty policemen dead and seventy wounded.

That was the spark that set Cairo on fire on January 26, 1952, a day that began with a mutiny by Cairo policemen to avenge their fallen colleagues, and came to be remembered as Black Saturday. A crowd gone amok set fire to British property, hotels, and foreign department stores, burning, shattering, and looting. At the end of the day, Cairo was smoldering in a cloud of black smoke. To this day, it is not possible to point to a single responsible party or organization.

Nahas' government fell, ushering in a period of great instability. For the first time since the birth of the nationalist movement, the events had targeted the king himself. Sadat later wrote, "The Cairo fire was a warning sign of impending revolution which, if it broke out, would destroy everything. It was definitely directed at the king and the political system."

At the end of the first year, I ranked near the top of my class of sixty, telegraphed my parents, and celebrated with my friends at Café Babel. I was very homesick, and felt a strong urge to return to Cairo, if only for a short vacation. I wanted to hug my mother and my little sister, who was about to turn seventeen. I wanted to retrieve the heady smell of Cairo, the dust, the blaring of horns, and clank of horse carriages. I wanted to walk to Ismailiya Square and rediscover the taste of Issaevitch's *foul* and *falafel* sandwiches. I wanted to breathe the air of Cinema Metro, walk to the Lycée and visit my childhood classrooms, feel the blackboard with the palm of my hand and smell the chalk and violet ink. I wanted to see my room and the instruments I had patiently assembled with my own hands—an oscilloscope, a frequency generator, a radio transmitter. I wanted to lean from the balcony and perhaps catch sight of Yvette absentmindedly leaning from hers. She would wave at me as she lovingly did the day I sailed to France.

I wanted to be reassured that my father had recovered from his stroke, sit with him at Groppi's, and tell him of my experiences at Sup'Élec and the Cité Universitaire, of the drab autumn, the bitter cold winter, and the discovery of spring in Paris. I also wanted him to explain the tragic events that unfolded in January 1952, when Cairo was set afire.

In his correspondence, he warned that we were on the verge of a revolution that might change the face of Egypt forever. He recommended that I spend the summer vacations in France. Yvette's family was planning to sail to France during the holidays and criss-cross the countryside aboard their Studebaker. Her father invited me to join their party, and I wholeheartedly accepted, never having had a chance to discover rural France.

On July 23, we heard on the radio that the 'Free Officers,' under the titular leadership of General Muhammad Naguib, had seized power and overthrown King Farouk. No one knew exactly which way the country was headed, including the Free Officers themselves, as attested by Sadat himself many years later.

I felt relieved that the revolution had unfolded without bloodshed, and that Naguib, who came across as liberal, had allowed the king, his wife, and his infant son to sail unharmed to Italy. The monarchy was not dissolved, and a regency council was put in place, the king having abdicated in favor of his son Ahmad Fuad. Their departure on board the *Mahroussa* was even accompanied by a twenty-one gun salute!

When classes resumed at summer's end, the director formally announced that Vincent Auriol, president of the Republic, would visit Sup'Élec on October 21 and award our school the 1939–1945 Croix de Guerre on behalf of its fallen students. A quarter of a century earlier, the school had been awarded the 1914–18 Croix de Guerre.

Thereupon, I received word from the director that he wanted to see me in his office. He had decided that the top three students would hold the cushion upon which the president was to pin the Cross, and asked me if I had any objection to being one of the three.

I was taken aback by that request. Would I be disloyal to my country if I accepted the director's offer? In his letters, my father reassured me that the French, who had not received any particularly alarming instructions from their embassy, were enjoying tea at Groppi and the debonair Cairo life as usual. French schools had reopened, and General Naguib was making every attempt to appease the foreign community by visiting churches and other symbolic venues.

I thanked the director, and courteously accepted.

October 21, 1952 was a very cold day, and an incessant icy drizzle kept falling as if to set the stage for a day of mourning and remembrance. The top student of our class, an officer in the French army, wore a khaki uniform and a light blue kepi, his chest adorned with two strips of tiny multicolored bands, as he stood at attention with the satin cushion resting on his forearms. The 1914–18 cross was already pinned down, slightly left of center. The second student and I also stood at attention in our dark suits on either side of the officer. A canopy had been erected in the courtyard with the president of the republic and the director in the forefront, surrounded by a learned assembly of officials, most probably the ministers of industry, reconstruction, etc. I had no idea who they were. Following the director's flowery welcome speech, the president took center stage and, in grandiloquent terms typical of the nascent fourth republic, congratulated our school for the electrification of the Donzères-Montdragon dam. In those days, reconstructing a France in ruins was top priority. Electrical power and radio broadcasting were about as high-tech as you could get.

Throughout the ceremony, I cursed the Paris weather, for I was literally shivering and couldn't keep my nose from running. Of course I wasn't going to blow it right there, in the middle of the president's speech! We had not been allowed to wear overcoats, and the woolen undershirt that my mother had thoughtfully packed did not prevent me from catching the worst cold of my life.

Perhaps France was not racist after all. Perhaps it had never ceased to be the land of human rights. Perhaps it was true that thousands of men and women had died in combat, in the Resistance, and on the roads of France, only so that the director of an establishment such as this might someday ask a young Egyptian if he *wouldn't mind* raising the school banner and receiving the Croix de Guerre on behalf of his fallen fellow alumni.

~ There is Something Rotten... ~

*Their troops marched through the streets of Cairo singing obscene
songs about our king, a man whom few of us admired but who,
nevertheless, was as much a national symbol as our flag. Farouk was
never so popular as when he was being insulted in public by British
troops, for we knew, as they knew, that by insulting our unfortunate
king they were insulting the Egyptian people as a whole.*

General Muhammad Naguib[55]

I remember King Fuad's frightening plastered-up handlebar moustache,
and my father's mixed feelings toward him, which I gleaned from his
hushed conversations with my mother. "Imagine a king who does not
speak the language of his countrymen!" Fuad spoke Turkish in the
palace, as did the entire royal family.

During Fuad's nineteen year reign,[56] Queen Nazli gave birth to one
boy—Farouk—and four girls—Fawziya, Fayza, Fayqa, and Fathiya—all
of whom could have been beauty queens not to mention real queens. In
memory of his mother Ferial, the king had wanted all his children's'
names to begin with the letter "F." Princess Fawziya later became
empress of Iran upon marrying the young shah despite her brother's initial reluctance, for Egypt belonged to the Sunni branch of Islam whereas Iran was predominantly Shi'ite.[57]

Farouk was born on February 11, 1920 in one of the four hundred
rooms that comprised the palace of Qasr el Qubba, amidst forty hectares
of perfectly groomed royal grounds.

Consistent with his ancestor Muhammad Ali's disregard for Egypt's
heritage—the viceroy had offered the two Luxor obelisks to King Louis
Philippe of France and three more to the British court[58]—Farouk had turned
ten without ever seeing the pyramids, much to the amazement of his English
schoolmates, who could not fathom such an incredible shortcoming.

Fuad saw to it, however, that his son, whom he did not like, be taught proper Arabic, a decision that caused surprise and delight among the common people, for it portended that the new king would look charitably upon their miserable condition. Since the days of the pharaohs, the Egyptian people looked to the ruler's benevolence to alleviate the burden of their daily lives.

Fuad died on April 19, 1936, and a Regency Council was put in place pending the young prince's accession to the throne. When he returned from England, Farouk candidly declared that a king was not fair unless the people enjoyed their lawful rights, that the poor were not responsible for their condition, that it behooved the rich to give to the poor, etc. The higher he raised the people's expectations, the harder he eventually fell.

In those days, ninety percent of Egypt's population lived in the countryside on less than five pounds a day, toiling on estates owned by an immensely wealthy aristocracy. That state of affairs did not deter the prince, shortly before his coronation, from embarking with his family on a vacation trip to Europe along with a retinue of thirty and 250 trunks.

In Egypt's history, 1936 was a pivotal year. In the face of King Fuad's sympathies for the Italians, the British sought to reinforce the sentiment that the fascists would be harsher occupants, and loosened their grip on Egypt, granting it increased autonomy.[59]

In September of that year, another momentous decision authorized general admission to the Egyptian military academy, which was heretofore reserved for the aristocratic elite, opening its doors to young men of modest social origin. Thus those very men who would overthrow the king sixteen years thence were allowed to become officers.

In May 1937, a conference was convened in Montreux, Switzerland, by Egypt and twelve European countries, putting an end to capitulatory rights.

Farouk's coronation was celebrated in July 1937 amidst unprecedented popular jubilation. Myriad of garlands of flowers and lights adorned the streets of Cairo, where triumphal arches were erected bearing his portrait surmounted by giant crowns. I even remember a large array of light bulbs spelling *Vive Farouk!* in French.

The handsome young king appeared on the balcony of 'Abdin

palace clad in a long white frock coat, his breast bedecked with a multitude of medals that caused my father to facetiously remark that he had certainly not earned them in class, where his performance was less than honorable. He had been turned down by Eton and one of Britain's military academies.

Sir Edward Ford, the king's tutor in 1936–37, said of him that he never read a book after his coronation, and that he had no respect for appointments, sometimes keeping him waiting for three hours or more. Being the only boy, he had been exceedingly spoilt by his mother, Queen Nazli, of whom it was said that she led a fickle life despite her husband's strict authoritarianism. She aspired to independence, had artistic inclinations, and was a rather enlightened photographer who processed her own work. She was extremely superstitious and partook of past-midnight spiritualist séances, often accompanied by her son, on whom that habit had a disastrous influence.

It must have been love at first sight when Farouk met his future wife Safinaz Zulficar in Europe, for their engagement took place one short month after the coronation, despite both mothers' exhortations. Farouk was seventeen and the future queen fifteen.

I vividly remember the wedding celebrations on January 20, 1938. Egypt had not witnessed similarly lavish pageants since the Suez Canal opening ceremonies sixty-nine years earlier. I, for one, had never before seen floral floats in such large numbers, crumbling under thousands of freshly cut flowers of all colors. In keeping with family tradition, the queen's first name was changed to Farida, meaning "unique."

Hitler offered the young king a black and red Mercedes coupe and George VI, king of England, immediately retorted by offering him a British-made automobile. Sir Miles Lampson, the British ambassador, offered Farouk two rifles, knowing his penchant for weapons. When matters turned sour between the two countries, Lampson would say, "Leave the boy to me." He once derided Farouk's request that the two canons placed at the entrance of the Yacht Club be transported to the Palace. Farouk consequently loathed the ambassador, whose disdain was enhanced by his massive build and arrogant demeanor.

In counterpoint, out of deference to his mother's French great-grand-father Soliman Pasha, Farouk expressed his attachment to France on more than one occasion. Monsieur de Comnène, director of the Heliopolis Lycée Français and the king's private French tutor, often invited him to the school commencement ceremonies, and the king graciously acceded. In a 1939 issue of *Le Temps*, Farouk addressed the following message to the French: "It is with great emotion that I address myself to France. I wish to tell her that I know and love her. I know her through her long and prestigious history, through her literature and her arts. I love her learned men, her peasants, her craftsmen. I love her elegance and the simplicity of her family life. I love her patriotism and generosity. I love her through her living and her dead, through Champollion, de Lesseps, and Soliman Pasha. I salute the country to which so many strong links join my Country and my House." Given Farouk's familiarity with literature and the arts, it is not unreasonable to assume that it was de Comnène or some other French-speaking courtier who drafted that message.

When Field Marshal Rommel's troops reached El Alamein, Farouk saw a God-sent opportunity to rid the country of the British, and overtly sided with the Germans, scoffing at Lampson. On February 4, 1942, the ambassador surrounded the royal palace with his tanks, demanding his abdication unless he appointed pro-British Nahas Pasha prime minister. That was the beginning of the end for Farouk, and Nahas as well.

Britain's victory over the Germans in the historic battle of El Alamein dashed Farouk's hopes and allowed Lampson's arrogance to increase tenfold. When Churchill and Roosevelt met in Egypt in 1945, a childish Farouk thought to upstage the British leader by sporting a longer cigar and adorning his chest with innumerable decorations.

The king attempted to present himself to the Arab world as Commander of the Faithful and legitimate caliph of Islam, but his numerous and indiscriminate sexual adventures soon became the talk of the town, as he gradually lost interest in state affairs. Queen Farida divorced him in November 1948 after giving him three exceptionally beautiful daughters—Ferial, Fawziya, and Fadya. The divorce caused immense consternation among the common people, that was later compounded by his second marriage to a sixteen-year-old commoner named Nariman Sadiq, who lacked the social graces. On the tragic day that went down in history as Black Saturday, a blissful Farouk was entertaining his high-ranking officers in celebration of his son's birth, while Cairo was burning.

He was known to play poker until the wee hours of the morning at the Automobile Club, and loose considerable amounts of money. On one occasion, having announced that he had a king of spades, he was courteously asked to produce it. Thereupon, he haughtily replied, "The king is I!" He probably had a premonition of his impending demise when he once declared that there would soon remain only five kings in the world—the four kings in the pack of cards and the king of England!

During the 1948 Palestine war, he allegedly participated in a ring that included high-ranking military figures who purchased defective World War II equipment, with the help of a certain Pulli, a palace electrician, and sold it to the army, costing the armed forces hundreds of lives. The Arab countries' humiliating defeat came to be regarded by the Egyptians as Farouk's personal defeat, and the scandal caused a handful of young front-line officers to vow to remove him.

Forsaken by the British and the Americans as well, he was forced to abdicate and sail miserably to Italy on the *Mahroussa*, the very yacht that took his exiled grandfather Ismail to Italy seventy-three years earlier, en route to Emitgan in Turkey. General Naguib, first president of the Egyptian Republic, later said that, as he was about to embark, the king confided to him, "You have anticipated what I was planning to do." During his forced exile, Farouk's obsession with women apparently never let up, causing Nariman also to divorce him and return to Egypt without the prince, leaving the fallen king in the arms of a third-rate Italian would-be actress. He died one month after learning that his youngest daughter Fadya, following in the footsteps of her aunt Fathiya, had married a Christian.[60]

Of the eleven monarchs belonging to Farouk's august lineage, from his great-great-grandfather Muhammad Ali to his son Fuad II, five remained on the throne until their natural death, four were deposed, one was strangled, and one never ruled, not counting Prince Ahmad, who drowned in the Nile (see above, under "En Route to Alexandria").

Other members of Muhammad Ali's dynasty, however, rendered eminent services to the country, among them Princess Fatima, Fuad's sister, who sold her jewels to finance Cairo University, or Prince Omar Toussoun, who donated considerable sums of money to fend off imperialistic aggressions directed at friendly countries such as Libya, Sudan, and Ethiopia. He was first to conceive a plan to send an Egyptian delegation to the 1918 Peace Conference. The delegation—*wafd* in Arabic— gave birth to the namesake party, which was to become the leading democratic party in Egypt under the leadership of Saad Zaghlul.

An erudite and prolific author, he was tapped by the British in 1914 to succeed Khedive Abbas, son of Hilmi II, whom they had just deposed upon declaring Egypt a British protectorate, but he categorically refused, allowing Prince Hussein Kamel, the khedive's uncle and son of Ismail, to sit on the throne.

Three years later, it would be the turn of Fuad, also a son of Ismail, to be crowned sultan, then king, of Egypt. The rest is history. Farouk succeeded his father Fuad, bringing Muhammad Ali's dynasty to a pitiful end.

God only knows what turn Egypt's fate would have taken had Omar Toussoun accepted.

⚬ First Job ⚬

A student asked me what had inspired me to choose the little known field of computers forty years earlier. I answered him that I had been inspired by Divine Providence—not in a dream, but in a map of the Paris bus system.

On June 18, 1953, the week of my graduation, the Free Officers suddenly decided to abolish the monarchy and proclaim the Republic of Egypt.

It dawned on me that Egypt's two thousand-year loss of sovereignty to foreign rulers had finally come to an end. Naguib was the first Egyptian head of state since the pharaohs!

The time had come to return to Egypt, and I eagerly looked forward to reuniting with my family and friends. My enthusiasm was rekindled by the recent events and the prospect of serving my country under the new leadership. I started packing the little that remained of my possessions, mainly books. My wardrobe had not been renewed since leaving Egypt two years earlier and was showing signs of fatigue. I bundled up what was left of my winter clothes and gave them to a distant friend who devoted much of her free time to the Salvation Army. I then sent a telegram to my parents announcing my graduation and my imminent return.

My father responded with a warm congratulatory telegram, expressing his pride in "a son whose success he had never doubted," but suggested that I take a well deserved vacation after seven years spent between Cairo University and Sup'Élec.

I understood the true meaning of his cryptic post cards when, in February 1954, the Revolutionary Command Council stripped Naguib of the premiership. Things were not as smooth as they looked, and inner conflicts within the Revolutionary Command Council were beginning to surface, announcing the oncoming chaos.

In the face of the popular outcry that followed his resignation, Naguib was shortly reinstated, granting freedom of the press and announcing his intention to hold general elections. The Anglo-Egyptian Evacuation Agreement was signed in October, which stipulated that the British would leave Egypt twenty months thence. Things looked brighter than ever . . . until an assassination attempt on Nasser was used as a pretext to strip Naguib of the presidency. The ambitious Nasser took over, immediately canceling the proposed elections. Naguib was arrested by the infamous Abdel Hakim Amer, and placed under house arrest in what used to be the country house of Zaynab el Wakil, Nahas Pasha's wife, where he suffered humiliation and ill treatment at the hands of the authorities as well as the guards.

~

I decided to remain in France, at least for a while, and started looking for a job, an enormous undertaking given the strained relations between Egypt and France. After a fortnight spent catching my breath in the wake of trying oral exams, I decided to start looking seriously for a job. I bought a map of Paris and the day's *Figaro* from the bookstore on Boulevard Jourdan, then sat on the terrace of Café Babel in the warm June sun and ordered an *express*. I browsed among the myriad job offers directed at young engineering graduates, looking up their exact location on the Paris map. My criterion was a simple one: which outfit was closest to the Cité Universitaire? Thereupon, I came across an American company exactly five bus stops away on the Petite Ceinture. "That's the one!" I said to myself. I applied, received a favorable reply, and showed up for an interview with the general manager. So much for my inspiration.

Little did I suspect the problems that lay ahead. Not being French, I could not be employed without a temporary work permit, and that could not be delivered unless I was already employed! Furthermore, I could not apply for the work permit without a temporary residence, which could not be renewed unless I was employed. Worst of all, Nasser's government required that I be issued a special kind of dispensation authorizing me to be employed by a foreign company! Talk about catch twenty-two!

The general manager was a Jew who had survived Germany's concentration camps. I feared he would be unsympathetic to the ordeal of a young Egyptian, whose country had been at war with Israel for five years. I don't know what strings he pulled, but in a matter of days the residence and work permit were granted and I was hired. I was assigned to Research and Engineering, the other openings falling in sales. That suited me well for I was never really interested in interacting with prospective customers or closing deals, and my sales talents were pitiful. In the family environment where I grew up, selling was not looked upon as a particularly honorable endeavor, let alone devoting your entire life to that purpose. On the other hand, I had been fascinated by science as far back as I could remember.

On my first day in the lab, I was handed a textbook that dealt with the design of digital computers, a subject not included in Sup'Élec's curriculum at the time—neither was the transistor for that matter! In the book, I discovered a special kind of algebra invented by British nineteenth-century mathematician George Boole to help him solve problems of logic. In 1938, a Bell Labs scientist by the name of Claude Shannon showed that Boolean algebra, as it was called, could be put to advantage in the design of computers. I was very excited by the field's novelty and set about writing memo upon memo, overflowing with original ideas. My essays, which were published internally, soon drew the attention of a Lebanese American who had just been appointed vice-president for Research and Engineering. I owe him an immense debt of gratitude for he was quick to extract me from the depressing environment that prevailed in the French lab, where my mathematical excursions fell on deaf ears and attracted only gibes from my peers. He offered to move me to the United States, a childhood dream of mine.

We were now in the fall of 1956, and my wedding date was set for December 29, in Marseilles. It could not be changed under any circumstances, my future in-laws having invited hundreds of guests and made elaborate arrangements. I decided to travel to the United States right away, look for a home, then return to France in time for the wedding and fly back to the States with my young bride. Marielle was twenty-one and I twenty-seven.

~ Three Births, Three Cultures: ~ Stéphane, Valérie, Olivia

The contrast between France and America was striking. Everything looked larger and cleaner, and everyone I met, whether at work or on the street, was curious about France and wanted to be reassured that I liked America. "How do you like it here?" they invariably asked, as though they feared the French had come to reject the very Americans who delivered them from German tyranny. I was not particularly inclined to defend France's versatility and nostalgia of lost *grandeur*, or embark upon a psychoanalysis of the average Frenchman. I kept reminding them that I was an Egyptian whose love of France was rooted in his education, if not in his experience.

My peers made me feel comfortable from the very first day and showed me around the lab's rambling premises. They invited me to their homes, a thing which had never once occurred throughout my student years in France. Their wives volunteered to help me look for a house, or "go house hunting," as they used to say.

The erudite atmosphere that prevailed in the laboratory belied the age-old prejudice that the French harbored vis-à-vis Americans in general, and their education system in particular, which they regarded as inferior to theirs. Most of my American peers were Ph.D.'s in their twenties, and I learned an immeasurable lot from them. Beyond their outstanding scientific credentials, most of them were versed in the arts, making them true renaissance men. I shared a little cubicle with Herb, a physicist who worked on artificial intelligence, a virgin field at the time to which scientists were beginning to turn their attention, convinced as they were that the computer, a kind of brain, would some day outperform human beings. He designed a program that enabled the sluggish computer to solve elementary problems of plane geometry. Another scientist, Professor Albert Samuel, designed a program that played an interesting game of checkers, prophesying that the computer would soon defeat the world's top chess players. Yet another studied voice recognition, and often put me to task uttering long lists of English and French words. (Either because of my accent or the program, the computer rarely understood me!) John Paul introduced me to the little known Japanese game of *go*, for which he had written a somewhat primitive computer algorithm.[61] A Belgian engineer, Bert, was struggling with a very hard problem, that of drawing images on a cathode-ray tube. In those days, there was neither computer screen nor mouse. One of my most brilliant peers, John Backus, invented a revolutionary language that allowed you to communicate with the computer using ordinary mathematical expressions. His breakthrough invention, known as Fortran, instantly conquered the world, making him one of the greatest pioneers of the computer age, on whose threshold we stood.

One of my papers was chosen to appear in the first issue of the corporation's research journal, but the galley proofs didn't reach me until after my wedding. Having missed the deadline, I had to settle for issue number two.

I stayed in a little ten-room motel that was managed by an iron-fisted bosomy Valkyrie and her little round ancillary husband. The room was impeccably clean and perpetually smelled of Cashmere Bouquet body soap. What a change from Madame Moralène's dingy furnished room and her out-of-bounds bathroom! The company authorized me to lease a Ford automobile that seemed inordinately large by French standards. Before long, I became familiar with power steering, power brakes, and automatic transmission. You are fast becoming a soft, pampered American, I kept saying to myself, but I enjoyed every minute of it. It took me a while, though, and one or two admonitions from the local trooper, to comply with the twenty-five miles per hour speed limit, and not pass a yellow school bus whose lights were flashing. It dawned on me that my years in France had turned an indolent Egyptian into a highly-strung, self-centered misanthropist. I therefore decided to slow my pace and enjoy the ineffable beauty of the winding little roads, so typical of American suburbia. The ancient oaks, the magnolias, the ponds, the smell of freshly cut grass, and the whitewashed split-level homes with their funny semi-cylindrical mailboxes charmed me. I was so dazzled when the maple trees turned red that I took picture upon picture, knowing well that the skeptical French back home would inevitably attribute the color of the trees against the Indian summer sky to the Kodachrome film, for it is a matter of common knowledge, *mon cher*, that the Americans, who know no subtlety, suffer from a natural tendency to exaggerate everything!

When December finally came, the French consulate in New York abruptly refused to renew my visa, no matter how much I pleaded. Nothing mattered in their eyes—that I had graduated from a Grande École, that I was employed in France by the subsidiary of a prestigious American Company, or that I was to marry a French girl on December 29. "Desolé, cher Monsieur," haughtily replied the consul, "but you do not seem to understand that your country is at war with France."

Egypt at war with France! How did that nightmare come about?[62]

The French consulate informed me that the visa might take several weeks before being granted, if at all. I decided to prepare myself to travel to France at a moment's notice, and the company agreed to transfer me to our Swiss laboratory pending the visa's hypothetical delivery. My in-laws pulled every string they could muster, as time was running out. As a precautionary measure, they went as far as making arrangements for a subsidiary ceremony in Switzerland, just in case.

My forced exile in Zurich lasted two restless weeks during which I reluctantly went to the laboratory every morning, confronted with icy roads and incessant snowfall, then returned to my hotel with nothing to look forward to but dull uneventful evenings.

The visa was finally granted on the eve of my wedding, forcing events to unfold at a much faster pace than planned. We rented a small Renault 4CV and spent a brief honeymoon in the south of France before getting ready to fly to America. We were still in the wake of the Suez aggression and gas was rationed, prompting some of our good friends to share their valuable coupons with us.

At the end of a rather long but otherwise pleasant flight on Air France— we had to refuel in Shannon and Gander—our Lockheed Constellation finally landed at Idlewild airport on January 17, 1957. We were met by a vice-president who whisked us away in a long black limousine to the New York headquarters, where a young secretary first accompanied my wife to the ladies' room, suggesting that she might want to "powder her nose," then ushered us into the chairman's office. He welcomed us with the words "I am told you are doing some interesting work in the labs and were quick to adopt our ways. If you wish to stay with us, only the sky is the limit."

That afternoon, I dragged my exhausted wife to the top of the Empire State Building, where we recorded our voices on a 45 rpm plastic disk that we later mailed to her family. Nothing could be mailed safely to Egypt, and my parents never heard our New York message.

The following morning, my young bride and I visited St. Patrick's

Cathedral. From the guide, we learned the precise height of the cathedral and its volume in cubic feet compared to that of Saint Peter of the Vatican, oblivious of the spiritual content of the impressive spaces. One visitor asked how much it had cost to build it, causing my wife to pinch my arm and raise her eyebrows. I don't remember the answer of the guide, who was surely prepared for a question of that nature; I only remember saying to myself that George Bernanos was right when he said that the machine age was the civilization of quantity, as opposed to that of quality.

A rented car was delivered to the doorstep of our hotel, and we merrily drove upstate, marveling at the snow-blanketed landscape. As I drew my wife's attention to the typically American homes along the Taconic parkway, she couldn't believe they were built of timber, with a telephone in every house and a car behind every garage door. In those days, the French telephone system was so primitive that half the population was waiting for a telephone line while the other half was waiting for a dial tone!

Our furnished house nested cozily in a wooded area, all of whose dwellers also worked for the company. Scotty and Dottie lived across the drive and befriended us the minute we moved in. He was in sales and wore a hat to work, something totally foreign to the French dress code. She was a lovely American housewife, typical of the fifties, with her thin waist and long ample skirts. They owned a black-and-white television and regularly invited us to watch the *Ed Sullivan Show*, *I Love Lucy*, *What's My Line*, and others, all of which afforded us an insight into American manners and customs of the day. On their way to church every Sunday morning, Scotty, Dottie, and their daughters Betsie and Leslie reminded me of the ads in *Look* magazine where a middle-class American family would be seen happily cruising in the latest model out of Detroit.

Life was easy. I was brimming with ideas, and my wife enrolled at Vassar College, where she made several friends, who often rode their bicycles to our modest home for chocolate cake and coffee.

In the summer of 1957, I was invited to deliver a paper at the Summer Institute for Symbolic Logic, which was being held at Cornell

University. There, I had the good fortune to rub shoulders with the giants of the field—Quine, Tarski, Church, Kleene, Rosser, and others. I learned an immeasurable amount from that erudite crowd, and I shall always be grateful to each one of them.

The summer was pleasantly warm, and the beautiful campus conducive to romantic endeavors. My son Stéphane was thus conceived in Ithaca, New York. In those days, there were no sonograms to let you know in advance whether you expected a boy or a girl. The unborn child was therefore referred to as Ithaca! Marielle was barely twenty-three, and insisted on having her child in Marseilles with her mother and sisters by her side, forsaking the godsent opportunity of giving birth to an American citizen. Be that as it may, some twenty-five years later, Stéphane, alias Ithaca, was granted a Fulbright as well as a George Lurcy scholarship, and received his Masters of Laws from Michigan University with flying colors.

We frequently had dinner at a nearby delicatessen, where the Rosen family introduced us to new culinary experiences, notably pastrami on rye, lox and cream cheese, bagels and kosher dills. When we told the owner that we were planning to have our child in France, Mrs. Rosen took pity on my wife, and asked us in all candor if they had good hospitals over there! We flew back to France a few days before the event and stayed at my in-laws' villa, where Marielle's innumerable relatives and friends visited us daily, eager to hear about the mythical United States and view our Kodachrome slides. My father-in-law had graduated from Harvard shortly before the depression, and one of Marielle's sisters was even born in Scarsdale, New York. My in-laws, who, strangely enough, never went back to the United States, were moved to tears when they saw the pictures of my expectant wife posing in front of the Tudor building they had once inhabited in Scarsdale.

François was a close family friend whose parents had died in German concentration camps when he was a small child. My wife's family was a kind of second home to him, his sister Aline, and his elder brother Pierre, who later became one of the staunchest and most prominent upholders of human rights.

That year, François, freshly graduated as a barrister, was appointed by the court to assist one of a dozen women who had had abortions and were being tried for that criminal offence. Also on trial was the doctor who had illegally carried out the operations. In the fifties, those who performed abortions, whether or not they were doctors, were referred to as *faiseurs d'anges*, or angel-makers, one of the cruelest and most pathetic colloquial metaphors in the French language. François insisted that we attend the collective trial and hear him deliver his first defense plea, but Marielle, who was within days of giving birth, was not particularly inclined to sit in a courtroom with her nine-month prominence, as if to scoff at those miserable women who had endured God knows what physical and moral ordeals. François insisted and we eventually obliged.[63]

Ten or fifteen minutes into the trial, amidst the prosecutor's outpouring of gory details, my wife experienced her first contractions. We rushed to the Clinique de l'Oasis, and half an hour later, on April 19, 1958, Stéphane Jean Joseph was born.[64]

On August 22, 1958, an agreement was signed in Zurich between France and Egypt, ushering in the beginnings of a return to normal relations between the two countries. The Lycées reopened their doors, albeit under Egyptian management, and sequestered French properties were partially freed.[65]

Like a cork on the surface of troubled waters, I kept bobbing up and down at the mercy of every mood-change in Franco-Egyptian relations. Having my passport renewed became increasingly difficult, and the consul general invariably urged me to return to my country and serve the new ruler whose large portrait hung above his head.

On May 19, 1959, I defended my doctoral thesis at the Sorbonne in the very amphitheater where Marie Curie had defended hers! I was obviously very impressed by the august setting, but dreaded most of all the French mathematicians in attendance. The thesis was based on my work in the United States and made little reference, if any, to modern French mathematicians. I doubt if the French had even heard of the Ithaca crowd!

(When my brother defended his doctoral thesis in Montpellier, which was based on his work in the States, he advocated a surgical approach to the treatment of cholecystitis, a severe gall bladder ailment. One pontiff in the jury scoffed at American practices—they were greedy savages, lancet in hand, always prompt to open bellies and charge exorbitant fees. In the opinion of the medical bigwigs of the time, French medicine was the best in the world. France was barely emerging from the dark years of German occupation and had been cut off from the "Anglo-Saxons." Very few French could read English anyway.)

In June, my wife obtained the *Institut des Sciences Politiques* diploma, in addition to her law degree. (Little did we suspect that our son Stéphane, who was one year old, and our yet unborn daughter Olivia would both follow in her footsteps.)

My father died in October of that year, soon after writing us a long letter of congratulations that was filled with an eerie sense of foreboding.

In the spring of 1960, we again moved to the United States. I was one of a handful of international employees to be familiar at the time with an emerging field called teleprocessing, that consisted in marrying telecommunications and computers. Anyone using the Internet nowadays takes that marriage for granted, but in the late fifties, it was far from self-evident and required special skills that few possessed. I shuttled back and forth between the United States and Europe, where I was often called upon to make presentations to major European airline companies who were eager to modernize their antiquated reservation systems by hooking up remote terminals to a central mainframe. Other prospective customers were forward-thinking banks, insurance companies, etc.

The Egyptian economy was in a shambles, and no one could anticipate what Nasser's next move was going to be.[66] In November 1961, his police arrested four respectable French diplomats, convicting them of espionage,[67] and forbade the entry of French citizens into Egypt. As a retaliatory measure, the French government recalled all French teachers and prevented Egyptian citizens from leaving France. Luckily, our little family had already left the scene, and I was able to pursue my research work in the United States.

In the spring of 1962, the Evian Agreement was signed between de Gaulle and the Algerians, sealing Algeria's independence and the tragic migration to France of thousands upon thousands of Pieds-Noirs, those Frenchmen who had felt as much at home in Algeria as their compatriots on the banks of the Suez Canal. Nasser, a staunch ally of the Algerian rebels, saluted the event by freeing the French diplomats in April, marking the beginning of a new era in economic, political, and cultural relations between the two countries.

In June 1962, Marielle was again about to give birth, and we decided to have our second child in the United States.

Around the middle of June, I was assigned by the company to do something or other in London. I called Marielle every afternoon to inquire after her pregnancy, which was quite advanced. On the afternoon of June 24, she said, "If I were in your shoes, I wouldn't wait much longer before coming back." I jumped on the evening flight, took a cab from Idlewild to Grand Central Station, and another from the little suburban station to our house. It must have been five in the morning when I finally fell in bed after kissing my wife and Stéphane. No sooner had I shut my eyes than Marielle nudged me two or three times in the ribs, announcing the onset of contractions. We rushed to the local hospital, where they immediately wheeled her into the delivery room as I collapsed on a couch in the father's room and fell sound asleep.

Minutes later, a nurse woke me up with the words "You are the father of a beautiful little girl!" She was holding the bundle in her arms and allowed me to place the palm of my hand over her little tummy.

At that moment, Valérie Pascale Isabelle painstakingly opened one blue eye, then the other, and no one will ever convince me that she didn't actually look at me and smile.

Toward the middle of 1963, the company offered me a three-year assignment in Japan, suggesting that we take an exploratory trip to Tokyo, following which my wife and I would make up our minds.

We returned to France for a short summer vacation and began preparing ourselves for the adventure, with our Spanish nanny Mercedes diligently helping us pack, knowing well that she might have to return to her native Spain should we accept the Tokyo assignment. The prospect of sailing back to New York on Steamship France was very exciting to all of us. We boarded the train at Gare Saint Lazare on September 13, 1963 and embarked immediately upon reaching Le Havre. I remember Mercedes lounging in the deck chair hugging Valérie against her chest in the gentle Atlantic breeze. Stéphane, who was five at the time, was terribly seasick the entire crossing and only found some respite in the ship's swimming pool, whose water remained level despite the ship's rolling and pitching. Shortly after landing in New York, we drove off to Virginia where lived my brother, whose wife Solange offered to keep our children during our short absence, together with our dear Mercedes.

In Tokyo, we stayed at the Okura, an exquisitely Japanese hotel, surrounded by delicately landscaped shrubbery and ancient stones.

November 23 was a Saturday. We had planned to spend the day in Kyoto, having heard so much about that city's ineffable beauty in the fall. The TV was on as we were getting ready, though we couldn't understand what was being said. An elaborate retrospective of Kennedy's life was unfolding, going back to his childhood, his PT boat, his wedding, his inauguration, etc. My wife asked, "What month was Kennedy elected? This must be the third anniversary of his election, don't you think so?"

Suddenly, I had a hunch something terrible had happened, for the speaker's voice was unusually solemn, sounding like a eulogy. I rushed downstairs and emerged in the lobby where Japanese and foreigners alike stood petrified. I asked the concierge what was the matter. His reply was "President Kennedy is dead. Very sorry." I rushed back to our room and told Marielle, who burst into tears and fell on our bed face down, repeating over and over that it couldn't be true.

We walked to the American embassy and stood in a long line of mourners, mostly Japanese, waiting for their turn to sign the condolences book between two Marines standing at attention. When our turn came, something inspired us to address our message, in French, to Jackie Bouvier Kennedy. We did not go to Kyoto that day.

~

We rented a lovely house, immersed in a genuinely Japanese section of town untouched by the pervasive westernization of other sections. Built by a wealthy Japanese, the house was designed to be rented to *gaijins* ('foreigners'), whose lifestyle was vastly different from theirs.

It is hard to believe that we had to import our own electrical appliances, something that today would be akin to carrying coals to Newcastle. Japanese industry was slowly recovering from the war and the country still lacked the luxuries that we took for granted in the West. The landlord offered us an antique Kakemono and a collection of original etchings, should we decide to leave the air-conditioners behind, as well as other valuable treasures in exchange for my tired Volkswagen Beetle! Importing our car and appliances was a hurdle race. Were it not for the diligence of our Japanese fellow employees, we wouldn't have even begun to understand what was required of us. Though I personally loved the feel of natural wood and tranquil Japanese lines, we had Western style furniture custom built for us. That was the accepted procedure in the company, in view of the rarity of these items.

While waiting for our house to become available, we rented a two-room suite in the Okura hotel. Every afternoon, the maids knocked on our door, shyly asking if we would let Stéphane join them in their quarters. They loved his big black eyes and happy disposition, and taught him all sorts of silly games. When we finally moved into our new home— Stéphane was five and Valérie not yet two—the furniture that was delivered bore little resemblance to what we had imagined. We defined its style as Nippo-Danish and learned to live with it.

Much to our surprise, we discovered that the streets had no names and that our address only consisted of the subsection of town where we eventually established our residence, after duly registering with the nearby police box and post office.

One of the first sentences my expectant wife had to learn for the baby's sake was "Yukkuri ite kudasai," an injunction that caused the taxi drivers to temporarily slow down before again speeding up, ignoring my wife's plea. The 1964 Summer Olympics were drawing near and Tokyo was undergoing a gigantic facelift that everyone feared would never be finished in time. In the wake of the fierce bombardments that had burnt the city to the ground, innumerable streets were yet unpaved. It seemed as though former landlords had reclaimed their property helter-skelter, leaving narrow passages between the rebuilt timber houses that required you to slalom between the electrical poles hastily planted on either side of the streets. "At last old stones!" my wife exclaimed as we drove past the Imperial Palace, majestically perched beyond Niju-Bashi Bridge, in sharp contrast to the surrounding pandemonium.

I shall never forget Shimoda in summer, Kyoto and Nara in the fall. We bought a beautiful color etching of the Golden Pavilion of which Mishima once wrote that nothing in the world equaled its beauty. The temple, standing serenely like a golden jewel amidst its luxuriant surroundings, irresistibly invites you to meditate in silence.

Marielle's delivery was drawing near, and I dreaded the prospect of having to drive her to the hospital when the fateful moment came, for Tokyo's topography was changing from one day to the next, erasing whatever landmarks I had identified during my weekly reconnaissance trips. Tokyo was a sprawling metropolis thrust by the Olympic specter into a frenzy of planning and replanning. No sooner had I charted what I believed to be a viable itinerary, than new roadblocks would be thrown up along the way, playing havoc with my plans and my nerves.

On the evening of May 16, 1964, ignoring my failed attempts, my wife summoned Mioshi San, our Japanese housekeeper, and asked her what to do in her urgent circumstances.

Minutes later, a fire department ambulance pulled up in front of our door, its engine running. Because of the dense clusters of wooden houses, Tokyo had more than once been the scene of tragic fires, causing the city builders to scatter hundreds of fire stations all over the sprawling city.

On our way to Seibo Bioyin Hospital, a fireman sat next to the berth upon which Marielle was lying , his right palm resting on her stomach, as he intently gazed at his wristwatch. Every now and then, he would exclaim "Dai jobu!" reassuring my wife that everything was just fine. When we reached our destination, I attempted to offer a monetary reward to the fireman but he stubbornly refused, bowed two or three times, and took off.

We called the baby Olivia Michiko Genevieve. Olivia, because we both liked the name, and I had fallen in love with Olivia de Havilland, alias Melanie, twenty-two years earlier when *Gone with the Wind* was shown in Cairo. Michiko, which means beautiful and intelligent, was the name given to the young Japanese imperial princess, and turned out later in life to fit our little girl perfectly. Genevieve is the name of the patron saint of the city of Paris we missed so much.

I had never seen a hospital as impeccably kept as Seibo Bioyin. (The Japanese nation is probably the cleanest in the world—they make a habit of daily dipping in scalding "Ofuros," those public baths where naked men and women blissfully wade side by side.) That evening, I was authorized to admire Olivia behind a large glass window, amidst a dozen babies in their minute cribs. With their perfectly round heads, straight black hair and sharply slit eyes, Japanese newborn babies resemble delicate *kokeshi* dolls, those familiar objects typical of a nation where the child is king. In their midst, I had no difficulty singling out a rosy-cheeked baby twice their size with light curly hair and big blue eyes.

Japanese parents, not content with taking dozens of photos of their own babies, begged me to let them photograph Olivia, exclaiming "Kawai, neeeh?" ('Isn't she cute?')

When we returned home, Mioshi San suggested that I pay a visit to the fire department, whose threshold no *gaijin* had ever crossed, and bring the firemen two or three High-Lite cigarette cartons as well as an assortment of rice pastries.

But the present that drew the largest number of bows and exclamations of pride was when I told them that we had named the baby Michiko.

Interlude
~ Life in the Multinationals ~

~ Executive Development ~

S hortly after returning to the United States, a company director named Frank asked me to make a presentation to a major British "prospect." A prospect is someone who is not your customer yet, and whom you are attempting to lure into becoming one. I spent an entire weekend preparing for the event, filling more than twenty flip charts with intricate multicolored diagrams. Monday morning, I put on my best suit, rolled up the charts, and boarded the New York train.

Several presentations took place in the morning, with four senior officials from the customer side in attendance, including their president, which meant that our own president also had to attend. We broke for lunch around twelve and were chauffeured in long black limousines to the Top of the Sixes, an elegant New York club. My colleagues and I were not allowed to indulge in alcoholic beverages during working hours—they caught up later in the day—and we therefore abstained when the maître d'hôtel took our orders. Our British guests were not encumbered by such rules and drank profusely before, during, and after lunch.

I was first on the agenda upon returning to headquarters. As I unfurled my presentation flip chart after flip chart, I had the distinct feeling that I was gradually loosing my audience. Ten or fifteen minutes into my speech, the prospect's president literally fell asleep, and our own president had to prop him up a few times by discreetly thrusting his shoulder against the guest's. I looked at Frank, begging for some clue as to what to do next. He repeatedly tapped his right palm with the tip of his left hand's outstretched fingers, but I miserably failed to get the message. In despair, he twirled his hand in the air as if he were turning some kind of virtual crank. It dawned on me that it was in my best interest to bring my presentation to a premature end.

We accompanied the guests to the elevators, after which Frank said he wanted a word with me. I dreaded his reaction, for you do not turn prospects into customers by putting them to sleep. We stood in the hall-way, his forehead almost touching my nose as if he were getting ready to strike a header—he was the spitting image of Humphrey Bogart, and played the part. He calmly said, "Look Gaz, the guys in the lab tell me you are a kind of genius, but I have no way of judging that. I'll tell you what I know, though. You are a lousy salesman." That blunt observation taught me nothing new, but in a company where the act of selling was the foundation upon which the entire edifice rested, Frank's statement was akin to a death sentence. He added, "You talked bits and bytes to a bunch of guys who understand nothing other than the airline business, but never told them how your bits and bytes were going to help them make more money." Frank was right. I had never before assessed my work in monetary terms. I could feel the sharp steely edge of the guillo-tine on the back of my neck when, against all odds, he lit a cigarette, took a deep draw and said, wrapping a cloud of smoke around each syllable, "You know what, Gaz? I'm gonna do you a favor. When you go home tonight, tell Marielle to start house hunting in Scarsdale, Hartsdale, Larchmont, whatever. As of tomorrow, you are my personal assistant. I'm gonna teach you some marketing."

That is exactly how my career unexpectedly veered from research to marketing. I spent a little over a year virtually carrying Frank's attaché case from customer presentation to top-level meeting, treading the thick mellow carpeting of executive offices and rubbing shoulders with presidents, executive vice-presidents, vice-presidents, directors, and other characters, all of whom gradually lost their luster and ceased to seem mythical. Not once was I impressed by anyone's dazzling intelligence, but I longed for the lab's effervescence and pervading acumen. It was all in your demeanor, your ability to socialize, and your command of a very limited set of acronyms such as PBT (profit before tax), ROI (return on investment), etc.

Toward the end of July 1963, Frank enrolled me in a four-week executive development program that took place on bucolic premises not far from New York, where they locked us up—there were fifteen of us—six hours a day around a large oval table. At the far end of the room stood a man who introduced himself as the moderator then fell eerily silent following that succinct statement. His silence soon became unbearable, and I wondered how long the suspense would last before he explained his presence in the room. We later learned that he was some sort of psychologist whose job was to observe each participant's behavior down to the slightest facial twitch. His secret agenda was to surreptitiously create the conditions for a leader to emerge from within the group.

Eventually, Fitz, a tall lanky fellow who possessed—and probably nurtured—a strong Texan drawl that perfectly matched his Gary Cooper–like demeanor, abruptly broke the heavy silence by banging his fist on the table and exclaiming "What the heck is going on here? What does that clown want from us?" Fitz was some leader!

I had just finished reading Desmond Morris's *Naked Ape*, where the author reveals the unexpectedly many traits we share with our simian cousins. In the eyes of our corporate psychologist, we were nothing more than a community of apes, with one major difference, however—there were no females. That, in my opinion, overshadowed the conflicts that eventually arose as a result of the moderator's deliberate efforts to thrust us against one another. In any case, I enjoyed my four weeks of seclusion. Conflicts eventually surfaced, with or without females at stake, and I ended up strongly disliking one participant, Art.

I have never ceased to be amazed by the American system's infatuation with case studies, a miserable substitute for real life experience. You are required to spend several hours reading the story of some corporate success or failure, trimmed with a multitude of graphs, balance sheets, and the rest, all of which is intended to give the case a semblance of reality, and legitimize the exorbitant fees charged by the moderator for his theatrical performance. You then convene with your peers and engage in an amiable debate of no consequence, reminiscent of the palavers they refer to in France as *discussions du Café du Commerce*. (Every little French town owes it to itself to possess one such establishment, alongside the Café des Sports, where idle customers volunteer their personal analysis of contemporary issues over a glass of wine or Pastis, each offering his original solution to world problems.)

I remember once remarking to the moderator, reputedly a university professor, that what he was preaching really boiled down to an apology for greed. I was flabbergasted by his reply "Yeah, right on! Greed, that's what drives the economy."

What I found really ludicrous was the management simulation game, where a computer is programmed to mimic the market your virtual company thrives in. Competing teams were formed, vying for leadership. At the outset, each player was assigned a specific role within his team: president, sales or marketing director, head of manufacturing or research, etc. You should have seen how eager the players were, each discharging his responsibility as if his company's life depended on it. For my part, I invented a new role for myself, that of press relations director. That position exempted me from having to take part in the decision-making process, and only required me to issue a virtual daily statement to the press. Believe it or not, a violent conflict once opposed me to my virtual president because my virtual press release did not reflect the company's virtual performance of the day. I tended my virtual resignation and returned to my room. As a precaution, I had packed two or three math books, a welcome change from that mindless exercise.

In one of the many games we played, we were each given five geometric cardboard pieces, rectangles, triangles, etc. No two sets were alike, and the game's object was for each player to assemble a perfect square by passing the pieces he did not need to his right hand neighbor while receiving new pieces from his left hand neighbor. The challenge consisted in *collectively* finishing the game in the shortest possible time. Chance had it that my initial set contained a beautiful little square. I immediately came to the triumphant conclusion that my part was done, and kept passing the pieces from left to right without looking, having blissfully disengaged myself from the collective undertaking. As it turned out, my piece was only the central element of a larger square that required four additional triangles to be completed. After a while, everyone had completed his assignment, with my missing triangles circulating round and round like a hot potato. Finally, Fitz angrily shouted in my direction, "Darn it, Frenchie, play ball for Chrissake." The wisdom of the Americans, I thought to myself, derived from baseball or American football, whose rules I was hopelessly unfamiliar with. Additionally, evocations of damnation and the Lord were not blasphemous, but a socially acceptable surrogate for other imprecations deriving from sexual activity. As for Fitz's judgment of the Frenchies and their lack of team spirit, he was dead right. Ten years in France had turned me into an irredeemable individualist.

Never before had I shared a room with an American, or seen one brush his teeth, shave, and walk around in his underwear. We were assigned a new roommate every week, affording each one of us a chance to cohabit with four vastly different individuals.

The first week, I shared my room with a chief accountant, a race I was not naturally inclined to befriend, but he turned out to be a very sensitive individual. He had lost a young child in an accident, and that wound in his flesh and soul made him exceptionally attentive to other people's miseries. I wondered if that loss had changed his outlook on the relevance of the myriad spreadsheets to which he was dedicating his life.

The second week, my roommate was a plant foreman whose limited vocabulary he put to use with extraordinary colorfulness. Never having managed anyone so far, I intently listened to his experiences, attempting to fathom some underlying philosophy. He obsessively dreaded the prospect of a union shop being set up in the factory, and used the foulest subset of his narrow vocabulary to run down union organizers.

My third week's roommate was the only one I loathed, namely Art. The moderator no doubt knew what he was doing, for the assignment of roommates was not done at random, and he had obviously taken note of our incessant confrontations. I understood that we were being submitted to some kind of test and resolved to make the best of my predicament. I tried to understand why we disliked each other so much but miserably failed, and disliked him even more at week's end. He was a cynical social climber of the worst kind. My week with Art reminded me of Jean-Paul Sartre's play, *Huis clos*, where one of the characters exclaims "L'enfer, c'est les autres!" ('Hell is other people!').

My fourth and last roommate was a salesman. At last, I said to myself, I was going to have a close look at that special kind of bird, so foreign to my culture. He was relaxed and debonair, played an excellent game of golf, and possessed an impressive collection of polo shirts and ample knit cardigans, an apparently essential attribute of the successful salesman–golf-player. He whistled with everything he did—smoothing his hair with brilliantine, putting on his checkered pants, or tying his shoelaces.

Every time he showered, he sang, "Fly me to the moon . . ." in a loud baritone voice that was not unpleasant to hear. The minute he moved in, he stowed his golf bag in a corner of the room then unzipped his leather suitcase, which was quite luxurious by my standards, extracted a framed picture of his wife and three children, and squarely placed it on his desk, whistling all the time.

I confessed to him the reason for my being there—I was a lousy salesman—upon which he told me not to worry for he was going to teach me a few tricks. The only pearl of wisdom I remember had to do with the art of spotting the weakest link in the prospect's decision process and inflating his ego by blowing hot air into his rear end.

I asked myself in earnest if solving a difficult mathematical problem was commensurate with the effort involved in selling, earning large amounts of money, and crushing competition, or if the latter only mobilized a minuscule region of our brain, letting the rest turn to fallow land. And yet, our research scientists were able to engage in abstract speculation only because my roommate and his fellow salesman were out there on the front lines, conquering market share. Perhaps one constant of human activity, I thought, was that intellectual elites, relatively shielded from material constraints but nonetheless immersed in the realities of their day (and who was more immersed in the bloody war between the Greeks and Romans, to which he eventually fell victim, than the great Archimedes himself?), were authorized to dwell on abstract objects not accessible to the common man, and formulate the paradigms of their time, providing their society with a necessary contemporary vision of the world. Other men, inclined by their different nature to build, conquer, and rule, would then translate that vision into progress or devastation. It is amazing how cohabitation with a salesman can turn one into a philosopher!

Following the graduation ceremonies, we decided to have dinner at a French restaurant, which turned out to have nothing French other than the maître d'hôtel's contrived accent and the flowery names given to the courses. When the wine waiter came to our table, everyone turned in my direction for it behooved the only Frenchman in the group to select the wine. Alas! I was only French by education and knew nothing about wine.

My very first exposure to that beverage came immediately after the war, from which we emerged verging on rickety, so stringent had the food shortages been. All these years, we had also been deprived of German and Swiss medicines, which in the eyes of the Egyptians were more effective than those imported from Great Britain. My mother bought several bottles of Tonique Roche, a Swiss tonic that was supposed to harbor extraordinary virtues. The directions printed on the label suggested that the beverage be absorbed pure, or mixed with water or wine. We never had wine at home, but my mother decided that nothing was too good for her children. If the Europeans drank it like that, and they were not better than we were, there was no reason why she should deprive her family of wine with the tonic. The effect of the concoction was immediate, and my mother always marveled at our sudden burst of buoyancy upon absorbing the syrupy beverage.

My second exposure to wine took place in the lovely Burgundy town of Autun, where my father-in-law and I once stopped to visit the beautiful twelfth-century Romance Cathedral, on our way from Marseilles to Paris. That night, we had dinner in a quaint little inn that catered to no more than half a dozen tables and served regional *cuisine bourgeoise*, of the kind they cook at home. The *patron* suggested Corton 1959 to accompany our dinner, and my father-in-law gracefully acquiesced. To this day, I remember the taste of my first kiss and that of Corton 1959.

My third wine experience occurred that night upon skimming through the American restaurant's wine list, when I discovered—O divine surprise!—the only wine I knew. I haughtily told the waiter "We'll have Corton 59." He showed up minutes later with a white napkin wrapped around his precious bottle. I didn't know much about wine, but had never before seen a bottle of red wine thus wrapped. He ceremoniously poured a little quantity in my glass and waited for my response as if it were a mere formality. In those days, American wine drinkers were not as sophisticated as they have now become, with California wines outclassing the best French vintages. I patted my lips with my napkin and drew a minuscule sip from the glass. It was not Corton 59! I courteously conveyed my doubts to the waiter and asked him to unwrap the napkin. Lo and behold, it was Corton 58! Little did I know that, as Corton goes, 1959 was one of the vineyard's greatest years, and 1958 one of the worst. The waiter apologized profusely and offered not to charge for the bottle. As for my friends, they were literally flabbergasted. To tell you the truth, so was I.

The moral of the story is that of the virgin bride who remains forever faithful to her husband. Namely, that the true connoisseur is someone who knows only one vineyard and one year . . . .

My grandfather, Habib Bey Gazalé, 1938   My father in 1924, aged 21

My mother, at
the age of 17,
dressed as
an Egyptian
peasant

My parents' wedding, October 23, 1926

Myself at age 4, in Zeitoun

With my father and brother Waguih on
Stanley Beach, Alexandria, 1936

With my brother and sister
in Alexandria, 1939

The apartment on Marietta Pasha Street, seen from the Museum gardens

The Lycée Français du Caire in 1981

In my room at the Cité Universitaire, April 1952

"Satisfécit" obtained in 1943 for ranking first in English, worth three hours
of "consigne" (detention), reduced to one hour following some mischief

Receiving the 1939–45 Croix de
Guerre on behalf of the École
Supérieure d'Électricité, Paris,
October 1952 (author on right)

Defending my doctoral thesis at
the Sorbonne, May 1959

My wedding, December 1956

In the Mena House garden, 1984

My mother and sister Marlène,
Virginia, 1984

My brother Waguih demonstrating a
surgical tool of his invention to our
brother-in-law Victor, Virginia, 1984

Muhammad in Luxor, holding pail and
postcards, December 1985

With Sister Emmanuelle,
Cairo, April 1993

My son Stéphane, 1986

My daughters Valérie (foreground)
and Olivia at the Pincio gardens,
Rome, in 1987

My granddaughter Clara, 2003

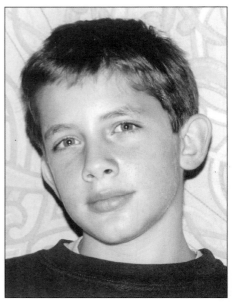

My grandson Fabio, 2000

With my brother (center) and my childhood friend Robert (who also fell in
love with Madame Moulin, our history
teacher), Paris, December 2002

My granddaughter Helena, 2003

⟶ The Cowboy and the Samurai ⟵

Cranes who cannot come back,
Cranes who cannot forget

The Asia-Pacific president, who was referred to as the Cowboy, not always admiringly, expressed himself with a strong southern drawl that no doubt reassured our New York executives, to whose ears it carried a ring of truth and unquestionable sincerity. With an accent like that, he was in no danger of "going native" and could be depended upon to hold sway over our foreign subsidiaries, the Japanese in particular. His folksy vocabulary was surprisingly limited for a man of his stature and his grammar rather unconventional. He used expressions such as "Let's don't do this . . . . That strategy ain't goin' nowhere . . . . You might could . . . ." I was somewhat baffled at the outset, but soon made a habit of recording his southern pearls in a little notebook. That exercise some-what relieved the boredom that pervaded the fastidious staff meetings and fooled everyone into believing that I was sheepishly noting down their mind-expanding contributions.

In contrast, I truly enjoyed working with the Japanese subsidiary, also headquartered in Tokyo, a stone's throw from our offices. I was warmly befriended by the Japanese and shortly familiarized myself with their customs. I did not attempt to learn the intricacies of their etiquette, for they did not favorably look upon the awkward aping of their manners by foreign visitors, such as bowing while exchanging calling cards. On the average, I found them better educated than the headquarters crowd, tech-nically as well as socially, aware of their rich cultural heritage, and infinitely more refined.

The Japanese subsidiary chairman, Mitsuyoshi San, belonged to an old aristocratic family. His heavy eyelids and long delicate fingers made him look like some medieval Samurai come alive. His subordinates, overwhelmed by his princely demeanor, bowed very low when addressing him, in deference not so much to his rank as to his symbolic embodiment of Japan's eternal traditions and values.

In the course of one of our staff meetings, one headquarters zealot reported that the Japanese chairman had committed the mortal sin of deliberately ignoring one of the intangible corporate taboos. I vaguely remember that it had to do with offering a discount to some academic institution, an otherwise laudable initiative in my opinion. His crime consisted of not filling out the myriad forms and securing the necessary rubber stamps from New York. The Cowboy no doubt felt his personal authority flouted and that made him fly into a rage, thundering "Ama gonna chew'im up!" Two days later, the chairman was summoned in the presence of a bunch of headquarters staffers who were looking forward to the replay of some B-movie where the lanky straight-shooting country boy invariably triumphs over the cunning little man with slit eyes.

Mitsuyoshi San was exactly on time, not one second early, for that would have afforded the Cowboy an excuse to let him simmer in the lobby; and not one second late, for that would have been offending to his host. Under the pretence that his inadequate command of English might not allow him to reap the full benefit of the American's imprecations, he was accompanied by the sales director, a World War II kamikaze pilot who had allegedly been on the verge of taking off on a suicide mission when his country capitulated. Be that as it may, he looked like a Sumo wrestler in Western attire, and I often wondered if his neckties were custom designed to go full circle around his neck.

Contrary to Japanese tradition, the encounter began with the Cowboy thundering and barking, forsaking the indispensable graceful amenities. The chairman sat imperturbably straight, his eyes barely open, without the slightest expression on his face. Every now and then, the Sumo wrestler would lean toward him and whisper something under his breath, pretending to be translating the admonitions. I well knew that they were exchanging private jokes, without either one batting an eyelash. At the end of his harangue, all of whose statements began with "I want you to do" this or that, an acceptable form in American culture but utterly detestable in any other, and in the face of his interlocutor's apparent indifference, the president finally exploded "Do you understand what I'm saying, Mister Mitsuyoshi?" I don't know if he meant to humiliate the Samurai further by referring to him as "Mister" instead of the traditional "San," but that also fell on deaf ears. Mitsuyoshi San nodded once then whispered something to his interpreter who declared, after noisily sucking air between his clenched teeth, his head slightly tilted to one side, "Mitsuyoshi San, he say thank you foah kindu lecommendation . . . ." Thereupon, they rose from their armchairs and serenely walked out of the room, the Samurai leading and the sumo wrestler trailing in his footsteps.

That spring, in the course of a visit to an auto manufacturing plant—I believe it was Toyo Kogyo—Takeshita San, the salesman in charge of the account asked me if I would be interested in visiting the nearby city of Hiroshima. I was well aware that the favor I was being offered was only rarely extended to foreigners.

We crossed Peace Bridge on our way to the memorial cenotaph and museum designed by Isamu Noguchi and paused in front of a large sculpture representing a man stooping over a baby as if to protect it from the blast, with another child desperately attempting to climb on his father's back. Beyond the immense rose bed, the awesome metallic dome structure that survived the bombing defiantly stood on the edge of the Ota-Gawa River, resembling the vestige of some medieval cathedral celebrating the spirit of man.

I had difficulty holding back my tears when we came to the children's memorial, shaped like an oversized three-legged bombshell upon which a charred childlike figure was crucified, with another child, Sadako, perched atop the dome, holding above his head a golden crane ready to fly off into the sky. A throng of impeccably dressed schoolchildren silently took turns at hanging long strings of folded paper cranes under the dome, amidst myriads of similar multicolored origami strings. Takeshita San explained that according to Japanese tradition, if a sick person makes one thousand paper cranes, that person will get well. Those who died in Hiroshima were referred to as "cranes who cannot come back," and those who survived as "cranes who cannot forget."

Thereupon, Takeshita San delicately picked up a fallen string and gave it to me saying, "Please remember Hiroshima."

Lorenzo or,
⌁ What is the Meaning of Culture? ⌁

The Italians are ill-tempered Frenchmen.

Jean Cocteau

Lorenzo picked me up at Milan's Linate airport. In those days, I was running the overseas operations of an American computer company based in the Boston area.

Lorenzo, the managing director of our Italian subsidiary, had established his quarters in an unusually large office in Milan, with a custom-designed circular desk that was literally wrapped around his person and made him look like the bust of some ancient Roman emperor erected atop a disproportionately massive round pedestal. He also sported a moustache, a beard, and an additional attribute in the form of a classic Jaguar 4.2 with leather interior which, as you would expect from a true Milanese, he drove at speeds unreasonable even by French standards. He would have looked ridiculous, owning a Jag and not storming past the Fiat midgets on the highway.

Lorenzo was balding at a relatively young age—he must have been in his middle thirties—which explains the thick beard. I have never ceased to be fascinated by those men who insist on proving that hair can grow somewhere on their skull, if not on its top. He was also quite short and slightly heavy, which explains the long, slender Jaguar.

Lorenzo spoke in a loud voice and articulated every syllable even more than the Italian language already requires. When you are not expressing yourself in your own language, you often tend to be louder than necessary, perhaps in the hope that volume, if not the words, will convey the meaning.

Lorenzo would have felt crippled with the windows up, even in the heart of winter. He needed to be prepared at all times to tell the other drivers what he thought of their driving skills, using one or more fingers of his left hand. He also needed to hear clearly and not miss a word in the event that one such driver elected to make the kind of discourteous statement that would surely reinforce Lorenzo's opinion that he was surrounded by degenerates all of whom had fallen victims to sodomy early in life. Following each repartee, he laughed good-heartedly, explaining that the bastard was obviously jealous of his Jaguar.

He used both hands to accompany his words as though he was sculpting them in the air between us, having developed an unusual talent for steering the car with his left elbow, which he stuck between the wheel and one of the spokes. Both his shoulders would be facing me, and except for a slight impediment in his left arm caused by the steering, he would become very articulate—mouth, eyebrows, hands, and all.

When recounting an episode involving a telephone conversation, he would fabricate a receiver with the three middle fingers of his right hand folded against his palm, and the thumb stuck in his ear. He would then hold the outstretched little finger at a distance from his lips that varied with the degree of confidentiality of the subject at hand, so to speak. At the end of the telephone conversation, he never failed to hang up his virtual receiver.

The episode he was telling me about that day infuriated him so much that he abruptly hung up on his hypothetical interlocutor and slammed the receiver on the gear stick. The car veered to the right, affording an unexpected conversation piece to the other drivers who instantly coalesced against my friend, sneering, and freely commenting on the disharmony between his size and that of his car, as they looked at me with angelic compassion. One driver asked him if he had won his driver's license in a raffle, and another reached from his window and offered Lorenzo a pillow with the suggestion that he stick it under his behind, in order for his nose to emerge above the steering wheel. I myself had toyed with the idea of offering him such a cushion, of the elaborately embroidered kind.

I sank my body into the comfortable seat so as to bring my nose to about the same height as Lorenzo's, so curious was I to assess how much of the road ahead he could see from that vantage point. I wear bifocal lenses and have learned over the years to walk without actually seeing my feet, which are blurred by the powerful half moon encrusted near the bottom of my lenses. It was probably the same with Lorenzo's driving: he had blissfully survived all these years without ever seeing the abyss beyond the hood, having probably developed an additional sense that allowed him to assess the distance from other cars by the look in the driver's eye, in much the same fashion as the hard of hearing read lips.

I feverishly searched for the seat belt's buckle but could not find it. Nobody used it anyway, and it had probably vanished without anyone ever noticing. It was not very manly to fasten your seat belt in Italy, and it would have surely offended Lorenzo to watch me buckle up as if I didn't trust his driving.

Needless to say, I could not concentrate on his story. I vaguely remember that it had to do with some uptight customer who was threatening to take us to court. According to my driver, the customer's jockey shorts were evidently too tight, and that was no problem of ours. He reassured me that the situation was under control, as he planned to offer that company's data processing manager a gold Parker pen. Lorenzo had an impressive collection of pens under lock and key in his bottom drawer, and they performed miracles. At that point, I was in no mood to engage in a discourse on ethics. My mind was concentrating on survival, leaving me at the very bottom of Maszlow's famous pyramid, which places survival at the base and self-esteem at the top.

As we came to an orange traffic light in the immediate outskirts of Milan, Lorenzo furiously stepped on the gas pedal. We were a good fifty meters from the intersection, and by the time we reached it, the light was bright red, with our car flying at no less than one hundred kilometers per hour.

"Lorenzo . . . the light was orange . . . . You should have slowed down, don't you think?" said I, half mad, half terrified.

But Lorenzo is also an educator, I failed to say. He did not bother to look in my direction but calmly declared, "In Ee-taly, orrrange means you have to go fast, because the light is going to turn red!" He was very composed, and his incontrovertible reply did not invite any further belaboring of the subject.

Thereupon, we came to a second traffic light. This time, it was unmistakably red. When we reached the intersection, Lorenzo did not depart from his calm, which was now akin to some kind of bliss. He went right through without changing the expression on his face.

"My God, Lorenzo, that light was red! Don't you ever stop on red?"

Lorenzo was calmer than ever, evidently trying not to lose patience with me.

"In Ee-taly, red means use your judgment!" That statement was so implacable that I decided not to challenge it. After all, he had lived to be thirty-five or -six and I could not see blood all over the intersections with mangled bodies hanging from traffic lights!

I pulled myself together and attempted to pursue our civilized conversation as if we were sitting in his living room, sipping Campari.

"Tell me then, Lorenzo . . . In Ee-taly, if you accelerate on orange and use your judgment on red . . . what do you do when the light is green?"

With fully semi-circular eyebrows and spherical eyeballs, as though he was getting ready to utter some unspeakable horror, he said, "In Ee-taly, green, you must be ve-ry ca-reful . . . . Maybe somebody using his judgment!"

Thereupon, I conceded that the only good judgment in Ee-taly is that of its aboriginal inhabitants. The judgments of other people, who drive though green traffic lights without taking infinite precautions, are incurably flawed.

It also dawned on me that as long as all Milanese drivers shared the same common values, namely, accelerate on orange, go on red and stop on green, *non c'è problema*.

We finally managed to reach his office unharmed. He stopped the engine, got out of the car, and nonchalantly slammed the door shut. I cannot say whether he actually parked the car or merely abandoned it in the middle of the road before blissfully moving away.

"Are you sure you are legally parked?" I asked—rather naively, I must admit—for that sort of unselfconsciousness can cost you dear in Paris. "Don't worry," he airily replied as we walked toward the building's entrance.

We broke at two in the afternoon, because I had asked Lorenzo if he wouldn't mind an early lunch. When we came out of the building, the Jaguar was surrounded by three carabinieri busily inspecting it from every angle and exchanging comments. All hell is going to break loose, I said to myself. Lorenzo was very composed as he approached the men and greeted them in a very civilized manner. Little did I suspect the Italian carabinieris' infatuation with sports cars. They pressed Lorenzo with a flurry of questions none of them had to do with his blatant misdemeanor. They just wanted to know how fast the car was, how many liters it consumed, etc.

Whenever the international gatherings took place outside the United States, local country managers took it in turns to organize them in their home countries, with attendees converging in large numbers from headquarters and other subsidiaries. We thus held meetings in London, Rome, Madrid, even Cairo and Riyadh, among a multitude of other capitals. Following a particularly long day of fastidious presentations, Lorenzo, host of the month, took the conference attendees and their spouses on a Rome-by-night bus tour. As we stood on top of Capitol Hill, he proudly declared, "Ladies and gentlemen, do you realize that this city was built exactly two thousand years before America was discovered?" (Luckily, no one asked why the Italians were bent on building nothing but ruins . . . .) For my part, I couldn't help thinking that when Rome was built, the Saqqara pyramid was itself two thousand years old, but I chose to remain silent, for Egypt, with all its glorious past, was once upon a time conquered by Julius Caesar and his Roman legions.

Thereupon our host decided to cut the visit short because the guests, who were beginning to show signs of intellectual fatigue, were anxious to discover the legendary Antica Pesa restaurant in the Trastevere, an old section of town across the Tiber. They enjoyed the food and Chianti but were otherwise disappointed, for they had been looking forward to the musical extravaganzas that American tourists are usually offered by outwardly jubilant *trovatore* clad in folk attire singing *Funiculi, funicula.*

⟿ Lorenzo, Ten Years Later ⟿

In Turin, I looked up my good old friend Lorenzo whom I had not seen for at least ten years, and who had been jumping from one company to the next, negotiating a substantial salary increase with every move. He was now employed by a large Italian auto manufacturer that had put a chauffeured car at his disposal after realizing that he was getting involved in too many collisions, some mechanical, and some verbal. Due to the abundance of business lunches that his position required, he had gained quite a bit of weight and now looked a true patrician.

He was in excellent spirits and laughed at the days when it was advisable to have sandwiches in the office whenever American visitors were around. Pure heresy in Italy, home of so many delightful culinary inventions. The restaurant he took me to was known only to connoisseurs, and we were greeted at the door with great deference. As we walked in, he waved his hand at this and that habitué. "I bet you the executives in Detroit have hamburgers for lunch and drink coffee out of paper cups," he said as we sat down. "That doesn't make their cars any better than ours," he added as he picked up his impeccably starched napkin and violently shook it in the air before sticking one of its corners in his shirt collar, concealing his expensive Italian silk necktie. That was a good omen, for it presaged succulent food and wine. I had to be careful though, for I had a rather long drive ahead of me. After kissing each other on both cheeks, I sat in my car and took off. I could see him in my rear view mirror waving his hand until I turned around the bend and he finally disappeared. I have never seen him since and often wonder what has become of him.

~ Pity We Lost India ~

That summer, I was invited by a major British company to run their French subsidiary. The company's history was rather complex; there had been mergers, acquisitions, divestitures, etc., all of which had resulted in an odd combination of cultures that meshed together helter-skelter, at least for a while. There eventually came a time when drastic strategic revisions had to be envisaged in the face of rapidly declining performance and melting profits. The board resolved to remove the entire top management tier and the chairman as well. We woke up one morning with a new chairman and a new managing director, who was described as a kind of genius from some other galaxy. Our woes would soon be over. All we had to do was wait for the *wunderkind* to concoct his plan and rescue our ship in distress.

I liked him for his acumen, his boyish appearance, and his disregard for the corporate establishment. He was a welcome change from the otherwise very respectable World War II veterans who, to be sure, had been capable of heroic feats both as engineers and soldiers, but were incurably hampered by the memory of their country's past grandeur.

Months later, we were in still greater danger of losing our major accounts in the face of the industry's brisk pace and the sluggishness of our response. I decided to travel to London and put my case to the management committee, an august cenacle of some twenty top executives seated around a large oval table.

The managing director was slouched in his armchair with his feet on the table squarely facing the poor blokes who took turns at presenting their case and taking the heat from the *wunderkind*. I never saw as large a group of executives doodling in silence, deceptively appearing to be taking notes. With extreme application, the man to my right was slowly filling an entire sheet of paper with the most intricate pattern, delicate as Flemish embroidery. After about an hour and a half of labor, I asked him if I could keep the drawing. He courteously replied that it was only half finished, because the sessions usually lasted three hours. That drew a smile from the man to my left, who overheard the exchange as he kept twisting and untwisting a paper clip.

Every now and then, one of them would mechanically nod and another slowly shake his head from left to right as if to signify, "Pity we lost India!" The British sense of humor was intact and expressed itself best in the face of adversity. When my turn came to move to the hot seat, I made my statement to the learned assembly in rather strong terms, though measured and courteous. I sincerely expected the managing director to appreciate my frankness and learn something from our real-life experiences, but my performance seemed to fall on deaf ears. I quietly picked up my notes and headed for the door, after thanking everyone for their attention.

As chairman of the board of the French subsidiary, my primary allegiance legally went to the mother-company chairman. The next morning, I called him from Paris where I had promptly returned, and informed him that I intended to call an extraordinary meeting of the board where I would tender my resignation. He had heard about the episode and expressed his regrets. He asked me not to do anything rash until we had had a chance to talk, and suggested lunch at his downtown London quarters.

The company rented a luxurious apartment in the elegant center of what was once the capital of the most powerful country in the world, and whose inhabitants had bravely endured the savage German bombardments thirty years earlier. I could not repress a feeling of genuine sadness as we drove past long lines of ugly buildings where once stood, I imagined, charming little houses with their legendary manicured lawns.

Our plane was late on arrival, and I asked the taxi driver to move as fast as he could. He took me through a maze of back streets, a real pity, for I loved the drive through Hyde Park, which invariably reminded me of Mr. Inglott, our English teacher. Time and time again, he would describe that mythical park to the inattentive bunch of little Egyptians that we were, his voice filled with nostalgia.

The chairman greeted me with a glass of sherry, and we proceeded to the elegant dining room. Again and again, he asked me not to leave the company, and made a number of tantalizing financial offers in my direction—stock options, golden handshake when the time came, etc. He was extremely courteous but my mind was irrevocably made up and I was just being polite. He told me to think about it and offered to have his chauffeur drive me back to the airport in his personal car.

The Bentley was stationed in front of the elegant iron fence that had miraculously survived the bombings. I walked to the car's side and waited for the chauffeur to open the door. As I sank into the comfortable and appropriately worn out leather seat, I felt an irresistible urge to mimic the condescention of English aristocrats, and asked him what his name was. I could not believe my ears when he replied "Jeeves, Sir." How could the British so precisely predict their children's destiny, and name them in anticipation of whatever trade they would choose later in life? Or did their name command that choice? As I reflected upon that mystery and pondered the meanders of the British mind, I marveled at Jeeves' perfect style as he took possession of the driver's seat.

The back of Jeeves' neck was congested and sweaty. "My God," I said to myself, "that man is the spitting image of the sergeant who kicked me in the rear end when I was a child!" I kept gazing at his neck, flooded with a deluge of childhood memories.

What a delight! Here I was, sitting in the back of that legendary British car whose interior smelled of leather and expensive cigars, and an *Englishman* was driving me, attentive to my slightest desires. The time had finally come to get even with the occupier. I bent slightly forward and, with the handle of my umbrella, knocked on the glass partition that separated the rich from the poor. Jeeves instantly slid the partition open and asked "Sir?"

God only knows the power of our subconscious mind, and how many of our choices are governed by the mysterious other self that inhabits each of us. Had I perchance joined a British company, then resigned, only to savor that moment? I suddenly changed my mind about going back to Paris that night, and decided to enjoy the London good life.

I conjured up my best Oxford accent and said, "The Savoy, Jeeves."

The next morning, I opened my window overlooking the Thames and, as if to complete my immersion in Egypt's past, there it stood, right under my bewildered eyes—Cleopatra's Needle! I had often dreamed of admiring it as I had the obelisk adorning the Place de la Concorde and half a dozen others in Rome, in addition, of course, to the handful still erect in Egypt.[68] I only remembered that it stood on Victoria Embankment, somewhere between Waterloo and Charing Cross bridges.

It was an exceptionally clear day. Westminster Abbey, Big Ben, and Cleopatra's Needle stood defiantly aligned as if to celebrate the spirit of man.

⌐ Harrods ⌐

That afternoon, I strolled in London for several hours. These were the days when Beatlemania ruled. On Carnaby Street, I acquired all sorts of trinkets that my children had begged me to bring back: tee shirts with the Union Jack printed on the chest, panties with the flag on the derrière, Beatles posters, Beatles pencils, and Beatles this and that. I then walked to Hamley's where I bought a little red double-decker bus and a variety of other typically English knick-knacks. In the Beatles' wake, anglomania ruled.

Nearby, I fell upon a stationery, where I browsed for half an hour or more. I love the smell of paper, of almond-scented glue, India rubber, and wooden pencils. When I was child, most school supplies had to be imported, generally from England.

I remember the excitement of our school reopening day. We would eagerly flock to La Phalène stationery shop and buy the prescribed list of supplies amidst hordes of other pupils, then rush home, our school bags heavy with the loot. For years and years, we thought that La Phalène was the name of the shopkeeper, whom we respectfully addressed as "Monsieur de La Phalène," though he spoke French with a strong accent that could have been Greek or Maltese. One morning, our pedantic French teacher, with his customary compunction, explained that the *phalène* was a kind of moth, and that the word could be either masculine of feminine.

His recitation of Alfred de Musset's little poem "Le phalène doré, dans sa course légère, traverse les près embaumés . . ." did not ease the pain. The insensitive French teacher had crushed our little house of dreams.

Our favorite brand of copybook was the hardbound Croxley's, whose paper was exceptionally white and smooth. With immense application, we would write our name on the little tag, then religiously half open the copybook, taking care not to crush it flat, and inscribe the subject matter on the virgin first page with our newly purchased ink pen dipped in the blue-black Higgins inkpot, full to the brim.

Though we frequented the Lycée Français and spoke Arabic at home, it dawned on me that England was very much an integral part of our fabric, despite our mixed feelings about the occupier.

I asked the shopkeeper if the Croxley brand of copybook was still around. When he replied "Of course, sir," I thought to myself that the British were incorrigible conservatives. That gave me a warm sense of permanence and even immortality, as time seemed to come to a standstill. Though I had no immediate use for the items, I purchased three copybooks that I decided to save for the day when I would sit down and write about my childhood.

I then walked to Harrods with nothing particular in mind, and there I aimlessly strolled down the aisles, politely replying to the attentive sales assistants that I was just looking around. Harrods is where the parents of our playmates purchased the cashmere jumpers that so well espoused the shape of their budding little breasts. Harrods is also where they bought Church's shoes for the boys and Laura Ashley dresses for the little girls. My father would never wear any cologne other than Atkinson's English Lavender, one of the few traits I inherited from him. I bought three large bottles of Atkinson's and went on.

It was early evening when I finally stepped out of Harrods. It was raining cats and dogs, as the English would say, a deluge that did not seem to affect Londoners. I opened my umbrella and walked to the curb, desperately trying to catch a taxi driver's eye. The doorman stood squarely in the middle of Bronfman Road, blowing his whistle to no avail. As I waited for a miracle to happen, a gentleman stopped behind me, forming a neat queue of two. He had obviously spent his entire life playing cricket and sipping tea at the Singapore Cricket Club or some similarly Victorian venue. He had every attribute of the city patrician—brisk colonial whiskers, bowler hat, striped trousers, and black jacket slightly pinched at the waist. He never looked at me, standing tall under his black umbrella. I discreetly scrutinized him from the corner of my eye, eager to ascertain whether he actually carried the *Times* tucked under his armpit. He was not showing the slightest sign of impatience, as we both stood stoically silent under the heavy rain.

Thereupon along came a young lady, visibly an expectant mother, who fell in line behind the major, shivering. He offered her the hospitality of his large umbrella as she mumbled, "How silly of me, on such a rainy day . . . ." Following an interminable wait, a taxi finally pulled up. Bowing slightly, I offered my turn to the young mother-to-be, assuring her that it wouldn't be long before the next taxi showed up. She was reluctant to accept my offer but I stubbornly insisted, and she finally yielded. With a discreet smile on her face, her eyelashes furiously fluttering, she said, "That's really very kind of you, Monsieur. Vous êtes un vrai gentleman." Obviously, my French accent had given me away. At that moment, the English major, without really looking at me, articulated in my direction, "Ghastly weather, isn't it?"

Though we had not been properly introduced, I was finally deemed worthy of a short comment—on the weather, mind you.

I politely replied, "Indeed!"

Thirty years later, I am writing these lines in my Croxley copybook.

⁓ Proper Corporate Attire ⁓

Don't tell anyone, but I ran the French subsidiary of a large American company for several years without ever utilizing the internal electronic mail system. That was before the emergence of the Internet, and the system we used was not particularly friendly. Moreover, I was instinctively resistant to the very idea of using a keyboard, and gazing at a screen all day. I belonged to the paper generation and enjoyed picking up my mail from the paleolithic in-basket, one piece at a time. I had also been trained to dictate, and did that best as I walked back and forth in the manner of an Aristotle teaching his peripatetic disciples.

During all my years with that company I was blessed with the most intelligent, efficient, and loyal secretary (she never revealed my computer illiteracy to anyone). She was Dutch, and that made her fluent in both English and French in addition to being highly organized. Her name was Mieke. Every morning, she turned on her computer and, by virtue of some black magic, fooled everyone into believing that I, not she, was on line. She would print out the incoming mail and bring it to me in my favorite form: hard copy. After mulling over its content, which was usually meager, I would dictate an appropriate response that she promptly dispatched to the sender along with the usual stream of people to whom copies were sent for information purposes. Mieke had an exceptional knack for translating proper English into electronic mail gibberish. She deliberately shattered my grammar and deleted any construction that Americans could have regarded as pedantic or literary. So we played the part and fooled the crowds.

Using the internal system was not compulsory, but you were sure to collect Brownie points if you used it regularly and kept open channels with your peers, jamming expensive telephone lines with trivia.

My American assistant Melanie was a mother-company veteran with several years of service in the various business units. She had been asked to serve as my assistant because of her familiarity with the corporate labyrinth, which, God knows, is vast. Initially, we had a sneaking suspicion that she was planted in our office in order to keep an eye on local country nationals, as we were referred to despite our brilliant credentials, in sharp contrast to those of the expatriates assigned to our office. She was nicknamed Miss CIA. Eventually, our suspicions were dispelled.

Every day at 3 p.m. sharp, 9 a.m. in the United States, she would turn her back to the door, bend over the telephone, and whisper under her breath for hours on end. She was keeping abreast in real time and with insatiable lust of who was promoted, who was demoted, who was being transferred where, and who was now reporting to whom. She was burning to share these savory morsels with me, alas to no avail, as I had no idea who the protagonists were of that unfolding human comedy and frankly, as Rhett would say, I did not give a damn. That frustrated her immensely and, perhaps for fear that it might badly reflect on her ability to tame the locals, she often reprimanded me for not paying attention to these cosmic events lest I became a social outcast.

The first person we hired was Claudine, a kind of girl Friday who, through hard work and unrelenting effort, successfully inched her way up the corporate ladder.

I was incessantly struggling with French bureaucracy, going from one hearing to the next. They wanted to find out why we wanted to establish a company in France, what our ambitions were, whether we were a threat to their indigenous industry, how many people we intended to hire locally, etc, etc.

Meanwhile, Melanie was doing her best to make top management comfortable with the idea, very novel to them, of establishing a subsidiary in France, in addition to reassuring them that we possessed the required moral credentials and concealed no hidden agendas. She organized a tour of executive offices back in the States, and introduced me to the key players, keeping her fingers crossed that I would project the right image. "Midhat," she would say, "I have come to know you rather well. Make an effort. Please don't blow it!"

When Melanie finally got through opening her cartons and organizing her universe, she unearthed a little booklet whose title was "Proper Corporate Attire." When she showed it to us, Claudine and I could not believe our eyes. We examined the pictures again and again, until Claudine glanced at me from the corner of her eye, and we both burst out with laughter. "Melanie," I said, "what on earth is *that*? Are the girls in the office required to buy polyester suits from some tacky suburban discount outlet? You are in *Paris*, for heaven's sake!" Melanie was really annoyed at me on at least two counts. First, she was dead serious about the manual and second, she had told me time and time again that it was not proper to refer to the women in the office as 'girls.' We had to say women. Needless to say, I never abided by that unmannerly rule. I was taught English by English teachers and regarded the term 'woman' as rather vulgar. A young person of the opposite gender was a girl until she became a young lady and that was that! My position was adamant.

Claudine was in the habit of wearing elegant, well cut pants. Parisian girls have a knack for unearthing inexpensive, perfectly sophisticated outfits that look like they were molded over their silhouettes by some inspired couturier. Melanie, on the other hand, invariably wore deliberately shapeless navy blue suits with longish skirts and the inescapable burgundy bow, straight out of the manual. Most of all, she never bared what little was visible of her legs, even in the height of summer, that Godsent time of year when Parisiennes grab every opportunity to bare as much of their figure as they can get away with.

Melanie firmly suggested to Claudine that she trade her pants for a skirt. I found that rather strange and difficult to reconcile with the women's-liberation culture that prevailed in the United States. Weren't liberated women referred to in our country as those wearing the *pantalon*?

Melanie never wore perfume either, and insisted that we treat her "like a guy"! These were her own words. She was strangely inflexible in the face of Claudine's stubborn reluctance. Wasn't she the guardian of corporate values? Her eyes full of tears, Claudine shouted, "Very good, I am leaving now while the stores are still open. I will buy a dress, and you will never see me wearing pants again! I'll even wear a chador if that makes you happy!"

The next morning was dismal as a wake, and I am sure Melanie will never forget it as long as she lives. Claudine showed up in a lovely cotton dress, with a print of tiny pink cherry blossoms. She walked into my office, greeted me with a contrived smile and left before I had a chance to compliment her on her choice and tell her how genuinely beautiful she looked. As she turned her back on me, I discovered that her left leg was a good inch shorter than her right. It suddenly dawned on me that she always walked with a slight limp that she concealed with extraordinary grace.

She went back to her desk, her light dress floating in the air about her, her back straight and her thick hair bouncing up and down with every step she took.

A few minutes later, she came back to pick up something or other in my office. I remained silent as she fumbled with this and that paper, all of which now seemed so irrelevant. She finally looked at me and said softly "I had polio when I was a child . . . ."

As soon as she left, Melanie stepped into my office. Without saying a word, she sat in the visitor's chair and wept.

When I was a child, we used to spend every summer on the Alexandrian seashore in order to escape the sizzling Cairo heat. That summer, we rode the train to Alexandria as usual, and no sooner had we reached our summer quarters than we jumped into our bathing suits and ran to the beach. My elder brother was sixteen, I was fourteen, and my sister Marlène had just turned nine. When we came home for dinner, her throat was very sore and she looked feverish. Two days later, she could not move her legs. When the doctor pronounced the word polio, my father collapsed on the floor. At that precise moment, I knew that as long as I lived, I would remember that day as the blackest in my life.

Several years later, Marlène married Victor, the most loving, courteous, and loyal husband I have ever come across. I owe him an immense debt of gratitude for looking after my sister and mother for so many years, doing more for them than my brother and I ever did.

As I was absentmindedly gazing through the window of a sports shop in New York, I remembered Claudine telling me that she loved to play tennis. That now sounded somewhat incongruous, but as I mulled over the thought, I was overwhelmed with a strange mixture of admiration and tenderness toward her, and decided to buy her the most sophisticated tennis racket in the store.

Several years went by. Claudine married her boyfriend, was promoted several times, and had a little girl. Mieke had a little boy, then a little girl, and was more cheerful than ever. Melanie no longer wore stockings in summer. Her skirts gradually shrank and the disappearance of her burgundy bow at last revealed her generous feminine attributes.

One hot summer day, the air conditioning system was huffing and puffing to no avail. As Melanie stood in my doorway, I opened the window to let in some fresh air. That caused a strong and sudden draft to sweep across the office. I sniffed the air, turned around and said, "Melanie, if that is Shalimar you are wearing, I hereby declare that you have just graduated from the Paris Finishing School. You may now return in peace to your country, for you will never be the same."

⌐ La Colombe D'or ⌐

When my turn came to organize the International Conference, I chose to hold it in the South of France. It was spring, and I had a hunch the guests wouldn't mind a three-day boondoggle on the French Riviera. The choice of that particular venue attracted many more executives than I had anticipated, all of whom suddenly felt a strong urge to socialize.

We booked the major part of a luxurious hotel perched at the foot of the historic village of Saint Paul de Vence. The lavender and mimosas were in full bloom, filling the air with an inexpressibly light fragrance. The meetings lasted from 9 a.m. to 1 p.m. and were followed by one of those culinary feasts whose secret only Mediterraneans possess.

By choosing that location, I was obviously doing myself a favor, but I earnestly wanted our guests and their spouses to catch a whiff of the air that the ancient Egyptians, Greeks, and Romans once breathed.

A hidden purpose of mine was to introduce the executives to Sofia Antipolis, a nearby science park that hosts a multitude of high tech companies and scientific laboratories. That location, by virtue of its clement weather, the availability of an international airport, and a good university, bears many similarities to the California coast and has come to be known as the French Silicon Valley. Engineers and scientists flock in from all over Europe and, once established with their families, seldom leave that little heaven. The park was founded by Senator Pierre Laffitte in memory of his wife Sofia, whose name means wisdom in Greek. *Antipolis* is the original Roman name given to the city of Antibes.

I wanted the company to set foot on the Mediterranean seashore and establish a research laboratory on the site, but met with persistent reluctance on the part of U.S. decision-makers.

France is often viewed by ill-traveled Americans as a kind of amusement park where people eat smelly cheeses and drink lots of wine. Suffice it to observe the way such people dress in the heart of Paris as if it were some kind of Atlantic City, oblivious to the aborigines who go about their daily toil in that busy, industrious city. Would any American in his right mind then seriously consider investing on the Riviera, of all places?

Real obstacles however, were the magnitude of the tax burden, the lack of flexibility when it comes to hiring and laying off, the minimum wage, the unrealistic thirty-five hour work week and five-week holiday, the mandatory retirement age, the never ending utilities and transportation strikes etc., etc., not to mention the legendary burden of bureaucracy, and the specter of left-wing trade unions.

Not altogether unjustifiably, many Americans regard France as a country of ingrate nationalists who harbor only detestation toward those who delivered them from German tyranny, leaving behind thousands of their gallant youths. I often jokingly tell my American friends that the French do not target them in particular: they are actually at war with each other, and the poor Americans just happen to be caught in the middle! After all, French youths eat MacDonald hamburgers, drink Coca Cola, wear Levi jeans and Nike shoes, dance to rock music, and use *Le web*. The more 'in' among them stuff their vocabulary with expressions borrowed from the American media industry such as 'star,' 'hit,' 'live,' 'best of,' 'making of,' 'one-man-show,' 'prime time,' 'nomination,' 'standing ovation,' 'has-been,' etc. Adding insult to injury, Disneyland Paris, derided by the snobs as a cultural Chernobyl, is visited twice as often as the Eiffel Tower[69] and Woody Allen was awarded the coveted Palm of Palms at the 2002 Cannes Film Festival!

As we strolled down Albert Einstein Street, I plucked a lavender twig and breathed its fresh sunny scent, then held it out to one of the visitors saying, "This is the perfume of Provence!"

He was engaged with two other colleagues in a furious debate that had to do, I believe, with some bloke from another business unit who had said this and done that, thousands of miles and several cultures away. Without looking, he seized the twig and absentmindedly crushed its little buds between his thick fingers as he angrily pledged to get even with the far-away bastard. He then let the flower drop to the ground without having ever been aware of the gentle twig, the tiny buds, the marvelous scent, and the soul of Provence.

Afternoons were free, and Melanie had organized optional programs for the guests and their spouses. The traditional Riviera bus tour took us to Monte Carlo and back. Upon boarding the bus on our way back to Sofia, some participants decided to forego the ride, declaring that they preferred to catch a cab and take the slow road home. Slow indeed, for most of them lost their shirts in the casino and did not show up till dawn.

The following afternoon, three distinct itineraries were offered to the guests. The first would take them to the center of Nice, the second to a nearby golf course and the third to the Maeght Foundation, the Picasso Museum, and the Matisse church. I retained the services of a distinguished local *bourgeoise* who volunteered to escort the ladies. She had spent several happy years in America and was delighted at the opportunity to reciprocate.

Most of the ladies went shopping while the others went golfing, most of the men went golfing while the others went shopping, and we had to cancel the third bus for which there were no candidates.

That evening, we dined at the Colombe d'Or—the Golden Dove— where scores of contemporary painters and sculptors had stayed at one time or another in exchange for their works. The walls were covered with paintings by Picasso, Braque, Chagall, and others, while sculptures by Cesar, Giacometti, and Tinguely adorned every corner of the place. The swimming pool lay under a squeaky metal sculpture by Calder and its entire rear wall was covered with a mosaic rendering of a dove assembled by Braque. The inn's entrance was adorned with a giant white dove sculpted by Picasso. We dined in the little garden, facing a large ceramic wall sculpture by Fernand Léger.

Oblivious to the surroundings, the guests noisily indulged in *apéritifs*, and by the time dinner was served, they were too tipsy to tell the difference between Madame Roux's cuisine and that of a New Jersey greasy spoon. A small handful however, admired the masterpieces and enjoyed the cool spring evening under the fig trees.

⌁ Benelux ⌁

We used to visit the U.S. headquarters regularly, where meetings would be convened whenever management had some cosmic message to deliver to the subsidiaries at large. Also invited were large cohorts from headquarters, in the hope that some of the overseas reality might rub off on them and, conversely, that subsidiary managers might benefit from their strategic acumen.

For hours on end, we would politely endure computer-assisted PowerPoint presentations that invariably rehashed how important Europe was to the company's future. One recurrent theme was that of 'Fortress Europe.' Headquarters dwellers had vaguely heard of the European Community, and persuaded themselves that we had concocted that device for the sole purpose of keeping Americans out since we were unable to compete with them on an equal footing. European economies were raising all sorts of regulatory barriers to impede American penetration. The Americans blissfully believed, however, that they possessed a reliable ally inside the fortress on whom they could depend as if he were one of their own. I am of course referring to the British Isles, that giant U.S. aircraft carrier parked outside Europe.

Unless they wished to be assigned to one of those foreign posts where they would lead the lives of pampered expatriates, most headquarters people didn't really attempt to understand European issues. The contrast between expatriates and local country nationals, as we were called, was glaring. They received exorbitant housing allowances that allowed them to rent large apartments in the most coveted sections of Paris, where they regularly entertained their fellow Americans. They also sent their children to the best private bilingual schools and enrolled in French courses for adults that barely allowed them to purchase their groceries after three years of residence. Their Filipino maids spoke English and French, and that greatly facilitated interfacing with the locals.

Expatriates were usually assigned to foreign posts under the assumption that the talents they possessed could not be matched by the local second-class citizens that we were. It is true that the most essential talent you needed was your personal network of acquaintances back in the States, and we badly lacked that advantage.

One of the paradoxes that American multinationals operating in Europe have to contend with is that the compensation of a subsidiary employee, which has to be consistent with local practices, is often more substantial that that of his own boss, if you discount freebees. Upon repatriation, the expatriate's pampered life comes to a brutal end and with it the freebees. Human resource development managers—or more appropriately human resource disposal managers—are aware of the redoubtable re-entry problem. The Space Program has provided them with a metaphor that adequately describes the poor blighter's fate upon re-entering the mother company's atmosphere. As he traverses the upper layers, to which he thinks he now belongs, he gradually feels the searing heat that accompanies his pitiful return to earth. He is now a foreigner in his own land who has drifted out of touch with the corporate planet. Worst of all, he is suspected of having gone native.

Since the end of World War II, the fall of the Berlin Wall, and the demise of the Soviet Empire, ever larger numbers of Europeans have taken to traveling throughout the continent, exploring its myriad traditions and cultures. Unbelievable as that may sound, today's Frenchmen have even come to like their British neighbors, to whom they no longer refer as natives of "perfidious Albion" or as *rosbifs* ('roast beefs'). Conversely, the French are no longer Froggies and the Germans have ceased to be Krauts. In sharp contrast, many of our company's historical American executives were approaching the ripe age of sixty without having ever left their own state, let alone the United States.

Most of the time, the conference's central topic was the latest reorganization. This manager would now report to that director, this director to that vice president, this vice president to that senior vice president, and so on all the way to the top. In my early days with the company, I was struck by the frequency of corporate reorganizations. One of my peers once surmised that our executives were the descendents of those Titanic survivors whose task had been to rearrange the deckchairs while the ship was going under.

Those who rose through the ranks were the most adept at keeping track of the earthshaking reorganizations, and finding themselves at the right place at the right time. You had to have *visibility*, and that required going through the motions with impeccable corporate style.

It also helped if you mastered the game of golf, and could mix cocktails in your backyard, as if that required some kind of oenological prowess. The meetings usually took place in pleasant bucolic surroundings, the number one criterion being the availability of a golf course nearby. Being good at that game authorized you to rub shoulders with high-ranking executives and give them a chance to know you socially, if not professionally.

Back in France, I always felt uneasy upon regurgitating to my eager associates what was said in the meetings. It was somewhat difficult, time after time, to justify one's absence from the office with a laconic "Oh, nothing much."

Following one memorable session where the subject of Fortress Europe was again rehashed, John Bright, a senior something or other who did not exactly deserve his name, pulled me aside, saying that he needed some advice. He had just been given overall responsibility for Europe, or perhaps the world, or even the universe.

We walked to his office, where he asked his faithful secretary to bring us coffee. Thereupon, he unfolded a large map of Europe, spread it flat on the table in the manner of a chief of armed forces, and said, "You see,

Midhat, my wife Mary is very excited about my new responsibilities and the prospect of traveling to Europe. She went to Rand McNally and bought me this map. Isn't it a beauty?"

"Indeed, it is very well done, sir." (Most educated Europeans will say "sir" when addressing a superior, particularly if he is older. That does not include those zealots who, the minute they join an American company, start aping their ways—playing golf, taking sides in American elections, showing pictures of their wives and kids, wearing yellow power ties, owning personalized coffee mugs, contriving an American accent, and going by first names.)

"Well, I have been studying it carefully, but despite my efforts, I couldn't find the Benelux. Isn't it part of the European Community? Would you show me where it is?"

I was literally flabbergasted and my embarrassment reached unprecedented heights. How was I to explain to that respectable sexagenarian that Benelux was not one country but three? How was I to extricate myself from that predicament? Why did he choose me, of all people, to deflower him? I cleared my throat a few times, mustered my courage and mumbled, "Hum . . . . Well, sir, Be-ne-lux is only hum . . . an informal acronym that we sometimes use in reference to Belgium, the Netherlands, and Luxembourg. Three very small countries indeed!"

A few weeks later, his administrative assistant, an arrogant young suburban know-all, called me in Paris, where he had never set foot, and informed me of the travel plans he had concocted for his boss. The first leg of his tour obviously took him to London, where the friendly climate contrived by the Brits usually reassured their American visitors and softened the cultural shock awaiting them on the other side of the Channel.

The company jet was scheduled to land at Le Bourget Airport, and we had to make absolutely sure that the formalities took place inside the airplane, not on the tarmac or in one of those customs shacks he had heard about. He also insisted that the guest be pre-registered at the Ritz and avoid the hassle of filling forms in the lobby. The assistant had heard of some places in Europe whose showers did not project from the bathroom wall, a shortcoming that forced the guest to hold on to the shower's knob with one hand while lathering his body with the other. That had to be avoided at all costs. We also had to make sure that the washbasins were equipped with a single faucet that delivered warm water, not those dual faucets that might cause the boss to scald himself. The suite had to be e-mail–ready, because the chief needed to connect with headquarters the minute he checked in, for fear that some momentous event had taken place while he was getting tipsy between London and Paris.

The administrative assistant had personally mapped out a tour of Paris, whose highlights he selected with the help of a Paris guidebook. With remarkable sophistication, he chose the Eiffel Tower, the Champs Elysées, and Montmartre. Moreover, his wife needed a female escort to take her shopping, preferably some American expatriate's wife. Finally, having heard of the Tour d'Argent, the young man e-mailed me the menu—numbered duckling, wine and all. In the course of the visit, which was to last two days, the boss expressed the desire to address French business leaders at the highest level, and we had to make the necessary arrangements. We also had to organize a quick informal get together with the subsidiary employees who, with the exception of the expatriates, were looking forward to the event with minimal anticipation.

I chose to hold the customer event at the Cercle Interallié, France's most sophisticated private club, whose ballroom was turned into a conference room for the occasion. The young ignoramus was bewildered by the eighteenth-century decorum. In case his boss became suddenly interested in what the large tapestry represented, he asked me to fill him in. I was tempted to mislead him, and tell him that it represented some episode of French history prior to the discovery of America, but charitably informed him that it depicted an episode of Racine's play known as *Athalie's Dream,* inspired by the murder of Athalyah, Queen of Judea. I did not belabor the issue any further because he was already experiencing enough stress as it was.

For the most part, my guests were themselves members of that exclusive venue and knew each other well. There was no particular seating arrangement, and they sat with whomever they chose to rub shoulders with. I explained to my boss that it would be appropriate if I personally greeted the guests in French and introduced him to the crowd. But he insisted on doing that himself in accordance with his administrative assistant's prescriptions, in the manner of a Napoleon snatching the imperial crown from the Pope's hands and placing it upon his own head. When everybody was finally seated, the boss rose to the podium, checked his fly, buttoned his jacket, adjusted the micro-phone's angle—he was six foot tall and the lectern had to be adjusted accordingly—drank a sip of water, cleared his throat, and opened with the words "Hi folks!"

Whereupon, my immediate neighbor, one of the leading captains of industry, discreetly leaned toward me and asked under his breath, "Qu'est-ce que c'est 'Folks'?"

~ Bill Hewlett ~

In memoriam

One man had a decisive influence on my life, though I met him only once. It was in the seventies on a Paris–Boston flight. He was absorbed in a maze of mathematical equations scribbled on a yellow pad as he qui-etly sipped his Scotch on the rocks. Having recognized those weird mathematical animals we call 'tensors,' I couldn't resist asking him what he was working on. He was attempting to solve a somewhat difficult problem posed by his son, an architect who had set his mind on design-ing an original geodesic dome resembling the double hump on a camel's back.

When dinner was served, I mustered enough courage to resume our conversation. Having told him which company I worked for, he exclaimed, "Ah! That's a nice little company in the Boston area, not far from Hewlett-Packard, where I work."

"I have always admired your company for its corporate culture and dedication to science. Are you a scientist by any chance?"

"I believe so. My name is Bill Hewlett."

"I am very honored to meet you. Let me ask you an indiscreet question if I may. How can you reconcile being at the helm of that impressive company and doing *that* at the same time? I mean solving difficult math problems."

"*That* is what keeps my brain alive! What is your background?"

"I have a couple of engineering degrees and a science doctorate."

"That's great! And when was the last time you read a science book?"

"Oh, it must have been ten or fifteen years."

"Listen young man, when we land in Boston, dump your suitcase in your hotel room and rush to the nearest bookstore. Get yourself a couple of good science books, and never stop reading as long as you live."

Having heeded Bill Hewlett's advice, I presently own several hundred science books in my personal library. When I retired in 1993, I decided to return to my frustrated passion, and jot down some of the mathematical ideas I had come across over the years. They eventually constituted the substance of two books that were published by Princeton University Press, the first in 1999 and the second the following year.

Bill Hewlett died in January 2001, unaware of the decisive influence he had on my life, as well as on so many others.

∽ Back To Egypt ∾

∽ Cairo Rediscovered ∾

*Monstrous hotels spreading the fake luxury of their eye-catching
façades; along the streets, whitewash over plaster daub; saraband of
all styles, rocaille, Romanesque, Gothic, Art Nouveau, pharaonic, and
most of all, the pretentious and preposterous . . . . Is that the Cairo
of the future, that cosmopolitan bedlam? My God, when will they pull
themselves together, the Egyptians? When will they understand that
their ancestors have bequeathed to them an inalienable heritage of art,
architecture, refined elegance, and that by giving it up, one the most
exquisite cities on earth is crumbling and dying?*

Pierre Loti, 1908[70]

In 1981, I returned to Egypt after exactly thirty years of absence. On
my way back from an assignment in Johannesburg, I decided on the
spur of the moment to stop over in Cairo for a few days. I asked my
secretary to check if a hotel by the name of Mena House had escaped the
great Cairo fire of 1952, and make a reservation in case it had.

Initially intended as a rest house at the foot of the Great Pyramid, the

Mena House was later purchased by wealthy Australians who transformed it into a hotel and named it after King Mena of ancient Egypt.[71] They preserved much of its Ottoman character but could not resist adding unmistakably Victorian terraces, croquet lawns, etc. The hotel register included one of the world's most extraordinary guest lists — Winston Churchill, Franklin Roosevelt, even the infamous Josef Goebbels.

On our way to the pyramids, we would dismount our bicycles to catch our breath and admire the Mena House's elaborate architecture and arabesque *mashrabiyas*.[72] The garden on the edge of the desert sagged under the magnolia and flame trees, its walkways lined with royal palms and oleanders. The Pyramids Road, leading from Cairo to the pyramids, was inaugurated by Ismail for the comfort of Empress Eugénie of France, first foreign sovereign to visit the lodge, in the course of the 1869 opening festivities for the Suez Canal. In return, she had offered the monarch acacia trees that were planted on either side of the majestic road. Legend has it that the khedive had schemed with the designer to bend the road sharply at some point, hoping that the empress, who accompanied him in her husband's absence, would be thrust against him, and press her body against his.[73] The acacias were eventually supplanted by eucalyptus trees, whose nonchalant foliage protected us from the blinding sunshine.

As I caught sight of Lake Nasser in the distance, the pilot announced that we were about to cross the Egyptian border. The new Aswan dam had given birth to an immense water reservoir that made its entry into geography books as Lake Nasser, changing forever the map of Africa. The last time I visited Aswan, I had traveled by train with my fellow students of the Faculty of Engineering on a field trip to the old British-built dam. Lake Nasser wasn't there!

From our altitude, we could clearly distinguish the narrow strips of arable land on either side of the Nile. The lives — in Arabic they say 'breaths' — of fifty million people depended on that thin silvery line, glittering brightly in the afternoon sun. Herodotus was right, I thought, when he declared that Egypt was a gift of the Nile.

As we approached Cairo, I was bewildered by the immensity of the city's sprawl into the surrounding desert. I hoped to catch sight of some familiar landmark, but could barely recognize anything. When the pilot announced that we were about to land at Cairo International Airport, I asked the attendant if that was Almaza Airport's new name. She looked at me as if I had descended from a different planet or another century.

In the forties, I would take the *metro* from Bab el Hadid station to Heliopolis then another to Almaza, and walk the rest of the way to the airport. My father had obtained a special pass from the minister of civil aviation that gave me access to the small airport, where I wandered about undisturbed, ignoring the "Do Not Loiter on Tarmac" signs. I loved the heady smell of varnish with which the fabric-coated wings and body were sprayed, making them taut as a drum. I had purchased a collection of "aircraft recognition charts," and could recognize the silhouette of every warplane, friend or foe. One Sunday, an Egyptian pilot offered me a ride on a de Havilland Tiger Moss, a two-seater instruction biplane, at the remarkable speed of 75 miles per hour—the first and most exhilarating flying experience of my life. Another Sunday, I stumbled upon a Spitfire that seemed abandoned in a remote area of the airfield, with the cockpit door open. I climbed on the wing, then into the pilot's seat, placed my feet squarely on the rudder bar and seized the joystick, my head full of heroic dreams. When the film *Spitfire* was shown in Cairo, I believe I saw it four or five times. It told the story of the fighter airplane whose pilots inspired Winston Churchill's famous testimonial: "Never before in the history of mankind has so much been owed by so many to so few." Leslie Howard played the part of Mitch, the aircraft's designer, and David Niven that of Chris, the gallant test pilot.[74] For several years thereafter, my nickname was Mitch.

When I emerged from the airbus and took a whiff of the desert air, my childhood and adolescence all at once unfolded in front of my eyes.

I asked the cab driver if he knew the Mena House. He replied, "Naturally, sir. No doubt the Pasha is living abroad." My question was akin to asking a Paris cab driver if he knew the Eiffel Tower. He had probably detected a slight foreign accent acquired during my prolonged expatriation. I explained that I had been away for thirty years, and were it not for my frequent visits to the United States where my mother, brother, and sister lived, I never spoke Arabic with anyone, except the Egyptian consulate people of the early fifties—so different from today's refined crowd—who endlessly harassed me once a year when the time came to have my passport renewed.

I could barely recognize anything: shabby buildings where once stood beautiful villas, unfinished concrete skeletons where fellaheen once cultivated orange groves, ill-kept streets, potholes everywhere. Was this the Cairo of my childhood? Where had the beauty and grace gone? Thirty years of nostalgia were blown away in the wind.

After about one hour of driving in the polluted air and incessant blare of horns, I fell tired of looking at the nauseating hodgepodge of houses, gaudy restaurants, and storefronts of all colors and shapes that lined the road. I asked the driver when we would finally come to the Pyramids Road. When he replied, "But this is it, Sir!" I was dumbfounded and asked him where all the trees had gone. He turned around in his seat and, shaking his head from side to side, his eyes filled with sadness, said, "That was a long time ago, serene Pasha." When the trees were uprooted, they were a century old.

I recalled my visits to Greece and Turkey a few years earlier. Athens suffocated in the exhaust fumes, and the Parthenon had all but lost its awesome charm amidst the hordes of tourists. Istanbul was devoured by the surrounding slums, the ugly camps erected by the Anatolian mountain dwellers, and the two bridges across the Bosphorus that scarred its once magnificent landscape.

The legendary hotel was still there, at the foot of the pyramids, not having changed in the slightest, except for the new wing in the back. As I strolled in the garden before checking in, I could perceive the massive silhouette of Cheops against the setting sun, bringing back hundreds of blissful memories. The sun was soon swallowed by Nout, the goddess of night, who would beget it at dawn, as it was in the beginning. I could hear my mother cautioning us not to touch the pink flowers of the oleander for they could make us go blind, as she made last minute adjustments to our attire before sitting up for tea in the wicker chairs of the garden terrace.

The next morning, I asked the taxi driver to take me to what used to be our apartment house on Mariette Pasha Street. It had become so decrepit that I didn't dare cross the threshold, so anxious was I to keep my memories intact. The Nubian *bawwab* ('doorman') had inherited the charge from his cousin Soliman, who died in the early fifties. He remembered my parents and inquired about my mother's health. "May God keep her and grant her long life! I have never known a kinder person," he said, his face and palms turned toward the heavens. I asked him, "Why are all the shutters closed? This looks like a ghost building."

"No one has lived here since the seventies. When the foreigners deserted the building in 1956 in the wake of the Suez aggression, cohorts of army officers and servants of Nasser's regime moved in from behind their cows. Abdel Hakim Amer, head of the Feudality Liquidation Committee, may they all turn in their graves, froze the rents, as if to punish the landlords. Your apartment now rents for a handful of pounds. In the seventies, the tenants moved to the newer districts such as Mohandessin, and the building fell into disrepair. On the roof, the maids' rooms have been transformed into minuscule dwellings that are rented out to the destitute. You will observe that most apartments on this street are empty."

"But who replaced those tenants?"

"No one. They are patiently waiting for someone to offer them key money to the tune of one to two hundred thousand pounds. As for the landlord, why should he invest in an asset from which he does not reap any benefit?

"Meanwhile, people are desperately looking for a place to live."

"You should take a look at the cemeteries. The living have invaded the burial vaults."

I crossed the museum's iron gate and paused for a moment in front of Mariette's mausoleum, then turned my gaze to the balcony from which I never failed to watch the sun's perfect ball of fire slowly plunge into the desert sands beyond the pyramids.

The museum hadn't changed noticeably—the same chaotic hodge-podge of treasures, too many to be housed in the cramped edifice built by Mariette in 1902. When were they going to build a new facility, commensurate with that formidable heritage, I asked myself. It seemed that the concrete-happy nouveaux riches only enjoyed crisscrossing the city with hideous overpasses, and disfiguring the Nile banks with monstrous hotels.

I then walked to the Lycée Français, where my childhood and adolescence were blissfully spent. En route, I attempted to catch sight of the landmarks that punctuated my daily journey to and back from school. Gone was the horse-carriage station near the museum's entrance, with the nauseating yet familiar bouquet you might expect from a dozen horses in the simmering Cairo heat. Gone were the English barracks, in whose exact location now stood the Nile Hilton. I remembered the day when, for some reason, I fell from my bicycle squarely in front of the barracks gate, which was perpetually guarded by half a dozen armed sentries. I felt extremely faint for a fraction of a second, having bumped my head on the asphalt, then lost consciousness. When I came back to my senses, I found myself lying down on a narrow bunk in the sentry box under a coarse khaki blanket, my elbows and knees smeared with iodine tincture. One of the soldiers said, "You fell in a stinkin' pile of Gippy horseshit. The nurse gave you a tet'nos shot, just in case. Your Raleigh is outside. Made in England, eh?" I thanked him and walked out of the awesome gate whose threshold I had never crossed before and would never cross again. Two weeks later, the terrible tragedy of February 21 unfolded in front of that very gate.

Midan Ismailiya was gone and with it Issaievitch, which served the best *foul* sandwiches in the world. Renamed Midan el Tahrir, meaning 'Liberation Square,' the *midan* was now inordinately large, having absorbed the barracks' courtyard. The blare of horns was deafening. It seemed as though everyone needed to announce his presence all around as if in the midst of a thick fog. When they functioned, which was infrequently, traffic lights were blissfully ignored by the drivers who slalomed through the pandemonium with incredible recklessness. I stood petrified on the curb as I attempted to cross the street, incapable of mustering enough courage to meet my impending ordeal. In despair, I asked a pedestrian how one crosses a street in Cairo. "Come with me," he said, as he wriggled between the cars in the manner of a Spanish toreador dodging the charge of a dozen bulls.

Having survived Midan el Tahrir's traffic, I had no difficulty finding my way to the Lycée. It was still there, its heavy wooden gate surmounted by a large GARÇONS carved in stone, with its once beautiful arabesque walls now blighted by a multitude of protruding air conditioners. The auditorium where the annual graduation ceremonies were held since time immemorial had been converted into a theater that, judging from the scruffy billboards, was not dedicated to the most refined repertoires. I walked around the corner to the main entrance whose threshold no student ever crossed unless summoned by the director in the presence of his parents, when he had committed some abominable crime. I carefully climbed the stairs, dreading to be reprimanded by the ill-tempered janitor. Much to my surprise, he rose from his worn out bench, set his waterpipe aside, then asked me, bowing and scraping, what might be the purpose of the serene Pasha's visit. When I told him that I was an alumnus who wished to visit the courtyard and perhaps one or two classes, he summoned a lesser employee, and ordered him to show me around and cater to my slightest desires.

For some obscure reason, the sycamore had been uprooted, carrying into oblivion the myriad little hearts amorously carved on its red bark by generations of adolescents in love. Our history teacher had explained that the sycamore, frequently mentioned in fables and legends, was known in ancient Egypt as the Love Tree. Otherwise, the courtyard had not changed, with the brass bell hanging in the same old corner. How we loved its ring when it signaled the end of the math class, and how we hated it at the end of the recess! We had nicknamed it the Inchcape Bell, having learned that little verse by Robert Southey, which emerged from the depths of my memory:

The Abbot of Aberbrothok
Had placed that bell on the Inchcape Rock;
On a buoy in the storm it floated and swung,
And over the waves its warning rung.

Mr. Inglott had chosen that poem to put us on guard against the hundreds of irregular English verbs. He would emphatically articulate:

To swing, swung, swung
To ring, rang, rung
To bring, brought, brought.

I knew exactly which class to visit. That of 1940–41, the year Robert and I fell in love with Madame Moulin. Alas! The old benches were gone, and with them my hieroglyphs. I asked the director if I could visit the archive room. She replied, wringing her hands, that its contents had been destroyed when the Lycée was nationalized in 1956. That year, they renamed my school "Liberty Lycée." In sharp contrast, the American University next door was miraculously intact, and Ewart Memorial Hall still seemed to serve its initial purpose. The AUC, I later learned, had become the alma mater of numerous Egyptian captains of industry and political leaders, among them Mrs. Suzanne Mubarak, Egypt's first lady.

⟞ From Luxor to Aswan ⟝

Every child of Adam must share the bread and salt with his fellow man.
Islamic precept

My children and I were leaning over the railing of the *Akhenaton*, one of several luxurious boats cruising up and down the Nile, as we observed the crew unload basket upon basket of fresh vegetables and fruits, noisily heckling one another. People were coming and going in every direction, sometimes stopping to shake hands and inquire about their families upstream. The boat had arrived the previous night from Aswan, and was getting ready to sail back that afternoon.

A dozen schoolchildren stood on the embankment, facetiously exchanging comments in French or English with the passengers, "Welcome to Luxor! Bon voyage! Ça va bien, mon ami?"

Across the street stood the Luxor Temple in all its majesty, with the lone obelisk flanking its entrance.[75] "I cannot believe all of this is true, Papa," said my younger daughter, "Here we are, in the heart of Thebes, the land of your ancestors. The Nile, the Luxor temple, the people—it has to be a dream." My son Stéphane was already absorbed in his *Guide bleu*, studying our itinerary and its landmarks—the temples of Esna, Edfu, Kom Ombo, Philae, and finally Abu Simbel. The need to understand the history and significance of whichever site he visits is one of his characteristic traits, whereas his sisters enjoy abandoning their imagination to the magic and mystery of places.

To the left of the temple stood the Winter Palace, where so many illustrious foreigners, among them Byron, stayed at one time or another. The Victorian landmark inspired Agatha Christie's *Death on the Nile* and the namesake movie was shot partly in that setting, partly in Aswan's fabulous Cataract Hotel, where wealthy British tourists suffering from tuberculosis flocked in every winter in the hope of an improbable recovery.[76]

Minutes after leaving the pier, we were thrust back three thousand years into the past. Green strips of arable land on either bank of the Nile, so narrow in places that the desert sand had worked its way to the water's edge. One could clearly fathom how the silt brought down by millions of successive annual floods had blanketed those miniscule strips of Libyan Desert to the west and Arabian Desert to the east.

The fields were greener than anything we had ever seen. With their tanned faces, their garb, their water buffalos and wooden ploughs, the villagers went about their chores resembling their ancestors down to the smallest detail—a pharaonic wall painting come alive. Their brightly colored robes rolled up above the knee, the women sat on the water's edge busy with their laundry, chattering, giggling, and waving back at us, while the children ran on the bank, racing our boat amidst a joyous clamor.

I lounged in an armchair on the deck and let the landscape unfold in front of my eyes. "This must be one of the happiest moments of my life," I said to myself, as the voice of Umm Kalthum emerged from the fields, the Nile, the skies, and the depths of time.

The passengers were French, except for three elderly American couples who seemed to be enjoying their voyage immensely. Upon learning that I was Egyptian and spoke English, they befriended my little family and loved to chat with my erudite son. He nicknamed their group "the National Geographic crowd" because they carried with them several back issues of that magazine. I remember once borrowing a superb issue featuring the raising of the colossal statues of Ramesses II as the new Aswan dam was being built.

Following our visit to the temple of Esna, we returned to the boat, ready to sail on to Edfu and Kom Ombo. An old, immaculately dressed Egyptian with a clean-cropped white beard was crouched on a mat at the foot of the gangplank. He was surrounded by a number of the musical instruments called *kamanga* that, apart from the quality of the materials used, perfectly fit Edward Lane's description in his classical *Manners and Customs of the Modern Egyptians*. (Lane's modern Egyptians lived in 1836, mind you, at the time of the book's first printing). The *kamanga*, he writes, "is a kind of viol. Its name, which . . . is Persian and more properly written kemangeh, signifies 'a bow-instrument'. . . . The sounding-body is a cocoanut [a gourd in this instance], of which about a fourth part has been cut off. It is pierced with many small holes. Over the front of it is strained a piece of the skin of a fish of the genus *Silurus*, called *bayad*; and upon it rests the bridge. The neck is of ebony, inlaid with ivory [of plain sycamore in this instance] . . . ." Whereas Edward Lane's bow stick was made of ash, the old man's was of palm stalk and the chord of horsehairs. He mastered the instrument with extraordinary virtuosity, drawing from the little gourd a poignant and nostalgic threnody that filled the National Geographic crowd with awe and admiration. In no time at all, they purchased his entire stock of instruments, then awkwardly climbed the gangplank with their precious acquisitions. Out of curiosity, I asked the old man

"Tell me, *ya Hagg*, how much did you charge for the *kamanga*?"

"One American dollar, my son."

"Do you realize that you could have gotten ten times that amount without the Americans batting an eyelash?"

"But they didn't cost me anything! Here and there, I pick up a fallen gourd or a palm stalk. The *hantur*-driver gives me a few hairs from his horse's tail, and that's all I need."

Obviously, the kind old man's notion of time was very different from that hammered in by management schools.

"And what do you do with the dollars?"

"Ali the taxi driver changes them for me."

Ali, who rubbed shoulders with tourists from all over the world and spoke English, French, German and Italian, was the old man's only interface with western civilization.

"How many pounds does he give you in exchange for one dollar?"

"Sometimes one, sometimes two. He says it depends on the banks."

"But for heaven's sake, don't you realize that he is taking advantage of you?"

"*Ma'alesh*, my son! I don't mind sharing God's bounty. Every child of Adam must share the bread and salt with his fellow man."

Egypt, I thought to myself, had lost nothing of the Osirian morals that governed the lives of the venerable old man's ancestors.

Just before reaching Edfu, the captain announced that a costume ball was scheduled to take place that evening, whose theme was—of course—ancient Egypt. The minute we landed, we were submerged under a swarm of peddlers noisily competing to lure us into their shops. "Costume ball tonight! You, madame, beautiful Nefertiti! Very nice, very cheap!" They were obviously informed of the impending ritual ball, and I have a sneaking suspicion that the captain received something in return. But that was all right, for none of the passengers was really taken in, and they were all looking forward to having a good time clowning around in pharaonic attire.

My daughters bought magnificent silk embroidered robes, ancient amber necklaces, regal tiaras, and golden sandals. As I browsed around, I stumbled upon a beautiful alabaster statuette representing an ibis. The carving was a copy of a votive offering to the Ibis-headed Thoth, god of wisdom and writing. There was nothing antique about it, but it was a beautiful piece of craftsmanship nonetheless, and Thoth was my favorite god in Egypt's pantheon. I asked the merchant how much it cost, in Arabic. He was somewhat taken aback, for I am told that I no longer look Egyptian, probably because decades of living amongst Europeans has rubbed off on my appearance. He replied, "For you, serene Pasha, thirty pounds." A preposterous price, serene or not. I looked him squarely in the eye and told him in perfect popular dialect, "Look at me and listen carefully. I have been living in Europe for the past thirty years, and am not in the mood for haggling. I have no taste for your primitive ways and no time for sterile back and forth bickering. Give me one price and that's that. All right?" He gave me a pathetic look and said apologetically, "Excuse me, serene Pasha. For you, ten pounds." I took the object, gave him ten pounds and walked away. Minutes later, as we were about to board the *calèche*, one of nearly fifty vying for a passage amidst an infernal gridlock of horses, wheels, peddlers, and tourists, my son approached me with the mysterious air of someone who had unearthed some treasure, holding on to a scruffy newspaper wrapped around his loot. Lo and behold! His ibis was the spitting image of mine. "How much did you pay for it?" I asked, fearing that some merchant might have taken advantage of a young European boy, ignorant of the language and the art of haggling. When I learned that he had paid only seven pounds, my blood boiled over. Not for a difference of three pounds, a trifle by European standards, but because I felt humiliated. I dashed back to the shop and blasted, "How dare you fool me into believing that ten pounds is a good price for that trinket, then sell it to my son for seven?" He looked at me unabashedly, tilted his head to one side, shrugged his shoulders, and turned the palms of his hands toward the heavens saying, "Look, serene Pasha. Here I am, quietly going about my business, when you come storming into my shop saying that you spent thirty years here and there, that our ways are primitive, that you have no time to waste because you are a very important man, etc. Therefore, I said to myself, 'By God almighty, I am a humble fake antique merchant from Esna who is going to screw the pasha from abroad!'"

Thereupon, he and I laughed to our heart's content. When I came back to my senses, I patted him on the shoulder and gave him twenty pounds, saying, "You taught me a lesson that well deserves the thirty pounds you attempted to wring from me in the first place!" He replied, "May God bless you and grant your son long life!" as he offered me a little alabaster scarab.

One of the passengers, Madame Naggar, an elderly Jewish lady who had forsaken her gracious Alexandrian life in the wake of the 1956 aggression, was on her first trip back to Egypt after all these years. She loved to reminisce about the old days and exercise what little was left of her Arabic with the Nubian waiters. Every morning, she would ferret around the dining room immediately after breakfast, collecting whatever was left over on the deserted tables—croissants, brioches, chocolate bread—and stuffing her booty into two large plastic bags. Upon disembarking on our way to the daily excursion, she would hail the little children, of whom there would always be a large number gathered on the pier and say, "I have some goodies for you . . . . Come and get them!" in her fractured Arabic. In no time at all, a bevy of little barefooted boys and girls would swarm around her like bees, take the loot, and run.

We reached Kom Ombo shortly before New Year's Eve. A gala dinner was served in the ballroom to the tune of a local orchestra that only knew how to play the tango, waltz, and fox trot, in addition, of course, to Arabic music. We were offered the inescapable belly dance where foreigners are invited to join the scantily clad fattish dancers and awkwardly ape their ways, the whirling dervishes, and the snake charmer whose slinky reptiles invariably draw strident shrieks from the ladies. Shortly before midnight, the waiters went around the room passing out silly cardboard hats of all colors, paper streamers, trumpets, and the usual New Year's Eve paraphernalia. Madame Naggar was bravely fending off an irresistible urge to fall asleep. She would doze off, come back to her senses, then doze off again, until the party was over and the last guest went back to his cabin. At that moment, she sprang out of her armchair and went around the ballroom collecting the abandoned streamers and piling the cone-shaped hats on top of one another.

The next morning, we were allowed to sleep late before visiting the temple of Kom Ombo, but Madame Naggar, who had risen early as usual, was standing on the pier, distributing her treasures to a gang of little children noisily scrambling for the funny hats, trying them on, and laughing.

When we returned from our excursion that afternoon, the children, as if they were responding to some call of the wild, popped out of the fields from every direction, brandishing the hats and shouting, "Nice hat! One pound! Merry Christmas!"

I could not believe my eyes and ears. The little scoundrels were actually selling back their own hats to a bunch of bewildered tourists. I gave one pound to a little girl who looked somewhat like my daughter Valérie, patted her on the cheek, and told her she could keep the hat. How can I forget the smile on her face?

A Nubian child might sell you funny little hats, but he is too proud to beg. He will enjoy your croissants and chocolate-bread not because he is hungry, which he is not, but because he is not different from any other child in the world.

⇌ Mothers of Egypt ⇋

In 1985, I decided to spend a short solitary vacation in Luxor. I was longing to once again immerse myself in that magical atmosphere so charged with history, walk on the promenade along the Nile, chat with the inhabitants, and lazily lounge in the Winter Palace's gardens, whose banyan and flametrees I knew so well. I also loved to browse around in Abboudi's bookshop with nothing particular in mind, and chat with the venerable old man, a true encyclopedia of ancient Egypt. He was perpetually seated behind his tiny cluttered desk at the far end of the store, and always greeted me by first name despite my prolonged absences. (I have never ceased to be amazed at the Egyptians' capacity to remember faces and names.) My gray hair entitles me to the title of *hagg*, which is deserved only by those who return from a pilgrimage to Mecca, but is often used as a sign of deference toward the elderly. The merchant is a veritable *hagg*, which I am not, but I do not dislike being addressed in that manner, which gives me the fleeting delusion that I am a Muslim amongst the Muslims.

At Abboudi's, I purchased exceptionally good reproductions of David Roberts' views of the temples as they appeared to him around the middle of the nineteenth century, half buried in the desert sand.

Abboudi also carried a large collection of ancient post cards dating back to the days when Howard Carter discovered the treasures of Tutankhamen, with naive "Greetings from the Nile" printed on the face.[77] The people still looked the same, as if time had come to a standstill in that part of the world, blessed by so many gods.

One afternoon around six o'clock, as I was taking a random walk on the promenade, I came across a little barefoot boy standing on the curb side, wearing a ragged *gallabiya* on top of an oversized man's shirt, and carrying a pail that looked disproportionately heavy in relation to his frail body. I asked him what he was doing, standing there with a pail. He replied that he washed cars (probably a full time job whenever dust blows in from the desert; however, the past few days had been exceptionally clear, and he looked idle and anguished).

"How old are you?"

"Eight and a half."

"Don't you go to school?"

"Yes, in the morning. I wash cars in the afternoon because my father is dead, God's mercy upon him."

"God's mercy upon him. And what is your name?"

"Muhammad."

With his big black eyes, Muhammad looked very much like my son at his age. (I need to temper that tendency of mine to find that every little Egyptian child I come across resembles one of my own children.)

"Did you wash any cars today?"

"No, not for the past three days."

"And how much do you usually charge?"

"One pound, but I have to give Osta 'Abdu twenty-five piasters."[78]

"Who is Osta 'Abdu?"

"He owns this part of the street, where the cars pass on their way to the ferry barge."

I dug in my pocket, and discreetly gave him a ten-pound note. He clenched his fist on the note and dashed off like a rocket. I figured that Osta 'Abdu was probably lurking somewhere in the neighborhood, and Muhammad had no intention of sharing the loot with anyone.

The following afternoon, also around six, Muhammad was standing near the hotel entrance.

"*Ahlan ya Muhammad*! What on earth are you doing here?"

"I was waiting for you."

"For me? How strange! And how did you know I was staying at this hotel?"

"I figured that a pasha like you had to stay at the Winter!"

"What did you do with the ten pounds?"

"I gave them to my mother. She told me to kiss your hand."

"You don't need to do that. I hope you didn't come to beg, did you!"

"No, never, by Allah! I just wanted to ask you if I could walk with you for a little while, for everyone to see us together."

I didn't ask any questions and seized his roughened little hand. We walked to the barge, where a bunch of children gave him sidelong glances, probably under the watchful eye of Osta 'Abdu. We turned around at the end of the pier and returned to the hotel. Muhammad said,

"May Allah keep you, *ya-buya* ('my father'). May I ask you for something else?"

"What is it now?"

"Would you take a picture of me? My mother doesn't have any."

"Of course, *ya–bni* ('my son')."

I took half a dozen pictures of Muhammad, with and without the pail. We then walked together to the photo shop at the foot of the Winter Palace, and gave the roll to be processed. "They will be ready tomorrow afternoon, God willing," said the shopkeeper.

The following afternoon at six o'clock, Muhammad was again standing near the hotel entrance, eager to get the photos. He seized the envelope, thanked me, and dashed home without opening it.

On the afternoon of December 31, Muhammad was standing in the usual place.

"What brings you today, Muhammad?"

"I only wanted to wish you well on the eve of the New Year. My mother baked these little biscuits for you. They are very good—stuffed with date marmalade!"

He reached in his pocket and gave me a washed-out French postcard representing, of all places, the Rochefort railroad station! I took the card and plastic bag and thanked him. "Come with me," I said, "and help me pick a present for your mother. You decide which."

The contrast between the populous area behind the hotel and the Nile promenade was striking. Storefronts overflowing with herbs of all colors and scents, craftsmen toiling in the street, merchants selling souvenirs and fake antiques, meat carcasses hanging in the open, vegetable and fruit stalls invading the sidewalk . . . .

He took me to a tiny clothes shop whose owner he well knew because he often washed his Mercedes. The man was sitting on a wooden bench outside the store, one bare foot resting on the bench and the other on top of his slippers. He was drinking tea out of a small glass and smoking a waterpipe, as if he had all eternity in front of him. Muhammad introduced me saying that the pasha needed to buy a dress for his lady. The merchant offered me a glass of tea, declaring that the store was my store, that it was an honor to welcome me on these humble premises, etc. I picked a navy blue *gallabiya* richly embroidered around the neck and sleeves with golden thread, as well as a pair of matching slippers, and asked Muhammad to carry the shopping bag as if he were doing it for me. The second we turned the corner, he dashed home as usual.

That night, the once-a-year countdown began ten seconds before midnight, with champagne corks popping off amidst a deafening noise and people cheering and kissing. I attempted to call my mother in New York, but the hotel operator replied that all lines to Cairo were busy, and suggested that I try later. I tried again and again, but the operator invariably repeated that there was "no heat" in the line or that the line had "fallen." After several unfruitful attempts, I finally went to bed, cursing the country's telephone system. It was the first time in more than twenty years that I failed to call my mother on New Year's Eve.

I was awakened in the morning by a knock on my door. The messenger boy delivered a telegram from Paris in which the children informed me, with immense sadness, that their beloved Teta had died shortly after midnight.

I flew to Paris in the afternoon, and found the children waiting for me at the airport. They hugged me, telling me softly me how affected they were. Aboard the plane to Washington, the Air France hostess asked me if there was anything she could do, confessing that she had sensed immense sadness in my eyes. She gave me a little orchid that I kept in my hand until we reached Dulles airport, where my brother picked me up and headed straight for the funeral home.

I placed the orchid between my mother's joined hands and kissed her forehead, which smelled of Arpège, her favorite perfume.

⟿ Fall of a Giant ⟾

In June 1947, my brother Waguih sailed to France and enrolled in the Montpellier faculty of medicine, reputedly the oldest in the world. I remember seeing him off at the pier, accompanied by a dozen family members—aunts, uncles, cousins, and sundry well-wishers—all of whom were vacationing in Alexandria according to an unchanging ritual. My childhood friend Robert, who like me had fallen in love with Madame Moulin some six years earlier, was also en route to Montpellier. (He studied chemistry and shared an apartment with my brother throughout their studies.) We lingered on the pier, waving our handkerchiefs until the *Cadio*, a Greek boat—actually a tired old tub—vanished beyond the horizon, leaving behind a thin trail of black smoke floating in the afternoon summer sky. Needless to say, both mothers were crying profusely, for in those years it took some ten days to sail from Alexandria to Marseilles, and international long-distance calls were not exactly the custom of the time.

Degree in hand, my brother elected to establish his residence in Fairfax, Virginia, where the warm climate somewhat reminded him of Egypt, and whose population was growing exponentially. It wasn't long before he founded the Commonwealth Doctors Hospital, as well as two private clinics. My mother, who proudly attended all three ground-breaking ceremonies, never failed to refer to her elder son as "My son the surgeon." Never mind me, with my useless science doctorate! His oil portrait, painted by a talented Russian named Marcos Blakhove, hung at the far end of the hospital boardroom.

One of my brother's clinics specialized in ambulatory surgery. The patient would enter the clinic in the morning, undergo surgery, then return home in the afternoon. Chances of early recovery were apparently enhanced by a procedure whereby patients convalesced at home, surrounded by their family and fed with home-cooked meals. Not to mention the economic advantage to the patient and the limited exposure to diseases acquired in the hospital environment—which are more frequent than you are led to believe. I loved to visit him in Fairfax and watch him perform surgery.

One winter afternoon, my brother was quietly cruising down the Nile with his daughters, when it dawned on him that an ordinary Nile boat could be readily transformed into an ambulatory clinic. The boat would sail up and down the Nile, traversing Egypt from end to end, stopping in remote villages whose fellaheen had no access to a nearby hospital. By coming to their doorstep, the hospital would reduce their natural apprehension and encourage them to seek treatment. One of my brother's basic stipulations was that treatment would have to be dispensed free of charge. To that effect, he would create a foundation, train the doctors and nurses, and volunteer his own time after retirement.

Literally obsessed by the project, he drafted the boat's plans down to the minutest detail, and even built a cardboard model whose successive decks could be removed one by one, revealing the hospital's infrastructure. Project in hand, he visited his old friend Hassan Shalakamy at his Imbaba shipyard on the Nile and shared the idea with him. Hassan was a self-made entrepreneur who had single-handedly established what was to become Egypt's major shipyard. He had acquired the immense stock of leftover steel that Egypt had purchased from the Russians in the course of the construction of the Aswan High Dam, and with it built his first Nile cruise boat, followed by dozens of others. If you embark on a Nile cruise, chances are you will be sailing on one of Hassan's boats.

The meeting of minds was instantaneous. The two men, who profoundly loved Egypt and had set their hearts on serving its kind, underprivileged people, agreed to jointly finance the project. Upon returning to the States, my brother scouted a handful of hospitals he knew well, and convinced his colleagues to donate part of their used surgery-room equipment.

On November 13, 1987—the sun was just rising—the telephone rang in my Paris apartment. My brother's wife in tears informed me that he had been brutally assaulted in his office, where he had stopped on his way home from the airport to tidy up some papers. His skull had been smashed. It was after working hours and everyone had gone home. Had it not been for Willard the handyman, who was mixing paints in the basement, my brother would have surely died. He had suffered no less than fourteen skull fractures and was lying in a puddle of blood when the man rushed to his side, having been alerted by the rumble above his head. Willard called the hospital and bound up the wounds as best he could. Minutes later, a helicopter landed in the deserted parking lot and my brother was whisked away to the very hospital he had founded in the sixties.

My brother was in a deep coma, and the prognosis was dismal. In the best of cases, should he survive, he would be severely brain-damaged. I noticed that his left hand was in a cast. He had evidently attempted to shield his head from the repeated blows on the left side of his skull. Even if he pulled through, the doctor said, he would probably never be able to practice surgery again, given the state of his damaged hand. Had Waguih not been tall and strong, he would have surely succumbed under the blows of his aggressors, who were two in number, judging from the footsteps they left on the snow outside. Nor would he have survived the invasive treatment administered by the flurry of doctors who bustled around by his bedside. They stuck a tube down his nose and another down the trachea. They fed him though a hole in the stomach and planted a tube in his chest to drain the excess fluid. Another drain was sticking out of his skull, to relieve the pressure on his brain.

Thousand of childhood images came to my mind, of Waguih dissecting rabbits and frogs, and of our afternoon strolls in Alexandria, where the carpenter, the cobbler, and the tinsmith would introduce us to the knacks of their trade in their small streetside shops. "When I grow up," my brother used to say, "I want to be a good craftsman." It was a blessing, I thought, that my mother didn't live long enough to see her first born son thus felled. But he miraculously survived.

The culprits were never found. The cardboard model of his boat has been sitting ever since on the mantelpiece of his Virginia home, side by side with the statuette that my grandfather had given him when he was a child.

⌁ Sister Emmanuelle ⌁

In 1993, the wife of an alumnus of mine, a prominent minister at the time, suggested that I meet Sister Emmanuelle, should I wish to do something useful for my country. Sister Emmanuelle, a Catholic nun, lived amongst the most destitute inhabitants of the monstrously sprawling city of Cairo, the garbage collectors, or *zabbalin*. A friend of hers agreed to pick me up the next morning at dawn near the gate of the Citadel, a stone's throw from where Sister Emanuelle had established her quarters and shared the life of the men, women, and children who toiled in hell.

As soon as we left the main road, I was overwhelmed by a pungent smell that became less and less tolerable as the car wriggled its way through a labyrinth of narrow unpaved streets, lined with tin shacks reminiscent of Brazil's *favelas*. The car finally stopped in front of one of the most eerie sights I ever saw in my life. Imagine a hole as big as a football field with a huge mound of black garbage in the middle, and clusters of little dwellings huddled against one another around its rim. We were in April, the sizzling summer temperatures had not set in, and yet the smoldering mound exhaled columns of grayish smoke that seemed to emerge from the depths of some volcanic inferno. The stench was unbearable. A band of little barefoot boys and girls in grimy clothes, their faces as black as the garbage itself, joyously raced each other to the top of the heap, sometimes vanishing behind the smoke. I cringed when I saw one of the little girls pick up a filthy plastic bag from which she extracted what must have been remnants of food and brought them to her mouth.

I was led to a two-story whitewashed building that seemed an island of salubrity amidst an ocean of squalor. The lady explained that Sister Emmanuelle had built the little edifice to house a school where the children learned to read and write, as well as a manual trade. Sister Emanuelle had also built a clinic in one of the three shanty towns where she spent her days amongst the *zabbalin*.

I stood on the balcony as I awaited Sister Emmanuelle's arrival, watching the incessant comings and goings of donkey carts laden with garbage and driven by little children perched on top of the foul-smelling heaps. My host explained that the collectors crisscrossed the city every day at dawn, then brought home their cargo and spilled it on the floor of their dwellings. After sorting the broken glass, tin and plastic containers, paper, cloth, and so on, they would dump what remained in the middle of the open space, where the good Sister had installed a makeshift compost machine that transformed the garbage into fertilizer.

Sister Emmanuelle was noisily greeted by a bevy of little boys and girls who clung to her habit, giggling and laughing. She knew every one of them by first name and inquired about their parents' health as well as their own performance in class, congratulating this one and gently reprimanding another. She wore a longish, gray robe, a head cover of the same material, a simple silver cross, and tired old tennis shoes. Her wrist watch was the reminder of a keen sense of urgency that never let up.

After we had been introduced, she vigorously seized my arm and said, "Yalla, come with me, I'll show you around," unabashedly using the familiar *tu* form in French. (The injunction *Yalla* is a contraction of *Ya Allah*, meaning 'O God,' and is an exhortation to move ahead.)

We visited the weaving classroom, where a dozen impeccably dressed girls seated at their looms turned their faces in my direction, each flashing two rows of healthy white teeth. "They are not allowed to cross the threshold," Sister Emanuelle said, "until they have washed their bodies and clothes. What we have done here is restore their dignity as human beings. You see, between those who work and those who don't, those who have and those who have not, there is an insuperable barrier of indifference, even hostility. Those who are excluded from society suffer most of all from the loss of dignity. They feel worthless and are despised more than they are pitied. Here, we want to give them a sense of self-worth they have never known."

We then went to the nearby school, whose courtyard was decorated all around with naively painted pharaonic motifs that exuded happiness. It was recess time, and the pupils swarmed around us from every direction. A little girl offered me a holy image she had probably received for being a good pupil.

We went back to the little building and sat around a small table with Sister Sara and two other colleagues, discussing the ways in which my friends and I could make ourselves useful. Sister Sara's devotion to Emmanuelle's cause was almost religious, and little could have been accomplished without her. Together, they were able to mobilize an army of staunch supporters, not the least of whom was Mrs. Suzanne Mubarak, the first lady.

At one o'clock, Sister Emmanuelle rose from her chair, grabbed my arm, and said, "Yalla, let's go." At the bottom of the stairs, she asked, "Do you have any plans for lunch?"

"No, none."

"Fine then. I feel like having grilled fish. I know a little restaurant on the Nile, not too far from here, but far enough from the stench. I am used to it, but I noticed that it bothers you somewhat." Indeed, the stench was still lingering in my throat and nostrils as it would be for several days thereafter.

The restaurant was simple, yet unusually clean, and probably catered to civil servants employed in a nearby administration building. The fish was superb, as well as the endless variety of *mezzes* that were served as a matter of course—*hommos, tahina, baba ghannouge*, etc. Sister Emmanuelle's appetite was surprisingly hearty for a frail woman of eighty-five. I was mesmerized by her piercing yet kind blue eyes behind her oversized rectangular glasses.

"Tell me, Sister, where exactly do you come from?"

"I was born in 1908 of Franco-Belgian parents and received a liberal education, spending my insouciant adolescence with a father and mother who adored each other."

"When did you join the congregation of Notre Dame de Sion?"

"I felt the vocation and decided to dedicate my life to God when I saw my father drown in front of my eyes and couldn't rescue him. I was twenty-three years old, and chose that congregation because of its profound underlying spirituality. I changed my name from Madeleine to Emmanuelle, a biblical name which means 'God is upon us.'"

"And did you discover the *zabbalin* right away?"

"No, that was not until I reached the age when one usually retires."

"What did you do in the meantime?"

"I taught for twenty-eight years at Notre Dame de Sion in Istanbul. Among my pupils were the two daughters of Ataturk—a great man who did a lot to emancipate his country. I then taught for five years in Tunis and another six in Alexandria, before discovering the shanty town of Ezbet el Nakhl in the suburbs of Cairo."

"Alexandria is my birthplace."

"You are very fortunate. It's a beautiful city, so charged with history . . . the Greeks, the Romans, the Copts . . . ."

"But how did you come across the *zabbalin*?"

"Not through my affluent pupils or their parents, who lived in a different world, but through a friend from the Vatican embassy who had taken pity on the *zabbal* who picked up the garbage from his home every morning, and decided one day to accompany him to his dwelling."

"Until today, I thought I was getting old, but it seems you have given me a new lease on life."

"You know, when I turned seventy-four, I felt that life was beginning anew. I moved from Ezbet el Nakhl to this place, where my wonderful colleagues created the Association des Amis de Soeur Emmanuelle. They presently assist more than 60,000 children all over the world."

"Did you gain any converts to the Catholic church?"

"I never mention God unless someone comes to me with a question, and make it a rule never to interfere with anyone's religious beliefs. A group of young Muslims once asked me to convert them to the Catholic faith, but I refused, because they were too young to decide for themselves. In an Islamic country, converting someone to a different religion is tantamount to uprooting a tree. I have never had any problems with Islam."

"What do you think of the situation in this part of the world?"

"I pray for peace."

"You are now barely eighty-five . . . what are your plans for the future?"

"Unfortunately, this is my last year in Egypt, because I have to obey my superiors of the Order and retire in France. It will be heartbreaking to part with these wonderful people, who have become my family. I will have to learn to live in an environment probably devoid of *joie de vivre*, of brotherhood, and of that intense happiness that transcends misery and is only begotten by love. Everyone in France seems sullen and surly; they are unhappy with the government, their working conditions, their car, their neighbor, the ozone layer, whereas here, lacking material possessions to agonize about, the people thrive on concern for each other's well-being."

"Meanwhile, Sister Emmanuelle, how would you like an assortment of oriental pastries?"

"I would love that!"

In recognition of her work, President Mubarak awarded Sister Emmanuelle the Egyptian nationality, and President Chirac of France bestowed upon her the Grand Cross of Commander of the Legion of Honor.

⌁ Bonaparte's Scientists ⌁

As for the learned scribes . . . they did not make for themselves
pyramids of copper with tombstones of iron. They were unable to
leave an heir in the form of children who would pronounce their
 name, but they made for themselves an heir of the writing and
instruction they had made.

Inscription on an ostracon unearthed in Deir el Madina[79]

Ever since the Napoleonic campaign, Egypt has exercised a strange fascination upon the French, verging on passion. It was one of Napoleon's
generals who discovered the Rosetta stone, and Champollion who deciphered the hieroglyphic alphabet. The Frenchmen Mariette and Maspero
founded the Egyptian Museum and Ferdinand de Lesseps inaugurated the
Suez Canal in the presence of Empress Eugenie. The obelisk of Luxor
adorns one of the most beautiful squares in the world and the Egyptian
department of the Louvre is the most frequently visited of all.[80]

Until Nasser's revolution, that passion was reciprocated by the
Egyptians. Over 150 French schools were scattered throughout Egypt:
Lycées, Jesuits, Friars, nuns, etc., making French the undisputed lan-
guage of the educated classes.

A dedicated civil servant and staunch francophile, my father had
insisted on enrolling me in the Egyptian and French departments of the
Lycée Français du Caire simultaneously, submitting me to a dual curriculum that required almost nothing less than a split brain. On the one
hand, I was required to read Montaigne, Voltaire, and Molière, and on the
other, I learned to decipher difficult medieval texts and memorize hundreds of verses in literary Arabic, a tongue no one currently spoke except
the most learned. Colloquial Egyptian is but a dialect derived from the
authentic language enshrined in the Muslim scriptures.

Where the chasm was really intractable was history. In one reading,

Jerusalem was conquered in 1099 by the crusaders following a three-month siege that took the life of no less than ten thousand miscreants, and in the other, the chivalrous Saladin, founder of the Ayyubid dynasty, bravely reconquered the Holy City in 1187, forcing the admiration and respect of the wretched infidels.[81]

On March 10, 1998, an exhibition entitled *Les Savants en Égypte* opened in Paris, celebrating the two-hundredth anniversary of Bonaparte's scientific expedition. The event took place in the Jardin des Plantes, France's renowned natural history museum, close to the Paris mosque.

En route to the museum in the proverbially congested Paris traffic, my thoughts were freely wandering as I attempted to fathom the mysterious and passionate relationship between France and Egypt. My mind kept shuttling back and forth between East and West, where surprisingly concomitant events of considerable magnitude were shaping the world to come. In 1389, the Ottomans defeated the Serbs in Kosovo while civil war was raging in France between the Armagnacs and the Bourguignons.[82] In 1453, twenty-one years after the burning of Joan of Arc, the Hundred Year War between France and England finally came to an end and with it English occupation of France. That year, the Byzantine era also came to an end when Muhammad II declared Constantinople capital of the Ottoman Empire and named it Istanbul.[83] (Egypt, however, was not to surrender to the Ottomans until 1517, following six centuries of Arab rule—by the caliphs—and two and a half centuries of rule by the Mamluks, slave-warriors imported from the Caucasus.)

I was thrust back into contemporary Parisian reality when it came to finding a parking spot near the museum. After driving around the block several times and illegally parking my car in despair, I finally entered the museum's august premises, where hundreds of guests were gathered on the majestic staircase leading to the exhibition. A small podium had been erected at the foot of the staircase from which three speeches were delivered, the first by the museum director, the second by the exhibition's curator and the third by the Egyptian ambassador.

That afternoon's event commemorated a decision reached by the French Directoire two hundred years earlier to the day, giving birth to the

Commission des Sciences et des Arts of the young Republic's Oriental Army.[84] Within a short three months, a contingent of 154 scholars, many in their twenties, joined the expedition. They were engineers, technicians, mathematicians, chemists, physicians, naturalists, architects, draftsmen, printers, orientalists, musicians, etc., led by outstanding scientists of the caliber of Monge, Berthollet, Dolomieu, and others.

In the course of the construction of Fort Julien near the town of Rosetta, an officer named Pierre Bouchard unearthed a slab of granite that eventually fell into the hands of the victorious British general. The Rosetta stone, which is kept in the British Museum, bears a Greek text along with its hieroglyphic and Coptic translations. That discovery, I thought, would have gone unnoticed were it not for the French scientists, who were quick to understand that the engraved text was a decree handed down by Ptolemy V around 196 B.C. They correctly conjectured that the hieroglyphic and Coptic texts were literal translations of the accompanying Greek text. Confirming Louis Pasteur's observation that fortune smiles on the prepared mind, the triple text enabled Jean-François Champollion to decipher the hieroglyphic alphabet.

At that point, I could not but ponder over the mysterious powers that guide the destiny of great men of genius. Who could have imagined that an adolescent boy from Figeac, a small town in the southwest of France, would some day decide to devote his entire life to a singularly focused goal . . . that of deciphering the Egyptian alphabet? With that purpose in mind, Champollion taught himself the Coptic language, which was spoken by the Egyptians at the dawn of Christianity and, having no one to practice it with, often forced himself to think in that language. At the age of 16, he delivered a paper before the Grenoble Academy in which he propounded the theory that the Coptic language was that of the ancient Egyptians. In 1842, the *Dictionnaire égyptien* was posthumously published by the author's brother following the publication of the first installment of *La Grammaire égyptienne* on December 12, 1835, the day Champollion would have turned forty-five.

As the museum director spoke, it dawned on me that I belonged to the fifth generation of Egyptians who still thrived on French culture after only three years of French military presence, and seventy-five years of British occupation.

The British may have discovered Tutankhamen's tomb, the greatest treasure ever unearthed, but they also bombarded Alexandria, occupied the country militarily, interfered in Egyptian affairs, dismissed monarchs, exiled political leaders or sentenced them to death, curtailed education and industry, engaged the Egyptians in bloody warfare, and most of all . . . most of all, they treated them with the most loathesome arrogance and contempt.

The short-lived French expedition, on the other hand, left indelible traces in the minds and hearts of the Egyptians, perhaps because of their shared rejection of the British, but surely by virtue of the cultural heritage that forever changed the face of Egypt. One thought leading to another, I remembered the disastrous Franco-British-Israeli invasion of November 1956, following Nasser's nationalization of the Canal. Operation Musketeer was the name given to the expedition, according to the derisory habit of giving names to battles, as if they were Hollywood productions. But it went down in our history books as the cowardly Tripartite Aggression, and marked the end of a golden era of friendship and cultural exchange between France and Egypt. My cherished Lycée Français was nationalized and my childhood friends scattered to the four winds, unable to forgive the French, and unable to hate them.

The curator then delivered an impassioned yet measured speech in which he recounted the expedition with bewildering erudition. Such had been my French teachers, modest, and erudite. Humble as an Egyptian scribe, he almost apologized for the breadth and depth of his understanding of Egypt's history, so wary was he of tiring his audience.

The third speaker was the Egyptian ambassador, a refined French-educated diplomat, whose grandfather and granduncle had both served as prime ministers in the forties and fifties. Somewhat taken aback by the director's unplanned invitation to say a few words to the audience, he observed, in his impeccable French and tongue in cheek, that it was odd indeed for an ambassador to be called upon to celebrate a military defeat inflicted upon his country. He nonetheless confessed that in the wake of the short-lived French expedition and the protracted British occupation, having to express themselves in English never prevented the Egyptians from dreaming in French.

⇐ The Obelisk and the Clock ⇒

I am watching a live broadcast of the annual July 14 parade down the Champs Élysées—Bastille Day, as the Americans call it. Thousands of people line both sides of the Champs Élysées, hoisting themselves on the tips of their toes or awkwardly aiming makeshift cardboard periscopes at the parading contingents. Amidst the throng of once-a-year French patriots brandishing tricolor flags, tourists flash their cameras, wary of missing anything. They will later tell their friends that the event was typical of the French, charming and cocky.

Suddenly, the camera's vantage point shifts to the top of a high crane, squarely behind the Place de la Concorde obelisk. The golden pyramidion atop the monument now occupies center stage, dwarfing the noisy pageant both in size and in historical significance, with the almighty French army parading at the foot of the obelisk.

I cannot but think of its lonesome twin still standing guard on the eastern side of Luxor temple's entrance. It is a heartbreaking thought, for Ramesses surely never dreamt that one of his obelisks would some day be transported from the bank of the Nile to that of the Seine, where it would stand battered by rain and drizzle amidst the exhaust fumes.

When he offered the obelisk[85] to King Louis-Philippe of France in exchange for a clock, Viceroy Muhammad Ali perhaps believed he was exchanging one timepiece for another. Contemporary historians, whose understanding of Egypt's history was meager, contended that the obelisks, several of which were erected in Egypt, served as sundials. One only has to observe the manner in which obelisks flanked the entrance of temples in pairs, as epitomized by the Temple of Luxor, to conclude that they were never intended by the Egyptians to serve as sundials or indeed any purpose other than to glorify the god Amun. On the base of one of the two obelisks that still stand in Karnak, just north of Luxor, Queen Hatshepsut recorded that "she built for her father Amun . . . two great obelisks of solid red granite of the region of the south; their upper halves of gold of the best of all countries."[86]

The Luxor obelisk was erected in the Place de la Concorde in 1836, one short year after Champollion published the first volume of the prodigious treatise that revealed to mankind the hidden meaning of Egyptian hieroglyphs. For that reason alone, I absolve the ignorant viceroy whose origins and personal history were so foreign to our Egyptian heritage. I also absolve the king of France for offering the Albanian a gaudy clock, in keeping with the colonial practice of offering glass beads to the natives in exchange for their gold. I am also grateful to French Egyptologists and Parisian city planners for crowning the obelisk with a golden pyramidion, hopefully setting an example to be followed by other countries, including Egypt.

But let us return to the protagonists of the Luxor obelisk's fate—an Ottoman viceroy deposed in 1848 for reasons of senility, and a French emperor overthrown the same year!

Viceroy Muhammad Ali was an Albanian military chief, born in 1769—the same year as Napoleon Bonaparte—in the Macedonian town of Cavalla. Appointed governor of Egypt in 1805 by the Ottoman sultan, Muhammad Ali felt such little kinship with Egypt's ancient history, that he once considered using the pyramids' stones to build a dam! Wrote Alain Blotière,[87] "The heyday of the great western pillage of ancient Egypt (following millennia of endogenous pillage), encouraged by Muhammad Ali, who saw in it the ransom to be paid to modernity . . . came to an end with that of the viceroy. The Zodiac of Denderah, the temple of Elephantine Island, Ounnefer's tomb in Sakkarah, the small temples of Esna, the Typhonium of Edfou and one thousand other marvels accompanied by tons of miscellaneous objects and mummies already occupied a place of honor in the museums and the *salons bourgeois* of London, Paris, Vienna, or Berlin."

Louis Philippe, the obelisk's recipient, was born Duc d'Orleans in

1773 and proclaimed king of France in 1830. His reign, referred to as the July monarchy, lasted until 1848, when Bonaparte's brother, Louis Napoleon, became president of the Republic, putting an end to the Orleans dynasty. Following the coup d'état of 1851, Louis Napoleon became Napoleon III, last French emperor.

And what happened to the clock? It was eventually installed above the ablution fountain in the courtyard of the Muhammad Ali mosque at the Citadel.

The punch line of that story is that, whereas the obelisk was more than once considered by the Parisians to be usable as a sundial, the clock never gave the time of day, not even for a second!

⟿ The Copybook ⟿

Guide us along the straight path,
The path of those upon whom Thou hast bestowed Thy Grace,
Not those who have incurred thy wrath nor those who have gone astray.
From the opening *Sura* (chapter) of the Qur'an

Throughout my university years in Cairo, Adel was undoubtedly my best friend. He came from a Muslim family of high-ranking civil servants, and I believe his grandfather had been a notable in the early nineteen hundreds. Adel had inherited from that august lineage a keen sense of service, and I knew in my heart that he would some day become a distinguished civil servant himself. Another close friend was Maher, who came from a family of ministers, prime ministers, ambassadors, etc. I believe he was of Circassian origin, and descended from Ottoman or Mamluk forebears, many of whom had lived to be one hundred or more. He vowed at an early age to preserve family tradition and become minister some day. In the five years of university that I shared with Adel and Maher, I believe I never heard either one speak ill of anyone or tell an unseemly joke, despite the prevailing and traditional bawdiness of university students and their legendary propensity to jest about every subject under the sun.

Kamal was different. He was the odd one out in an otherwise highly respectable family, and his language was singularly coarse. He played an excellent game of tennis and comfortably thrived among the children of the ruling families at the Gezira Sporting Club or the Alexandrian beach of Sidi Bishr.

Adel drove his father's Lincoln Cosmopolitan and often picked me up on his way to the Faculty of Engineering, which was located in Giza, not far from the pyramids. Classes would be out at two in the afternoon, and we had to take infinite precautions as we climbed into the sizzling hot car during the summer months. We had lunch with our families, then took a short nap before getting together later in the afternoon, usually in Adel's apartment. After being served ice-cold Coca-Cola by his Nubian *sufragi*, clad in the traditional white *gallabiya* with the wide red belt around the waist, we would exchange comments about the latest American films being shown in town, or last Saturday's dance at the Sporting Club before reluctantly plunging into our books.

One morning, we were taking a physics lecture in the main auditorium when I experienced a sudden and violent attack of sinusitis. These episodes were caused by a combination of pollen and dust that often befell Cairo in spring, and I was particularly allergic to both. The pain in my left eyebrow was so excruciating that I felt as though my eye was about to burst out of my head. I told Adel that I could no longer withstand the pain and would have to leave the auditorium. Slightly bowing, I cautiously climbed the steps leading to the exit.

One hour later, Adel showed up in the infirmary where I had taken refuge, asked me how I was doing, and handed me the copybook I had left behind.

He then helped me to his car and dropped me off as usual. Back in my apartment, I opened the copybook and discovered to my great amazement that Adel had taken down the lecture notes in my stead. His handwriting was strikingly poised and regular compared to mine, and the pages he had filled were like an island of serenity amidst an ocean of chaos. I rushed to the phone and thanked him profusely, but he refused to let me go on and just said, "Midhat, don't forget to bring your copybook tonight, as I need to copy the lecture notes into mine." That evening, I suggested to Adel that I copy the notes myself. He accepted, saying with a chuckle, "I hope I'll be able to read your handwriting!" I had a vision of two knights out of our history books incising the skin of their palms and pledging eternal loyalty as they mixed their blood.

I left Egypt immediately after graduation and only carried with me the bare essentials. Among them was the physics copybook.

Thirty years later—in 1981—I checked in at the legendary Mena House, next to the Giza Pyramids. Before unpacking, I called the front desk and miraculously obtained the telephone numbers of my three university colleagues. Maher had been appointed a minister by President Sadat. Adel was a top-ranking civil servant, and Kamal had turned into a wealthy tycoon. They looked slightly older and heavier, but I would have had no difficulty singling them out of a crowd of thousands.

Ten years later, I was running the French subsidiary of a major U.S. corporation. Ahmad, Adel's elder son, moved to Europe, and I was able to convince him to join our company. Another young person we hired was Diane, an authentic member of the staunchly Catholic *noblesse bretonne*. They fell in love and decided to get married.

Ahmad's parents, who had been exposed to interreligious marriages in cosmopolitan Egypt and were exceptionally open-minded, loved Diane, and welcomed her on the spot. Diane's parents were similarly open-minded and loved Ahmad, though there was no precedent in their family of anyone marrying a non-Catholic. Their family tree could be traced all the way back to the days of Joan of Arc!

Adel's health was failing, making it impossible for him to attend the wedding reception in Paris, which I promised to go to in his stead. Tradition in France has it that a friend of each spouse read a personal statement on behalf of the younger crowd. Pauline, Diane's closest friend and also a Catholic, read the following words:

In the name of God, the Compassionate, the Merciful.
Praise be to God, Lord of the Universe,
The Compassionate, the Merciful,
Sovereign of the Day of Judgment.
Thee do we worship, and Thine aid we seek.
Guide us along the straight path,
The path of those upon whom Thou hast bestowed Thy Grace,
Not those who have incurred thy wrath nor those who have gone astray.
Amen.

Following a brief pause, Pauline told the gathered crowd, "Dear friends, the text you have just heard is the first chapter of the Holy Qur'an."

Naming their first-born child, a daughter, was not an easy matter, as both Ahmad and Diane wanted to honor their respective cultures and family traditions. Inspired by some divine providence, they called the baby Jehanne. That is how Joan of Arc's name was spelt in the fifteenth century, and the kinship with President Sadat's wife's first name, Jehan, was quasi-miraculous. In her memoirs, Jehan Sadat confessed that until the age of eleven, she believed her name was Jean, for that was how her English-born mother addressed her.[88]

Unfortunately, our beloved Adel left us before having had a chance to see his first grandchild. His wife Laila flew in from Egypt to get acquainted with Jehanne, and the young couple seized that opportunity to have us both for lunch at their suburban home.

I went back to my cellar and looked for the physics copybook, which lay intact at the bottom of a carton where it had sojourned for more than four decades. I carefully opened it as one opens a relic, and showed Adel's handwriting to Ahmad and his mother, which they immediately recognized with considerable emotion.

I recounted the episode, and offered the copybook to Ahmad.

～ Amazing Grace ～

Nothing evokes my childhood serenity as vividly as a muezzin's
recitation of the Qur'an, or the Ave Maria that my mother used to sing.

It was one of those evenings that are touched by ineffable grace. As she took bow after bow on the stage of the Cairo Opera House, Nadia pressed an enormous bouquet against her chest. She was being given a standing ovation, and I thought the applause would never end, as the public asked for encore after encore. Nadia had offered them arias from Bellini's *Romeo and Juliet,* Rossini's *Barber of Seville*, and others by Rachmaninov and Tchaikovsky, in addition to Gershwin's *Summertime*. She confessed that, not knowing the Egyptian public's taste, she had settled on an eclectic repertoire.

I knew she was exhausted. Her health was rather frail and she had flown to Egypt the previous night. The minute she landed at Cairo airport, she was whisked away from one reception to another, and could not muster enough energy to fend off the legendary Egyptian hospitality, which can be overwhelming at times. It was her first trip to Egypt and one of the first out of Bulgaria, where she had studied music in the miserable environment brought about by the communists.

The next morning, she woke up just in time for a luncheon in her honor to which I was also invited. It was past four o'clock when she finally managed to escape. She was flying home the next morning and was desperate to see something of Cairo.

For some inexplicable reason, the Egyptian Antiquities Museum shuts at four with its fabulous treasures, not the least of which lie in the rambling Tutankhamun gallery and the awesome Mummies Room. The pyramid area also shuts at four, only to reopen at night for the Sound and Light shows. I therefore decided to give her a glimpse of Islamic Cairo, then take her to the pyramids at eight o'clock, in time for the show.

En route to the Citadel, we came to Ibrahim Pasha Square which, for all I know, is now called by some other name, most references to pashas having been obliterated by Nasser. As we drove past a hideous multistory public parking facility behind the pasha's equestrian statue, I asked Nadia if she could guess what building stood in that exact location thirty years earlier.

She was dumbfounded upon hearing that it was the Royal Opera House, built by Khedive Ismail for the inauguration of the Suez Canal in 1869. The building had survived a little over a century when it burned to the ground in 1971, engulfing its fabulous costumes and stage settings. The Opera House where she sang the previous night was not the original edifice, but a gift from the Japanese Government, inaugurated by President Mubarak in 1988.

Khedive Ismail had asked Verdi to compose an opera to be premiered in the course of the Suez Canal celebrations, but the proud musician initially refused. Verdi, a champion of justice and liberty whose spirit was molded by the humanistic ideas of the time, was not willing to write an opera on demand, let alone for an oriental absolute monarch. He finally gave in to an offer of no less than 150,000 francs in gold, and set about composing *Aida*, based on a libretto authored by Auguste Mariette, the father of Egyptian archaeology and founder of the Cairo Museum.

Verdi did not compose his opera out of thin air, but thoroughly studied what was believed to be ancient Egyptian music, based on a study of Coptic liturgy and a compendium of ancient Egyptian instruments.[89] *Aida* could not be completed in time for the event, and was not performed until February 2, 1872 at the Scala de Milano. Instead, *Rigoletto*, composed in 1851, was offered to the public. Little did Ismail suspect that Rigoletto, inspired by Victor Hugo's *Le Roi s'amuse* ('The King Frolics'), depicted a libidinous monarch who seduced every beautiful woman within his reach, eventually causing the innocent Gilda, whose part Nadia often played, to fall to her tragic death.

The Citadel, built by Saladin in the twelfth century, was also closed and could only be visited on the outside. The nearby Muqattam Hill offered a breathtaking view of Cairo, with its countless medieval buildings scattered amongst a dense cluster of dust colored dwellings, crisscrossed by a labyrinth of narrow streets. From that vantage point, Mariette wrote, "The surrounding calm was extraordinary. In front of me lay the city of Cairo. A thick heavy fog seemed to have befallen the city, drowning every house to the top of its roof. From that deep sea emerged three hundred minarets, like the masts of some submerged fleet . . . . To the west, drowned in the dust and the setting sun, stood the pyramids. The sight was grandiose and absorbed me with a violence verging on pain . . . ." I explained to Nadia that the Arabic name *el Qahira*, meaning 'the Victorious,' was given to the city because the planet Mars was in the ascendant when the foundations were being laid near where the garrison town of el Fustat ('The Camp') once stood, northeast of Babylon. Unlike Damascus or Baghdad, the city was spared the savage Mongol invasion, and what remained of el Fustat was set on fire in 1168 to deny it to the Crusaders.

As she silently gazed at the thousand-and-one-nights scenery, I could see the reflection of the setting sun in her beautiful black eyes. After a long silence, she turned to me and said, "You know, Midhat, an artist is a kind of medium. Strange though it may seem, all of this reminds me very much of my country. Perhaps not the city itself, but the people who dwell and toil in it. I can feel their hearts throb in my chest. I understand why you love them so much."

"In all likelihood," I replied, "your sentiment is inspired by the common Ottoman heritage that our countries share. Both Egypt and Bulgaria were under Ottoman domination for over four centuries."

We drove past el Azhar, the oldest Islamic University in the world, and parked in front of the Sultan Hassan *madrasa* (college–mosque), Cairo's unquestionable Mamluk masterpiece. We then walked to the Rifai Mosque,[90] and asked the custodian if he would let us in for a few moments. Luckily, Nadia always carried a large shawl for fear that she should catch cold and harm her voice. She covered her head and bare shoulders, and we crossed the gate with infinite respect, having taken off our shoes. I cautioned her to carry the shoes in her left hand, for the right was dedicated to the nobler tasks, such as eating, greeting, and touching holy objects. I also explained that it was not until the nineteenth century that non-Muslims were allowed to cross the threshold of a mosque, the strictest being el Azhar and el Hussein.

As we came upon the tomb of Sheikh el Rifai, a saint in his lifetime, I suggested that she touch the sandalwood screen, for that was believed to bring happiness and fulfillment.

The man then ushered us into a room where lay the tombs of King Fuad of Egypt, his son Farouk, and his mother Ferial, alongside that of Muhammad Reza Pahlevi, last shah of Iran. He said with contained anger, "The entire world abandoned the shah to his tragic fate. We Egyptians shall never forget the day when, in the wake of the 1973 war against Israel, Egypt's oil had dwindled to almost nothing, threatening the very livelihood of our people. Upon being informed by Sadat of the imminent disaster, the shah ordered Iranian tankers out at sea to steer a different course and sail to Egypt, supplying the country with 500,000 barrels of oil. After having been a rampart against fundamentalism, the ailing monarch was considered a political risk to the West and to his shortsighted former friends. Anwar el-Sadat not only offered him shelter, but also gave him a state burial in defiance of the free world. May they both rest in peace on this hallowed ground!"[91]

He then led us into an immense room, exactly beneath the apex of the mosque's magnificent dome, and introduced us to the muezzin, a white bearded patriarch whose eyes were filled with kindness. I explained that the foreign lady was an opera singer, and the muezzin offered her warm words of welcome. He drew our attention to some unique architectural details and helped me decipher the verses on the walls. Nadia was bewildered by the monumental proportions of the mosque's interior, its forty-four giant columns, its dazzling ornamentation, and gilded ceiling. "Do not attempt to count the different varieties of marble," said the muezzin "for they are nineteen in number."

He then asked me if the singer would care to hear him recite a Qur'anic verse. With the first notes of his chant, Nadia and I were petrified. It was as though his voice emerged from the depths of the Middle Ages, filled with love for the Prophet and awe in the face of God. She listened intently, and tears ran down her cheeks.

When he fell silent, Nadia begged me to ask him if it was at all possible for her to sing in that holy place. He hesitated a little, arguing that she was not Muslim, but eventually yielded, for we were all children of Abraham, and peoples of the Book. Nadia joined the palms of her hands, raised her head as though she could see the Heavens beyond the dome, and sang Gounod's *Ave Maria*. Her crystal voice wrapped itself around us from every direction and its reverberation suspended every note as if it were to last forever. Over and over, the muezzin murmured "Subhan Allah, Subhan Allah . . . ." ('Glory to God, Glory to God . . . .').

My eyes blurred with tears, I saw the ceiling of the Sistine Chapel blend into the mosque's majestic dome.

We thanked him profusely and walked out of the mosque into the setting sun. Nadia squeezed my arm and said, "Midhat, you have offered me the most beautiful musical moment of my life." She added that under any sky, liturgy is the most deep-rooted cultural component of a man's making. Hadn't Gregorian chant played a more decisive role than Charlemagne in uniting the Holy Roman Empire?

It was also the most beautiful musical moment of my own life, which was not nearly as rich as hers, and I doubt if I shall ever experience anything like it again.

~ Notes ~

1 Midhat J Gazalé, *Gnomon: From Pharaohs to Fractals*. Princeton: Princeton University Press, 1999, and *Number: From Ahmes to Cantor*. Princeton: Princeton University Press, 2000.

2 In *Les mémoires d'outre tombe*, part 3, 2L19, ch. 3.

3 At the request of Muhammad Ali, the Frenchman Antoine Barthélémy Clot, a doctor from Marseilles, founded a hospital in the Cairo suburb of Abu Za'bal. The title of bey was bestowed upon him by the viceroy for his dedication during the cholera epidemic of 1831.

4 The Ottoman Empire's sovereign and highest Islamic authority, the padishah or sultan–caliph, resided in Istanbul. He appointed non-hereditary pashas, or governors, to rule the empire's provinces (*pashaliks* or *vilayets*). The title borne by Muhammad Ali (1769–1849) was viceroy of Egypt. His grandson Ismail changed his title to khedive in 1863.

5 The Earl of Cromer, *Modern Egypt*, New York: Macmillan, 1908, vol. I, xvii–xviii.

6 Around A.D. 40, Saint Mark founded the Christian church in Alexandria, where he died a martyr in 68. His body was snatched by the Venetians in 828 from the Church of the Bucolians in Alexandria and enshrined under the Basilica of Saint Mark in Venice. His relics were partly restored to

Egypt more than eleven centuries later, and kept at Cairo's Basilica of Saint Mark. The first to embrace the new faith were the Alexandrian Jews, whose number was very large. The new Christians were bent on obliterating the Greco-Roman heritage, causing numerous conflicts with the local communities. One is struck, upon visiting the temples of Upper Egypt, by the Copts' determination to erase pagan symbols, often super-imposing the Coptic cross (which somewhat resembles the Maltese cross) upon the reliefs. The word Copt, *Qibt* in Arabic, derives from the Greek *Aiguptos*, meaning 'Egyptian,' which in turn derives from the pharaonic *Hat Ka Ptah*, or House of the Spirit of Ptah.

7 From the *Memoirs* of Fakhri Abdel Nour, co-founder of the Wafd party, comrade-in-arms of Saad Zaghlul, and father of the learned Amin Fakhri Abdel Nour and the late Saad (d. 2003) (Cairo: Dar El Shorouk).

8 With the help of Dr. Abdel Salam el Gindi, who was also fluent in both lan-guages.

9 "My Habib," Habib being my grandfather's first name. *Habibi* also means "my beloved." .

10 Naguib Mahfouz, Egyptian writer, was awarded the 1988 Nobel prize for literature (Naguib Mahfouz, *Respected Sir*, translated by Rasheed El-Enany. Cairo: The American University in Cairo Press, 1987).

11 Edward Lane, *An Account of the Manners and Customs of the Modern Egyptians*, 5th edition, 1860, Cairo: The American University in Cairo Press, 2003.

12 Others are: *dubara* for double two; *dosa* for double three; *durgi* for dou-ble four; *shish-do* for six-and-two, etc.

13 The Lycée was designed by French architect Victor Erlanger.

14 The American University, as one would expect, was privately owned and operated, whereas the Lycée was founded in 1909 by the Mission Laïque Francaise, an organization founded in 1902 by the Alliance Française to promote French culture throughout the world.

15 The word *pschent* derives from the Demotic *skhent*, and refers to the dou-ble crown worn by the pharaohs to symbolize the unification of the Upper and Lower Kingdoms.

16 Richard B. Parker and Robin Sabin, *Islamic Monuments in Cairo*. Cairo,

American University in Cairo Press, 1985: "The tomb [Soliman's] is a charming pavilion of cast iron, much in need of repair . . . . Nearby lies his widow (d. 1894), the Dame Maryam. Her tomb is unremarkable, but her story is romantic. She was a young Greek of great beauty. At the time of the Egyptian expedition to Greece (1825–27), Soliman rescued her from a boat which was to take her and other women to Alexandria, and married her himself."

17 Cinema Metro was designed by Italian architect Paolo Caccia Dominioni.

18 Fava beans and chickpea fritters. Falafel, whose birthplace is Egypt, is called *ta'miya* in Cairo and *falafel* in Alexandria.

19 Now Hardee's, an American fast-food outlet.

20 Christian Cannuyer, *Coptic Egypt: The Christians of the Nile*. London: Thames & Hudson, 2001.

21 In 420, Nestorius, Bishop of Constantinople refused to regard the Virgin Mary as mother of God, for she had only begotten the *human* person of Jesus, whereas Cyrillus, the monophysite Patriarch of Alexandria, argued that Jesus possessed a single nature, both divine and human. Amidst bitter rivalry between Constantinople and Alexandria, the Council of Chalcedon deposed the Patriarch of Alexandria in 451, and the Coptic Church broke away from the Byzantine. With the schism, the Coptic Church became the national church of Egypt, albeit with strong Greek and Byzantine influences, and continued to appoint its own bishops in defiance of Constantinople. Today, the 110th Patriarch of the Coptic Church is Pope Shenouda III.

22 Ever since the genocide perpetrated by the Turks, the Armenian community in Egypt had been very large, particularly in Alexandria. They were mostly craftsmen, and frequented their own churches and schools. Their community was characterized by discretion and unflinching solidarity, perpetuating their native language and traditions. Following the 1948 war against Israel and the bitter defeat inflicted upon the Arab coalition, most European communities, including the Armenian, began leaving the country never to return.

23 The word comes from the Turkish *torgoman*, meaning 'translator'; the word also gave birth to the French *truchement*, meaning 'go-between.'

24 Little did I know that, decades later, I would publish a book on the subject: *Gnomon: From Pharaohs to Fractals*, Princeton: Princeton University Press, 1999.

25 Samir Raafat, "When Doctor Goebbels Comes to Town," *Egyptian Mail*, January 1, 1999.

26 The Muslim Brotherhood (*al-Ikhwan al-Muslimin*) was founded in 1928 by Hassan el Banna under the banner "God is the Greatest, and praise be to God," and Young Egypt (*Misr al-Fatat*) in 1933 by Ahmad Hussein under the banner "God, King, and Country." Both parties were pro-Nazi, whether they predicated their philosophy on a fundamentalist interpretation of Islam, or on a chauvinistic reading of Egyptian history. Young Egypt even possessed a paramilitary organization, the Green Shirts—the Egyptian flag was green—patterned after the Hitlerjugend. Hassan el Banna was assassinated by the secret police in 1949. Ahmad Hussein was jailed following the 1952 burning of Cairo, then released and arrested again in 1954. He was released in 1956 and withdrew from public life. He died in 1982.

27 Ahmad Maher formed a new government in 1943 following the dismissal of Nahas, and was assassinated in February by a Nazi sympathizer. Egypt did not officially declare war on Germany and Italy until a 1944 vote by Parliament.

28 Sadat escaped from the prison infirmary in 1944 and was jailed again in 1946 in the wake of Amin Osman's assassination. He had founded the Free Officers secret organization shortly after his 1938 graduation from the Royal Military Academy. The group was later taken over by Nasser while Sadat served his prison term.

29 Anwar el-Sadat, *In Search of Identity: An Autobiography*. New York: William Collins, 1978.

30 Women's Army Auxiliary Corps.

31 Mussolini boasted that his armies were equiped with eight million bayonets, a claim for which he was often derided.

32 Navy, Army, and Air Force Institute.

33 The two terrorists, Eliahu Bet Souri and Eliahu Hakim, shot Lord Moyne and his driver at point blank range in front of his residence on Hassan

Sabri Street (where the famous Four Corners restaurant stands today) in Zamalek, one of the most upscale districts of Cairo. The men, both in their twenties, then took off on their bicycles, only to be arrested minutes later by a constable who happened to be cruising on his motorcycle and was alerted by the sound of the shots. The terrorists' object was to force the British to put an end to their mandate on Palestine and refrain from interfering with Jewish immigration into that country. The Stern Gang, to which both terrorists belonged, was under the control of Itzhak Shamir. Both men were briskly tried and hanged. In 1945, a plaque was dedicated in the Anglican Cathedral in memory of Lord Moyne. In May 1948, the British withdrew from Palestine, and Ben Gurion announced the establishment of the State of Israel. The terrorists were proclaimed Heroes of the State of Israel. Their bodies were exhumed from the Jewish Cemetery at Basatin near Cairo in 1975 and buried on Mount Herzl in Israel, where Itzhak Rabin, then prime minister, sent them off with military honors.

34 Quoted in Selma Botman, *Egypt from Independence to Revolution*. Syracuse: Syracuse University Press, 1991, p.48.

35 Edward Lane, *An Account of the Manners and Customs of the Modern Egyptians*, 5th edition, 1860, Cairo: The American University in Cairo Press, 2003.

36 Forty-five years later, historian Selma Botman would write: "That Europeanized Egyptians had a considerable edge in education is undeniable; their literacy rate was fourteen times greater than that of the overall Egyptian population in the first decades of the twentieth century. But foreign language institutions provided students with more than a mere facility with Western languages. They also conveyed, through both classroom experience and social interaction, modern notions of class, nation, art and politics distilled from European and American history . . . ." (Botman, *Egypt*, p.92).

37 Following that tragedy, Nuqrashi resigned the premiership, only to return in December. Two years later, in December 1948, Nuqrashi was assassinated after banning the Muslim Brotherhood, who were perpetrating terrorist actions in the wake of the severe losses suffered by the Egyptian army at the hands of the Israeli.

38 In the preface to *John Bull's Other Island.*

39 In 1925, King Fuad founded the university named after him, which was renamed Cairo University following the military *coup d'état* of 1952. Having graduated from that university when it still bore the king's name, I find it somewhat unfair that he should be remembered only for his ill-considered resistance to the nationalist movement, not for his substantial contributions to education.

40 Mit Abul Kom is the village where Sadat was born. Maybe Ahmad and Anwar played together by the canal when they were children.

41 Samir Raafat, in the May 15, 1997 edition of the *Cairo Times*, recalls that Wallace Beery's *Bad Man Bascombe* was being shown that day.

42 Robert Koch (1843–1910) was the discoverer of the anthrax spore, as well as the cholera and tuberculosis bacilli. In 1894, in the course of one of the most virulent epidemics in England, Dr. John Snow established an incontrovertible correlation between water wells infected with human faeces and the incidence of cases in their immediate vicinity. Koch was awarded the Nobel prize for medicine in 1905.

43 On January 15, 1951, the Egyptian representative at the World Health Organization demonstrated that the 1947 epidemic had been introduced by way of the British troops stationed in the Canal Zone.

44 As these words are being written, Egypt's population borders on seventy million. Literacy has climbed dramatically, and infant mortality has decreased similarly, thanks to the efforts of the government, alas contributing to the present overpopulation.

45 The microbe, which is absorbed by mouth, progresses through the stomach then adheres to the intestinal walls. Its survival in the digestive tract is favored by a lowered stomach acidity that can be caused by a number of factors, not the least of which is undernourishment. Toxins are released into the capillary vessels, causing abundant loss of fluids.

46 If they were not Parisians, those students who frequented the Latin Quarter had no choice but to dwell in little hotels or in dingy furnished rooms rented from the inhabitants. That state of affairs discouraged foreigners and non-Parisians from studying in Paris, and the number of enrolments in the Sorbonne actually began dwindling in the early twen-

ties. In 1925, a wealthy industrialist by the name of Emile Deutsch de la Meurthe donated ten million Francs, a fortune at the time, toward the construction of a little hamlet designed to welcome three hundred students. More *pavillons*, as they were called, were built over the years by foreign embassies, where they housed their own as well as a prescribed quota of other nationals. I had the good fortune to be admitted to the Pavillon des Provinces de France, which was particularly hospitable to students from developing nations such as mine which lacked a *pavillon* of their own.

47 Third Republic: 1870–1940. Vichy Regime: 1940–1944.

48 Pierre-Jean Deschodt and Francois Huguenin, *La République Xénophobe*. Paris: Jean-Claude Lattès, 2001.

49 Sophie Wahnich, *L'Impossible Citoyen, l'Étranger dans la Révolution Française*. Paris: Albin Michel, 1997.

50 The word derives from the Greek *metoikos*, whose roots are *meta* ('outside') and *oikos* ('dwelling'), and applies to someone who is not in his house. In ancient Greece, the word referred to those who lived in Athens without enjoying citizenship. In France, the derogatory *métèque* applies to foreign residents of Mediterranean origin whose appearance is disquieting.

51 Prince Louis de Broglie (1892–1987) was the originator of the theory of Wave Mechanics and 1929 Nobel laureate in physics.

52 On August 26, a historic Anglo-Egyptian Treaty was signed between the British and an Egyptian delegation, within the framework of the Anglo-Egyptian military alliance. The treaty recognized Egypt as a sovereign nation. The catch was that Britain would continue to "protect" Egypt in case of emergency. Its 10,000 troops would be limited to the Suez Canal Zone in time of peace, with Egypt granting them the military facilities required to protect their lines of communications. The treaty also put an end to the Anglo-Egyptian Condominium of Sudan, leaving Britain in full control. Sir Miles Lampson, British High Commissioner, was designated ambassador and the British Supreme Command of the Egyptian army came to an end. In September of that year, another momentous decision instituted general admission to the Military Academy, opening

its doors to applicants of modest social origin. Thus those very young men were allowed to become officers who would overthrow the king sixteen years thence.

53 The British had pulled back to the Canal Zone in 1947.

54 Site of the Anglo-Iranian oil refineries.

55 Muhammad Naguib, "Egypt's Destiny," in Botman, *Egypt*, p. 44.

56 Fuad's reign covered the critical *entre deux guerres,* from the end of World War I to Ethiopia's invasion by Italy. Though he was not a democrat by any stretch of the imagination, and consistently appointed servile governments, he stands out, together with his father Ismail and great-grandfather Muhammad Ali, as one of the great modernizers of Egypt.

57 The Shi'ites, or 'partisans' of Ali ibn Abi Taleb, son-in-law of the Prophet Muhammad and third caliph, adhered to the principle of hereditary succession of the caliphs. Their leaders claimed to be the descendents of Fatima, the Prophet's daughter, hence the name of the Fatimid dynasty, which ruled Egypt from the tenth to near the end of the twelfth century A.D. On the other hand, the Sunnis, or followers of the Sunna or 'Way' of Muhammad, believed in succession by consensus, given their tribal origins. Egypt was re-converted from Shi'i to Sunni Islam by the great Saladin around 1175.

58 Among them Cleopatra's needle, which was found in Alexandria, whence its fanciful name. It can be admired on the Victoria Embankment in London, opposite the Savoy Hotel.

59 See note 54.

60 Princess Fathiya married a Christian in San Francisco in 1950, with the assent of her mother, Queen Nazli. Both were expelled by Farouk from the palace, and Queen Nazli died in San Francisco in 1978, after the princess was murdered by her former husband.

61 The word "algorithm" derives from al-Khawarizmi, the Arab (actually Uzbek) inventor of algebra. It refers to a succession of operations, arithmetic or otherwise, where each step derives from the preceding steps according to a prescribed set of rules.

62 One of Nasser's pharaonic ambitons was to fulfill the age-old dream of building a colossal dam in Aswan, a few kilometers upstream of the obso-

lete British-built dam, to be financed by the International Bank for Reconstruction and Development. On July 19, 1956, John Foster Dulles, the American secretary of state, declared the Egyptian government insolvent, and in the face of the Soviet Union's increasing influence in Egypt, the United States and Great Britain withdrew their offer of financing. That marked a turning point in Egypt's modern history. On July 26, from his balcony overlooking Muhammad Ali Square in Alexandria (a highly symbolic venue since its bombardment by the British fleet), a humiliated Nasser took the world by surprise as he announced his decision to nationalize the Suez Canal, arguing that the move would enable Egypt to finance the dam on its own. A secret meeting took place on October 22 in the Paris suburb of Sèvres between Guy Mollet, Christian Pineau, and Maurice Bourgès Manoury of France, Selwyn Lloyd of Britain, and an Israeli delegation consisting of David Ben Gurion, Shimon Peres, and Moshe Dayan. On October 28, Israeli troops entered the Sinai Peninsula and landed their paratroopers a hundred kilometers east of the Canal. British bombers all but destroyed the Egyptian air force, and French and British paratroopers landed in Port Fuad and Port Said. In retaliation, the Egyptians paralyzed transit through the Canal by scuttling forty-five ships in its waters.

63 The doctor was sentenced to five years in jail, and the young women to three-month suspended sentences each. Thanks to the unrelenting efforts of Simone Veil, minister of health, abortion was legalized in 1975.

64 Joseph was my father's first name.

65 Following the May 13, 1958 uprising in Algiers by the colonial French, who demanded that Algeria remain French territory, President René Coty appointed General Charles de Gaulle prime minister. Maurice Couve de Murville, who had been ambassador to Egypt from 1950 to 1954, was appointed foreign minister in 1958 and partially repaired the severely damaged Franco-Egyptian relations. In December 1958, de Gaulle had a sweeping constitutional reform approved, and was elected first president of the Fifth Republic. Diplomatic relations between France and Egypt, which had been interrupted in 1956, were restored in April 1963. Couve de Murville was appointed prime minister in 1968, a position he held until de Gaulle's resignation in 1969.

66 Sadat later wrote, "The economic legacy Nasser left me was in even poorer shape than the political . . . . We had, with crass stupidity, copied the Soviet pattern of socialism, although we lacked the necessary resources, technical capabilities, and capital. On the first day of January 1957—when our London reserves were released and all foreign concerns nationalized—our economy was at its best. Hence the public sector came into being with assets of not less than 1000 million pounds. If we had started off properly, we would by now have been a great power . . . . However, our socialism began to be tinged in practice with Marxism. Any free enterprise system came to be regarded as odious capitalism and the private sector as synonymous with exploitation and robbery. Individual effort came to a standstill, and from this stemmed the terrible passivity of the people that I still suffer from to this day . . . . They expected the state to provide them with food, work, housing, and education. Indeed, having professed to be socialist, the state was expected to provide citizens with everything they needed without their having to make any positive effort at all. It was that shrinking back from active individual enterprise that came to be regarded as odious capitalism and the private sector that marked the beginning of our abysmal economic collapse."

67 One of the diplomats was André Miquel, who later confessed that his stay in prison had changed his vocation from diplomat to professor. He is among the most erudite French intellectuals, speaks and writes Arabic fluently, and has written innumerable books on Islam and Arabic literature.

68 Cleopatra's Needle is an outright misnomer, for the obelisk and its twin were originally quarried by the great Tuthmosis III in the southern Egyptian town of Aswan nearly fifteen centuries before Cleopatra was born, then erected in Heliopolis. As was customary in those days, Ramesses II appropriated the monuments two centuries later and had his own name carved on two of their sides, but left them standing in Heliopolis. Around 13 B.C., nearly twenty years after Cleopatra's suicide and the assassination of Caesarion, son of Cleopatra and Caesar, Emperor Augustus ordered the architect Pontius to transport both

obelisks to Alexandria, where they eventually flanked the entrance to the Caesarium. Clepoatra's Needle's twin was later erected in Central Park, New York.

69 Disneyland drew over 12 million visitors in 2001.

70 In "La mort du Caire," *Le Figaro*, February 22, 1907.

71 During the Predynastic Period (ca. 4000–3200 B.C.), the communities bordering the Nile united to form the Kingdoms of Upper and Lower Egypt. During the Archaic Period (ca. 3200–2780 B.C.), King Mena (Menes) of Upper Egypt conquered Lower Egypt and unified the kingdom, with Memphis as its capital.

72 Wooden openwork windows that allowed the women in the house to look out through the interstices without fear of being seen.

73 Robert Solé, *L'Égypte, passion française*. Paris: Éditions du Seuil, 1997.

74 Mitch, alias Reginald Mitchell, died of exhaustion and ill health in 1937 at the age of forty-two, having seen only his brainchild's first prototype, but with the knowledge that the Royal Air Force had placed an order for three hundred.

75 The obelisk's twin stands in the center of Place de la Concorde in Paris.

76 We owe much of our knowledge of Egyptian arithmetic to the patience and dedication of Arnold Buffum Chace, principal author of *The Rhind Mathematical Papyrus*, published in 1927. A. Henry Rhind was a Scottish antiquary who suffered from tuberculosis and sojourned in Luxor in 1858, where the dry warm climate attracted wealthy European tourists. There, he purchased the papyrus that now bears his name and which was acquired by the British Museum following his death. Other fragments of the papyrus, which were sold to the American collector Edwin Smith, later turned up at the New York Historical Society. Smith, who lived in Luxor, also purchased the two most famous medical papyri, today known as the *Smith Papyrus* and the *Ebers Papyrus*. They came from a clandestine find in the Ramesses II necropolis. In those days, tomb plunderers abounded and sold their loot to shrewd receivers. One of the manuscripts was later sold by Smith to the German Egyptologist Georg Ebers and is named after him.

77 The treasures were discovered in 1922.

78 *Osta* refers to someone who is proficient in his trade or manages a group of people. One pound equals one hundred piasters, and was worth around 65 U.S. cents in 1985.

79 Deir el Madina is the southern Egyptian town near Luxor where the architect Senenmut built Hatshepsut's magnificent temple. The inscription is from Andrea McDowell, "Daily life in Ancient Egypt" in *Scientific American*, December 1996.

80 More recently, French archaeologist Jean Philippe Lauer spent his entire career giving life to Saqqara; without Christiane Desroches Noblecourt's unrelenting efforts and the funding by UNESCO, the temple of Abu Simbel would have disappeared forever under the waters of Lake Nasser; Jean Yoyotte of the Collège de France rendered invaluable services to archaeology, rediscovering the treasures of Tanis, among other achievements; Jean-Yves Empereur and Jean-Pierre Corteggiani raised from the depths of the Mediterranean what remains of the Pharos . . . to mention only a few.

81 The first crusade was launched in 1095 and the seventh ended in 1249 with the debacle of Mansura, an Egyptian town where Saint Louis, king of France, was made prisoner. He died of the plague in Tunis in 1270.

82 King Charles VI of France having fallen victim to dementia, Henry V, king of England, seized that God-sent opportunity and, with the help of the Bourguignons, defeated the Armagnacs in the memorable battle of Agincourt (1415). He was later recognized as legitimate heir to the throne of France.

83 Constantinople was the name given to Byzantium, later renamed Istanbul. A pact was signed between François I, king of France, and the sultan of Constantinople authorizing French merchants to buy and sell anywhere in the Ottoman Empire, in addition to granting them tax exemption. Disputes between Frenchmen and locals were settled in presence of the official consulate interpreter, whereas disputes among French residents were arbitrated by their own consul according to French law. That pact was referred to as the "Capitulations," not because it sealed some Ottoman diplomatic defeat as the name might suggest, but because the pact was comprised of a number of chapters, or *capitula*. In 1802,

shortly after France's defeat at the hands of the British, a treaty was signed reconfirming the Capitulations, and Mathieu de Lesseps, father of the immensely famous Ferdinand de Lesseps who designed and dug the Suez Canal, was appointed consul in Egypt. In May 1937, a conference was convened in Montreux, Switzerland, by Egypt and the twelve European countries that enjoyed capitulatory rights. The capitulations were abolished, and, in 1949, mixed courts were finally abolished. That year, incredible as that may sound, Egypt was finally allowed to set up embassies and consulates in foreign countries for the first time in its long history.

84 The Directoire was the executive body installed under the 1795 Constitution, which appointed ministers and military chiefs. The Directoire's decision establishing the *Commission des Sciences et des Arts* was taken on March 16, 1798. Napoleon's expedition began on July 2, 1798 with the landing of 54,000 French troops in Alexandria. The French were eventually defeated by the British and forced to repatriate the remaining 20,000 French survivors on September 3, 1801. Adding insult to injury, the harrowed Frenchmen had no choice but to be shipped home on British vessels, having altogether lost their fleet.

85 As a matter of fact three obelisks, not just one.

86 Labib Habachi, *The Obelisks of Egypt*, Cairo: The American University in Cairo Press, 1988.

87 In his introduction to Prisse d'Avennes, *Atlas of Egyptian Art*. Cairo: Zeitouna, 1991.

88 Jehan Sadat, *A Woman of Egypt*. New York: Simon and Schuster, 1987.

89 The study of Coptic liturgy was compiled by French composer Felicien David and the compendium of ancient Egyptian instruments was assembled by André Villoteau, a member of the Napoleonic expedition.

90 The Rifai Mosque was begun in 1869 under the reign of Khedive Ismail, and suspended in 1880 under the reign of his son Tewfik, two years before the British bombarded Alexandria and occupied Egypt. Tewfik died in 1892 and was succeeded by his son Abbas Hilmi II, who was deposed by the British in 1914, the year World War I broke out. Construction of the mosque resumed in 1905, and was not to be termi-

nated until 1912. The decorations were executed by Max Herz, who was, as a result, elevated to the rank of bey by the khedive.

91 When he married Princess Fawziya in 1939, Muhammad Reza Pahlevi was crown prince (shahpour) of Persia. Despite the specter of war on the horizon, the fairy-tale wedding was celebrated with unprecedented pomp. The princess, a teenager, was considered one of the most beautiful women in the world. The crown prince was barely one year older. The sterile marriage was not a happy one, and the princess eventually returned to the royal palace in Egypt. The shah remarried, first to Soraya Asfahandiary, then to Farah Diba. In 1979, the shah was overthrown and became very ill. When none of the countries that had befriended him, among them the United States and the Arab monarchies, offered him asylum, President Sadat welcomed the emperor and his wife to Egypt. The shah died near Cairo in August 1980. Sadat was shot down on October 6, 1981.

❧ Index ❧

One of A Kind

Making Things Happen

Third Edition

By
Tony Moore

Copyright © 2022 by Tony Moore.

One of A Kind
Making Things Happen

Third Edition

To order additional copies of this book, order contact Amazon.com

ISBN-13-978-1544678818 Paperback

For more information about the author and his other works go to:

https://oneofakindbook.com/

FOREWORD

T HE REASON I decided to write my book was not for personal gain (even if all my friends bought it—both of them!) but as a calling, I felt I had to answer. I am in fact just an ordinary person with an extraordinary ability to make the most of the situations that I found myself in both good and bad.

I have often thought about how truly lucky I have been throughout my life, even in the toughest of times, so I decided to write my story in the faint hope that you will read my story and be inspired to make the most of your life too.

I truly believe that all of us are given divine gifts, talents, when we are born to enable us to manage our lives, deal with the problems, risk failure, or achieve our successes, if we choose to do so. We are also given divine help in the form of the very small voice that stays with us all our lives and is sometimes so very hard to hear against the "noise" of life and living and the crowded noise of our jumbled-up thoughts.

Although I eventually learned to listen to this voice, which is not inside your head but is right in the middle of your being; I didn't learn to "hear" the voice until I had made many, many mistakes along the way.

I also know that I have been blessed with some brilliant friends who have been there for me in times of great difficulty. Even after a lifetime of not seeing them since school or where we worked together in earlier jobs that we had shared when we were just starting in our twenties, many are still in touch and we still remain close.

I have been gifted on three occasions with dreams that foretold to me what was going to happen and how I should deal with the imminent or upcoming situations, which I will explain later in this book. When I was dreaming of each of the three dreams, I was aware that I was being told something important. With each dream, I knew I had to remember everything and had to say what I had seen out loud.

I have also had a spiritual experience while in my local church, in Greenwood, of all places. To this day, I cannot explain it, except to say that what happened did happen; it was very real and it proved to me beyond the shadow of a doubt that God exists, that he is real, and that he is there for us if we know to ask for help.

So, why the title I chose? It's as if my life has been made up of a never-ending series of short stories that have run on; sometimes overlapping and sometimes as a series of single events, stories that made me, "make things happen." Not that knowing what I know now makes me brilliant (though I probably am brilliant); but what I do know, as a thinking and genuine Guinness-drinking bloke, is a lot about a little and making extraordinary things happen is what I have succeeded at. Now, that I have fully explained my title, on with my book.

ROSINA

None of us get to choose the conditions under which we are born, we, therefore, have to make the most of the hand we are dealt with, regardless.

I WAS BORN in Northampton, England and my mother, Rosina, was a Catholic, from a large Irish family of seven sisters and five brothers, a mother and father and grandparents, but I was not to find this out for decades into my 60s. My mom was pretty, with dark wavy hair and dressed, on the times I saw her, in light pastel colors. I'm sure I would have loved her very much if I had known her, but unfortunately, I only saw her three times in my life.

At that time, in England, there was an epidemic of tuberculosis and unfortunately, my mother had TB when I was born. Of course, it didn't mean much to me at the time, except that I couldn't live with her for fear of catching the highly contagious disease.

I can't imagine how she must have felt having had to give me, her first and only son, into the care of the Middlesex County Council for my health and well-being.

Probably a part of her was happy that I would be looked after, but a part would have been sad as well at having to see me go away. For my friends in America, Middlesex isn't a lifestyle choice, but an area of Greater London, the London County Council, or LCC as it was, was the governing body of Greater London responsible for all things that moved (or tried to) in the Greater London area.

I was born with TB as what is known as a "TB contact," which left a large scar on my lung. So I was moved out of my mother's home in Acton in West London, where I lived with my mother for a very short time before they found me a place for me to live by the sea at Lowestoft in Suffolk with a Mrs. Bleby.

The only times I ever saw my mother after I was moved to Lowestoft in Suffolk to live with Auntie, as Mrs. Bleby became to all the little children she was blessed to have in her care. When I was three years old I traveled by train from Auntie's house in Lowestoft with Tessa, my surrogate older sister, Auntie's daughter.

We left Lowestoft on the early-morning train and we had breakfast in the Pullman car along the way. I was excited at having breakfast on the train, while watching the world go by and gazing out of the window, looking up at the patterns that the steam made as it billowed above our carriage. The train was pulled along by a powerful steam engine that made the trip to Liverpool Street station in a few hours.

We traveled by tube from Central London to Acton, where my mother lived and I remember meeting my mom in a bungalow there.

Although it didn't seem strange that after spending only a day with her we should leave to get back to Lowestoft, I was sad to leave her. I thought that I may never see her again, even though I was so young. She gave me a whole box of soft mints to eat along the way, which, being only three at the time, I promptly dropped as I boarded the bus and had to scramble to try to get them all back in the box.

Lowestoft was now my home although I wanted very much to know my mom, which was not to be. When I saw her that time, she was dressed in a pastel pink dressing gown and seemed to be very tired. She was slim, with very dark wavy hair. She was quite petite and very graceful. She called my name softly, as I went to her and held her small hand in mine. She spoke to me, asking me how I was telling me how tall I had become and how proud she was of me. I didn't understand all that she said, but I loved the sound of her voice; it was pleasant to listen to, though often she was asking Tessa about my new life at Auntie's. She became quite breathless at talking as the TB had gotten a real hold of her.

We left later that same day and, as I found out much later, I wasn't as sad as I could have been as I was very happy living with Auntie and my very large family and I had all the space anybody could ever possibly need. I remembered looking back at her as she stood in the doorway, waving to me as we left her. We caught a cab to the station and I looked out the back window to keep seeing her as long as I could waving to her the whole time. She finally disappeared as we turned the corner, I would never visit her again.

I asked Tessa if we could visit my mom and she said, "Yes, of course, dear. We'll meet her as soon as your mother is strong enough."

The last time I ever saw her was when she traveled from a sanitarium, where she had been moved to from her house in London, to see me at Lowestoft. Her journey, like mine, took some three hours by train and Auntie had her picked up from the station.

My beautiful, but now very ill, mother had come to see me and when she arrived at Lowestoft she watched me playing, through the window in our large nursery, at the back of the house overlooking aunties' large garden. She traveled with her new husband of ten days, though I only vaguely remember him, as she watched me from outside the large bay window while I played with all the other children. I remember looking out through the window and waving at her after Tessa told me she was my mother and that she was here to see me.

I can only imagine how happy yet sad she must have felt, but at the time, I thought it was perfectly normal. Normal is, after all, only relative to what you're used to, isn't it? And since I had never really spent time with my mother or knew anything more than what I had been told by Tessa and Auntie, I had nothing to compare what a real mother should or could be like. What I do know is that if Auntie hadn't cared enough to go out of her way to make this meeting happen, I would never have had known anything of what my very own mother was like.

She stayed outside for a little while watching me through the window and smiling at me the whole time; she was supported by her new husband, standing next to her in the cold March air. I went over to the window and placed my hand on the glass as she did the same so that we could both touch hands through the glass—my tiny hand and her very small hand. She was smiling the whole time, as I sat on the ledge of the bay window and looked at her the whole time she was standing with her small hand on the window. She left shortly after that and sadly, I was never to see my mother again as she died of TB shortly after. She had managed to see me one last time before she died.

My mother was not rich-in fact, she was rather poor and at that time, to be an unwed mother was a difficult issue and was, to a large extent, swept under the carpet.

Now, however, being a single mom is not a big deal and it is much more prevalent than it was then. But to all the children having to grow up with one or no parents, it is a difficult thing to deal with and can continue to affect them their whole life.

In my case, though, I was gifted with the ability to cope and to do well and climb up after each fall, and to succeed whatever the difficulty.

This was one of the many gifts I seem to have been given, along with a good sense of humor to help me along the way.

Auntie told me years later that my mother's last wish was that I should not remain a Catholic. Though my mother was Irish and definitely from a strong Catholic family, she didn't want me to remain a Catholic. I can only surmise that through her ordeal of having a baby and having TB life must have been very difficult for her or that perhaps, as I always suspected, there was another reason why she left her entire family, but more of that later in my story.

So, despite having a huge family still living in Northampton, who under different circumstances could have helped her, my mother wanted nothing to do with her family. So her husband, Charles Willatts, carried out her wish. As for me I lived an entirely different life than that which I may have lived had this not occurred. My mother lived another life as well along with her sister Peggy. I am not sure if they ever got back in touch with her family or not but now it doesn't matter.

The only reason I knew of her sister, Peggy, was from an old photograph of my mother with her sister, which was given by my stepfather to my daughter Georgia when she went to visit him. He was still living in the same house that I had lived in for a short while after being forced to leave Lowestoft to live with my stepfather in Acton. In the photograph, the two of them were together riding bikes with another man who was a close friend, but I don't know who he was except that his name was Bill Giddings. Years later, I often thought about these things in my past; but life goes on, so you either move with it or get stuck at that point in time, but I was not a person to dwell on things like this.

In 2018 I was to find out I had family on my father's side when I was contacted by a cousin living in Texas, but more of this later.

When things happen that you can't control all that you can do is learn to accept what Is while doing your best to manage the situation.

AUNTIE

Sometimes someone will come into your life to make an eternal and positive difference!

I WAS MOVED to Lowestoft where Mr. Bleby who became known as Auntie lived. Auntie was everything one could imagine that a proper English lady or a great aunt could and should be. She was the stuff that an empire was built from.

Auntie was larger than life and as nature would have it, she was also a rather large lady who often wore huge flamboyant hats whenever she went out. Auntie had perfect English diction, sounding like Joyce Grenville, the famous storyteller and actress at that time. Her speech was perfect "Queens English." She would always call me "Tony deah" or "my dahling Tony" and would call me that right up until her ninety-second birthday. But there's a lot more to talk about before that time comes!

Auntie was my true guardian angel, placed into my life by none other than God or maybe by one of God's angels. It's the only explanation I can think of. You see, Auntie was not a true blood relation but was the choice of the London County Council in their infinite wisdom. So you see, even local government can get it right sometimes! But not all the time as you will see later on.

No one messed with Auntie; what she said was the way it would be. She would stride through life absolutely and completely sure of what she was doing and where she was going. She was, to me, absolutely the perfect surrogate mom any boy could ever wish for. Shakespeare once said, "Give me a child to his seventh birthday and he's mine for life." So Auntie had me up to age eight and she was to be the biggest influence in my life.

Auntie was extremely protective and always made sure you found plenty of things to do, or she would find them for you. "Go and play in the bottom garden" or "Help Mr. Moore with the gardening" or "Why don't you find something to do with your beautiful day?" And we did in case she found it for us.

When I say "us," I mean Beatrice, William (Beatrice's brother)Mary Brookes, John Hoey and me. We were inseparable right up until I left Auntie at eight years old; But more about Beatrice later.

You could hear Auntie's voice all over the house; although she never, to my recollection, shouted. She just had one of those voices that carried and it pierced through the highest wind or the noisiest of surroundings and definitely carried from the kitchen all the way up to the top of the house, three floors up.

I loved Auntie as I never would or ever could love any other person in my whole life and I could never have made it to where I am now without her strong, never-wavering help and sound advice.

Apart from being who she was to me, I can honestly say she was a very clever and wise person. She believed in fairies and believed that every time a baby is born, a fairy smiles. And when good people die, they "go to the fairies," which was her way of saying they went to heaven. She was very tolerant of children but completely intolerant of adults, especially those who behaved badly. Though as I said she was very proper, she was also very liberal in her ideals. She helped me always and gave me her wisdom until I was well into my forties. To me, she was like the queen is to England—always there in the background and always doing the right thing.

Auntie's first husband was Nunky, who was quite old and was the retired headmaster of a very large public school in Scarborough. She called him "my darling Nunky," and they had two children. Her son was John Bleby, who was, to me, an ethereal figure that would appear once in a while when coming home from Cambridge University or the army.

When John came home, all the nurses would go wild at his stories of travel and university life. John studied veterinary medicine and became a vet. He even went on to become a veterinary surgeon to Her Majesty, the Queen. I believe he looked after some of her many horses and used to go to the Royal "Tattoo" to look after the horses there.

Auntie's daughter was Tessa Bleby. Though I seldom saw John, at least not until many years later, I spent a lot of time with Tessa. To me, Tessa was like an older sister and was at that time still at school. She went to St. Mary's Convent on Kirkley Cliffs, right on the seafront, perched on a high cliff overlooking the sea. That was my first school when I was five years old. Imagine that! Me taught by nuns! I remember very little of that school except that it was very strict and was a rather large gray austere building overlooking the sea.

Auntie's house, at 35 Kirkley Park Road in Lowestoft, Suffolk, was huge and she had decided, years earlier, to use it as a children's nursery or a children's home for young children, from one year to eight years old, who for one reason or another couldn't live with their parents.

To her, this was perfect. She had twenty or more children at that time. I remember even at that time being in love with Mary Brookes (at four years old). I have a photo of Mary and me standing in the middle of the main staircase in our pajamas which I included here. Mary was holding a doll; I was looking on—Mary with her beautiful blonde hair and me with my very dark and curly hair.

I don't know to this day why Mary was there, but I knew absolutely that I did in fact love her as only a four-year-old boy could! Mary had the most beautiful blonde hair and lived with us, with me, for seven years. I never knew when she left, but I missed her a lot. I did know that Mary had left never to come back into my life again. I tried to find her through Facebook and Friends Reunited but was never able to find my beautiful Mary Brookes ever again.

Some were children of diplomats who were eventually picked up to live again at their real homes, while others like me had no home to go to except this home. The funny thing is that this was to be the theme of most of my childhood. I was there for convalescence and to be able to breathe the clear, non-smoggy non-London air while living by the sea.

Kirkley Park Road

Kirkley Park Road was a quiet street along the coast from Lowestoft, just off the Pakefield Road. It was one street back from the sea. The road curved and had very large houses all along, each one set back with its own driveway and each built to its own unique design, probably in late Victorian times. Ours was constructed of red brick and was three stories tall.

Each was large enough to have its own servants' quarters or large enough for the very biggest of families. Number 35 was Auntie's house, set back from the road behind a wide, sweeping graveled driveway. It was a very large house with a large front door set back in a brick porch.

There were two large bay windows at the front that continued up to the second floor on either side of the front door.

The house had three very tall floors; the children's bedrooms were located upstairs off a wide spacious landing. There was a babies' nursery in the front downstairs inside a glass conservatory with colored panes of glass that amplified the daylight, making it very bright inside.

To the right of the drive was a garage complete with concrete steps down to a pit for repairing the cars. Above the garage was the "apple loft," where, originally, apples from our orchard were picked and were placed there to ripen. Now, however, it was converted into a very comfortable apartment, or flat, that I stayed in many years later, as a young teenager when I went to visit Auntie. The smell of the apples had over the years permeated into the very woodwork of that loft and hung in the air like being in an orchard.

At the side of the house, just past the large stand-alone garage, was a long-graveled path leading through the top garden and on into the lower back garden.

On the first floor, there were two large bedrooms at the front of the house that could sleep around eight to ten children each. One was "the pink room," and the other was "the blue room." The pink room was where I spent my very youngest days. The blue room was where I slept as I got older, from three years old. Across the large landing was the "Snuggery," Auntie and Nunky's lounge. It always smelled of brandy, wood fires and pipe smoke. I loved the smells in that room and sometimes crept in there during the day to breathe in the beautiful aroma of the room. It was surprising I didn't take up a pipe or cigars at the time as I loved the aromas emanating from within their private sanctuary.

The Dollhouse

Just outside the Snuggery was the largest dollhouse I have ever seen. It stood at the top of the main stairs on its own pedestal and was beautifully made and very detailed. It was a three-story house with front doors, back doors, sash windows that opened, lights that lit, servants' quarters in the loft and tiny handcrafted furniture in every room. Even down to the detail of cups saucers and plated pictures on the walls, the dollhouse was painstakingly accurate in every detail. The walls had wallpaper, the stairs had a stair carpet and in some of the rooms, there was a chandelier.

I have never ever seen such a beautiful dollhouse and once many years later, when I was visiting Auntie in Scarborough with Sue, my wife, Auntie asked me what I wanted from her estate when she "went to the fairies."

I told her there was only one thing that I would love to have, I told her it was the dollhouse. She looked at me and said, "Would you look after it, Tony?" I remember telling her that I would and that I would rebuild anything that was broken and that I would probably place it in a museum so thousands of children could enjoy it as much as the other children and I always had. Unfortunately, though, that wasn't to be as the family wouldn't allow that to happen and instead left it broken and in disrepair. Some things are never valued or meant to be left as a legacy for others.

In Aunties house, on the first floor, there were also several bathrooms, a nursing station with an airing room and a long verandah outside that overlooked the west-facing garden. The verandah was the width of the large house and in summer, some of us, who were older (maybe four or five years old) were allowed to sleep there at night. I mention west-facing because not only did it have a magnificent view of the bowling greens, the enormous greenhouses and the bottom garden; but we could also see the sunsets from there. And even at that age, I loved just standing, with Mary and Beatrice, quietly watching the sun setting across our beautiful garden. I would stand there for hours, often by myself, just looking at this beautiful sight.

Apart from the very large sweeping main staircase, there was another set of servants' stairs leading to the upper third floor, where Auntie's bedroom, the nurse's bedroom, bathrooms and Tessa's bedroom were located. Between these rooms, at the top of the upper stairway, was the tank room where there was a hoard of the most interesting stuff you could ever imagine. There was a very large model yacht that was as big as I was, train sets and all kinds of things that had belonged to Nunky or John and Tessa and could never be thrown away.

Tessa's bedroom was where I spent many nights when I was older and I slept in Tessa's bed. I loved Tessa; she was the kindest gentlest girl I have ever met. I can never remember her raising her voice, only that she was so kind to me. She and Auntie would take me out with them into town to go shopping, or down to the beach for the whole day, or out into the garden. Tessa was the best older sister a boy could ever wish for and we spent so much time together.

Above Tessa's bed was a pastel painting of a baby sleeping. She used to tell me that it was me as a baby and although I didn't know if this was true, it really didn't matter.

The room, being at the very top of the house, had a sloping ceiling that formed part of the roof and had huge wooden beams along the ceiling. It was decorated in pastel yellow and white and was always very neat. The bed was in one corner to the left next to the front window that looked out onto a stone-turreted balcony outside both Tessa's room and the nurse's windows along the roof. I imagined that I was living in a castle and often looked out over the stone-turreted balcony.

I spent a lot of time in the kitchen "helping" the cooks as they prepared our meals on two large ranges. One range was an "Aga;" the other was an eight-burner large gray gas range for preparing the food for all of us children. Just off the kitchen was the walk-in pantry loaded with everything you could imagine. Next to the kitchen was the breakfast room or dining room.

We had the complete set of blue "Willow Pattern" tableware all housed in a very tall glass-fronted cupboard and there must have been hundreds of pieces placed there in the breakfast room.

The "breakfast" table was a very large solid oak table that sat sixteen with ease when Auntie was entertaining guests. Dinners were at 7:00 p.m. and were fairly formal in that we had to dress properly, wash hands and be on our best behavior. I would always eat with Auntie, Tessa, John when he was home and the nursing staff. It was these times that I picked up much of the local gossip and what was going on in our house with all the children and staff.

That was my home for the first eight years of my life—laundry maids, kitchen staff, gardeners, nurses and a full house of children. One could never say it was quiet; in fact, it was the opposite—absolutely teaming with our daily life. Often the nurses would invite their boyfriends over for drinks or a party at night. On some of these times, I would hide under the table in case I got caught and if I did, it was straight up to bed, from a very stern Auntie.

Tessa was fine with me being there, but Auntie would send me upstairs with a stern comment.

Auntie The Boss

Auntie was a   larger-than-life English lady who managed a staff of kitchen maids, laundry maids, two gardeners and a full staff of nurses. Though a large lady, she was good-natured, at least toward me, but sometimes she could be quite severe. She was the most intelligent woman I have ever known and had a way of seeing things that were unique. She also had a way of describing things that would happen if you did something wrong without thinking it through; she was always right.

Everyone respected Auntie, no one ever crossed her—at least if they did, they wouldn't get away with it for long. Although she was quite strict, she had a very kind side for her "babies," as she called us. She would never tolerate fools or idle chatter about nothing. The nurses were all very respectful of her and she ran a very tight ship.

In summer, Auntie would invite hers and Nunky's numerous friends to play bowls on the bowling greens in the back garden. They all got dressed up in white, wearing all the correct clothes to play all afternoon in the sunshine and have drinks and afternoon tea. I would sometimes watch them from upstairs on the verandah, wondering how the bowling balls seemed to know when to turn in toward the little white "Jack."

They all laughed or shouted out when someone won or knocked a close ball away from the small white "Jack."

Auntie was a working mom and would direct all of the daily routines in the busy household. She would direct the kitchen staff on what to cook, often helping them prepare the food. She would discuss with old Mr. Moore what he was to take care of that day; she would direct the nurses on which children had special needs that day and in fact, managed the whole house like a general in charge of her own army.

The only times I ever saw her get serious was when the family doctor, Dr. Mc Nab, came 'round to see one of the children if they were sick. Dr. McNab was an elderly gray-haired Scottish doctor who always looked the part, a little like Dr. Finlay's father in the TV series, he always dressed in a three-piece suit with a pocket watch that he used to check our heart rate with.

Auntie had a soft spot for Dr. McNab. She loved him coming round and would talk to him for hours about a situation concerning one of her children. But she was very matter-of-fact about the problems the children had and always let him do his work, but often she would tell him what she thought might be the trouble. When Auntie spoke, no one interrupted, not even dear Dr. McNab!

I went back to see Auntie as an older child around nine years old and later as a teenager, long after I had left the nursery as I had so many happy memories of living at Lowestoft with her and the "family" there.

Auntie never changed; she was always exactly the same and was as sharp as a pin even in her nineties. I listened to whatever she had to say and often she would sit and talk as if I were an adult, asking me what I had been up to and how my job was going and what London life was about for me.

She often played bowls in summer on our bowling green that was so perfect that when I watched them play, from the verandah, though now being older, I still didn't get the game. I could see the balls rolling long and very straight. I used to watch in wonder at how they knew the rules and would shout at each other in glee as the game went on. Sometimes the balls would roll straight and then twist inward toward the "Jack," while other times the balls would roll straight without bending in.

I asked her how the balls knew when to turn as they did. She told me that it was something called "bias," which of course made it clear as mud to me back then.

Behind the bowling green were two very large greenhouses for growing just about anything you could imagine, from oranges, tomatoes, to grapes on old vines that stretched right across the glass roof of the greenhouse. There were also all kinds of fruits and vegetables that were also grown there. I loved the warm smell inside the greenhouses and would watch Auntie or the gardeners doing all the work to grow anything we needed. The air inside was always warm, humid and strong and rich with the smells of the vegetation and the many things that we grew in there. Behind the greenhouses was a potting shed and the boiler house, where a lot of "other" things went on, nothing at all to do with potting; but you'll have to ask the nurses all about that.

Other than the greenhouses, we also had our market garden that we called "the bottom garden," where we grew our own vegetables and we had an orchard with apples, pears, fig-trees, peach trees, plum and cherry trees. We even had a pond where we kept geese and had an area where we kept chickens. I climbed up the trees to get the fruit, often throwing down the ripest to William or Beatrice, when on holiday there as a teen.

At Christmas or Easter, Auntie would ask old Mr. Moore (no relation) to get us a good-sized goose for dinner and I would wander down the garden to sit quietly and watch him pluck all the feathers off. I was happy to just sit there chatting with old Mr. Moore, marveling at how huge the pile of feathers came from just from one goose.

"Where do all those feathers go?" I asked him one time. Old Mr. Moore replied in his broad Suffolk accent, "Buggered if oi knows, but oi do knows they've all gotter come off in toim fer dinner. Otherwoise, you'll all be going 'ungry, an Auntie'll have moi guts fer gar'ers." He let me try to pluck one of the feathers out, but it was determined to remain where it was. I didn't think of the goose as dead; it just was there being plucked, ready for lunch.

Mr. Moore was our general handyman, he cycled to the house every day from Pakefield, about five miles along the coast road, regardless of the weather. I never knew his first name, but as far as I was concerned, he was "old Mr. Moore." He was a wiry man—not tall but very strong, with his shirt sleeves always rolled up, revealing naval tattoos on his arms—and was good at everything from fixing things, polishing the shiny hardwood floors, cleaning the windows and gardening. When he polished the shiny parquet floors, in our main hall, the smell of fresh polish was so fragrant it would drift through the whole house. He did that always on a Tuesday morning, so when I smelled the fragrance of fresh polish anywhere throughout the house, I knew it was Tuesday.

Mr. Moore always called me "Little Tojo" for some unknown reason, based on his extensive knowledge of the great Japanese emperor of the same name.

These times living with Auntie were the very best I ever had it didn't bother me at all if this was my home or, as it turned out, a borrowed home where I was fortunate to live for a time. Summer lasted forever, winters were always fun with snow everywhere and we played in the sea in all weather. I loved to be at the sea, especially in the rough weather clinging on to Auntie's, Tessa's, or Nurse Rosemary's hand while the huge waves crashed over my head. We spent all of our free time at the beach and it didn't matter if it was summer autumn or winter, when Auntie said, "Beach time today, Tony deah," that was what we were doing.

As if this wasn't enough, we also had a beach hut right on the beach promenade where we could make tea, get changed, or take shelter when the weather got rough or when the weather turned suddenly as it often did and started to thunder and rain. I loved the sea, especially when spending days there with Auntie, Tessa and the nurses and always with my surrogate sister, Beatrice and her younger brother William.

As I said, there were many children there and we were like a huge family. Beatrice and William were lucky enough to live with Auntie except for a few years away before it had been decided to return them to Boreham Woods, where their mother lived, as the authorities had done with me being returned to Acton to live with my step-father.

Sadly, their mother was in a mental hospital and was deemed incapable of looking after them. So they were sent back to Aunties home. All through their childhood, they lived in Lowestoft as a normal family. I, unfortunately, could not as the Middlesex County Council in their infinite wisdom decided to move me back to London, at eight years old, but that's another story.

The day that Auntie and Tessa came to give me some "very sad news," I was five years old and was lying on the floor, painting with my paint pallet on the upstairs landing next to the dollhouse, which was my favorite place. She came up to me and said to me, "Tony deah (that's how she called me till the day she died at ninety-two), I have some very sad news about your darling mother. She died this morning, bless her and she has gone up to the fairies." She held me close as she told me, "You shouldn't be sad." Adding that "She's in a much better place now."

I didn't know what to think as I had seen my mother only 3 times. I was very sad, but it didn't sink in to me.

She told me years later that when I was told that awful news, I answered, "Well, that's how it should be then, isn't it, Auntie? She was so very ill, adding I'm sure she will be all right, don't you? After all, she is in a better place now." And I continued painting. Sadly, it meant little to me since I had only met her three times and life for me was so full and my mother by that time was only a distant memory. But the photos I have of her tell me a lot about her.

When I was four years old, I became seriously ill with meningitis. In fact, I was on death's doorstep. Auntie and Dr. McNab didn't think I would make it back to the nursery after I was taken away in an ambulance to spend many weeks in hospital. Tessa bought me a pair of blue slippers and left them at the bottom of my hospital bed, just in case.

I recovered and was returned to Auntie's where I spent many long boring weeks lying in bed. I laid in bed and spent all day looking out of the large bay window at the sky and the red chimney pots of the house over the road, which was all I could see for weeks and weeks. The illness was serious and I had to recover completely; so, for so many weeks, I could not get out of bed. But I had managed to deal with my TB so this was just another thing.

ADHD? Or Just Loving Life?

I never slept more than two to three hours a night and was probably the very first child to be diagnosed as hyperactive." I have never had more than two to four hours of sleep a night in my whole life.

How lucky I was, though, to have had such a huge bedroom to be in when at night I couldn't possibly sleep as I wasn't at all tired. So Auntie's fix for me (Ritalin wasn't invented yet) was to leave me to go to sleep in a large wooden playpen with pillows inside (just in case I did nod off)where I would spend night after night rocking it and bumping it along the floor from one side of the large bedroom to the other. The bedroom was about thirty feet by thirty-five feet. Once I got to the other side of the room, I would turn all my stuff around to face the other direction and bump the cot all the way back, continuing on until morning.

On her ninety-first birthday party in Scarborough, Auntie told me that they would always hear a bang followed by a scrape, which was me sliding around the bedroom in my wooden cot. And they would take turns to check up on me, if the noise stopped, whoever was on night duty, all through the night, night after night, to make sure I was OK.

It was during that time that I had my first nightmare or maybe it was a dream, which I have remembered even to this day and to me it was very, very, real. I was sitting in my playpen when all the other children were asleep, in the middle of the night, when a huge tiger entered the bedroom and padded silently and slowly past me. As he passed by, he looked straight at me, gazing with huge unblinking, amber-colored eyes. I watched him in numbed silence as he slowly passed close by me, so close I could reach out and touch him, but I wasn't scared; I knew he wouldn't harm me and when he stared at me, it was as if he knew something about me and didn't want to share it. I only saw him once but remembered my feelings and the sight of him slowly moving past me in the bedroom as if he was guarding all of the children.

Decades later as I was writing my book I decided to look up online to tell me what this dream meant. Here's what I found out. "The dream of a tiger is about how you can spiritually grow yourself to become immune to traumatic events in daily life. Think about your life for a moment. Imagine a life free of fears, crazy demands and above all else free from dissatisfaction. The tiger has appeared to help you move forward into a journey that is free from the stress and pressures of the world. The tiger appears in dreams when you know secretly you have negative energy within but you hold the internal wisdom to heal yourself. Maybe this was how I managed to deal with everything as a child and the many events I was to face later, as you will read, here in my book!

When I was around five or six, during a very hot summer night while we were sleeping on the verandah, John Hoey, who was a little older than me, was telling us that he learned at school about what a mile was. "What's a mile then?" we asked him. He looked over at the back garden to a neighbor's garden and said, "It's as far as that." We all looked and thought what a long way a mile was. In fact, that was only a couple of hundred yards or so, but it's relevant, isn't it? At our size, it was a very significant distance so for days afterward, I made sure everyone else knew what a mile really was. It was anything from "over there past the back door" to "as far as you can see anything."

During long summer days, Mary Brookes, Beatrice and I would go down to the bottom garden, beyond the orchard, to where there was an old open gypsy wagon painted in faded pink and light blue, which used to be pulled along by horses. We would play there all day long, never troubled or worried and with no one to bother us.

These times were soon to be gone forever, as the Middlesex County Council decided that, despite Auntie's stream of letters and telephone calls, I should be moved back to London to live with my, now widowed, stepfather in Acton, West London. They decided that she had too many children there and that she couldn't adopt me as well as Beatrice and William.

Auntie decided to adopt them both as she thought that they would fare better with her than in a children's home or in a foster home after their mother had been moved into a mental hospital. Though I didn't know it then, she was right, of course. Beatrice and William's mother was in a psychiatric hospital and had been for many years. William was a little slow at understanding things, maybe a little autistic and was very quick to temper throwing hysterical temper fits. Beatrice and William were at that time quite close as I recall, as they, like me, were used to living at the nursery. William took a lot of handling mainly because of his quick temper.

But with all the help and care Auntie and the nurses gave him, he would at least have a fair chance to manage his life.

Auntie made the difference to many children; I was lucky to be one.

DARK TIMES

It's sometimes not the problems but how we deal with them.

I WAS EIGHT and a half when I was moved back to live with my stepfather who had married my mother shortly before she died of TB, just around the time she had come to see me that last time at Lowestoft. She met him in the sanitarium, where he survived and sadly for us both she didn't.

I have a photo of my mother on her wedding day and I could see years later when Auntie gave me that picture, that her coat was too large for her because at that time she had lost weight due to her illness, but she looked so pretty and had a beautiful smile, which I always thought was just for me.

I don't to this day know why I was moved back to Acton from Auntie's large home in Lowestoft, but it was to become a very dark time in my life. I was like a toy robot; all you had to do was point me in a direction and off I went wherever I was told to go.

When I moved into my stepfather's tiny flat from Lowestoft, I couldn't believe how small it was. It was an upstairs flat at number 39A Cumberland Road, in Acton and had a bedroom, living room, a kitchen and a bathroom. We had to go up the stairs through a tall door to get to the flat.

It was what is now called a row house, one of a long row of houses built in Victorian England. He lived with his mother (whatever her name was), who was, I swear, truly a real witch. She was a miserable old lady and always got me into trouble, telling tales about what I had supposedly done that day. I definitely became unmanageable; I wore out my shoes, probably because they spent the money on themselves instead of replacing my worn-out shoes. I stayed out on the streets all the time after school rather than spend time in that horribly miserable flat.

I went to a day school a few streets away, sometimes I would be taken by his mother and most times; I would walk there myself, at eight years old. The flat was tiny and seemed to always smell of paraffin, which was used, in a small heater, to heat the freezing place in winter. I hated it there and prayed every night that Auntie would come to get me.

My school was nasty as well and quite rough. I seem to remember the school's name was Derwentwater Primary School which was close to where we lived. I recall even now how horrible it was and how I regularly got attacked by the other boys because I spoke nicely (thanks a bunch, Auntie). This was where I started to learn to look after myself.

One day, as I was leaving school to go home, his mother was meeting me from school when I was attacked and knocked to the ground as several of the boys jumped me by the boys' toilets where I was kicked and punched repeatedly.

I had never ever experienced this and was certain it would never happen to me again. I had bruises, a bleeding nose, two black eyes and torn clothes. I was eight years old. Anyway, she was waiting for me along with all of the other mothers who were horrified at seeing me come around the corner from the inner playground crying. They said, "He's got it written all over his poor little face." And all I could think of then was how do I get rid of the writing that was apparently on my face, though I couldn't see it when I got home later. I was concentrating on hiding my face from everyone as I walked home in case they would see the writing that I was now convinced was all over my face.

The next day, I was called in front of the whole class to point out the boys that did it, but I didn't want to cause myself more embarrassment.

All I wanted was to move on and not to remember what had happened. I never told on who they were and was placed under the care of an older girl who offered to look after me at playtime. I didn't need any help and had all but forgotten what had happened but was never bothered by them again.

These were the darkest times in my childhood probably because I was desperately unhappy there. Sometimes I was caned across my hand while being made to stand on a chair facing the kitchen window with my arm stretched out in front of me. I know it hurt, but I refused to let either my stepfather or "the witch" see that it hurt. I would simply go to the happy place, in my mind and imagine being back at Auntie's, while staring straight ahead, looking at the rooftops and chimneys. I hated it when I heard him coming up the stairs from work in case I had done something wrong that I didn't know about.

All that had to happen for me to get into trouble when he came home was for his mother to tell him that I had been swearing or had run off, or I had stayed out playing on the streets or had been seen by her spitting on the road. (Where did I learn that little gem?) Yep, I learned a whole lot of neat things in my early Acton life that I never learned at Aunties!

I subsequently played out on the street from school time until dinnertime as I was certain that I didn't want to be in that horrible tiny flat alone with her. Even if I wasn't allowed to go out, I didn't want to spend any time at home, so I stayed out after school as long as I could find things to occupy my time either on the streets or in the small park at the bottom of my road.

It was hard to imagine moving from Auntie's in Lowestoft, with all that I had there and all the friends and people who I loved, into a small flat with two of the most miserable, unhappy people I had ever met. I do not recall them ever laughing or ever being happy with me there, but I never knew why. I do know that whenever the council caseworker came around, they were really nice to me, telling me not to talk unless spoken to or asked to speak. I soon got the hang of mentioning how often I was smacked just before my caseworker came 'round in order to get sweets "a little bribe" for keeping quiet.

Funny how things turn out, years later when I was thirty-three, I had a wine bar in Ealing, not far from Acton and a woman who used to be a regular in my bar told me she worked at Elizabeth Arden in Acton. She told me of a very tall, horrible security guard with red hair who was always nasty to the staff, shutting the gate if they were late or locking the gate if they didn't leave on time forcing them to go and find him to unlock the gate. She told me his name was Willatts! Unbelievable, it was the same man. As I recalled, my stepfather worked as a security guard at Elizabeth Arden! I couldn't believe my ears as she told me what he was like at work. They called him "Hitler." Yep, that was him all right! So I didn't exaggerate it; he was an unhappy miserable man everywhere he went.

He was very tall like a lurch and had thinning curly reddish hair and large gangly hands with large gangly feet. What on earth did my lovely mother see in him? I prayed hard every night while lying awake in bed, that Auntie would come to get me and take me back with her to my real home in Lowestoft.

I was free when I was out of their flat and I could do whatever I wanted to do. I used to cross the main road and go into the park to play with Rex. Rex was a huge white Pyrenean Mountain dog who was bigger than me. I would wait for him for hours until he arrived with his master. To me, everything was "par for the course." And despite not liking where I was living or the rough Acton school that

I had to go to, I had Rex to play with; so everything for a short while each day was fine. Well, as luck would have it, my prayers were eventually answered.

An Angel Comes To Visit

One sunny afternoon when I was playing with Rex in the park, which was called Springfield Gardens, I heard this very familiar voice calling from the park entrance. "Tony deah, is that you?" It was my very own Auntie. She had come in answer to my prayers.

"What on earth are you doing here by yourself, Tony deah?" as she was looking around at the park and at me playing there. I was so happy I couldn't speak as I ran across the park and held her as tightly as I could with both hands in case she disappeared, or in case I was dreaming again. I chatted non-stop and held on to her tightly, not daring to let her go.

Only Auntie could arrive in a completely strange place, in a huge city like London and in a town like Acton and ask anybody who she passed on the street, "Do you know my little Tony?" and believe it or not, as she told me years later people knew me from her description and she was not surprised at all. I had introduced myself to anyone that passed me along the street. What a moron I must have been.

She was told that at this time of the day "Tony is always over at the park playing with a very large white dog." I was now nine years old at the time when I heard her calling out to me from right across the park from where she was standing at the entrance, next to the wrought-iron gate. She gave me one of her huge hugs, squeezing the breath out of me as she lifted me off my feet. I kissed her again and again, as we were standing in that park. I begged her to take me back with her to Lowestoft. I held her face in my hands, as she bent down to hug me and I thought, *you really are my angel from heaven.* "Have you come to take me home, Auntie, please, please, take me home with you?" I asked her repeatedly on the walk back to my dreary little flat.

That was the only time I ever saw tears in her eyes, although I didn't understand why. She said she would see what she could do and asked me to take her to where I lived. "What are those people thinking," she said, "leaving you to play by yourself on these wicked streets?" I told her, "I'm OK, Auntie. I have plenty to do and there's always Rex," as I pointed over the park to where my beautiful Rex was sitting quietly watching us. "He's my special friend and I play with him after school, huge, isn't he? I wish I could have a dog just like Rex?"

We walked back to the flat with me chatting the whole way clinging to her hand, afraid she would disappear again. Once back at the tiny flat, Auntie told the witch who she was and that she would wait until Mr. Willatts came home to speak to him. She told Auntie how bad I was and how much I swore, that I wore my shoes out and that I cost a fortune to keep. She told Auntie all about my bad behavior. She probably thought Auntie would agree with her or give them money for keeping me! Auntie told her that she had brought me up for eight years and I had never behaved like that at all. It was funny, Auntie told her, "I don't know you and I don't want to, but a good idea right now would be for you to stop talking while I wait here!"

Well, as soon as "he" got back, Auntie tore into them both, "How dare you treat Tony like this? Look at him you've made him into a scruffy urchin. Of course, he wears his shoes out, he's a little boy and that's what little boys do, deah and I should know as I have dozens of them." I was clutching her hand for dear life, hiding behind her dress, peering around her to look at them both and begging her, "Please take me with you please, please" But they were having none of that. They got hold of my other hand and yanked it hard away from her, trying to pull me back as they started pulling my arm in the other direction. I was stuck in the middle, trying to get them to let me go, kicking and struggling with two battling grown-ups-them on one side and Auntie on the other side. She was worth both of them and more besides! I remained like that stretched out between them, while they both fought their battle to keep me.

I was trying to get them to let go and I was yelling at them, "LET ME GO, LET ME GO," screaming for all I was worth, "I hate living here. I don't want to be here. I want to go home with Auntie RIGHT NOW!" Auntie was telling them, "He's clearly very unhappy here adding "I have all the space and these things you're telling me are not the Tony I know at all." They would have none of it and I couldn't understand why, since they seemed to dislike me as much as I disliked them, but they didn't jump at the chance to let me go.

But in the end, Auntie had to let me go. As she left, she promised to do everything in her power to get me back. She left that evening and I was desolate as I watched her leave and walk away down the street, knowing I had to stay with these people. I cried later that night, which is something I never did and prayed to God that I would be able to go away from here and be happy again.

Prayers Answered

Well, as luck would have it, a move was soon to be a reality when my prayers were answered. Shortly after Auntie's visit, when I was nine and a half years old, my stepfather gathered all my things (my worn-out clothes) and we walked down the road to the bus stop. He was in silence the whole way on the bus ride from Acton to where we were going in Hanwell some 5 miles down the Uxbridge Road and said nothing at all to me while we were traveling. My stepfather didn't even tell me where he was taking me, as we sat on the bus in silence.

I had no relationship with him and never saw him as a father figure or anything else for that matter. Well, what a surprise! I was being moved into a children's home, an orphanage, at number 82 Oaklands Road in Hanwell, some forty-five minutes and a million miles away from their tiny flat in Acton. I couldn't care less where I was as long as I never ever saw them again.

We walked from the bus stop to number 82, but I didn't have a clue what this was all about. I just walked in silence with nothing to say. I refused to hold his hand and we walked along the street.

When he left me standing in the doorway of what I realized was an orphanage, he did so without saying anything to me at all, not a single word, not even goodbye, which was fine by me, another door to close in my life. Apparently, Auntie's prayers on my behalf were answered but probably not in the way she planned (I'm sure God has a sense of humor).

Closing that door in my mind on this pain was one of the tools I had been given and was my way of dealing with all of the things that would happen to me as I grew up. This was a tool that I often used to deal with all the bad things that I had to deal with and it stayed with me as a way of dealing with life's many tests and trials yet to come. I learned that When you ask for help you have to accept the help that is given.

The Orphanage

82 Oaklands Road was an orphanage, a children's home that had some eight kids—all boys—and was in another smaller house; but

this one had several bedrooms. The mistress of this place was called Mrs. Bumford! She was a large, homely woman who looked after all her boys. I don't have many memories of that time, except that her cooking was always very bland and tasteless. We always had loads of greens and cabbage and I hated greens. Though Mrs. Bumford was OK, the place had no love and no good things at all going for it except that we were all there together as a sort of temporary foster family. I shared a bedroom with four other boys.

While I was there, I had to go to a new school called, "Oaklands Road Primary school which was just across the road from the children's home. It was an old Victorian building, very austere and was built of gray stone. It had very tall windows and a large concrete playground.

It was known by all the staff that I was from *The Orphanage*, which meant little to me at the time as I couldn't care less what they thought. I spent most of my time in my own little world and for the most part, managed to shut the rest of the world out. I did, however, soon see an advantage in that the dinner ladies, as we called them, all felt very sorry for me, for some reason that for the life of me I couldn't understand, they always gave me loads of extra food.

I don't know if they knew I was always hungry, which I always was, or that I looked thin, which I probably did. Anyway, they were very nice to me and I looked forward to school dinnertime when I could load up with enough food to last me till the following day. I could even have seconds and thirds before others even had the first course. I especially loved the pudding, which was banana custard or chocolate custard and I loved the skin. I always asked them to save it for me, which they always did. I got the feeling they looked forward as much to see me as I did to seeing them and they were happy to give me all the food I wanted. Funny, this was going to stay with me throughout my childhood and well into my adult life. I knew that if I ate my food fast, no one could take it off my plate. Every day was like a mini battle being fought, with the battlefield being the school canteen and my plate. I would line up with all the other kids, get my plate and hold it forward for each dinner lady to dollop on whatever was for dinner that day. We would pass down the food line until we got to the end then move over to sit at a table. Most of the time, I sat by myself, as no one would sit with me, because I was from "the orphanage." I didn't mind that as I could eat fast and go for seconds and thirds, often rejoining the line to get more food.

On weekends at Oaklands Road, the radio was usually tuned to the BBC Light program, when I had to listen to current hits like "Que Sera Sera," and other songs that I tried to sing along with. I loved music and could get completely lost in a song. I didn't care what I sounded like, but when I sang, I was oblivious to anything else.

Weekends, at the Oaklands Road orphanage, were also very interesting for another reason. Young married couples arrived on Saturday mornings and afternoons, as potential foster parents for some of the boys. They came into the home, to meet whoever they were there to see, then took them away for the day or for the weekend. No one ever came for me, as I knew no one at all here in London and I was nearly always alone there at weekends, which was fine by me as I could play with any of the toys and no one was there to stop me as they usually did when they were present.

I had no toys of my own to play with and never had. I loved playing with the Hornby 00 Gauge wind-up train set, as the electric train was not for me to ever touch. However, on weekends, I played with it all day long in the back room, when no one else was there. I loved the smell of the electric sparks that came out from the wheels whenever it went over a join in the rails. I didn't have to ever wind it up and it would run on and on around the track. The detail was amazing, the engines were so realistic and the maroon and cream passenger cars reminded me of Lowestoft and the train ride when I went to see my mother. I often pretended I was on that train going back to Aunties.'

After several months of living there, life for me settled down, again, then one Saturday afternoon, a young couple came to the home while I was playing in the back room. The young lady, Joyce, was very pretty with dark wavy hair, reminding me of my beautiful mother and was quite tall, slim and very well dressed. Joyce had a kind face and was smiling at me the whole time. Her husband was Herbert (Bert). He was very elegantly dressed in a dark pinstriped suit and they both seemed interested in talking to me.

They both knelt down next to me and started playing along with me and the train set. They had come to meet a boy called Freddy Weekly, but he was out that day. They met me by accident and started talking to me instead of leaving. They were asking me why I was there alone and what had happened to my family. I told them my mother had gone to the fairies, which was as it should be since she had been "very ill with TB, you know." I hadn't a clue what TB was, but people seemed to know all about it and it saved me from having to explain further.

The Whiteheads, which was their name as I understood from Mrs. Bumford, came again some weeks later and were looking again for Freddy. Well, Freddy had once again already gone out that day and as usual, I was there by myself.

I would most often get the electric train set out to play with and on this second trip, I recognized them. They asked me if I would like to go out with them for the day. Of course, I said, "Yes; that would be OK if Mrs. Bumford said it was all right." I whispered to them to ask if I could eat lunch with them as the food there was not very nice. They laughed and said, "Yes, of course."

We went out from Oaklands Road to their home in Boston Manor and their house was much larger than the foster home. The house had three bedrooms, two rooms downstairs and a small front garden with a longer back garden. The house was brightly painted in red and white and was located halfway down on the left-hand side on a respectable quiet street called Clitherow Avenue and the house was number 107.

I spent many weekends thereafter that, staying first on Saturdays, after which they would both take me back to Oaklands Road Hanwell on the trolley bus. As time went on and we became better acquainted, I got to stay with the family for whole weekends. Bert and Joyce had a son, Richard, who was two years older than me and seemed OK; but I wasn't sure about him yet.

Richard told me, one night, he had wanted a brother and thought that I was probably going to be his new brother. I didn't mind at all since it was better than life at the children's home and I really liked my new foster parents, his mom and dad. I said to Richard, "OK then, I'll be your new brother," not knowing what a brother was supposed to do, but if it meant leaving the children's home and living here instead, then that was fine by me.

Some months later, their visits became regular events for me, which I looked forward to, especially when I could go to my "new family" for the weekend. One day sometime later, Joyce asked me if I would like to live with them permanently. I said I needed to ask permission, but if it was OK with Mrs. Bumford, it was fine with me and that was that.

I was so excited to be moving out of the children's home for good, so I simply left there, no goodbyes and no fuss, just another door to close behind me as I moved on. Freddy's loss was my gain, although he had found another couple to stay with, so it was not a real loss for him. I never saw Freddy again, nor did I ever go back to see that orphanage again ever! In fact, this part was more difficult to write than other parts as it had few memories for me and I had little to say about that time except being dropped off and eventually being found by the Whiteheads.

I seemed to have put that place in a separate part of my mind, so "closing that door" was very easy. I saw that things happen for a reason and being there got me away from my stepfather and even if it was a children's home, it didn't matter to me. I just fitted in wherever I was and made the most of whatever I had to deal with at the time. My belief in God was unshakeable and I knew I must have had a whole host of guardian angels looking after me to have been so lucky as to have Bert and his beautiful wife Joyce to come into my life right at that point, just when I needed them, now I was ready to move on.

I had to stand on my own at a very young age, this stayed with me always

MY NEW FAMILY

I entered a period of calm in my life.

LIFE BEGAN TO settle down for me and I was beginning to have somewhat of a normal life. I started at a new school, Fielding Primary School, though I stayed there for only a few months before moving on to Fielding Junior School. Soon it was summer when I could do anything, play all summer long and go back to my very own home. Each week, Joyce used to give Richard and I pocket money. I hadn't a clue what it was for as I had never needed money, but she bought me some sweets with the money and they were kept in a jar on a high shelf in the larder—licorice, Flying Saucers, Sherbet Lemons, fruit salad's penny chews and anything I wanted.

Richard had his jar marked with his name and I had mine. Most of the time, I was so busy I forgot all about the sweets, so Richard took mine as well as his. I didn't mind, nor did I notice until I had none left in the middle of the week. At that point, repeatedly, mom would ask me if I had already eaten all of my sweets and when I replied, "No, I haven't touched them," she would step in and take sweets from Richard's jar and would give them to me. The shelf was too high for me to reach so I would have had to ask Joyce to reach them for me.

Richard always said I owed him his sweets back, so I would give him some of mine from time to time. I had never had any possessions of my own at that time, no toys that were mine and certainly I had never had sweets, so it didn't matter that much and I thought if Richard needed mine, he could have them. After all, it was his house. But mom, as I got to call her, was angry that he took them.

I remember we even went on summer holidays to Broadstairs where there was an incredible ice cream shop with hundreds of, "knickerbocker Glories" all lined up on a wall for us to choose which one we chose.

After summer I moved up from Fielding Primary school to Fielding Junior School. That was when I began for the first time to have real friends. It was there, at Fielding, that I met my lifelong friend Ian Howard. Ian had a house about a mile away from my house at number 5 Southdown Avenue and he had a younger sister called Annabelle. Ian and I began to be best of friends and spent all of our time together. We were to remain friends all our lives, although we didn't know it then of course. The two of us joined the Cub Scouts and even sang in the church choir at the huge "St. Thomas the Apostle" Protestant church on the Boston Road.

We were together all the time and would meet up at his house or mine and would go out every Wednesday night to choir practice at the church. When we weren't at choir practice, we went to the Cub Scout hut, on Friday nights, which at that time was in an old wooden hut next to the church. Later when we became Boy Scouts, we went to a purpose-built hut down Trumpers Way in lower Hanwell, some three miles from our houses.

Ian's mother was a famous actress, *Peggy Evans*, though it meant little to us at the time, Dad certainly knew of her acting and told me she was a film star. She was very beautiful and was tall, had long blonde glamorous wavy hair that would cascade down to her shoulders. Ian's mom was always very kind to me and always let me see Ian whenever I wanted, which was almost all the time.

Peggy had starred in a film called *The Blue Lamp* with Dirk Bogarde and Jack Warner. She was often seen on television doing her famous scream as Jack was shot outside a cinema by Dirk Bogarde, who was playing the role of a small-time thug. Peggy would come running out of the cinema look at what her boyfriend, Dirk, had just done, as Jack was slowly sinking to the ground, having just been shot and she would scream at the top of her lungs.

Ian and I would watch the clip whenever it was on and recite word-for-word what Jack and Peggy said in that scene. "Drop it and don't be a fool" Ian would say and I would reply, "I'll drop you. This thing works. Get back, get back, I say." Well, apparently, he didn't get back because Dirk shot Jack dead right there in front of the cinema. Jack Warner's name in the film was *Constable Dixon*, the police station was at Dock Green, the real station was at Paddington Green in west London. That scene was played over and over again for the next fifty years and it caused the same stir of emotion because it was the very first time a uniformed policeman had been shot on screen. Boy were they all in for a surprise nowadays; sadly, it happens both in real life and in movies every day.

Jack went on to star in a very long-running TV series of the same name, *Dixon of Dock Green*. I watched that show for years afterwards; even though it was in black and white. It was always on, on, Saturday nights at 7:00 p.m.

Ian, Annabelle and their mom didn't have a lot of money all the time I knew Ian, but they got by just fine. Ian's dad was a famous comedian called Michael Howard and was on a radio show every lunchtime, in a show called *Workers Playtime*, which was played in all of the factories all over England. Michael had divorced Peggy shortly after Annabelle was born. Peggy got a little help from "Equity," which was an actor's union; but it wasn't much and I don't think Michael ever helped her out with Ian and Annabelle.

Money and possessions meant nothing to me or to Ian. We had all we needed, our friendship, plenty of fun, both our homes and loads to do. We were inseparable throughout our childhood and on into our late teenage years. We learned to sing and play guitar, but that is a later story.

Life for me at last was now very normal. I loved school, I loved my new home, I loved my new family and I loved all my new friends. The school was magic and was the best school one could hope for. The teachers and the atmosphere at Fielding Junior School were the best I would ever know. Many years later, I met all of my school friends online through a Web site called *Friends Reunited*. I kept in touch with Janette Andersen, Linda Miller, Carolyn Davies, Iris Nunn and many more. In some way, it proved to me that all of these things had happened.

Our favorite teacher was our music teacher, Mr. Woodcraft (Woody Woodcraft) and he was a truly gifted music teacher.

Mr. Woodcraft had a teaching method where he would describe a complete piece of music to us before playing it on a large wooden gramophone that he wheeled in front of the classroom. He would describe a scene from *Peer Gynt in the Hall of the Mountain King* or the *William Tell Overture* or the *Fingal's Cave* (part of *The Hebrides Suite*), or *Peter and the Wolf*. Then after half an hour of a detailed description of the music, what part each of the instruments in the orchestra played and what the music represented. He let us hear the piece of music, playing it in front of the class and we could fully understand all that the music had described.

I loved these music lessons and he was to influence my life forever. It was through him that we were all fortunate enough to have had a complete understanding of how music was written and why it was written, of the "movements" in a piece; how it progressed through to the finale. Music lessons involved a large music sheet with colored musical notes denoting which instrument would play each piece.

Christmas was magic, the whole school was decorated and every window in the large school hall was painted with Christmas scenes from the Bible and from Christmas carols. Each class got to choose what their painted window represented.

Each class was given one of the large windows in the school hall for them to paint their scene. Some, of course, were better than others; but our art teacher would make all of the paintings seem perfect. We sang carols at morning assembly and I loved the beautiful hymns and carols that we sang. The excitement of waiting for the Christmas holidays lasted for the whole month of December when the weather was starting to get cold.

My birthday signaled the beginning of the Christmas season and I was happy that it was on December 6th for that reason. The walk from my house to the school was almost one mile and sometimes Ian and I would meet at the bottom of my road, which was on our way. We walked to school together, then at the end of the school day, we walked home together, parting at the bottom of my street, after dawdling and chatting about the day's events. We were in no hurry. Then he could go on to his house and I to mine.

We all loved the time there at Fielding and even now, though my school friends haven't met for at least forty years, many of us keep in touch through Facebook and other sites.

On Sundays in summer, Mom, Dad, Richard and I went to the Lyons Sports club in Acton as Dad worked for J. Lyons & Company at their head office in Cadby Hall in Central London.

The club was just for employees and their families and was incredible. The club had an open-air swimming pool, playing fields and almost every sports activity you could think of. There were soccer teams, rugby, tennis courts, bowls and every sports activity one could imagine.

Joyce loved to play tennis and would play for hours on any of the many courts there with her friends, sometimes singles and sometimes doubles. Richard and I would sometimes swatch her play; she was a very good tennis player. Life was so good then and I wanted nothing else. My guardian angel had once again looked after me.

I had many new friends to play with, Brian Phillips, Brian Pinder, Ian Howard. Peter Fothergill (who has sadly passed, too young). Brian Phillips was a sturdy, or as his Scottish kinfolk would say a "brawny," boy with red hair, freckles and a very kind character. Brian Pinder was also much bigger than me (as were most of my friends) and went on after school to join the army (101st Airborne). We all played together or cycled about the streets and did whatever we wanted.

On Saturday mornings, we went to the Northfields Odeon to watch *Saturday Morning Pictures*. It was thruppence and lasted for three hours.

We all sat together to watch *Mr. Pastry*, the *Lone Ranger*, *Superman*, *Laurel and Hardy* many other short film episodes, some in black and white. Brian Pinder got us sweets from his dad's sweet shop on the corner of Northfields Avenue and Devonshire Road. We all sat there shouting at the screen as some villain was up to no good or when the Lone Ranger rose on his horse and said, "Hi-ho Silver away," whatever that meant but we all shouted it out with him.

Summers were of course endless and we always found things to do. I pretty much went on with my life doing all the normal things boys do. On Sundays, if we weren't going to the Lyons Sports Club, Dad would go to the local pub for a lunchtime pint, or two or three. He took Richard and I and we would both have an 'Orangina' each, which for both of us was a real treat.

The pub, the Royal Hotel, was an enormous Tudor building in white, with black beams all over the rather stylish front and sides and was located right at the corner of our street. It had an interesting garden with a miniature zoo. There were parrots, monkeys, a donkey and other little creatures.

We spent lunchtime there till Dad had had his pint or two. Then we'd all walk home where my beautiful mom had made roast beef or roast lamb for lunch. I loved Sunday lunch with the whole family together, though often Mom would get cross with Dad for getting back at one-thirty when lunch was at 1:00 p.m. I never understood why lunch on Sundays was at 1 pm when Dad never got back before 1.30. This became our Sunday ritual; it made me smile . . . my normal family.

Another Door To Close

I now had my perfect family; everything else was behind me and I was at last happy. One warm sunny Sunday in summer when I was now 10 years old, Mom and Dad took Rich and me to dad's sports club. So we all set off together with me swinging between Mom and Dad's arms, excited to be meeting all of their friends. The sports club was three stops on the Piccadilly line from Boston Manor to Acton Town, where we changed trains, to get another train to Sudbury Hill station where the sports grounds were located.

After a short walk to the Boston Manor Tube station, we took the Piccadilly line to Acton Town then changed tubes. When we got to the sports club, Dad would smoke his Players Weights and played cards with his friends, always with a beer next to him, while Mom played tennis with her friends. I made as much noise as I could with other kids or simply stayed with Dad and watched him, fascinated as he played cards. Richard, being older than me, hung out with his friends, when we usually stayed until it was time to go home usually around 3:30 p.m.

That day we boarded the tube for home and arrived at Boston Manor station shortly after 4:00 p.m., as we usually did, with me swinging happily between Mom and Dad as we walked home together in the afternoon sunlight of a warm summer's day.

As we reached the corner of our street, Mom suddenly stopped walking, complaining of feeling a little giddy and lightheaded, so she asked me to stop swinging as she sat down on the low wall at the corner of our road. Dad told Rich and me to go on home, saying they would follow as soon as Mom felt better. She looked so pale as I had never seen her before.

Later were both told to go 'around the corner 'and wait at a friend's house until Dad called us home. Early that evening, we were both told to go home to see Dad. The Cuttings, who were our very close family friends, where we spent the remainder of that afternoon, took a phone call and became very serious, telling us we had to return home. I could tell something was wrong as they weren't smiling and seemed so very sad.

As Richard and I walked home, we were talking about Mom, wondering what was wrong with her as we had never seen her so pale before. When we arrived home only a few minutes later, Dad was in the front room, looking pale, trembling and looking terrible. I couldn't imagine what was wrong. I had never seen a grown-up look as Dad looked at that moment. He asked us to join him in the front room as he sat heavily on the couch. He gathered his strength and looked at us both long and hard before telling us, in a now cracking voice, that Mom had died that afternoon of a brain hemorrhage.

Mom had died right there, on the corner of our street while sitting on that low wall. Richard and I never saw mom again, she was gone, just like that! I wish I had kissed her goodbye or told her how much I loved her, but life isn't like that. We never get the chance to change the past and I would never get that chance again. We were both scared and shocked we didn't know what to do.

Richard screamed at the news and sobbed his poor heart out, his whole body shaking in the pain of his lost mom. I was very sad too but not in the same way Richard was. I had no idea really what this all meant, but what I did know was that my life would probably change yet again. I went up to my room and sat on the bed, scared of what might happen to me now. I closed the door that day and prepared myself, once again, to move on to whatever was next in store for me. I was getting used to this news and was very sad at this; but at the same time, I knew had to just deal with it.

I felt once again desolate and alone but had no one to really talk to, so I had to keep my emotions to myself as Rich was immersed in his own sadness and Dad was, well, Dad and didn't ever show us his true emotions, so I didn't want to bother him though it broke my heart to see him this way. I was also scared that if I cried or got on his nerves, he might place me back in that awful orphanage. So I remained quiet. The curtains in our front room were drawn closed meaning there had been a death in the house.

The funeral, several days later, was a very sad day; though I must confess it didn't really sink in as it did for Dad and Rich. I never went to the funeral and instead was parked with relatives for the afternoon at our house; the atmosphere was awful.

I was scared, as I had been through this before. I prayed again that God would look after me and not let anything too bad happen to me. I had no idea what would happen to me now that Mom was gone; but what I did know was that I missed her very, very, much. Her passing was so sudden. It never impacted me until many months later. I thought I had all that I needed and I was just getting used to what must have been a normal life in a normal family and once again I had to "shut the door" and move on. I had no choice.

I had no idea how serious it was to be for me; my life was about to change again at 10 years old. My father was alone now with no partner to help look after Rich and me. He was my stepdad (number 2) and may not be able to keep me as a single parent with a full-time job, looking after two boys with no help. I worried a lot about the possibility of being placed in another children's home or orphanage but tried not to think about that possibility as, if this was to be, I could do nothing about it.

It was at this time that Ian's Mom, Peggy Evans, came 'round and asked Dad if I could go and live with her, Annabelle and Ian and perhaps she could adopt me, saying that Ian and I were like brothers anyway. Dad, of course, told her that it wasn't possible and so, Ian and I never became real brothers. But in truth, we were every bit true brothers even more than Richard and me.

A family shares everything, including loss and it is at these times of loss that we pause our lives before we can move on.

AUNTIE SIS

Some people we meet may never know how well we see them as we may not be in a position to tell them at that time.

 D AD HAD A sister in Manchester where he was originally from and invited her to come and stay with us to help him cope. Auntie Sis, as she became known to us, moved down from Manchester to live with us and did everything for us; she cooked, did our laundry, cleaned and looked after all of us, including Dad. She reminded me a lot of "Ena Sharples," a character from way back in the now long-running *Coronation Street*, having the same appearance and accent; the hairnet and even her mannerisms were the same.

The only change I saw was that once every three months, the county council, in their infinite wisdom, sent a caseworker to see how I was doing. She was a very calm tall lady, with dark hair and her name was Mrs. Osborne, though I never knew her first name. She would always talk to Dad and then to me, then she would talk to just me alone.

I never really understood the purpose of these meetings, but I knew that Dad was always a little nervous before she came around. She would ask me about school and my friends and about how my life was at home.

I was fine, although I did become more of a loner at school. I talked about it with Ian, but we both would start laughing at something or other and life would move on. Aunt Sis being with us enabled me to remain at our house and enabled Dad to cope with bringing two boys up without a mom as long as Aunt Sis stayed with us.

Gradually, things returned to normal and I remember saying to Ian one day when we were walking home from school, "I suppose I should be grateful. I have now had two moms and two dads in my life, but you've only had one." Ian didn't say anything that time and we walked home in silence. Richard changed after Mom had died and became harder to live with and never ceased to remind me that Joyce was his mom, not mine.

Though his words stung, I understood why he said that, though I could never show him that it hurt as it would give him more ammo!

I understood how he felt and felt so sad for him, though there was nothing I could do about it. But at the end of the day, I had lost two moms by now, he had only lost one; so, as I saw it, he was much better off than me.

Richard became angry and aggressive and little things seemed to upset him very easily. I guess it was grieving that he needed to get through. There were no "counselors" and no programmed grief counseling at all for us, so we just had to "grin and bear it" with a "stiff upper lip."

Dad never showed his grief to us, but I remember that he seldom smiled after Mom died and seemed to be going through life mechanically. However, one day, two years later, he told us there was a woman that he liked at work and he was going to bring her home to meet us soon.

He had married beautiful Joyce fairly young; they had known each other since high school and were perfect for each other. It's times like this that I often wondered where God was and why we were given such difficult things to deal with. I did realize though that if a person has an easy life, they don't have anything to develop or test their strength of character.

Boy, I suppose I should have been Mr. Universe in that case, but that's life, so I just learned to deal with it.

When Dad got ready for work, he always wore shiny black shoes that he polished every day. He also wore a striped shirt with a separate white collar attached with a stud, a dark pin-striped suit, a toned-down tie a bowler hat and an umbrella. He looked every bit the London businessman and I looked up to him and admired how elegantly he always dressed. He did manage to keep all of us together and I loved him for that and for everything else he did for us. Aunt Sis was a lovely person and although she was old, she managed to keep us all well and helped Dad a great deal, doing all that she could to help him look after the family. Aunt Sis, I love you still!

The stiff upper lip that my stepfather wore, showed us he had great inner strength.

SCHOOL - STUFF OF A 10-YEAR-OLD

If something looks too good to be true, it usually is.

ONE DAY, WHEN Ian and I were walking home when we were in the fourth year at Fielding Junior school, we spotted a huge bright red apple on a tree in someone's garden behind a wall next to the school on Wyndham Road. This red apple was all by itself in a garden hanging on a single branch high up behind a high curved wall, which was on a bend in the road. The wall separated the garden from the street and had a smooth side with bits of broken glass set in the bricks along the top of the wall.

So as we were walking past, day after day, we decided that the apple was made for eating and it was all alone on the tree and would probably taste delicious. At that time, "scrumping" (another word for stealing apples from other people's trees) was a perfectly normal thing for kids like us to do and besides, that particular bright red and ripe apple had been hanging there for weeks . . . all alone and by itself.

It never occurred to us that the tree had no other fruit on it, nor that the apple was huge and looked exactly the same every day as we walked home from school!

So on our way home from school one day, we decided that one of us (me) would climb up the wall, grab the apple and toss it down to the other (Ian) then we would both share it. So after carefully looking up and down the street to make sure no one was around to see what we were about to do, Ian gave me a leg up and I climbed up the wall.

The wall was around eight-feet high; it took us several attempts as we kept bursting out with laughter. I finally climbed onto Ian's shoulders then onto his head making sure I stood on his face to get high enough for me to just reach the top of the wall, chuckling as I heard him spluttering and making other noises as I climbed on his head and face. I climbed up onto the wall and shinned along the top, minding the broken glass all along the top of the wall to reach the tree.

With adrenaline pumping, I climbed onto the branch, stretched out holding onto the branch and slowly edged my way along to reach for the apple.

Of course, while I was up there completely exposed, Ian wasn't keeping quiet; he was shouting at the top of his lungs to anyone who was around to hear: "Tony Moore who lives at 107 Clitherow Avenue is stealing your apples and he's taking that huge red one. Help, police! Tony Moore... I told you not to do it . . . that's STEALING." He was in fits of laughter as he was shouting out to the "hopefully" empty street.

Bloody great, I was up the tree loudly whispering down to him, "Shut up, stupid, or we'll get caught." I am doing the hard work; he is making it worse! I grabbed the big red apple but couldn't move fast enough, frightened that someone would catch me up that tree. But I was both laughing and cross at Ian for blowing my cover and as usual, we both burst out laughing. I could hardly move for laughing so hard. Anyway, before I climbed down the tree, I shouted that I would keep the apple and eat it right up there in front of him if he didn't shut up. I then held the huge red apple in front of me, polishing it on my school blazer to emphasize the point and making out that I was about to take a big bite, so he finally stopped shouting.

I tossed it down to Ian who was waiting on the pavement. I then jumped down and we both ran as fast as we could, laughing the whole time as we both ran away from that house. When we were at safe distance from the house, we ran down an alleyway where we decided to share our spoils in the form of the huge red apple. Since I got it down, the first bite was mine and as I bit into the huge red apple, it broke completely apart, falling into many pieces onto the ground. The beautiful apple that we had been ogling at for weeks was made completely out of clay and tasted disgusting as I spat out the pieces all over Ian!

The whole thing was a hoax. Just great! We laughed and laughed all the way home and took some of the pieces to show Janette and Roisin O'Connor, at school the following day, what had happened to us the day before.

Ralph and the Guard Dog

Our scout hall was at the bottom of "Trumpers Way," a long mostly unlit lane which meant that we had to walk home with other Boy Scouts from our troop which was the 7th Hanwell Scout Troop. Ralph, one of our friends, a rather plain slightly overweight kid who wore milk bottle bottom glasses, would sometimes come home with

Ian and I as he was scared of the dark road and anyway three is better than two.

One night, on our way home, we were walking down Trumpers Way and decided to stop at the film props yard to take a look inside. The yard was behind a long sliding steel door that was twelve inches off the ground and slid open and closed along a long steel runner at the top while the bottom of the long steel door hung free.

The yard was halfway down Trumpers Way and was in a very dark part of the lane. We used to peek inside, to look at all of the neat stuff that was inside, behind the big steel sliding door. Inside, it was an amazing sight, there were many film props, army trucks, field guns, a helicopter, parts of airplane fuselages, army Jeeps, etc. It was, of course, a film set junkyard; but to us, it was a treasure trove of the coolest stuff an eleven-year-old could ever see.

We decided that we would take a closer look inside, but Ralph didn't want to come in with us, so we told him to wait by the sliding steel door and keep a lookout just in case, it was around 8.30 pm. So as Ian bent down to slip under the door and was just over halfway through into the yard, I started barking like a guard dog as loud as I could, making Ian jump out of his skin. I swear he completely left the ground as he was crawling in on all fours and had just cleared the door. He wasn't amused as he quickly changed direction to crawl back under the door to get back onto the street.

I burst out laughing to see him so scared. "you idiot! That's not funny," he said. "I could have got hurt on that door." But I was laughing so hard that he began laughing as well. As luck would have it, apparently, I said something in dog talk that started off the real guard dog, which we had no idea lived there, in a tirade of really fierce barking at us. We could hear this barking starting from deep inside the yard as this huge brute began barking back at us. The dog rounded a corner from behind an aircraft fuselage and was a huge black German shepherd. He was chained to his doghouse by a huge steel chain that we could see glinting in the moonlight as he ran back and forth, straining at his leash.

We both legged it as fast as we could, but when he didn't come after us, we both slowly crept back and knelt down, peering under the sliding door, to see why and we realized he wasn't coming as he was still securely chained, or so we thought. So we started barking back at the dog who was heaving and straining even more at his chain, trying to get to us.

I really think that all barking is to get the attention of other dogs then, as dogs bark they start thinking about what they want to say. When that happens, I believe other dogs can subliminally hear whatever it is the dog is thinking and speaking at the time.

Anyway, that's just me and it didn't matter what I was thinking as it made no difference to what was about to happen. We just knelt there laughing and barking back at the huge dog under the sliding door; while Ralph, now scared shitless, was shouting at us to stop as he stood some way back along the road nervously looking at us and at the way out up the lane.

After several minutes of the dog barking and us, attempting to have a conversation with the dog, by barking back, the bloody brute broke free and we saw him come bounding across the yard toward us, getting bigger and bigger as he got closer. The three of us legged it as fast as we could back up Trumpers Way, looking back over our shoulders as we ran.

Now Ian and I were certainly not gentlemen and we ran as fast as we could, getting past Ralph who was flat-footed and was not by any means as good a runner as we were (we had had more practice at running away). As we passed either side of him, the huge dog was getting far too close for comfort. Just then, we came up next to a large lorry that was parked on the side of the road. "Quick!" I shouted to Ian. "Let's get inside the cab."

We both leapt up onto the running board and prayed that the door wasn't locked. As luck would have it, it wasn't, so we quickly grabbed the door handle and leapt inside, slamming the door behind us.

Once we were safe inside the large lorry, we both slowly moved our heads up the door so that we could sneak a look out of the window, only to see poor Ralphy being grabbed by the huge dog and was being taken down by his leg. Ian and I were so scared at this point we could only look on with bated breath, mesmerized at the sight, with noses pressed hard on the truck window. We watched as the huge guard dog grabbed poor Ralph at the back of his knee and expertly twisted him down. Ralph, of course, screamed at the top of his lungs as he fell to the ground. Once Ralph was down, the dog then looked up to see where we had gone; We were trying to distract the dog, he then saw us and jumped up at us, snarling and snapping at us at the window, not reaching us as we were now safely in the cab. We knew we were safe and began snarling right back at the brute. He then lost interest in us and ran back past poor Ralphy, who was now lying sobbing on the road clutching his knee. The dog went back under the door and back inside the yard, ignoring Ralph who was moaning and crying on the ground.

We listened to poor Ralph as he was crying after having been bitten. We should have felt really bad, but once again, we looked at each other and started to laugh and we couldn't stop laughing, having a mixture of adrenaline, fear and relief mainly at the sad fact that we were better runners than Ralphy.

As we gingerly stepped down from the truck, Ralph was still lying on the ground, lit by the yellow light of the one and only street light on Trumpers Way. Ralphy was still moaning and clutching his leg. We helped him up and looked to see the damage. "Not much muscle there, Ralphy thank God, otherwise, he would have had even more to bite on," Ian said. "We were trying to get to you, but the door just locked on us and it wouldn't unlock until just now."

The damage wasn't really too bad though, but he did have the beginning of a huge bruise with perfect teeth marks beginning to show and though. We were still trying not to laugh as we were being as sincere as we possibly could, but we couldn't stop laughing though we felt sorry for Ralph. Poor Ralph, once he realized he was OK, he started laughing and crying too, more out of relief than humor. We kept on looking at his leg, admiring the perfect set of teeth marks at the back of his leg as we walked him limping home.

Ralph was a good sport and we agreed that we couldn't say anything to anyone as it was Ian's fault, as I kept telling Ralph while pretending to give Ian the evil eye, saying if not for him, we wouldn't have gotten into trouble at all.

Autumn Leaves

On our way back from choir practice one Wednesday evening in October, we were playing in the autumn leaves along the Boston Road. As we had nothing else to do, we decided to stack as many leaves as we could outside a large house on the corner of my street. Laughing at our brilliant plan, we began to stack a huge pile of leaves right outside the door, which was the side of the house on Cardiff Road. We had no idea who it belonged to except that it was fair game for our little prank. Finally, after some thirty minutes of "leaf stacking," we had stacked the leaves to an impressive height of at least six feet high. When we were finished we admired our handiwork, ran to the corner, and hid to see what would happen.

We were very proud of our leaf-building abilities and were carefully peeking around the corner at our handiwork. All of a sudden porch light went on and two men came out and stopped dead at the sight of our huge 6-foot pile of leaves outside their door. I turned to Ian and said, "Let's be really cool and slowly walk right past and pretend we know nothing about it."

I said to Ian. "OK, but no laughing and I mean it," as we casually started walking slowly past the house, whistling as we went, being very careful not to look at the huge stack of leaves or the two men staring at our handiwork from the lighted front porch. We were doing great, as we quite casually began to cross the road, next to their house, that is until Ian looked at me and I looked back at him at the same time. That was it. "Don't do it," I whispered forcefully at him. "Don't you dare laugh." But all our cool vanished, as we tried desperately not to laugh. Well, it didn't work. "OYE YOU," one of the men shouted! "run!" I shouted as we legged it off down the street, chased by both of the men. The older of the two gave up after chasing us some two hundred yards farther down the road and went back to the house.

As we were both laughing and running as fast as we could, the remaining man was getting closer and closer behind us. I remember shouting to Ian, "Behind you," as we used to say at Saturday morning pictures when a villain was about to pounce on the good guy; but this time, the good guy was behind the villain. Ian laughed even more and now couldn't run because of it.

As we reached a corner, we split up, Ian went straight ahead down Boston Road, a stupid move as I constantly reminded him later; while I turned the corner and ran off down another side street and into an alleyway that ran behind the houses.

I heard Ian get caught when he shouted, "It wasn't me! It was all Tony's idea," nothing new here! He was collared by the house owner and was frog-marched back to the house, being dragged along by the man holding Ian by his coat collar. As for me, I collapsed in nervous laughter and had to catch my breath before checking out what had happened to Ian.

Talk about something embarrassing! Ian was dragged back to the house, by his collar and had to face the music. He had to clear the whole lot up, which took him at least an hour. They made him clear up their whole front garden of all the leaves there as well as placing all the leaves into big bags. I waited before creeping back to see if he was ok. As I got close, I peeked out from around the corner at Ian having to shovel all the leaves up. I watched him for a while, making sure there were no other people from the house around, but I couldn't stop laughing at his bad luck.

I called out to him, "Psst," from my "safe distance," but he ignored me and pretended he couldn't hear. I called again, "Psst, Ian, you missed some over there behind you." He, needless to say, was not amused at all. "I'd like to help," I half-shouted, half-whispered, "but I'm so tired from all that running and getting away," to which he gave me the evil eye. I stayed though till he finished and knocked on the front door to let them inspect his cleaning up. We walked home together.

I told him that if he hadn't run straight ahead, he may have gotten away; but some of my wisdom falls on deaf ears. Ian was tired from all that leaf clearing and having to shovel them all up into bags. "You know," I said, "if we had played our cards right and if you hadn't laughed so much, we could have charged them two and six for cleaning up that mess."
But unfortunately, he didn't see the funny side!

Carol Singing

Since Ian and I were both in the St. Thomas's church choir, we could both sing all the words and harmonies for all of the Christmas carols that we learned in church. So we decided on the way back from choir practice one cold evening in mid-December, just before Christmas to try our hand at carol singing to make some extra cash. At that time, in many of the streets in London, there were lots of carol singers and though some were really bad some, I have to admit (like us) they were really good, as we should be since we were part of the church choir.

We got the carol book from church and tried it. At the first house first, we couldn't sing for laughing so much and had to run for it. As time went on, though, we got better and went from door to door singing some terrific harmonies, or so we thought and as the doors opened, we would continue singing, over mouthing the vocals as we had been taught by our choirmaster Mr. Gosling and we even asked for requests, as we found that this upped the ante, getting us more money for our efforts.

We made loads of money and promptly went to the off-license at the side of the Royal Hotel just along from my house to buy as many sweets and pop as we could carry. Though it was freezing, we would sit down and scoff as much as we could eat. We even made up our own words to some of the carols and pretended we were singing in Latin which was a blast.

Ian and I were as close as brothers, but we were also quite competitive, so while carol singing, we would always try to out-sing each other, getting louder and louder. Ian's mom and my dad always thought we were at a late choir practice for Christmas, but we had to make sure we didn't sing too close to our own houses or that Richard didn't get to know; otherwise, he would have wanted some of my money for keeping quiet.

Christmas was always amazing, we were so busy at Scouts and at choir practice twice a week and at weekends in December, we would sing around the local old people's homes and children's hospitals in Hanwell with a small group from the choir. I loved doing that to see the faces of the patients who were always so happy to see us and anyway there were the nurses! We would compare notes as to which nurse was the prettiest and if there was a really pretty nurse, we would sing our very best, drowning out all of the others in the choir.

On Christmas Eve, there were always two services, one at 7:00 p.m. and one at midnight and because we were part of the choir, we were both required to be there. At one of the side chapels in the church, there was a nativity scene with stars and a desert looking just like the real thing and there was a manger with three kings, some animals, a field of sheep with the shepherds and the small town of Bethlehem. It was quite beautiful. All was well at the church until several months later when the vicar decided to have an affair with a local builder's wife, who was always coming to church on Sundays sitting in the front row she was very attractive. He was quickly moved on and we got a new vicar.

For the most part, we were so busy all the time we practically never watched TV. We did watch *Fireball XL 5* and *Four Feather Falls* or *Thunderbirds*. On Saturday nights and I loved *Doctor Who* and *Dixon of Dock Green.*

Saint Paul's Cathedral Choir

Ian and I were picked from our church choir to sing Handel's "Messiah" at St. Paul's Cathedral as a Christmas Special, which was to be broadcasted over BBC radio live that Christmas. We were picked because we could reach "Top C," which for us was a breeze and was the top note in the Hallelujah chorus. We both traveled together on the tube from Boston Manor to St. Paul's and walked the remainder of the distance to the cathedral.

We practiced from October to December in 1962 and the final recital was over three nights the week before Christmas. We were part of a large London Choir that joined the St. Paul's choir for the event, which we sang together with a bunch of apparently famous and professional sopranos, altos, tenors and bass singers who each had the solos.

In front of us was a large orchestra that accompanied our singing and we were conducted by Edouard Nies-Berger a famous conductor and choirmaster at St. Paul's!

We rehearsed every Tuesday evening and as the time to our performance came closer, it became Tuesdays and Thursdays. We robed in one of the crypts under the huge cathedral.

Queen Victoria and Me

Next to where we got changed into our choir clothes was a huge iron funeral carriage. The carriage was made to be drawn by six huge Clydesdales, it had four large-spoked wheels and was all made of black cast iron. The top that held a coffin was very ornate, but we thought it must have been very, very heavy to pull along. We sometimes laid on the platform, pretending to be dead while trying to imagine what it must have been like to actually be in it, but hopefully, we would never find that out.

It had one great use for Ian and I, though, as somewhere to put our sandwiches on during the break. There we were both sitting on the driver's seat, munching away when the Dean of the cathedral came over and told us off for desecrating the carriage. We couldn't understand it; it was old and was not in use at the moment, so what was the big deal?

As we were to find out, the funeral carriage was made for Queen Victoria and her husband Prince Albert, though little did we care about that except that it was great for keeping our sandwiches on while we were practicing and for sitting in the driver's bench seat while eating our sandwiches during the break or when the conductor was going through stuff with the orchestra. Sometimes, no matter how hard we try, we just can't seem to do the right thing!

Anyway, as the time drew near, we were ready for our performance and we were both placed in the front row. Right in front of us was the orchestra and we were next to the cellists.

Finally, it was opening night and Ian and I had agreed to out-sing all of the rest of the choir, which was some fifty people. We pretended that we had a volume control in front of us when we sang the "Hallelujah" chorus. We could both reach "top C" with ease and decided that on that refrain we would gradually get louder and louder as we reached the crescendo, building up to the highest note of the entire performance.

The cellists in front of us all watched as we began the "Hallelujah" chorus refrain, "King of Kings and Lord of Lords" and although we both sang it "normally" on our rehearsal nights, we turned up the volume on the actual performance night to see if we could hear ourselves on the radio following the broadcast of the performance.

We sang the chorus so loud and with so much gusto as we both turned our fingers as if we were turning our volume control up each trying to outdo the other. We were mouthing the words perfectly with really exaggerated syllables like true professional singers. We were grinning from ear to ear as the cellists in front of us were glancing at us out of the corner of their eyes at our outstanding and perfect pitched high notes, or so we preferred to think.

At the end of the performance, we all went down to the crypt, when the conductor told us that was one of the best he had conducted, especially the "Hallelujah" chorus, which was in no small part down to Ian and I.

To sing in Saint Paul's Cathedral and to sing Handel's "Messiah" as choir boys was, even for Ian and I, a huge honor and we were happy that we had been given the opportunity. The special sandwich cart, in the form of Queen Victoria's funeral carriage, placed there just for us, was the icing on the cake and ever since that one Christmas, I have always loved Handel's "Messiah." And when I hear the "Hallelujah" chorus, I go right back to that one moment in time eating our sandwiches on Queen Victoria's funeral carriage.

The London Fog

The London Fog was very real back when I was a child and came down so thick you couldn't see anything three feet in front of you. This was no ordinary fog; this was "smog." Still, there was no getting off school, so we had to walk there anyway. The Internet hadn't been invented, so there was no banner at the bottom of the screen telling us that school was out because of the fog.

What I used to do was to walk along the edge of the pavement with one foot on the road and one foot on the pavement, counting the side roads along the way and having to get right up close to the street signs, which were always located on someone's front wall on the corner of each street. It was unusual being out in that thick "pea-souper." There was absolutely no sound as the fog or, as it was called "the smog," was so dense it deadened all sounds. I quite liked it as I could see if I knew the way to school as if I was "blindfolded."

There were no cars on the roads when the smog came down as none could drive through it; so all was very, very still and even the birds couldn't fly in that thick smog.

The smog was caused by the burning of coal in all the London homes which gave off nasty smoke into the air and when the air pressure was low, with no wind, the London air could not move the heavy, yellow smog which came down. As I walked through it, I used to sing at the top of my voice any song I wanted on the way to and from school and pretended to be a pop singer. I knew all of the words and I was certain that I was an impressive singer; but if I wasn't, I didn't care anyway.

In the early 60s, all the London houses had to change their fires over to clean-burning, or smokeless coal, so London would be rid of the smog which was a killer at the time. This was called the "clean air act," and all of our fireplaces had to be converted so they could burn the clean-burning coke instead of the hard and rough natural coal.

In winter, the flatbed coal truck would slowly pass by traveling down all of the streets, the coalmen would deliver huge heavy black sacks of coal into our coal shed at the back of the house. The men were always covered from head to toe in black coal dust and they wore a leather hat with a neck and shoulder cover that would come down from their head at the back to protect their neck from the sharp pieces of coal in the bags. They would heft the bag that weighed one hundredweight, onto their shoulders from the flatbed of the truck. Sometimes even one on each shoulder then tip them into our coal shed.

The Winter of 1963

One winter's night, in 1963, the snow came down so thick it was three feet high and stacked up all over the streets in drifts. I loved it, no school. I did, however, have my paper round and turned up to do it walking the first footprints in the brand-new snow at 6:00 a.m. on our road. I was the only person out on that day but Richard didn't bother to do his. The paper shop manager was so surprised to see me he gave me double the money for each bag I delivered. I made out like a bandit; off I went to deliver the morning papers trudging through the thick snow. It took me all day and after each round, I went back for another bag of newspapers, getting two and six for each full bag I delivered door to door.

I loved the fresh new snow and loved being the first and only footprints along the now completely quiet roads. Normally, I made ten shillings for the week; but on that day, I made two pounds, which was amazing to me. I bought a new Dinky toy, which I had been looking at for months. It was a silver and black Bentley Continental complete with very real-looking jeweled headlights and suspension that steered if you pressed on one side while rolling the car forward. It was my best toy and was very real-looking. I kept it for years.

When the snow came down like that, I loved all of the white trees and covered streetlamps. The lamps cast a bright glow in the night and all the world was quiet and still. I even remember the lamplighter who would come 'round our street to check on the streetlights in case any did not light. He always had a ladder with him, wider at the bottom and narrower at the top. I watched as he placed the ladder the arms at the side of the street lamp that went out from the lamp and climb up to check on the lamp or repair it if it didn't light properly.

Sometimes I would just go out of the house when I saw him coming and walk with my friend the lamp lighter, chatting as we walked together down my street. There was never any danger at night and at that time London for me was perfect. The lamplighter told me stories of the things he had seen while lighting the lamps and I was fascinated to listen to his stories. Though he was old, at least to me, he climbed up every lamp he needed to without ever getting tired. He wore a flat hat, a scarf around his neck, a coat over his overalls, a pair of leather boots and his name was Tom.

Once every month, we would hear the rag and bone man calling as he came slowly down all of the streets. "rag 'n bone," he would shout, which he repeated as he rode slowly while sitting behind his horse on an old cart full of old broken bicycles, washing wringers and any bits of metal you wanted to give or sell him if he wanted to buy. If not, he would take it anyway for free.

Also, there was a gypsy knife sharpener who would slowly go down the streets, on a gypsy caravan pulled along by a cart-horse. The milkman would also deliver milk and groceries, billing us every week from a book where we had our own page. Our milkman, whose name was Ron, would arrive early in the morning and deliver bottles of gold top, silver top, or blue top milk from Job's Dairy along with any other dairy items we asked for. The service was a little more expensive, but after all, it was delivered door to door and Mom would leave a note in one of the empty bottles that were left outside the front door.

If we missed or needed anything, I would cycle all around the streets to find where the Job's Milk's electric milk float was located to get butter, eggs, or anything we had forgotten to place on the note. I knew his rounds by heart and where to find him at any time of the day. If he was heading back toward my house, I would wait until he set off and hang on to the back of his van while riding my bike for a free lift; he knew I was there but didn't mind at all.

Everything had its own special smell—the night, autumn, the snow, the early morning, our church, the coal, autumn and the London fog. I could close my eyes and know where I was by the scent of it.

As time drifted on and because of Mrs. Osborne, my caseworker from the Middlesex County Council, I had been allowed to go back to Lowestoft for my holidays, which gave Dad a break and gave me some of my roots back again. I loved visiting Auntie and now that I was older, while Beatrice and William were living there, we found plenty to do all summer long. The nurses were becoming more interesting to me now and one nurse in particular called Maureen, who was eighteen seemed very interested in me. I still have a photo of her in her nurse's uniform at aunties. We went out a few nights together and walked along the beach at night.

Beatrice, William and I would go to Kensington Gardens to go on the electric boats which were just up the road from Aunties house

I also had my best "other friend," Beatrice and we did everything together like brother and sister. We would go to the beach, spending all day as often as we could there. Auntie would sometimes take us out in her little car "Arabella," which was a 1937 black Austin Seven convertible, down the coast road for afternoon tea.

Auntie even taught me to drive Arabella when I was just eleven years old. I have a photo that Beatrice took of me driving the car around our driveway until I accidentally left the lights on a caused a flat battery. The car was difficult for me to drive as it had a crash gearbox requiring that I double de-clutch to change gear up and down, but I could only just see over the bonnet. That summer I practiced my driving skills, turning, reversing (though it was difficult for me to see over the folded hood) and became fairly good at maneuvering Arabella. That was one of the best summers at Aunties.

I never let my difficult past affect my having fun!

ANOTHER MOM

A new broom sweeps clean!

TWO YEARS AFTER Mom had died Dad told us both that he was seeing a new girlfriend. Rich and I were enthralled at this news and immediately bombarded him with questions about her. "What's her name? How old is she? Is she pretty? Are you going to marry her? When will we meet her?" Well, after several months, we finally got to meet Jill, Dad's new fiancée, one Sunday afternoon in April. We both got up to the bay window at the front of our house to see if we could see her walking with him down our street.

Dad was forty-two, Jill was only twenty-one. Richard was fourteen and I was now twelve. Jill had red hair and was quite attractive; Richard was mixed in his feelings about her as he was seeing her as replacing his real mom, Joyce. For me, she was my third mother so it was OK by me. But for Richard, it was just two short years since his mom had died. I think he was both excited at having another mom living with us and upset at the short time since she passed away.

Jill came round more often and eventually stayed weekends, arriving on Friday after work with Dad and leaving with him for work on Monday morning. Jill introduced us to her younger sister, Avril, who was a blonde and very different from Jill. She also introduced us to her mother and father whom we called Nan and Pop. I liked both of them, especially Pop. He was very much like a grandfather I had never had; in fact, I didn't know what having a grandfather was really like, but I knew I liked him.

Dad and Jill got married on May 23, then Jill moved in with us permanently from then on. All was well for a while at least. Jill was quite intelligent and did crosswords and read the *Manchester Guardian* and the *Telegraph*.

Jill was quite a strong and dominant personality and soon began to rule the house. Dad seemed happy to have a partner to help him and to be a companion to him. They sat together doing crosswords in the evenings.

I loved Dad; he was very kind and did all he could to stop Richard and I from fighting. I too was very strong. Actually, on reflection, I was stubborn and would never give in and we often got into fights after school. Looking back, it is obvious now that we were both reacting to the events of Mom's death and her replacement by Jill.

Jill and Auntie Sis didn't get along at all, from the moment Jill moved in. Jill was always complaining about her to Dad when he got home from work. Jill began a campaign to get rid of Aunt Sis, even though she had looked after Richard and I for so long after Mom died and had looked after Dad in his very needy times.

Auntie Sis had cooked, cleaned and did all our washing and we never even thought about it. She used to ask me to get shopping, cycling down to Hanwell to get groceries. Aunty Sis had been a real surrogate mom during these years when I was nine to twelve years old until she came up against Jill. Sis had left her home and her life in Manchester to come down to London to look after us all when dad asked her to.

Shortly after Jill had come to live with us, Richard and I heard sobbing from Aunt Sis's room. We knocked and entered and saw Aunt Sis in tears. We wanted to know what was wrong. "I am moving back to Manchester," she told us and continued sobbing. "She (Jill) doesn't want me here anymore and I thought this was my home." She gave your dad an ultimatum, her or me." I didn't know what to do for her. I was so sad, but I could do nothing about this. One didn't question Jill about these things as it would lead to a screaming and shouting fit, which by the way happened quite often.

Finally, only a few weeks after that tearful day, the day came when Aunt Sis moved out. She kissed us both goodbye and walked off down the street in her coat and her "Ena Sharples" hat, never looking back and never to return. I was never to see my lovely Aunt Sis again.

Dad called Richard and I into the front room only six months later and told us that Aunt Sis, his sister, had died. Rich and I knew she had died from a broken heart. I never forgave Jill as I knew what she had done to orchestrate minor issues that she had created to make Aunt Sis look like a troublemaker. I often thought of Aunt Sis and hoped she was in a better place there with the angels. Jill didn't bat an eyelid and life went on, another small door to close but I missed Aunt Sis.

I soon realized that life just keeps moving on and there's nothing we can do to stop it. For me, as I have said before, it was all normal that people around me either died or went away and I was after all quite used to it by now, as these constant changes were after all part of my early life.

Life at home settled down once again but living with Jill in the house was very difficult as she didn't get on with either Richard or me.

I couldn't help feeling that Dad had been conned into getting married and spoke of this to Rich. He thought the same but also said, "She's here to stay and as long as Dad is happy, that's all we can hope for." I, of course, thought about what he had said and agreed with him, which I didn't do very often.

For two years, life moved on with Jill, Rich and me battling over every little thing. Life got difficult with Richard and I fighting almost every night when we got home from school before Jill or Dad got home from work.

In winter 1962 Dad became very ill with bronchitis. London had had a bad winter with heavy snow and fog. Dad soon became too ill to go to work and was taken to hospital five miles away. He stayed there for what seemed like weeks and weeks. I cycled over to see him every Saturday afternoon after I had reluctantly done my mammoth number of chores and saw him steadily getting worse.

He was let out of hospital in December to spend Christmas at home with us. Little did Rich or I know that this was to be the last Christmas we would ever have together as a family with Dad.

I thought that all would be OK again at home, not realizing God's plan for me had changed yet again. Immediately after Christmas, Dad was admitted back into hospital but this time into an intensive care unit in Acton Hospital. Again, I went to see him as school had commenced after the Christmas holidays. But now he was in an oxygen tent and looked so very weak he couldn't recognize me. His breathing was very shallow and ragged and seemed to be getting worse and worse.

His condition worsened into double pneumonia, affecting both of his lungs, making his condition extremely serious.

I went back to school after New Year, but then on January 7th, I was called to Mr. O'Brian, the headmaster's, office, which was normally to get the cane; but this was different. "You have to go home immediately, Tony. Your father is gravely ill," he told me, so I left school immediately and walked home. When I got home at around 10:00 a.m., Jill, Rich and I went immediately to see Dad, leaving by taxi as we had no car at that time.

When we arrived at Acton Hospital, the atmosphere was all wrong for me; the nurses and hospital staff were calm and spoke softly to us. I was told I could go in and see Dad, this time though he was gasping for every breath he took and could not focus at all but was staring and gasping. It was awful; my lovely dad, who I loved, who had looked after me and had fought to keep us together, was so sick now. He didn't know I was even there. Jill and Rich came in, a few minutes later, to join me; but Dad died at 11:00 a.m. while we were there with him. I felt desolate once again, so sad now at losing Dad. I remember putting my arm around Rich and saying, "It's just you and me now." We both disliked Jill and we did not look forward to spending time with her without dad.

Once again, I had no one to talk to about how desolate I now felt at losing another parent. I loved Dad; he was everything to me. I loved him for keeping us together and being able to keep me in his family. But once again, I kept my feelings to myself and once again, I now felt completely alone and had to find a way to close yet another door and move on. I wouldn't allow myself to show how I felt, I didn't know how to as I was becoming used to having to move on from people I loved who were gone.

Life to me seemed like a series of turbulent events, just as I was learning to trust people who were close to me, they were yanked out of my life. I didn't understand what I may have done wrong, so I just kept going and had to put these bad things behind me.

The day Dad had died, Jill took us home and told me to go back to school "immediately," as I was not needed at home. I couldn't understand, that on leaving school to go to see Dad, I was now returning without a Dad. I walked slowly back to school in a daze and arrived just after lunch minus one parent.

I was numb with the loss and found it difficult to focus on anything at school. I sat there quietly keeping to myself, thinking about Dad not being with me anymore, not wanting to show my emotions in front of my class, even if I knew what emotion I should feel and I was not going to cry. I was deeply sad but was afraid that if I showed how I felt, I would show everyone my true feelings and I couldn't do that because I had to be strong, always!

During that afternoon break, on Monday, 7 January, I was walking with one of my friends, Tommy Costello, I told him that my Dad had just died "this morning at 11:00 a.m." (always the details).
He stopped and looked at me, in shock, saying, "Tony, you're kidding. Your dad just died and you're here at school." I said, "Yes, that's what I had to leave school for. I went to see him in hospital one last time and sadly he just died right while I was there."

Tommy said he was so sorry and said, "Why are you back here at school, Tony? If my dad had died, I would be at home." It's funny how you remember some things as clearly as if they had happened just today, but I remembered this one thing in that way and even exactly where we were when I told him. I appreciated his concern but asked that he please keep it to himself as I didn't want to appear needy or weak. I kept up the brave front while feeling empty inside. I blamed Jill for this feeling and could never, ever forgive her for not letting me be at home that morning with Rich to help us both get through this very sad time, but Jill didn't care it was now about her.

I didn't want to go home from school that day, as it was so sad at home and the atmosphere was dreadful. Rich was crying his eyes out and was sobbing the whole time. The curtains were closed in our house for the second time now. Jill seemed to cope just fine and took complete control of all matters. Rich and I didn't know who to talk to or what to think.

We did have each other and spent hours in our bedroom together over the next few weeks, just sitting there saying nothing, putting a wall around us of quiet thoughts with our memories. That was one of our really close times together. I closed the door in my mind, as I had done each other time someone I loved had died, or when I was in that awful place with my stepdad in Acton. I had to move on with my life once again I had no choice; though I was scared that I might be moved into another children's home but I would cross that bridge if it happened.

Life Without Dad

Life once again slowly settled down for me. I began to go out at night and skipped going to Scouts and instead found other things to do instead. Just what I need, I remember thinking—a little fun in my life and I made new friends at my school, Bordeston Secondary Modern School for Boys."

Jill was up to her old tricks and went to work in the mornings, leaving home at 7:00 a.m. and locked me and Rich out of our house to wait for school time on the street, which wasn't until eight-thirty. The neighbors didn't like that and let me wait inside their house as soon as she turned the corner if it was raining.

I had other plans though and took the front door key out of Mom's handbag and had another one cut at the hardware shop on Boston Parade just down the road from our house. I kept it well hidden in the front garden hidden from Jill. Rich and I would sit on our small front wall, wait till she went to work, wave goodbye like good little boys; then as soon as she went 'round the corner at the top of our road to catch the Piccadilly line tube at Boston Manor station, we would get the key out from under a stone in the front garden and let ourselves back into the house. Many good and interesting things were to be found under a stone in a front garden as you will see later.

One of my new friends, Wally (his real name was Alan Walsh), became great friends with me and we would go out and climb into people's backyards, go scrumping for apples, often getting chased out of people's gardens by dogs or house owners (I was always being chased).

Generally, we did as much as we could to have fun. Wally only had only a mom and no father. I didn't know why and didn't ask.

I was, however, going down the wrong path now, angry at how I was treated by Jill after losing Dad and I lost interest in many things I had loved before. Ian had been moved out of Bordeston by his mom and started going to Hounslow College, so he wasn't around at school anymore and before he left, he was having math tutoring by our teacher, Mr. Cardiff.

The next thing I knew was that I had to start going to the Ealing Child Guidance Center in Ealing Broadway. That was a hoot. I had to look at all these stupid cards with smudges and blobs of black ink on them and tell a counselor what they reminded me of. "A dog crapping," or "Just a blob," or anything I could think of that was not what I thought they wanted me to say. I don't know where this led to; but I was aware that Mrs. Osborne, my child care officer, came 'round to see me more and more often.

Finally, one Saturday morning, Jill told me I had to go away to boarding school in Cheltenham and would be leaving after the summer holidays. I spent months begging her not to make me go and offering to be a good boy, though I wasn't a bad boy, I was just reacting to what she represented. Rich and I knew she had married dad to get the house and we also knew there was nothing we could do about this.

Nothing made any difference; I was going and that was that. "So how often will I be home?" I asked. "Summer holidays, Easter and Christmas and that's all and only if I decide that I want you back," she told me.

Shortly before I was to leave for boarding school, Pop, Jill's father, died. I was once again sad that yet another person that I loved being with had died. Pop committed suicide and I never knew why. He was a printer and had bad eczema, maybe that was it, but I closed that door and moved on. I spoke to Rich and said to him that he would have to be alone now in the house with Jill. He didn't like it, but there was nothing he could do. I realize now that Rich must have been scared of what was to happen to him, though I didn't realize it at the time.

When circumstances are out of our control, we have to 'go with the flow' and do our best to make good of the things that life throws at us in order to get by and move on with life.

BATTLEDOWN MANOR

Another dramatic change in my childhood that I would deal with it regardless.

SEPTEMBER 1993 was being shipped off to boarding school. Jill said goodbye at the front door, kissed the air and told me how to get to the coach stop, a two-mile walk, to the Uxbridge Road, so off I went. I struggled with my suitcase and made it to the coach stop, having to frequently stop along the way to put my case down for a rest. I wish they had invented wheels for cases at that time. The black-and-white coach finally arrived and off I went to boarding school. The journey was around four hours with a stop halfway at Stokenchurch in the Cotswold's.

When I arrived at Cheltenham's main bus terminal, I was met by a tall military-looking man with a handlebar mustache, his name was Bernard J Ward and he was the principal of Battledown Manor. Mr. Ward asked me who I was, ticked off my name, then informed me who he was and told me to "go and wait by the car." The car was a beautiful black Jaguar Mark 9 and looked like a Bentley. The Jag, as we called it, had red leather seats and had a unique smell of leather and petrol and I loved it. It had walnut trays that folded out of the back of the front seats. Two other boys were on the black-and-white coach with me, but I didn't know them yet.

So three of us were taken to "Battledown Manor" in Charlton Kings, just outside Cheltenham, we arrived late afternoon on a Sunday in September 1963, me, Bobby Galvin and Seamus Noon.

The boarding school was a large-old manor house on acres of wooded and hilly grounds. Battledown Manor sat on top of a hill and looked very imposing as it stood solitary looking out over the Cotswold Hills. It was huge and had leaded widows all 'round on every window with gray flag-stoned walls. A large oak front door was set back into a large grey stone porch. It got its name from a battle that had taken place on the hill behind the school six hundred years before.

My first impression once inside was of a big difference from what I was used to at home. I suppose this move was because Jill Wanted me out of the house. Well, whatever. I was here now and had to get on with it. One of my gifts was to be able to deal with sudden changes and new places to live in and to call "home" and now helped me once again and so here I was and I had to deal with it.

As I entered the main hall, I saw it was paneled all the way up the great staircase and all the way onto the first floor. There were old paintings on the walls and the image was exactly as one would have imagined a boarding school to be. I thought as I looked around, *this will be home for me now, so I might as well make the best of it.* Outside the main house, at the back, was a courtyard where stables, outhouses and a flagstone-paved backyard next to the stables, overlooking the kitchen and "wardroom."

Above the stables was a large apartment. The roof of the stables was covered in moss and the main house had several tall chimneys on the roof. At the back, in the courtyard was the entrance door that we were to use which went into the "wardroom" where all our shoes, coats and hats were kept and where we were expected to change before entering the manor. The "wardroom" led through into a large kitchen with an Aga cooking stove. The kitchen was always warm and inviting and I liked it in there (that was where the food was).

I was immediately shown to my dorm, on the first floor, sharing it with several other boys. I was told which was my bed then I had to go downstairs when the gong sounded, for dinner. Dinner comprised two half slices of toast, a cup of tea and a poached egg! I was starving, having traveled from Ealing on a four-hour coach trip. We then had to stand up and be introduced to all the other boys.

I sat next to a Black boy called Bobby Galvin, who had arrived earlier that day with me but who had been at the school for six months and knew the ropes. Bobby and I quickly became friends and I learned that he was from inner-city London and was there because he had no real home anymore, as his dad and mom couldn't look after him. I decided not to ask any questions.

Two of the older boys there were Shaunty Bahador, who came from Hanwell close to my home and David Dadsie, who didn't like me on sight. Bobby warned me to stay clear of these two older boys as they were trouble. Like I cared!

Well, life settled down for the next period in my life. I was to attend a local school in the lower, poor part of Cheltenham, where I was quite different from the local boys. Many of my new friends from day school didn't even have socks and often came to school wearing jeans and no school uniform at all because their parents did not have the money. I wasn't used to that since it was an absolute necessity at Bordeston school in Ealing.

I cycled to my day school from Charlton Kings, which was a ride six miles all downhill, across the other end of town, all the way to school and of course six miles uphill all the way back.

I was placed in a class where the local boys seemed dim to me. I was classed as eighteen months advanced for my age, big deal; it didn't help me at all. It made my schoolwork boring as I knew all of the stuff being taught having done it eighteen months before!

So anyway, Dadsie and Shaunty picked on me most of the time and I always gave back as hard as I got it from them. After all, I had been used to an older brother who had taught me how to look after myself.

Dadsie would often lie in wait for me while I was walking through the school and would pounce when I was unaware. It would always lead to a fight and we would both be in trouble. Apart from that though, things settled down quickly for me and I got used to being thrust into a completely different lifestyle of life at boarding school.

To get to the school from the main road meant walking up a long tree-lined lane called Greenway Lane that was unlit at night. I went to night school activities for art and other stuff, which I didn't mind at all as it got me out of Battledown Manor and meant I could be alone to and from Elmfield School where my evening classes were cycling there and back.

I loved cycling to and from school at night and would walk up Greenway Lane, listening to the wind in the trees and watching fascinated at the way the nighttime clouds moved silently across the sky, lit by the moonlight. Sometimes I would just sit quietly at the side of the road and smell the scent in the air listening to the small night sounds all around me. I often shone my cycle lamp out across the fields to see the many pairs of eyes caught in my beam. I would then switch it off and switch it back on to see which eyes had moved, only to freeze again and stare at my light beam.

I was only scared of the dark at first, then I realized I could "tune in" to the night and my surroundings and I wasn't afraid at all. I became at one with the night sounds and if I moved quietly, I became part of everything around me.

At my new school, they were fascinated with my very proper and excellent English, thanks to Auntie and would listen intently as I talked noting the difference between my accent and their west-country accents. However, there was a gang of around seven rough kids, led by a boy named Robinson. Well, Robinson never led any trouble directly but always steered the others to cause trouble, especially for me as I was from London and different.

One day, in January, that first winter after I had arrived, it had been snowing and we were all walking back from football even though the fields were frozen. I was smashed in the side of my head by a piece of ice thrown at me full force by a little red-haired loudmouth called Ginger. Though it hurt like hell and made my ear bleed, I stopped walking and turned to face him. and his buddies as they all caught up with me and my friends. When he got alongside me, I said very quietly, "If you do that one more time, I'm going to knock you out."

"Oh yeah?" he said loudly to impress his gang, "You and whose army?" At which point, my two friends, Dave Soule and Nigel Rich began to distance themselves from me they didn't want a fight. I remembered someone, maybe my brother Rich, saying to me to always go for the loudest and biggest and take him out first.

Ginger looked at his "gang" who were daring him to do it again and picked up another piece of ice and threw it as hard as he could. It caught me in the side of my head again, so I turned toward him, not showing any sign of what I was going to do, I walked right up to him slowly and deliberately and punched him as hard as I could, catching him full in the face. He went down like a sack of potatoes, with his nose broken and with blood all over his face. He laid there in the snow, out cold.

I then turned to the others that were with him that had been leading him on and squared up to all of them and as cool as I could, though I didn't feel cool at all and looked Robinson right in the eye. I pointed right at his face and said, "What about you? Do you want the same too?" And as I said it, I moved right in his face, daring him to do or say anything. I was at the point of not caring now as I had committed and as Rich once said to me, "Tony, once you commit, you can't back down . . . ever!"

No one had ever squared up to these kids and they were now unsure of "the new kid." Fortunately, they backed down. I didn't think I could take them all, but I knew one thing: if they decided to start, I would take Robinson right out in the first second. Images of my time being beaten up in Acton flashed before me and I knew "that's not happening to me ever again."

After that though we became good friends and Ginger treated me with respect. He told me later that he didn't know what hit him, saying that I was so fast that he wouldn't ever do that again. But I was not out to prove myself and told him of what had happened to me when I was eight and I told him I would never let that happen to me again. I didn't like that feeling afterward though as I never have liked hurting anyone, but sometimes in life, you have to make a stand.

I got in with another bad crowd in Cheltenham, who I used to go out with on "wanders." My new friends were John Brown and Dave (I never knew Dave's second name or even if he had one). They came from very poor families and never had money, socks, or sometimes even a shirt, only wearing old worn-out jackets. John Brown was a scruff with dark curly hair, while Dave was a blonde scruff with a mop of wavy hair.

During these "wanders," they would case out a block of flats to break into them to steal things. They could be in and out of the flats in what seemed like a few seconds. They would come running out to where I was standing, then we legged it down the road as fast as we could. Though I never broke into anyone's house, I loved the excitement of being with these two. We had fun doing everything and anything we wanted. I took a change of clothes and kept my uniform in my duffel bag so no one would recognize my school. I had to change again on the way home before I got back to Battledown Manor.

Rewarded For Excellence.

After that first year at my new school, I was awarded a holiday to Austria over Easter for getting excellent results at school. It was to be a three-week holiday, leaving by train, from London through France and on to Austria high up in the Alps. I was with a load of other children who had also won the trip. It was brilliant as I had never been abroad before. We stayed in a mountain hotel high up in the Alps in a town called Innermanzing. My trip was because Mr. Ward had put a good word in for me with the Ealing County Council after seeing my excellent school report. The ultra-cool part was that there was a local Gasthof (hotel and bar) where we could order beer, at fourteen years old! Smooth! Once again, I found myself loving the food and at breakfast, we had chocolate-flavored semolina, which I loved and once again, I managed to get seconds and thirds enough to keep me going till lunchtime. Each evening, a group of us would go to the local Gasthof to have some beers and have a good time. We certainly didn't get drunk and we were treated like young adults for once, which was very different from how we were treated at our different schools.

Rich At Last!

One sunny afternoon, as me, Bobby Galvin and Michael Shepherd (another boy from Battledown Manor) were walking back from the local sweet shop, we saw a van parked on the side of the lane with the back doors open. Inside there was a chocolate display box, the kind that would normally have lots of bars of Cadbury's chocolate in. The three of us looked around and saw no one inside the van or anywhere near.

As we were deciding what to do, Michael suddenly reached into the back of the van and grabbed the box, whereupon we all legged it up Greenway Lane as fast as we could. We ran up the lane, along our long driveway and into the woods next to our school. We sat on the ground behind the low Cotswold wall that surrounded our old swimming pool in the middle of the woods.

Excitedly, we all peered into the box as Michael opened it up and saw not chocolate bars but loads of money! There were bags of coins, pennies, half-crowns, tanners and two bobs, all in separate little brown paper money bags. There were also lots of banknotes a whole stack of them, and a pile of checks.

We couldn't believe our luck. "Let's count it all and split it three ways." We all agreed, not even thinking about the consequences of what we had just done. The total of the money we had just pinched came to three hundred and eighty-four pounds, which in 1964 and for a bunch of boarding school kids on two and sixpence pocket money a week was an absolute bloody fortune.

Well, pretty soon, we realized what could happen, so we warned Michael, saying "Don't get caught and whatever you do, don't spend any of it at the local sweet shop down the road. Otherwise, she will call the old man and we'll all get caught."

So we hid the box, with all the money inside, behind a stone in the wall by the old swimming pool. The Cotswold stone walls comprise of flat Cotswold stones laid on top of one another to a height of about four feet high and were not ever cemented.

Our wall was around the concrete swimming pool, in the middle of the woods and was a perfect hiding place.

We began to pull stones out of the wall until we found one with a space behind it big enough to hide our stash and placed the stone back into the wall with the box of money hidden behind it. We marked our "stone" with a scratch mark.

Later the next day, which was Sunday, Bobby and I went to the wall in the woods and took several bags of coins. I don't know what Bobby did with his, but I cycled on down the hill toward Cheltenham and hid the bags of money in several front gardens, inside hedges or under stones where they would not be found. I hid around fifty pounds in all, remembering which front garden's I hid the money in.

Well, I went to my day school and took John Brown and Dave out for a slap-up lunch at their favorite café, saying to the waitress, "The lunch is on me." I did this for two weeks, buying them things they wanted and enjoyed doing it. We bought fountain pens, lighters, bottles of cider, cigarettes and anything we wanted. Though I didn't smoke initially, I learned very quickly. I had loads of stuff, as did Bobby, but we didn't know what Michael did, until later.

Around three weeks later, as I was coming back on Saturday afternoon from a "spending spree" with my friends from the bad side of town, I walked through the front door only to hear that one sound that can freeze the blood "Tony Moore!" I heard my name being shouted as I entered the main hall, so I looked around.

There sitting at his desk in the front hall was Mr. Ward, our principal He strode over to me and grabbed me by my collar, dragging me through the hall and into his study shutting the door behind us. There sitting on the sofa was Michael and Bobby. Michael was crying and I knew what had just happened.

The old man, as we called Mr. Ward, asked us what we knew about a large amount of stolen money taken from the back of a van some four weeks before while parked along Greenway Lane one Saturday afternoon.

I attempted to deny all knowledge of this heinous act and began talking as fast as I could to deny everything. "It wasn't me. I was never there. How could you think I would do something like that? I don't know what you're talking about."

Well, just as I was getting into my full stride of complete and utter denial, Bobby quietly told me that they had told the old man everything. "He's even been to our secret hiding place and has got all the remaining cash." "All of it?, great" I exclaimed. "So what happens now?" I was cool as a cucumber.

"The police are on their way from Cheltenham police station and will be here in a few minutes," the old man said. He sat and stared at me for a long time. "I thought better of you, Tony. I didn't believe you could be part of this massive theft," he said. I couldn't think of anything to say, so I said nothing at all. I was, however, furiously thinking, *How can I get out of this?*

I can honestly say I wasn't scared or intimidated by the two huge cops that arrived to interview us, but I had no idea what was going to happen.

They took us downtown in a black police car and split us up into different rooms to be "interviewed." On the way downtown, I very quietly said to Bobby and Michael, "Whatever you do, don't tell them about the booze or the cigarettes, otherwise, we'll be in even more trouble." Once at the police station, a rather drab place with opaque windows between each room, linoleum floors and old drab metal furniture. We were to be interviewed about what we had done.

They began to question me, so I had to make up all sorts of stuff I had never bought as I still had about fifty pounds stashed in various places.

Eventually, as I couldn't tell them all of the things that I had bought with the money—the cigs and the booze—I had to admit that I had money stashed in various places along the route into town from the school.

"All right," they said, "show us." So off we went for the long walk back to Charlton Kings. A police car was following us, with me walking between the two cops on either side. As we walked along the way back to Battledown Manor, I stopped and told them, "There behind that wall in the front garden under a big stone on the left" So in they went and lifted the stone and underneath it, there was a bag of cash. Then farther along, I stopped again and told them, "Under the hedge on the right," they reached under the hedge and found another bag.

In all, I had twenty hiding places for my "stash." By the time we were finished, they were both chuckling and were truly amazed that I could remember all of the places where I had hidden the money.

Finally, when I had managed to account for most of what I had said I had spent, they took me back to the school.

When we arrived back, the old man was both furious and intrigued at the audacity of what we had done. Audacious or not, we were gated, grounded, for a month and we had to do chores. My chores were potato peeling for the whole school and shoe cleaning every day and every weekend for four weeks. I sat by myself in the kitchen, peeling whole sacks of spuds, or again out by myself in the wardroom shining shoes. I manage to get covered in shoe polish, black, brown, or oxblood all over my hands on my face as I wiped the sweat from my forehead and all over my clothes.

Well, I still had around sixty pounds left, which I had accounted for in my statements to the two cops, but still had hidden away This all happened around eight weeks before we were to break up for summer hols. I knew we would be searched just in case we had stashed money for the holidays so I hid my money in two places, one was in my sock, carefully rolled around my ankle. The other was in my Brownie 127 camera, inside where the film was supposed to be. At the back of the camera was a small red window showing you how many pictures you had used. So I carefully rolled the banknotes inside the camera around the film winder and stretched a one-pound note across the red film window so that the "number 1" fitted right behind the small red window. I then very carefully closed the camera and reviewed my handiwork; it was perfect, undetectable, and showed that there was picture number 1 in the frame ready to be used. Boy, would I make an excellent master criminal or even a master spy! Even Dadsie and Bobby had a new respect for me after knowing what we had done. Michael though was sent away to another school as he had a history of stealing stuff that went way back. We were never to see or hear from him again.

The last day of school finally arrived before summer hols. I had my final stash well hidden in my sock and in my camera. As I was sitting at breakfast, on the last day of school, next to Bobby (as always) I was feeling rather nervous. The old man was sitting at the head table and kept looking at my feet making me even more nervous.

Then his voice boomed out across the breakfast room, "Tony Moore!" I froze when he said, "Stand up, boy." So I stood trying to be cool as I could. He looked at my feet directly where some of my stash was stuffed down my sock. "Why are your shoelaces untied, boy? Tie them up and get on with your breakfast," he said loudly. I looked down and saw what he had been looking at the whole time, my as usual untied shoelaces. I bent down, relieved that it was just that and not that he had seen my stash so I re-tied my shoelaces, carefully checking out my stash and flattened the money in my sock, pushing it further down.

We left school for the summer holidays and I was taken to the black-and-white bus station in Mr. Ward's beautiful black Jag. I was so happy and relieved I could hardly wait to get home and spend my last stash. I was going to have a summer of all summers and I was rich beyond measure!

Once home, Jill read me the riot act, saying nothing good would ever come of me! Rich, however, wanted to know if I had any money left. I knew he would go through my things to find any money I had left. He never found my money and I had the best holiday I ever had, with loads of money to spend all holiday. I bought as many sweets and comics as I could and bought a one-foot-high stack of used Marvel comics, negotiating a deal with the shop owner. I spent the next week reading comics and eating sweets. Brilliant!

The Burning Hedge

During my last year at Battledown Manor, I had the chore of mowing the front lawn with Bobby on our motorized walk-behind mower. So we went and got the lawnmower from where it was kept in the stables behind the school along with the five-gallon can of petrol and walked them both to the large sloping front lawn in front of the house. We set the petrol can down next to the long hedgerow that separated the front of the school from the front lawn. As the manor house had been built on a hill overlooking Charlton Kings, the view was imposing, with a clear view of some fifteen miles to the Malvern hills on the horizon.

Well, we started to mow the large front lawn in stripes. When we got partway through mowing we decided to have a smoke break. We crouched down hidden from view of the school, behind the hedge on the freshly mowed grass and sat down to smoke. I brought the cigs and Bobby, the matches. As I lit up, gazing over the fine job we had done, though some of the mowed lines were, in fact, a little crooked, I tossed the match over my shoulder and began to enjoy the moment, after all the work was quite hard and the lawn was huge. As luck would have it and unbeknownst to me, I threw the match behind me and it landed right in the open can of petrol.

What a brilliant shot! But what happened next was nothing short of "explosive!" All of a sudden, we heard a whoosh as the petrol can exploded into flame. We both jumped up fast as we could not sure what to do. The fire immediately caught the whole front hedgerow alight, as the flames shot up high into the air. The flames were as high as thirty to forty feet as they ignited the very dry old hedgerow.

We both started yelling, "fire! fire!" But we needn't have bothered though as the flames shot straight up to the level of the upstairs windows and could be seen from as far as the Malvern's, which must have been fifteen or twenty miles away.

Everyone came rushing out as Mr. Ward immediately started barking out orders like a real professional fire chief. "Quickly now! You boys, go and get water in anything that will hold it, make a supply chain and fast!" The flames burned so hot and high that they began to bow all of the leaded windows outward all over the front of our school. "The damn windows are melting!" Mr. Ward shouted and we all worked even more furiously to put out the fire. Bobby and I quickly put a story together that a spark must have ignited the petrol vapors. The fire was so hot and the flames were scary, it was like looking at a column of sheer flame thirty feet high.

Well, eventually, the flames were put out. and we surveyed the damage. The once beautiful old hedgerow was now a series of smoldering stumps that separated the half-mowed lawn from the Manor. Worse still, the front bay windows were now uneven and severely bowed out by the heat. Though we didn't get into trouble, too much, we were however gated again and had to do even more chores. There was no proof of what we had done by smoking; so we got away with it. Bobby's face and my face were now both the same black color as I was covered in soot from head to toe.

I visited Battledown Manor many years later with Ian and the windows were still all bowed outwards; but the hedgerow had been superseded by a row of rose bushes, which I thought was a vast improvement on the original hedge, so I knew it had happened and it was not a figment of my imagination. The rose bushes were a great improvement, so apart from the windows, I thought our handiwork was an improvement.

I learned also that fires are bloody scary!

A LAST VISIT FROM JILL

If the actions of someone you know don't make sense, it's because what you know is probably not the entire story!

SOME WEEKS BEFORE Easter in 1965, now 3 years since dad had died, Jill wrote me a letter announcing that she had decided to come to Cheltenham to see me for a weekend. She had never shown any interest in what I was doing at school, but it was OK that she would come to see me, as long as she brought me money or sweets. "I can only spend a day there as I am far too busy and must get back to Ealing," she announced on arrival at Battledown Manor.

Once she arrived, she made a brief nod to me, kissing the air between us and promptly went into Mr. Ward's study where she stayed for a while, leaving me standing in the hallway with no greeting at all. When she came out, she seemed very flushed and informed me she had to go back to London immediately and promptly turned on her heel and left just like that. I thought, *OK, I guess she didn't want to see me after all*. There was no love lost between us and as long as she wasn't telling me off, shouting at me, or demanding that I do chores, I was OK with that.

Sometime later on a Saturday afternoon, shortly after that whirlwind visit, when Mr. Ward was making a curry, he called me into the large kitchen and asked if I would like to help him. This was a huge honor as I loved his curry and none of us boys had ever been asked to help him. He was preparing the most incredible chicken curry in a huge pot and was leaning over the Aga range as he started talking to me. This time, he wasn't talking at me as he usually did but was talking to me as a grown-up.

"Tony," he began, "what would you do if you had the money to do something with?" I replied, "Depends on how much money we are talking about," I said "Well," he said, "what if you had, say, one hundred pounds? and of course, I realize that with your past escapades, this is probably a paltry sum, but what if it was yours and it was legal?" As he said the word "legal" he turned to look at me. Now one hundred pounds was a lot of money at that time, so I thought for a while and replied, "Probably I'd buy a scooter." I waited for his mood to become "normal."

"Alright," he said. (what!) "But we'll have to have some ground rules about this if we go ahead." I couldn't believe what I'd just heard. "Sorry, Sir, did you say yes?" He ignored my response and continued, "You must pass your driving test and learn to drive it properly, do you understand?" I immediately agreed!

"Where is the money coming from?" I asked. "Let's say it was a gift well deserved," he said and looked at me with a long serious and thoughtful stare. He went on to explain that it was money from Jill and left it at that.

I couldn't think why she would ever give me money, but I was to find out pretty soon. I thought nothing of it and couldn't wait to tell Bobby my news.

My First Set of Wheels

This was now 1975 and in England at that time, we had mods and rockers. I was definitely a mod. Mods were those that liked fashionable clothes and cool hairstyles wearing long parka coats, with a hood often edged with fur. They all drove around on modified Vespa's or Lambretta (Lambo's) scooters.

I already had a parka and used it when I was cycling into town. I was fifteen and was just old enough to drive a scooter. Mods were everywhere. The other group, the rockers, rode motorbikes and wore leather gear. Though I liked motorbikes, I liked the mod look much more.

Well, I was going to move up from being a look-alike mod, riding a pushbike, with my full-length parka complete with fur on the hood, to a full-fledged, fully loaded mod and with my own scooter!

I told Bobby and the news got all over the school, suddenly I was the coolest boy in school. Dadsie hated it, but I was fine with that. There was nothing he wanted more than a scooter and I was getting one.

So I spent the next weeks poring over the Exchange and Mart making sure I did it when Dadsie was around so he would be so envious. I was looking for a scooter that I could afford. Finally, I settled on a model LD, which was a Lambretta and a very plain one at that, looked like something an old man would be riding, I knew I would do it up with high-chrome exhaust pipes, crash bars with loads of mirrors all over the front. It would be so cool and I would be one of them, an actual mod with my own wheels.

After I bought it, I drove it carefully up the driveway and into one of the stables at the back ready for its transformation into my very own mod mobile! I took it apart and began planning the transformation of my very plain "Lambo," converting it into my mod mobile. It cost me fifty-seven pounds and with the money I had leftover, I transformed it into my dream machine. I bought the best, noisiest, flared tube silencer I could find and fitted it to the engine. It fitted to the cylinder head and went upward at an angle from the side of the scooter sticking up in the air with a wide chrome tailpipe that was flared out toward the end and made a sound you could hear for miles, with a sweet spot that roared.

I modified the engine a little to get more speed, by removing the cylinder head and filing out the cavity and it could do eighty-five miles per hour, plenty fast enough for me. It was weird though, not having to cycle to move along; all I had to do was twist the throttle and away I went. So bloody cool!

I never felt so proud as I did when it was finally finished, it was all my own work and I made my first trip out from the Battledown driveway. I cruised slowly, not wanting to make any mistakes as all of the other boys were out front watching me, or upstairs peering out of the upstairs windows. Mr. Ward came out to survey my handiwork and harrumphed when he saw all the chrome. He did say though that I had done a fine job, but that I must be careful driving it as he thought they were a little unstable. "Such tiny wheels," he remarked, looking at what I had done to improve the drab little machine.

The scooter was red, white and black and had chrome everywhere; I had to be careful not to open up the throttle too much in front of Mr. Ward as he might finally flip. I met some of my school friends in downtown Cheltenham who also had scooters, so we rode all over town in a small group, making a very loud noise.

On weekends, we would go out in a convoy of up to six scooters, all done up with mirrors, crash bars and loud silencers. Mine was the coolest as I had spent the most time doing it up and had the most chrome (that was the measure of a truly brilliant scooter). I can still feel the eyes of all those watching us as we rode through town, noisy like hell but so cool. As we rode, we leaned back, with our feet riding on the edge of the running board looking very cool.

A learned what it is to succeed even in a boarding school

ANOTHER HOME

When one door closes another can slam in your face.

A FEW WEEKS later it was half term, between Easter and summer hols and I went home for the week this time but not on the Scooter as I had too much stuff to carry home. I got off the coach in Hanwell and dragged my suitcase home, a walk of about two miles, reaching my front door at 107 Clitherow Avenue.

I knocked on the door, a lady who I didn't know answered it. "Hi," I said, "who are you?" As I promptly went to enter my house, walking past her and into the front hallway. "I live here," she said. "Who are you?" I dropped my bag in the hallway and turned to her as she said, "Oh dear, I think I know who you are, you're Tony, aren't you?"

As I stood there in the hallway, she told me she had bought the house from a Mrs. Whitehead and had moved in several weeks before. "Oh," I said, "well I guess that's that." (I was shocked but didn't show it) I picked up my bag and promptly left. I didn't want to make any more of an issue, though I was acutely embarrassed and felt stupid, but I wanted to be away from there as soon as possible. "What will you do? Where are you going?" she called out as I quickly walked off down the street, what used to be my street, but now it was no more and so this would be for the last time. Another door to close!

So let's just hold on a mo! I'm fifteen, just got home from boarding school at half term, someone else has bought my house, moved in and I have nowhere to live! Worse still, no one had told me! I felt stupid that I didn't foresee this happening or that, it was the sole reason for Jill's quick visit, not to meet me but to see Mr. Ward. She had said nothing at all to me at that visit, though she did tell me in a phone call later that she had met someone else and maybe living with him sometime in the future.

My home once again was gone, so I did the only thing I could do. I walked around the corner to my friend Brian Phillips's house and stayed there for the holidays. They were shocked at what had happened but readily agreed that I could stay. I have been blessed with good friends who have truly loved me and have helped me at my times of most need, there were many of those, while I was growing up.

I told them what had happened just before Easter and about the quick visit by Jill, her very sudden departure, about her not talking to me since and they couldn't believe it. I also asked them not to say anything to the children's department, as they would send me back to boarding school.

So another door to close, what had once been my lovely home, one that had allowed me to leave the orphanage with Me, Rich, Mom and Dad, was, for me, once again now gone. It was time for me to close this door and move on. Well, I was used to that by now, but it didn't make it any easier only that I knew I had to move on and could never go back.

Never looking back was too hard, it forced me to only look forward, but in doing so I was ready for the next step even if I didn't know what it was going to be.

A CHEF FOR J. LYONS & CO.

We always remember our first job.

I MANAGED TO GET a job when I was fifteen, during the holidays, working as a chef in one of J Lyons new hamburger restaurants in West Ealing. It was to compete with the Wimpy Bars that were springing up all over the place. The regional manageress who interviewed me knew Dad very well and told me what a great and kind person he was to work with, adding that they all missed him very much. She also told me how Jill had pursued him every day when she worked in the same office as him, never letting up until she finally snagged him.

I always found it amazing how pieces of information came to me from unusual sources and when that happened, from completely "out in left field," I always knew it to be true information.

I got the job because of Dad and I learned to cook from a chef called Hassan, in full view of the customers. He taught me how to break eggs with one hand (I was proud of that) without breaking the yokes. Though I had to admit it cost J. Lyons dozens of eggs while I was practicing and I have to say though that I hope they were not looking at the bottom line, as I managed to break the yokes of at last thirty eggs while attempting to break each with one hand.

I also learned how to manage several orders at the same time (my first multitasking job) and how to present the food I had prepared so that it looked appetizing. Ian and his mom came in for lunch some Saturdays while I was there, I looked very professional with my tall white chef's hat, my white high-collared mandarin style jacket and blue pin-striped chef's pants.

I got to eat all the food I could sneak under my large hot plate grille and take out the back to eat it when we had a quiet moment. I liked the job and I liked seeing all of the customers come in and I especially liked my new pay packet every week.

At that time, there was only the Wimpey Bar in West Ealing that made hamburgers as it was fairly new in London at that time. J. Lyons was trying to follow the new style of "fast food." It worked well as we were always very busy, but when the holidays ended, I went back to school, saying my goodbyes to Hasan and the staff, never to return to that job.

Back To Boarding School For The Last Time

I WAS NOW a senior at school and had all the privileges of being a senior. I could drive my scooter and could go out more or less as I wanted, which was even better. Mr. Ward now treated me as a grown-up.

I asked him what had happened when Jill came to see him. He told me that she had dropped it on him only when she arrived and had told him she would not be moving until I had left school and only after I had found somewhere else to live once I found a job.

He also told me she had told him how bad I had been and how ungrateful and nasty I was to look after. He told her that I was a very normal boy and that I was a pleasure to have around.

WHAT? he said that about me? Then he said, he meant it. "Yes," he said turning back to me, "of course, you got into some fine troubles, but you were never a problem for us and after what you had dealt with before you arrived here, you were fine, Tony."

He told me he that told her to leave Battledown Manor immediately! He also told her to get out of his office there and then and never call Battledown Manor ever again!

Wow, good for you, Mr. Ward. I never thought you would be sticking up for me, but thanks! Many years later, in 2019, I was contacted by a Facebook group, Battledown Manor" run by some ex-schoolboys, who I was very surprised and happy to meet up with again. I also had several conversations with Stephanie, The Ward's daughter who was no older than 6 or 7 years old when I left in 1966. Now she was all grown up with many memories. Steph and I will meet up sometime soon and we are both looking forward to that meeting.

My first job, paying taxes, was a curse I would have to bear until retirement!

MY FIRST REAL JOB INTERVIEW

Being truthful during an interview meant I was given the opportunity that would change my life and everything is related!

I HAD BEEN LOOKING for a job in London after I got back to school for the last time and had traveled from Cheltenham to do several interviews in and around Ealing. One interview was with a company called Taylor Woodrow, a large multi-national building contractor that had an apprenticeship program. This meant I could go to college and get paid for being at work as well. So I wrote off to the company and got a letter back saying that I was welcome to come to London for an interview.

The interview was with a Mr. Peter Purvey, an older man who was very kind and eventually became like a grandfather to me. I think he had a soft spot for me and always treated me well. I grew to love him like a father figure as he later took a personal interest in my career.

At the interview, I was shown around the company. I saw the biggest truck-mounted cranes, tower cranes, bulldozers and some of the biggest contracting plant machinery I had ever seen. I was hooked and couldn't wait to start. The heavy equipment attracted me and being paid to go to college was a godsend for someone like me who had nothing else at all. It was another example of divine intervention at the right time and just when I needed it.

I finally left school and was so happy. I was free to live a normal life, or so I thought. That final Saturday, when it was time to leave, was warm and very sunny when Brian Phillips, Ella, Albert and his sister Lynne all came to pick me up from school, like a family of my own. I had known them ever since I was nine years old and next to Ian, Brian was my other best friend. They arrived in their Morris Minor Traveler and all my stuff was loaded into the back. I said my goodbyes and thanks to Mr. Ward and his staff and left as fast as I could, never looking back. It was the end of a very surprising event in my life, but just another door to close.

I finally headed back to my other friends and a new life back in London. I never looked back at the school as I rode off on my scooter and was glad to have left there forever. I moved in with the Phillips as my home was now long gone and started my first job. I had signed on to an apprenticeship, which was to last for five years and would finish when I was twenty-one years old.

Life with the Phillips was great; we made homemade elderberry wine, went camping for weekends, built a two-person canoe and generally did family things that I liked to do and I was like a second son to them as well as being a very close friend to Brian, who was the same age as me and who I had been at school within Fielding and Bordeston.

They had a cleaner who came 'round twice a week, as both Ella and Albert worked full-time who liked me but became upset when I jokingly told her not to get too close to me as most people who were close to me had died. Ella explained that this was just my sense of humor.

Ella worked in Hanwell at the most beautiful, thatched cottage in old Hanwell, where her company *"Pictorial Charts Educational Trust"* was located. This was a fascinating place located in a large barn at the back of the beautiful, thatched cottage next to a small lake in the garden. The company produced and distributed the many colorful wall charts and educational posters that went into schools all across the country. Brian and I worked during the summer with Ella there to earn some cash when I was fifteen before I took on a full-time job.

I made money in the strangest of places and always had fun earning it.

ANOTHER PLACE TO LIVE

I was finally on the treadmill, earning and paying taxes!

W HEN I CAME back from boarding school, at Easter I was sixteen, it was April, I had my GCSEs in art, math, history, science, English Lit and English Language and geography and I didn't need to stay on until summer, because I had already finished my GCSE exams and got all seven with good grades, I was set. I was now a full-time apprentice at Taylor Woodrow, which was located in Greenford. There were around twenty apprentices hired each year. I was an engineering apprentice, which paid me and paid for a college course, whereby if I went to college I would get my standard pay for attending. It was too good to miss.

Peter Purvey, my manager, was nice to me and wanted to know all about me being in care (which I never talked about) and asked me about boarding school and had talked to my counselor as he was concerned about whether I wanted to do this job. I hated talking to people about my past as they always had the same look, which I didn't understand or want, so I kept my answers to an absolute minimum.

Mill Hall

I had to stay at a hostel because I had nowhere else to live at 16, years old, thanks to Jill, it was called 'Mill Hall' and was a place for bad kids but I was not one of them! It had a bad reputation and was located on the other side of Southall at Norwood Green. I hated it and disliked the insipid pseudo-military warden-like man that ran this with his insipid wife.

I suddenly found myself living back in a dormitory with seven other boys, all of whom had been placed there by various authorities. But I was there simply because I had nowhere to live and no money to rent a flat, having just arrived back from boarding school.

I had to line up before breakfast, have my bed made to the satisfaction of the old man and had to put up with the strictest rules and regulations. This was like being in Borstal or a halfway house and I had no business being there and I was very angry at the Council who dumped me there! But as was explained by my new caseworker,

Mr. Brown, "It's the only place we have for you, Tony, so you will have to stay there until you are eighteen, " Two long years

Worst of all, I had to relinquish my pride and joy, my scooter, as I was told, "It is unfair to the other boys that you should have a privilege." The scooter was placed inside a locked shed and that was that. I had also started my five-year apprenticeship with Taylor Woodrow and so had to go on the bus to work, while my beautiful scooter was locked in a shed!

The place had the most ridiculous rules and regulations. We had to buy a suit, a pair of light blue jeans (no more bleached bell-bottoms for me) and a pair each of black and brown shoes. It was a miserable time for me and I hated it, especially as I had done nothing wrong to get there.

On weekends, we were allowed to go out; but unless we had very special permission, we had to be home by 11:00 p.m. I was even given an allowance but it was from my own earnings!

I had to go out and buy a boring suit, light blue jeans, white T-shirts to wear with the "light blue jeans" that I hated wearing and generally, I had to conform to become exactly the same as all the other boys. If we went out in Southall, you could tell the Mill Hall boys by the stupid light blue jeans they all wore around town.

Sunday mornings were the worst. We all had to sit in the "communal" living room and suffer one of the old man's lectures about how to behave and what to think. He would always end up saying, "There can never be a winner without a loser. There are always ten times as many losers as there are winners. And if you are all here listening to me, then you are all losers" Well, not for me! I was certainly not ever going to be a loser! I bought my own clothes and stashed them in my hiding place, under a bush on the way out of the place and got changed once I was out of the hostel. To say that I hated it there would be to underestimate how I really felt.

The rules and regulations were simply ridiculous. I just dealt with it and knew I would get out of there one way or another. As for my scooter, I found where they kept the key to the shed and got a soap image made and got a spare key made at a local hardware store.

On weekends, I watched and waited till no one was around after all the boys had left for the day and took my scooter out of the shed to roll it down the curved driveway, out of view, walked it quietly down the road before getting on and *freedom at last.*

They never had a clue as I never mentioned the scooter at any time while I was there and the shed was never opened. It made me feel really good to put one over on their stupid rules. I rode it loud and fast through Southall and Ealing, wearing my crash helmet so no one could see it was me and I nodded to all the other mods, as I went to join Ian on his scooter and we went out together.

I learned to rise above an awful situation and to have fun anyway!

STARTING MY APPRENTICESHIP

Sometimes you just know that you have made an important decision about your life and this was one for me.

I STARTED MY job at Taylor Woodrow as an apprentice, along with nineteen other boys. I did all the overtime I could as I hated going back to the hostel and wanted to stay out as long as I could. I planned to either run away from there or leave within one more month.

My first pay was six pounds a week (ten dollars) and I thought I was rich. Think about it, I could go to the pub (illegally), I was earning money and I was *independent* at last! well, at least for a short time. I was now an employee of Taylor Woodrow and began my 5-year apprenticeship and little did I know it then, but the skills I was to learn were to take me through my entire life.

I was learning skills of being able to fix things, repairing engines, electrical, auto mechanical while working on all kinds of equipment.

On my first day, I was introduced to the rest of the apprentices together in an apprentice workshop. The way it worked was that as we were given jobs to do either with other apprentices or with fully indentured engineers and we were each able to contribute to the company in return for being able to be trained and go to college; it was a good system.

I was to work "my time" as an apprentice in each department from light-engineering, engine workshop, cranes, heavy contractor equipment and in the machine shop. I got to work on Caterpillars, huge Ruston Bucyrus heavy lift cranes, Rolls-Royce diesel generators, Drott, International Harvester, Lister diesel engines and just about everything used on a large construction site was for me to work on.

It was a fantastic job; though the pay as an apprentice wasn't that good, the experience was incredible and I was taught by experts. My pay would increase every year and with milestones, I could achieve more along the way.

What I liked the most was when I was placed in the auto repair shop working on brand-new cars that belonged to executives. Part of my job was to convert these new executive cars from dynamos to alternators, fit radios into brand new fleet vehicles, fix small problems and I even got to set the cars up onto our "in-house" dynamometer where I could set the car wheels on the huge, long rollers and drive up to one hundred miles per hour on the testbed to assess brake horsepower and the brakes if we had replaced them.

It was the coolest thing and at every opportunity I had, I would take one of the cars I was working on onto the dynamometer, finding any excuse to do so.

The Royal Free Hospital-200 Feet Up

One February I was working in the crane section when I had to go to the new Royal Free Hospital, that they were building in Hampstead, to fix a tower crane that had a frozen jib end pulley. It was the pulley right at the end of that long arm you can see high above the ground on tall tower cranes. I had to climb up two hundred feet to the long straight jib of the crane wearing a "fall-harness" that was strapped around my waist then fixed to a horizontal safety rail that ran along the jib. I had to walk out slowly to the very end of the jib and lubricate the gears at the end, removing ice that had stopped it from working. I was working with an ex-marine sergeant major called Stan, who was an ex-army physical training instructor a fitness freak and was always telling us how we were all weak and couldn't keep up with him. So out we went—him and me—and I said to him, "So you think I couldn't handle this job then?" And he said, "No way." That was a challenge, wasn't it?

"OK, I'll go up and I'll go by myself." And he had to agree but insisted I wore the safety harness. It sure was a long way up and I had been shown how to place the fall protection harness on around my waist and legs and to attach it to the safety rail that ran along the length of the jib. I climbed up all the way with the can of lubricant grease and very gingerly reached the high cab where the operator was sitting in his small square windowed box. I told him that when I freed up the pulleys, he should go through the silent hand signs for a "trolley in," "trolley out," and to lift a test load that we had set on the ground near to the crane.

The hand signs were clenching and unclenching my hand, for slow, then making circular motions with my fingers pointing up or down for lift or lower and I would remain on the end of the jib. He told me he thought I must be crazy to go out onto the jib, especially on a freezing cold February morning.

I slowly walked out onto the jib, holding on to the safety rail, sliding more than walking out to the end. I looked down. Fuck! It was a long way to the ground, two hundred feet up and there was nothing between me and the ground at all. I was wondering if birds get dizzy!

I hated heights, but if there is nothing connecting me to the ground, I was sort of OK. I could never stand on a tall building and look down as it always made me woozy, but I could stand on this jib, weird, huh!

I knew I was being watched by my partner, Stan, so off I went to reach the end of the fifty-foot-long jib. I reached the end and the wind was gusting the whole time. I was freezing my arse off as I surveyed the job at hand. Bloody hell! what the hell was I doing up here at all? I wanted danger money, but fat chance of that!

I had a great view of London though and looked out at all the scenery as I could see clearly over to the post office tower. I finally reached the end of the jib and greased the pulleys and I gave the signal for trolley in and trolley out, which he did.

What I didn't know though was that a tower crane leans backward when at rest, because of the counterbalance weights on the other end of the jib and when it lifts a load, the end of the jib drops at least six feet as the load is picked up and rises again when the load is released. I got to see this firsthand and from above and looking down at, well, nothing at all. When he "slewed" left or right, it felt like I was on a huge merry-go-round, spinning at the end of the jib. I had never and even since experienced anything like this as I was perched on the end of the tower crane. By now there was a small crowd of workers below me.

I could see our tiny little van and all of the building site two hundred feet below. But I did it and that shut Stan up for good! After I slid back to the crane's cab, driver thanked me and gave me some hot coffee. I was wondering what makes a person want that job sitting all alone in a cab like this way up there.

He asked me why I did this, so I said, "I should ask you the same question." We laughed and saying goodbye to my new friend, I began the long climb down. "Good job, Tone," my partner said. And we drove back to Greenford in total silence. I couldn't talk anyway as the adrenalin was still pumping high in my veins.

I also got to work on huge Rolls-Royce sixteen-cylinder diesel engines used as power generators, stripping them down and rebuilding them from scratch before placing them onto the testbed to certify them as ready to be used. Of course, I could never work on them by myself, only with an experienced engineer.

I even worked on the very first Jaguar XJ6 belonging to one of the directors. No one had ever seen the car and I was at nineteen years old, fitting a two-way radio in. I got to take it out onto the street and took my overalls off as soon as I left the company grounds, so I could pretend that the car was mine (as if!) I drove it through Greenford and into Ealing with everyone staring at this superb new Jag XJ6.

Funny though, I loved doing my job as an apprentice and learning for me was fun. I had no idea that all of this was to be so important for my future and would affect whatever I did with my life. I was moving gradually forward in a direction that would take me onward through my life-learning skills, that I would need, right through everything I ever did.

There was an artist who worked there, called John, a slight man with reddish hair, that I got to know well and every opportunity I had, I would sneak over to his hut to watch him at his work. John was a signwriter; he hand-painted all of the huge signs that Taylor Woodrow had all over the world. I was fascinated to watch him making his perfect lettering on walls, signs, trucks and anything that needed a sign. I asked him if he enjoyed it and he told me that if he had to paint one more man pulling on a rope, he would scream! That was Taylor Woodrow's corporate signature, four men pulling on a rope that signified teamwork.

I laughed and asked him why he did the job then. He told me his first love was art, but that it would never make enough money for him to live on, so this was at least working with paints and brushes; so for him, it used a tiny part of his skill and he could paint in his spare time.

For extra cash, I used to make small model figures, which I welded or soldered together out of nuts, bolts and pieces of metal. I sold them to local gift stores, or I made them for friends.

John's Mom and Dad were having a twenty-fifth wedding anniversary and he liked what I created. He asked me if I would make something special for his parents as an anniversary gift from him to them so I made two figures holding hands, walking together while passing a twenty-five-year milestone placed on the road next to them. I made them out of metal with round ball-bearing heads. For the lady, I made a large hat and for the man a cane and a top hat with coat tails. I placed it into a box that I also made and wrapped it in a piece of blue tissue paper, making it fit properly, before giving it to

John. He loved it and agreed to paint me a picture in return and we swapped many items like that, I kept all of his paintings as I thought he was a very gifted artist.

I was working for Taylor Woodrow, singing at night and making enough money to live on, while I was making and selling small models. I was by that time beginning to be an entrepreneur.

I stayed at Taylor Woodrow for the five years needed to complete my apprenticeship, I got my degree and decided that I didn't want to remain in that business and I didn't want to become a specialist mechanic.

What was so cool to me as a schoolboy was not so interesting for me now that I had completed my five-year apprenticeship. I even learned to be an auto electrician or what we called an "auto-sparks," and the expert that taught me was none other than Jimmy Marshall's brother. Jim was the founder of Marshall Amplifiers, now seen on all of the rock concerts behind the bands from the Who to Elton John, Led Zeppelin and many others.

At that time, Jimmy Marshall was just beginning to build his iconic Marshall stacks and had a small shop selling guitars, drums and amps in Hanwell, near where I lived. I was introduced to him, but at that time, he only had a fledgling company. I bought my first guitar from the shop in Hanwell. Jim had the same illness I was born with, TB, but his childhood was worse as he had to wear a body cast throughout his childhood.

Anyway, his brother was Fred, (at least that was what Fred told me) and Fred had a limp, could hardly walk and seemed to me to be at least sixty when I was apprenticed to him. He called me "Tone" and directed me to do all the work while he told me exactly what to do. I liked him a lot and looked forward to my workdays while working with Fred. Fred showed me how to troubleshoot and fix almost anything electrical on many different cars, vans and lorry-mounted cranes that belonged to Taylor Woodrow's fleet.

I got to drive many of the cars off the premises and 'round the streets to "test-drive" them if we had installed the two-way radios; though most times, there was nothing wrong with the cars and they definitely didn't need a "test drive." Still, it was one of the perks with the job and meant I could pop out to get breakfast from the local café.

I moved through each of the workshops, working for up to six months in each while I was going to college on a one-month at a time block release at Uxbridge Technical College in order to take my degree (*City and Guilds*, parts 1 and 2). I had no car at that time. I couldn't afford one, as my pay was so very little and I needed it to pay the rent at Paddy Gallagher's Mom's house after I had left Mill Hall at 18 but I had my scooter.

Oops!

While I was working in the crane section, I got plenty of overtime and often worked Saturday mornings for extra cash at time and a half. I was still only seventeen and one Saturday, as I was finishing off the electronic "Wiley Safety System," which was an audible and visual warning system in case the operator overloaded the crane's lift mechanism which was triggered off the tension in the steel ropes of the crane by two pulleys arranged over and under the steel ropes. A heavier lift put more tension on the pulleys which triggered the alarm. I had just finished working on it that Saturday morning, when there was hardly anyone around, so I took the huge truck-mounted crane for a "spin" around the yard.

It was so cool; I had full control of this huge beastie and was determined to put it through its paces, so off I went driving it up to the backlot. They had just opened a brand-new paint spray shop that could paint complete vehicles and mine was scheduled to be painted the following Monday. The new spray shop had been featured in the monthly *"Taywood News"* and had photos and articles on the advanced technology adopted, something called negative attraction spray system that made the paint go onto the structure and not all over the shop.

So there I was, cruising around the huge yard, pretending to be a professional crane operator at seventeen with no HGV (heavy goods vehicle license,) and honking the horn driving all over the yard. I even went to the outer perimeter and parked up and extended the telescopic jib fully, looking out of the rear sky-roof window in the cab, while admiring my handiwork. I set a test load on the ground, locked it onto the cranes hook, set the outriggers to stabilize the truck then lifted the test load, placing it carefully back down . . . way cooler still!

Noticing the time, I retracted the jib, locked it in place and drove it back to the workshop. Halfway back, I had a great idea and decided to park it in the spray shop so it wouldn't have to be done on Monday. I honked the horn to let anyone who may be inside know that I wanted the automatic doors to be opened and they began to open.

As I drove the crane into the spray shop, I heard a huge "CRUNCH" and bricks and bits of debris came showering all over the crane and the cab. Little did I know that the crane was too big and I had completely smashed into the brand-new and soon-to-be officially opened automatic doors of the equally brand-new super-duper paint spray shop.

Well, fuck it! I was in serious trouble now. What I thought was a fairly empty workshop on a Saturday morning was suddenly full of people running toward me. They came from everywhere, including the manager. I stepped down from the cab and surveyed the damage. Oh shit! Where the top of the entrance doorway was, there was now a huge hole.

The top of the automatic door was bent and twisted and bricks were still falling while my jib was poking right through to the inside of the building. I was devastated at the damage I had done. Funny how quickly a great day can be ruined. Ever noticed that? I did and how!

I was sent home and was told to be in the manager's office on Monday morning. I had a lousy weekend and thought I would surely be fired.

When Monday came, all of the other apprentices were laughing at me and joking about my superb driving skills, I didn't think it was funny at all and was wondering how I was going to get out of this one. I was summoned to the plant manager's office and Peter Purvey came with me. There were several of them there and a representative of the union as well. I listened to their statements as they read out the extent of the damage I had done and the approximate cost of repair.

I had never gotten into any trouble there and had a completely clean apprentice record, not even a missed day or even a late day. Peter Purvey told them I was an exceptional apprentice, that I should be given a second chance as there were other things that needed to be considered in my case. I was certain he was referring to my background and he was making sure that he defended me and put me in a positive light to them.

I was asked to explain myself, so I told them that I was trying to save time on Monday by parking the crane inside ready to be painted. One of the managers said I should make sure that the door is open first. They laughed but I wasn't laughing as I didn't want to lose my job but had nothing to say in my own defense, so I said nothing. I did apologize several times and offered to pay or to fix the damage I had done. I mentally calculated that I would probably have to work one hundred hours a week for at least two years to pay for it. I had to wait outside while they conferred about how serious my damage was.

They all agreed that it was after all an insurance claim, adding that they would probably make the door higher as a result. I was however given a three-day suspension without pay but would not be fired. I asked if this would go on my apprenticeship record. The union leader told me that if I maintained a clean record and didn't do anything else stupid, over the next twelve months, it would not go on my record. I felt lousy though as I had caused so much damage while trying to be cool.

Outside, I thanked Peter and assured him I would be more careful in future and left to begin my three days off. I called Ian and told him what had happened and he was as surprised as I was that I still had a job there.

At that time, we were just starting to sing and we learned to play guitar so that we could both earn money while we were at college; otherwise, I would honestly have starved at weekends.

As it was, on many of the weekends while I was an apprentice, I had no food at all, so I would try to keep some food from the canteen on Friday and try to make it last right through the weekend. I managed the three days off and practiced guitar, learning some new songs to make use of my time.

I enjoyed my apprenticeship and had even been presented with several awards from Taylor Woodrow for achievements along the way—best apprentice, best-made tools, etc.

An Indentured Craftsman

I had spent 5 years at Taylor Woodrow, from sixteen to twenty-one and had become a fully indentured professional craftsman. I could, if I wanted, work anywhere in any blue-collar or engineering job; but I didn't want that. Only six of the twenty that began the apprenticeship with me finished and I was one of them.

At the final ceremony, when Frank Taylor came down himself to address us all and to award our Indentured Apprentice certificates, I had asked Auntie to come as many of my fellow apprentices had parents and family there and I had no one except Auntie.

We were each asked to make something that would represent our skill at these annual awards and all of the exhibits were placed on tables, along with a small card in front to say who had made the exhibit, to be assessed and awarded points for skill and workmanship. I made a set of Trammels (God knows why as I've never used them) and also made the metal box for them including a green felt interior that held the trammels in place. I have to admit they looked very professional.

Trammels are used for scribing a precise circle on metal, for perhaps permanently marking, or for cutting out the marked area and could be attached end to end and locked in place together to make a circle as wide as three feet in diameter. So now you know what a trammel is. I won the award for the best-made tool. For that, I got another certificate and £100. Cool, huh!

Auntie had come to watch me receive my indentured papers and I introduced Auntie to John's family, my other friends, and managers and she was like the Queen Mother in every way. I was happy she was there with me.

At one annual award ceremony race car driver Graham Hill, the Formula 1 World Champion, was to give us all our awards for excellence but couldn't make it. Instead, his beautiful wife came and when she gave me my award, I thanked her, squeezing her hand in mine.

She told me she wouldn't have missed it for the world as her late husband always talked about the importance of apprenticeships in the racing world. She was so elegant and so beautiful; she admired my work. Cool, huh! I still have a photograph of getting that award, when Auntie was there too, to see me complete what I had started out to do five years earlier, as a young school leaver and straight from school. She was so proud of me and having her there at that time was as good as having any real mom, I imagined.

I left Taylor Woodrow after completing my apprenticeship to become a professional singer with Ian and our singer Dee Anderson and never looked back.

While working for Taylor Woodrow, I had gone from a young boarding schoolboy into becoming a young man, independent, with a career, a degree and I was now a fully indentured master craftsman. I didn't realize it then, but I could work anywhere with that, even thirty years later in the United States I could have used my skill there to be a professional "Journeyman," as it is called in the United States, meaning I would have been hired in preference to others not having been an indentured apprentice.

I had learned auto-electrical work on cars and trucks, heavy equipment hydraulics and I could rebuild engines, even sixteen-cylinder Rolls-Royce engines. I had worked on all sorts of large cranes, tool and die making and how to think through problems and how to solve them. I have used the skills I gained there throughout my whole life and these skills have both saved me a fortune and made me a great living ever since. Having that apprenticeship was the sole reason I gained my green card in 1993 while living in the United States. Later I found out I was considered to be a "professional" with an E-16 classification from the US. government immigration department meaning as far as the immigration board was concerned, I was a "person of extraordinary talent." Cool huh!

Something that took years of hard work was worth it in the end!

JIMI HENDRIX LIVE

I was there when Jimi performed live!

I Was There in 1967, as I had complimentary tickets to see Jimi Hendrix playing at the Finsbury Astoria and I was in the fourth row from the front while watching him do something no one had ever done before. He actually set fire to his Fender Stratocaster guitar.

Unbelievable! I was so close and was right there watching him as he, being completely spaced out, placed his guitar on the floor in the middle of the stage while squirting it with lighter fluid and setting the thing on fire. Brilliant! I knew I would remember this night forever and hoped I would see him again live; but unfortunately, I never got to do that as he died of an overdose on October 5th, 1970. *What a waste*, I thought, but then there was that moment in time for me when I did enjoy his music live at one of his concerts.

I had to find a place to live when I left Mill Hall so I looked around for a cheap flat. I found one just off Northfields Avenue. It was a single bed-sit room at the back of a house where an old lady lived with her two sons. The sons were aged eleven and seventeen. I don't remember the older boy's name, but his younger brother was called Paddy Gallagher.

Now Paddy was a real street tough guy and was already going the wrong way at eleven years old. I liked Paddy though and we got along really well. His mom was not well and I used to do small errands for her. My room was very small, but I was independent, it was mine and I had all I needed there and anyway, it took me out of that awful place, Mill Hall.

If I got too hungry while I was living at Paddy's Mom's house, which was almost every weekend, I called Brian Phillips to see if his mom and dad could use some help in their pub in Islington. It was always OK for me to go there as they were like family and Brian and I were close friends. I could do lots of work there to earn my food and I liked that, so I went by tube over to Islington on a Friday afternoon after work, to work at their pub to earn my food. I loaded shelves, kept the bar clean, worked the cellar, and helped Ella out in the kitchen.

Pirate Radio

As I was now a Mod, possessing everything I needed to be recognized as one, I used to listen to the two pirate radio stations—"Radio Caroline" and "Radio London" (Wonderful Radio London)—and these stations were both amazing to listen to. They were new and played the latest rock and pop bands that the BBC (Beeb) wouldn't play. They played the Kinks, Cream, the Rolling Stones, of course, the Beatles, the Animals, Pink Floyd and The Who. They played all new pop and rock music, much of which was seldom if ever, played by BBC.

The Beeb as we all called it, was so stuffy and had no passion for what it really was—*"a popular music radio program"*—there to entertain us and to play what we, the peasants, wanted to hear. It was as if we should feel privileged to accept all of the programs the government chose to put out for us and to grin and bear it. *Wow*, lucky us!

The *"BBC Light Program"* was the only "popular" (not pop) channel that we could listen to and the Beeb was part of the government who were definitely not interested in entertaining the public unless of course you were being entertained at "Her Majesty's Pleasure," which was something entirely different. I use the term popular very loosely since the only other program was Radio Luxembourg, which faded in and out the whole time and mostly couldn't be heard at all!

These two independent radio stations, Caroline and London, were playing requests, making jokes, conducting interviews with rock musicians, were advertising cool new stuff and were doing live chats on the air. The stations were broadcast from two ships moored off the English coast and were not licensed by the government who had to license all broadcasters.

Of course, both of them applied for and reapplied for, broadcasting licenses from the government; but naturally, the government would have none of it and refused to grant them a license to broadcast their programs based on no reason at all.

They continued regardless while trying to appeal against the government's refusals. They broadcast from 1964 till 1966, perfect for a new young MOD eager to listen to all of the new music that was being played at the time. The Who were our standard-bearers and sang about being a MOD. They had hairstyles like ours, short and spiked on top and longer at the back and were often photographed in the same clothes that we chose to wear.

Everyone listened to these two pirate radio stations Caroline and London; if you didn't, then there was only a very faded Radio Luxemburg that often faded right out of sound. I listened to Radio Luxembourg on a small crystal radio set complete with earphones that I made from old bits and pieces in my bedroom at night under my bed covers.

The adverts that these now called "pirate Radio" stations played caused a major stir as the advertisers could target their audience very precisely, unlike the Independent TV that catered for a much broader audience. Sales of the products advertised on Pirate Radio increased very quickly. They advertised hair products, makeup, chewing gum and a myriad of other previously unheard-of new products that younger people wanted to buy. This single event started radio advertising and paved the way for a new style of television ads that would be the basis of advertising for the next fifty years.

Apart from this, the music and interviews were "here and now" and not managed by a committee of stuffy government employees that knew little of, or cared for, or understood the new market for pop music and young people's products.

The government in its infinite wisdom, at that time, began a campaign using legalities aimed at preventing "that sort of music" and "those sorts of people" from being able to broadcast on "its airwaves."

Eventually, due to the rising popularity of these now "Pirate" radio stations, the government passed "an illegal broadcasting law" under a new maritime law that made these stations illegal so that they could then board the pirate radio boats and shut them down, even though they were in international waters.

But at the end of the day, what actually happened was that a quiet revolution had just occurred. These two pirate radio stations had caused a chain of events that would enable better broadcasting standards and eventually the breakdown of BBC's stranglehold on all radio programming in Britain.

The BBC had to accept that its formula for radio broadcasting at that time was old and tired and that it did not meet its own standard of being accountable and meeting the needs of its public, license-paying, audience. Quite apart from that the pirate stations were fantastic and alive and were doing for us what no other radio programs before had done.

They were asking us what we wanted to hear and then playing it with live feedback on what people thought right there on the airwaves. The "live call-ins" were funny, we could hear ordinary people chatting on the radio to the DJs and the DJs were talking back at them, saying what they wanted to say and not bothering who was listening and certainly no one was criticizing them for their opinions and they were being very natural while on-air.

Talking To Pirate Radio

One part I loved listening to was when they were asking people on the shoreline to flash their headlights if they were listening from the mainland. Then they would talk, on the airwaves, live and find out through a series of questions answered by the flashing of headlights onshore the names and music preferences of the listeners. It was fascinating and we all felt truly connected through these radio stations and we were able to communicate live on the airwaves— even as far as being able to get the names of the people in the cars and referring to them by name, it was amazing!

Quite apart from this, they were part of the times we were living in—fashions from Carnaby Street and Kings Road, *New Musical Express*, Twiggy, miniskirts, new short hairstyles (club cut, Paige boy and MOD crewcuts), the new rock culture, discos (these were new also) this was the very beginning of "flower power," which was soon to become the ultimate in nonviolent radical change. So, Mr. Gandhi, you were remembered. We listened to you. After all, we followed your lead and did the same when we created a silent revolution.

Radio London was my favorite. I listened with my friends in places like Hyde Park, as they were telling us they were to be shut down. We listened as Radio Caroline was telling us that they had been "boarded," and we listened as they told us they were sinking in the ocean off the coast.

We were shocked at what we were hearing in real-time news right as it was happening (forty years before CNN did the same) I listened sadly as I heard the last broadcast of "Wonderful Radio London" in its unique electronic sounding slogan, which was repeated continuously until 3:00 p.m. that day, in the middle of summer, 1967, then faded out forever.

I knew when I heard this that history had just been made and also that I had been part of the audience hearing what was going on at that time. They had played music by Cream, The Who, Pink Floyd Jimi Hendrix, Long John Baldry and Chicken Shack, all of which would never have been given airtime on the Beeb.

A Final Epitaph for Pirate Radio

These pirate stations, as the government referred to them, did make a difference. They started a chain reaction that was to change the British and European music radio broadcasting scene forever. They had given a challenge to the government and although the government had won the battle by force and in refusing to grant licenses, they had lost the war.

Several years later, licenses were granted for other broadcasting stations like Capital Radio, which was modeled exactly like Radio Caroline and Radio London. Capital Radio was a commercial station with adverts, live talk, chats with their audience and even some of the DJs from the "pirate" radio stations had come over to join them.

Capital Radio had begun, several years later, with Kenny Everett and Dave Cash to head up their lineup in the important morning "drive-in" program. "Kenny and Cash," as they were known, were brilliant together, zany, up to the minute and they held that spot for many years, placing Capital Radio as the most listened to radio station in England, giving it a very firm foundation that was to endure for decades as it still is some 50 years on.

Great going, Radio London and Radio Caroline! You really did start something very special and like all truly great things, your endowment to the broadcasting scene, the music scene, fashion and up-to-the-minute issues lasted a lot longer than your initial concept!

Buckingham Palace?

Since I was now a mod, I decided to paint Ian's scooter, which was a Vesper "GS," with large "bubbles" on either side. I painted it into a complete Union Jack. His mom, Peggy, didn't want that at all; but with persistence, she finally gave in and we began to transform Ian's bland-looking boring machine into a true mod mobile'

I marked out the red, white and blue Union Jack with masking tape on the front panel, going from the handlebars right down to the front mudguard. I marked out a Union Jack on each of the side panels, as we both began to paint the scooter.

When we had finished, it looked truly amazing a complete up-to-the-minute, high fashion "mod" scooter. We showed Ian's mom and she had to agree that it looked great.

This was now summer 1967 when the best music ever was out on the airwaves. The Beatles had just released their *Sergeant Pepper* album, Small Faces had released "Ichigoo Park," and Procol Harum had their huge hit "A Whiter Shade of Pale" (though I never understood the words). The music was unbelievable! Pink Floyd was all over the airwaves even the Beach Boys had an amazing hit with "Good Vibrations." Now well into the charts.

The music, that summer in '67 was the best ever, with hit after hit every week and later all subsequently became pop and rock classics. Off we went, the two of us, riding through Ealing with our loud silencers making a huge racket as we drove by. We had to make sure we throttled back whenever we rode around close to home though; otherwise, Peggy would have made Ian use a "normal" silencer.

One weekend, I borrowed the "mod" machine to drive down to Selsey-Bill on the coast to meet a girlfriend, Anne Shepherd, there. She was staying with a girlfriend at her aunt's house.

Anne was the daughter of my doctor when I was living at Mill Hall in Southall and was the light in my life at that time. I was crazy about her, but because I was living at Mill Hall, when we met her father forbade her to go out with me. I never understood why that was, but it made no difference to us; we still saw each other whenever we wanted to, while she was finishing off at Notting Hill School for Girls, which was an exclusive school in Ealing.

I was so cool, at least I thought so. I had my full parka coat with a fur edging around the hood and a Union Jack on the back, a Union Jack crash helmet, a Union Jack scooter, a tent and all I needed to be completely independent.

I camped in a field near where Anne was staying with her friend and we all went to the beach together every day. Donovan's "Catch the Wind" was number 1 for a while and I just had to look the part. Even my jeans were bleached in rough broad stripes all the way down front and back, I also wore a pair of small "John Lennon" round sunglasses with my long hair worn down past my shoulders.

Anne wore a pair of heart-shaped rose-tinted glasses and I thought she looked just like Mary Quant in her tiny miniskirt, her slim figure, with her dark hair cut in a Paige boy style. We looked great together and I took Anne and her friend on the back of the scooter, one at a time, of course, to different places on or near the beach. I stayed for a week with them and we had a great time there, going to the bars, the beaches, the shops taking them on the back of my Mod scooter.

On the way back from spending the weekend with Anne, I stopped at a petrol station where the attendant came out to fill my scooter with two-stroke petrol. At that time, you had to fill it with one gallon of petrol then have the attendant put three squirts of "two-stroke" oil put into the tank to make "two-stroke" fuel, which is a mixture of oil and petrol. You then had to swish it around in the tank by rocking the scooter side to side.

As he was doing this, he said to me, "Boy, you're patriotic, aren't you, with all this Union Jack stuff?" I replied without even thinking "I have to be patriotic because of where I live." He said, "So where do you live then?" I told him, "At Buckingham Palace. I live at Buckingham Palace, of course."

He stopped what he was doing and looked at me incredulously and said, "You're kidding, right?" I said, "No, not at all. My dad's a butler to Her Majesty the Queen and we both live in the servant's quarters and this is the only way he would let me ride this into Buckingham Palace if it was painted in patriotic colors."

"Well, I never," he said, "I must tell my wife that I've met the son of the queen's butler." Well, I couldn't burst his bubble, could I? I let my little (or huge) white lie stand and drove away grinning from ear to ear.

Later on, I took Ian to Selsey Bill and we both drove our scooters for weekends there, sleeping in doorways of offices along the way. One morning though, at around 5:00 a.m., we were woken up by two local policemen who stopped to wake us up asking, "What the hell are you two doing here? Move along." We had to move along and find somewhere for breakfast. So much for "life as a mod."

So, what the hell is a mod? Well, I was one at sixteen. I wore bell-bottom jeans with striped bleached lines down each leg (bleach poured directly onto the jeans while lying in the bath), long black hair down to my shoulders and a parka coat with a fur-trimmed hood. And I rode a modified motor scooter all over London. I also had a striped jacket in red and black stripes. We would go to a "meet" where all of the other "mods" were hanging out. Mods were the forerunners of "punks" as they went on to become. Most mods had short hair cropped close, but I didn't.

My scooter had twenty mirrors on the front and sides, at least six spot lamps and a beautiful set of chrome crash bars with a high backrest.

I had a Union Jack crash helmet and I was "in" with the "in-crowd." I looked very cool (or at least I thought I did) and dressed exactly as I wanted. We listened to the Who, Cream, Hollies and all of the current music and my striped jacket was just like one the Who wore.

On weekends, some of the mods went down to Brighton to fight with the "rockers" who were exactly the opposite of us. Rockers rode motorbikes and wore leathers, rode around in gangs, listened to Elvis and to us they generally looked old-fashioned like something out of the 50s. We bought our clothes from places like Lord John or Mr. Howard in Carnaby Street and Kings Road or Biba in Kensington where I used to frequent every Saturday morning. I loved the music, the styles and the up-to-date fashion that was "in" at the time.

I was always interested in wearing the latest fashions and of course, so were the girls I went out with at that time. Twiggy had just begun to make a name for herself in the fashion mags. She was the absolute girl version of us mods and I loved her waiflike look and short-cropped blonde hair and she had the biggest eyes I ever saw. I thought she was the sexiest girl on the planet and she is still beautiful!

The clothes we were wearing were bell-bottoms, shoes eventually with ridiculous platform soles, wide blade ties and shirts with "penny round" collars. We wore big striped shirts, flower power shirts and even paisley patterns (which I have hated ever since) while listening to Mamas and Papas, Beach Boys, Edison Lighthouse, Christie's Yellow River all of which were my favorites at that time. While we were doing straight pop and rock style music, the Philly Sound was emerging from the United States with full strings, harmony, horns and keyboards. The Motown bands I loved were Temptations, Four Tops and the Isley Brothers. I thought the musical arrangements were so much more advanced than what we were doing in Britain. But still, our British music seemed to be the most popular.

The Beatles and the Stones were producing hit after hit after hit and their music was truly amazing. The Beatles occupied the top 5 slots in Britain's Top 10, which no one had ever done or has ever done since. We were so lucky that we were in our teens when all this new music hit the charts and we were part of the music revolution.

First Man On The Moon

It was while I was working at the pub for Ella and Albert in 1969, in Islington, that Brian and I watched the first lunar landing that year with Neil Armstrong, Edwin "Buzz" Aldrin and John Collins, who was the command module pilot.

We were sitting in the pub on July 20, which was a Saturday afternoon, watching TV in the now-closed bar after the morning session and before we opened up the bar for the very busy Saturday evening session. We watched as the small landing module approached the moon and began to slowly descend. We heard the distance to the surface being called out as it continued with its descent. We sat in awed silence as the black-and-white scratchy images of their lunar module slowly descended to the surface of the moon. We listened to the soundtrack indented with a "peep" after each sentence in the communication between Houston and the astronauts.

We watched the descent of Neil Armstrong as he climbed awkwardly down the steps of the landing module in his silver spacesuit, ready to step onto the surface of the moon. We watched in utter silence and with breath held as he took his first step onto the moon. I was so moved at what I was watching that I couldn't breathe, worried and praying that nothing would go wrong at the very last moment. We listened as he announced to the universe, *"That's one small step for man, one giant leap for mankind."* We cheered at that and again watched the reruns and the commentary on TV in the bar.

Cool, huh, to have witnessed that too and live on TV actually as it was happening. I was watching as history was being made right there on TV and right before my eyes. Earlier when I was younger I had gone to the Great West Road, with the Phillips' to watch as Yuri Gagarin, the first man in space, drove past us, waving at us as we watched him go back to Heathrow for his return to Russia in a convoy of VIP cars.

What a rich teenage life I led, so many events the memories of which will last forever.

My Mother, Rosina May, as I remember her
taken on her wedding day not long before she
passed away

Aunties house 35 Kirkley Park Road, in Lowestoft

The back of Aunties house, with our climbing frame on the
right background and the bowling green in the foreground. The
verandah is looking over the garden.
There is another part of the garden behind the camera

Top From the left: Auntie, Auntie's sister, Zannie Nurse Rosemary (sitting) is in front on the left. I am not sure who the other nurse is. I am 2nd child front row from right.

The climbing frame in the garden. I am leaning out of the frame in the lower right, with black hair. Beatrice is the girl sitting with her hand in front of her face, in front of me. Mary Brooks is in the lower left inside of the frame,

Me (front right) and Mary Brooks (standing on the
left) on the stairs I loved Mary Brooks at 3 years
old

Me learning to drive in 'Arabella' Aunties 1937 Austin Seven at age 12
complete with a 'crash gearbox' as Auntie put it, "so you can learn to
drive properly" Picture (blurred) as taken by 11 yr. old Beatrice

Back Row: Tony Moore, Robert Jones, Kevin Cromer, Brian Parkes, Michael, Prior, Robert Mc Ghee, Ralph Herbert, Michael Bulmer, Robin Reece
Second Row: Peter Fothergill, Ian Howard, Christine Putnam, Adele Rosevere, Lesley Goring, Rosamund Want, Linda McFarland, Linda Shepherd, Christine Jaks, Madeline Arnette, Diane Rodgers, Russell Gordon, Robert Gwyther
Front Row: Roisin O'Connor, Monica Newman, Janette Andersen, ?, Margaret Hall, Mr. Hughes, Carolyn Davis, ?, Vivian King, Susan King, Iris Nunn

The Snow Queen 1960

The cast of 'The Snow Queen' at Fielding Junior School. I am kneeling on the right side front (looking at the photo) of the front row Ian is at the top row on the right (looking at the photo) of the Snow Queen

Jane Henley before we met (third from the right) as a
poster girl for the film The Belles of St Trinians

Norwell (Noz) Roberts, QPM; at his investiture of the Queens Police Medal for services to the Metropolitan Police after his retirement.

Norwell Roberts in his Metropolitan Police Uniform

f Project Facebook INORWELLROBERTS IAMNORWELLROBERTS
Community, Film and Theatre

Norwell (Noz) Roberts, QPM;
*Courtesy I Am Norwell Roberts
Community Films*

Auntie in 1988 in Scarborough, with her MG Midget, she often drove it down to London and always loved driving.

Jumbo Fiske, OBE (1905-1977), the greatest herring skipper of the twentieth century, a legendary fisherman. His two trawlers, the "Suffolk Venturer" and "The Suffolk Warrior," were part of the Lowestoft fleet. I went on his boat whenever I visited Lowestoft if he was in port. His daughter, Rosemary, was one of the nurses that looked after me to age eight and whom I stayed in touch with all my life.

Ian and I playing at The Old Swan in Battersea with 'Blind Bob' playing Bass
in the background. Adrian played with us here.
(*Low light Photo taken by Ray Chapman*)

One of my Apprenticeship award ceremonies, my
boss and father figure Peter Purvey looking over
my shoulder behind me.

Getting my apprenticeship papers at 21-years old. I
was now a fully indentured apprentice after 5-years
which I started when I was 16-years old

My "Frogeye" Sprite

Four faces of aging that led to me finding my
father and my long lost siblings.

Me with the very talented Vick Elms, who sadly passed away in 2017.
Vick was formerly with the band 'Christie' famed for their number
one hit "Yellow River," and who was married to Dee Anderson our
first girl singer.
Photo by Ray Chapman

'Dressed For Business As Usual'
This was the advertising image of me that went
'global' The pen I was using was a Mont Blanc I won
for having a technical article, I wrote, published in a
magazine.
Courtesy Tony Yates, Publitek

Stardust by Parfums Llewelyn

1.7oz Eau de Parfum Spray

3.4 oz Eau de Toilette Spray

Stardust For Men After Shave Balm

tardust

t for Men

fums Llewelyn

Moisturizer for Men

After Shave Balm

1.7oz Gift Set

3.4oz Eau de Parfum spray

Our "Stardust Award" for the *Links Fund* and *The Women's Fund of Indiana*. The actual award was an engraved crystal replica of our beautiful bottle designed by world-famous Marc Rosen of New York

Our Wine Bar artwork as designed by our
talented, and sadly late friend Carolyn Mann

My late friend Tony Holland as I remember him
from our wine bar days. He was a highly talented
writer and inventor of East Enders and the writer
for the Z Car series

LEARNING TO SING

When we have to, we learn really fast how to make money to survive.

MY FLAT AT this time, cost me four pounds a week and I had practically no money left over for food or petrol, so I had to work as much overtime as I could get. This became a real problem for me and one weekend, Ian and I discussed that we both needed money and agreed that since we could both sing fairly well, we should learn to play for money, cash, gelt, or readies. So, we practiced and practiced and learned as many songs as we could. We learned folk songs by Peter, Paul and Mary; Bob Dylan; Pete Seeger; the Kingston Trio and Simon and Garfunkel.

After some six months of practicing every weekend and some evenings each week, we were finally ready to play to an audience, or so Ian's Mom thought and we rode our scooters to Uxbridge where there was a folk club behind a pub called the Load of Hay in Uxbridge, well, actually Hillingdon. We plucked up our courage and played as guest artists, our first actual gig in a folk club at the back of the pub and in fact, we became guest singers there for more than a year. I think we sounded a lot like the real thing as we had always learned to sing harmonies and could play and sing like Simon and Garfunkel. We learned all of their many hits and we built up a repertoire of more than one hundred songs. We practiced over and over again until we knew all the words by heart.

This was to become the most important part of our teenage life as we were both at college and both needed the money. My daytime job, as an apprentice, went well but didn't pay me enough so Ian and I began to play pubs and clubs all over London, becoming better and more professional the more we played. We gained a reputation as well and had a fan club of regulars who followed us around everywhere we played.

Cezara

I met Cezara when I was nineteen. Cez was a stunningly beautiful Polish girl with long ash blonde hair and light gray eyes. Cez, as I called her, had several brothers that were a lot older than her. Zbyszek who lived in Australia, Joe who lived in Kensington and Lolek who lived in South London, none were married and all were very independent.

Cez had an elderly mother who was a fantastic cook and could cook any Polish dish ever created, though she could not speak English very well. As for me, I could pronounce two things in Polish perfectly: the names of Polish food and swear words! So I learned all about the Polish way of life, along with some perfect phrases that I can never repeat in good company. I also loved the Polish food - *Galumpki (pronounced Gwumpki), borscht, pierogi* and I could cook some of these dishes myself, but not anywhere close to what Cez's Mom could do. By the way, if you love food as much as I do, then you have to be able to cook it to be able to have it whenever you wish. So I learned to cook fairly well; French, Italian, Polish and Indian and thanks to Brian Phillips's family, my boyhood friend, I even learned to cook several Scottish dishes.

In 1969, the Rolling Stones were playing at Hyde Park when Brian Jones had recently drowned in his swimming pool. Cez had a flat in Mayfair at the time, so we both went to Hyde Park with some of her hostess friends, from the nightclub where she worked, to see them play in Hyde Park. It was a very hot summer's day on July 5 and we were both very close to the stage, as they released thousands of butterflies in memory of Brian.

Cez was working as a nightclub hostess at the Crazy Horse and the 800 Club and was making more money than I ever did at the time. Despite how well Cez and I got on, as good and very close friends, I knew it wouldn't last as I had no vision of marriage with Cez and I still had way too many things to do.

We often went to a Polish club in South Kensington's Exhibition Road called Ognisko, after I had finished performing and if she had a night off from the 800 Club.

Ognisko was a Polish drinking club that was open till the early hours and was somewhat old-fashioned inside but was a great club where the drinks were dead cheap. It was like stepping back in time though, being with all the Polish crowd. The club looked like and felt like a Second World War club that you would see in a black-and-white movie. The Polish people that I met at that time were all heavy drinkers and seemed to always be drinking vodka, getting drunk almost every night, ending up falling about all over the place.

Cez and I were an item; we went on holidays together with Ian and his then-girlfriend Sandy. I took Cez to visit Auntie in Lowestoft, for a weekend, which was a disaster as Auntie got on Cez's case and made her very uncomfortable. To this day, I have no idea why she did that, but sometimes Auntie was a little unpredictable.

We lived in a flat right in the heart of Ealing Broadway, which was close to all the Ealing life and was within walking distance of all the pubs and clubs. I shared a flat with two friends Mike and Colin, whom I had also shared a flat with previously. Cez shared a basement flat with her school friend Eva in the same building. We lived together there for about eighteen months and we settled in to what for me was a boring home life. I was now singing full-time and was performing at the Penthouse in Mayfair, the Old Swan on the Thames at Battersea, working men's clubs and many other places all over the south of England to make enough money to live on.

Cez often left for work at around 9:00 p.m. and didn't get home until around 5:00 a.m. or later, depending on how busy the club was that night.

The difference between liking someone a lot as a friend and loving someone is the difference between a girlfriend and a wife.

US AND THE EQUALS
(OR THE OTHER WAY AROUND)

When you meet people on their way up you hope fame never changes them.

ONE GIG THAT our manager Reggie Perrin landed us for was as a backup band to "The Equals" who were just about to launch their single *"Baby Come Back,"* which went on to become their first big number 1 hit. We met them while both of us were sitting in a waiting area at a record label, the name of which I can't remember, but I do recall it was in Wardour Street in the heart of Soho. We were both there to meet with the A & R (Artist and Recording) manager that Reggie had set up for us.

We were sitting in the waiting room and talking to several members of the band and we started talking to a great guy called Eddie (Grant). Eddie wanted to know what sort of music we played and wondered if we might like to support them in an upcoming gig just outside London.

The gig was at the Watford Top Rank, which was a huge venue, holding thousands of people, just off the M1 near Watford North of London and we readily agreed.

At the Top Rank, the stage we were performing on was very large and wide and had a turntable set into the floor. We even had a complete set of stagehands and sound engineers to assist us. We were supposed to set up behind a large panel in the center of the rotating stage that separated one-half of the circular stage from the other, out of view of the audience.

Then when we gave the nod to the stagehands, they would start the turntable going as we started playing our opening number. Well, as luck would have it, Ian set the gear too close to the outside of the turntable (I'm sure it was Ian's fault) and as it started to turn, on the biggest gig we had ever managed to get, our amps and speakers started disappearing behind us. As we came into view of the mega audience, we were both scrambling to get our gear back with us as it disappeared behind the turning stage. Well, the damn thing kept turning as we came into view of our audience. Can you imagine seeing this as part of the audience? The sound starts, while the band is facing the wrong way as they came into view. The gig went well despite this, many members of the audience that came up to us afterward asked for our autographs.

We learned that for a really big performance, always check it out first!

SIR ADRIAN JOHNS

Sometimes we only get to meet a special friend for a very short time.

ONE OF OUR friends was Adrian Johns, who Ian had known for many years as Ian had always gone on holiday to Newquay in Cornwall and Adrian was from that area. So they would meet up in summer when Ian went there for the holidays. But now as we were all at college at the time, Ian doing pure math at Brunel, Adrian at Imperial College taking Physics in London and me doing Mechanical Engineering at Uxbridge Tech. Adrian needed the extra money to help him get through college, which was the same for us also. Adrian's mother was bringing him up in Cornwall and he had a brother called Julian who looked a lot like John Lennon and even had the same round glasses as John, with similar long hair.

Adrian had a West Country accent and seldom, if ever, talked on stage and definitely didn't or maybe couldn't sing. But as he, like us, didn't have a lot of money, we asked him if he would like to play with us in the band.

Adrian was a gifted guitarist, learned the songs easily and played with us for over a year. He also played on our demo album that we cut in a studio in the southeast end of London.

Adrian didn't have a car, so we had to pick him up in either Ian's old Ford Anglia Estate car, or as luck would have it, in my very small yellow Frogeye Sprite. My frogeye was quite small and three guys plus guitars was a real stretch in a strictly two-seater sports car. So I put my guitar and Ian's in the small trunk, which was an open space behind the two front seats and had no hatch or boot lid opening, so anything that was put in the "trunk" had to be slid in by leaning the seats forward in order to get to the "boot" or trunk space. I drove and Ian sat on the passenger seat but the only way we could get Adrian into the car was with Adrian sitting on Ian's lap. Now Adrian was very tall, around six feet three and the only way we could get him into the car was to have his head sticking out of the sliding passenger side window, while he was sitting slightly sideways on Ian's lap.

So, there we were—the three of us—Ian and Adrian on the passenger seat and me driving, a guitar laying half across my lap with poor Adrian's head poking out of the side of the little yellow sports car. As we drove from South Kensington, where Adrian's college was, to Battersea Bridge where the Old Swan, our current gig, was located, I began to see how funny this must have seemed. London streets are not that wide and the oncoming traffic moved very fast, as did I when I was driving. So, with Adrian's head sticking out of the car, I began to see the funny side of what we were doing and what it must have looked like to anyone else seeing us pass by and I started to drive as close as I could to anything we overtook along the way.

It got worse and if I overtook any double-decker bus, of which there were several we passed along the way, I made sure I hung the car right next to it, driving at the same speed as the bus. And just as we got level with the large spinning bus wheels, I gradually moved the little car with Adrian's head sticking out the side, closer and closer till his head came alongside and practically grazed the wheels. He couldn't get his head back into the car as there was no room whatsoever and he was frantically trying to grab the steering wheel from me, without being able to see inside the car, to get the car to move away from the fast-moving and spinning bus tires. He was yelling at me, "Moore! What the fuck are you doing?"

Of course, I would never let anything bad happen; but it was so funny. I also slowed down if the bus or truck's exhaust pipe was sticking out on Adrian's side of the car, to make sure he got blasted with the exhaust smoke while pretending of course that I hadn't noticed by carrying on a conversation with Ian. Such is life, into every life, a little rain must fall and for Adrian, riding in my car we were his downpour.

Now taxi drivers in their black cabs were notoriously rude to other drivers as they picked up and dropped off their passengers, or cut in front of us other drivers, believing themselves to be the divine users of the London streets. So I drove right up alongside one, at the traffic lights waiting for the lights to turn green and started honking my horn making as much noise as I could. The taxi driver looked around to see what the trouble was. He eventually looked down at the tiny yellow sports car sitting next to him at the traffic lights, he saw Adrian's head right next to his cab staring right up at him.

The driver looked as though he was going to kill Adrian, so Adrian, pleading, shouted up at the taxi driver, "It's not me. It's the idiot driver." But I just kept honking from the safe side of the car shouting, "Get out the bloody way." The taxi driver was not amused at all and shouted at Adrian, "You better f*#k off then, mate, or I'll get out of this cab."

Adrian was desperately trying to apologize to him. Have you ever seen anyone physically "shrink"? Well, Adrian did just that as we passed too close to the lorries, (trucks) and buses. Needless to say, when we arrived at the Old Swan, Adrian's hair was a sight, blown all over the place with soot on his face from being so close to the exhaust pipes of the trucks, lorries and buses that we had driven alongside on the way.

Our drive took us around forty-five minutes from Imperial College to where we were playing in Battersea, so we had all the time in the world to have fun, unfortunately, at Adrian's expense.

Well, after the gig, Adrian refused to get back in the car ever again with me driving and said he would feel safer walking, getting a cab, or getting a bus home. So I pleaded and pleaded with him and promised, looking him right in the eye, while promising on my mother's life, that I would not do it again under any circumstances. "I'm so sorry," I said to them both.

So very reluctantly, giving me the evil eye the whole time, Adrian got back into my car, once again sitting on Ian's lap with his head poking out the side window and off we went back from the gig in Battersea to Imperial College. Well, once they were both back in my car, they were mine! I did exactly the same all over again and started laughing like a witch, all the way home, with Adrian cursing and yelling at us both. Ian, of course, was laughing his head off with me, with tears rolling down our cheeks and we finally let Adrian out of the car once we arrived at his college after I made him promise not to hit me. This was, of course, all in fun and we loved playing our music with Adrian on lead guitar.

After the three of us finished college, Adrian told us he was thinking of joining the navy, "The navy," we both said in unison, "what a complete waste of time." And though we tried to convince him otherwise, he went ahead and joined up. We wished him good luck and we agreed we would all keep in touch. That was the last time Ian and I saw Adrian for three decades!

One day I got a call from Ian who said to me, "Do you remember Adrian who used to play lead guitar with us?" "Of course, I do, he left to join the Royal Navy," I replied, immediately recalling our journeys to and from our gigs, with Adrian, in my little yellow sports car. "Well, go onto Wikipedia and look him up and give me a call."

I looked up his name and there right before me was Sir Adrian Johns, second sea lord of the Royal Navy, Vice Admiral of the Royal Fleet, having been knighted by Her Majesty the Queen for outstanding services to the navy and for the country.

I was amazed to see Adrian's face smiling out at me on the Wikipedia page along with a complete chest full of medals, a very sharp uniform, and a biography, while I was recalling the gigs we had done and the rides in my tiny Frogeye Sprite. I called Ian back and said laughingly, "We told him it would be a waste of time to join the navy. Now see what he's done." But we were both so proud of what he had achieved.

What you should know, is that the Royal Navy is one of the most traditional of the armed services and to rise that high, coming from a single-parent family, having to have a scholarship to get through college, is in itself a stunning achievement. Normally, you would have come from a naval family with a long tradition of achievement in defending the Realm from the marauding hoards on our high seas. When I looked up "Second Sea Lord," I saw a long line of sea lords going back to 1830 and the last name on the list, at the time I read the article, was marked Adrian Johns, marked 2005—with a dash next to his name and no termination date, as he was the present second sea lord.

He relinquished his position as second sea lord and vice-admiral of the Royal Navy when Her Majesty the Queen appointed Adrian to become the governor of Gibraltar in 2009. He was taken there as the guest of honor on board a naval vessel and presented with the Keys of Gibraltar.

I went online and found the address of the governor of Gibraltar and decided to write a letter to him.

August 29, 2010
Dear Adrian,
I doubt that you will remember me, but Ian Howard yourself and me played in a band while we were all in college. You were at Imperial College taking physics, Ian took pure math at Brunel and I took mechanical engineering at Uxbridge while completing an apprenticeship at Taylor Woodrow.
You were exceptionally good at lead guitar, as I recall, we played at 'The Old Swan' in Battersea together where, once after a very scary drive in my very small yellow Frogeye Sprite with you sitting on

Ian's lap with your head sticking outside of the small sliding window, you vowed never to get in a car with me again.

Sorry for that, Adrian and I note your hair regrew after me driving far too close to the buses we overtook on the way to the 'gig with your hair brushing the tires of the buses and lorries along the way.

You also played on our demo album. I was so happy and so very proud when I saw your amazing progress with your career in the Royal Navy. Ian and I have kept in close contact over the years and he called me to ask me to look you up on Wikipedia.

I read with great interest your meteoric rise through the ranks and your knighthood leading to your present appointment as Governor of Gibraltar. Congratulations, Adrian. You haven't changed though, in your picture, but undoubtedly in other ways, you must have as a result of your immense responsibilities and the weight associated with your official capacity.

As for me, I moved over to Indianapolis in 1991 with Alfa Laval having managed their global customer service operations in Brussels. After leaving them I started up a fragrance company which we sold and then became General Manager and CEO of a glove company of all things. I designed and built firefighting gloves including one which is presently the most widely used in the US and Canada. I was asked to take part in the US Army's Rapid Field Initiative in 2004, after the beginning of the war in Iraq, to be part of a group of specialized manufacturers and advanced materials specialists, to help redesign the apparel for the US forces.

I designed, among other things, a glove for the US Army which, after being shown at the Pentagon, is now installed in every U.S. GI's kit bag and me a Brit!

Life is sometimes so strange, isn't it Adrian and very exciting with your success in the Navy, Ian's success in his music businesses and my diverse career we all scraped through. I am married to Sue for 22 years with 2 girls living in Ealing and 2 boys living here in the US.

I am writing a book, which I hope will inspire young people to reach their potential based on all the things I have been so fortunate to have done, but which pales compared to your success.

However when you consider that the three of us, you Ian and I, had somewhat difficult upbringings we have all done exceptionally well despite that, or perhaps it was because of that that we three succeeded.

I realize this may never get to you, but in case it does I would love to hear about the things you have done and I'm really glad you didn't take Ian's and my advice not to join up but to stay in the band!

Yours Sincerely,

Your friend,

Tony Moore

I received a reply from him very shortly by e-mail:

Tony,

Thank you so much for taking the trouble to write. It was great to hear from you and I can only apologize for taking so long to reply. I had been meaning to put pen to paper but then decided to ask Ian for your e-mail address—undoubtedly a quicker means of communication to and from the colonies!

I feel very guilty that I only caught up with Ian just over a year ago, just before we moved out to Gibraltar. It was 35 years since I'd seen him (and you) and the stupid thing was that we lived in London for the last 13 years—so close yet we never met.

Anyway, we had a terrific catch-up session at his place and had a really good laugh about your old frogeye Sprite. I remember only too well tearing along the roads perilously close to the parked cars and buses with my head stuck out of the passenger window—some problem with the heater I seem to recall!

I was fascinated to hear about how life has treated you—evidently not too badly and certainly very interestingly. I would never have put you down as a glove man, but there you are—life is never predictable. You know the three of us ought to catch up with each other again and, as I keep telling Ian now, none of us can afford to wait another 35 years or whatever the interval is. I may be out in the US (Iowa) next year for a wedding; if it works out well, I'm hoping that we can spend a week or so traveling—perhaps there's an opportunity there. But in any case, a warm welcome awaits you (and Ian) in Gibraltar—maybe we ought to have a musical reunion!

Whatever happens, let's ensure we keep in touch this time.

With warm regards,

AJ

His message back was as if no time at all had passed between us in more than thirty years.

That's the thing with friends; time doesn't matter at all and we are all still the same people we were then as now.

Well, congrats, Adrian. Way to go! I hope we meet up again sometime soon, but hopefully not in another thirty-five years, maybe one day when I come over to England to see my family; but after Ian and I talked a bit, we decided, "Don't call us. We'll call you when we need you as a lead guitarist again.

I recognized in Adrian the same drive Ian and I had and he, like us, stuck to what he loved and he also, made it no matter what. You will know yourself by the friends you keep so take a look around you, what do your friends say about you?

THE PENTHOUSE

Bob Guccione was" one of a kind" as well and was a highly successful gentleman when I met him.

W E WERE PLAYING in a pub in Mayfair called the Kings Arms in Shepherds Market in Mayfair, which was close to the Penthouse Club, when Bob Guccione came with several of his gorgeous "Penthouse Pets" and sat in the upstairs bar opposite us for a while listening to our music. That evening we found it difficult to remember our words and even more so to remain standing while he and these 3 incredibly beautiful girls were sitting opposite us. Each of them wore extremely short micro-mini skirts or hot pants and during our break, Bob came over to talk to us. He told us who he was, but we knew already, as Ian had seen his face in his *Penthouse* magazines (which as I recall he was always reading). He asked us to play at his club and invited us in for drinks later that night after we had finished at the pub. We went as his guests to see where we would perform.

His house band, "The International Trio," was off playing on the QE 2 for a six-month gig. So we got to play at the Penthouse club, in the International Room, where the best-looking girls we had ever seen now worked and believe me, there were loads of them there every night. They were his "Penthouse Pets" and were often featured in his *Penthouse* magazine as centerfolds!

We were able to recognize some of them with their clothes on and they were very similar to *Playboy*'s "Bunny Girls" at the Playboy Club, which was just down the street and had recently opened not far from where we were playing in Shepherd's Market.

The Playboy Club was opposite Hyde Park and the "pets" wore very tight body-hugging costumes that started halfway down their boobs and finished at the top of their very long legs. Their tops were very low cut and they also wore dark fishnet tights, with high heels that finished off their costumes . . . perfectly. I said to Bob one night when he came down to hear us, that we'd do this gig for nothing; but to get paid for being in the Penthouse Club was such a blast! Bob, looked at me and offered to let us play for nothing if that was what we wanted, but we told him the "No! Money was fine." He laughed at that and said " I thought so too"

Our gig was from midnight till 3:00 a.m., depending on how busy the club was. One night, one of the "pets," called Julia, came up to us and stood right in front of me as we were singing. I had noticed her from the first night but also thought that the girls were probably off-limits to us. Julia stood right in front of my face, as we were halfway through a song, that she had no ride home and wanted me to take her home after the gig! I said I'd think about it and after about one nanosecond said. "OK!"

I took her home to her flat in Fulham, which was on my way home from Mayfair. Julia was great fun to be with and we went out together for a few months. I would go to the club on Sunday mornings to pick her up in my sports car; I remember thinking, *Life Just doesn't get any better than this*, as I was driving through London in summer, in an open-top sports car, with one of the most beautiful girls in the world, a "Penthouse pet," sitting next to me with her long hair blowing in the wind!

Bob Guccione, to me, was a hero and the drive it takes to reach the top in any profession is the same drive that sometimes offends others.

LADY PENELOPE

Sometimes you can just get lucky; after all, every success has a little luck!

WE DECIDED TO advertise for a girl singer and advertised in the trade mags. We came across a beautiful blonde called "Dee Anderson" who we auditioned for. Dee was a stunningly good-looking girl; she wore the shortest hot pants we had ever seen. She had very sexy legs and a very pretty face. Dee was slim, petite and had the great voice to go with it. In short, Dee had the complete package and was perfect to join Ian and I.

Dee, as we found out later, was the daughter of Sylvia and Gerry Anderson, who had created produced and directed all of the *Supermarionation* TV series: *Twizzle, Torchy, Thunderbirds, Fireball XL-5, Supercar,* Joe 90 and many more children's TV shows since the late sixties, going back as far as *Four Feather Falls,* which Ian had watched while we were in junior school.

We used to practice singing with her sometimes at Ian's house and sometimes at her mother's house in Gerrard's Cross just twenty-five miles west of Ealing.

At her mother's house, there were alcoves set into the walls, all the way up the sweeping staircase, with the actual puppets that were used in the TV series. I was fascinated by the detail in every model. I was looking at Mike, Virgil, Brains and of course, Lady Penelope, from the *Thunderbirds* series and every costume had the tiniest stitching and each was finished right down to the smallest detail. Brains even had a small pen in his top pocket along with a tiny pair of glasses. When her mom wasn't around, I used to make Parker, the chauffeur, bonk Lady Penelope, much to the disgust of Dee, who was petrified in case her mom came back into the room.

Singing with Dee brought us some class and a third part harmony, which we needed and enabled us to do more complex three-part musical arrangements. Dee was married to Vick Elmes, who was the lead guitarist with a band called Christie, we even sang some of their songs. Christie had just had a number 1 hit in England and all over Europe, a couple of years earlier, with *"Yellow River"* and were currently away on a South African tour. Christie also released other songs *"San Bernardino"* and *"Iron Horse,"* but these didn't do as well as "Yellow River."

Dee sang with us for a long time and was a true professional with the most amazing "stage presence," adding a third dimension to our sound. Together with Dee, we did some big shows backing people like Ruby Murray, who although now is no longer singing having retired a long time ago, at that time they were headliners and were still big names in the British music scene.

I decided to make our stage costumes, for our cabaret gigs, as we had no money to buy them with. We went out and looked at fabrics and finally settled on bright pink satin for the trousers, with white satin baggy shirts. I made the trousers for Ian and me I and Dee, of course, had the shortest " pink hot pants" ever made and looked stunning in whatever she wore, so I made her hot pants with the small offcuts leftover.

During one gig with Dee, we were playing in front of a large working men's club in North London that was packed with people who had come to hear us as we had been billed for several months.

We were playing one Sunday in a lunchtime show when, at the end of one of our numbers, we all kicked our legs into the air together (God, did we actually did do that stuff!) Unfortunately though, as we did this on that particular day, Ian's trousers were a little too tight and as he kicked his leg as high as he could, exactly as we had rehearsed it, his trousers split all the way from the front zipper to the back waistband right at the crotch.

Dee and I heard a ripping sound and looked 'round at a very red-faced Ian. He immediately felt "quite free." Dee and I burst out laughing but had to continue with the song, luckily, he was wearing underwear, so it could have been worse.

You should have seen the women's faces on the front row as they ogled the scene. Ian, of course, was bright red and tried to lower his guitar to cover his underwear in case the fly opened. Unfortunately for him though, the guitar strap wouldn't let it drop down far enough to cover the split in his trousers, so there he was kind of crouched over as if he was dying to go to the bathroom trying to make the guitar hang lower. In fact, it wasn't the guitar that was hanging lower at all. We quickly finished the number and Ian had to rush back to the dressing room to change.

Together with Dee, we also got gigs in many variety shows and reviews. They were always fun to do, mainly because we only had to sing four or five numbers and were getting paid more than we usually did playing all night in clubs and pubs.

Our fans came with us everywhere to support us all the time. Christmas was the greatest time of all and we had several Christmas songs that we played—Slade, John Lennon, Wizard and many others—and we were good at getting people dancing and singing along with us. We were in high demand and had to be booked up for New Year's Eve and Christmas Eve months or even a year in advance.

Our favorite gig though was the Old Swan in Battersea, where we played overlooking the river Thames and sang there off and on for three years.

Ian's girlfriend was called Sandy, who, as I recall, loved animals and was obsessed with dogs. I thought Ian would marry her, but that wasn't to be. I was still with Cezara and the four of us used to go on holiday together in Cornwall. We booked a cottage to stay in and all drove down together. Life for us both was so easy and at that time we seemed to be able to do whatever we wanted.

Dee Anderson and I have remained close friends, we follow the successes of our true friends with great pride.

MOIRA

Making a difficult choice to end a relationship as good friends is better in hindsight

It WAS AROUND this time when I started working at Alfa Laval, I was singing almost every night when I met Moira. Moira was eighteen years old with naturally beautiful long blonde hair. She was working at Beecham's just down the Great West Road near my office at Alfa Laval. We met in a local pub, one lunchtime when I was with some work friends though I'm not sure which pub it was as there were so many close to my office.

Moira was gorgeous, so I just had to go up and talk to her, though I wasn't sure if she would talk to me; but I didn't care. It was worth a try anyway. So I went over to her and we started to talk. We arranged to meet a few days later, at lunchtime in the pub. I told her that there was a job going at my company as a secretary to one of the service directors if she was interested in applying for it. Well, she was interested and she applied for and got the job as a personal assistant for a service director called Jim Henderson, who was a little scatty but a good bloke.

Moira was the most stunning-looking girl in the entire company. She came into work often in short miniskirts, which of course were very "in" at that time and sometimes she also wore a pair of metallic maroon knee-length boots, which coupled with her natural light honey blonde hair, worn down past her shoulders, made her devastatingly beautiful.

All of the guys working there, in the offices, wanted to go out with Moira; but she was quite shy and would only talk to a very few people. I was the lucky one that she did talk to.

Although her first name is Irish, she was very much a London girl. She dressed beautifully all the time and had a nice lilting voice with a sexy laugh that was always just under the surface. I seemed to be able to make her laugh a lot back then.

Our paths crossed while I was working in the spares office, as she often came in to check on something or other for her service team. I knew she could have done it over the phone but took the fact that she came into my office instead to mean one of two things; either she needed to get out of her boss Jim's office, or she wanted to come into my office to see me. I of course chose to believe the latter.

She was very kind, very thoughtful and better still she paid her way, not letting me always buy the drinks but insisting on paying for them as well, unlike most other girls I knew then. She took life and her job quite seriously, which is more than I can say for myself as I was just a clown. We went out together for about nine months, during the time she worked there, but we very seldom, if ever, met at night. I was always playing and singing all over London and I had little time for a steady girlfriend at that time, which was not what Moira wanted.

Moira told me one day that she had a boyfriend and she was considering marriage. I saw our relationship as mostly daytime friends, almost like brother and sister, but I didn't think of a permanent relationship at that time, with anyone. Moira would have been the girl I would have married if I had been in a different frame of mind, but life was too busy and there were too many fun things to do to ever consider getting married.

I knew that she wanted a permanent relationship with me and I knew that she loved me and that she was telling me this to see what my reaction would be. I also knew though that I was not the right person at that time for her as I had so many things I still wanted to do and didn't want a permanent relationship at that time. I certainly never wanted to cause any problems or ever hurt Moira but knew that if I did go out with her on a more permanent basis let alone get married to her, at that time, it would have ended in disaster and it would have been caused entirely by me.

Moira wanted more from her relationship with me and after her boss, Jim, was transferred to the States to run a service operation in Lake Geneva in the Midwest, in 1973, Moira left Alfa Laval, never to return. We did, however, still meet up occasionally for a lunchtime drink, to catch up on things, for a long time after she left, though by now she was happily married. We became very close as time went on long after both she and I had left Alfa Laval and later Moira became my soul mate. We have remained friends ever since, she in London and me in the States and although we never meet in person, we have kept in touch for over forty years.

A break in a relationship for honest reasons can make friends forever.

JANET

A femme fatale once in your life is being on a rollercoaster!

I WAS DRIVING a red MGBGT at the time and decided to change it for a different one. So I started looking through Exchange and Mart and eventually found a late model automatic. I arranged to meet the seller, outside Alfa Laval's offices in Brentford where I worked, the seller turned out to be a French girl, I took the car for a test drive and asked all the right questions and decided to buy her car. The next day, I bought the blue MGBGT from Janet and we became friends. We talked over the phone for several weeks before actually meeting up again and began going out together.

I went out with Janet for two tumultuous years and can honestly say that she was the one person that taught me all about girls and how a boy should act when going out with a girl. One detail though, Janet was married and had a son called Toby, who was five years old and, at that time, this was a fact that I was not certain about at all.

She told me she was divorcing her husband, Richard, a minicab driver, adding that they didn't get on at all well and that he sometimes hit her. Janet had a very sexy French accent that she could turn up or down at will and the amount of her French accent always depended on what she wanted from whomever she was talking to. She was very elegant, beautiful in fact, tall and slim with long brown highlighted hair. She had such a magnetic presence about her that when we went to restaurants or clubs in London, she would always turn heads as she entered.

She loved the attention she got and made sure when she moved everyone noticed her. Her family was from Toulouse in Southern France, she had a sister called Katherine, "Kati." Janet was blessed with incredible looks and the charm to go with it.

I became infatuated with her and we went out all over the place, to clubs, restaurants, parks, art galleries and anywhere she wanted to go to and I learned how to act cool (cooler than I thought I already was) and learned what sophistication was all about. Yeah right!

"Tonnie," she would say in her very French accent, "ow you do dress so droll; you look like a plouk. I weel take you out and pick out some cloths that soot you more." "What's a plouk then?" I asked her, she told me, "Plouk is a word for a peasant... just like you." And I used the word a lot as I liked the sound of it. "Plouk" was a perfect word.

So we went out to buy new clothes and I changed my "look" just like that! I was so bloody gullible. She had me wearing horizontally striped French-cut T-shirts, a black neck scarf and flared jeans. I thought I looked like the character "Falconetti" from *Rich Man, Poor Man*, a current show on TV of the time. Janet looked a lot like Barbara Streisand—not only because she had similar features but also because she acted like her too. At least she acted like the parts Streisand played in the movies she was acting in at the time, movies like *The Owl and the Pussycat* with Walter Matthau.

Janet had also done some modeling for a magazine so I guessed she knew about fashionable dress sense. Once for my birthday, when I was twenty-five, she took me to the most expensive restaurant I had ever been to—"The White Elephant"—on the river Thames and gave me my birthday present, which was a solid silver very chunky bracelet with the letters of my name *TONY* cast into the links of the bracelet (It's in the photo of me with Vick Elmes).

It was beautiful and unique, I loved it and I still have it. I had never seen anything like it and apparently, as she continued to inform me, "Eet kem from a very expenseev and excluseev designer gallerie in Paris. So you see ow much I love you, Tonnie. I av made you into a not-so-plouky person . . . all by my leetle French self." God, how could I not fall in love with that!

Things at her house, with Richard, got progressively worse and she convinced me to drive her to her home in Toulouse. "Eet will be so much fun, Tonnie. I can teach you ow to speak French like a true Frenchman and we can live in the south of France together." Well, for me, that sounded great and I could do with a change of scenery.

So we moved on our plan. She began to teach me French and I was a good learner. I seemed to have a knack for languages, or so I thought. I was also learning to speak the absolute worse slang phrases imaginable and come out with them just at the right time, just as I had with Polish phrases with Cezara.

I was now a multilingual swearer. I could swear with the best of them in three languages—Polish, French and of course English.

Janet had a health issue though, causing her to go into a freeze-like trance that she called Tetany, which was some kind of illness that caused her to collapse on the floor completely stiff. This was not a problem for me, as it happened very infrequently. When it happened though, she had to take some dark brown liquid that she always kept in her purse in a sealed glass vial that had to be snapped at one end to get the liquid out. I had met some of her friends from Toulouse when they came over to London just after Christmas in 1974 and we got on very well.

There was Jean Louie and Jackotte, Eve and Michel and Georges. When they came over to visit her, at her house in Pinner, I was introduced to them and they looked so cool. They each wore a different style of hat and dressed very "French" in dark corduroy trousers in colors that matched their hats. For example, Michel had a pair of light brown cords and a brown fedora, Jean Louis had a gray pair of cords and a gray beret, while Georges wore dark brown cords with a dark brown hat.

I tried out my newly learned French, which they thought was hilarious; but because I did try to speak with them in French and I tried the many slang phrases as well as conversational French that I had been taught by Janet, (I blamed my lousy French on my very bad teacher).

They all came over just after Christmas, in late December and we took them to clubs and pubs all over London.

Jackotte and Jean Louie were quite wealthy and had their own farm. Eve was a gifted artist while Michel was the absolute rough and ready French male chauvinist; but I liked him a lot, especially since Janet often called him simply "the plouk." Georges was single and though I never knew what he did for a living they had all known each other since school. I envied that part as they were so alike and were so much fun to be with—my "French crowd."

The French Connection

I was by now crazy about Janet and was quite prepared to do anything to help her. So in summer 1976, I met with my personnel manager and told him I had to take a temporary leave so that I could take my girlfriend back to her family in France.

My HR manager agreed, so Janet and I left London to drive down to Toulouse in my blue MGB-GT, initially for a vacation. The weather that year was the hottest summer we had had in Europe for decades, with eight weeks of very hot sunny days and temperatures in the nineties. We drove my car down through Paris to Rouen in perfect weather, which became hotter and hotter as we drove south toward Toulouse. Janet wanted to show me how beautiful her capital, Paris, was; although she constantly reminded me, "Toulouse is of course much more important than Paris."

We passed through Le Mans, so we could drive "The Strip" where the famous Le Mans Twenty-Four-Hour race is held and having a sports car was great. We drove like a GT racer through some of the most beautiful countryside I had ever seen. We passed through the Loir Valley where it was so hot we stopped and went for a swim in the Loir River. We then went on through Clermont-Ferrand which was high up in the Massif Central Mountains. Clermont-Ferrand was an expensive ski resort with a casino in the middle of town.

Janet had her way and insisted we meet the mayor of Clermont-Ferrand, who was quite taken by her and he made some phone calls for us to stay in a beautiful hotel overlooking the town with the mountains in the background.

I loved it! That was typical of Janet, to make last-minute arrangements at the highest level. That night, we got into the casino, compliments of the mayor and had a blast. I knew nothing of gambling and was quite naive, compared with Janet. She showed me how to play roulette, blackjack and poker. She won at everything, while I lost! The casino was fabulous, with old money and the rich from all over France who went there for weekends.

We then got back onto the road to Toulouse the following day, heading east through Brive-La-Gaillarde then to Limoges where we tried the local wine on our drive south. The most beautiful place we passed through was Uzerche, on our way down from Limoges, where the local wine was incredible.

The town was very pretty and had a river running right through it. The local shops restaurants and bars were so quaint and we had lunch while in Uzerche and I hoped one day to go back through there. Little was I to know that my wish would come true, but that's later. We lived on local wine, local saucisson (French country sausage) and local cheeses that were delicious. We eventually drove through Montauban and finally arrived at Toulouse, "The Rose City," called that because of the rose-colored roof tiles and the pink brick that the town was built from.

Although we were not staying in Toulouse, as her friends lived just outside in a small town called Bruguières, just to the north of Toulouse.

I was introduced to Janet's parents as her "friend" who had brought her home from England. Her mother was a very attractive well-dressed and elegantly "chic" lady who taught English at an "Ecole du Langue" in Downtown Toulouse. She was the "in-charge" head of the family and while her father, an Englishman, was pleasant, he said very little to me. He seemed very different from her mother and was from somewhere in the Midlands, judging from his accent.

I didn't want to stay with her parents, even as Janet insisted that I should. I felt uncomfortable not being Janet's husband. Eve, (pronounced Ev) and Michel insisted that I stayed with them, so I moved my stuff into Eve and Michel's home in Bruguières, which was only a twenty-five-minute drive out of town.

I grew very fond of Eve and Michel and loved their house. They had two hunting dogs that were kept outside always, whose names were "Boogie" and "Patou" and their house had a beautiful view to the South of Andorra, a tiny country that borders France and Spain and is located in the Andorra Mountains.

In the evenings, we could watch the thunderstorms that often occurred in the high mountains around Andorra where the warm air from Southern France met with the cooler air off the mountains.

Eve and Michel became very close friends with me, with Michel taking me with him into the local village every evening to meet his friends at the local bar. I became well known and was often asked to play guitar for them all. We had many parties and I met lots of Eve and Michel's friends from all over the south of France.

Eve lived a very "country" lifestyle and lived for the day and always made dinner arrangements spontaneously. They had two children: Olivier, who was eight years old and Isabelle, who was six years old. The children were a lot of fun and I was the superstar who played all over London and was apparently "famous" there, according to Janet. Well, I was well known, but not famous.

So, I sang for my supper, whenever they wanted me to, which I was happy to do. I even got gigs in some of the local restaurants and clubs in Toulouse. I didn't make a huge amount of money, but it was enough for me to get by and allowed me to buy petrol for my car and to help Eve pay for food. I was even in a local music magazine with a picture of Ian and me. Eve and Michel were not well off at that time when Michel was often away on sales trips all over Southern France.

Michel came from a large family who lived on the same plot of land with an open-air swimming pool placed between Eve and Michel's house and his parents' house. His older brother, Bernard Nicolas, was a news announcer with "Canal Plus," a nationwide TV station. We often saw him announcing the evening news on TV where he was broadcasting the day's events his wife at the time was Josiane.

I stayed mostly with Eve, while Michel was away. I helped her with the family and rode around on her little moped. That was a blast in itself; though it didn't go fast, it was fast enough for me, especially since the local drivers were so bloody dangerous and drove so fast that I took my life into my hands whenever I got on the thing. Often they would come right up behind me and blast their horns to let me know they were passing regardless of a bend, a narrow lane, or whatever.

They would shout out, "hey, Englese, ow is the queen," so bloody funny as I was quite well known in the small village of Bruguières and several times I was forced off the road and into the ditch, which was a real hoot!

Needless to say, after some three weeks of vacationing in Toulouse, it was time for me to get back to work.

The drive back was fast and the weather was still very hot, one of the hottest summers on record. We arrived back in England and I dropped her off; it was now September and soon the weather would change.

I went back to my job at Alfa Laval and got back into my routine of singing at night while working during the day. Life was good and I never seemed to have time for anything else as we were playing six nights a week and working five days.

Things with Janet at home got steadily worse. she wanted me to take her back to France to live there permanently; however, she had met up with an old boyfriend who stayed at her house for a few weeks, someone she had apparently known for many years. His name was Jean Georges and to me, they seemed very close.

I didn't care though as I was not the jealous type and believed in our relationship. By now, my French was pretty good but one afternoon while the three of us were playing Belote (pronounced Boulet), I heard them both talking quietly in French as we were playing, she was saying, "Mais je t'aime plus mon chér" to Jean Georges, or something very close. I told her later that I had understood what she had just said. She began a lengthy explanation that it was another French expression that meant they were just friends and nothing more. But I knew better. She eventually married Jean Georges so my misgivings and my understanding of what was said turned out to be true.

Shortly after this incident, she decided to move to France permanently. I discussed this with Ian and we agreed that I would set up gigs for us to play there and he would come over and join me to sing to a French audience.

We drove over in late September and I moved back in with Eve and Michel, while Janet and Toby moved in with her mom and dad in downtown Toulouse. We found Toby a local French school, where he began to attend, with me taking him and picking him up. I had no experience with looking after a seven-year-old but gave it my best. It was a difficult time though and I began to have doubts about our relationship and whether I could make it there and could not, as time went on, think I could live there permanently.

I could speak a little French and I was improving day by day. I had to find gigs in restaurants, bars and clubs by myself. Janet's mother had given me a job teaching English at her private school, but I didn't like it much. Janet's mother didn't like what her daughter was doing and made it clear to me I was unwelcome.

Janet was finding it very difficult to live back in France and this was the cause of numerous and increasing problems between us.

Meanwhile, as I had been living there for a while, Alfa Laval was contacting me to see if I would come back to work and as money was getting very tight for me and the gigs I did manage to get did not pay that well, certainly not enough to support Janet and Toby, so after some careful thought, I decided to return to London and to leave Janet to her back in Toulouse with her family. I had not seen her for three months. Eve and Michel were true friends, even after I left them and we have stayed in touch for many years.

After I left France and had finished with Janet for good, I sent them some money for Christmas in a letter I wrote, telling them that this money was for all of them to spend or squander on whatever they wanted for themselves and not to be used for paying bills. Eve told me years later that as she read it out to Michel and showed him the money, he cried at what I had done. I told her, "No, not that, Eve. I only wanted to repay some of the kindness you both showed me while I was living there." It was such a small thing in return for all that they had done to help me. We were and still are true soul mates.

As I was to find out years later, Janet moved back in with Richard for several years, but I had moved on.

One tumultuous event that taught me so much and I discovered w whole new me!

GOING SEPARATE WAYS

Music or business!

IT WAS AT THIS time after I had returned from France, that Ian told me he had started a business and that was why he wouldn't come over to France despite me getting gigs and having articles written about my playing.

Ian's business was a second-hand records and tapes business with Alan, a friend of ours. He had opened a small shop in Putney called Music Market and was planning to open more shops as his business grew.

I had looked forward to moving on together in music and I had planned for us to sing in France for as long as we could.

"Look," Ian said one day when we were talking about his new business and I wanted to know why he hadn't told me about it, "there is a space for your name on the letterhead if you want to join us." I knew though it wouldn't work and that if it was meant to be, we would have done it together already.

This was the point at which Ian and I stopped being such close friends and started moving in separate directions. We didn't see or contact each other much over the next thirty years, as both of us moved in different directions. More of Ian's exploits later. I knew that Ian's actions would never allow us to be close friends ever again.

It is a tough decision to make—that you are not going to make it big in the music business by performing, although many of the artist managers and agents that had heard us play had wanted to represent us and move us up in the music business with performances and even recordings.

One manager had even started making plans that we should become the next "New Seekers," but we didn't like that idea. I was now twenty-six and decided that if I was meant to make it, it would have happened by now.

I had written several songs and Brian Longley, who was managing *Christie, Edison Lighthouse,* and other bands at that time, wanted me to sing the songs over to him as the band *"Middle of the Road"* were looking for a follow up to "Chirpy Chirpy Cheep Cheep," a terrible song that had made it high in the charts.

Brian had played them my songs and they liked one called "Penny Farthing." The deal though was for 25 percent of the net and I knew that by the time he had taken his cut and all of his expenses were taken out I would have nothing left, so I declined. Brian certainly knew the business and was managing several other bands at the same time.

I decided that since I had a degree in engineering, I had better start using it and start focusing on my job, which by the way was taking off and I was getting a good reputation in the company, not that I thought much about that as I always focused only on what I was doing and not about what others thought of me.

Knowing the difference between being a good performer and having the star quality required to make it in the entertainment business is hard. It's worse though to continue in the belief that you are better than you really are!

JANE

Comes a time to settle down.

 JANE AND I MET at the Queens Silver Jubilee party at "The Haven" pub in Ealing on June 6, 1977, when everyone in England had a street party to celebrate the queen's twenty-fifth anniversary.

We began dating soon after, as Jane had recently divorced from Lesley, her first husband. Jane had a young daughter, Amanda, from that marriage and Amanda was only eleven months when Jane and I met. I liked Amanda immediately as she was such a quiet little girl with light blonde curly hair, she and I became instant best friends. Jane and I had been dating for several months, during which time I often moved between my pad and her apartment, which was located in a very expensive part of Ealing.

At that time, both Jane and I had good careers, so money was never a problem. I worked during the day at Alfa Laval and during the evenings I was playing at pubs and clubs all over London. I think I could have become a taxi driver with so many places I knew how to get to all over London.

After we had been going out for several months, she asked me if I wanted to move in with her as it would be cheaper for both of us. I was a little concerned about whether Les, her ex-husband, would make it difficult; but as he had been the sole cause of their marriage break up and was living with another woman, Jane told me he had nothing to say in the matter. So I moved out of my very cool and trendy little bachelor pad in Acton and moved in with Jane, in Ealing.

Life went on for the both of us and it seemed we were always having parties, going to parties, or spending late nights at the Haven pub. Often at weekends, even during the week, the proprietors of the pub, would close the bar and allow us to drink after hours. We would play music and party like there was no tomorrow. On Sunday afternoons, we used to go to a club on Kings Road in Chelsea, which was always packed.

My boss, Peter, lived directly opposite the Haven Arms and was amazed at how I could be in the bar till 3:00 a.m. and still get into work at 8:00 a.m., but never be late and definitely never tired. "How on earth do you do it?" he often said, even now, in retrospect I don't know either.

If we didn't end up at the Haven, we would all go on to "Maddox," which was a nightclub in Ealing Broadway and was the place where the Rolling Stones, The Who and many other bands first began to perform in the early '60s. At that time, though, it was called the Ealing Club.

But the club had never changed, only its name. It was a downstairs dive bar and was very busy on weekends with long lines outside with people waiting to get in after the pubs closed. We always went to the front of the line as we were well known by the owners. Maddox was open sometimes all night. The managers were also very good friends of ours and were always happy to see us, as we usually brought in a crowd. Amanda was well looked after by Eve or Mimi and Alice, who were Jane's aunts, or even Rene, who was Lesley's mother and Amanda's grandmother. Amanda loved staying with Meme and Alice and was never a problem.

We were inundated with babysitters, especially since Amanda was so good to look after, in fact, they would often argue over who was to look after her. Eve was the manageress of Russell and Bromley, a high-quality shoe shop in Ealing Broadway. So we got all our shoes at a discount; needless to say, I had loads of really good shoes.

Jane and I were to become friends for life, a great outcome for us both.

VISION INTO REALITY

It's the planning that turns a vision into reality.

THE THREE OF us became an instant family—
Jane, Amanda and me. I was working at Alfa Laval, in the "spares
department," while Jane was in the film business. Jane was an
actress, an extra, a stunt double and a hand model, all at the same
time! We decided to buy a house in Hanwell, as Jane wanted to live
near her mother Eve, Meme and Alice. Meme and Alice were
Amanda's aunts on her mother's side of the family and both lived
downstairs in her mother Eve's house in Drayton Bridge Road in
Hanwell.

Eve had a lodger, Bill, who was a Geordie who had lived with her
many years and who spent all of his time in a Catholic club in Ealing.

Meme and Alice had looked after Jane for many years and were old
family friends. We bought a cottage in old Hanwell in Clairville
Gardens. The house was a two-up, two-down, but with a large
kitchen overlooking the garden. I decided to completely remodel the
house and knock through the front and back rooms to make a larger
open plan room with arches.

I had help from Brian, a local builder. Brian and his wife, Barb,
became good friends with us both.

We knocked through the rooms, added an arch across the ceiling,
then took the door out between the living room and the kitchen and
built a bar under the stairs. When I had finished, it looked very
modern and had a lot of character. Nothing was too difficult for me
to do. I did electrical work, plumbing, floated walls and even re-did
the ceilings.

While I was standing on the stairs, halfway through the work, with
Brian and Bill who was Jane's mother's live-in friend. I noticed
some black specs on the back of my hand. I wiped them off, but they
reappeared, so I looked up to see the upstairs ceiling, above the stairs
forming a black and rapidly growing crack right above us. "Run" I
shouted to Brian and Bill, as we legged it as fast as we could outside
the open front door just as the entire ceiling collapsed right where
we were standing only seconds before.

The idiot we hired to replace the water tank in the loft had cut right
through a ceiling joist to get the new tank into the loft. The weight

of the now-full water tank on the unsupported ceiling joist brought the whole lot crashing down. Smoke and dust from over a hundred years in our loft all came right down in an instant and we were left coughing and spluttering as the dust cloud came billowing out of the front door.

The three of us looked like Black men with white eyes and as we stood outside our not-quite-finished first home, we burst out laughing, leaving white streaks on our faces as the tears, partly from the black soot in our eyes and partly from laughing, left their tracks down our faces.

The centerpiece of our remodeling work was the kitchen where I decided to make a suspended kitchen table, which would be hung from a four-inch-square beam dropped down through the ceiling above.

I went upstairs and measured the floor and took up the floorboards. I made an exact four-inch-square hole in the ceiling, next to the big wooden ceiling joist, I cut the same-sized square hole in the concrete floor in the kitchen below. I measured and cut a breakfast bar that would have a suspended round table with a square hole in the middle that I hoped would fit together and would enable the square pole to go through the breakfast bar from above coming through the ceiling, through the round table with the square hole cut in the middle and on into the square hole cut into the floor.

When I finished the work, I checked once again for the umpteenth time; then I slid the wooden beam through the ceiling and through the bar as it slid through right into the square indentation in the floor. It looked great and the whole thing went together perfectly. It was such a perfect fit that it had to be tapped in with a hammer. The overall look was exactly as I had planned and gave the house a unique modern look. The breakfast bar was suspended from the ceiling and was attached to the work surface seemingly as one entire piece. Brilliant! As luck would have it, it worked beautifully.

I learned that when we spend a lot of time planning we are more likely to succeed!

MY LITTLE BROTHER

This was to be one of the saddest friendships in my life.

OPPOSITE OUR COTTAGE, in Clairville Gardens, a friend of ours, Carolyn, who was a very talented artist who lived together with her two children, Adrian and Sarah and had moved in shortly after we did.

Adrian, who was eleven years old, was in the "Corona" drama school for stage and music and whenever I got home from work, he always came over to spend time with me. I used to take him and Amanda out with me. Adrian loved making his plastic models with me or he would help me make one of my own in my very limited free time.

Adrian would come over to our house and bring his model kits to get me to show him how to make them or paint them. Adrian was like a younger brother and was always interested in whatever I was doing.

Adrian was a really sweet kid, always polite, always interested in everything and I became very close to him like an older brother. I used to take him to the Model Shop in Harrow where we would both spend all Saturday morning looking at the possibilities of what he and I could make together. Adrian's sister, Sarah, was also a very sweet girl; but I spent more time with Ade (as we called him).

Another Brick In The Wall

One day when Adrian came home from school, he told me he had been singing with his class on a new record by Pink Floyd for a soon-to-be-released album called *Another Brick in the Wall*. He and his class had sung the children's chorus. At that time, Pink Floyd was huge in England and once again, we never knew how big that single would eventually become.

Several weeks later, I went with a friend of mine, Lenny Lewis, to the "Konk's" recording studio at Muswell Hill, which was owned by the Kinks. While we were there, we heard the, not yet released, fully expanded single, *Another Brick In The Wall*, from the album on a forty-eight-track reel to reel master tape of the single from their latest album *The Wall*. This was before it was to be mixed down and put through a compressor and a limiter, which were two processes in the final mixed-down sound ready for releasing their music.

The music was played on the 48 track "reel to reel" tape machine on the studio's huge monitor speakers, which was exactly as it had all been recorded by the Floyd and was the "raw." Sound. As we were listening, our Tee shirts were being moved by the huge bass line—boom de boom boom boom, which was moving our chests along with it. It was incredible the sound and the recording. I had never heard such a unique single before that and we knew it would become a huge hit after listening to it.

As we know now, *The Wall* is a rock standard and is as good now as it was then! Sadly, several years later when I met a much older Adrian, now in his early twenties, he had become a very changed person and very different from the great kid I knew when he came over to our house. Adrian went on to do some acting and was in several films and had a potential career but later, when he was 18, he chose instead to join the army.

He now had a child of his own and very sadly, he committed suicide because of what is known to be a very treatable mental illness, called "Manic Depression."

I still think of Adrian all the time, especially at Christmas and if I hear Pink Floyd's best-ever single *"Another Brick in the Wall,"* I always listen for his voice so in a way he is always with me. I realized how easy it was to see only the bad things, when you are in a chronic low depression, you don't see the good things. Adrian had been in several movies and had great career potential in the film business. Sadly, that was not to be for him.

Carolyn Mann, his mother, who was a great friend of mine, sent me this message when I contacted her after a gap of over twenty-five years to ask her permission to place Adrian into my book.

Here's what she said, in an e-mail, about my little "brother" Adrian and me:

"I remember how fond Adrian was of you and of course vice versa—you added something to his life that was essential for him—I always knew that the presence of a really good adult male figure was what he not only wanted but needed. His relationship with you was so important—thanks so much for that—I'm really touched by the inclusion of "Ade" in your book and of course, your life."

I was happy that while our circles touched, I was able to be with him in his very short time on this earth. I find it hard even now to think of how sad he must have felt to take the route he took, but part of me is happy also that he is in a better place than many.

In the words of Dick Lewis, a high-flying police officer at New Scotland Yard, whom I also met after a twenty-plus year gap in 2011 in Brighton he said "Tony, some people are wired up wrong and there's nothing we can do about that. At some point, they will do the inevitable and we can't protect them from themselves forever." Sadly, though, Dick was referring to his daughter who took her own life while she was excelling at a university with a beautiful life before her. She had also suffered from depression.

I was so very happy that Carolyn's message could be included as she is not only a gifted friend of mine with her art but also has had to put up with her own share of life's difficulties and like me, my dear and very talented Carolyn is still standing!

Carolyn wrote a poem for Adrian (Ade): *Fat Black Plastic Sacks*

Fat Black Plastic Sacks

Fat black plastic sacks surround my bed
delivered to my door by his sad and distraught friends
each bag enclosing proof of his terrestrial life
his suits, his shoes, his socks, his shirts,
his rambling crazy midnight notes are here with me
and here am I
encircled for three years within this ring of tactile memories
their secrecy and comfort colluding in my denial.
And now
as if from a chrysalis, I emerge into the light of day
and I must face these horrors
these demons clutching at my heart and lungs
so I can live and speak of him again
and speak of him as one would speak of any child
whose tiny body clings to love
to smile its pleasure into its mother's eyes.
Methodically, for many hours I move among this treasured trove of earthliness
to sort, to save, to allocate with folded tissue' d care

until I'm done
then crouched in genuflection and wet with anguished tears
I feel a sudden rush of wind blow past my face
A breeze as if from nowhere encircles me in his cool remembrance.
When Carolyn had finished going through the black plastic sacks of
Ade's life, left by his friends, after a period of three years, a cool
breeze
blew through the room; though no doors or windows were open as
if he was now free as was she.

*We will never forget you Adrian your charm, your humor, your
too-short life!*

STAR WARS IN THE MAKING

Sometimes, the simplest experience, seeming to be quite normal at the time, becomes a momentous event on reflection later on in life.

WHILE JANE AND I were at the beginning of our relationship, I would often drive up to Boreham Wood Studios, where Jane was working on a new movie called *Star Wars*, as Carrie Fisher's "stand-in." I left my office to drive as fast as I could to Boreham Wood studios, where, with my name left at the gate by Jane, I could go right on through to the film set. Jane was always very natural with her "film friends," and they were a great bunch of people.

We sat at a standard canteen table, no-frills, we had a canteen lunch with Wookie, Darth Vader and several of the other characters who were in that day's shoot.

They were good fun to be with and when "on set," no one did the "star" thing at all; no one knew how big the film was going to become as it was only in the filming stage of the first Star Wars movie when I went to see it being made. I loved standing behind the camera and watching, the acting in quiet fascination, without any special effects, which were to be added later on.

To this day, I can still see the particular scenes that I had seen first-hand being filmed while standing with Jane behind the camera.

One day while I was standing quietly behind the camera, watching a scene where the small spacecraft belonging to Hans Solo had landed in what was to be a swamp, though when I was there it was just an empty studio floor with tape markings all over. Actors came running onto the ramp, pretending to fire prop guns at some enemy that I couldn't see. I have to say it looked very "lame."

Now at this time, there was no *Star Wars* film released as yet and though it was a new "sci-fi" movie, no one had any idea how it would look or how big it was to become. And I had never heard of George Lucas before that film but standing next to me was none other than George Lucas, the director. He asked me what I thought of what was being filmed. Now at that time what I was watching, with no special effects seemed very lame. So I turned to Mr. Lucas and said in reply, "Great. I suppose, though, I have to say your imagination is probably a lot better than mine." Mr. Lucas went on to explain some of the plots at that point in the film, so I told him I couldn't wait for it to be released so I could see what he was explaining.

I was mesmerized by the way that the crew got everything together. Anyone wanting to know what "controlled chaos" really looks like should see a film crew at work. All is crazy until the "recording now buzzer" goes off, after which you could hear a pin drop.

As a scene finished being filmed, the cameraman or director would see that something needed changing and would make a simple statement like, "The key is off a little. Bring it around."

Then all hell would let loose as they made the corrections for the next shot. My full congratulations to all of the actors as they had to repeat the same scene over and over again until they got it right to the director's satisfaction.

In one scene, George Lucas was getting quite cross at Wookie for not moving his head correctly when he made his growling sound when talking to Hans Solo in his beaten-up space cruiser. They had to do that one piece of the scene over and over again. Finally, George went over to Wookie and showed him what he wanted, mimicking the correct movement.

After the film had been completed, Jane and I went to the *Star Wars* premiere in Leicester Square, where I was reintroduced to a lot of the crew, who greeted Jane as an old friend. The film became legendary and was absolutely a classic from the moment it was released, we couldn't believe how the special effects had transformed what we had seen being filmed into what was now the finished movie.

When we were courting I also went to meet Jane on various other film sets, if I wasn't playing somewhere, including the set of the first couple of *Superman* movies, where we sat with the late Christopher Reeves while we were having lunch. I was watching the scene where he flew past an airliner's pilot's window and waved at the pilot and copilot, while they were flying the plane.

That scene was filmed over and over until it was acceptable to the director. Superman, Christopher Reeve, was in a big harness and was reeled back and forth in front of the cockpit windows, in front of a huge fan to give the effect of the high wind as he was flying while keeping up with the airliner and did the same wave with as many slight variations as could be managed with each successive take.

Christopher Reeve was a kind and very ordinary man, working for a living, with no "star" image of himself; almost as if he knew at that time how privileged he was to be doing what he was doing. Jane and I often talked to him over our lunch dates while eating lunch in the canteen during the filming. It was so sad to hear he had passed on October 4th, 2004, but to us, he left a legacy that will survive for decades.

An American Werewolf In London

One day when I was working at Alfa Laval, Jane called me and asked me if she could use my car to go uptown for a "night shoot" in a new movie called *An American Werewolf in London*. I said, "OK, no problem. I'll use yours." Jane, at that time, had a very small sports car, an "old English white" MG Midget convertible. So that night off she went to work and wouldn't be back until just before dawn.

Several days later when I got my brand-new company car back, after she had borrowed it for driving to the set, I noticed that there were spots of red flecks all over the windshield and bonnet (hood).

I asked Jane if she knew what it was, as the car was only a few weeks old and was perfect when she took it to the shoot. "It's nothing," she said," just flecks of blood." "WHAT!" I said. "Has someone had an accident in my car?" I asked as I began to inspect my one-week-old company car in more detail while Jane just looked on saying nothing.

"Well, OK, then," she finally began, "if you really want to know what happened, I was a pedestrian, running away from the werewolf, as he came out of the cinema in Piccadilly Circus and your car was used in that scene. It was in a staged accident where it was covered in blood all over the hood; the windshield had cracks placed all over it when your car had crashed into a bus." I immediately went outside to see if there was any damage; of course, there was none at all.

"So," I said, "let me get this right. If anyone at Alfa Laval takes a look at that scene and they recognize you, they'll also see my present, (not to be for long if they find out), company car, covered in blood, with you dead on the bonnet." "Fraid so," she said. Now I have to say that getting information out of Jane when she didn't want to tell you something was like pulling teeth!

"Anyway," she added, "I had them drape my leg over the number plate so no one could see it was your car." "Well, that's OK then, I s'pose," I added and that was that.

The funny thing is I often see Jane in small bits and pieces of British-made films; she was a redhead with a mass of curls that were unmistakable. Many years later in 2012, Amanda found an old film poster of a film called *The Belles of St. Tinian's* on Google and posted it on her Facebook home page. The film was a comedy about a very rough girls' boarding school and Jane was, at eighteen, one of the so-called belles.

It was often like this with Jane, when we were dating and then when we were married: she was always either with no work for months or in work for weeks or months. Sometimes, my work colleagues or friends would tell me that they had seen her in this film or that. Even some of the modeling work would be in a newspaper or a magazine.

Funny thing, when we were looking for a mortgage, from Abbey National, there was Jane on a full-page advert in the *Observer*, for none other than Abbey National looking as if she had just got engaged to whomever it was that was standing next to her in the ad! Neither of us knew it was going in the paper; but there it was, a full-page ad featuring her for the same mortgage company that we were looking to get a mortgage from!

To see a movie during filming, and as a finished product, is to see true magic happening. It is the same magic to create anything that has never been done before.

VICK ELMES BRIAN CONNOLLY AND ME

The moment when talent comes together unexpectedly is a memory forever.

I MET DEE again and her husband Vick Elmes when he had left his band *"Christie"* after their number 1 hit with *"Yellow River"* and had several other hits with 'San Bernardino' and 'Iron Horse.' Vick was the lead guitarist and harmony vocals behind Jeff Christie. Jeff Christie had quit the band to begin a solo career and Vick was now playing gigs solo.

After meeting with Vick, when he returned from a world tour when the band had split up; Dee suggested that we should perform together, as the sound would be much better than as single musicians. So we practiced in their flat in Chiswick for several months and then began to play as a duo. Vick was a brilliant guitarist and at that time the Eagles had just released, *"Hotel California"* with one of the best guitar solos of all time played by Don Felder and Joe Walsh.

Vick could play that solo note-perfect and with the exact same sound and not as a dual guitar solo but by himself. He was that good!

The crowds that we played to loved it and always called out that we sing, *"Hotel California."* Will Chichester, who used to work with me at Alfa Laval several years earlier, was himself a pianist a bass player who played drums for us so now we were a trio.

Vick though had one little problem with alcohol and was rapidly becoming a serious alcoholic, which sometimes manifested itself during gigs. Though I understood why he had this problem, as many performers do, after having to deal with the downside after the fame and fortune was over, then to perform in pubs and clubs. Vick wrote and performed a score for our former singer Dee's parents, Sylvia and Gerry Anderson, for their new series, *Space 1999*; but now he was becoming more depressed.

Dee and Vick were moving toward divorce and I hoped that the music would keep him together; but sadly, I was to be proved wrong. Dee and I spent many hours trying to get him to seek help, but he had to decide that for himself. At that time, he, like so many others in his addiction, didn't agree he had a problem.

One night we were playing in a pub in Gerard's Cross when Brian Connolly, lead singer of *The Sweet* came in to hear us play along with an entourage of friends and another band member. During the break, they came over to talk to us wanting to jam together with us. We quickly made up a song list that we could play with Brian.

Vick never broadcast to our audiences who he was and preferred to go *incognito*, maybe because he was embarrassed at not being right up there at number one. Anyway, the pub was packed but no one knew who was playing until we did one of Brian's songs. Brian, unfortunately, did not have his legendary long blond hair at this time as he was going through a similar situation as Vick and was struggling with his addiction, which at that time left him looking very different from what people would remember with his legendary long blonde hair.

However, that one night, when Brian opened up his vocals and let go with his unbelievably great voice, the packed bar began to realize who was singing; not only that but also both Christie and the Sweet had each reached number 1 across the whole of Europe. The gig was amazing and Vick told me on the way home that it reminded him of playing like that together with his friend Joe Cocker, which I would have loved to have seen.

I will never forget that one night when I was lucky enough to have been playing and singing with Brian and Vick. WHAT A NIGHT! We jammed for almost the whole set!

Sadly, Brian died way before his time; but that one night for me was a life highlight. Brian made truly great music and I'm certain our audience that night were still talking about it long after that one magical night!

Later though, as Vick, Will Chichester and I were playing at a club in Chiswick, Vick had an alcoholic meltdown in front of a packed club where our fans, had come from all over London to hear us play. He arrived thirty minutes late and was trashed.

We got him onto the stage and hoped the music would sober him up, but it didn't. He was standing next to me on stage, smashing at the strings on his guitar and making such an awful noise that I turned his vocals off and his guitar right down. After only a few numbers, I had had enough and looked over to Will who was shaking his head. Vick was swaying at his mic stand next to me and could hardly stand up so I switched it off and we left the stage, I had to apologize for Vick. I can say that I died a thousand deaths that night, as anyone who has had such disaster in front of an audience understands; but for Vick and I, the party was over. Dee and I were very sad to see such a waste of pure talent go out in this way.

I remember him proudly telling me that when he cut the soundtrack for the TV series, *Space 1999,* he did it in one take, to the amazement of the entire orchestra that was playing with him in the studio as they laid down the theme tune. He said that he arrived, set up to play, made sure his guitar was in tune and when the red light came on did the whole solo in one take. As soon as the producer gave him the nod, he packed up and left, leaving a stunned orchestra in the studio.

Dee and I didn't ever see Vick again. One last thing about the great side of my friend Vick: he used to do a whole skit on the *Muppets,* where he took on all of the voices of Kermit, Fozzy Bear, the two old men and it was so good that he could have been one of them.

Years later in 2001, James was dancing with a troupe from the Dance Refinery, where he had been attending for several years and was at a national dance contest in Myrtle Beach. His troupe was dancing to *The Sweet's* hit *"Blockbuster."* I told him when I saw him dance to it that I had sung with Brian Connolly, the lead singer with *The Sweet,* for just one night in England but I'm certain he still doesn't believe me!

One day unexpectedly, Dee called me to tell me Vick had passed away, my friend Vick died on 11th April 2017.

I contacted Jeff Christie and loved his obituary, of our friend Vick Elmes, which said, *"I just learned that Vic Elmes had died in April this year, which came as a shock to me. Vic was 70. Vic was with me right at the beginning of those glory days from the early '70s when Christie was enjoying massive success and topping charts worldwide. He was an accomplished musician who made a valid contribution to many of those early recordings, emerging later as a songwriter in his own right and later including the odd film credit on his musical CV. We traveled the world together and shared good times and bad times, but making music was always the bottom line, making friends and some special memories along the way."*

Rest in peace my dear friend Vick Elmes I hope we meet again one day.

I prefer to remember someone at the top of their life's achievements, as hitting the bottom can so easily happen to any of us.

THE VILLAGE WINE BAR

Creating something new is harder than it looks

J ane and I were now married when a friend of ours, Paul, who was an accountant to an electrical shop in North Ealing, told us about a business that was for sale and was near "The Greystoke" pub. He also told us that his brother had mentioned that the owner may be interested in selling the business, or that he may let someone take it over as he was looking to retire. I found the location, a few days later, as I was driving through North Ealing and stopped, parked my car on Queens Drive, then for no particular reason sat in my car and studied a parade of shops next to "The Greystoke Arms" pub where the electrical shop was located.

I was thinking that this location would make a great wine bar. I don't know why I thought that, but I did. So I went over to the electrical shop located between a pharmacy and a flower shop. Above the parade of shops were apartments; the "parade" had some twenty shops from "The Greystoke Arms" to the very busy North Circular Road and the location was excellent.

I entered the shop and while I waited for the owner to come out to see me, I looked around and saw that it was a perfect size for a bar with a large window looking onto the street.

It had a wooden grid hanging below the ceiling, upon which were hundreds of lighting fixtures hanging there.

I was imagining how I could convert it into a wine bar when the owner came out to ask me what I wanted. He was an elderly man, slim tall and with white hair, obviously Jewish and I asked him if he was interested in selling his business. "Maybe," he said, "but out of interest, what do you want it for?" "I think it would make a great wine bar," I replied.

"Hmm," he said, "a wine bar. Do you know much about them?" "Yes," I said," I do know a little and I know this would be a great location. It's perfect, just off the main road, plenty of passing traffic, with no other wine bar anywhere close."

He seemed interested so we talked about it some more while standing outside his shop, which was clearly not very busy at the time we were talking. He told me his health was forcing him to think about retirement and that he had considered selling. As we talked, he became more thoughtful and seemed to like the idea of not having to work in his shop much longer.

The day was very sunny and I took that as a good sign. He told me he would have to speak to his wife Sally, adding that he'd call me back in a few days. He called and had agreed to let us go for a change of use and to convert it into a wine bar.

I didn't wait a moment. I went home told Jane all about what I had seen and immediately started to draw out how it could look. I drew the bar, the window, the seating, I even designed wooden paneling all around the bar area. The concept took on a life of its own, as we began making up lists of what we needed to do to get it started.

A friend of ours was Freddie Barrett, who owned several "off-licenses" (retail wine liquor stores) and was often advertising on radio and TV. Freddie's son was Hugh Barrett, who owned Barrett's Liquor Store in Ealing Broadway was also a friend of ours. I went to see him to seek his help as we had often met for drinks when we were out in Ealing and we knew him quite well.

Hugh offered to set us up with some of his wine suppliers and even offered to help with the wine list. There was so much to be done and we had never had a business of our own before. There were the legal issues of getting a resale alcohol license, wine suppliers to be found, capital that we would need to start up and many more things to do.

A few days later, the owner called me and said that he thought it would be a great idea to convert the shop and told me he would work out the contract with his accountant Paul and we could go in any time we wanted to see what needed to be done. Jane went in more than I did as he seemed to like her. I took measurements and began to make my sketches into reality by adding a scaled drawing of the floor layout, to estimate the bar size, how many customers we could fit in and what it would take to make the change of usage from a retail electrical store into a wine bar.

There was one thing we couldn't short cut and that was the license application. This had to be dealt with through the courts, so we needed a specialist licensing attorney whose specialty was license applications. Once again, Hugh helped us by giving us the name of his license attorney. Hugh was a fantastic help and got us wholesale wine and beer prices, as well as the names of good suppliers that he trusted and found contact addresses and phone numbers for us.

I met with Paul, our soon-to-be accountant, and asked him what I needed to do to get finance. He gave me a shopping list of things, bank references, business references, cost estimates of equipment to buy, conversion costs, rent and utilities, wine prices, and even a sample wine list to take to the courthouse to present pending our license application. We made a complete list of all that we needed to get done and began assembling all of the items.

Of course, we thought, Ealing could easily handle another wine bar, as they were the latest trend in entertainment and pubs didn't cater for everyone especially women who wanted to go out together with other women friends to drink and meet. The pubs were fine, but women didn't go in them unless with a friend, usually a male, but seldom with other female friends as the pubs were not so good for them.

We were going to do this come hell or high water; we were determined to go ahead.

Sometimes when things are meant to be, they fall into place with ease, it was that way with this new business venture. We didn't tell many people about our venture and quietly proceeded to get all that we needed to be done, completed.

We called our new best friend, the licensing attorney and we had to pay him money upfront. He told us that we needed to make a scale map of five hundred yards all around the prospective location and mark out every pub, restaurant and off-license within the marked area to make it complete and easy to read. He set up the license hearing, which was to be at Brentford County Courthouse, the area authority for license applications. He also told us that the other license holders would object, especially the Greystoke, as it was only fifty feet from that pub. The date was set for July 7, 1981.

I got hold of the potential wine distributors and we began assembling a wine list of red and white wines. We needed a house red and a house white and were told that these would be our most important wines, ones that customers would measure us by and the wine that we would make the most profit from.

I asked a friend of ours, Carolyn Mann, who I mentioned earlier who lived opposite us and was the mother of my young friend Adrian. Carolyn was a talented graphic artist so we asked if she could help design our menu and wine list covers.

She did and we chose one that was an ancient etching by William Blake of Saint Michael, with one hand holding his bowed head and the other on the hilt of his sword, which was resting point down. He looked to me like he had a really bad hangover it was perfect. Carolyn not only designed the menu, but we also used the same design for the label of our house wines.

My next task was to see if we could get the finance required to open the bar. I went to see my bank manager at Barclays Bank where I had been banking since I started work at Taylor Woodrow, some fifteen years earlier.

I had prepared everything—cost schedules containing all of our work from wine costs, the capital expense for tables, chairs and conversion estimates, glassware—in fact, everything we had worked on. I made cash flow forecasts, with three estimations—a minimum, medium and maximum sales revenue.

I met the manager at 10:00 a.m. on a Saturday. My bank account was in good shape and I felt confident about my numbers. He didn't even look at my folder, but instead told me that I should think about staying with my day job and to remain in stable employment and not change anything.

I couldn't believe what he was saying, so I asked him if my numbers were wrong (though he had not even looked at them). Was there something I had missed? Did he know a reason why this would not work? He said my numbers looked good, but he didn't think it was a good idea to go into business for myself.

I was pissed off with his blasé attitude and his simple denial with no explanation, I stood up and told him what I thought of his response and told him I would open my new business regardless with or without his help, adding that I would be changing my bank on the day I opened my new business.

Well, it was back to square one. We met for drinks later that night to talk it over. For me, it was a minor setback. We then set up a meeting with the bank manager at the Allied Irish Bank in Ealing Broadway.

A few days later, I met with the bank manager, who was a tall Irishman and was great to discuss my business concept with. His staff were nice and apparently already knew why I was there.

He came out, immediately shook my hand and took me through to his office. I sat down and showed him my folder containing all our background information and all of my numbers along with the sketch I had drawn of how it would look. He looked through all of my calculations, estimates, wine list, my cash flow projections and told me that the numbers looked good and asked me where I thought our true numbers would be. I said I thought it would be all three, great at weekends, quiet during the week and we would average at the middle numbers. He agreed and said that they still looked acceptable. I only needed £12,500 to get started when he gave me an over-draught facility that would only be charged for the amount that we used. We were now game on!

That meeting took just fifteen minutes and we now had our funds. I told him we would be moving our accounts from Barclays but didn't tell him that they had refused. One thing though, it depended on our ability to get our license, so he said the money was there ready immediately but advised me to wait until we had the license. We wanted to open the bar in time for Prince Charles's upcoming marriage to Princess Diana, which was set for July 21, 1981, in London.

Our Day In Court

We never met our license attorney in person until the day of the hearing, which was set for July 7 at 9:30 a.m. at Brentford Courthouse. Jane and I went to the courthouse, with all that we had prepared in a thick folder we finally met our man. He told us what to expect and that several big breweries had grouped together to oppose us, along with all the local pubs from Ealing Broadway to the Greystoke.

I was optimistic but also annoyed that they had "ganged" up on us, Jane was angry at the opposition trying to stop us from opening our bar. "Why would they care?" she said. "Our business will be small by comparison; it surely cannot offer any serious competition to them, after all, they had huge breweries backing them"

Anyway, we had to sit through a load of prior items, ranging from bar brawls, license renewals, police issues related to pubs that we knew were always having fights and were having their licenses opposed for renewal. We sat there through it all and became increasingly nervous as we waited for what seemed to be hours.

Our time finally came, when we had to go through and sit in the witness box; it felt like we were criminals. The judge was very good and had moved along at a fast pace, but he seemed fair. He told us right up front that he wanted to get this finished before lunch, as this had been a very busy session.

He notified the court that he was reviewing a new license application made on behalf of a Tony and Jane Moore and asked if there was any opposition. The attorney who had introduced himself to us in the antechamber rose and informed the court he was opposing the license application.

This was it, pass or fail at this point; everything we had done had led us to this point and now it was out of our hands and into the famous British legal system.

I was first up and the cross-examination began. "There are approximately twenty-five pubs already in Ealing, with at least three wine bars, plus another twenty restaurants that have been satisfying all of the local needs," the opposing attorney opened loudly for all in the court to hear. "What makes you think that Ealing needs yet another bar?" He demanded and he then went straight on with several rapid-fire questions that were designed to trip me up. He didn't give me time to answer any of them, before bombarding me with more questions. He wanted to make me seem like I was fumbling, but I had put too much into this and was not going to be tripped up now, especially by this ruse and by such a bombastic rude attorney as him.

I took a deep breath and prayed to God to help me get through this ordeal without fucking it up too much just this one time! I began to answer the first question and took my time talking over him as he wouldn't stop with his tirade of questions. The judge intervened and told him to allow the witness to answer the questions. "That's OK, your honor," I said, "I have a good memory and I can answer all of his questions, but only one at a time," I told the court. "Your first question was how did we know there is a need?" I said. "Well, this past year, beer sales have grown at only 2.2 percent and spirits sales had declined by 4 percent. And the national alcohol sales growth has been 6.2 percent, which is higher than both of these numbers, which would indicate that neither are meeting the needs of the market." "And exactly how do you know this? Is it based on fact or purely conjecture on your part?" he huffed to the large assembly in the court.

I paused before dropping the other shoe, "Well, actually," I began slowly, "these are published numbers from a publication that you, in fact, represent, the Licensed Victuallers Association's annual report."

"Prove it," he sneered. I then produced the publication, from out of my folder and asked if the judge would like to see it.

A court bailiff came over and took the publication from me and took it directly to the judge, who began leafing through my evidence. "And how did you come by this information?" he asked. I replied, "I work for a company that designs breweries, supplies equipment to all manner of the wine, beer and food industries." And I got the information through my company. The court found this very funny, as a murmur ensued throughout the courtroom. I looked over to Jane and she winked, happy that we had scored a big one.

The judge announced that since this was a trade publication, that the opposing attorney did indeed represent, it was admissible and asked if we could move it along while taking a slow and deliberate look at his watch while peering at our opposing attorney over the rim of his half specs with one eyebrow raised. The opposition attorney then arrogantly looked over our wine list and tried to tell the court that the local pub was able to offer all the wines that people wanted and could meet the demands with ease.

I went on to explain that "Wine consumption had increased by 300 percent in annual sales," and I asked if he knew what the percentage wine sales had been in any of the pubs he represented. He ignored my question, so I asked the judge if he could please answer my questions as I had to answer his. The judge was clearly enjoying this exchange and agreed. "Do you have that information by any chance?" the judge asked him. "Actually, I do, but it's not here with me," he said. The judge was not impressed and went on, "Well, if that's all you have, let's move it along."

"I would like to bring Jane Moore to the witness stand," he said. I whispered to her, "We've got this," as she passed me and nervously entered into the witness box, I added a "good luck" as she passed by me on her way to the front of the court to sit by herself in the witness box.

He was just as nasty to Jane and started asking her about what food she was going to make. Jane answered, going through all of the things we had discussed over the many weeks of preparations.

"The Greystoke has an extensive food menu. Why would people want to eat at your bar?" he asked sarcastically (he was just doing his job). Jane was no fool and began by praising the excellent food that was available at the Greystoke, saying that she and I had often eaten there and probably would continue to do so. I had to smile at her deftness in taking the wind right out of his sails by her over pleasant and so sweet demeanor.

"Nevertheless," he said, "why would they choose to eat your food?" He demanded testily as he was getting nowhere with her. Jane smiled and answered, "Because we will be cooking it fresh daily."

"And exactly what will YOU be doing in this bar of yours?" stabbing his finger at Jane as he asked.

"Cooking," she said, looking right at the magistrate as if it was a stupid question. She was brilliant and the whole court laughed with her.

The judge finally intervened and said, "I've heard enough. If that's all you have, we're finished here." He smiled at Jane, asking her politely to step down from the witness box.

"On reviewing, all that I have seen and heard here, I'm granting this license," he said, adding, "I wish you both the best of luck with your new venture and I may even drop by to try some of your, personally cooked food." He smiled. "You will be very welcome," Jane replied as we left the courtroom, not believing that we now had overcome our last hurdle in starting up our business.

We were jumping up and down outside and shouting, "We did it. We did it," shaking our attorney's hand. Just then, the other attorney came out and offered his hand to mine "I knew you would get this," he said. "It was a predetermined win for you both." I didn't want to shake his hand though.

"Why were you so rude?" Jane asked him. "It's just how things are done in license cases like this," he replied. "We do this to see how much you know about the business and to see if you can argue your case. You both did very well and if you need a good attorney in the future, I would be happy to represent you in any future issues." I took his card and couldn't wait to get out of the place.

We went straight to "The Haven" and had a bottle of champagne to celebrate. The news was out now and would be published in the local paper along with the name of the bar, the location's address and our names; it was a legal requirement. A week or so later, many of the locals were asking about our new venture and when it would be open. I had only three weeks from that day until the anticipated opening day to manage the complete change-over from an electrical shop into a new wine bar.

I called into my office and took my three weeks' vacation (I had five weeks in all) to begin the work. It was July 1981 when we finally began to see our new business venture begin.

I proudly pasted the drawing I had made on the wall showing what I wanted our bar to look like. I had two friends help me to do the work. One was in the film business with Jane; the other was just about to join the Royal Navy. They both worked hard and I gave them each jobs to do, paying them by the hour. Many of our friends came in to see how the work was progressing. As we worked. many passers-by popped in to ask if this was going to be the new wine bar and when the bar would be open. I worked late into the night, often not finishing until three in the morning in order to complete the work as soon as I could.

I had never made wooden paneling before, but it seemed straightforward and so I began at the back wall and worked my way forward, making each of the wooden wall panels and measuring for the next. It looked very professional when I had finished. I had to cover it with a thick coating of flame-retardant varnish to meet the fire code.

The ceiling was covered in a crisscross of wooden beams, two feet apart, that we used to place film props like old cameras, film lighting, clapper boards and props. I began to transform it from the place it used to be into what we wanted it to be, a new wine bar in Ealing.

We painted the ceiling all black, so it would effectively disappear and not show the smoke stains that would inevitably start to form when the bar became busy.

Day by day, it became increasingly like my sketch and was gradually taking shape. Finally, we took delivery of the wines and put them all either in the fridge for the whites or in the large wall rack I had placed behind the bar for the reds. Finbar our Irish friend built the brick bar as well as our secure outhouse for our stock.

We were ready for the opening day set for Saturday, July 25, 1981, and we finally got clearance to open the bar complete with our license and fire permit, which we proudly placed on the wall at the end of the bar.

Opening night finally came, it was summer after a year of hard work when we were open and packed with people out in our garden and out on the street in front of the bar. The *Ealing Gazette* was also there, snapping away; we were too busy for an interview, so they agreed to come back during the week.

One thing though, the kitchen and the painting of the toilets were not to be finished for another three weeks and required another coat of paint and some small finishing off items. There were curved bars on the back windows in the kitchen and toilets that the previous owner had put in place to protect all his electrical stock of lights and fittings.

We realized that everything our clairvoyant friend Peggy had predicted, had in fact happened exactly as she had foretold it two years before, but it wasn't until we were opened that Jane and I saw the truth of her words.

Peggy had told us she saw us having a restaurant of some sort and it may be in a converted stable because it had bars on the windows, but not bars like a prison, these would be ornate, curved bars.

What she had described was exactly what had happened, even down to the detail that we would be open before we were completely finished but the additional work would take us 3 weeks to complete.

This was uncanny in the fact it was exactly right and she was a gifted clairvoyant.

Another thing she told Jane in her meeting with Peggy, one day, was to tell Jane to let me know not to contact my stepbrother, as he never cared about me and did not want to be contacted again. At what she told Jane I was stunned and I realized that, on reflection, it had always been me who had reached out to Richard and never the other way around. So, sadly, I never contacted Richard again and now many years later I have no idea if he is alive or not, but I agreed with Peggy, I had been wasting my time keeping in contact with him.

I knew from my childhood that if I worked hard enough and planned it all out I could "make anything happen"

GEORGIA

The birth of a daughter! THE event of our lives.

ON OCTOBER 23, 1982, Georgia was born and I had to rush Jane off to Queen Charlotte's hospital for the birth. The weather that morning was beautiful—dry, warm, very sunny and all of the autumn colors were on the trees. Georgia arrived with little fuss, as she was eager to get started with her life, which was her trait all through her life.

She was born with a mop of very dark hair and she was definitely a Moore; there's no mistaking that fact!

We took her home and now Amanda had a younger sister to look after. Amanda was a natural and loved Georgia from that very first day. Amanda and Georgia were to be very different as is often the case with sisters. Where Amanda was quiet, laid-back and nonjudgmental, Georgia was a go-getter and had to have things her way most of the time. She was a perfect addition to the family and with the help of many babysitters, we managed to work at the bar as well as look after both of them. She was a beautiful little girl, just like Amanda and from the moment she was born, we became very, very close. She loved being in the middle of everything and as she grew up, she was a real compliment to her older sister Amanda.

Many times as she and Amanda were going through life's difficulties as we all do and I remember saying to them both that they should be their own closest friends. As time moved on, they were in fact and still are the closest of friends.

Problems Upstairs

The wine bar had to be open on time every day regardless of staff, illness, or any other thing that happened. We opened at 11:00 a.m. until two-thirty weekdays and till 11:00 p.m. weekends and this had to happen each and every day. We decided to have music five nights a week and the music brought in more trade, one problem was the people living in the apartment above the bar began complaining, nicely at first but continuously even on nights when we had no live music. Eventually, we were visited by the local authorities who took sound readings upstairs with a "noise level meter." We thought we may be closed down, as they told us that we needed to have better soundproofing to prevent the noise from getting upstairs. We tried to find someone that knew what to do and couldn't find anyone ready to take on the task.

Jane had friends in the film business and knew of some film crew carpenters that may be able to help. She put the word out and a few days later, one of the crews of "chippies" called her and agreed to take a look to see if they could fix the problem for us.

They were truly amazing. They came in, looked at the ceiling and told us that this was easy to fix and they would start immediately after they had finished the film they were working on. One night at closing time, a whole bunch of them arrived, six in all. They put a complete drop ceiling in just two nights. They called it a "moving mass" ceiling and placed beams around the walls, with thick rubber mounts so that the new ceiling would rest on it and as the sound made vibrations, it would be trapped as the ceiling took up these vibrations and prevented most of the noise from going farther up to the flat upstairs. It worked and they were a great bunch of workers. They completed the job—no mess, no fuss in and out—and we were so relieved the problem was solved.

Eventually, the people upstairs realized they would not get rent-free accommodation from us, as they were trying to do, so they moved out, another problem solved!

Our sales were on target and we were doing well. The music was always varied from soloists, duos and even four-piece groups. We had a small stage at the front window and when there was no live music, we placed tables there right in the window. We were rocking! We were always in the press and we always took care of the local reporters; in fact, we had more press than any other bar in West London.

The news articles were positive and we always called the papers to let them know what we were up to in weeks to come. We advertised in the local cinema; many people came in because of our advertising.

Once every couple of months throughout the year, we organized a French, German, Italian, or Greek night. We decked the bar in flags and paraphernalia representing that part of the world and made a one-night-only special menu from the country we were representing.

We also brought in new wines from each country and the idea worked well. These nights were always booked solid, packed wall to wall with several "turnovers" of diners.

My favorite night, of course, was the French night, when we prepared a huge pot of "Moules Mariniere" and made sure we left the front door open so that the aroma of wine, garlic, fresh lemons and seafood wafted across the pavement. Slick, huh! But it worked and it worked well and even more people came in, having smelled the cooking all the way down the road.

We were quite a small operation though and we wanted a bigger place, but that was not possible with our location. After we opened and the first article came out in the papers, a full-page and with our photo standing outside the front window of the bar, our secret was out. The following week, Bo Wirsen, my managing director at Alfa Laval, came down to my office to see me and showed me the article, asking if I was leaving the company. I told him no, telling him that Jane was running it during the day and it would not affect my work at all. I invited him to come and have a drink with us and he agreed to do just that. In fact, several of the Alfa Laval directors came in for lunch. I always worried if our service and food was OK. I needn't have. Jane did a superb job and looked after them as she had always done.

Frank Sinatra

Later after a year or so, Jane and I were invited by one of our customers, Ash an Iranian who had escaped Iran when it changed from being Persia under the Shah. He was a film distributor and had tickets to go to the Frank Sinatra concert at the London Palladium. They were fabulous tickets and we were in the second row from the front with all the stars. Carry Grant and his wife were sitting in front of us; Cubby Broccoli, the producer of all the *James Bond* films, was next to us; Dudley Moore was two seats down and Roger Moore was on the other side of us.

In the intermission, all of the press descended to the front of the theater and began taking photos of all the stars sitting around us. I said to Jane and Ash, "I bet all of the people looking at these pictures in tomorrow's morning newspapers will be asking, 'who are all those people sitting around Tony and Jane?'" We had to laugh and when we went outside for some fresh air, during the break and we bumped into Dudley Moore who immediately recognized Jane and asked how she was and what she was working on.

Jane and Dud chatted a while before the buzzer went off for the second act. Jane later told me she had been working with him on *The*

Hound of the Baskervilles, unfortunately, Dudley didn't run too much; so as Jane was the same height and build, she did his stunt doubles, so the running scenes where he was getting away from the huge hounds were actually Jane.

Buddy Rich was backing Frank Sinatra, playing the drums and did an amazing act when he began playing a drum solo as Frank left the stage for a short break. He started with a drum solo played on his drums then moved across the stage playing the mike stand, the floor, then right down the stairs leading from stage right to the front row of seats, moving right across the whole row, playing the armrests, people's heads sitting there, the handrails and back up the stairs stage right, across the stage floor and finally back onto his drum set to a now standing ovation. He never missed a beat and kept the rhythm going the whole time. It was amazing to see. I knew this would be the only time I would ever see Frank Sinatra performing live.

Assault Of Course

We decided to have a charity fund-raiser for our chosen charity, multiple sclerosis and we had arranged to see if we could use the army's assault training course at the military base in Aldershot. We called them and told them what we were doing and they liked the idea, especially the part when I mentioned that we would be having around twenty to thirty mostly eighteen—to twenty-five-year-old mainly single girls with us.

We planned it for weeks and hoped the weather would be good; we called the local Ealing Gazette (as always) and arranged for everyone to be picked up outside the bar on a Saturday morning in July and took them all down to Aldershot barracks in a big bus.

The day was to end with an auction for our charity, back at the bar and we would show a video of all of us on the assault course. So off we went at 6:00 a.m. The weather was perfect, as it had been all summer—hot and dry—and we arrived right on time at seven-thirty.

I had spoken to the camp commander and asked if he could make it as realistic as possible, to which he happily agreed. There were climbing ropes, high beams, climbing nets and terrible-smelling pools of mud that they had freshened up with more water to make them even more disgusting.

There were around forty of us altogether, many were local police who were regulars in our bar. Our favorite friends were Richard Lewis and Bob Lewis, both very Welsh and John Done, whose father was an infamous Welsh poacher and who had been in jail many times for his highly effective poaching skills.

John like his dad had often been poaching ducks on Ealing Common at 3:00 a.m. using his police squad car's headlights to mesmerize the poor ducks while catching them and taking them home to the police section house to cook them. Also, we had several ex-SAS and other military regulars with us, who showed us all how easy it was since they had been doing these assault courses as part of their military training.

Everything went off well and we had plenty of footage of the girls and the guys climbing up rope ladders, crawling under nets, shinning up logged inclines; they were falling into the muddy pools while attempting to do all the activities on the course. They were continuously falling into the mud and all the while, the real-life drill sergeant major was yelling at them, telling them how sissy they were and they were no good and weak and not fit for the army. This caused them to start laughing even more and, of course, they all failed the course miserably.

The more he yelled, the more they kept failing. By midafternoon, everyone was covered in stinking mud from head to toe. Finally, we said our goodbyes to the camp commander and his team and invited the soldiers back with us to the bar; many of them came.

Later that night, after we were all cleaned up, we held an auction for our charity and the bar was completely packed, spilling right out onto the street, again. We raised £3,000 for the charity, just for having a lot of fun. DHL had donated to us a free return ticket JFK to Heathrow on Concord. Another donated a bottle of Louis XIV cognac (worth hundreds) very rare bottles of wine and many restaurant free dinners for two or four. It was one of those rare events where everything fell into place, when people that we knew, from suppliers to customers to friends gave with considerable generosity. Needless to say, we were in the local papers again.

Planes, Chutes and Crosses On The Ground

Later we had another such event where we all went parachuting for charity down in Kent and although I had already done this before, we decided to see who could land closest to a white "X," which was placed on the ground in the middle of a field next to our big crowd of onlookers that had traveled with us to see the jump.

We had spent the weekend training and learning how to jump and how to open the chute. We all suited up and got ready and were carefully checked over by the jumpmaster everyone was in great spirits.

The weather was dry hot and sunny, as it had been all summer long and after we climbed in the twin-engine stripped-out plane, we each sat around with our backs against the fuselage.

Next to me was the open door, a big square hole in the side overlooking the back edge of the wing, which was fine when we were taking off; but when we climbed high up in the sky, it was a strange feeling to be looking straight down at the ground way, way down. We climbed up to our altitude and things looked very different on the ground as I gazed out of the doorway. We circled around the general area of the drop zone when the jumpmaster dropped some bright orange markers to check the wind direction and speed and to decide where our drop zone was to be set.

We banked around and headed across the zone at a height of around five thousand feet. Then a buzzer sounded as we all lined up next to the big square gaping hole in the side of the fuselage. It was just about now that each of us were looking at each other and thinking, *"Why the hell are we jumping out of a perfectly functioning aircraft?"* We looked out of the open door at the ground below, reality bites just about here.

One by one, we all jumped out, shouting and screaming in nervous excitement as we left the safety of the plane. I watched them as each of them stepped out of the aircraft then all fell away, rapidly shrinking as they fell, one by one and I looked on as they descended toward the ground. One thing is for absolute certain: once you leave the plane, there's only one thing to do, fall and keep falling until you reach the ground.

I was last out, to make sure the rest were all out OK and as the jumpmaster nodded, I leapt out of the plane, forming an "X" with my body to gain control of my descent and to make certain that when I pulled the ripcord, I wasn't upside down. If this happens, the chords can run between your legs and as you can imagine, the sudden halt in speed, from 120 mph to less than 15mph in a split second! It would be very painful and if that happened to me I would probably be able to reach those high notes I reached when I was a soprano in the choir!

We were told that the first thing to do was to make sure our chute was opened properly with a complete circle above our head. The next was then to get our bearings, take a look around making certain to look up to make sure no one was above or directly below. I free fell for around five or six hours, though in reality, it was probably less than ten seconds. Then I prayed loudly, figuring I was closer to God right at that moment than I had ever been and pulled the chord to open my chute. I heard a loud rushing as the silk sped out of the backpack and was suddenly yanked up to where God was probably sitting, looking on in amusement at my utter stupidity.

The feeling is amazing; the wind hits you first, it hit me full in the face, as I left the safety of the plane, Next, the sound of rushing as I picked up speed headed in one direction . . . down, down, down.

My free fall came to an abrupt end as this all happened in a split second. I remembered to look up again, to make sure my chute had opened fully. What if it hadn't? What if it wasn't a full circle? What if only part of it had opened or the chords were tangled? Everything rushed through my mind along with my life, which was by now flashing before me!

I opened the chute at around two thousand feet when the buildings were as big as my fingertip. As soon as my chute took my weight, I yelled at the top of my lungs, YEaaaaaaah," as my descent slowed and I began floating gently down. Now I could look around to see the beautiful sight of the ground far below and more importantly the perfect shape of my chute. I looked at the sky all around me and above me and relaxed for the three-day fall to earth. I could turn the chute in any direction and began to guide the chute toward the field and the tiny "X" no bigger than an X written on this piece of paper from this height and seemingly dangerously close to all our friends below in the field next to it. I gradually began to get closer and turned the chute around at about fifty feet to turn into the gentle 5mph wind by pulling on one side of the chords to slow the forward momentum of the chute, which was now about fifteen miles per hour down to around 5 miles per hour. I saw the "X" right below but didn't see the high clump of grass right under my left foot.

As I landed, I kept my ankles together as I had been trained, but I felt my ankle crunch as my left foot landed on the clump and twisted as I came down. *Bugger that!* I thought as I began to get up grabbing the chute as I arose.

Determined not to let it show, I walked slowly back with the others carrying my chute back to the barracks. We were all laughing as we all returned with no mishaps but my ankle was getting worse. Many of those present had taken pictures and videos of our descent, we couldn't wait till later to see them all at the bar. As I drove back with Jane, I decided to head for the hospital on the way back to Ealing.

Jane drove me to the local hospital to have my ankle looked at. I was still high on adrenaline, so it didn't hurt so much. I saw the doctor who told me it was definitely fractured and would need pins. "I figured as much," I told him and I explained that we had a huge charity function that night and asked if they could hold off with the cast for my ankle. They reluctantly agreed but gave me some incredibly strong painkillers, Vicodin, warning me that these pills were so strong that I shouldn't drink with them. *Yeah right*, I thought, *I'm running a bar*. And I left with only a bandage around my ankle. I played it down when we arrived as the bar was packed again from door to door and all out on the street, with hundreds of our customers and friends ready for the auction that we had planned to begin and we had a very busy evening with live music and videos of our exploits of that day.

The evening was another huge success and was once again the local papers contained photos and comments about the jump and the money we had raised for charity.

Once back at work a few days later, now wearing a cast on my leg, my managing director, Bo Wirsen, came down to see me in my plaster cast and asked me to promise not to continue with any more dangerous sports as they didn't want to lose me! I of course agreed.

Microlites In A Suit!

One afternoon a year later as I was driving back through Oxford, on my way back home from a business trip I noticed some little "Microlites" aircraft circling above. They seemed tiny and had various shapes—some looked like small-motorized hang gliders and some looked like motorized dragonflies but all had brightly colored wings. I was fascinated and decided on a whim to go and get a closer look for myself.

So I drove onto the small airfield and parked up at the end of the runway, sitting in my car in case someone started shouting. This was way too cool to miss, so after a while, when no one seemed to care that I was there, well, actually there seemed to be no one around, so I drove around to the hangars and met a couple of flyers there. Both were standing at a workbench next to a couple of Microlite aircraft.

"Fancy coming up for a ride?" one of them asked me. Without any hesitation, I said, "Are you kidding? Yes." So he got me a form to fill in. "What's this?" I asked. "Oh, just a waiver, in case we crash," he said, "just in case." So there I was in a pin-striped business suit, white shirt and tie, dressed for business "as usual," climbing into the smallest aircraft in the world.

It was a funny-looking thing comprising a triangular base made of the flimsiest aluminum frame with a motor mounted on a small platform up and behind a plastic double seat, the backseat being set higher than the front seat. The motor was mounted right behind the upper seat with a large propeller at the back.

"OK," my instant new "best friend" in the world, my personal pilot told me (his name was James, by the way, which was all it could be for someone with a handlebar mustache and a leather "Biggles"-style leather helmet on), "this is the prop just behind your head." He casually informed me, pointing to a wicked-looking eight-foot propeller. "You will sit in this high seat right here and I'll be sitting in the seat below and to the front of you," he went on as I climbed into the flimsy little aircraft.

Not for one moment was I afraid or did I think of the danger; it was way too cool. "Just one thing," he mentioned as I climbed in, "the takeoff may be a little bumpy, so hold on." I looked around at what to hold on to, but there was absolutely nothing, no handle, no beam, or anything that remotely looked like it would do so I grabbed the edge of my seat, holding on for dear life.

He walked around behind me, switched a few things on, then grabbing the prop with both hands he turned the prop, which instantly began spinning with the loudest noise I have ever heard, like a huge angry buzz saw and it was about one foot behind my head. Very cool!

He climbed onto his seat, in front and just below my seat, so I could see in front of him as he began to push a small pedal down and grabbed hold of the horizontal metal bar in front of him which was attached to the large wing. We began to move across the grass under power. It was very bumpy as we moved across the grass to the runway. I was amazed that this one propeller was able to move us along so fast.

We reached the end of the runway, which comprised of a mowed grass strip about a quarter-mile long when he turned and asked me if I was OK. He realized I couldn't hear him, so he simply gave the thumbs-up and I returned the sign.

With that, he pushed down on the pedal, more like a stirrup, the roar became ten times louder behind me and we began moving faster and faster along the grass runway. Bumpy was an understatement, my teeth were rattling and the tiny craft was shaking and rattling as we continued to build up speed and I prayed that if it broke apart it would be better to do it while we were on the ground than up in the air! I was hanging on for dear life, to the edge of my "plastic" seat, thinking that it probably wouldn't do much to save me if we fell out of the sky. As he pushed forward on the "A" bar in front of him, he pushed the throttle hard down, making the tiny engine scream even louder till it hit the "sweet spot." We immediately lifted off. I think we were doing around seventy to eighty miles per hour as we lifted off, but it felt like 150! Suddenly, all the shaking stopped as we left the ground, then all became calm and serene, except for the noise of the engine.

We climbed very fast in our little triangular craft, higher and higher, so fast I couldn't believe how fast we climbed, circling as we went and I could see the ground getting smaller and smaller behind us. The hangars looked like tiny matchbox models; I could no longer see my car. We got to a height of around five thousand feet and throttled back to cruise. Now I have flown many, many times before that and have always had a drink, a stewardess, windows and toilets, not to mention a tough hard fuselage all around me. Not so now as there was only him (my new best friend) and me, a plastic seat molded for two people, a very loud engine and a wicked propeller right next to my head. I loved every minute of it. As we flew in circles, diving, climbing higher and higher, turning on a dime and doing all the tricks he knew; I felt liberated, free as a bird and it was the closest thing to flying by oneself.

I now knew how lucky birds are—they were, by the way, far below us. The pilot turned to me and shouted above the roar of the engine, which seemed only three inches behind my head and the noise of rushing wind, he turned to me and asked, "So what do you think?" I said, "Amazing! Bloody amazing, I love it!" I shouted back, laughing he told me that was how he saw it too and that he loved being up there high above the ground.

The sun was setting and the sky was lit up in all colors of red and orange as we sailed across the evening sky free as a bird . . . literally.

The few clouds there were, seemed lit from behind by the setting sun and the whole scene was unbelievably beautiful and somewhat surreal. It's times like this that I think to myself that's where God is, right there in that amazingly beautiful sky and I've always thought this, whenever I see a very beautiful sight like this.

All was calm, as I had now tuned the buzz of the motor out of my mind and I was gazing around at the new sights now seen from an entirely new perspective. As he turned the little craft, the ground below spun beneath us. I had never seen this before, as the sun moved around us as we turned full circles. That was the only way I could tell how fast we turned, seeing the sun flash across my field of vision.

After around forty-five minutes of cruising, doing the bumps, turning, climbing and diving, he began the descent and we banked around as we made our way back to the runway. The funny thing though, the slow motion of the altitude suddenly becomes a ground rush as you get to around thirty feet above the ground. I gripped the seat until my knuckles were white as we touched (or rather thumped) down, now I was tingling all over.

We powered back to the hangar; I was talking my head off about the experience. He and the others there were laughing with me, remembering their first trip up in one of these, as they swapped stories and I listened. I thanked them all and invited them to the bar for a free drink any time they wanted and left them, driving home still tingling all over.

I met Rich St. Clair in "The Bell," one of my local Ealing pubs, later that evening and he asked me how my day went. I proceeded to tell him what I had done earlier that day. "Funny you should ask because, on my way home, I stopped off in Oxford on the way back and decided to go up in a Microlite." "Bloody typical," Rich said and followed by adding as an afterthought, "as you do, I suppose, as you do. Just a day out of the office; anything else?" "Nope," I said. "I did some work, visited a few customers, drummed up some business as well, but I've forgotten what it was now." and we both laughed and continued chatting.

I was kept busy all the time, working by day at Alfa Laval running a sales department and at night in the wine bar and I kept it up for eight years. My work at Alfa was going very well, my business was booming.

The wine bar was doing very well also and we managed both, working as a team, in one long and continual "shift."

Amanda and Georgia were happy and came in many times on weekends or played in the wine garden while we ran the bar. I would get up for work at 7:15 a.m. at the office then come back to the wine bar with a change of clothes in the back of the car. I would go into the kitchen and open the bar at 5:30 p.m., getting changed in the back with the clothes I had selected that morning, ready for my second job.

We stayed open till eleven and if we had a good crowd, we didn't get home until 2:00 a.m. or 3:00 a.m. the following day. Sometimes I would love it and sometimes I would find the hard work relentless. We had plenty of staff, but we still had to be there all the time. Either Jane or I were always in the bar, every day. This was not for the lazy or faint-hearted as the hard work was nonstop, but it was what we had wanted to do; it was foretold to us. And despite it all, we loved the bar and especially the crowd that we had come to know. I had drawn it out on paper, built it exactly as I had drawn it and worked at it day after day to build it up into a very successful business. The great thing about the business wasn't the furniture, the décor, or the location but the wonderful locals, Kiki, Ash, little port-drinking Jeffrey, not to mention the villains like Scottish Jack, the robbers, the fraudsters, the cops, the actors, the stuntmen, the camera operators, even my overseas work colleagues who came to see when they visiting me on business.

All were a part of our rich tapestry; one that we were interwoven right through it so much so that we could never get away far enough to see the whole thing or visualize all.

Would I do these things again? I doubt it but I did it them one time!

My beautiful friend Richard St. Clair sadly died of cancer in 2017 following a heroic fight. I miss him, his friendship, his humor and his music. He was a fighter until the very end. We will meet again one day; of that I am certain!

THE BIRTH OF EASTENDERS

A chance conversation can lead to a momentous event.

Early EVENINGS WERE the best, especially in summer when we could leave the front door open with the evening sun slanting its rays along Madely Road and along Queens Parade outside. I sometimes sat outside at one of the tables on the street and listened to our music drifting out to where I was sitting, which for me was mostly new wave eighties bands like Spandau Ballet, Bronski Beat's "Small Town Boy" (we knew little Jimmy Summerville, the lead singer, who used to be a barman at Pete's Wine Bar in Pittshangar Lane), Fade To Gray, ELO and of course Fleetwood Mac. At these early times, we had time to get things organized before the hordes came in wanting our undivided attention and wanting to know where Jane was and if she was joining me later, of course, she would as she always did every night.

It was during these quiet times in 1983 that one of our bar staff, Chris, who had become a good friend and who was also a hairdresser in a small salon opposite the bar, introduced us to a close friend of his, Tony Holland. He was a screen playwright and had co-written *Z Cars*, a popular TV show in the early seventies.

Tony was a quiet, elegant man in his mid-forties, with an introspective air about him that made you lean forward to listen as he spoke. After a few months of coming into our bar, he began to outline his new brainchild for a brand-new TV series. Tony was tall and slim, with a well-trimmed beard, though not a full beard, more like one an artist or jazz musician would wear.

It made him look like an artist or a college professor teaching probably English. When he spoke, we just had to listen in case we missed something and he spoke very carefully with a soft voice, thinking about what he wanted to say before saying it.

Tony began coming in to see us and became a regular at the Village. He sometimes came in with another lady, Julia Smith, who was a BBC TV studio producer and they came in more often, he began to tell us that he had a concept to write a TV series that was to be all about London street life, barrow boys, pubs, wheelers and dealers and all the things that happened day today in London, following not a single street but a whole area and would probably be set somewhere in the East End of London. He told Jane and me that his idea was that it would be an ongoing life-like drama, similar to *Coronation Street*, but a London version.

As time went on, it became increasingly obvious that this may happen. He announced to us one day, over his usual bottle of house red wine, that his new series would be called "*Eastenders*," and that he was starting production as the writer.

We often sat with him listening to the as yet unfinished storylines and the concepts for each character, going through some of the storylines with him adding bits here and there. Sometimes when he came in, he would sit, with a bottle of wine, to tell us of a problem he had with one of the characters or that the storyline was stuck at a particular point. We all sat around the table and, with more and more wine, began discussing ideas for solving his script problems with the story. We thought our ideas were brilliant, though I'm not sure that Tony shared all of our solutions, maybe some ideas though.

Tony was a very perceptive person and could see things in people's characters that others missed, he could characterize people's nuances and build them into a truly three-dimensional part. None of us at the time had any clue just how big it was to become and now, 40-years on, it is still running and is still as popular now as it was then probably even more popular than it was in its first season.

Well done, Tony! What a great contribution you made for all those seemingly real-life characters and all of the people's lives you made just a little bit more bearable as they looked forward to watching your epic series day by day.

Tony, the careers you created for your actors, film crews, producers and writers. You could outdo even the biggest corporation and if that wasn't enough, everyone that worked with your show enjoyed it immensely. Not many people could say that about the company they work for or had built from scratch.

When I went back to London after a thirty-year absence, after living in Brussels and Indiana, I still caught some shows when I returned to Hanwell, just to see what was happening as if it were real life and I was seeing old friends again.

To see the characters that were still in the current show from the original episodes as I had seen it then all those years ago and seeing them as they now looked, like me; they were now older, wiser, a few more lines of wisdom on their faces, with a little less hair, some aging better than others. Why is that? Watching the series occasionally now in my present-day when, from thousands of miles away, takes me right back to a specific time earlier in my life and reminds me of the words from one of the saddest but truest songs, *"Landslide"* by Stevie Nicks: *"Time grows bolder, children grow older I'm getting older too,"* and seeing all the characters again now as if in a three-dimensional "snapshot" with me looking on while looking with one eye in the mirror, seeing if I had changed that much too. Unfortunately, I had as well, so much for that!

The big "normalizer," that eventually reduces everyone to look the same in old age even as we all did when we were born. Maybe that's what it's all about, the big equalizer proving to us that as we get older we look all the same, filled with life's experiences marked with the lines on our face and it doesn't matter what we've done in the meantime as it is now all in our past.

We can only pass on so much, after which we are all just somewhere in the past to others. Boy, it makes you want to live life to the full and not waste any time. I even saw *East Enders* when I was traveling around the United States and while I was staying in so many boring hotel rooms, which seemed to be my life's destiny while working within the United States. When that happened, it always seemed to prove to me that these things had truly taken place, in my earlier life.

It proved to me that I was there when it happened and I remembered when and exactly how that series had been born, maybe even contributing to these events, as a bystander, in some small way.

I sometimes felt like a real-life Forrest Gump, while writing my book, having to get all my thoughts and in particular my deeds in some semblance of chronological order. I seem to have been always there at the time somewhere in the background, or right in the middle of it, being part of the most incredible change in human history; viewing it and, like so many others born into this time period, adding small pieces to help it along the way. How lucky I was, in fact as we all were, to have been born at this time, in this century and to have seen these changes as if we had been watching our own epic series taking place.

Tony Holland sadly died on 28 November 2007, aged sixty-seven, but what plays he created! I am so very happy that we passed by each other during our time here, like two ships passing in the night, bright lights in a dark starlit ocean. We will all miss you, Tony, but thanks for the truly great shows and for making all our lives that much better in being able to be totally immersed in your daily saga of

Eastenders! Whoever thought it would rival *Coronation Street* and would still be one of the top TV shows in the world after thirty years.

Thanks for the good times, Tony, I'm so very glad we spent as much time as we were able and I still think the story about radiation poisoning was a brilliant storyline, but sad you didn't go for it!

Tony Holland's legacy of Eastenders is still showing and will live on for a very long time!

MORE CHANGES

Change is a fact of life; things never remain the same so we must get on board for the ride.

THINGS BEGAN TO get a little tough for both Jane and I, working at night in the bar and for Alfa Laval by day while traveling to Europe, the Middle East and everywhere in England, building up my Alfa Laval business model.

The business I had started in 1980, the "customer service marketing" operation, had now really taken off and the Swedish senior management was beginning to see some great results from my work.

I was invited to Sweden to meet with the business unit heads in Tumba just outside Stockholm, where the corporate headquarters of the company are located.

Jane was invited too and came over with me to Stockholm; but it was, to say the least, a tough few days. We had been drifting apart for some time and were now looking at divorce. I hoped that maybe the offer of a new beginning would help heal things between us, but it wasn't to be.

We had both made mistakes in our marriage and Jane had no intention of ever moving away from London as her life revolved around Ealing and she didn't ever want to relocate.

I, on the other hand, didn't want to stay living in London as I knew my destiny was somewhere else. Even when I was at school in geography lessons, at age eleven, I would open the book to the map of America and imagine what it was like to live in places with names like St. Louis, Denver, Cheyenne, Los Angeles and San Francisco. All of these places I had heard of in the cowboy films I had watched as a child, now held a mystery for me and way back then, I wanted to know what it was like there.

The names were so different from those places that I knew of with names like "Scunthorpe" or "Wolverhampton" or "Rottingdean," which were in part beautiful towns but just didn't have the same pizazz as those names I read in the pages of our school atlas. I realized when Jane and I were in Stockholm that sadly we had so much of a gulf between us now that it would be difficult or impossible to rebuild our lives back together. Conversation was difficult, Jane was distracted the whole time we were away and since she had no intention of ever moving away from Ealing, any future I had was elsewhere not living my whole life in Ealing.

The night when Jane left Stockholm to return to London was the saddest I had ever had, but I could see no way back and I had to shut that door and begin to move on and come what may it could only be forward and never backward.

I don't want to go too much into the reasons for our divorce, but suffice it to say, we both made mistakes and it was an inevitable result. We had both agreed, after that trip to Sweden, that we needed to get on with our lives and we were both looking at separation.

When I returned to the wine bar, Noz Roberts called me and asked if we could meet for a drink; We met in a pub in Southall, where he was well known and as the night wore on, he asked me, "What do 'you' want, Tony? Do you want to try to make it back with Jane or do you want a divorce?" He added, "The choice at the end of the day is down to you, mate, so what do you want to do?" I thought he had been talking with Jane, although I wondered what that conversation may have been like, Jane had already moved on and had a boyfriend, so my decision was a straightforward one.

I already knew what my answer would be, so I told him that there was no way either of us would be able to pick up the pieces. I remember telling him that marriage was like a beautiful crystal vase that held beautiful flowers that you could change as the seasons changed; but once it was broken, even if it was repaired and repaired well, it would never look as beautiful. There would always be a crack that showed the damage every time the light shone through it. And even if it was repaired, the slightest knock could shatter it again.

While we were going through this, I still had a lot of travel in support of my job and had considerable pressure to keep up the momentum of my work.

My problem was that I loved to work and loved what I was developing, doing whatever it took to get ahead and to "prove" myself; though for the life of me, I had no idea who I had to prove myself to! The business, though serious, was fun and we made sure we did have fun every day!

My business at Alfa Laval grew bigger and more important, it provided a cushion for me and now the company had built a brand-new service facility in Brentford and we were all moving into a very modern ten-story office building along the Great West Road, just next door to our old offices that the company had been in since the early 1920s. Our new office was the now-closed Brentford Nylons building. Brentford Nylons used to advertise continuously on radio and television "ad nauseum." But now they had closed down, leaving their 10 story building empty.

I now had a full sales operation, compliments of my mentor Bo Wirsen plus a marketing secretary. My highly talented group of young salesmen were Mike Corrigan, Richard St. Clair, Mark Pacey, David Pollard and Steve Harlow.

I trained each of my new staff in marketing and sales and had completed the hiring within a three-month time frame. Each person had developed their own marketing plan for sales and marketing activities.

We unofficially called our department the "Big Bucks Department," and we even had a dollar bill enlarged to nearly two feet long and pasted on the glass door of my office, much to the amusement of Bo, but to the seeming annoyance of the other managers.

Our office was on the mezzanine floor above the spares office overlooking the Great West Road and the M4 motorway in a corner location that was open plan. We were doing well as each of my team went about their jobs promoting a wide variety of newly developed service products, many of which we had "invented" and were selling well.

Our business, "After Sales Marketing," was to become very important in the company as it applied to all of our installed equipment, whatever age, wherever they were located and in every one of the countries that Alfa Laval operated in. What I had started in 1980 was now a fully operational business unit with a budget, sales, strategic marketing plans, a full sales team and a complete range of highly profitable service products that we had developed and were still developing.

The reason that we were able to make such a success of this operation was entirely because of our managing director, Bo Wirsen.

Later, after leaving the company, Mark Pacey, who was one of my team, ended up in prison for fraud and sadly David Pollard another of my sales team later died of brain cancer.

The Middle East

I received a call from a telephone operator in Saudi Arabia, of all places and she asked me to identify if I was Tony Moore, working for Alfa Laval in London. I said yes, she then asked me to be ready to accept a call the following Friday at 10:00 a.m. from a "field telephone" in a location called Al Jubail in Saudi Arabia and that I was to wait for the call next to the phone I was presently using.

When I received the call, it was from two ex-British Steel Managers calling me from a "field telephone" via a satellite link (brand-new at that time). They had both left British Steel to work for Saudi Iron and Steel in Al Jubail near Dhahran on the eastern side next to the Persian Gulf. They had some of the biggest plate heat exchangers Alfa Laval had ever made at that time and had called me to set up a service plan for them similar to that which I had done for them in their former UK British Steel operation.

They explained that they were now managing the maintenance and production operation for this newly formed Saudi company and wanted the same service that I had developed for them at BSC some years before because they could never shut the Saudi operation down. The Saudi government was using some of their oil wealth to divest their wealth in oil money by diversifying into new markets in order to be more independent of imported products while building up an improved infrastructure, which would in itself become a new export market for them.

The deal was worth more than £1 million in sales it was highly profitable and was the largest order my department had ever received. Bo Wirsen came down and awarded me the sales prize for landing that order. I got a great prize for that little gem, a beautiful Dunhill gold watch with a jet-black face and gold numbers that was only a few millimeters thick. I still wear the beautiful watch today, remembering when I received it from a very happy and smiling Bo Wirsen.

To Sweden Again

I was summoned over to Sweden to explain how I had got the Saudi order since the Swedish head office was responsible for all international sales and it was not a UK market that I should have even been involved with.

Bo told me to go over and explain what I had done and how I had won the order, telling me, "It's always easier to seek forgiveness than it is to ask for permission." I told him, "I am not giving them the order as we won it fair and square." He simply said to me, "Go over there, Tony and see what happens." I had no problem going over to see what they wanted but I certainly had no intention to give my watch back!

I had been to Sweden many, many times; but I had never been summoned at such short notice by such senior staff as the head honcho of the Thermal Division.

After I arrived in Lund in southern Sweden, via Copenhagen, where the thermal business unit was headquartered, I was shown into a large conference theater with seats arranged in ascending rows in a semicircle around a raised stage with a presentation projector set on a pedestal and a huge screen behind.

In came the business head of the thermal operation, Sigge Haraldson, whom I had heard of but had never met before that point. He was followed by several others, including a design engineer called Lars Åke Johansson, who I had never heard of but who would become a key figure in my immediate future. There were six other department heads who sat around with notepads and wrote copious notes during the long meeting. Lars was a tall, slim blond-haired Swede with a serious disposition. Lars was the opposite to me, where I was at that time brash and somewhat irresponsible, making quick decisions and going with a hunch, Lars was serious thoughtful completive and slow to react, typical of the design engineer that he was.

I was introduced to all these senior directors and asked to tell them about my Saudi order. I told them of the new products and services that my small department had developed and how my small team was winning new customer service business within the UK operation. I told them this could be repeated in all countries where the company operated in. Eric Annestrand, the Business Unit manager, told me he already knew about us as they had been measuring how my small operation was outselling all of the other market companies.

He then put a slide up and showed me a graph of global sales for the past four years, where all of the other country operations were showing moderate sales increases. He then overlaid the UK sales, which went up at a staggering rate of increase every year and was more than double the sales in all of the other countries.

What they wanted was for me to show them how to develop and market a technical service business into all of their other countries.

I was shown a potential market opportunity in the Middle Eastern countries, as that was what had piqued their interest, including Saudi Arabia, Kuwait, Iraq, Iran, Dubai, Abu Dhabi and other smaller countries in the United Arab Emirates. I was amazed at this turn of events.

The outcome of this meeting was that I should collaborate with Lars Áke Johansson and visit each of these countries together with him to develop each market as well as my UK market.

They would pay my UK company for my time as a consultant, with some of the resulting sales would come back to my UK operation so that my home office could gain from my extensive time in the Middle East.

I came home on a cloud. I had now been given an international market to go after but I still had my UK operation as well. Instead of being berated for taking the Saudi order, I had been promoted.

I thought I was busy before but was soon to see how busy I would be in developing the new markets in the Middle East.

I learned never to assume an outcome but to rely on my abilities.

SUE

To make one relationship work is better than a hundred that don't.

IT WAS AT this time, after Jane and I were nearing the completion of our divorce, that I met Sue while out in Ealing with my sales team. We were out for the evening, in Ealing, when a friend of mine, Jan Friday (Jan), came into the bar. She saw me with my friends, celebrating winning an order (like we needed an excuse). Jan at first didn't want to join us as she had taken a few days off without calling in to her boss. Like I cared! Jan worked for the divisional head of our marine department.

She introduced Sue to us, then Jan asked me not to tell her boss that we had met her that evening, just in case it got her into trouble, as if I would. Anyway, Sue and I started talking together and we got on very well and I found Sue easy to talk to.

Anyway, I invited Jan and Sue to meet up with us later at "Maddox" a nightclub in Ealing and they both agreed.

Sue was a slim and very attractive girl with a "mane" of beautiful curls that were highlighted in streaks of blonde and light brown and she possessed a great 'earthy' sense of humor. I had never seen her around, but it turned out that although we had never moved in the same circles she knew many of my work and personal friends.

My close friend Richard St. Clair and I met up with Jan and Sue in "Maddox" at 11.30 p.m. that night, as Maddox was open until 3:00 a.m. long after the pubs had closed. Maddox used to be "The Ealing Club," where the Rolling Stones and The Who first started playing there during the early '60s.

Now, however, the club was a popular members-only late-night hangout. I had a membership since I knew the owners who had been regulars at the Village Wine Bar. I usually went there in a crowd of friends after we had closed the bar but never before midnight as it usually picked up around 1:00 a.m. Sue, Jan, Rich and I all met up later that night, listening to the DJ playing Hamilton Bohannon, Gloria Gaynor, Kid Creole and the Coconuts, KC and the Sunshine Band and all of the eighties "club" music. Sue and I were getting along great and after that, we started seeing each other more. We were in fact both going through a divorce at the same time, me with Jane and Sue with her ex.

I eventually moved out of our house in Bruton Way Ealing, after we had sold it as part of our divorce. I moved in with Sue into her ground floor flat in Acton for a short while when we were looking for our own house. Jane now had a boyfriend who eventually moved in with her in her newly purchased cottage in Hanwell.

Sue's flat was quite small but it had plenty of room for just the two of us with her black-and-white cat called Pickle.

Things began to settle down for Sue and me as well as for Jane and her boyfriend; we began to look for a house and had been looking all over from Ealing to as far as Wembley and Pinner, an area of around fifteen miles.

We eventually found a property we liked and, of course, as usual, I was in the Middle East while the negotiations were taking place.

I was also in the process of selling my home, as well as the wine bar, so Jane and I had to coordinate closely with each other.

Jane and Sue got along fine, as our divorce has nothing to do with Sue and I. It was while these negotiations were going on that I had to make a call to our solicitor in Ealing to set up the purchase of one house and the sale of the other while I was away in Dubai.

The phone call from Dubai cost a staggering £350 ($500), during which I was agreeing to the purchase of a new house and the sale of our old home in Bruton Way. Anyway, the home that we both liked was in Wembley and was located in a large Tudor estate of similar homes. Our house was a corner house with a front and rear garden as well as a wooden garage on the side. It had leaded windows with large bay windows on the ground floor and the upper master bedroom. There were three bedrooms large enough for Amanda and Georgia to come and stay during weekends.

The street was tree-lined with beautiful tall lime trees and was a nice quiet suburb with a park at the bottom of our road. It was perfect for us. The house was newly painted and was, of course, black and white, making it look every bit the Tudor style it had been designed to be.

We took Amanda and Georgia to see the new home, they both liked it so it was decided this was to be our first home together.

Jane and I had now completed our divorce. Sue and her ex had not seen one another for over two years and the divorce "Decree Nisi" had been granted over a year before, so a final "decree absolute" was inevitable. I continued with the purchase and Jane had also found a beautiful cottage in old Hanwell in St. Andrews Road.

Jane had enough money from the divorce to be able to buy her home, almost totally for cash, but she chose only a minimum of mortgage payments. At that time, I had the deeds to her mother's house in Hanwell, from which I owned half together with Jane. I had agreed with Jane that if we could both manage an amicable divorce, I would hand over my half of Jane's mother's house back to Jane so that she could sell the downstairs apartment and keep any money from that sale while allowing her mother to live there. I also agreed to let Jane have the Beemer (BMW 528i), which I had been mostly driving, as I now had a company car.

Sue and I lived in Sue's apartment for about three months and she had a close, family that I was introduced to a short time later. There was her mother Sylvia, her dad Maurice, her younger sister Lesley and her brother Paul. They became family to me, accepting me even though I was not Jewish, which they all were.

We completed the sale of Bruton Way and the purchase of Oldborough Road and we finally moved in, with Amanda and Georgia helping us to get the move completed as a way of getting them used to the new arrangement. Amanda was now eleven and Georgia was four.

Soon after we had completed moving into our new home, I was off again to the Middle East for another three weeks. Jane and I had decided to sell the wine bar because I had decided that after our divorce, it would become more difficult for Jane to manage Amanda and Georgia while running the bar. In fact, I had made this a condition of our divorce settlement just for this fact. I knew that as they became teenagers, it would be increasingly important for Jane to be there for them even if I could not because of my extensive travel.

I felt that our divorce was going to be difficult for Georgia and Amanda to deal with, without adding to this by Jane having to manage the bar as well as managing babysitters and nannies and with me being often gone away on my many business trips overseas.

I also felt that they would need more attention from us both as times may get difficult for them entering their teen years. So we sold the bar. What we had started for very little more than a couple of months' wages when we opened the bar was now worth twelve times as much as "a going concern" with an excellent reputation.

The downside was with Amanda and Georgia who would have to now deal with a broken home, something that was now unavoidable.

This was, for us both as in any divorce with children, the worst part of it all and we would have to manage that as best we both could. We had agreed that I would have them every weekend and even during the week if needed or if either Georgia or Amanda wanted to stay with me.

While Amanda quietly accepted our decision to divorce, Georgia was excited at the possibility of having two homes instead of one. At her age, she couldn't see any downside. Amanda was more retrospect about the situation and things for her became more complicated, as I'll explain later.

I told Amanda that I wanted them both to remain best friends and be closer to each other than even their mom. As I saw it, they would always be there for each other as sisters and friends. That wish came true as they are still each other's closest friends and while they argue like cats and dogs, they are nevertheless extremely close.

A Visit From An Arab Sheik

One of my business contacts in Saudi wanted to come over to visit and to see London and our facility in Brentford. So I made the arrangements for him to come over and asked if he would come to see our brand-new facility while dressed in his traditional robes. Imagine what that looked like when he arrived at the Brentford operation complete with his flowing white Arabian Emirati traditional robes, his red and white patterned Ghutra covering his head with his black woven traditional Saudi Igala on top of his head.

I told him it would look so cool to our staff and as he was quite young, he loved the idea, especially when I told him that he looked like a very rich oil sheik. We both laughed and I liked Ahmed a lot and I knew the feeling was mutual. He may have been a rich sheik, but I didn't ask about that.

I took Sue to meet my Saudi Arabian visitor when he arrived as he was staying at the Hilton in Mayfair. Sue and I both picked him up at his hotel. When you are in Saudi, it is very polite to introduce business friends to your family; so in fact We took him to Trader Vicks under the Hilton in Mayfair; he had no idea that Sue was Jewish. Neither would it matter to him, but since Ahmed was an Arab, we decided that we wouldn't mention that small detail.

I proved, work can be fun, if we want it to be.

ROME LADY IN RED

Sue was the one for me and Rome was the best place to see it.

I WAS KEY speaker to address a conference in Rome, on my way back from the Middle East and had arranged to come back to London via Rome so that I could be at the meeting. I told Sue about it and invited her to meet me at the Hotel Michelangelo and bought her a ticket to meet me in Rome.

I flew from Dubai to Rome and caught a taxi from the airport making my way to meet her in the hotel lobby. Of course, we had no cell phones at that time; so once the arrangements had been made, you had to hope nothing had gone wrong. I arrived at the hotel and waited for Sue to meet me in the lobby and called up to her room to let her know that I was here.

When she came out of the elevator, she looked like the most beautiful girl I had ever seen. This one moment for me was a moment in time I knew at that very moment I would never forget. She was wearing a brightly colored summer dress in white and red, with many brightly colored flowers on it and her hair had highlights that seemed to match her dress. As she came out of the elevator, she took my breath away, I was stunned. Her mane of curly hair had caught the late-afternoon sunlight as it came in dappled light across the lobby from the windows and shone, lighting her and the whole lobby up.

I told her she looked stunning, to which she replied, "I suppose I do after looking at all those Middle Eastern women for the last three weeks with their long black robes with veils hiding their faces."

We went out on the town to several street cafes and bars, enjoying every moment. We found a family-run Italian restaurant. but then, they all were. We sat down outside in a small-raised garden to order dinner and wine.

After we had ordered, Sue got up to go to the bathroom while I ordered a bottle of red wine. After the wine arrived, I sat while waiting for her to return, before ordering our main course; but after half an hour, she still hadn't shown up.

I asked the waiter if he had seen her, he said yes, she was out back, so I went to find her and to see if she was OK.

Well, I found her sitting at a huge table in the kitchen with the family who owned the restaurant; Sue was eating and drinking with them, while I was sitting out front waiting for her before ordering dinner!

"Hi, darling," she said, smiling. "I was looking for the bathroom and made a wrong turn, ending up in the kitchen when they invited me to join them and sample their food, but before I could say no thanks, they made a space at the table and sat me down." They were all laughing and talking to Sue in Italian and broken English, offering her their wine and samples of all of their food and she was having the time of her life. This is what I love about Italians, their hospitality.

She was laughing too, even though she couldn't understand what they were saying; but then she didn't need to. She was having a blast and I realized at that moment, seeing her there at the table, that Friday night in Rome, tilting her head back laughing and enjoying herself, with her eyes alight with happiness that I had at that moment fallen in love with her.

I loved her spontaneous laugh and her ready sense of humor and especially the way she looked that night. The song by Chris De Burg, "Lady in Red," would from that moment on and forever be my special song for Sue, reminding me of how beautiful Sue looked that night in Rome. Whenever I heard it played, it would always take me back to that one moment in time when she came out of the elevator, in the Hotel Michelangelo, with the evening sun glowing in her hair and her highlights shining matching the color of her eyes. I knew I would remember all of the details of that night forever.

A song with so much personal meaning is a memory forever

TONY YATES

Even the most boring of jobs can be fun, with a highly talented team

To market my Alfa Laval business which was gaining ground and I sought the help of a London-based and highly talented advertising company called "Publitek." The account manager was a friend of mine called Tony Yates, who I knew because he came into my wine bar. Tony's company had been mainly in the pharmaceutical business and had been responsible for one of the world's most effective pharmaceutical advertising campaigns ever. They had marketed and advertised Zantac for Glaxo and Publitek's concepts had helped to place Zantac into the *Guinness Book of World Records* as the most prescribed drug in the world. So I figured if they could do that for an ulcer drug, I wonder what they could do for us.

"Into the Guinness Book of World Records?" I said to Tony when he told me of their success with Zantac. Anything to do with Guinness was good enough for me," I told him laughingly. In case I forgot to mention, Guinness was my favorite beer. Did I mention that? So we began what was to be an exceptionally good partnership to help promote my marketing operation. We had such a laugh dreaming up ideas for brochures, adverts and some very zany concepts. One of the concepts we came up with was making replicas of the rubber gaskets used in our heat exchangers but made from licorice, with the idea being to promote "a sweet deal on Regasketing."

Another idea was a dice loaded with gold-plated chocolate money to "sweeten the deal and save big bucks" and even a box of bath salts to help take away all the fatigue from managing engine room problems onboard the world's shipping if they were not using our "preventive maintenance."

All of these concepts had been packaged and shipped all over the world to our marketing companies that I had been asked to set up as "duplicates" of our first operation in London. The concepts had been a huge success as no one else had ever done this kind of marketing for these types of products, the service, we had put together became a resounding and global success.

After each of our successful ad campaigns, we went to "Yates Wine Bar" (no relation) in London's West End to celebrate.

A Silent Movie

Later on, when was working from Brussels, we decided to make a movie to promote "preventive maintenance," which by any measure was a very boring product to advertise. Tony and the team at Publitek came up with a brilliant idea to make a five-minute movie with no words using "mime" accompanied by grunts and a few noises of things "happening" as the movie moved on. We had an "infinity" studio where there was no backdrop at all, only a black background. In the foreground was an entire company made in a straight line with the opening scene showing a very pleased CEO and behind him, a wall chart showing climbing sales and profits; while the CEO, complete with his handlebar mustache, was lighting a big cigar.

The camera pans to the right to a machine with white boxes going in on a meshed conveyor belt, representing production units, entering into a packaging machine, which then breaks down with a siren going off as the machine stops. Meanwhile, the previously happy CEO was now in a rage with the wall chart showing sales drooping down to the floor and the company founder, his dad looking like a much older version of him, looking equally enraged.

As they call for our service, again in mime, the machine starts up again and all is well; but the production manager, who didn't use our service before the breakdown until it was too late, leaves to go home. But his car won't start, meaning that he should use "preventive maintenance" on his car too.

Needless to say, with no words at all, the short movie was shown all over the world in every market company and the film was a huge success, thanks to Tony and his team.

My Famous Reputation

Some thirty years later, in 2014, I decided to reach out to Tony and began to search on the Internet from the United States and found several companies in Richmond, in the advertising media, that specialized in pharmaceuticals, companies that he had either owned or started up. So then I sent an e-mail to the general e-mail address of one such company called Pan Advertising, saying that "I used to work with Tony Yates at his former company, "Publitek," adding that, "they probably would not have heard of me." But I asked if they knew how I could get back in contact with my old friend Tony Yates as I was now living in the United States.

Well, I couldn't believe it when I got an e-mail back from Ben, who was the managing director and used to work with Tony at Publitek. I remembered him and, yes, he remembered me very well. He went on to tell me in his responding e-mail that I had become "a legend" in the advertising world because of some of the crazy things I had done. He recalled to me that one story was that I sent four bottles of champagne back while celebrating a new campaign in "Yates Wine Bar" because the bubbles were too big. "WHAT? Are you kidding,?" I replied. Then later after I got in touch with Tony, he confirmed that and some other stories that I could not possibly repeat even in this book.

Tony Yates, not surprisingly, had been awarded an honorary doctorate at a prestigious London University for his work in the specialized world of pharmaceutical advertising.

I was so proud to learn of his achievements and we spoke of meeting up again when I came over to London next time.

I also learned that it's sometimes the life achievements of others who we had the privilege to work with or to have come into contact with who inspire us to do what we can do and to do it as well as we can possibly can.

Tony, my good friend, was one of those exceptional people that I was privileged to work with. I was very happy that we had managed to keep in touch and was stunned to hear of Tony's working career and all that he had achieved. He was the best! Tony was now a Ph.D. and I was happy to read about his achievements. What a team we made working together, Thanks, Tony!

If the right personalities, talent and skills can be put together and work as a team, everything is possible.

A GUNNESS WORLD RECORD

Sometimes, I really am an idiot!

WHILE I WAS traveling to the United States with Lars, we began our trip in Houston and the date happened to be March 17, which meant nothing to me at all, being from London but it was St. Patrick's Day. Anyway, from there, we went on to New Orleans and we ended up on Bourbon Street at Pat O'Brian's Pub just off Bourbon Street. Lars told me we have to try a Hurricane, which is a drink I had never heard of before.

We had one each, in a tall tulip-shaped glass with some wickedly tasting cherry drink inside. I drank mine down fairly quickly and said to Lars, "Mmmn yummy. Think I'll have another." "I'd take it easy if I were you," he said. "These are very strong drinks." Anyway, I had another and then another after that.

Finally, when the two of us left the bar and turned onto Bourbon Street, it hit me and I started to see double and had to hang on to the lamp post in order to stand up. "Fuck," I informed anyone and no one at all, "What the hell was in that drink?" I looked over and saw that Lars was as bad as I was.

We both staggered off down the street and looked for somewhere to get something to eat so that we could feel better. We found an open-air hamburger place farther down the street and sat down in a vague hope of actually being able to order something from the menu.

I couldn't even talk and we started to giggle while trying to read the menu. I had to read it with one eye closed, because when I opened the other one, it refused to see the same menu as my other eye and kept looking somewhere else, which made us both laugh hysterically.

We finally ordered by pointing at a customer sitting at a table nearby who had a very large cheeseburger. "One of thosh," I said, not looking up with my one good eye. "Me 'shwell," uttered Lars. "Sho two more of the shame." I informed our waitress as we were both now quite drunk. She understood and we both ordered a large pitcher of iced water, each, as well.

We ate our food with some difficulty, then tried to get up without seeming too drunk and staggered out of the restaurant. We made it back to our hotel, where we were both sick.

The next day, we were heading up to New York on our way home when I received a call from British Airways who informed me that my Sunday afternoon flight back to London had been canceled but the call was to inform me that they could get me back from New York on Concorde if that was OK. "Let me think for a second," I said to the girl on the other end of the phone. "I suppose that will have to do," I said, as she started laughing adding, "I should think so. I work for British Airways and I have never flown on it, so enjoy your flight, Mr. Moore. It's on us."

I couldn't wait to tell Lars and he was so envious he could hardly speak to me and all the way back to New York, I kept dropping the name Concorde as we chatted on the flight from New Orleans to JFK, just throwing it in the middle of our conversation. "Did I mention I'm flying Concorde, by any chance, Lars?" I said while nudging him and winking.

As we parted at JFK, I made sure to ask an official, "Where is the Concorde lounge?" right in front of Lars just to rub it in. As we parted, Lars said, "Have a great flight and don't forget to tell me what it was like." "What's what like?" I said, pretending not to know what he was talking about. "Oh, you mean flying on Concorde?"

I said, sounding innocent. "Of course, I will. I can't wait to see what it's like to travel at twice the speed of sound. Are you flying coach, Larsy? Shame . . . still, if you feel a bumpy ride, then it's probably me in Concorde passing you by at twice the speed of sound." He glared as we waved goodbye.

I arrived at the Concorde lounge, it was amazing; there were canapés with caviar, shrimp and lobster, as well as a drinks cart with the biggest collection of the best brandies and aged single malt whiskeys I had ever seen and that was before we even boarded. Well, we finally began to board the aircraft and I was very excited to be boarding the world-famous Concorde.

Once inside the doorway, there was the flight deck with a pilot, co-pilot and a flight engineer who sat behind them facing the side. In front of him was a wall of gauges and switches. He saw me looking and said, "Impressive, isn't it?" "Yes," I replied. "I have never seen anything like it." He then pointed to a long slot in the panel in front of him that went up to the low curved ceiling and told me, "See that slot? When we are at Mach 2, it opens up to nine inches wide." "Why is that?" I said. He replied, "Because the aircraft stretches that much because of the drag on the airframe." "No," I said. "Are you kidding me?" He said, "Tell you what, when we are up to speed and the seat belt signs are switched off, why don't you come up to the flight deck and take a look." "Cool," I said. "I definitely will do that. Thanks." And I went on to my seat.

The seating inside the cabin was in two rows of two large gray leather seats, very luxurious and very high class. There was plenty of legroom, as one would expect from such a luxury aircraft.

As we began to take off, it was very bumpy, a bit like being in a very fast sports car with a tightened-up suspension. The speed of acceleration was incredible as the four Rolls-Royce Olympus engines throttled up faster and faster for takeoff speed.

Now in most aircraft, you get used to the rate of climb and the angle of climb. In Concorde, it is twice as steep and it feels like you are almost vertical feeling the incredible power of the four Rolls Royce Olympus 593 turbojets. As we climbed higher, there was a green digital gauge at the bulkhead of the cabin that showed all of the passengers the rate of climb, which was spinning furiously fast as we climbed so rapidly. We soon reached 38,000 feet, which is where most passenger aircraft normally flew; but we were continuing up to twice that height.

Meanwhile, the gauge began to show our speed in miles per hour and as a percentage of Mach 1, which is the speed of sound. It began reading 0.8 Mach 1, then 0.85 Mach 1, then 0.9 Mach 1. The ground speed was also showing alongside the "Machmeter." And we were now exceeding 650 miles per with our ground speed continuing to increase to a staggering seven hundred miles per hour while still accelerating past Mach 1.

I was trying to feel or listen to the sound barrier as we went through Mach 1, but sadly I could feel nothing. The speed continued to increase as we continued upward while the digital gauge now showed our altitude as well. We were now at one thousand miles per hour and still accelerating; it was simply incredible.

Our altitude was still climbing to more than twice that of any other passenger aircraft. I was stunned at it all as I watched the Machmeter now showing 0.8 Mach 2 continuing even faster. We finally leveled off at 65,000 feet or more than twelve miles high. We had now reached 1,420 miles per hour and at that altitude, we were now faster than Mach 2. The gauge finally stopped spinning and settled at our speed as well as the distance flown and how far we had yet to go.

The seat belts sign finally went off and I was invited to see the "stretch" panel in front of the flight engineer in the flight deck. But on my way, I decided to go to the bathroom, which faced sideways to the aircraft.

As I stood in the tiny bathroom, I suddenly had a brilliant idea— what if I stood facing the direction of Concorde and peed in the direction we were flying. I would be peeing at more than twice the speed of sound and faster than Concorde flew. It was difficult, to say the least, but I was determined to manage it and looked at my watch to begin the calculation. I peed for almost two minutes, dragging it out; I estimated the rate of flow as fifteen miles per hour. That meant I peed for a distance of sixty-one miles and at 1,435 miles per hour, at a height of 65,000 feet and at more than twice the speed of sound! Bloody cool!

I was so proud of myself and couldn't wait to inform the flight engineer of what I hoped would be my astounding new world record.

The stewardess took me to the flight deck. At that time, passengers were allowed to enter the flight deck with the captain's permission.

I walked to the front of the aircraft and noticed that the sky color was a deeper blue than I had ever seen on my many flights in the past, maybe it was our high altitude.

The flight deck, for me, was truly incredible. The panel in front of the fight engineer had opened up to a gap of at least nine inches where it had been closed before when we were on the ground. He showed me the gauges and the famous "droop snoop" at the front of the aircraft, which drooped at takeoff and landing for the pilot to see where he was going while on the ground.

He also showed me a second hardened glass composite that had come up in front of the windshield as the air pressure was so high that it would have glowed red hot at this speed and altitude. I began to tell him what I had done in the bathroom, telling him of my rather unique calculations and estimations of time and distance. At this, all three of them looked 'round at me as if I was mad, so I said, "No, really I did this and I think it may be a world record. What do you think?" The copilot shook his head and started laughing. "You did what?" he said, then thought for a moment, turned to me and said, "You know, you may be right. I can't think of anyone flying this high and at this speed and in this type of aircraft actually thinking of doing such a thing."

The fight engineer told me that there was no aircraft in the world capable of keeping up with Concorde. "What about some of the military fighter jets?" I asked, he replied, "Not even those that can fly at Mach 3 or higher, as they can only sustain that speed for about twenty minutes because of the rate of fuel burn," adding that once they began to chase Concord it would be hundreds of miles further away at 1420 miles per hour. "we (Concorde) could keep this speed up for three and a half hours, there is no other aircraft that could ever do that."

I went back to my seat and enjoyed the flight, which took us three hours and ten minutes to Heathrow from New York's JFK airport, wondering along the way, if I had peed over the longest distance and the fastest time in the world as I rechecked my calculations. I reasoned that astronauts were after all in space and not within the earth's atmosphere. On that basis, I reasoned, I probably had a fair chance.

I would never forget that flight and on leaving we were all given a double pack of "Concorde" playing cards in silver and blue, a certificate showing the date and time of the flight, which the captain signed for me (which I still have).

I wrote to Lars and told him what I had achieved all he said was "Only you would even think of something like that." The aircraft was Concorde number 004, the fourth one to have been built. Concorde is now out of service sadly, but I am happy that I had the experience and that I did what I did and I still wonder if I would have made the *Guinness Book of Records*, though I never contacted them with my stunt. They probably wouldn't have got it.

Another Job

As a result of my work, I was promoted and I was sent to meet Professor McDonald at his faculty at the Cranfield School of Business, just north of London. Malcolm had trained the company in Strategic Market planning.

I attended an intensive course in marketing learned how to make a three-year market plan, including a market and competitive survey; strengths, weaknesses, opportunities and threats (SWOT) analysis; a one-year business plan and a three-year market plan complete with a financial projection leading to a profit and loss statement on my business.

Whew, that's it? Anyway, soon after I began my new position, I realized that what Bo wanted was not what my new divisional head wanted. I hired a New Zealander, directly from Professor

McDonald's faculty, who had recently achieved his MBA. His name was David Foreman and he and I would work closely together to create a market plan for the newly formed division.

So we both began our mammoth task of converting my new sales division to complete a strategic market plan and hit our first roadblock, in getting my new sales team, to tell me all that they knew of their market in the form of a market survey.

The reason we hit this roadblock was that none of them had a clue about their market, size, or structure despite having, in some cases, worked in their "specialized" markets for a decade or more.

This was to be a real problem and one that I went to my new boss to discuss.

I was amazed to see his response, which was "You were given the job. You deal with it." I could see he wasn't going to help me. We got most of the job completed except for two salesmen who refused to comply and vehemently refused to have the company, as they put it, "look over their shoulders to see what they were doing." I told them that since they were employees of the company, the company had every right to demand of them anything that they wanted to win increased business, which after all was what they were paid to do. These two were not as good as they thought and really did not know their market.

I had all that I needed except for these two pieces of market data and went again to my new boss to let him know that unless I was to threaten them with being fired, there was nothing I could do to force the information from them. I also told him that it didn't matter since I could effectively leave out their particular information with a footnote saying that these two areas were unable to produce the necessary information and that their area was to be left blank!

He saw what I was telling him that these two had no idea of what their market structure was, thus, they were order takers, not order getters.

I was aware that something was going on, but I didn't know what except that our main competitor, "APV," had an advertising campaign showing that they were "lean and mean" and were a slimmer fitter organization and were capitalizing on the "Black Friday" that UK operation had just come through, where 45 of the food division sales and support staff had been fired. I was the manager following this event.

45 of our friends and colleagues each had a red card on their desks with a simple message saying come to HR at 2 pm, or 2.25, or 2.30

by our HR director (who will remain nameless). That afternoon both our company our customers and our competitors were stunned that we had fired 45 people all on one Friday afternoon.

When your boss is not supporting you, it's time to move or be moved!

AN UNFORTUNATE MEETING WITH

H.R.H PRINCE PHILLIP

Even the simplest of fixes can be disastrous!

ONE OF MY functions in my new position was to organize the various events that Alfa Laval sponsored and one particular event was the "Royal Shire Horse Show" in Peterborough, which was one of the events that Prince Phillip attended in person.

The event was one of the nonregistered or informal events that various members of the royal family can attend without being on the public calendar.

When I say informal, there is nothing informal about the event, which is a show for shire horses that are owned and used by the big breweries and shown around the country.

We received a formal invitation to the show and we at Alfa Laval were to present, along with Prince Phillip, a cup for the "Pairs in Hand," which meant two horses pulling a brewery dray. There are also 6-in hand, 4-in hand for pulling larger brewery drays. Along with our invitation, we sent a card containing the "dress code" and "Royal Etiquette" explaining how we were to address the prince if we were ourselves addressed by him. Men were also shown how to bow, while Sue was shown how to curtsy.

There were three apparent dress codes: "formal dress" for the Friday night's dinner when Prince Phillip would arrive, "informal" for the dress code for Saturday night's awards dinner, "very informal" for the dress code while at the show itself. Informal meant a business or lounge suit, while very informal meant a shirt and tie as well as jacket and trousers; but they didn't have to be a suit.

As for the formal meeting, we were told that in the first response, should Prince Phillip address us, we were to answer his question ending with the phrase "Your Royal Highness." If he engaged us further, we were to end with "Sir." Sue and I drove up to Peterborough for the show and I had a formal evening suit, or tuxedo, while Sue, who was seven months pregnant with our soon-to-be son Nicholas, had a two-piece evening suit. But when we arrived at our hotel, this pregnancy was soon to be very apparent.

As we were dressing for the formal introduction dinner, Sue discovered that her black velvet two-piece evening suit didn't fit her.

Unfortunately, nature had done its normal thing in preparing my darling wife's body for her upcoming birth event by enlarging her boobs to a size 38 double "D"! She was still not showing anywhere else at all, but her boobs were now quite enormous! She couldn't close her jacket. So, no problem for me I called down to the front desk and obtained a couple of stout safety pins to fix her now gaping jacket. The fix was perfect . . . well, almost.

Off we both went to the dinner and waited for His Royal Highness to arrive, which he did shortly after we did. He was shown around the large dining room and was introduced to the entire event's sponsors, which included us. He came over to us and asked about Alfa Laval being a Swedish company when horror of horrors! As Sue quite correctly began her perfect curtsy, the stout safety pin that I had placed reverently and purposefully in her jacket, to hold her boobs in, suddenly let go!

Aaargh! Out popped her beauties, all of them, in their bountiful perfection and glory, wobbling and bouncing as they leapt out of their tight confinement right in front of Prince Phillip's face as he leaned over to take Sue's hand as she curtsied. "Oh my," he said, as he couldn't help seeing both of her 38 double D's bouncing out in front of him. "Oh no," said Sue, giving me her evil eye as she quickly tried to grab them both as well as her jacket, a hurried motion in an attempt to limit the damage. To Prince Phillip's credit, he smiled at her and moved on. As he did so, Sue was standing there clutching the front of her jacket, attempting fruitlessly to prevent them from obtaining even more freedom.

We fixed Sue's jacket and got ready for our next meeting with HRH the following day at the awards ceremony to present the cup to the winner of our event. When we were presented to the prince again, he looked at Sue and smiled at her saying, "Oh yes, my dear, I remember you very well!" And Sue was mortified that he remembered her for her perfectly formed "'38 double D's," which, only a few months before were more reasonably sized and not nearly so outrageously bouncy as they had, unfortunately, become while being presented, along with my darling wife, to Prince Phillip.

As for me, I didn't fare much better as I had no suitable necktie for the Saturday's events and had to buy a hideous one from a market trader at the show. The only tie available was a full-color shire horse tie that contained the most hideous, with what seemed to be, almost full-sized color prints of the real and fully grown shire horses, yeeugh and one of them was so big that I could only see its arse on the front of my tie as the rest of it was around the back, a fine way to present one's self to the queen's husband.

The tie was all I could find there, so I had to wear it in order to meet the dress code, but I noticed that Prince Phillip had an almost identical tie as well, so I didn't mind so much. But one difference was that the horses on his tie were a lot smaller than mine and probably a lot more expensive!

The only thing I can say is that we were the proud sponsors of "The Pairs in Hand," which although was a meaningful term in the fine dictionary of the Royal Shire Horse Society, for us and Prince Phillip it meant something else entirely!

My confidence in being able to fix anything, under any circumstances, proved not to be as good in reality!

DRESSED FOR BUSINESS AS USUAL

How a simple ad campaign uncovered hidden agendas!

Our biggest competitor had a series of adverts that were being placed all over the world and were causing a lot of controversy in our markets and with our mutual customers who were telling us they either liked or hated the ads, which, either way, meant they were very effective.

In the Middle East, the ads were unfavorably viewed as each advert in the series of around six or seven in the campaign showed a naked man or woman, viewed from the side, crouched while "getting set" at a starting line just ready for a race around an athletic track. I knew that in Middle Eastern countries, public nudity was entirely unacceptable in any form, especially on public advertising like this.

I called Tony Yates and told him I had a great idea for a response campaign called "Dressed for Business as Usual," with a picture of a very well-dressed senior manager on the phone calmly taking an order or talking to a customer.

Tony discussed it with his creative team, took a look at the APV adverts, then called me back, saying it was a great idea and could he and his team come to our offices in Brentford to discuss it.

He came to meet me and my boss to show us the new advertising campaign. During the run-through of the new campaign, they explained that the so-called Black Friday was our way of emerging stronger and more than ever ready for new business. He then opened an artboard showing an artist's impression of a manager well-dressed in a suit and tie while sitting at a desk, with a pen in hand, taking an order over the phone. In other words, a direct hit at the nudity of our competitor.

My boss loved it until the next statement came out. "This should be a real manager, not a hired model," Tony added, my boss reluctantly agreed.

"So, who better than your own general sales manager - Tony Moore." at that, my boss said that he didn't agree and that we should use a generic, which would have a longer ad life in that if anything was to change, then the ad would have to be pulled. I have to admit I missed that little "cue" as to what was being planned.

Tony argued that it would be a false statement if it wasn't a "real" manager, adding, that our competitors would soon respond once they found out that it was a "hired" model, it would be even more embarrassing for us and could leave the door open for them to respond negatively toward us.

I listened and was curious about what it was all about as something was not right. Tony finally had his way, as he usually did and I was to be in the one-full page advert, shown in beautiful high definition through a black-and-white photo, taken with a large-format Hasselblad and was to be placed in every one of the many food, dairy, business and major news media as well.

I went to the studio in London, we took the photo in only two takes. I wore a light gray faintly checked suit with a striped tie and a white shirt; actually, it was my Armani shirt that I had bought for my wedding with Sue.

The photo of me that we had taken was now plastered in magazines and printed news media all over the country and was titled "Dressed for Business as Usual," with the Alfa Laval logo visible underneath.

As if that wasn't bad enough, I got a call from our Swedish Head Office's Marketing Department who wanted to know who our advertising company was and if I minded them using this campaign all over the world. I put them through to Tony and he readily agreed "for a fee" to let them use the campaign.

So there I was now featured all over the world in magazines in just about every language and in every country where our competitor had advertised with their "nude" campaign and I was right there on a full page, "Dressed For Business As Usual" ad that was far superior!

As I was to find out shortly afterward, the reason that my boss didn't want my picture to be used was that he was trying to get me out of his department. To this day, I don't know why and I didn't then, nor do I now care as what transpired next was truly remarkable.

The HR director (HRD, as I shall call him, who shall remain nameless called me into his office for a series of meetings to discuss how I was doing in my department. I had two meetings a week for around three weeks, during which he probed as to whether I was still in touch with Bo or not, and then I smelled a rat.

During one such meeting, he showed me a resume that he had just received from a headhunter and read it out loud to see what I thought of the candidate. As he read from the resume I commented, "Wow, that's someone that we could use," adding, "He seems to have great credentials. Maybe we should hire him?"

HRD looked at me and replied, "We already have, Tony. Why don't you take a look at this front page? It's your resume!" I snatched the resume front page, which was missing from the document he first gave me and saw that it was my own resume! FUCK! It was the resume that I had sent to a headhunter in London, who had then stupidly sent it to my own damn company. "You really have no idea what this is all about, have you?" he asked.

Of course, I knew what it was about, I had put two and two together which was why I had made up my resume; but I certainly wasn't going to show my hand to him and chose instead to reply, "I have no idea what you are talking about, but I have to get back to my office, as I have a ton of stuff to get done." And I turned and left without waiting for his response, fuck him! Outside, I was braving it; but inside, I was furious at being caught looking for another job.

I had nothing really to say to HRD on my way out but told him of the micromanagement style of my boss, adding that he had consistently failed to support me since I was given the position. "And by the way," I pointed out, "I never asked or applied for that position. I was given it by Bo Wirsen!" On my way out, HRD said, "Tony, you realize that this is a serious situation, so you'll have to leave it with me to decide how best we manage this matter." My response was, "Fuck you! Do what you want, I honestly don't give a damn!" I didn't tell Sue about all of this as I didn't know yet what would happen, though I had a good idea; so I thought I should wait to tell her when a decision had been made.

I went out that night with Dave Foreman to a pub in Ealing and we talked about the probable outcome, which for me was "stay or go"! I told Dave not to worry, that I would make sure he was OK and that he would be fine; but I suggested that he should begin to distance himself from me from this point on "just in case." Dave, bless him, didn't want to do that and instead told me that he had plenty of other positions available to him and could go to any other company with his MBA.

The following day at lunch in our canteen, I noticed that one of the HR managers, a very attractive woman whom I liked, called Anne, who had always been very straight with me and my department, was staring at me across the large canteen. It was one of those pieces that don't seem to fit in at the time but which "registers" with you at a deeper level, as confirmation of what it meant. In other words, an "aha moment." But I now knew or had a damn good idea of, what was about to happen to me that I was soon to be fired. I continued with my lunch, with my mind racing. I was now listening to what Dave was talking about with only half an ear as the rest of my mind was both sad and excited at the prospect of a new beginning. Typical of my mental agility, resulting from all the stuff I had had to deal with, I began to imagine myself in another and far more exciting career in a yet-to-be-named new company.

I felt good about my future prospects and imagined myself being interviewed for a new 'dream' job. I was also thinking of all the successes I had achieved—After Sales Marketing, Middle East business, the French business with Sandrine, setting up a new department and of the huge orders I had won and the ground-breaking business concepts I had started. I thought of all of the things I had done for the company and knew it made no difference in the end, what was to be, would be and there was nothing I could or was interested in doing about it. Mentally I had "crossed the bridge" and had closed the door on this company ready to move on.

"Crossing the bridge," was to say that I had switched off from this company and was now looking to my next job, whatever that would be. That afternoon, I was called up to the HR director's office and was told that my position was being changed and that I was being made redundant; that they had decided not to have a GM but instead have a series of territory managers instead. I was not shocked at the news and felt elated at the chance of having a whole new career in an entirely new business and began mentally to make plans as to what I wanted to do, while I was not listening to the boring comments that were being made by he who shall remain nameless "Another door to close." I stood and without a word left.

I left my office immediately and went straight home to let Sue know what had happened. She was shocked and was asking me about the mortgage payments and all of the other things that needed to be paid. I told her I had severance pay, adding that we would be fine, but I didn't care at all as I was very excited at what may happen for me next.

The only part I would miss was my old work friends, as I had known them now for fifteen years, but I had to only think about my next opportunity.

A few days later, as I was having a leisurely coffee and mulling through the newspapers looking for headhunters and job opportunities, I received a call from none other than Fred Grubb, the company chauffeur!

"Is that you, mate?" he asked me, I told him it was, recognizing his strong east-end accent and wondering how in hell he got my number. Now Fred always sold me boxes of cigars which he got from his many visitors while picking them up and taking them around London; while they were visiting Bo and the UK head office while Bo was managing director. Fred and I were good friends (friends in low places), Fred often told me all the gossip when I went to see him downstairs in his tiny office while he was waiting to collect a visiting VIP or drop them off. I always took time to talk to everyone regardless of their position in the company.

"Fred," I said, "why are you calling me? You know I was made redundant a few days ago?" "Yes," he said, "but you're not going to believe what has happened since you left."

He went on to tell me that Bo had heard what had happened, while he was in a board meeting with the main board in Sweden and that he immediately left the board meeting, called Fred to find out my home phone number, to call me later that afternoon. Fred told me, "Boy, have you got friends in high places, Tone." And he told me that Bo had arranged to fly over from Sweden immediately to find out what the bloody hell had happened (Bo's words) in his former UK operation.

I got the call from Bo while he was in Sweden, he asked me to tell him exactly what had happened. I told him that I had been spending 80 percent of my time in management meetings, even meetings to discuss meetings, that I had not been supported by my boss and had been left to deal with major issues with no support from him. Two salesmen (Bo said he knew who they were) refused to do what was tasked and my boss allowed this, but I did not (leaders lead). I also told him that because of the many meetings, I had completed the market plan with great difficulty, having to do most of it in my own time. "As a result," I said, "I had my resume out and had been actively looking for another job when it suddenly appeared on the HR directors desk." Bo listened and didn't comment at all until I had finished.

"That," said Bo, "was very unfortunate as HR director, he should have resolved it." He added finally, "Tony, you don't go from all you have done for this company to becoming seemingly incompetent in only four months. That's simply ridiculous." He then got very serious and asked me to promise that I would not take another position until I received a call from him directly as he needed to find out what had been going on as soon as his back was turned. Bo was now the President of the Alfa Laval group of companies sitting at the head of the board of directors of our $7 billion company.

I promised but added that I would not have a problem finding another job, to which he replied, "That is not what I and this company want," he said finally. Later when Sue got home from work, I told her of the conversations with Dick Grubb and with Bo.

A few days after that, I got another call from Bo telling me that he had arranged for one of his senior managers to come over to my home and to discuss an exciting opportunity for me within the company, adding that I was to keep this confidential. As for me, I had prepared to move on though and was not sure that I even wanted to stay any longer in that company, as I was certain that there were other jobs I could get that would not have as many politics as this one seemed now to have.

Sure enough, a few days after that phone call, Fred arrived in the company limo with a very tall Swedish man, another Lars, who came into my home to discuss a new position for me. Funny thing, he was so tall he had to stoop to get into the front room.

I invited Fred inside as well, but he winked and declined, saying he should wait outside while we talked things over.

Promoted

A new position was outlined to me to head up a new project for developing and implementing strategic market planning for the entire company and would involve me collaborating directly with Professor McDonald and his team for two years or however long it took to complete the process.

He told me that they had taken my UK plan for my food operation and found it to be complete and well presented. He also said that Professor McDonald had remembered me from his tutorials and thought I would be the "champion" for getting this global project off the ground.

"Your title will be " International Marketing Manager" and we've set aside a travel budget for you, which will be more than enough to complete the task. You should begin as soon as possible and plan to have visas and whatnot for visiting the company's major markets." I asked him which ones. He replied, "All of them. There are around thirty major market countries from Australia to Japan, most of Europe and across Canada as well as North and South America."

I went from being laid-off to having a promotion. I said I would have to think about it, then he invited me over to Sweden to meet his senior staff and to go through what would be required and what my responsibilities would be in more detail before making a final decision.

So I had a first-class ticket to Stockholm sent to my home and was to meet none other than my nemesis, the "HRD who shall remain nameless," at Heathrow Airport to travel with me. He met me at the airport and once we were on the way over, he started telling me how there were two types of powerful people in any company or even in the running of a country or government.

There were those with "formal" power and those with "informal" power, he explained. While some people had a position and title with all the power that went with that position and title, others had a reputation and a following based on achievement and success. And in these instances, their "informal" power was far more powerful than their leaders.' He told me he had no idea how big my power base was explaining that I had more power than all the leaders in the UK operation. He said finally, looking directly at me, "I got this one wrong Tony, I won't make that mistake again!" But I noticed he did not apologize unless this was a sort of lame apology.

But I was more interested in what I was to hear in Sweden. I didn't trust him and never would after what he had done and I had no interest in being "buddy, buddy" with him now. I spent the rest of the trip pretending to read the airline magazines and, for the most part, ignored him from then on for the duration of the trip.

We arrived in Stockholm and were taken by the company limo to the corporate offices in Tumba, a town just outside of Stockholm. David was making small talk while I was just gazing out the window and wondering if I should accept this new position or continue with my plans to leave the company and start a new career.

We finally arrived and were ushered into a large meeting room, where I was seated at an elegant long table while my former HR Director chose to sit on one of the chairs placed around the room, away from the table and me.

Several business unit heads came in and I was told that Bo would be calling in on a conference call later on. Each of the business unit directors, there were 7 in all who each spoke of their plans and how they would be prepared to assist me in my new role. I was to visit more than thirty countries and was to go and train each operation on strategic market planning, leading to a summary plan containing the direction for the company's global business for the next three years.

This was a huge undertaking, so I asked if I could have some help to get this task done. Lars, who headed the meeting (yes, another Lars), and was the person who met me in my home, told me I would be working with two MBAs from Professor McDonald's faculty and they would assist me with the task.

This sounded unbelievable and very exciting. I had traveled, but not like this. They were all explaining what they wanted for their respective business units, I took copious notes and after several hours, Lars let his secretary know that we were ready for Bo's call. He came on the speakerphone and suddenly, everyone sat up to listen, not saying a word, as Bo told all who were gathered that this was a very important project and one that would change the direction of the company. He also told me that I had a direct line to him should I require his assistance on anything at all and that I should give him regular updates. This, I knew, was to let the business unit heads know that I was being supported from the very top. HRD sitting nearby said nothing at all in the meeting but was probably making many mental notes!

So I agreed to take the job and Bo thanked everyone for taking time out of their busy day to take part in the meeting with me. He added that he and I would be speaking later.

We left the offices for our return flight back to London. When we were seated on the plane and once we were airborne HRD said to me, "You know, Tony, I had no idea that you had such high-level support in Sweden." I replied that I had no idea either, which was no lie.

He then went on to tell me that if I hadn't taken the job, he would have been automatically fired as soon as he touched down at Heathrow.

He looked at me and said, "Tony, you knew all along what it was about, didn't you?" I said, "If you're referring to me being fired, of course, I knew what was going on. That was why I was getting my resume updated and sent out and by the way, I already had several interviews already lined up. I added, "That headhunter who sent you my resume, by mistake, was going gangbusters to make amends for what he had done and didn't want to be sued by me for unprofessional conduct."

I had no more to say to him. He was a political player and had just scraped through keeping his job. We sat in silence all the rest of the way back. He had no more influence over me and could never affect me in any way in the foreseeable future. We had both learned a lesson from this: mine was that hard work pays off. He was a political player and was one who usually survived I never trusted HR departments after that.

The difference between informal and formal power was something for others to learn from as I already had it!

NEW HORIZONS

This one meeting, with the best there is, was to help me forever! All I had to do was to listen and learn.

FOLLOWING MY acceptance of my new position, I went to Cranfield to meet Professor Malcolm McDonald and on arrival, he took me to his office and sat next to me in front of his desk. He said to me that it had been the most stupid thing he had ever seen in a Fortune 500 company: that someone who had been promoted for a job well done, given the task of preparing a strategic market plan for his new operation, was then fired for doing it, with no help in between. I was surprised at how much he knew, so I asked him how he knew this.

He said that he and Bo shared many ideas for the company, adding that he admired Bo's management style and they had outlined this new position, adding that I was a "shoe-in" fit for the task.

I then met my two new partners, Ian and Yvette, both of whom were graduate MBAs and both had been in consulting and teaching market planning for several years. Ian was a tall slim man of around thirty-five with dark hair and a well-trimmed short beard; while Yvette was a sharp, slim attractive blonde in her late twenties. We were going to get along just fine as we swapped contact information ready for our new assignment. Together with Malcolm, we outlined the plan for the mammoth task of making a three-year strategic plan covering thirty countries.

Malcolm outlined to us some of his ideas for how to get the job done and how Yvette and Ian would interface with me. We split the world into east and west. I would travel with each of them. Ian would take the west, including all of the Americas and Canada; while Yvette would take Europe, Australia, New Zealand all the way north to China, Japan and Russia.

Initially, I used an office in the Alfa Laval building and hired an assistant who had two young daughters, Kate and Mauve, who were the same age as Amanda and Georgia and were close friends.

She and I worked together very well and she was very efficient; but as for me, I didn't want to be in the Brentford building anymore, so I moved to work from home and hired Sue as my assistant. It worked out very well. I was traveling all the time yet could call Sue from anywhere in the world, part private and part work.

An Interesting Dinner Party

One night Sue and I decided that since we had recently re-decorated our house and had just finished installing a brand-new all-black dining room suite, we should have a dinner party for our close friends.

It was to be on a Saturday evening and we invited Tony Yates and his fiancée Liz, Rich St. Clair and his girlfriend, Dave Forman who was to accompany Lesley, Sue's sister with Sue and me. The dinner would christen our beautiful dining room, which was decorated with gray walls, gray velvet curtains and a brand new black dining table and chairs.

I had the idea that we should do it properly and have the men wearing tuxedos and the women wearing evening gowns. Sue and I worked at the menu, which included individual champagne cocktails, hors d'oeuvres comprising Danish Aquavit and Russian canapés with salmon, caviar and cream cheese on black Russian rondels of bread. We also planned the main course of spiced chicken fillets with fresh steamed vegetables and a dessert of truffles and cream-filled crepes that Sue made and to finish off with vintage Port with blue cheese on light wheat crackers.

Now my brilliant idea included the aquavit that I had been given during a trip to Aalborg in Denmark. This was the famous and very expensive 'Linje Aquavit' (pronounced linni) which was Aquavit that had been matured in old sherry barrels while traveling in a ship's hold, during which it had to pass over the equator twice.

On the back of the label was the date of the voyage, the name of the ship where the ship sailed from and where it sailed to, very cool and very expensive. However, the dinner started off extremely well, with everyone arriving by cab to our house and being offered a champagne cocktail on arrival. Sue, bless her, had been slaving over the stove the whole afternoon and had together with me prepared a fantastic gourmet dinner.

After we had finished the cocktails, in our front room, we then all moved into the dining room and all were seated around our brand-new shiny black table.

"OK," I announced, "here's how we do this," holding up my special bottle of aquavit and a large platter with my caviar canape's which had been freezing all day in the freezer along with the shot glasses. "I'll pour out a shot for each of us, you knock it back in one, followed by eating one of these canapés." We all loved the idea, so I proceeded to pour out a shot for everyone, adding, "To make it more interesting, each time we raise our glasses, the next person on your left will announce the next toast, which will be starting with 1987 and moving backward until we either fall over or can't remember what the next date is." Everyone laughed and we began.

There were plenty of canapés and plenty of aquavit; however, before this, we had each had several brightly colored champagne cocktails, compliments of our newly purchased and very colorful cocktail recipe book and, I forgot to add, that the aquavit was extremely strong. Sue left the table to quickly finish off preparing the main course; meanwhile, we were all knocking back the very easy-to-drink second bottle of fine Danish high-quality aquavit. Tony Yates's fiancée, Liz, was sitting opposite me wearing a very low-cut black dress, not easily concealing her ample boobs. Each time we told a joke—and myself, Tony and Rich were wickedly on form—she would laugh, which made her boobs jiggle inside her low-cut evening gown.

Suddenly, it dawned on me as to what she reminded me of and I immediately, without forethought, which was by now impossible as we had already reached somewhere in the seventies in our backward toasts of each year, announced my stunning revelation. "I know what you remind me of Liz," I said looking at Liz's boobs, "your boobs remind me of a road worker, working with a pneumatic road drill with his pants half off his arse." I was laughing. "His arse cheeks look just like your boobs jiggling." And we collapsed in fits of laughter. Liz, however, didn't see it that way, saying, "Ha, bloody, ha, very funny," and she proceeded repeatedly to stab the back of my hand with her fork.

Tony, though nearly crying with laughter, tried to grab her hand to stop her, as I was laughing and howling at the same time while moving backward on my chair to get out of the way of her murderous fork-wielding hand, as just then my chair collapsed under me with a very loud "crack." I ended up on the floor while clutching onto the tablecloth as I went down. As Tony reached over to grab her hand, she pulled away backward and they in turn both went back on their chairs, which also made a very loud cracking sound and they both broke their chairs also.

As Tony tried to help her in a somewhat badly aimed "grab," he managed to grab her left breast, which immediately freed itself from her totally inadequate fine black fabric, low-cut gown, revealing itself to all. She went backward, with Tony who by now was falling on top of her, with her legs up in the air on either side of his torso.

Rich then said through laughter, "Hey, both of you, save that stuff for upstairs, not at the dinner table." And we laughed even more. My sides were now hurting. That did it! We were by now all nearly crying with laughter, no doubt helped along by the malicious mix of champagne and aquavit. Liz then tried to get up, but the drink had its way and she fell forward onto the table, unable to move any more.

So Tony and I helped Liz upstairs and placed her onto our bed, quickly returning to the dinner table.

Sue bravely returned with the main course, glaring daggers at me and we attempted to finish the dinner, though without any luck. We had to bring in two more chairs for Tony and me to sit on as Liz was flat on her back, now passed out in our upstairs bedroom.

We never made the main course, sadly, Sue was furious with me for that, blaming me for the events of the evening. We were still at the table at 1:00 a.m. and we made a valiant attempt to eat the chicken, for several hours. But try as we did, we couldn't finish it. Dave and Lesley stayed the night and we had ordered a cab for Tony and Liz.

When the cab finally arrived, Tony and I helped Liz down the stairs, to the waiting cab, driven by an Indian with a turban. As we came down the stairs, both getting in our way as we stumbled down, with Liz between us, once again, her dress gave up the task of trying to contain her ample breasts. As she leaned forward, her boobs fell out of her dress, as Tony and I got her out of the house down our path toward the waiting minicab.

The driver looked over and saw two very large creamy white breasts coming toward him, seemingly suspended in midair, as the black dress beneath them blended with the night's darkness on our pathway, her boobs were gleaming in the clear moonlight. "Oh gor blimey," he said, in his strong Indian accent, both shaking and nodding his head at the same time, while Tony and I were busy trying to stuff them back into the dress. It was like trying to get two melons into a shoe bag, almost impossible.

Tony was still trying as I helped shove them both into the cab and said, "G'night, mate. Hope you had enough to eat." Tony was concentrating on the job at hand, with Liz like a rag doll completely unaware of the events of the evening.

I went back indoors and straight up to bed collapsing half asleep thinking, *"I'll deal with everything tomorrow."* I was out cold. I awoke the next day feeling hungover and crept downstairs flabbergasted at the now very evident damage done the night before. I really did feel bad, when Sue came down sometime later as I was attempting to clear up. "Mornin, darling," I said, trying to look much more cheerful than I felt. "I thought our dinner party went well if you ignore the actual food." Sue wasn't impressed though and looked daggers at me, saying, "I spent hours cooking that dinner and it was ruined," looking at all of the wasted food and dishes piled up on the worktop.

"We never even made the main course," she said furiously. "Well, there was that" I said lamely adding, "Still, it was a good evening." I was still hopeful that I could get her in a good mood while hiding my damaged hand with the prong marks on the back. I had tried putting all the dishes in the dishwasher to clear up but had not succeeded, as I was feeling really bad seeing all of the half-eaten food.

"Why don't you go back to bed," Sue told me like the Trojan she was, "since you are useless here and I can get this done faster without you than with you." I was feeling hungover, so I had to go back upstairs. The following day, we went to the large furniture store where we had, only a week before, bought the dining room suite from a very happy salesman, only this time it was to return the 3 broken chairs.

As we entered the large store, Sue opened the doors for me as I followed her in with the three broken chairs lying on my outstretched arms like a sad black shiny pet.

As we entered the store, all of the previously very eager and willing sales staff miraculously disappeared, melting behind all of the brand-new furniture. We made our way to the back of the store, with Sue leading the way and the chairs and me following, to explain to the manager that we had simply had a nice quiet dinner party with a few close friends when the chairs collapsed under us. I got the chairs replaced and couldn't mention the true reason they had failed. So much for that! It was a long time before I was allowed to have another dinner party after that, but I was still forbidden by "she who must be obeyed" from ever making cocktails or drinking aquavit before any future dinner party. Oh well, into every life, a little rain must fall!

To keep the peace, I agreed not to have another party at least for a while but added the caveat that as long as we didn't mix the drinks that should be OK. Sue said nothing but was still furious with all of us.

All I can say about this is sorry Sue!

A SECOND MARRIAGE

A simple question can lead to a life-altering answer.

SUE AND I were out for an evening walk to the park at the bottom of our street, in Wembley, when she told me she was pregnant and I knew I would have to decide to get married. I just hadn't thought about a second marriage up to that point.

This was no reflection on our relationship, but we were so busy with everything day to day that we hadn't got 'round to it yet and anyway, I was traveling around the world with my new job. There was only one choice to be made and that was that we should get married; we loved each other, so that was that. We decided to get married in April with a registry office marriage, since we had both had big church weddings and we wanted a smaller affair with family and friends.

I invited Auntie, of course, and she brought John and his young girlfriend, Jane, who was several decades younger than him and all of Sue's family came too. Although the weather was dreary on our wedding day, we were very happy.

The funny part was when Auntie met Sue's Aunt Sally, who was quite stuck-up and always had been. Auntie was introduced to Sally and, as if right on cue said, to Aunt Sally a total stranger, "Isn't your Susan lucky to be getting married to my dahling Tony?" To which Aunt Sally who was completely taken aback said, "I'm sure it's a mutual thing." At which Sue immediately took Auntie's elbow and steered her away to introduce her to our friends in order to avoid a crisis. After the ceremony, we all went back to our house where we had a catered reception and thankfully it had finally stopped raining.

A Life Lesson

That afternoon, Auntie came to join me in our garden and said to me, "Tony deah, what is it that you really want? What is the "thing" that you will have that will tell you that you have finally arrived or have finally made it? I had no idea what the question was or how to answer, "Is it a Rolls, is it a big yacht, or a huge mansion, or maybe to be a millionaire? Look at what you've done, a wine bar, a great career, you've traveled all over the world; so what's next for you Tony?" I had no idea what my answer would be as I had never thought about "things" as being important, so I replied, "I don't know yet, Auntie, as I've never really thought about it. But I will now and I'll write and let you know my answer." "And then you can tell me when you get whatever it is that you want," she said with absolute certainty.

Around a month after our wedding, I thought of what a measure of my success would be while I was mowing the lawn outside in our back garden. As I was mowing our lawn I thought, *What if I had a house with a garden big enough that I had to have a riding lawn mower to cut my grass?"* My perspective at that point was from living in London where all of the back gardens are made to basically the same width of your house, which is around thirty to forty feet wide and anywhere in length from around ten feet in a small garden, to one hundred feet in a more expensive London home.

Our garden, being a corner house, was wedge-shaped and was around ninety feet long. So, my perspective of life and success was from a viewpoint of living in London in a fairly typical London house.

So I wrote to Auntie and told her of my decision in being able to answer her question, to which she replied simply, "That's nice, Tony deah. If that's what you want, let me know when you get it." I laughed at that, thinking, *Yeah right, like that'll ever happen.*

Pregnant At Sea

When Sue was seven months pregnant with Nicky, we went on holiday to St. Georgios island in Greece, as she was still not showing at all. One very hot day there, we decided to rent a small boat with two friends that we met there to have a picnic in a quiet cove somewhere along the coast. We sailed in our small four-seater converted rowing boat with a hopelessly inadequate outboard motor attached to the back, for around forty to fifty minutes when we spotted a perfect cove that could only be reached from the sea.

We pulled in and got the boat out of the water and up onto the beach. The weather was perfect, with blue skies and a warm breeze. After we had been there for several hours, swimming, snorkeling and sunbathing before we decided to leave for home.

But by now the weather had changed drastically and a strong wind had now blown up. The sea, which was only hours before, calm as a millpond and shades of blue, was now black with very high waves.

We headed out from our small cove and out into the bay to head south for home, but as we went out from our somewhat protected cove, we saw just how bad the sea really was. As we continued south, the waves by now were getting steadily worse and worse and our little motor couldn't get us over the crest of each wave.

I told the other three to don their life jackets only to find that there were only three anyway, so I didn't have one. Sue being her normal self said jokingly, "Ay, ay, Cap'n," as if she didn't care and was not too worried.

I, on the other hand, was beginning to get very concerned at our predicament as the sea was getting rougher by the minute and the waves were now well over eight feet high.

We had been traveling for about three-quarters of an hour when I guessed we were somewhere close to our bay "St. Georgios." The waves had become so high that we couldn't now see which direction was land, so I had to go by the wind direction and the direction of the waves coming over us as I was scalloping our tiny boat over the waves. Water was beginning to come into our open boat and we were now getting into serious trouble.

We rounded another bay and I looked ahead to gauge if we could make it across this bay and around the point ahead of us to where I thought our home bay was just around the other side. I estimated this on the length of time we had been sailing, but I didn't know I was in for a big surprise.

That little, small voice told me to "heave to" into the small cove that was to our starboard side and not to risk going across the extremely rough bay. The sea was now completely black, we were in the middle of a squall with huge waves crashing onto and into our boat. Our outboard motor was hopelessly inadequate and was unable to power us up and over each wave as I tried in vain to head the boat bow first into each huge wave. If I didn't, we would have been capsized and though I didn't know much about sailing or boating, I knew that we had to face into the waves and not let them broadside us.

I listened to that small voice and told them all that I was heaving the boat too, whereupon Sue laughed and said, "What the hell are you talking about?" I said nothing but knew that I had to get us out of this storm as soon as possible as the open boat was taking in water from the huge waves that were crashing across our bow.

I pointed the bow directly toward the small sandy cove and luckily we made it there, in a now waterlogged boat, where, looking like four drowned rats, we all got out of the boat to wait out the storm.

A little while later, a brightly colored water taxi arrived to take three people that had been nude bathing behind us, off the cove and home. I shouted across the water at "Adonis," the blond, curly-haired, cocky taxi driver dressed in shorts and a leather open-fronted vest and asked if he could take us too.

I will pick you up in a little while he told me as he gunned the huge double inboard engines to leave with his three passengers. We watched him as he went crashing over the waves and disappeared around the point into the ocean.

Some two hours later, he returned to pick us up. "£70," he said before we could get on we had to agree. We all got into his boat, which had a ski pole set in the floor at the stern end. Sue and the other girl that was with us grabbed the ski pole and were told to hold on as we took off at full speed across the bay.

Now Adonis to begin with was showing off to the girls that he was in complete control of the powerful ski boat, but pretty soon it became clear to us all that this was not going to be a picnic as he had to grip the wheel with all his force to steer the boat through the now extremely dangerous waves. We went across bay after bay and we were a lot farther out than we thought and nowhere close, as I had thought to our bay.

When we left that morning, the breeze and the currents were with us and we had covered a lot of ocean. But now, as he was steering the powerboat up and over each of the relentless waves, the boat with all of us in it, came crashing down as he too was scalloping the boat over the waves. We were going up with each swell then crashing down the other side, as each of the wave crests passed under our keel.

By now, "Adonis's" had white knuckles gripping the wheel. I'm certain he was thinking, *I hope we can make it OK.* We were sailing for over an hour of crashing through the stormy sea and we were being pounded into our seats by the rough weather. As our boat went up over crest, we were pinned to the floor; but when it came crashing down, we were smashed into our seats, every time.

We finally made it back to our bay where we all very shakily got off the boat, at Agios Georgios, thankful to still be alive and all of us had no feeling at all in our bottoms as a result of the extreme crossing.

Once on land, Sue was out for blood, she went striding straight over to the rental shack to have words and to have it out with the owner there. I thought I would let Sue handle this and stood back to enjoy the fireworks. "How could you rent a boat out to us with only three fucking life jackets?" she shouted at him. "There were only three of the fuckers but there were four of us, so why didn't you fucking well tell us there was a fucking storm headed our way, huh?"

He was taken aback by her anger and apologized to her profusely and told us he thought we would be OK. " You fucking thought? I'm fucking seven months pregnant!" she shouted at him, pointing to her completely flat tummy. I hoped he wouldn't say what I thought he would say next, because if he did, she would hit him. Well, he gave us half of our money back and was annoyed at having to go to pick up his boat; but we took the money straight to the beach bar and had a stiff brandy there.

The funny thing was that his girlfriend, standing next to him as Sue was ranting at him, knew me from the Village Wine bar and had been in to see us many times and here we all were in Greece, arguing over a very near and potentially fatal mishap. Still, we were all OK, though shaken up a bit, we were none the worse for wear.

The storm had passed and now, at seven in the evening, it was as if nothing had ever happened. The sunset, which could have been our last, was beautiful.

I knew that had I not listened to that very small voice, we probably wouldn't be sitting in the evening sun enjoying a brandy. We felt lucky to be alive and to look at the beautiful evening sun you would never have guessed the alternative outcome. Life's like that: one moment, all's well; the next moment, everything can change and sometimes forever.

After our harrowing journey at sea, we are lucky to still be here!!

NICKY IS BORN

Nothing remains the same after your child is born.

NICHOLAS ANDREW WAS born on August 29, 1988, at Wembley Hospital after Sue had an eighteen-hour labor. Seems he was quite comfortable where he was. I had been out the night before she went into hospital on the 26th with a friend of ours, Caroline, at the Michael Jackson concert at Wembley Stadium that Caroline had booked tickets for months earlier. It was his Bad Tour Live in London (August 26, 1988). Sue couldn't go with her so she invite me instead. The concert was the one with his spectacular white sequined glove and the now globally famous "moonwalk." With his white sequined socks, he was fantastic and the concert was packed that night.

Sue and I went to the hospital on the 26thth and Sylvia and Maurice had come over to stay to look after Georgia, while I went to stay with Sue for the birth of Nicholas. The labor lasted eighteen hours, which was a very long time; but Nicky was born at 9:10 in the morning of August 29th. We brought baby Nicholas back home into his well-prepared room and to a very expectant pair of grandparents and with Amanda and Georgia close at hand.

We were a family with one more addition. Sue didn't know how to prepare formula or any of the other things that were now a very central part of our lives, so I showed her how. I taught her how to mix, heat and test the baby formula mix.

Sue was a fast learner and did just fine. Georgia and Amanda were both very excited at our new addition as were Sylvia and Maurice who were very happy that their oldest daughter had given birth to a son.

Nicky's birth changed everything for us both as we now had a complete family at home, no more freewheeling at nights and no more unplanned nights out. We did enjoy taking Nicky to the park and spent time teaching Georgia to ride a bicycle around the same time.

Sue decided that she now wanted a dog, not just a silly lap dog but a bearded collie of all things. We all went to a kennel in Chertsey to pick one out. The kennel had six or seven young black-and-white

Beardie puppies and as we were standing there with Georgia, Amanda and a very little Nicky in tow, one of the puppies came over to me and nuzzled my leg as I stood there watching all of their antics. "It seems he has picked us,'" I said and picked him up. "He's beautiful," Sue said and we bought him there and then, taking him home with us. Sue named him Ben and we loved him as all families should. Ben grew up right alongside Nicky, becoming Nicky's buddy all through school. We took him from London to Brussels and then on to Indianapolis, so he was a true globe-trotting "Beardy."

My children would have what I never had, a family of their own.

A NEW JOB

Hard work will always pay off!

Soon after Nicky was born, I began to plan my travel arrangements, literally going around the globe to North America, South America, Canada, Northern and Southern Europe, India, Australia, New Zealand, up to Japan and back via Russia. All in all, I would be traveling to thirty-three countries in the space of two years.

I would visit each of the more than thirty countries at least twice. I would go once to train them in conducting a market audit and to train the local management on the development of a three-year strategic market plan. The second was to review what they had done and to summarize with them all that they had to undertake, as a "sounding board," and to provide advice as I was the subject expert. The project was a "doozie" for me, as I was learning from two of the very best in marketing that there were in England. In addition, I had a direct helpline to the "Prof," Professor Malcolm McDonald, for any help I might need along the way.

The amazing thing was that as we progressed through our meetings with the senior management of each market company, we began to become good at assessing what was in need of improvement within each market company we visited.

I always thought that really big companies, with assets in the billions, like ours, spanning almost all countries around the globe, managed their sales with a high level of skill and efficiency! Not so!

The issue was that our products were so damn good, they were extremely well designed by the Swedes, having a very high level of technical know-how in the manufacture that they almost sold themselves. So as a result, the company grew because of this fact and despite the sales efforts that in many instances seemed to do their utmost to lose business!

Bo wanted a more systematic approach where each market company had to analyze their market, showing a SWOT analysis as well as a market size and a competitor analysis. They had never done this before, so our job was to train them in the MBA techniques for doing this. This was to be an immense task for the three of us. We learned about the markets for our global operations very quickly. In some market countries, the staff had absolutely no idea of any of the critical information that they needed to make an effective strategy for sales, let alone increasing market share.

We did encounter some interesting customs though; for example, in India, Yvette had decided to arrive a day earlier than me and had attempted to begin the audit process before I had arrived. Unfortunately, in India, the protocol is such that they would not allow her, a female, English and she, a visitor, to begin until I had arrived the day later. Poor Yvette wanted to leave India immediately and to let them "stew," but I had to talk her out of it, though I did sympathize with her. We had to start the next day and she had to remain very professional and put her emotions behind her to get the job done.

India had our only female managing director, Leila Poonawalla, who was an effective talented and competent leader. I got on very well with Leila as we had been introduced several years before when she had just joined the company after graduating from university. Our first meeting was in Brentford when I was just starting with my new marketing department when she came to meet me.

I liked Leila a lot and thought she would have made a great political leader for India if politics allowed it; she was that good. She ran a complete manufacturing facility, making centrifugal separators with more sales managers in more sales regions than any other country operation we had and she did it very well.

I found after that meeting that Indian people are both perceptive and very intelligent, with incredible memories for data, names and detail. By contrast, in Australia, we arrived after some eighteen hours of air travel from London, got there for a normal and preplanned start at 8:30 a.m. and then had to wait until after 10:30 a.m. before the managing director and some his staff ambled in to begin their working day, which they did over the next several hours.

Yvette and I sat there with a pot of coffee, in the board room, drumming our fingers while waiting for the senior managers and sales staff to show up. Needless to say, that was the reason that they were underperforming. I had to call Bo to let him know what we had seen. Big changes were made one month after we left that first meeting, the Managing Director and several of his managers were fired.

In Brazil, they had a strike for the factory workers because of Brazil's hyper-inflation; but the strike, Brazilian style, was to samba music being played out loud on a truck with the biggest bloody boom box I had ever seen. Everyone was dancing, at the entrance to the factory, while they were on strike; it was funny and you had to love their style. Brazil was in the throes of massive inflation rated in the thousands of percent, which meant that wages agreed on Monday was not enough to live on by Friday.

Japan was very interesting too we got to travel on the Shinkansen, (bullet train) from Tokyo up to Nagoya, which regularly traveled at speeds up to 320 km/h (200 mph). We had lunch on the train with a beautiful backdrop of Mt. Fujiyama in the background. The train was as smooth as silk and the scenery was very beautiful. The mountain (Mt. Fujiyama) looked like a painting of what a "perfectly symmetrical" mountain should look like and as seen through the train's very large picture windows made the whole experience rather surreal. We visited the Sapporo Brewery.

The president of Sapporo personally took us around and explained that if he or anyone else saw something wrong they had to stay and fix it and not leave the problem until it was fixed. That year, I traveled to all of northern and southern European countries to New Zealand, Australia, India, Japan, Brazil, Argentina, Venezuela, Panama, Colombia, Chile, Mexico, the United States and Canada and to every European country. I went to each country at least twice. It was a, round the world trip, that most people would have loved. The work was good fun and was a great change from being stuck in one office. By the way, I found out that my old boss in Brentford, who had tried to get me fired, had been demoted to a tiny cheese-making operation in the southwest of England with a total staff of...7 staff. A far cry from the large department he had been running before.

Brussels

After I had completed the strategic marketing project, finalizing on a very detailed summary to the board, during which Yvette helped me make the final presentation, I was offered a new position working with another of my old work friends, Christer Kraftling. Christer and I had worked together in Brentford way back when I was only twenty-three. He was married to Annette, who also worked for Alfa Laval for a while. Christer and Annett got married in Acton when I was going out with Janet and we were both witnesses to their wedding. I still have the photo of the four of us. Christer, Annett,

Janet and me. We were so close that they named their first son Tony, after me. Cool, huh!

Christer, on our way over to Sweden after my big presentation to the board, offered me a new position in his newly formed marketing department based in Brussels. As my dream project had now concluded eighteen months after I began, so I now had to get a new position within the company and this was a perfect next step.

Sue and I left for Brussels after settling our affairs in London. We had decided that we should rent out our house in Wembley and placed it through an agency to keep it occupied while we were away. The house was in excellent condition, so we knew we could rent it out easily. I went over to Brussels to check it out and to see our new office, which was located in a large brand-new house around twenty miles to the south of Brussels. Sue came over with me to take a look at rental homes, of which there were hundreds since Brussels was a major center for NATO and SHAPE (Strategic Headquarters Allied Powers Europe), as well as the headquarters for the European Parliament or EEC as it was called then.

The town that we chose, Overijse, was a few miles just west of Brussels and north of Waterloo, where Napoleon made his last stand and was a Flemish town. The interesting thing about Belgium is that there are two distinctly different languages there; there are the French and the Flemish. People speak both languages as well as English, so they learn it at school; however, neither want to try to speak the other's language and all documents are in both Flemish and French, as well as English.

For the life of me, I cannot fathom why anyone would choose Brussels as a European headquarters for anything with all that going on. Added to this, neither the French townspeople nor the Flemish townspeople get along with each other very well. This manifests itself in the fact that each town and street name throughout Belgium has to have both the Flemish and the French name written and if the town is Flemish, that version of the name of the street or town goes on top with the other underneath and vice versa if it is a French town. Talk about stupid! So every day people go around and paint out the alternative language version of the street name, leaving only their version of the street or town's name on the sign.

The house we chose was a three-bedroom with an L-shaped living room, which angled into the dining room. The main reason we liked the place was the tidy garden and the L-shaped living room. We planned the move for September 1989 when Nicky was thirteen months old and had found a Chinese couple to rent our house, so all seemed well. Everything was moved into our new home. I made sure that Amanda and Georgia came over for their half term to be with us. Jane needed the break and we loved having them with us. They flew in from Heathrow and were escorted on and off the aircraft by an airline chaperone. We picked them up from Brussels airport and took them both to the new house. Needless to say, they were both excited. We took them into Brussels and to the "Grand Place," which was a very beautiful part in the center of Brussels. the Grand Place has an old cobblestoned square surrounded by very old and tall, beautiful buildings.

Sylvia and Maurice also came over for the holidays and loved being there with us, especially with the children Amanda and Georgia; we had a house full of life. In the garden was a strawberry patch placed over a small kidney-shaped pond that had been covered over to support the strawberries The location of our house was perfect and even had a pub right at the bottom of our street, which served several hundred different beers as well as Guinness on draft; that was the one for me. This was perfect. We had all that we needed and very near us were many other "ex-pats" from England, Scotland, the United States and many other countries. This was to be very important for Sue as I was going to be traveling all over the globe with my new position.

After we had been living there for around a year, we cleared out the strawberry patch in the back garden and I worked on a pond that was under it, resealing it until it was leakproof, then filled it up with water. My repair worked and the water didn't leak out; so Georgia and I, while she was over for the summer holidays, chose seven various colored small fish to place in the pond. Georgia was so excited as she had never had a fish pond before. I asked her to name the fish, which took her several hours and finally, she came up with names like "colors" and "silvers," very imaginative! I bought a jukebox for the house as Sue and I had several hundred singles from across the sixties, seventies and the eighties.

The jukebox worked well and was located in our dining room and we used it every time we had a party at the house.

Fortunately, with so many new friends, Sue had plenty to do and had arranged for little Nicky to attend a local day school where he was learning to speak in Flemish! He used to come home and say something to us both, waiting for a response; but she could not understand what the hell he had said. "English in the house, Nicky, please," she told him. Nicky, now only two years old was doing well at learning both languages Flemish and English.

After a year of living in Brussels, I made arrangements for Sue to come with me to meet Eve, Michel, Jean Louis and Jackotte in Toulouse for a long weekend. The flight from Brussels to Toulouse was only just over an hour. I hadn't seen Eve and Michel for ten years. I had called them in advance to see if they would have us there as guests. I needn't have worried; they were over the moon and were very excited that I was coming back with my new wife Sue.

They all came to meet us at the airport and greeted both Sue and I like long-lost family; it was all I hoped it would be and we stayed there for several days. It gave them a chance to get to know Sue. Michel and Eve had arranged a gourmet dinner for us at a local bar and restaurant in the town center of Bruguier's where they still lived.

The dinner was incredible and showed me how much I meant to them both and in their book, anyone who was a friend of mine was also a friend of theirs They asked about Jane, as they had met her many years before when I took her and a very young five-year-old Amanda with me to meet them. We told them that Jane and I were still very good friends and they sent her their love.

We met up with all of my old friends who came over to see us at Eve and Michel's house when I had lived there and we were made to feel like celebrities. We sat outside on their patio just like we had before, all of us together laughing and talking and eating till the early hours catching up on all that we each had done in the twenty years since Janet and I were there. Now Sue had been able to meet my friends and they were all happy to have met her.

Though we only stayed in Brussels for two years, it was a turning point for us both, as we had now left England, our home country, to begin a lifetime of living abroad.

Amanda and Georgia came over to stay for every school holiday even though I had plenty of reasons to go back to London to see them both often. Many other friends from London came over to see us for long weekends, so we never felt far away from home. The drive was only three hours plus the channel crossing.

True friends are friends forever!

AN UNFORTUNATE MERGER

Huge egos can make huge mistakes!

IN 1993 WHEN everything was going well, Alfa Laval had merged with another company Tetra Pak, also a Swedish privately held corporation, which was of equal size as Alfa Laval. Both companies were around seven billion dollars in sales and were similar in structure except that Tetra Pak was owned by the Rousing brothers and focused on high-speed packaging for drinks and liquids for human consumption. As time went on, both companies, across the globe, were to meet one another to see how the other half worked and as we met each other, it became very clear to me that the cultures of the two companies were vastly different.

Alfa Laval was an engineering-led company with managers that had been in the business and learned the company's finances and products. Tetra Pak had mainly hired young MBAs, fresh out of college, as managers in the United States and recruited around two hundred every few years when they wanted new General Managers, of which less than five would remain. This to us manages seemed a complete waste of time and resources.

If two Swedish companies in similar markets could be more different, these two were. Alfa Laval had a culture of careful and conservative management, having been founded in 1883 by Gustaf de Laval and Oscar Lamm and had a standardized budgeting process. We flew coach and rented average or appropriate cars.

Tetra Pak, on the other hand, flew first class and often hired limousines to visit their customers. Another difference was our US. customer base: we had 2,500 customers in our food-based sector within the United States, providing the same sales volume as only a few dozen high-speed packaging customers of Tetra Pak.

Bo Wirsen was now CEO of the $14 billion company and personally came over to meet us in our small (by comparison) Greenwood operation with senior members of the Tetra Pak corporate staff.

One purpose of his visit was that he wanted me on his "Tetra Pak" team asking me not to remain in the Alfa side of the business. Urban didn't want to join Tetra Pak and instead moved over to Alfa Laval on the East Coast, moving to Philadelphia while I stayed with the Tetra Pak organization based out of Chicago but living in Greenwood.

Later when Urban didn't get the president position of Alfa Laval US., he resigned from the company to start up his own consulting company. I never saw my friend Urban again, though we often traded Christmas cards together. I have to say that I didn't like the way Tetra Pak did business and the extravagance they lavished on their market, but it was what it was and that was that.

Soon after the merger, in a phone call from my new Tetra Pak CEO, I was informed that I was promoted to General Manager and was to take over five of their technical service divisions as well as running my own. I went from managing one division to managing six divisions with an increased staff as well as my own operation.

I got an immediate pay rise and was moved from being a vice president of a single operation to a General Manager of multiple operations, which accordingly was a much bigger position.

Next thing was that the company wanted me to shut down the Greenwood operation after it had only been opened for a few years. I was shocked and wanted to know why. The reason was that they didn't want a separate organization in Indiana and instead wanted it all under one roof in Chicago.

They Never Knew!

I discussed the impending decision to close Greenwood with Linda, my secretary and we agreed that I had to try to stop this closure if I could. I had to stop this madness because if we shut down Greenwood, at least sixty-five of my staff would lose their jobs and I knew all of them personally. So I had to do something about it.

I began by gathering all of the State and city info I could on housing costs, factory overhead costs, wage comparisons and even flight delay costs of Indianapolis compared with Chicago. I got information on comparable taxes, property rates, average wages in both places and even how much of the time the roads were congested in Indianapolis compared with Chicago.

I went to a corporate meeting in Chicago to present my case. Only my secretary Linda knew of my visit and the reason why as I didn't want anyone from Greenwood to know in case I failed to keep our Greenwood facility open.

I made my case with information from the FAA, the Governor's office, the local town hall and even several trades unions based out of Indy. In fact, I went with reams of statistical data all aimed at comparing our location in Greenwood to Chicago.

I presented a careful set of arguments one by one as an attorney would in managing his closing arguments. I won the case hands down. The senior board, over from Sweden, decided to keep the Greenwood operation, eventually making it an America's Center of Excellence where it remains to this day. It grew into a major production facility building complex and high-tech aseptic processing modules that were shipped all over North and South America.

No one to this day knows how close they all came to losing their jobs but Tetra Pak didn't care at all about that. Neither did my staff know the work I had put into trying to keep that facility open. Urban had been moved on so that fight was mine alone to undertake. I won the day and for me, that was the important thing.

Though I won the battle, I lost the war which, for me, meant moving my family to the company's location in Kenosha Wisconsin.

For the next two years, I had to travel up to a place called Pleasant Prairie in Kenosha Wisconsin, which was the location of our head office. We called the place 'K'nowhere' as that was what we thought about that location at that time as Kenosha where our office was located on Lakeview Parkway, had nothing close except a large power station with plumes of steam coming out of the huge cooling towers. I told Sue that we were expected to move to Wisconsin and she said, "If you think I'm going to eat cheese and brats (famous Wisconsin bratwurst sausages) while wearing lace hats surrounded by Amish people, you can forget it!" I tried several times to broach the subject with her, but it always ended in an argument, as she refused to even consider a move, so there was little I could do.

To win the battle and lose the war is sometimes better than to never take on the fight at all.

NOZZER THE COZZER

THE HIGH FLYING ROZZER

Big help from a big man

WHILE WE WERE still living in Brussels, I received a phone call one day from Wembley police, asking if I owned a house in Wembley and they went on to give me the address of my house. I said yes but added that we had rented it out to three elderly people.

They asked me if I was planning to come over to Wembley and if I did, would I call in to talk with them. The drive over was only four hours, including a hovercraft trip across the English Channel so that Friday, I went to the police station at Wembley.

After I arrived, I went over to Wembley Nick and met with several detectives who began to ask me about the house, how long I had been away, were they paying rent, could I provide proof of payments, etc. After a while, I became uncomfortable with the general direction that they were going with their questions and asked them, "What's all this about?" I asked them. They began telling me that I had rented the house out to three well-known criminals who were involved with a scheme of major credit card fraud!

"WHAT!" I said in disbelief, telling the investigators that they must be mistaken. "They are all around sixty years old plus," I said, but they confirmed what they knew and went on to explain how they worked their scheme.

They told me, "They rent a house then make sure they get onto the electoral register at the town hall. This is one of the checks that are made by credit card companies before issuing a new credit card. They then get electricity and gas bills in their names with their address the same as the home they have rented."

They went on to explain, that after being accepted for one credit card, usually Visa, they make small purchases from it immediately. They then pay off the card in full within the first month as this makes their automated credit rating with the card very high. Next, they apply for all of the other cards including Amex, Diners Club and repeat this activity, paying off the small opening balance immediately. Then comes the scam; they max out each of the cards with purchases and have around three to six months before anyone notices that they are scamming the card issuers.

I got it, but it didn't get me out of the uncomfortable feeling that I was being questioned in case I knew of this, which of course I didn't, though I have to admit it was a great scam. I told the detectives that I had met my renters only three times and each time I had to tell them the exact time of the day I would come by to check on the house. I added that once I had noticed a huge pile of dog food and other stuff stacked high in the dining room, though I thought it was strange, I thought it may have been something to do with their line of business. That part at least was true as it was part of their business which was illegal.

I asked the detectives at this point if they knew Noz. They stopped at my question. "Noz who?" one of them asked. "There is only one Noz Roberts," I replied. "You know Noz Roberts?" one of them asked and I replied that we were old friends. "OK," said the lead detective, "let's see how well you know him then!" And they made the call to my friend, "Nozzer the cozzer the high flying rozzer!" as we called him (among other things).

I watched their faces in amusement as they got hold of Noz, who by the way was at a secret meeting at his Freemason's lodge. They all looked over to me as they were answering his rapid-fire questions about me, which I found highly amusing. "Yes, he does. Yes, he is. OK then, that's fine, we'll put him on." They were answering his rapid-fire questions over the phone. "He wants to talk to you," one of them said sheepishly, as they now looked at me in a completely different way as I took the phone, Noz and I both started laughing at the fact that these detectives were questioning me. The interview was terminated by Noz and I was free to leave.

I agreed to meet with Noz the next day, making sure they heard our arrangement as I now had a real problem, which was how to get rid of these fraudsters who were renting my house. We parted with them asking me about my famous wine bar that Noz used to frequent when he was at Acton police station, which he frequently talked about. I left the police station at around 7:00 p.m. after some three hours of grilling, amid profuse apologies and thanks for my help and for coming back from Brussels to meet with them along with comments on the fact that I had been right I did know Noz and very well indeed.

Two Ways to Leave

When Noz and I met, I told him of my problem in getting these thieves and scam artists out of my house. If I did it the correct way, it could take a year or more with a loss of any rent, during which time they could trash my house and my cost would be very high.

Noz said to me, "Leave that to me, Tone. Tell me your address and we'll deal with it!" We arranged for me to meet the following day at 6:30 p.m. when I told him that they were usually home at that time.

I waited over the road at six-fifteen to watch the house, my house, while waiting for Noz to arrive. Now one thing I should mention is that Noz was built like a "linebacker," black as the ace of spades and huge at six feet six inches tall with arm muscles the same as an average man's thighs.

Noz was the very last person you would think of as a cop; if you were to see him, he was well into rap music and had a car tricked out with two huge boom boxes on his back shelf. I heard him approach when he was at least a mile away from the thumping boom, boom, boom of his music as it was being played out over the incredible stereo in his car. I knew where he was exactly as he approached and could hear his wheels screeching as he rounded the curve at the far end of my street.

He came into view with one very large arm hanging onto the roof outside his car window nodding his head in tune with some rapper piece or other. I smiled at his arrival, at the sight and sound of my friend, when he jumped out of the car. "Hey, Tone," he said as he gripped my hand in his huge bear paw of a hand. "So which one's yours?" he said. I pointed to my house on the corner.

"OK," he said, "here's what we'll do. You ring the bell and when they answer the door, you step aside and leave the rest to me." "OK," I said, "this is your show." We both went over the road and I rang my doorbell. I could hear them coming down the stairs inside and could also see them through the glass of the front door window. "oo iz it?" one of them asked in a squeaky voice. "It's only me, your landlord," I shouted through the still-closed door. "Is everything all right?" one of them said. And I replied that all was OK, but I had left something in the house (them).

As they opened the front door, I stepped to one side and Noz quickly stood in the doorway, immediately blocking out all of the light with his huge six-foot-six frame, looking like a huge "bouncer" and said, "I am a friend of the owners, as he showed his police warrant card, they know what you've been up to and they want you out of their house, so I'm here to let you know that there are two ways you can leave this house. They were stunned as he was talking and they were gaping at him looking him up and down. The first way, Noz continued, is through the front door with all of your shit, right now! "What's the other way then?" they asked to which Noz told them "the second way is through the upstairs window So what's it to be?"

I had to stop myself from laughing as these three weedy old fraudsters looked at each other in total shock at what had just been said on this nice sunny Saturday evening in a very warm April. "We w-w-will leave through the f-f-f-front door if, if it's OK with you," one of them said, as they scrambled upstairs to get their stuff. "Give me your keys," Noz told them in a stern voice that if I didn't know him better would have had me quaking in my boots.

They were out of my house in less than twenty-five minutes with all their stuff. Noz made a note of their car registration number for further use. I had brought with me a new set of locks and changed them immediately. After they had gone, we both burst out laughing, recalling their dismay and shock as they began to get it! We both had a drink at one of Noz's local haunts and caught up on all that had happened since we had closed our wine bar. He told me how he really missed it and I agreed as I did also, but things sometimes change, so did people.

Noz and I have kept in touch for more than thirty years and met in person a few years back. We both have remained close friends. Noz is one in a million, literally. He was awarded the Queen's Medal (QPM) for services to the London Metropolitan police force on his retirement several years ago. He now spends all his time doing charity work for underprivileged kids all over London.

He sent me photos of his investiture when he was awarded his QPM in his bright yellow waistcoat and tailed tuxedo, looking on top of the world and he deserved to feel like that.

I am very proud to know such a truly wonderful person as Noz, especially knowing the many trials he had to go through in his early career that would have surely made a lesser man quit and choose another line of work, but not Noz. He, like me, was never a quitter and I still laugh at how he dealt with things. When Noz was awarded his Queen's Police Medal in 1996, Prince Charles told him, "We need more people like you." And he was right. Noz is now Norwell Roberts QPM (Queens Police Medal).

Overcoming Racism in The Met

As I am writing this, The Norwell Roberts' story leading to his stunning QPM award, was filmed in a short documentary, "I AM NORWELL ROBERTS QPM" a biographical short film drama about London's first black Police Officer and the racism he faced.

Nowell, "Noz" (né Nowell Gumbs) rose above all the racism and stayed focused on his job as London's first black police officer. He told me of some of the things they did, like cutting off the buttons on his uniform just before parade and many other stupid and racist things. Noz was in tabloid cartoons and was even on the cover of Private Eye and in newspapers in America in the Southern States, the headlines read 'London gets first negro cop.

But Noz was made of much stronger stuff than they were and was promoted to Detective Sergeant which was his position on the force when we met at our wine bar in Ealing.

Another accolade he received was at the Hendon Police Training Academy where they named a training room after him. I was so proud of my friend when he told me this.

Hats off to you mate, my lovely friend, my now famous, gentle giant who I am honored to have included in my book and who am also honored to call my friend.

And as a last comment to you Noz, Prince Charles was right when he told you, "We need more people like you!"

Some people simply doing their job, while overcoming racism is something well worth the award given by royalty.

A NEW MEMBER OF THE FAMILY

Brussels was a stepping-stone for things to come.

AFTER LIVING IN Brussels for two years, my marketing job was completed and Alfa Laval had acquired a competing company based in Indianapolis called *Equipment Engineering*. This small company had been reverse engineering (copying) our spare parts and was busy selling them to our customers at half of our prices all across the US. and other countries in the "Americas." Including Mexico, Canada and South America.

I was offered a position as vice president of a new company, Equipment Engineering, which would mean moving to the States and after discussing it with Sue, we were once again on the move.

As we were busy preparing for our move to the United States, Sue, who was pregnant for the second time and was finally beginning to show at eight months, was busy getting all the things she needed for our new family addition.

I redecorated the bedroom for our soon-to-be new arrival; we had decided to have the baby in a big hospital in the ancient town of Leuven just twenty minutes away from Overijse. Sue had had a miscarriage while we were in Brussels and was nervous about the upcoming birth in case anything went wrong.

Leuven was a beautiful town with a large hospital and a world-renowned university. All over the town were tall buildings built in the eleventh century. Each of the buildings had sculptures of saints and important figures from ancient history as well as other historical figures and all were exquisitely carved all over the front of each building.

The town center had cobblestoned roads, which made for very bumpy driving and I commented to Sue that if she had any difficulty giving birth I would drive her at speed over these cobblestones, just to help. What I loved about the town, apart from all the beautiful buildings, was that it was the home of the more than 600-year-old *Stella Artois*, which was another of my favorite beers. Anyway, once when we had gone there to see the town with Nicky, I made sure we drove past the brewery just so I could say that I had been there.

David Forman who had worked with me in Brentford and who had come over to work with me again in a new marketing role in Brussels had become a close family friend. He often came over to stay for weekends at our house and we often went to the local pub at the end of my street after work even if it was only on the days when I was not traveling.

One Monday night, we had decided to have a beer on the way home from the office as Sue had invited David to have dinner with us that night. We drove from our office to arrive at the pub, at the bottom of my road, when, as we swung into the car park we nearly drove right into a barricade that had been placed over the entrance. WHAT! They had closed my local pub, just like that!

What a bummer! Dave and I got out of the car and walked around, but sure enough, there was a sign written in Flemish and French, saying it had closed *"Ferme!"*Closed down for good and our pub had been sold. Fortunately, a short time later, it reopened as the *"Mexican Grille,"* not really anything to do with Mexico or Mexican cuisine, but it was an all-you-could-eat buffet, where you chose what you wanted and cooked it yourself on one of several large open charcoal grills.

This at least compensated for the loss of my "local" and whenever we went there, usually in a small crowd with our friends, we men always offered to do the cooking while loading ourselves up with numerous jugs of beer that were included in the cost of the meal, for a small additional fee.

We went up to the bar and ordered as many jugs of beer as we each could hold, usually around four or five each, as each jug only held just around one liter. We placed them on the shelf over the grill ready to drink while we cooked dinner. As we explained to our wives, "cooking on these hot charcoal grilles was very hot work, so we have to keep ourselves hydrated!"

We were nearly always tipsy before we sat down to eat, so dinner was a lot of fun whenever we went there. I should mention that in Belgium there are reported to be over six hundred different beers available and each one has its own unique glass. I just thought I would mention that.

So every time you order a beer, you get the special glass with it, which I thought was really good marketing. I decided when we left Belgium we would take as many beer glasses over to the United States as we could pack.

That last Christmas, in Brussels, was spent with Lesley, her current boyfriend, and Georgia who both came over for the holidays. Amanda who was now a teen sometimes didn't want to come but instead chose to stay in London with her friends, which was fine by me, as long as she was happy.

In 1990, I had to go over to Indianapolis with Sue to meet the new company and all the staff at their Christmas party, which was in downtown Indianapolis in the Grand Union Station. Though Sue was seven months pregnant, she didn't show at all and despite being tired from our long trip from London, we were ready to meet my new company. She always amazed me with her resilience.

We arrived late afternoon, on Friday, December 15 and Sue had a chance to rest for only a few hours before we were to leave to join the company Christmas party and to be introduced to all my new staff.

Sue wore a long evening dress in deep green, which was stunning and she looked a million dollars and I was proud that she was my wife. When we arrived at Grand Union Station, where the company party was being held and which was a short distance from where we were staying at the Embassy Suites Hotel, we were amazed at all of the beautiful decorations inside the grand ticketing hall.

There were two huge, twenty-foot-high Christmas trees; each was decorated in silver with what must have been a million lights. All of the main halls of the station had been decorated with garlands and lights, the whole effect was beautiful. There were crowds of people in the old station; the décor was old-world with gas lamps and restaurants in the main hall and it all looked very festive. One thing I was to learn about the United States was that they did everything on a huge scale . . . no half measures there!

As we went up the stairs and entered the upstairs party, all heads turned to see Sue; I had met them all previously, but they were all intrigued to meet her. We were shown to our table where the previous owner, Bob Behrens; my new secretary, Linda and my new boss, Urban Swensson, the new CEO and their respective partners were all seated there to greet us.

After we all made the introductions, we sat down and had a chance to relax. Sue was overwhelmed at the company who were all there for the Christmas celebration but she was used to me and company Christmas parties, though here I had to be on my best behavior as I now had an important role as the new general manager.

We met Charlie, a realtor, the following day to look at houses and we couldn't believe what we were looking at. Compared with our house in London and Brussels, which were three-bedroom houses and very nice ones at that and what we were now looking at were mansions for the same cost as our London home, only three years before.

All were decorated with thousands of Christmas lights outlining the windows, the houses and the front gardens. There were even lights on the rooftops. We had never seen this before and certainly, at that time, in Brussels or in London, there were none of the Christmas decorations that we were seeing in Greenwood, Indiana.

After we had returned to Brussels, the time came for our new baby boy to arrive and it was March 9th when I got the frantic call that Sue had broken water while in a restaurant with several girls on a girls' night out.

They brought her quickly home and wished us both good luck as we sped off to the hospital as fast as we could. On the way though, with each contraction that Sue had, she grabbed the steering wheel with all her might. I nearly crashed the car several times in trying to prize her vicelike grip off the steering wheel while attempting to negotiate the winding twisting roads along the way.

When we arrived, the nurses began babbling in Flemish to us, refusing to speak English and we couldn't understand a word they were saying. This really pissed Sue off as she was dealing with a rapidly approaching childbirth, so she let them know in very loud, very fine swear words, which they pretended not to understand, while all the time their faces were getting redder and redder.

The birth, this time, was very fast and our son, James Alexander Moore, was born, without any mishap on March 10th.1991 Although we still couldn't understand anything of what they were saying, at that moment, we didn't care. All was well with the now-growing Moore clan.

Sue stayed in hospital for a day longer then I picked her and our newborn son and took them home. Over the next few weeks, we were inundated with visitors who had come to see Sue and our new baby James. I was now just a side issue!

Big Hats In Brussels

Not long after James was born, before we left for my next assignment in the US. after I told Auntie about our new addition to the family, she announced that she would come over for a week, with Nurse Rosemary, to give Sue a break. I was very happy at that as we had a spare bedroom with two beds that they could both use and there was plenty of room for my two oldest and dearest friends.

I went to the airport to meet them with Sue, Nicky and our new baby James; they arrived right on time. Auntie breezed through customs, sporting a bright blue large-brimmed hat and a matching outfit. Rosemary was wearing pink and another big hat, making them stand out from all of the other "gray" passengers. I heard her calling across the entrance, "Tony deah, there's my darling boy!" And she came rushing over to give me a huge hug with Rosemary in tow and I was so happy to see them both after such a long time.

When we all arrived home, Auntie did what Auntie did best: she completely took over all of the cooking, all the cleaning and all of the preparations for our two very young boys. Sue was very happy at that and was told in no uncertain terms that she was to rest completely for the whole time that Auntie was staying with us.

We took Auntie and Rosemary to the Grand Place, in the heart of Brussels for afternoon tea, the weather was very bright and sunny. She once again sported her very large-brimmed hat as did Rosemary, as we sat outside in the afternoon sun with Nicky and James at a table at a café in the "Grand Place." The waiter came over and was soon put to task as Auntie quickly informed him exactly what we were all to eat and drink, I watched in amusement as he quickly got the message that she was, as usual, entirely in charge.

I loved it and I loved Auntie. I went over to her at that moment and put my arms around her and told her, "Never ever change, dear Auntie. I love you just as you are." I went over to Rosemary and told her the same as we were both so happy that they were here with us.

The whole time they stayed, Sue had a much-needed and well-deserved break and loved every minute of it. When they left, wishing us good luck in America, we were left once again as a small family ready to move for our next big adventure; but Sue had some renewed strength and was back on form.

We left Brussels finally on April 26, 1991, for London where we were going to spend two weeks there before moving on to Indianapolis for our new life in the new world. We stayed at Sue's parent's home in Ealing. Nicky, who was nearly 2years old attempted to put a cookie in their VCR! This was the first of many things our mischievous Nicky was to do throughout his childhood.

A DREAM BECOMES REALITY

I learned that a dream can in fact become a reality proof that the universe works with us.

W e moved to the US. on May 5, 1991 and spent the first night in a hotel as our most needed personal items had been flown in a half-container, arriving the next day. I had shown Sue videos of various homes I had viewed as she had been too pregnant to fly. The home we had both settled on was a palace and was only a couple of years old having a three-car garage, five bedrooms and a huge living area.

While we were waiting for our things to arrive in Greenwood Indiana, I gave Sue the garage door opener and asked if she would like to have a look 'around while we were waiting for our things to arrive from the airport. She pressed the larger of 3 buttons and as the door began to open, sitting right in the middle of the huge empty double garage was a "Sears" rider lawnmower!

I couldn't believe it. I had apparently made it at last! "It's here," I said out loud, the riding lawnmower is here I don't believe it!" I said. Sue looked at me as if I was crazy. "What on earth are you talking about?" she asked me. "Of course, it's there it's a lawnmower."

I reminded her of my conversation with Auntie several years before when she told me to let her know when I "had made it," and in answer to her question, I told her my success would be realized when I had a home with a garden so large I would have my own riding-lawn mower to cut the grass around my house.

I knew at that very moment that she had been right and that although I didn't feel any different right now, I had got something I never knew was possible from my perspective of a future success while living in London. I had told Auntie; a rider lawnmower would be the "thing" telling me I had finally made it! The interesting thing was that amassing money was never my goal(just as well).

I wrote to Auntie and told her my news, sending with my letter a photo of Georgia and Nicky sitting on my lap as I was now mowing the grass around my house, to which she said simply, "So what's your next goal, Tony deah?" and once again, I had no idea my wish would come true., Maybe my next dream is to be a millionaire, maybe if pigs could fly!

Sue had her hands full with our two young boys, Nicky and James, while I was immersed in my new job.

Urban and I got along very well and we made a great team. We decided to move the company from its ramshackle and leaking building in South Indianapolis into a brand-new multimillion-dollar facility in Greenwood, Indiana, some twelve miles south of Indianapolis.

We both worked at the design and the new building was completed, with seventy thousand square feet of floor space, forty thousand of which was for the workshop and thirty thousand for the offices. For the next few years, we were busy the whole time with work and home. Amanda and Georgia both came over as did Lesley and Sue's Mom and Dad, for summer, for Christmas and any time they wanted.

We had plenty of room for visitors and had a complete suite upstairs of our "ranch-style" home, with 2 bedrooms and a bathroom. Urban and I turned that little company "Equipment Engineering" around from a $7.3 million operation into a $19.6 million business in the space of 20 months.

We were rocking and a subsequent survey by an outside, independent consulting company showed that Alfa Laval had now moved from being last in "perceived value" by our customers into becoming the number 1 preferred service provider. It didn't just happen, but Urban and I worked hard to make this happen. We each got on with our work and knew what we had to do. In my case, the excellent result was where I intended to take the company and with my strategic planning, I took it right there, exactly as I had planned to do. I had laid it out, as I had been trained to do by Professor Mc. Donald and then implemented my plan.

The Indy 500

Soon after we had moved to our new premises in Greenwood Indiana, we got involved with the Indy 500 race, as a race team sponsor. Every year in May, we took as many as one hundred customers to the track for the time trials. These took place two weeks before the actual Indy 500 race and were the time trials that all the race teams considering entering into the Indy 500 had to complete before being able to qualify for the race. Each team had to bring their race cars up to perfection and could use the track for two weeks before the race in order to achieve this.

The teams then set up their cars for the qualification time trials in which each team has to submit their Indy race car for examination to ensure they met the race qualifications. Then the track was closed for the "fastest four laps" of each car separately. The fastest times were entered showing their position on the starting grid of 33 cars, set according to their average times for the four solo time trial laps or qualifying laps.

It was a lot of fun and I got to know our team and many of the technical settings that our team *"McCormack Racing"* were using. On race day, we met our VIP customers in Greenwood then took them in a convoy of five large fifteen-seater vans complete with a police escort all the way to the track.

On race day, we were allowed to go right through red traffic lights and cruise at high speed over sixty miles per hour past all of the thousands of race fans along the twenty-mile distance from Greenwood to the Indianapolis Speedway on the east side of Indianapolis.

We had arranged for breakfast at the track and then a group seating for fifty seats right at the start-finish line. The atmosphere was electric with a packed stadium and a show that only America could put on. There were marching bands, thousands of balloons released there was even a flyby of the U.S. Air Force, which was always very moving.

The race was a five-hundred-mile race of tough endurance race for the cars, the teams and the drivers and normally lasted around four hours depending on how many yellow lights or accidents there were.

I was at that time, in 1992, one of the first people to have a cell, or a mobile phone; it cost a staggering $1,100 and was a flip phone made by Motorola.

Few people had a cell phone at that time mainly because of the cost, not surprisingly and when I took it with me to the track in a clip mounted on my belt in case I needed to call the office. At one time there were three attractive girls standing the other side of the fence, by pit row as they each lifted up their T-shirts and flashed their boobs at me while asking me if they could call their friends on my mobile phone. I declined but I did take a peek.

I called Georgia in London, during one of the many days at the track during the time trials and told her where I was. "That is so cool, Dad," she said. "Can I talk to a racing driver then, Dad?" She was ten years old at the time and just as she said this, our driver, Jeff Woods, came walking back from turn 1 of the track. This was during the 2-week testing period where all the racecars are allowed on the track to make adjustments to their car set up ready for the race.

Our car had broken down on turn one, so he got out and walked back to our pit area. I told Georgia to hold on as Jeff approached me, he stopped to tell me what had gone wrong with the car and I asked him if he wouldn't mind talking to my daughter in London. Jeff looked at the phone and said, "Sure, I will. What's her name?" "Georgia," I said and passed the phone over to him.

"Well, hi, Georgia," Jeff said to her and listened for her reply. "Hello, Georgia, are you there?" he asked again and still no reply. After trying a third time, he passed the phone back to me and said, "I think she's gone," "I doubt it," I said and took the phone back from him as we walked together back to the pits. "Georgia are you there?" I asked and she said, "Dad, was that a real race car driver?" I told her it was, but she was speechless and couldn't think of a thing to say to him! We both walked back to our pits together while I was talking to Georgia, but she never did talk to a real live Indy 500 race car driver!

A KEY DECISION

After making a carefully considered big decision; never second guess it.

ONE EVENING AS I was watching Nicky play football (soccer) at a rare time when I was at home and not in the office at Kenosha on a Wednesday night, I thought to myself I want to be able to bring my children up right here and not keep moving them all over the States as soon as Tetra Pak makes another knee-jerk decision, seemingly at the drop of a hat. With the merger of Alfa Laval and Tetra Pak, it was clear that things would change, which meant any of us could be moved anywhere and at a moment's notice that was Tetra Pak's disjointed decision making.

I made the choice not to move and come what may, I decided then and there that if this cost me my job, then so be it. Maybe it was time to move on from this company. I wanted to be able to spend time with my family and more than that to let Nicky and James have life-long school friends without being moved from location to location at the whim of my company, which was the way Tetra Pak managed their business.

I also wanted to take control of my family's future more than I could do while working for such a mercurial company that, under the Tetra Pak umbrella, seemed to bounce people and families all over the place with absolutely no care as to their family's happiness or stress.

Sue refused to even consider a move, especially to Wisconsin; even though she had never been and knew nothing about life in other places in the States. I told Sue of my decision, made at the side of the soccer field while watching Nicky play with his teammates. Her decision not to move was mainly because she simply refused to move again; but for me, it was to allow Nicky and James to have life-long school friends that I never had apart from Ian. I had decided that I should start looking for another job. After my decision, I "crossed the bridge" and everything inside the company, from that moment on, looked different to me.

An Unbelievable Coincidence

During the time I was working in Kenosha, where our head office was, traveling up and back Mondays and Fridays, I rented a house and shared it with two of my colleagues who also had to be relocated to the head office, George and Blair. I had hired both of them into the company in Greenwood and we made a fine trio.

I was once again traveling the whole time but found that one very cool part about Wisconsin life was that there were loads of pubs there seemingly on every corner. This at least meant that we had places to go to in the evenings, a small ray of sunshine in a bad time for me. I found a local dive bar called "The Cavern." The bar was down the road from our rental house and we went there frequently midweek.

They got to know me there and being English certainly helped, they told me that there was another local who talked just like me. They told me they would introduce us both when he next came in. I thought that to most Americans I had met so far, I may as well be Irish, Welsh, Australian, or a New Zealander and thought nothing more about it.

A few months later, I was introduced to the person they told me about and it turned out that he did in fact come from London. His name was Matthew (Matt) McCoy, and as we began to talk, I asked him where in London he had come from. He replied that he had lived in Ealing. I was now interested to see if he knew the same places or people that I knew. I asked him "what school did you go to?" he replied, "Fielding." I told him "so did I!" I then asked him, "So what teachers do you remember there?" He told me his favorite was his music teacher, Mr. Woodcraft! I couldn't believe it as we both said, "Woody Woodcraft" in unison. He went on to tell me that Ms. Hunt was still the headmistress and many of the same teachers that I remembered were still there.

Unbelievable! Here I am in the middle of nowhere—Kenosha, Wisconsin—and I meet someone who went to the same school as I did.

I asked him if he recalled seeing the many black-and-white photos all along the wall outside Ms. Hunt's office on the entrance wall to the main hall. He told me there were loads of pictures there, so I asked him if he had seen some pictures of a school play called *The Snow Queen* and he told me he had. When I told him that I was in that picture and another next to it, he recalled seeing the photos. I told him of the very happy times we had at Fielding and he had the same experience. I asked him what he was doing here in "Knowhere-Kenosha!" and he told me he was forming another band.

He was in a famous punk band called "UK Subs," which were around at the same time as the Stranglers. We shared stories about the various music and bands that we had played with and that evening was surreal for us both. He told me that Fielding Junior School had a really good reputation and was a highly sought-after school, although he was probably ten to fifteen years younger than me, he had enjoyed the same things I had.

Mr. Woodcraft had made a big difference to many of us as children and was a truly gifted teacher. He taught us what music was really about and we got it.

To this day, many of us old alumni still have an exceptional understanding of music because of his teaching. The best I can do is to remember our beloved Mr. Woodcraft in this book by saying, "Mr. Woodcraft, you really did make a difference, thank you for all you did."

A Prophetic Dream

Around this time I had a strange dream and it was so clear to me after I awoke I realized every scene in my dream was crystal clear and I knew while I was dreaming that I was being told something important, but I didn't know what it was at the time.

In my dream, I was camped between two tall buildings, not skyscraper tall, but older four- or five-story houses with steps leading up to the front door as in the style of a Chicago townhouse. Between these two tall houses was a grassy space where possibly a third house could have been. On this grassy space between them both was a tent that I was living in.

Looking up, I noticed, standing on the street, a work colleague of mine, Frank Schmitt, our technical director who was standing looking at me, not saying a word. I called out to him to say hi, but he said nothing at all to me and instead turned his back on me and walked away. I couldn't understand why he did this, but the dream was in dark colors and the atmosphere was remote and heavy for me.

When I awoke, though, I had no idea what the dream meant but I knew I could remember it all with perfect clarity.

Little did I know that this was one of several such dreams where I was being shown something very important and I was either being warned or advised of what was about to happen around me and that

I would know when the time came that the dream was forewarning me of events though I didn't yet know what they were to be. It was not until several months later that the events of that dream became clear to me.

The Best Management Compared

During what was to be my final few months working at Tetra Pak, I took part in a corporate decision to be part of a study where they had brought in a Canadian consulting company to evaluate each of the 7 main sales and marketing divisions. This was to see how the divisions were being managed and to see what changes may need to be made for more success within Tetra Pak USA. From my experience with the other GMs, they all needed to be replaced!

After the team of consultants had been to each of the other divisions, they finally came to my department and asked me how I ran it and what key information I had to manage my operation. At that point, I had a very large organization of sales, order handling, spares and technical service.

I asked that they first meet with my staff and ask them those questions then come back to me, as I had trained them all and they should be able to answer any questions about their individual markets.

After a few days of meetings with my sales staff, the consultants came back to me and told me how impressed they were with the knowledge each of my sales team had about their market structure, their individual goals, and key accounts. They asked me for a copy of my market plan and took the documents to show our CEO.

They told us all that my division was the best run operation in the company and was a model of how a marketing and sales operation should be run. I had to laugh as I knew that the company would be making a move on my position, so there was no way they could say my operation was in trouble. In addition to this, I had managed to turn a $1.2 million loss-making operation into a $400k profit another factor refuting their intent.

It was one of my salesmen George who told me, a few weeks later, he had been shown a new organization chart and my name was not on it. I knew then that I was being moved out and decided to wait to see it through.

After a year of living in Kenosha, during the week while still living in Greenwood, I was eventually called to the head office and was given an ultimatum.

I went there with my accountant, as we had both been summoned and were called into the board room. I was told to either move to Kenosha or be fired. I had already decided not to move, so I was fired.

The strange part of it was that as I came out of the board room and walked down the corridor, in the large open plan office, I passed my colleague Frank's Schmitt's office, which was between the board room and my own office thinking I would say my goodbye to Frank. I had known him for nearly fifteen years, but as I approached him, standing outside his office, he turned his back on me and shut his door to me. Though I was surprised that he should do this, I didn't care as I had made the decision to move on and had "crossed the bridge" many months before.

It was on the way back to Greenwood that I understood the meaning of my dream. The two tall buildings were my offices in Greenwood and Chicago and because I had decided not to move, I was camped between the two places—one building was representing my Greenwood office, while the other was my Chicago office. In my dream, Frank, who I had never crossed words with ever before, turned his back on me that day on May 5, 1997, when I left Tetra Pak.

It was an immense relief not to have to work there anymore, like a load being lifted off me and I threw a huge leaving party at our house for all my staff. The corporate attorney, John Felzan, called me a few days later and asked me not to make any rash decisions as to my future (the second time these words were said to me).

John and I had spent a lot of time together preventing possible lawsuits against the company over the non-supply of spare parts to our competitors and we had managed to stave off a potential major lawsuit as a result. John told me, off the record, I had a potential and successful lawsuit against Tetra Pak for age discrimination and unfair dismissal. I had already seen an attorney of my own to check out my legal status.

I told him that I already had an attorney, to which he asked me to give him time to put a really good package together and asked me to think about what I wanted. My attorney told me that I could go for a loss of wages for the remaining time I would have had a career at Tetra Pak ($1.6 million). One key item, against their firing me when I could easily have remained where I was without my location ever being an issue against doing my job! Another was the recent consulting group study that found my department to be the best-run operation in the entire U.S. group, having turned a loss-making organization into a profitable one; They gave me a letter summarizing their positive findings related to my operation. So, they had no other reason to let me go as my refusal to move did not in any way impair my ability to do my job because I traveled around the country for 60 percent of my time.

John came back with a package totaling two and a half years' full pay with full benefits and averaged out bonuses, plus unlimited time with a very expensive outplacement agency.

He told me that Tetra Pak had ignored the fact that I had been in the company for twenty-five years and had an outstanding career having launched a global business, so this had become a major issue underlying their ill-thought-out and badly implemented decision as related to me. Their decision was purely based on a power struggle, obstinacy and nothing to do with my work. I discussed this with my attorney and he asked if I could survive with a two, to three-year lawsuit, so I had to agree that I couldn't.

I signed the non-compete agreement in order to get the severance pay. John told me he had enjoyed working with me and told me they were really afraid that I was the one person with enough skill and knowledge who could start up my own company and compete with them, as I had set up the marketing operations worldwide.

I laughed at that and told him I would never consider competing against the company as I wanted to get into a completely different type of business and never wanted to be involved with the equipment industry again.

Sue and I took a much-needed vacation before I began to consider my next move. As the saying goes, "The world was now my oyster."

When it is time to move on just do it and close the door on the past

STARDUST

Investing in a startup requires more than passion and hard work.

AFTER A BREAK of a few months while I was attending the outplacement agency, I was shown how to make excellent resumes and I started attending several meetings downtown to network with both entrepreneurs and investors. It was at one of these meetings that I met a very tall black lady called Cynthia Prime. Cynthia asked me to visit her at her company on the north side of town where she was a headhunter.

I met with her a few days later, when she began asking me about what I wanted to do next. I explained that I wanted to either start up my own company or buy one. It was then that she told me about her husband, Phillip Prime, who had recently retired and who used to be the "nose" for Elizabeth Arden. He had developed several very well-known fragrances—Chloe, Red Door, Lagerfeld for Men and Burberry.

I used to wear Lagerfeld for Men and liked it. She asked if I would like to meet her husband to discuss a new fragrance company that had a fragrance called "Stardust," named after the famous Hoagy Carmichael song of the same name. We met a few days later and Phillip was a tall, retired olfactory scientist, as he called himself and was looking to start up his own company.

After a few more meetings, they made a pitch for me to invest in their as yet unformed company and help them to get it off the ground. I told them both that what I wanted was a job, something long-lasting and something interesting, but completely different from what I had been doing.

I asked them for some samples of their Stardust fragrance and Phillip gave me ten small vials or "testers" to show friends so that I could get their feedback. I told Sue about the opportunity and she was as excited as I was about launching a fragrance company. Now Phillip and Cynthia made it very clear to me that they were both very religious and in fact at each meeting we had they ended up praying. I thought this was a little over the top, but it was fine by me. Sue passed the fragrance vials out to her friends and they loved it; not one person had a bad thing to say about the fragrance. I called Phillip to set up a meeting to discuss how much was needed to launch Stardust and what the next steps would be. Most important to me was my role in this company and what my level of investment might be since I was not about to invest without being in a management role.

During the next meeting, I asked them about their prior company and if there was anything I should know about it before I invested. They both told me about a prior company called "My Choice" that they still owned, which was a design company involved with the design of the first Stardust bottle. Cynthia showed me the bottle, which was a glass orb with a woman sitting on top wearing a long flowing robe with her hands running through her long flowing hair. It looked a little "retro," and I told them that I thought the detail of her face and hands, though important, would be difficult to replicate with production molds when the company got up and running.

Phillip smiled at that and said that he thought so as well. I had struck a nerve as Cynthia began to defend her design. I explained that although I knew nothing of fragrances, I did know about manufacturing and as they had spent six years trying to get this company off the ground, in all probability, the bottle design may be part of the problem.

I had to be honest with them both and I told them that this being Indianapolis, the middle of a very conservative Midwest, meant that to get a large investment behind two Black people may be another issue and that while I was fully OK with my potential investment and had every belief in them both, others may not be, so we needed to find a management company to head up the investment drive.

We met with an investment company in downtown Indianapolis, Bernard & Associates, headed by John Bernard who seemed very interested in taking up the project. He passed us on to a young partner in the company an MBA grad called Tim, who was to be our assistant in getting the company off the ground.

I asked how much was required to make a new design of the bottle as I wasn't prepared to invest in their "orb" concept. Phillip thought $25,000 would be enough for the famous Marc Rosen in New York to come up with a new design.

Due Diligence

Before placing any cash into this fledgling company, I asked Phillip and Cynthia again if there was anything else I should know about their past company *"My Choice"* and asked them for a financial statement from that company. Phillip gave me the name of his accountant who was somewhere out in Greensburg. So I called and set a meeting then drove out to meet him the following day. When I got there, the office was closed, so I called again and got the answerphone. I waited for over an hour, but no one showed up, so I left and came back. I thought at the time that this was strange since I had made an appointment.

I told Tim about the aborted visit to find out what had happened with My Choice and we agreed that once the company was funded we would have a proper board and that both he and John would be there to help us build it up, so I thought nothing more about it.

After signing an agreement, set up by Bernard and Associates giving me shares in the company, I gave the company part of my severance from Tetra Pak to get a new bottle design made. We went to New York to meet the designer Marc Rosen in his Manhattan offices. He showed us all of the designs he had made for other fragrances.

I was impressed by his knowledge and his very well-known designs. He had designed the "Red Door" bottle, "Catalyst for Men," the "Perry Ellis" collection, "Fable," "Heaven Scent," "Lelong," and many others. He was a unique and gifted designer and was probably one of the best in the world.

We were very lucky for him to take on our project to create our new bottle design. Marc agreed that Cynthia's bottle design did not go with his interpretation of the Stardust name. He also explained that he saw it as a modern fragrance with a starlit bottle that would be bright and would be exciting, unique and not so much in the "retro" mode. We left it up to Marc to come up with our new design and left for Indianapolis later that day. We named our new company "Parfums Llewellyn."

Bad Advice

I had $100,000 which I intended to invest in this fledgling company in order to get us off the ground. The money was from a pension fund that Tetra Pak had insisted I take into the United States before the end of 1997. The company had invested it for me in an account in Switzerland, but I had to give them details of my account before December 31, 1997, as that was the end of their fiscal year. I spoke to Phillip and he put me onto an attorney that he knew downtown to advise me on how to make this payment into the company as an IRA rollover to legally avoid tax on it as an investment income.

He advised me to set up a separate account and move the money through this account and into Parfums Llewellyn and marked the check "IRA rollover" as advised. So I did what the attorney suggested to the letter and invested the money, becoming only the second investment the company had. This was partly to get us moving and partly to attract other investors.

The money came through from Switzerland at the end of 1997, so I did what I was advised, passing the money through into the company for preferred shares.

I had my hands full as we needed to make production and financial projections along with the estimated timeline and how much capital investment we needed to get Stardust off the ground. Financially, Sue and I were fine as I still had a year of salary from Tetra Pak left before my money ran out.

A few weeks later, a very excited Marc Rosen called us to say he had found the perfect bottle design for Stardust. It was unique easy to cast and was exactly what he had envisioned. We went to New York to see what he had come up with and were stunned at the bottle he had created.

It was a prism with a triangular shape that leaned back slightly, having a flat glass face that reflected light, throwing off "starlight" prisms of light. The cap would have a midnight blue oval center, which was the shape of the universe with tiny stars set in surrounded by a brushed silver oval surround.

We loved it! It was perfect and had come from a concept from Tiffany's in New York where Marc was passing by and noticed in the window a beautiful crystal paperweight that sent out sparkling light as he passed. He told us that as soon as he saw it he knew that it should be our Stardust bottle and bought the paperweight there and then.

Next came all of the costing for the bottle, the cap and the packaging, which I took on and placed the details onto a large spreadsheet that would form the basis of our bid for startup capital. The cost of the molds was staggering at over $120,000 for the bottle the cap and the perfume bottle. But it was a necessity, so we moved on as these would become assets of the company.

Phillip was busy working with Firmenich in Switzerland, who were going to make the bulk fragrance essence and ship it to wherever we were going to get the filling done. I was busy like hell but I loved it. I was working many times all night, getting everything ready for the capital investment push. I prepared a PowerPoint presentation, with all that an investor would need to see, images of the bottle, the price points, where our market was and what the cost of operations and production would be. I prepared everything and made the presentation time less than fifteen minutes, leaving time for discussion.

I now had enough detail to estimate the costs of the bottle and fragrance with shipping costs and now needed the packaging costs. I found several packaging companies and sent out the package designs to get that moving while I was searching for contract-filling companies.

Finding Investors

I finished the investment presentation and after several meetings with John Bernard, Tim and Phillip, we made slight changes, while Cynthia prepared a bunch of investment packages.

Tim, myself, John and Phillip came up with a stunning list of potential investors who may be interested in our startup. Our list included basketball stars, attorneys, TV celebrities and a previous owner of the National City Bank. Phillip and Cynthia had decided on the price points and that we were to only target the top-tier stores like Bergdorf Goodman in New York, Saks Fifth Avenue, Niemen Marcus, Jacobson's, and Nordstrom.

Tim and I were concerned that there were only 350 of these "top tier" stores, that Phillip insisted we focus on, whereas the second tier had 3,500 stores. We brought this to Phillip's notice, but Phillip insisted (stubbornly) that with the high price point of $95 for a 1.7-ounce, $135 for a 3.4 ounce and $300 for the 50-milliliter perfume these were the only stores we should focus on.

The prices were high, but I used them in my financial projections, as I had no idea if this was a good or a bad price point. I did know however that Phillip had been in the fragrance business for over thirty years, so we bowed to his knowledge.

I now had everything ready for our next step, which was to find $2.5 million for the launch.

I checked my final projections again and all was correct, at least as far as a financial projection could be. I designed a spreadsheet so that we could work with any number of stores and simply plug in new cost numbers at any month after the launch as any potential investor may need to see our break-even point.

I wanted to be able to provide financial arguments right there and then during any presentation. But, every time I sent the information to Phillip and Cynthia, she spent hours trying to correct the grammar (my grammar was perfect) So I finished it myself and paid for thirty sets of Stardust folders made in brushed silver and blue with our new logo, which incidentally I had designed at home. We had our list of investors and practiced our presentation in front of John Bernard and Tim Tichenor. After a critique, we were finally ready to move forward.

Tom Binford

I had been introduced to Tom Binford, who was famous in Indianapolis, being one of Indianapolis's most influential men; Tom was a civil rights leader and had been involved in many civic, philanthropic, cultural and political aspects of the city and state. Tom was highly respected and was a well-thought-of person who was valued for his wise counsel, personal and financial support, and sincerity. He led a consortium to buy the Pacers basketball team in 1975 and served as its president and general manager for one year from 1974 to 1975. He was instrumental in getting the Colts to Indianapolis and also served as the chief steward of the Indianapolis 500, presiding over its transition into the Indy Racing League or IRL as it is still known today.

Tom headed his own investment company and was an investor himself. I met him with Phillip and Cynthia who told me how close they were to Tom so we arranged to make our presentation to Tom. Tom said he would think about it and asked me for my contact information, which I gave him.

A few days later, Tom called me and asked me to meet him for lunch, which surprised me. I went to meet him and another colleague Tony who was part of Tom's company. During lunch, Tom began to explain that he knew of "The Primes" as acquaintances but not more than that and had never had any business dealings with them. He went on to warn me not to invest because of his name being used by the Primes. I asked if he would be investing and was surprised when he said probably not! This was not the first time I had seen a crack in the Primes' story as told to me but saw it more as Tom warning me to be careful in dealing with the Primes. I asked Tom if he trusted John Bernard and Tim Tichenor, he replied, "Absolutely!"

They will never steer you wrong, you should listen to John he knows what he's doing." I didn't ever talk of this to Cynthia and Phillip but did have a talk with Tim about it. Tim said that all investments had elements of risk, adding that we would have a serious company behind us to carry us through.

Phillip and Cynthia were name-droppers for sure, but Tim said, "Let's just get on with this and find the money elsewhere." But I was stunned at Tom's honesty and thought that I should be more wary in future. Over the next eight weeks, we met dozens of investors and gradually got commitments for $1.3 million, which was, according to Tim, enough to get us off the ground.

As Tim advised us, "It's easier to get more money when you have a finished product than a mere concept." I liked collaborating with John and Tim as they were both straight shooters and I knew I could trust their judgment, so we prepared for the launch of our new company, Parfums Llewellyn with our first fragrance "Stardust."

The Launch of Stardust

We now had some cash, though not all that we needed, but enough to get our first production run completed. We had bottles being made by Bross in France, caps being made in Georgia, fragrance made by Firmenich in Switzerland and packaging from a company out of New York. We were already an 'International company. I found a small contract packaging company in upstate New York, through reading the trade mags, with the capacity to fill enough sets for us to launch the product. The company was Sicilian-owned and I went there to meet them.

They agreed to package our fragrance saying, "The only thing is Tony," one of the owners told me in a broad Sicilian accent more like the Mafia, "is that when we do it, ya gotta pay for it, capisce?" Yes, I got it loud and clear, fearing that if I didn't I probably would never be found again.

We purchased all the components we needed for the upcoming launch. We then had decided to take on a cosmetics marketing and sales expert and after some weeks, we found Don Hilgeman, who had a great resume with many well-known cosmetics and fragrance companies as well as having exceptional knowledge of the buyers at the biggest high-end store chains where we intended to sell in to.

Don and I got on very well, we split the work between us, with Don taking all of the front-end sales and me the production. We began to get the company up and running with supplies to be delivered to our offices in downtown Indianapolis where I would do the assembly of the two-component cartons for the two sizes of bottles. The perfume was to be placed inside a beautiful box to make it worth the $300 price tag.

Our offices were on the eighth floor of the Guaranty Building, where we had an office suite a warehouse space and a board room, right on the circle in the very center of Indianapolis. We launched into Bergdorf Goodman in New York as well as Jacobson's on the north side of Indianapolis.

My task was to get all the filling and packaging finished, Don's was to get the in-store displays ready and Cynthia's was to get some handouts ready for our launch.

The Launch of Stardust

The date of the launch was set in late November 1998 in New York, then on, Sunday, December 6, in Indianapolis, which was my birthday.

We all went to New York and Bergdorf Goodman's staff met us at the entrance and led us to the made-up counters all decorated in silver and blue. They took us outside and showed us the store window featuring Stardust as the centerpiece of their most important window. What a display! and on New York's Fifth Avenue, of all places. We were not only in the most famous of all stores for our launch but in the most prestigious window in the entire United States and featuring our Stardust fragrance.

It was an unbelievable sight to see our conception realized into a finished product. I was proud of all that I had done to make this happen. Marc Rosen came to the launch with his wife Arlene Dahl, who graciously greeted us and talked up the fragrance, doing what film stars do in public which was to act the part.

The next step was the launch at Indianapolis, in Jacobson's on Eighty-Sixth Street, right at the entrance to the mall. I had a limousine to take Sue and several friends from our house to the store on the evening of 6 December 1998.

There were eight of us in the limo and when we arrived at the store, I couldn't believe it—the whole front of the mall entrance was lit up with stars moving across the entrance, across the car parking area and even across the sky! It was an awesome birthday present. We all went into the store on a red carpet that stretched from the car park right into the store.

As we entered Jacobson's, the CEO came out to greet us; Tim, John Barnard, Phillip, Cynthia and Don were all there with me. There was a stage set up in the middle of the store with a microphone, local TV crews were there to video the event for the local news. During the evening, Phillip got up and was introduced by Jacobson's CEO and he and Cynthia thanked everyone. The evening was a tremendous success and we were so happy with all that we had done, so far.

Don came up to me later that evening and said, "These two are fucking incredible. They behave as if this whole thing is about the two of them and not about all of the rest of us who have managed to get Stardust launched!"

I agreed with Don but didn't think too much about it. Sometimes people do things without thinking! We gave Marc a sample of each of the finished products and he agreed to get us several Factice bottles for the stores. The Factice was a supersized bottle a foot in height that was for display purposes and was filled with alcohol colored to match the fragrance.

We had plenty of products for the number of stores that we had initially and Don's job was to get us into the remaining stores on our list. As time moved on, we began to get into more stores; but we couldn't get into Nordstrom, which was a key store. We all went up to Seattle for a meeting with the "Guru" of the US. fragrance world, Dale Crichton, who was the fragrance buyer for Nordstrom. We had a specific ten-minute window to present our fragrance to Dale and a team of around twenty-five others.

We went to their Seattle head office where we were given a room with around thirty chairs facing a long table where we were to place our fragrance products and make a presentation of how it would be launched, what gifts, (spiffs) we would be giving customers, the price points and everything that Dale and her staff would need to know.

At the presentation, there were a total of ten other new fragrances competing with us. We had carefully rehearsed and prepared our ten-minute presentation and each of us knew our part well. We had this one chance to get in and we had left sample vials, placed inside a small "Stardust" card, on each of the chairs. At the allotted time, all twenty-five of them entered and sat down to listen. Cynthia was first up, at her insistence and she wasted five whole minutes on cause-related marketing, talking about women's causes but not the fragrance. I could see we were losing the crowd and looked over at Phillip hoping he would have the balls to cut her off and get on with the real presentation. But now he had little time left to present the fragrance after Cynthia had wasted all our allotted time.

Dale was gracious, it was clear that she knew the fragrance business and had insight, when she asked that we reconsider our cause-related items, as these were secondary to the fragrance itself. She quizzed us on the high price points, we left that up to Phillip to answer. She thought the fragrance was good but rather sweet and a little heady.

Her last comments were for us to focus on what the fragrance was all about and the "spiffs" and marketing tools like advertising and in-store giveaways rather than women's causes which never sold the product. We weren't ready for Nordstrom yet and needed to get more publicity and some sales before we would be ready for them.

We headed back to Indy for a regroup, Cynthia had arranged for the *Indianapolis Business Journal* to do an article on Stardust; but the article did not mention anything about the team that had put the company together, only about her and Phillip. Although I was in the office the day the writer came in with the photographer, this was all about Cynthia her ego and no one else, Don was there also, after we were up and running, but I was the one who made this happen and was not included. This was the second issue that caught me off guard and I thought back to Tom Binford's discussion and warning to me. I had seen people behave like this before and now knew this company was doomed to fail because of Phillip and Cynthia. This was to become a serious problem later on when the Primes showed their complete incompetence at running a company.

To be part of any creation of a new concept is to make our own history.

HELPING MY DAUGHTERS

Family comes first and always will!

IN 1998, DURING my weekly call to talk to Amanda and Georgia, Jane told me that Georgia was not going to school and had been absent for most of the term. I felt I had to try to help when she told me that she would not be allowed to finish her GCSE exams because she had missed so much time off school through truancy. The GCSE exams were the same as a graduation exam in the United States, with the difference being that in England you could take exams covering all of the subjects. Some of the final score was based on coursework during the year and some were based on the final exam results.

Just around this time, I had a conversation over the phone with Amanda; it was one of those phone calls that I knew I was being guided to have. Jane then told me that Amanda had anorexia, adding that she had hidden it well for several years. In Amanda's last years at school, she had suffered from anxiety attacks and sometimes I had to drop everything and go to pick her up from school. I was aware that she did have some issues to deal with, but I thought this was all behind her.

A Shocking Truth

During one of my weekly telephone calls to Amanda, I was asking her, as I normally did, how her health was. I made a joke to her that her behavior was as if she had been abused as a child, but I was certain that this wasn't the case as she had been with me as her father all the time. At that comment, she suddenly broke down on the phone with me.

I could have bitten my tongue off and wished that I hadn't said that. Nevertheless, Sadly, I had unwittingly hit the nail on the head, she was sobbing on the phone. I didn't know what to do, no words I said could comfort her. I was devastated at the implication of what I had just found out and was in shock myself.

Sue could hear the change in the conversation and asked me what was wrong. I covered the phone and asked Sue to take the phone from me and talk to Amanda, which she did as she too had similar experiences when she was younger.

Despite being so busy with Stardust, I decided to leave immediately for London to help Georgia and Amanda. I flew over to London and met both of them as I knew Jane needed my help without delay.

As soon as I arrived in London, I went with Georgia to her school Drayton Manor and we met with the headmaster together, though Georgia didn't want to. I told him I had flown over four thousand miles for that meeting and thanked him for seeing me. Jane had said it wouldn't help, but me being me, I had to at least try!

I asked the Head Master to please allow my daughter Georgia to sit her exams, as she had promised to go to school every day until the exams. He agreed to let her sit them, provided that she attended every single day. I spoke to her afterward to try to get her to see that this was important and that she had no chance in life if she didn't bother. Well, she did bother; she took the GCSE exams and got good grades in all six subjects, which showed she was able to do it almost with ease.

NHS at its Best!

Next, I had to go to see Amanda's clinic in Acton with her. She was nervous about me being there, but I told her I loved her and I would move heaven and earth to help her. That was why I came over from Indianapolis to help her.

We went to her meeting into a room with opaque glass windows, a vinyl floor and a row of seven metal seats set in a semicircle. Amanda was to sit in the one chair facing the other seven. She begged me not to say anything but to listen, so I told her I would do my best.

A group of doctors and counselors filed into the room for Amanda's meeting; there were seven in all and they sat opposite her on their appointed seats.

"So… good afternoon Amanda and how are you today?" one of them wearing a white coat asked her while making notes on a clipboard, though about what I had no idea as nothing had been said at that point! "Fine, thanks" was all Amanda said. I said nothing. "So how are you doing with your eating, Amanda?" another asked. "I'm doing fine, thanks," she replied again. "Good, good," he said to her. The meeting went on like that for around twenty minutes, achieving absolutely nothing. I could see that my darling Amanda was nervous at the meeting and clearly this was not helping her at all. "Good, good," one of them said, "So that's all for now. We'll see you in a month, OK?"

After remaining quiet, I could stand it no more and said to the group, "I'm sorry," at which Amanda shrank in her seat, not knowing what I was going to say but I held her hand in mine and said quietly, "don't worry, darling." "And who are you?" one of them said. I replied, "I am her father, I have flown four thousand miles to be here to see what help you are giving her and from what I have seen here so far, it is as I suspected, not much help at all!"

They asked me where I lived, so I told them, after which one of the "white coat" group told me that I should take her with me to the United States as their help for these illnesses was far better than what she could get from the NHS.

I told them I couldn't accept their logic because if they were happy with the status quo they were therefore helping to make these kinds of situations worse. I asked them who among them was in charge of this kind of therapy and how on earth did they justify this to themselves as professionals?

They told me they do the best they can. "That's not good enough," I said, quietly emphasizing my point. "Simply asking Amanda how she is doing isn't helping my daughter. There are no milestones, no weekly guidelines, so how will she ever measure her success or failure with this?" They wanted to move on and were becoming uncomfortable with my comments about their poor performance as doctors and counselors.

I could see that we were getting nowhere, so I took Amanda's hand and we left with no goodbyes or thanks (for nothing). I told her that she shouldn't bother to go there and stress herself out anymore as it was not something that was helping her.

Amanda told me several years later that my flying over to help her made her realize that she had to beat this herself as I had shown her that I would do anything to help her, but she also knew I couldn't do more than be a source of strength behind her. What she did do was to learn to become a Reiki healer, so that she could help others and by doing that, I think it helped her a lot and she eventually made it through.

Amanda is fine now and doing well. Eliza Jane's (Ellie) birth also helped her as she now had to be there for her baby daughter and she knew she couldn't let Ellie down ever. This is one of those things that although never goes completely away and as in Amanda's case, maybe managed to a "normal" or almost normal situation.

No matter what I was doing at the time I was ready to support my daughters immediately as Auntie had always supported me.

TROUBLE ON THE HORIZON

Stubbornness at the top can ruin everything

O N MY RETURN to the States to continue with our start-up, Cynthia had got us into a televised women's league, conference, downtown at the conference center in Indianapolis and had asked that Don and I take Stardust there and sell what we could but also get our name better known among the delegates. Though we had placed a full-page advert in *Vogue* magazine for a couple of months, each placement had cost us $50,000 for a one-page insertion. We couldn't do many of those as sales couldn't support it yet. Don and I carried more than three hundred of the EDP and perfume ready and took it to the conference center. Phillip and Cynthia had tickets to go into the conference and were on one of the top tables, partly to spread the word (we hoped) and partly to get better known within the group as potential Stardust customers.

We lugged tables and boxes of fragrance up to the mezzanine floor where the conference was being held and commenced to set up the tables with hundreds of cartons stacked up in pyramids outside the main door, so everyone could see the display. When we were satisfied with our display, we waited around until the conference had finished.

At around half-past ten, they began to leave the conference, so Don and I prepared to start selling the fragrance having waited from six-thirty for over four hours until the conference was over.

As they all began to file past us, several came up to ask about Stardust; we sold one or two of the fragrances, though not close to what we would have liked. We spotted Phillip and Cynthia coming out with a group of people. But both of them walked straight past us without turning their heads, acknowledging us, or looking at the setup that we had carefully prepared and instead they continued walking right past us and walked straight on!

Don and I were dumbfounded and were speechless at what had just happened. "Did you see what I saw, Don?" I said, he looked on at them both, shaking his head. I was angry, but my controlled anger was nothing compared with Don's. As we prepared to dismantle our display, Don told me, "That's it for me. I am done with these two bozos. Who do they think they are? All this work and they didn't even acknowledge us!"

I was concerned at what Don was saying and asked him if he was serious. He replied that we needed a "come to Jesus" meeting with John Bernard and Tim to discuss what had just happened and what was going wrong with the company. Don and I were doing all the work while Phillip and Cynthia were not following any work-like protocol. They seemed uninterested in the fact that we had other people's money, including my own, invested and were not even bothering to come in during the week before lunchtime then leaving around 3:00 p.m. having done nothing for the company. Don began to get us into more stores and sales began to climb. For that first year, we were hitting our targets.

But Cynthia wanted to buy expensive giveaways that our cash flow was insufficient for what she wanted and these were to be free not adding a dime to our bottom line. She wanted a very expensive box wrapped in silver with a blue base, which she had priced at well over $5 per box to be given away free.

I researched this, even though this was an unnecessary cost but found another version exactly the same, that I could get made up for less than $1.50 each and refused to get the more expensive version as it was a freebie and we couldn't afford it. So, Cynthia went around Don and I to get what she wanted and it cost the company all of the meager profit we were making at that point. Our costs were still higher than our sales, so we had to be very careful until we became more profitable, but Cynthia had no concept of what running a company involved.

As for me, I was just happy that I had managed to do all that I could to get this company off the ground, a little hard work was no problem for me as I had been doing this all my life.

Some people are destined to screw up any chance of a lifetime!

AUNTIE ONE LAST TIME

Making this trip was a priority, more important than anything else!

I TOOK TIME off, from our busy launch, to go to see Amanda and Georgia in London as I hadn't seen them for quite a while and to go to Auntie's 92nd birthday at Scarborough as I had missed her ninetieth because I was looking for work at that time. Amanda and Georgia now had a business together and were both Reiki masters.

I didn't understand Reiki but I knew that it was something to do with "grounding" the psyche of people and I understood that they could heal people suffering from many psychosomatic illnesses depression, headaches, anxiety and without the need for chemicals.

Georgia and I went for breakfast, lunch and dinners together and spent all the time we could in each other's company. I love them both as much as is humanly possible, but I am still living so far away from them both.

Georgia and Amanda took me to a shop they owned, called "Enchanted," in Northfields and their shop was thriving. Apart from the Reiki, they were also selling paintings by local artists, uplifting greeting cards and many other crystals and "healing" stones to their customers who believed in these things.

Georgia and I traveled to Scarborough to meet Auntie for what I knew to be the last time I would ever see my guardian angel here on earth. Amanda couldn't come as someone had to run the business, but she was fine with not coming.

At Aunties birthday party we met many of the people who had looked after me as a very young boy, at Lowestoft. Nurse Rosemary, Nurse Iris, John and of course William who was now grown up but was under the care of Rosemary. Auntie's other relatives were all there too. But not Beatrice, since she had moved to Australia she had little to no contact with the people who had looked after her, a very angry Beatrice who showed no gratitude for all that Aunty and Rosemary had done for her.

They all remembered me from my time at Lowestoft when I was only four years old. Georgia loved being with Auntie as she knew what she meant to me; Auntie really took to Georgia as if she was a granddaughter of her own.

The party was a great success and John had found an old day book that the nurses had to fill out every night while working for Auntie. He opened up a page mentioning me and my nightly activities. He read it out loud to the amusement of all that were there. "Tony was up again all night, talking and singing at the top of his voice. God, I could kill him! Why doesn't he ever sleep like the other children? Thank goodness it is nearly morning at last when my shift will finish!"

I couldn't believe it! There was proof that I did exist somewhere else after all. Georgia and I loved our time together as it was a precious time that we treasured and being with Aunty one last time was, for me, a pilgrimage I had to do.

I left to go back to Sue, Nicky, James and Ben our dog, back to the fragrance business, hoping I would see her again but in my heart knowing I probably would never see Auntie ever again.

I wanted to say goodbye to thank someone special in my life for all that she had done. I knew we would never meet again.

STARDUST - MOTHERS DAY

Commitment is to 'stay with it' no matter what!

W E HAD OUR first in-store deadline to meet for Mother's Day, which in the fragrance world was the second most important in sales to Christmas. We began a planning meeting in November for a March shipping deadline; 5 months and plenty of time with Phillip, Cynthia, Don and I and Tim sitting in. We set up an operational plan for a new product line of gift sets, comprising a body lotion, bath gel and moisturizing lotion. This would involve having some of our fifty thousand bottles "frosted" to differentiate the body spray from our EDPs.

Don headed up the meeting and we delegated the tasks to be completed. Phillip was to complete the lotion formulations; Cynthia had to complete the verbiage for the side of the packages with small pamphlet inserts. The inserts were to explain the basis of each product and the fragrances, etc., and would be inserted into each Mother's Day gift box.

My task was to get all the components sourced, designed, purchased, and manufactured and the packaging for the gift boxes, which were to hold the three-item gift set, containing a body lotion, a bath lotion in new silver and blue tubes and a body mist spray in an opaque version of our EDP completed which were to be shipped by early February.

Don would take care of the "sell" into our stores, which now totaled around fifty doors, but we were still short of our goal of 200 of the 350 top-tier stores, mainly because of the high price points.

My part went smoothly and we met several times over the next few months to follow up on the progress and to ensure that all was moving ahead on schedule and according to plan. For Don and I, this was exciting; Cynthia, however, had done nothing on her written insertion piece as yet, but we still had two months before we would need them.

I found a company to make the new tubes in Barcelona, Spain and Phillip had to agree on the color of the silver for the tubes. I was working with an English guy in Barcelona, so business discussions between the two of us was easy.

Phillip had finally agreed on a color for the tubes and signed off on the sample in late November. But now we needed more cash to manage the up-front costs for purchasing the components. I got together with Don to put together an estimated sell though and cost/profit summary, which if all went well would show a good profit for this, our first, Mother's Day gift set program. The first sample tubes came in during December with an eight-week delivery and were made to Phillip's exact color requirements.

Philip now decided to change the color to a darker shade of silver because he had changed his mind. I thought that he was being belligerent as the slight color change wouldn't make a damn difference to the product or the display inside the boxes and was exactly what he had signed off on.

We were becoming tired of the stupidity behavior of the Primes who, now the hard work was on in actually running our company, still didn't bother to come into the office before eleven-thirty or much before lunchtime, if at all. They did nothing for us when they did show up but Phillip insisted that the color of the tubes be changed, so we incurred additional costs associated with the color change and our supplier although trying to help was confused as to why we made the change after production had begun. So we paid an expensive penalty!

In the meantime, Cynthia had insisted that we purchase 250 gift boxes, a cost of $1500 much-needed cash, just to house a small vial of fragrance set in a card plus a small booklet of poems to be given away free. Our problem was the cost that for her version was now $6 per box, which Don, myself and Tim warned her was far too expensive and would take us into the red.

I refused to sign the purchase order and instead had another box, which was identical and was an in-stock item, so it was very cheap to buy. It was a three-inch square box with a silver top with our logo on it.

Don, Tim and I agreed to purchase the low-cost boxes at less than a dollar each as they were a standard stocked item. I added our logo on the front for a few cents each from a local printer and we were ready to go. In the meantime, Cynthia had gone around our necessary but tight purchasing system and had ordered her boxes directly with no money to pay for them, no permission and signed off by Phillip which none of us knew about until her damn boxes arrived. Because of the pair of them, we were now heading for a nightmare. She got Phillip to sign the purchase order without us knowing.

A Turning Point In Parfums Llewellyn

It was now January, we had four weeks left to get everything together for the ship date of the end of February to make the in-store deadline of the third week in March as promised by Don, some 5 months earlier.

We had another planning meeting with Don, Phillip, Cynthia and me and we updated our production timeline on the whiteboard checking that each of us had completed our tasks. The timeline had been placed on the board back in November when we decided to have a new product line ready for Mother's Day on May 11th.

My part had been delayed because Phillip had changed his mind about the tube color, but the formulations had been completed. I couldn't get the tubes finished because we were still awaiting Cynthia's verbiage to be written on the tubes, which by now because of the tightness of the timeline was too late.

At this important meeting, Don asked Cynthia to let us see her wording for the new packaging. This was now 3 months into our launch deadline; she told us that hadn't written a single word as she didn't have the time. We sat there in stunned silence, but Don was having none of it. He turned to Cynthia and said to her, "Cynthia, you knew the timeline. It's been on that board since November and it's now January. We all agreed with it together and I have now placed my reputation and our company's reputation on the line by promising that we would have the gift sets completed by the end of February and It is now February!" Don and I were pissed! "Why haven't you even written a single thing?" We waited for her reply, so he asked her again, while Phillip just sat there saying nothing. Instead of answering him, she just ignored the question and started humming a hymn, closed her eyes and began rocking to her tune back and forth with her head bowed.

I was furious and could see all my hard work and investment money going down the drain at this moment in time. I looked at Don, we both sat there in stunned, angry silence.

I asked her, "Cynthia, did you go ahead and purchase those expensive boxes that we agreed not to buy because of our limited finances?" I got no reply, but she continued humming and rocking back and forth on the seat like a child would when it knows it's done wrong. Was she even sane? Her stupid boxes had all arrived along with the boxes we did in fact agree to purchase, there was no discernable difference worth wasting our money on her purchase.

I was done with the Primes and wrote verbiage to go onto the tubes, so we wouldn't miss this deadline, even though Cynthia had not done a damn thing what I wrote was just fine.

Don and I left the office and went over the road, to Nicky Blaine's for a drink as it was now gone 5:00 p.m. "I think we are fucked, Don and if we are, it's my money not any of theirs that will be gone and I'm not going down without a fight." I then told him of being dissed at the opening and being left out of the news article when I had done all the hard work in getting the company off the ground; placing the seed capital to have the bottles made, making the financial projections and setting up the investor presentations before Don had come on board. It was my money only that got this company off the ground as the Primes had no money to invest!

He told me then that he had been very aware of Phillip and Cynthia's attitude regarding the company and to me but couldn't understand why. "Did you ever fall out with them?" he asked, I replied, "No never, not once, not even a crossed word in fact it was me who got the company the first seed funding!"

I told him that Phillip was blaming him for the lack of sales, so Don told me that the main reason we did not have more doors than we did was because of the high price points that were way too high. "I knew it!" I said. "I went to Nordstrom and Von Maur to look at the price points for all of their fragrances. They were all in the mid-seventy-dollar range." I asked Don to get me the sales statistics of a leading fragrance and if he could do that, I would analyze the data for an upcoming board meeting scheduled for three weeks ahead.

We were in a precarious position now and had limited funds to get things moving forward. He agreed to get me the data. "The Primes are going to cause this company to fail," he said and I agreed with him. Later that evening, Tim came in to join us in Nicky Blaine's, which was our "early doors" venue for an end-of-work drink. We told Tim of the issues that were going wrong. He asked us both, "Would either of you like to run the company?" I answered not but added that Phillip and Cynthia were now a liability to us in their total lack of responsiveness, fiduciary responsibility and leadership. I felt sick to my stomach at what I was seeing and kept thinking back to what Tom Binford had told me and now for the first time could see the end of Parfums Llewellyn and not even John Bernard and Tim Tichenor can stop it happening.

A week later, Don gave me a large computer readout of the sales data I had asked for related to "*Angel*" the number 1 fragrance in the

USA. I took the readout and began immediately analyzing the data. I worked once again right through the night and made up a spreadsheet of all the data, preparing it into a chart to be presented to the board the following week. I was amazed at what I saw. Out of thirty-seven products (SKUs), four made up more than 85% of their sales; all four were refillable and all were priced at below $72.

I sent the data to Don and he wanted me to present this data to the board the following week as he thought his days were numbered because of the lack of sales.

During our first financial year, we had made it to second place in national sales, as the second most purchased fragrance in the stores we were in, but that was short-lived as we were now struggling with repeat business because of the high price points that Phillip had set for our products.

The problem was that we had relied on Phillip for both the price points of our line as well as the closure style for our bottle, both were wrong! Phillip had ordered all "crimp-top" bottles that could not be refilled. In other words, when the fragrance was finished, the beautiful but empty bottle had to be thrown away. I knew from Sue that many women like to get either something off the next purchase or to be able to refill their fragrance bottles at a reduced price.

The purpose of the next board meeting was to get enough money for the completion of the launch of our new Mother's day product line and for our salaries.

All of our investors were there, in the board room at Bernard and Associates. Don began the presentation ending with the fact that our price points and being nonrefillable were the reasons we could not get into more doors. He then asked me to present my analysis, which I did and ended with two conclusions for the board to hear. The first conclusion was that we were far too expensive to get a second buy-through of existing customers or to increase our market penetration; the second was that we did not have refillable bottles. This meant that every customer had to pay for a second expensive bottle of Stardust while throwing away the empty bottle.

They all looked to Phillip and he said that for our fragrance, the prices were good, telling them that it was Don's job to get us into more doors. We were at a stalemate, but we got the additional funds for the completion of the Mother's Day gift sets.

It was during that board meeting that Tim and John also revealed that they had got the final financial statements of the Primes' former company, "*My Choice,*" that there had been amounts of money owed to suppliers, to the young woman who spent hours or weeks designing their "orb" design as well as the IRS who had filed an injunction and now had a lien on their property. So much for their fraudulent religious honesty!

Anyway, the tubes arrived late because of Phillip's color change, so I had to scramble to get all of the hundreds of empty tubes and the lotions hand-carried to a contract filling company in New Jersey to begin the job of filling. I had to work through the night alongside their production staff, mostly Mexican, to help them get the job completed on time. By midday, the following day the job was complete and all of the tubes were filled. I now had to take ten huge boxes back to Indianapolis.

I came back to Indy with ten huge cartons of filled tubes of lotion that I had to lug to the airport in New Jersey and then from Indianapolis airport to our eighth-floor warehouse to begin assembling the 1,100 gift boxes, which we had already sold.

I asked Phillip and Cynthia for help but got none! I was at the warehouse packing the 1,100 boxes by myself as I wanted to make sure that all went out on time. The entire warehouse was filled on every surface of all of the long tables we had with 1,100 empty gift boxes, which I had to place two tubes and a frosted bottle of body mist and a small "PL" logo sticker to seal each box. I started work after I arrived back from New Jersey and worked all night to get the task done on time. I was dead tired but felt I had to get this job done if we were to succeed with the launch, paid for by our investors.

By Monday, everything was ready to ship to all of the doors we now had. I then began to design a small conversion piece for our "crimp-top" bottles to make them into screw-top versions so that we could make them refillable.

I designed a small, brushed silver, top that would crimp onto our existing bottles with a small rubber seal that would not leak. I then researched all of our suppliers to find an inexpensive clear glass bottle that would hold 50-milliliter or 1.7-ounce of refillable fragrance. I found one and it was perfect and would cost us only $5.25 for each complete bottle of refill fragrance complete with packaging, which we could sell for around $50, a not too shabby profit.

I had a design and engineering company on the north side of town to make up and evaluate my design, they said it would work without leaking. I also designed a small cartridge-based 10-milliliter purse spray that we could present with a beautiful perfume spray plus two extra push-in refills. It was a fantastic concept and had never been done before. This would be a low-cost EDP spray option and would enable our market to have the EDP in a small convenient purse spray.

In effect, I had developed a very acceptable solution to our problem that we could work with that would be at the right price and highly profitable for us.

I told Don and he asked that I show Phillip the concept so when Phillip came in a few days later, as he now seldom came in at all I told him I had something to show him.

As I showed Phillip the concept and explained what it could do for us, in converting the crimp-top bottles into simple screw-top version, he got up and left the office with me in midsentence, throwing out over his shoulder as he reached the door, "it won't work and I don't like it." I watched him leave, knowing that this company could never ever succeed with him in it. Phillip and Cynthia were a fucking nightmare and had deceived us all with their lies, non-action, fake religious beliefs (not realized in their actions), and their laziness! The reason he didn't like my design was because it was an acceptance that he had made a mistake with our bottles and we now had thousands left unused!

Don came in the following week when we found that we didn't have enough cash to pay our wages! I was sitting behind Don when he asked Tim where his pay was and was told there was no more cash. As I sat behind him, I saw his neck become bright red as he got so furious at not being paid. "That's it for me," he said, "I'm suing them for everything." And he walked out never to return.

As for me, I had given the company eighteen months without pay in getting the company launched and had invested more than $100,000 plus my unpaid time, only to be dissed by the two people I had given their life's dream, and now our company was broke, having spent all of the invested money for the most part in fifty thousand of the wrong bottles because of Phillip's incompetence! I felt sick inside.

My dream had gone up in perfumed smoke, along with my hopes that were now dashed to the ground; but I felt that I had to work on helping the investors and doing what I could for my company as they had invested in the company partly because of me.

After another two months, working with no pay, I stopped coming in at all and told Tim and John that in my opinion Phillip and Cynthia were the sole cause of our demise, adding that neither of them had the experience stamina, mental capacity, or ability to work in the company that they had convinced us all to fund.

I left the company and began legal action to get my three months back pay as there was no way I was giving them that as well. I saw an attorney; we filed the lawsuit against the company two weeks later and I got my back pay.

Tim came to see me and told me the board had looked at my numbers again and had checked for themselves, all I had done to get this company off the ground. They agreed that I was "right on the money." They asked me through Tim if I would come back to run the company as president and COO and if I did, they would all support me financially to finish the job.

The downside was that they could only pay me half of what I needed to keep my house and pay my bills. I had already used up my severance pay, giving them my unpaid time and it would mean selling our house and moving into a flat. I now had a tough decision to make. I considered everything; how I had been treated by the Primes; how Phillip would still be the majority owner and therefore in a position to still ruin the company as he had done with his limited knowledge of the industry; how he had led us into having a great product but in the wrong price point and with the wrong bottles, which was the most significant problem we now faced.

I had given it all I had and had even had the insult of having to pay out another $37,500 in taxes because of the recommendation of the tax attorney, that Phillip had told me to see, which had also proven to be a complete waste of time as his advice was wrong!. Though I followed his advice to the letter, I had to pay tax on my investment in the company. To that point, I had put in more than any of the other investors and had done the most to get this company started, which at the beginning I was happy to do. I gave a total of eighteen months of unpaid work and had worked the hardest remaining fully committed throughout to get it going plus I gave the Prime's their start-up cash.

I told Tim I couldn't do it financially and that I couldn't work with the Primes and as long as they participated in any leadership capacity, the company would unfortunately fail.

Tim asked that I take time to reconsider and eventually, reluctantly, I decided not to have any further business with the incompetent, lying, and lazy Primes. We parted ways but I kept in touch with Tim when I needed references and he was very happy to do so.

Some nine months later, Tim called me to tell me that he had set up an important meeting with a large sales agency that wanted to promote Stardust into thousands of stores at the midlevel market, which was what Don and I had wanted to do from the onset. He had arranged for Phillip to go with him to this important meeting.

They met at the downtown office and Phillip, true to form, left his car on the circle with the engine running and his keys inside the car. Needless to say, after the police had been called to get into Phillip's car, they missed the flight, the meeting and the important deal was off. Tim told me that that was the final straw. Phillip was banned from having any more function in the company, banned from the offices and he was no longer a president or anything within Parfums Llewellyn.

I had to laugh at that, as Tim, like me, had done so much and had been let down same as me! The company was sold on to another fragrance house, so the name Stardust continued. I got my money back, well, most of what I had invested; so really, I lost my time and a lot of effort.

Lessons Learned

I learned a valuable lesson in that hard work alone doesn't cut it; that in a start-up business, everyone must work their hardest and not leave it up to only a few. The most important lesson was not to be blind-sided by someone's apparent and highly visible "faith" with open prayers and little else in the form of, "doing and not just saying." In other words, I will only trust people who "walk the walk, don't just talk the talk," especially when faith was used for the sole purpose of getting what they wanted. The Primes are two people who should never be trusted.

I was so concerned at my deep feeling of dislike for both Phillip and Cynthia, still believing that they were both basically good people though misguided in their beliefs that I went to see my pastor Greg Ponchot to ask him if my feelings were wrong against the Primes.

I sat with Greg a few weeks later and told him of the whole situation from start to finish and especially my feeling of being deceived by the Primes as I am certain that all of the other investors had been too. His reaction was very clear. "No," he said, "you are not wrong to feel angry. What is the basis of your anger? Was it that you had not succeeded with the company or was it that you had been deceived?"

"I was deceived," I said. "Completely taken in by their apparent religious beliefs, their prayers at work and at meetings and I believed them to be a good investment mainly because of that."

Greg told me that he had been brought up in a family of missionaries in Africa, saying that both his parents were missionaries that had planted churches and started building schools. He went on to explain that many of the local "so-called" preachers drank heavily and were notorious womanizers on Saturday nights yet breathed fire and brimstone of bigoted righteousness from the pulpit on Sundays while adorned with the trappings of being a religious leader. He told me that these were often traits of such people as the Primes that wanted to demonstrate their fervor to others as a way of becoming accepted.

The company was sold, I got most of my investment back over time in the form of tax deductions each year for my lost investment. So in the final outcome, I didn't lose that much and I did learn that one business I am not interested in was the fragrance business. Time to close the door and move on, I was not feeling good about the lost opportunity, but I had done all that I could do and in fact got the company up and running.

I learned never to trust anyone who places faith before honesty.

JAMES THE DANCER

James is very much like me; determined to make it.

SINCE HIS EARLY days at school, my son James had, since age five years old, decided that he wanted to dance and dance he did, right through school and on to college. When James was only eight years old, he was dancing for the Ballet International, a professional dance troupe based in Indianapolis. The role he initially landed was as a party boy in the story, to dance on stage at Indianapolis's Murat theater in their production *The Nutcracker*, which they performed every Christmas.

He did this for two years before landing the principal role as the lead boy Fritz. This was a wonderful achievement for him as he auditioned for it against over fifty other boys. Each Christmas, we took many of his school friends to see him perform and when we went to the opening night that first year, we were so proud of what he had achieved.

The rehearsals started in October and involved either Sue, myself, or both of us taking him downtown to the rehearsal studios every Saturday morning. Although he had been in many, many competitions while learning, what we hoped would be his trade, at the Dance Refinery in Greenwood, this was a professional validation of all his hard work.

I should mention that James was a kind quiet gay boy at school and had to put up with the "jocks" teasing and bullying him all through his primary and middle school; but instead of complaining to us, he dealt with it for years by himself and stood up to these ridiculous bullies. We eventually found out about it when he came home one day after putting up with it for many semesters. He was angry and certainly not allowing himself to continue to be victimized. We took him to the school and made a formal complaint to the headmistress. She reacted immediately by summoning the boys' parents to the school and informing them that the school was considering legal action against them. Needless to say, the school, Center Grove, had a very strong successful choir and performing arts program in place and had won the state and national championships for seven years in a row; this kind of intolerance could never be accepted especially with such a strong arts program.

We were very proud that James had managed to deal with this for such a long time and he had not wanted us to interfere. However, that is what we are here for and we could not and would not let him deal with this any longer without our help.

The school made it clear that the behavior would never be tolerated and if they did one more thing or stepped out of line one more time, the school would be taking legal action against the parents. Wow, that was a positive action. James was very well-liked by all, but these few stupid jocks, of redneck parents that knew no other way but to be completely intolerant of anything or anyone that was different than them.

Every summer, we went with James and Nicky to Myrtle Beach for a national dance contest in which contestants from all over the United States and Canada took place in four days of dance contests.

James was talented and had every intention of going on to college to become a professional dancer. He had never swayed from his dream. So it was up to Sue and I to make sure that we supported him in his desire to be a professional dancer.

All of this plus the many other contests and recitals, that he regularly took part in, made him very confident indeed and he loved being on stage in any performance. As I am writing this, James has recently opened and is managing a new cabaret, comedy and jazz club in downtown Indianapolis called "Almost Famous."

Way to go James you will always be a success!

If ten percent of all the words that we say to our children sink in then their future will be the best it can be.

AUNTIE MEETS HER FAIRIES

Some people, we are lucky to have met, leave a lasting legacy way beyond their life and we who are left behind are better people for having known them.

ONE SUNDAY AFTERNOON, in 1996, John Bleby called, telling us that Auntie had died of a brain aneurism. I was very sad, of course; but Auntie had been preparing me for this day for many years. I was happy for her and happy that she had done so much good for so many orphaned and terminally ill children. She had adopted William and Beatrice, providing them both with a home of their own when they had nothing at all except a life in and out of foster homes. She had also taken in terminally ill children to nurse them and to make their so short time with us here on earth as happy as possible, knowing that they would pass away long before their time. These were the children at the bottom of the pile that no one wanted or really cared about, except for Auntie.

As for me, she had asked that I not be sad at all as she had done all that she intended to do with her life and was ready to go to the fairies.

I didn't cry at the sad news but celebrated her amazing life and quietly thought about all that she had given me, her trips to be with me for my wedding, to both Jane and Sue and her visit just to be with me when I got my apprenticeship papers at Taylor Woodrow.

I thought of her visit to help Sue in Brussels when James was born and I thought of the hundreds of phone conversations I had with her from the States just to let her know that I cared about her and that she was never far from my thoughts. She told me, over and over again, not to be sad when she "goes to the fairies" as she put it, so I wasn't as sad as I could have been. She was after all, in the words of Churchill, "The stuff that Britain was made of."

Auntie is buried in a small church cemetery, in Scorby, just outside Scarborough and I have a photograph of her sitting among her beautiful flowers in a blaze of colors in her garden, smiling at me in the picture. It makes me happy to know that she is just fine! It also made me happy to write this about her and in this way to thank her for all she had done. Without her love, her guidance and her wisdom I could never have become the person I am today. She will be joining all the other angels, some becoming angels in heaven but for auntie, she was always an angel here on earth, my guardian angel, sent to guide me just when I needed it most taking care of my formative years and it was her guidance and love that enabled me to be the person I am today.

Auntie was an angel, who helped so many young lives including my own while she was here.

A DIVINE MOMENT

One experience in less than a second can change everything we know.

PART OF THE theme of my book and my life explained in it is based on my unshakable belief in a divine presence. This is by no means a simple blind faith though there is nothing wrong with that. For me, it is based on reality and being open to things that happened to me and around me, most of which affected my life and some that affected others in events that I could see unfolding.

Not long after we had to move, from our beautiful home, I went to my local church almost every month, after an absence of decades where I was simply too busy with life and survival to even bother. Anyway, as I explained rather lamely to myself, I went three times a week as a boy, while singing in the choir, so I figured I had earned a leave of absence.

However, one Sunday morning as I was standing on the upper balcony of my local and packed church, during a hymn which I didn't really feel like singing, as I was not "feeling it" at the time, I was looking around at all of the congregation standing and singing their hearts out while I was standing not singing but miming the words while daydreaming.

The thoughts I had now were saying to me, "I don't belong here with all of these really good people" and I was gazing around the packed church as I thought, I'm certain that they are all far better people than me.

All of a sudden, as I was lost in my thoughts, a tingling feeling washed down over me slowly from the top of my head like fingers moving slowly down my body and as this happened a voice—very, very clear and very loud said to me, "You do belong here, Tony. You belong here." The voice was not in my head but in my middle and to say that I was stunned would be an understatement; I was shocked and stood very still looking around at all of the people, almost expecting a glow to be above my head. I became very calm and knew at that very moment that whatever happened to me in the future and whatever had happened in the past, God was aware of me, little me, of no significance whatsoever and had spoken to me very directly and I heard his voice and knew then that my belief in a divine presence, in God, was based on absolute truth.

I was in shock at the depth and meaning of that one moment. Was what I heard true? The more I thought about that very simple sentence and the feeling I had at that instance, the more I knew that it was true and it was real and it had happened to me.

That one simple but profound moment would validate all that I believed to be true and I didn't care what anyone else believed at all. I now knew the whole truth and that was enough.

I went home after church and told Sue, looking carefully at her reaction. She believed that I believed it, but I knew that she was one person who, if she did have a belief, never discussed it, sadly.

This proved to me that God is real and whether it's cool or not to admit it to others, (not cool for the most part these days) for me it is an undeniable fact.

KEEPING OUR HEADS ABOVE WATER

Sometimes, we just have to keep moving forward

After WE LOST everything through bankruptcy as a direct result of 911, we were now living in a rented house and I was struggling to find another job that would get us back on top. For one year following our bankruptcy, I took on many jobs in order to feed my family. I was a car salesman in January and February, I hated it! I was also a "Living Trust" advisor, but I did learn all about living trusts! I was also a mortgage broker, at a time when mortgage sales were going through the roof.

I also traveled with a close friend, Greg Dallas, who I met when I was a consultant for the company he was working at called GK Optical. Greg was bringing in three-quarters of that company's entire sales. He and I were good friends and he helped me start up a company which I called "Optasia" which was in the professional Optometry industry that Greg had many years of experience with.

I developed a computer program, with a couple of friends, which enabled people who needed eyeglasses to see what they were going to purchase. Up to that point, as soon as they took their glasses off to try on a new frame, they couldn't see what they were choosing because their prescription was not in the sample frames!

My program comprised a computer with a flat-screen onto which was fitted a high-resolution camera that took six photos of the customer trying on up to five new frames, plus one photo of their existing frame. The customer could now compare how they looked in their new frames while wearing their own prescription glasses, comparing each with his own pair.

The system sold like hotcakes and it made a great profit for both me as well as the client. I then found a company in New York that made high-quality animation software showing how Polaroid lenses work seemingly sliding the polarised lens over their vision (on-screen) to see how they work compared with just tinted sunglasses.

We also had an animated Transitions lens piece, showing how they go dark with the sun; A no-line (graduated lens) bifocal and tri-focal lens piece that showed how these lenses work as if you are looking through the glasses showing how each field of vision, near, mid and distant view, was now clear to the wearer, but with no ugly line across their lens.

The most important piece to our program showed how "Anti Reflective Lenses" (AR) worked, for eyeglass wearers, especially while driving in rain and in the dark making their vision much safer to drive while wearing their glasses.

I did a licensing deal with the animations company and added the animation programs to my software making it easy for opticians to up-sell their customers into frames they loved to wear and with high tech products like AR (Anti-reflective) coatings that made them look younger.

My Optasia system had a payback to the eye doctor of only two months and increased their sales and profits significantly. I did very well with this company just when I needed something to help pay our bills. But, despite this, the sales though very good, were not consistent enough for me to rely just on my Optasia business and some months I had no sales at all so I needed a full-time job.

Necessity is the mother of invention and for a while, my company "Optasia" led the field in the retail eyeglass industry!

BACK TO WORK AGAIN

When we are suddenly out of work, everything else goes out of the window until we find another job!

I RECEIVED AN e-mail from a headhunter in Florida, while I was running my Optasia business, asking if I was interested in joining a company making specialized racing apparel and gloves this was October 2002. I was intrigued and responded that maybe I was. I received several more e-mails concerning a company looking to hire someone with my skills as general manager to run the company on behalf of the owners who were all quite old and all in retirement.

I checked out the Web site for the company called, *The Glove Corporation,* to find out what the company profile was like and saw it made firefighting and industrial gloves. I was told that there would be a series of interviews with the family members that owned the company, that the interviews would be by phone and that if I was successful this would end with a face-to-face interview in Alexandria north of Indianapolis where their head office was located in Indiana.

The phone interviews were arranged, with three of the family members making up the board of directors. These interviews went on over two months as they were apparently hard to get to one place at the same time, which as I would find out later was a common trait.

I found out during these telephone interviews that the company had been around for some eighty years and had been a family-run business ever since. The current president, Frank Sturm, was now seventy-five years old, had run the company for thirty years and was, in their opinion, incapable of managing it presently.

Sue was in London, visiting her family, at the time of my interview and we were now living in a rented house, after our bankruptcy. I called her while she was over there and promised her that I would get this job no matter what. So, the interview was set up and I drove to Alexandria which was seventy-five miles and one and a half hours drive to the north of Indianapolis.

The town of Alexandria where the office was located was a dump with several now closed and rusted old General Motor factories, a bunch of poorly maintained houses and a high street of mostly closed-down shops. Still, I didn't care as I was out for the kill. I was determined to get this job.

I arrived at the building, for my face-to-face interview, which was located in the very center of Alexandria in Indiana, at the crossroads in the middle of town, in a large old partially dilapidated building.

The Glove Corp headquarters was a large square three-story red brick building with its top floor comprising of mostly partially boarded-up windows and looked quite sinister. The entrance was an unmarked black door, under a squeaking, swinging rusting old sign, straight off the high street, if you could call a bunch of closed-down shops a high street, the building was located between shops on either side of the Glove Corp's entrance door. To the left was a small rather sad computer repair business, to the right was a fire equipment sales dealership.

I entered the door, a little late I might add and went up the squeaky, uncarpeted, plain dusty wooden staircase that creaked with every step and entered the office on my right through a tall door at the top of the staircase.

Once inside, the office was not too bad, but only three people were working in the "head office." I was shown into the boardroom where seated around a long plain wooden boardroom table were several people that I would eventually get to know "very" well.

Present at this interview was Rob, the thirtyish tall, slim police officer and a part-owner nephew of Frank Sturm, seated at the end of the table who was an elderly man and was the president and chairman of the board; Allen, the same age as Rob but heavy-set with dark circles around his eyes giving him somewhat of a piggy appearance; another elderly man called Mr. Rae, though I didn't know why they were so formal, in calling him "Mr. Rae instead of using his first name. He was the accountant and also present was Sharon Summers, who was the office manager.

During the interview, I gave it everything I had and made sure I answered all of their questions properly even asking them if I had answered their questions satisfactorily, something I had learned from poring over the many job search sites while learning how to manage interviews.

As the interview progressed, I gained momentum and realized that this was it, I gave it all I could to give the best impression of myself. During the interview, I showed them a box of "Stardust" perfume, telling them that in a way this was the same as gloves, (yeah right) in that it had a number of components that came from several suppliers and all went together to make a finished product. They understood what I was saying though and I think that small demonstration was key to getting me over the finish line and to being offered the job.

The interview lasted around two hours and was interesting. They all told me that the company had a great future under the right leadership but also that they were not certain of the future as the company had been losing money for several years. Allen Town said nothing during the entire interview, so I understood by that that he had probably wanted the job, just a feeling.

After the interview, I felt certain that I had the best chance possible and called Sue, telling her that the interview had gone well. The next day I called the headhunter, who turned out to be the wife of Joe, another family member who owned 25 percent of the company.

She asked me how I thought it went and I told her; she then said that subject to a background check, I had the job. I couldn't believe it; I would be back in a proper job after several years of trying anything and everything to make ends meet so that we didn't starve.

Talk about a tough time, that in the year 2002 I had seven jobs to make ends meet: a car salesman, a living trust salesman, a certified computer training company general manager. I had even launched a start-up digital imaging company, worked as a salesman for a UK imaging company and had worked with Sue for a few months as a mortgage broker as well as a consultant for a plastics company.

I had managed to keep our heads above water and we seemed to be able to just about make ends meet throughout. I called Sue, who was still in England and told her my good news; she gasped in relief as I told her "I nailed it, I got the job."

"When do you start and how much is the pay?" she asked. I told her that I would be starting on my birthday and would be paid weekly. The money was less than what I had earned at Alfa Laval before I left, but after all, we had been through it was better than nothing. I had agreed to a low start in salary, as a gesture to the company, but agreed also that if I exceeded their expectations and succeeded in turning the company around, they had to increase my pay as a result. They all agreed.

I then got a call from the headhunter who had found me the position, now just two days before I was to start my new job, telling me there was a problem as I had filed for bankruptcy. My heart fell; maybe I wouldn't get the job after all, but I wasn't about to lose it for something that wasn't my fault.

I told her that "If the company sees this as an issue, after the events of 9/11, then maybe I wasn't right for the company and then neither was the company right for me." I remember saying that I didn't want to have baggage in starting a new position running a small company like this especially when it was out of my control.

She was OK after that and told me that it would be all right for me to take the job and that she would not mention this to the others. Anyway, my background check was fine as I had never been in any trouble ever.

I started my new job, as general manager of *The Glove Corporation*, just around my birthday, on Monday December 2, 2002, driving from Greenwood to Alexandria, earning half of what I had earned some ten years before and having to drive seventy-five miles each way to and from my new office, a total of three hours' drive time every day.

I was nevertheless elated to have a new job, at last, I didn't care about the money or the drive. I was going to make my mark in this new industry! Gloves! Are you kidding? What the hell did I know about gloves? Oh well, I was certain I would make my mark and also that I would give this my absolute best shot.

We were so broke that I had to buy a car, a light blue Ford Taurus from a "buy here pay here" dealer in the seedy part of town. The "buy here pay here" was a no-down payment pay as you drive business that if you failed to make even a single payment, they would come around and repossess the car even if you had paid 95 percent of the total cost. The car though was fine and drove well; I even named her "Blue Bessie," and she never let me down once, although, she did overheat in summer, so I had to drive her with the heater full on in order not to overheat the engine.

The first issue I was to face was that the board wanted me to fire Frank Sturm (CEO and President) as my first action only a week after I arrived. I refused to do this for them, telling them that they should have done this as a board action and that having read the articles of incorporation I did not have that power.

I liked Frank and understood that he had run the company under the direction of the board, for more than thirty years. He had done exactly what they had asked him to do; that is all except being able to make a profit for them mainly because they had never allowed him to make any investment in the company. I worked with Frank, giving him a chance to help me as much as I could although he did nothing at all to help me during the first months of my leadership in his family's company.

Rob had decided to work with me to make sure that Frank didn't try to undermine me doing, what was his job prior to my hire.

The company was around $4 million in mainly firefighting glove sales but also they made industrial and special protective gloves used for welding, firefighting, driver, rope rescue, industrial work gloves and many more.

The company sold its products to a wide range of more than three hundred privately owned fire and industrial distributorships throughout the United States and Canada with sales going as far as Australia and South America.

They had seven main distributors who took 5 percent of the sales value in their respective territories to sell our gloves. After I had begun to gain market knowledge, I could see that the industrial glove business was dying because of very low-cost imports from China and Asia. I estimated that we would lose this business within two to three years unless we could do something about it.

The industrial sales were a quarter of their total sales and were in very low-priced gloves that were not profitable. The fire-glove market had higher price points with eight models that were each required to be annually certified to meet the NFPA certification requirements for the firefighting industry. The annual certification was extremely expensive and took around four to six months to complete every year. After completion, the gloves were allowed to contain an NFPA certification label inside.

This was a necessary part of being in the firefighting market and something that we had to comply with annually. To pass the annual NFPA certification, we had to send out hundreds of pairs of gloves in different sizes, swatches of materials and numerous carefully filled-out pages of paperwork for every style of glove we made. Sharon and Keith, my managers, had been used to this as they had both been doing this long before I joined the company. I was to have my work cut out if I was to be successful in turning this monster around!

Behind The Office

Behind my office on the second floor in the old, dilapidated building, was a pale green double door leading to a now closed-down factory where the once busy shipping department was located with long tables for shipping goods. The large wooden floored room housed among other things old outdated, disused and broken computers, printers, hundreds of files in dusty cabinets, and old brochures that could or should have been tossed away years earlier probably going back as to just after the earth cooled. There were boxes and boxes of the worst-made gloves I had ever seen with sizes that were wrong, poor quality and with left and right hands of differing sizes. I hoped that these were not what was being shipped out to customers now.

Everything was "hoarded"—all the old stuff all being kept for no good reason; it was so negative to the forward movement that I was going to bring to the company.

There were welders' gloves, electrical linemen's gloves, freezer gloves, firefighting gloves, work gloves, leather aprons, leather spats for welders to protect their feet and many, many different kinds of gloves that I had no idea what they were all for.

Though it was fascinating to see, to me the building and the boxes of old badly made products were all like an anchor, tethering the company to the past. This old stuff was now totally irrelevant in today's business environment, yet none of it had been let go by Sharon and she was an anchor to the company who focused on the past, not the future.

In the other front office, my office, were old desks, scattered around, faded black-and-white maps on the wall and old posters from previous advertising campaigns. It was awful and I decided that no customer or supplier from this point forward would ever come to Alexandria to see this mess.

Bats And Guano

The upper floor of our building was infested with bats so bad that they had called in a team of specialists to get rid of the hundreds of bats living there. It was so bad up there that their droppings corroded the large old freight elevator electrical wiring, causing it to frequently break down. It was disgusting, on some days, bats would be seen in our office and the staff would freak out asking me to get rid of them.

In the rear of the now-disused shipping office behind the double doors, was a very narrow creaky wooden staircase leading to an upper 3rd. floor which was all but completely dilapidated. It comprised of mostly boarded-up windows and a ceiling that had mostly collapsed and was now partly held up by wooden batons nailed roughly and haphazardly to the ceiling beams, seemingly by an amateur handyman to hold up what was left of the ceiling. There were large, dilapidated areas that showed the wooden laths where the ceiling and wall plaster had fallen off. There was black mold around the walls, missing plaster, heaps of pigeon and bat droppings which were all over the floor and on the old sewing equipment.

There were many old Singer sewing machines and folds of material left as if they had been quite suddenly abandoned like on the "Marie Celeste," left exactly as if the workers had vanished into thin air.

It was creepy in the closed factory, behind my office and there was the added junk that the Sturm family had seen fit to use as a dumping ground for their old disused smelly furniture which had no value at all; rusty, filthy old hairdryers and old torn settees faded and filthy with stains all over, broken tools, old rusty chairs, a rusted-up drum kit that was probably crappy when it was new. I hated all this junk, it was indicative of how the family saw their business, nothing important just for use as and when they wanted it as a dumping ground for their old junk and to take out whatever money they could without having made a single investment in decades!

The Glove Factory

Frank took me by car to the factory which was just as bad as the head office and was located at Heber Springs in Arkansas. I met the managers, Pat and Keith, along with the eighty-five-sewing staff, all sitting in straight lines facing the blank gray walls with opaque windows, all of whom seemed at that time fairly disdainful of my position, not surprising since they had seen numerous managers come and go.

The factory is comprised of a single-floor building set in a grass field with no outside lights and only some badly laid stones as a way of allowing cars to park at the facility. Inside there were heaps of old moldy leather of all kinds and all colors; some of which, as I was to find out, had been there for more than ten or fifteen years, showing evidence of either rats or mice with droppings on the floor by the pile of leather.

What was it about this company that they had to have creature droppings all over their operation in both the head office as well as the factory? There was not even a staff canteen, only a set of old plain tables located near a rusted window that had not been cleaned for years. The steel beams on the ceiling were all covered with at least six inches deep of dust and knap from the leather sewing and dirt that had accumulated over the past fifty years that the factory had existed in that location.

I asked Pat if the building had ever been cleaned, she said not that she knew of but added that this was clean compared to when they first arrived there some five years before.

As I sat looking around having a coffee, while meeting with Pat and Keith at the dining area, bits of dust and dirt was falling off the ceiling beams onto us and the table. The mood was bad, no one seemed happy to be there. There was no air-conditioning, only some old "chicken" hatchery coolers comprising of four, four-foot-wide, square "down shafts" which came down through the roof and when utilized would blast out air that had been only slightly cooled by water pipes running across the airflow coming in from the roof. These blast coolers made no difference at all to the heat inside the building and in summer the temperature got as high as 110 degrees and with humidity of 95 percent, making it even worse.

It got so hot in the Arkansas summer that the factory had to close at noon because of the heat from June right through to September. Those that sat at their sewing machines within a ten-foot radius from each down shaft had to have a piece of cardboard set in front of their workstation to stop their work from blowing away.

If that wasn't bad enough, when it rained hard, there was a torrent of water that flooded through the front office where Keith's desk was as the land grading outside the factory was so poor that the drainage was right through the office and foundations. When it rained, which it did with a vengeance, the roof leaked all over the factory and had to have buckets placed on the sewing tables and floors. The staff even knew beforehand, where to place the buckets!

When I discussed this with Pat and Keith, they told me that the owners and Sharon had never let them put in air conditioning or a canteen or especially re-grading the outside to prevent flooding, Sharon said, "What do they need all that for, open the doors and let the fresh air in and why do they need a break room anyway? They are there to work not to rest." Or they were told to use buckets as it only rains sometimes and the cost was too much to pay out of slim profits.

Unbelievable! What a mess I had got myself into. Still, I also knew it couldn't get worse than this, so I would make it better. This factory had been neglected for more than thirty years, with no investment and all of the meager profit, if any, had been taken out in the form of monthly dividends by the owners leaving only a slim operating capital enough to last for two months, not more.

The sewing machines were mainly old Singer chain-stitch machines that were new in the 1930s and there was not much that seemed much newer than that. Some of the Singers even had mechanical operating systems that were at least seventy years old. What a compliment to the Singer Sewing Machine company that these were still in operation. There were some industrial Juki and Mitsubishi's dotted around as well and these were very good machines.

There were two lines of leather cutters totaling thirteen in all and all were men who stood in front of mechanical "clickers" that "clacked" loudly as the large mechanical arm was swung into position by the cutters and snapped down onto the glove pattern dies. The "clickers" were placed onto a steel table with a plastic cutting board onto which the large pieces of leather, some as big as half a cow, were placed to be cut into glove components.

The factory produced around five hundred to one thousand pairs of gloves each week and only half that in summer, partly because of the early closing due to the summer heat inside the factory and partly because of the sales of fire gloves being slow in the summer.

All factory purchases had to run through Sharon who had only ever been in the glove factory a couple of times in her more than forty years of service with the company.

She believed that when the factory ran out of leather, which they did nearly every month, they should make something else instead even if they had no other orders to be made. (let them eat cake!) She also believed they were "saving" money when the factory staff was laid off, but she knew nothing of the cost of shutting down the factory with all of the operational costs remaining and with no production from which to cover these costs.

It made no sense having a large factory in Arkansas, with eighty-six staff and a head office in Indiana with only three people, especially as their work could easily have been managed in the factory.

What a great business to run; it certainly couldn't get any worse. According to the customers I spoke to, we had less than one year before we would shut the doors forever because of diminishing sales.

A Mic in the Light

One day, some nine months after I had started work in Alexandria, I came back from getting something to eat while continuing to work over lunch which I always did, when Sharon told me that Frank had been "fixing" the light above my desk. I told her that the light didn't need fixing as it worked fine but said I would take a look. What on earth was he up to? I climbed onto my desk and above it was a strip light with a plastic cover. I flipped open the cover and let it swing down, as it did so I noticed a very small black object attached to a wire hidden inside the light fixture.

I started to gently pull the object down and saw to my amazement and utter disbelief that it was a tiny microphone that had been hidden up there at some point by Frank. I stared at it in disbelief, what the hell! I was stunned and stood there looking at it for several minutes.

I called Rob who was on police duty that afternoon and asked him to come to the office immediately. He told me he was in his police uniform but would be off duty later. I told him he probably needed to be in uniform and needed to be here as soon as possible and yes he should probably be in uniform.

Rob arrived fifteen minutes later and came rushing up the steps, three at a time, into my office. "What the!" he started to say, but I put my finger to my lips telling him not to say anything and pointed up to the light fitting.

Rob being over six feet tall reached up and swung the cover down at which point the tiny microphone now dropped out and onto his head as I had pulled some of the wire through which made it drop lower this time.

Rob was furious. "What the hell!" he shouted and began pulling all the wire out of the false ceiling in my office. Imagine what it looked like, both of us standing looking up pulling yards and yards of microphone wire down, with ceiling tiles flying in all directions as we followed the long wire out of my office, pulling the wire down from where it was hidden above the ceiling tiles, straight across the board room ceiling next to my office, across the hallway with the wire bundle I was holding getting so big it was becoming difficult to hold.

The wire continued straight into Frank's office going across his ceiling down the sidewall, where it had been carefully hidden in with a load of other computer wires running down his wall until it finally descended under his carpet and ran straight into his desk drawer! Unbelievable!

Rob got increasingly angry as Frank, his uncle, watched the now-enormous bundle of wire that I was holding in both of my outstretched arms while Rob was now in his office pulling up the carpet to expose the wire hidden underneath.

All the while Frank was standing in his office, arms folded, with his hand stroking his chin while he looked on bemused at what was rapidly unfolding, looking on as if all this was nothing to do with him. "What the fuck have you done, Uncle Frank? What is this? A mic running into your office from Tony's office?" Rob shouted at him, continuing on, not waiting for a reply. "I can have you arrested for this, it's illegal to record someone's conversations and phone calls and I'm going to arrest you right now!" Rob shouted.

I asked Frank how long this had been there. "Oh, that's nothing to worry about," he said to both of us. "It's been there for ages, I just never bothered about it," he said rather lamely in an "aw shucks" kind of voice.

I left Frank's office, Rob followed me back into my office where I told him point-blank, "I'm not working with Frank anymore, I have tried to work with him but he does nothing at all and I refuse to have him in my office, president or not, I can't trust him anymore."

I turned to Rob and told him that he had better deal with this and fast, as legally I cannot since I am not an owner and this was unacceptable behavior from someone who I was supposed to fire immediately after joining. I reminded him that I was the reason Frank was still there, saying that he was useless to the running of the operation and had done not one single task I had given him, hoping he could help.

The next morning, I had a conference call with Rob and Joe, who both wanted Frank, fired immediately. "Fire his damn ass!" Joe growled into the phone, so I told them that if they did this it would lead to a lawsuit that the company would lose as a result of illegal dismissal of a board member and owner. I had read their articles of incorporation; a chairman or president could only be removed following a decision of the board. Also, I told them that they have to get an extraordinary board meeting set up giving Frank forty-eight-hour minimum notice.

I explained to them both that we had to do this by the letter while we needed to accomplish very strict guidelines with an offer of removal and the reasons why, plus a timeline during which he could disagree with the offer, a vote and a severance agreement.

I immediately sought the advice of a local corporate attorney and began the preparation of the severance agreement. Rob wanted to use the opportunity to buy Frank out of the business an opportunity that showed me another side of the "family." As for me, I was only interested in getting Frank out with the minimum of fuss.

It took several weeks to get a draught severance agreement; the content of which gave Frank twenty-one days to sign or disagree with the offer, after which time the offer, if not taken up, would be withdrawn.

I cautioned Rob that he needed to call a board meeting, take a vote, to make sure that Frank understood what was being said. I also told him to repeat everything three times, give Frank the agreement, and encourage him to seek advice of an attorney. The offer was extremely good, I saw to it that it was fair, though I knew Frank would ignore it as that was a family trait.

The board meeting was called and Rob followed my instructions to the letter. Because of this, there were no legal ramifications when it had been done correctly. Frank had no legal possibility to sue the company which was something I wanted to avoid at all costs.

Frank, of course, ignored the offer to pay him for his shares according to a fair market value along with an offer of full pay for eighteen months. He was stupid; he left it until the twenty-second day after being told he had twenty-one days and called Rob to discuss the agreement. Rob told him it was too late; the offer was now off the table and Frank was out. I knew from past experience with this that when done correctly, it was like nothing had happened; everything went smoothly and I also knew that the family had just learned a valuable lesson.

A New Direction

With Frank gone, I had the full reins in the running of the company, so I began by analyzing the revenue stream looked hard at the production costs and saw that the factory costs were high, prices were low and the profit was very, very slim.

I loved the analysis, having made this a skill that I had fine-tuned having been taught by the best there was and knew this was the key to understanding how the company performed, which would lead to how to fix it.

The office staff, of three women, was somewhat negative to work with, but I would deal with that later, not now. The company had lost a third of their distributors without even knowing it and had two business segments: one was firefighting gloves and the other was industrial gloves—both of which were unprofitable.

After my analysis, I created a market plan from which I would develop the "big fix" for this small company. It was clear that we would lose the industrial market to low-cost importers that could sell gloves at less than our leather cost alone.

The company had seen better days and was living in the past. Sharon repeatedly told of days in the past when the company had many sewing operations in that head office building, but something told me this was not entirely true as I could see no sign of any wealth, only old and dilapidated furniture and equipment that even when new was probably the cheapest they could get.

I started by trying on the many gloves we made and found them to be of poor quality, wide seams, differing in fit between the right hand and the left hand of the same pair of gloves. This was because the final inspection comprised a couple of old women whose hands were too small for the larger sizes we mostly sold and therefore could not possibly see how the large and extra-large gloves should have fitted.

The company did have an ISO 9001 quality system, but this did not reflect the poor quality of the end product. The firefighting gloves had to be certified each year by a third-party testing facility, but they frequently failed repeatedly to pass the rigorous NFPA annual tests because of the poor leather quality, since there were no technical staff able to remedy this and the company often used the cheapest inconsistent quality leather they could get.

The good thing though was that the company had been well known in the industry and I believed I could turn this around, but it would take a lot of very hard work to succeed.

I met with the independent sales rep agencies first to see if I had their support, as well as their promise of support provided I started improving our products and position in the market.

The Turn-Around

I began by re-engineering the gloves, as that would immediately improve sales, after realizing that many of the components in our gloves did not fit together and that the finish of the cuffs and seams in our firefighting products needed improving significantly as there were loose threads all over the finished product.

I reengineered the firefighting glove patterns and "walked" each of the patterns to see if the seams of the components were matched up to each other which in many cases they weren't. I also modified the glove design by changing the position of the little finger crotch and the thumb in order to make it fit the hand better than it did.

The results were astounding; the sewing staff found that they didn't have to "work" the leather, which was their term for making the components fit when the pattern was incorrect which was extremely tiring to the operator in trying to get the sewn components to fit together to sew each glove. When they did this, with bad patterns, the gloves became twisted and didn't look good.

The staff was beginning to understand that my methods were different from my six predecessors and they could see that the gloves seemed to be easier for them to sew now.

We had a fifty percent annual staff turnover through new hires not wanting to stay in the company as it was a "sweatshop," and I had to turn that around as well as all the other things that had to be done.

I also designed several new gloves, showing the market that Glove Corp was getting its act together at last.

My days were filled up, working hard to improve the company, leaving home at 6:00 a.m. and arriving home at 7:30 p.m. while driving 150 miles a day to the office in Alexandria and back. Still, I didn't mind at all as I was happy doing what I do and I was even happier to have a job that paid me.

Elks With Holes in Their Hides?

In 2004, just as things were, at last, turning around and our business began to improve, we began to get our biggest-selling glove made from elk skin being returned from firefighters all over the country saying that they had simply fallen apart. What had happened was that the leather was "tender" and was simply becoming full of holes having no strength, yet we didn't know why.

The problem got steadily worse and affected all of our Elk skin firefighting gloves. Fifty percent of our sales were gloves which were made of Elkskin, which was imported from Finland and were showing problems. We were getting gloves back by the dozens, so I called our competitors to see if they had the same problem. They told me they didn't though I was later to find out they were not telling the truth. What a surprise! A competitor not admitting they had a problem!

We contacted our leather importer who told us that we were the only ones having this problem, which I didn't believe so I decided to fly to Finland to visit our tannery in a place called Kokkola up on the northeast coast of Finland toward the Lapland border right on the edge of the Arctic Circle. I flew via Helsinki and then took a small plane to Kokkola where I met Ekki whose family had owned the tannery for four generations. I wanted to meet them face-to-face to see what the problem was.

Ekki picked me up from the hotel and I was shown around the tannery. They told me the problem may be the freezing of the hides while they were left outside in the months of the freezing weather in the Finnish winter. That night, I took Ekki out to dinner in a local restaurant and pub. Ekki's idea of a nice evening out was to get blind drunk until he fell over bursting into song while lying on the floor. The funny thing was no one seemed to notice as all of them were doing the same thing; it was like being in Sweden all over again. But unlike Sweden which only had two domestic beers, when I was there, Pripps number 1 and Pripps number 2, Finland had some great beers!

I left Finland, hoping that my visit would spur them to improve their quality of leather to us. But it was up to me, in the end, to find a solution to win the confidence of our customers again.

Don't trust what your suppliers are telling you if the likely outcome is going to be very expensive for them to fix!

AMANDA

No matter how important my work was it took no precedence over my daughter's immediate needs.

O N MY RETURN from Finland, I came back to the States via London where I met my darling daughters, Amanda and Georgia, as I hadn't seen them for several years since I had left Parfums Llewellyn. I stayed over for several days and the break was very welcome. They took me to their favorite place in the world, the ancient city of Glastonbury. I could see why they loved it there as it had an atmosphere of England in older medieval days. There were small shops selling what to me were "alternative medicine" items like herbs, spices, prayer bowls and mixtures of all cultures of religious and homeopathic medicines.

I was surprised though that when I took them both to a local Italian restaurant, Amanda did well, but after eating only half of her food she had to place her plate on the floor and out of her view. I could say nothing; she knew that I knew she was still fighting her anorexia. I had no intention of putting her on the spot with this and wanted her to feel my support in not saying anything negative.

Sometimes less is more so I held her hand and kissed her there were tears in her eyes. But we both managed just fine. I said a silent prayer for her that she would win her fight with this awful mental illness. I remembered going over to England while at Parfums Llewellyn to help by supporting her in joining her at the meeting she had with her doctors and councilors. Still, I had to admit she looked much stronger now than she looked back then.

Later when she gave birth to Ellie, (Eliza Jane), she had more to focus on, as baby Ellie had been born with a problem with her feet, involving her having to undertake a series of arduous operations all through her young years in order for her to walk. This gave Amanda something else to focus on and caused her to leave her anorexia behind her. Thank goodness for that.

Amanda got past her anorexia and managed it on her own which showed us all how strong she was in dealing with this deadly condition. She was also the reason why Georgia and herself began their business which was to last for 16 years with their shop

Enchanted. I loved spending time in their shop with them to see their success. If they succeeded in this once they could, if they wanted to, succeed again and again. They are both, a chip off the old block!

Sometimes we teach our children ways to be successful that only become apparent years later.

STARTING AGAIN

When we set our minds to the future, not the past, it was amazing how quickly we can gain everything back that I lost.

AFTER WORKING FOR the Glove Corp. for only eighteen months after we had filed bankruptcy, we were able to buy a new home, so we began looking. Sue hated living in rented accommodation although I didn't mind it; I was in no real hurry to get into another mortgage as I didn't trust the mortgage companies.

We found a perfect house close to the school where James and Nicky were attending. The house was a two-story Tudor-style home on a hill in an older edition surrounded by a golf course. The house had a basement and a kidney-shaped swimming pool in the garden. What I liked was the bay window in the kitchen that overlooked the garden. It had a large stone fireplace and was exactly what we had been looking for.

Looking for a new home after bankruptcy gave us both something to look forward to rather than living in a beautiful but "rented" home.

The garden had been modeled for a TV program called HGTV and had been completely landscaped including the pool. The kidney-shaped pool had fiber optic lighting that could change color in the pool at night moving from pink to green to blue and to white and it even had two planters that were fountains on the side of the pool.

We both loved it and decided to buy it, as the price was at that time far less than it was worth only two years before because of the housing market slowing down. Sue managed the paperwork and got us a mortgage after only a few months when we happily moved in. I would never again mind mowing our lawn.

So in the end, these 8 years of my life, although being the hardest time of my entire working life, enabled me to get through the worst time and still come out in great shape.

For me, this episode ended very well, we now had everything back that we had lost. I achieved all I intended to despite a group of nasty owners who did eventually, through their own stupidity lose the one thing that had been in their family for 90 years. But as I said, somethings are never meant to remain past a life expectancy, because of the negativity they create that becomes their company. I was now back in a good place and more than ready to move on!

I learned not to waste my energy focusing on what was, but to focus on what will be. We now had everything back that we lost but now we valued it all much more.

NICKY AND STEVENS JOHNSONS DISEASE

When a son is critically ill nothing else matters except to help him get well at all costs.

THINGS WERE GOING well at home and at work and we were finally getting everything back in place. It was Christmas that year, when Nicky, now fifteen, was on some mild medication for acne that was sulfur-based when I noticed that he had come out in spots and his eyes were itching.

I took him to our doctor, Dr. Jeff, on New Year's Eve, Jeff thought he had "pink eye" prescribing him with "Sulphacetamide" which was another sulfur-based medication.

Later that evening, Sue and I could hear Nicky struggling to breathe so we rushed in to see him. He was covered in spots, was wheezing, and couldn't breathe. We took him directly to the hospital where he was immediately admitted overnight. He got steadily worse and worse and by the early hours he had come up in blisters all over his body. One of the doctors told us she thought he had a disease called Stevens-Johnson's disease; he was getting worse by the minute.

He was taken by ambulance to Riley Children's Hospital downtown with us driving behind him, very, very scared of what could happen to our poor son, Nicky.

Sue and I were beside ourselves with this and had never seen anything like it.

As he lay there in the intensive care assessment unit, lying on a gurney in the middle of the emergency room; we could see that Riley was moving into an emergency care mode and in less than five minutes he was surrounded by all of the specialists including eyes, ear nose and throat, dermatologists, internal medicine specialists. All were deadly serious and all were consulting with the head administrator whose job it was to accumulate the incoming information and between them all to arrive at a direction of treatment. Meanwhile, poor Nicky was getting worse and where one of the nurses had touched him to get a pulse on the side of his neck using two fingers, he had now right before our eyes a blister the size of a very large grapefruit forming.

He was looking terrible as his body was reacting to the intake of sulfur, which he had a violent reaction to. Sue was by now sobbing while we were both looking at our son who was dying right in front of our eyes. His face was bright red and swollen and he now had blisters all over his body, on his face, his body, his eyes, under his fingernails in his ears and all over his mouth and digestive tract.

It was decided to treat him as a severe burn patient, so they took him immediately to the intensive care where we were told he would get far worse before he got better. We were very scared and prayed for him as we sincerely believed he may die from this. We were also told that there was no medication to treat this disease, but that it had to run its course.

The most important thing, we were told, was to make sure that he did not get any infection on his body as that would result in scarring. I sent a message that day to the church; in a note I wrote to our pastor Greg Ponchot for them to pray for him to survive this horrific illness.

Over the next four weeks, both Sue and I spent as much time as we could with him in the ICU and although I had to run the company, I made sure I went to see him directly from work every single day. Sue went to see him during the days also and spent almost all of her time there including sleeping in his room every night for the first two weeks.

We had to wear a mask, a hat, plastic overalls and plastic over-shoes to see him in his intensive care unit as the risk of airborne infection was very high. Nicky now had blisters over 97 percent of his entire body and was having difficulty seeing as the blisters were on his eyes and under his eyelids.

He had to have an intravenous food line inserted through his nose and a drip into his chest with medication for pain control. Nicky was placed on a specially constructed air bed with covers that were changed several times a day, as if this wasn't bad enough, he also had the risk of losing his sight. Sue made damn certain that every day, five times a day, the ophthalmologists came in to scrape under his eyelids to prevent any scar tissue from forming. Even writing this makes me deeply sad for my beautiful son. He also lost the sclerotic coating on his eyes. He lost his fingernails; toenails and the blisters were all in his mouth and down his throat.

We had never experienced anything like this and for the first two weeks, he didn't know we were even there.

Gradually though he managed to show his strength of willpower and could talk to us about overcoming his disease. The road to recovery was long though, but at fifteen years old, he was strong enough to make it through. When our friends, Ros and Tim, came to see him, Tim broke down and cried at seeing our poor Nicky lying in the intensive care unit in such a bad way, his face swollen up and covered in blisters, his skin coming off all over his body.

That Sunday, I knew I needed more help than what Sue and I could manage, so I informed the church where they held prayers for him when they heard about how he was and there was a gasp as many of the congregation knew Nicky from being a little and mischievous schoolboy.

Greg Ponchot, my pastor at New Hope, came to see him in hospital and I know that it made a very big difference; it also made Nicky very happy to see him as it gave him some divine help from above in his struggle to beat this. One Sunday afternoon, our close friends, Jerry and Jacque, came to see us and just turned up at the hospital, Sue and I were very pleased to see them both and they told us that many people were asking about Nicky at the church and his school.

Our friends brought round food for us as neither Sue nor myself felt like cooking and by the time we got home from the hospital, we were both worn out. It was these little things that helped us get through this extreme situation.

Nicky was in the ICU for four weeks and slowly, because of the excellent care he received at Riley, he began to get better. During the last week, he was allowed to take a bath to help him slough off the dead skin all over his body. The bath had a hydraulic chair to help him in and out as he was far too weak to stand, let alone get in and out of the bath.

He had to be taken to the bathroom, in a wheelchair, but when they helped him out of it and into the bath chair he was like a little old man. He could do nothing by himself at all. The bath was special and had purified warm air jets under the water, to help him with oxygenating his body to help it heal as it also sloughed off his loose skin. He had to keep spitting out the layers of skin inside his mouth where blisters had been. As big chunks of it came off we knew though that he was gradually getting better.

At last, we brought him home, but he was very weak and would have to recuperate for another three months while at home in order to become well again. The result of all he had been through was that he stopped caring for himself when he was told that he may never be able to wear contact lenses again, because of his eyes not, at that time, having a strong enough sclera over them.

The whole illness changed him and he didn't care about himself, but over time we knew he would get over it. He blamed our doctor for not diagnosing his condition correctly and for giving him the additional sulfacetamide eye drops. That most definitely took him over the edge and caused his dramatic and horrific reaction.

He then had to have tubes inserted into the corners of his eyes as his tear ducts had closed over because of scarring of the thin tissue around his eyes. They were eventually removed, but he still had a little redness in the corner of one eye.

We explained to him that we were happy that he had recovered so well after the terrible illness. After two years we found out that he could wear contacts again, so there was, in the end, very little outwardly visible from his bout with Stevens-Johnson syndrome. But what he had to deal with was inside his head. Later this entire episode led to Nicky's addiction.

It is at the worst times that families are often at their closest.

FIXING OLD PROBLEMS

Necessity is the mother of invention!

BACK AT THE Glove Company, we received a letter from Underwriters Laboratories, or UL as they were better known, telling us that three major firefighting glove companies all had a serious elk-skin problem that needed to be fixed. So, my competitors, as well as my tannery, were lying, they did have the same problems as we had but of course, had been telling the market that it was a Glove Corp issue in order to cost us business.

We were losing business fast and it was time to do something about it. It was clear as to what had happened: the "firefighter" glove that we marketed had become a huge success. As a result, our competitors had also decided to make and sell their own version of our elk-skin firefighting gloves.

I had to change this I had to find a way to reduce our dependency on elk skin or to change from a "suede" to a top grain leather on the back of the glove where the problem would be eliminated since it was impossible for an elk to have holes in his skin and our problem was only with the suede. The suede is split from under the outer or top grain leather and depending on the thickness of the hide it allows you to have one split grain or suede cut from the hide. You can only ever have one split for each hide and tanners know that you cannot take a second cut of suede from any hide as the middle split often has weak spots where the grain becomes vertical for some reason leaving the leather very soft and weak.

I got to work to develop a new "top grain" cowhide leather glove to replace our Elk skin gloves, which would fix the problem and give the glove a completely new look hopefully letting our customers know we had not only fixed the problem but had improved the glove at the same time. I helped develop a new tanning process to replicate the soft feel of the cowhide to become similar to the elk skins.

The total loss for Glove Corp was around three-quarters of a million dollars that year not to mention a loss of many customers right at the point where we were gaining market share after years of decline. All the positive work I had done in reengineering the gloves was now at risk. The problem with the elk skin was caused by nothing more than greed from the tannery.

The problem was that there were only a limited number of elks "culled" each year in Scandinavia and the increased need for elk suede from the US. fire glove manufacturers had resulted in the only supplier making double splits instead of a single split from each hide. This resulted in a middle split which always contained weak leather that fell apart. The strength of leather is through the crisscross pattern of the fibers within the hide. A middle split has areas where this doesn't happen and instead, the leather fibers are straight and as a result, has no strength.

I introduced a new glove with a "top grain" outer leather shell and after rushing to get it certified, our increased sales began to reduce the damage that had been done. I stood behind our market and replaced all gloves that were damaged, even replacing many that were not, but had been supplied together with some that were bad.

We replaced in total six times the number of failed gloves returned to keep hard-won customers from leaving us. If they bought thirty-six pairs and had a problem with only one glove, I replaced all thirty-six pairs to keep their confidence in the company.

This leather problem affected our profitability and we were lucky that it didn't close the company down. But, because of the immediate action taken in reengineering a new product, we were still in business though barely.

The board was not impressed at the loss of profit and didn't bother to understand that we were very lucky that we still had a company at all as this had affected all companies selling elk-skin gloves. All the board cared about was the monthly profit that they could take out. "You'd better get this fixed and damn fast!" growled Joe in the board meeting following my redesign of a replacement glove.

The First Lean Glove Company

I had to reduce manufacturing costs significantly if we were going to be able to stay in business as the company was barely breaking even every month in summer from June till September because of the low demand in summer for fire gloves, there was nothing I could do about that. It was a seasonal factor in the fire industry. I contacted the Arkansas Department of Economic Development to see if they could help us. Then after coming to the factory they told us that we needed to introduce LEAN manufacturing, which was a very advanced form of production started by the auto industry, to increase production without increasing costs.

After going to several seminars on the LEAN process, I decided to introduce this into the company as fast as possible. We began the process in April 2004 and had it completed by July 2004, which was itself a small miracle. Together with all the staff we cleaned the factory, painted all the machines, threw out all of the old leatherworking weekends to complete the daunting task.

We moved everyone into production teams and the new LEAN process was a huge success for us. When we had finished the process, we had successfully reduced costs by 30 percent, reducing the number of gloves we made. I also moved the operation away from "piece-work" which only a few of the staff were able to do well but most could not.

Piece-work forces staff to work flat out as fast as possible all day long with a very low base pay, each worker having to rely on a bonus based on how many units they made. The problem was that since most of the female sewing staff could not work fast enough to get their high production-based "piece" rate bonus, set deliberately high by Frank Sturm, many years before, they were instead on base pay only which Sharon and Frank had kept to $6.30 per hour, this was not enough to even keep any family in food and clothing.

The only way they could make money was through sewing at high speed, for eight hours per day. Many could not even feed their families on what Glove Corp paid them, but what did any of the owners care about that! They were the ones that had kept their staff down and below a livable wage. I hated what this had done to the hardworking staff they had in their factory, now my factory.

I changed this archaic system, leftover from the last century and instead I got all my staff onto a production bonus while increasing their base pay significantly I then added a quality bonus on top of that. They now worked in teams together reaching a common production and quality goal that was easily achievable.

We measured each of the standard sewing times it took to sew every glove component and made the "standard time" based on an average sewing speed that they agreed they could manage all day long. This by the way was slower than the speeds set by Frank, but his system caused huge quality errors, mine would not.

If they were able to sew to the standard time, they would make a good bonus and considerably more than they were getting before. I set up a new wage scale which gave them increased incentive points of base pay plus extra pay for time served in the company.

The factory now looked good, had a good atmosphere and was operating very well; people were finally smiling and the atmosphere was becoming much more positive and nothing like what it had been under Frank and Sharon!

Some Technical Problems

I now had to develop a new breathable barrier for the inside of our firefighting gloves and began work on this immediately. Our moisture barrier was not breathable and W L Gore who had a large share of our market had refused to sell us their breathable moisture barrier. Which was inside all other US. made gloves.

I found a UK company making a flame-retardant blood-borne pathogen barrier that could go inside our firefighting gloves. We met at Kings Lynne in Norfolk. The company had a breathable barrier that was far superior to our existing barrier. After months of development, working on adhesive issues, we finally had a breathable barrier, but their quality was inconsistent, which made their barrier often pull out of the glove, a problem that had dogged Glove Corp for years before I joined the company, a problem that Frank had never resolved.

So I needed to develop a new adhesive system and I needed it fast. At that time there was a huge manufacturing show in Germany. One of my contacts, from the UK, called me and gave me details of a system that he had seen there that could be used to get a better adhesion for the barrier and lining inside the gloves.

After months of development, I had finally designed a system that would work extremely well and that would allow us to get a thinner, more flexible barrier inside our gloves with a unique adhesive system that would, in turn, allow us to make firefighting gloves with better dexterity than any on the market. More importantly, it offered a superior end product than any that existed.

The system I developed was state of art and would never allow the lining to pull out of the glove. We now had a superior product to the mighty gorilla, the Crosstech® brand and we had a far more technically advanced glove system that would revolutionize the firefighting glove market. We had fixed all problems in one go; we had a new breathable barrier and a new advanced adhesive system.

A Board Like No Other!

I presented the new system to the board to get an agreement to purchase the new adhesive system, but the board, as expected, was reluctant to spend the money. I explained that we would lose our glove business because our gloves had always suffered from a bad reputation for liners pulling out. I had already spoken to Rob to get his support.

With Rob's help, the board reluctantly agreed to buy the new system which we immediately set up.

I called the new system *"Glove Bond"* and began to market the system to all of our customers, making cutaways of the glove so that they could see how the new high-tech design worked and to explain to the firefighters our new and unique improvements.

Our market share began to climb significantly, however, staff issues were still a problem in Heber Springs since the new hires did not want to work and despite the pay and health benefits we offered, they were always quitting.

We were still replacing 50 percent of our staff annually which meant we were always training new hires. I think that it was a problem of the area we were in, an Arkansas problem, and something I couldn't change without moving the factory to another location.

Our new glove system was winning increased business and I had innovated another new process which was a high-temperature labeling system where instead of having a huge NFPA label sewn into each glove that got in the way of getting the fire gloves on and off. Our new label used a flat flexible label that was bonded onto the glove and couldn't be removed—another first for us.

Hard work does pay off but only when coupled with focus, vision and a determination to succeed no matter what!

A MILITARY OPPORTUNITY

My strategic plan was now in operation exactly as I had envisioned it years before.

IN 2003, ONE year after the invasion of Iraq, I was contacted by the Research and development headquarters of the U.S. Army, in Natick Massachusetts, who informed me that I was the only "certified" glove designer in the entire USA!

They wanted me to take part in a new military program called a Rapid Field Initiative or RFI to improve the handwear and uniform apparel for our forces now fighting in Iraq. The technical committee I was to join included W L Gore (Crosstech), DuPont, Nomex, Kevlar and many other advanced materials manufacturers plus a few glove importers and we were all charged with designing and producing better apparel for our military.

During the first meeting, we were asked to place our cell phones on the table in front of each of us. When we did this the meeting leader showed us a mobile phone used at the beginning of 'Desert Shield' and 'Desert Storm' war just ten years before. It was a large bag phone; we all laughed but the point, as he explained to us, was that weapons and warfare had changed as much as these phones have changed. We all got the message loud and clear!

I was one of a very few glove makers and the only certified glove designer in that technical group and I liked the challenge. During these meetings, I met with many manufacturers who made various military clothing from boots to Kevlar bulletproof vests and body armor.

Glove Corp was the first and only LEAN manufacturer in the United States, making gloves and because of this some of the military R & D staff wanted to come down to meet us and to see our factory. We began making, under contract, combat and other military gloves which were very advanced, high dexterity multi-material gloves and required a far better sewing technique than that which we had been used to while making gloves in the industrial and firefighting market.

I had meetings with the entire factory staff, early in the mornings to win the staff over and to explain that if we were to survive in glove making in the United States and if they were all to keep their jobs, we had to learn new skills and widen our knowledge.

We began to manufacture these new gloves for Camelbak and Wiley X and were now advancing our methods into becoming the best in the United States. The Camelbak glove was difficult so they sent someone to get us started who had no idea how to sew at all. Still, we moved forward into very high-end products. I was then asked to design a new "light duty utility glove" that would eventually go into every kit bag for every GI in the U.S. Army and I was given several samples from which to design a new glove.

I started designing the new military glove and finished it in 2006, sending samples to the R & D headquarters and their management team who were responsible for acceptance of the new glove products for the army.

After evaluating the new glove in their labs at Natick they ordered three thousand pairs to be sent all over the world for field testing by the military personnel who would be wearing our designed gloves. I told our board during one of the bi-monthly meetings about the new opportunity, but all they wanted to know was how many and what would be the profit.

This was all they wanted to know about with any of the things we were doing in their company and for the next three years during any board meeting they would continuously ask me "So where's the military order?" One owner, Tom, another family member, and a complete idiot, even accused me of taking the design somewhere else! We were steadily rebuilding the operation and improving our production methods. But we still had problems with staff losses every week. Pat and Keith had grown in their knowledge of production but still needed all the help they could get.

Keith had managed operations in Jamaica with nine hundred staff making shirts as well as in Mexico with five hundred staff. Pat, his wife, had been in manufacturing and had been in the front office when I took over the company.

As time went on, I promoted Pat into the factory to assist Keith where she had been key in implementing LEAN and had grown as a manager with more responsibility.

Keith was a good manager, who wanted to retire and didn't need the job or the money but Pat wanted to continue to grow and to learn more about advanced production methods. Neither the head office nor the board and owners had any idea how hard Pat and Keith worked, every day to keep the factory running neither did they even care!

In an effort to fix this disconnect, after many years working together in this disjointed way, I instructed the 3 head office staff to come to the factory to see all the improvements that had been made there. I gave them three months' notice, but as the time approached, they grew increasingly more negative about the visit. I knew that they had given the factory such a hard time over the years, through ignorance, that they had painted themselves into a corner. I cared nothing of the situation caused by the head office staff and told them that if they backed out they would be looking for another job, period!

They finally decided to go under the threat of being fired and I drove them by car as none of them wanted to fly.

We arrived at the factory at around four in the afternoon and as soon as we went through the entrance Sharon made a comment to Pat and Keith who had spent hours upon hours, evenings and weekends, in cleaning, painting, reorganizing and completely transforming the operation. Sharon's comment was heard by all those that were within earshot that she "saw nothing different" and that it looked the same as she had seen several years earlier!

She didn't care for the factory or the staff that paid her wages! Our customers had seen the turnaround, so had the Arkansas Manufacturing Systems staff who had been instrumental in getting us into LEAN as well as the Arkansas Department of Economic Development who had seen the considerable improvement, but apparently not Sharon!

I had had enough and asked the board to allow me to replace the three head office staff and to relocate it to Heber Springs. I showed them that it would save us $9,000 a month in unnecessary costs and that none of the head office staff had any knowledge that was worth keeping as they never had offered anything that would help improve the company. The board flatly refused to allow me to make the very necessary changes, which was strange in that these costs savings would go directly to them. I thought there must be another reason.

We "apparently" kept losing money or at best, breaking even, despite all the cost savings that I had made in decreasing factory costs by 33 percent while increasing the profitability of the gloves we were now making, eliminating all the non-profitable models. Nevertheless we were at best, breaking even and not making a profit which did not make sense to me. Where are the profits going?

I was for the most time fighting the continued negativity coming from the head office staff. They didn't communicate with each other despite sitting no more than ten feet apart for decades. I had too much to do to keep this company moving forward.

It was, to say the least, an uphill struggle working to improve that company, but I wanted to do what I set out to do, despite the nasty board and owners, to make it the biggest glove operation in the United States—that was my personal goal. Boy, this was the worst job I had ever taken on!

Sometimes it is the accumulation of good work that leads to unexpected rewards.

VACATION WITH GEORGIA

One week with my daughter would bring decades of memories

GEORGIA CALLED ME, while I was in the middle of everything, to see if we could have a holiday together and wanted it to be in the States. I thought what a great idea! She and I could spend some great time together and as I had customers on the northeast coast that I had planned to visit I could certainly take her with me. I arranged to fly her over to Boston where I would pick her up and I would mix business with pleasure in a trip to Maine.

She told me she was three months pregnant and this would be the last time for a very long time that she could be a single girl and able to have a holiday with just me and her.

I began to plan the trip, so I looked for hotels finding one that was, according to the online brochure, right on the beach. I called and asked the owner, who was Australian, "Are you saying that the hotel is right on the beach?" And he said, "Yea, mate, right on the beach." "So, it's right there with no other building that you're not mentioning in front between your hotel and the beach?" "No, mate nothing." "So, if I book it, there's sand coming into the room as it seems in the brochure?" "Yes, yes and yes." He said, "Now either book it or not, but let me know either way," I booked it and hoped he was telling the truth. I next had to book a car, so I rented a convertible and hoped that the weather would hold; it was after all the middle of summer.

Georgia finally made it and I couldn't wait to see her, as it had been some two years since we had seen each other. I was very, very happy to be spending a whole week, just her and me. As she came through Boston Airport, I met her at the passenger exit from the international terminal.

We hugged for at least an hour and just stood there letting the world go by as we both said nothing just to let that one moment linger. I wished Amanda could have come too, but unfortunately, that wasn't to be. We picked up the convertible, a white Sebring, which was going to be perfect for our week together as we headed north from Boston and up the coast toward Maine. We decided to meet up with Annabelle, Ian's sister who I had not seen since she was a teenager and who now lived in Newhaven which was about an hour north of Boston.

Annabelle and her family, lived in an artsy house close to the coast and later that evening we all went to walk along the beach; Annabelle her husband, Forest, Georgia and myself. Georgia wanted to know all about my childhood and Annabelle talked about Ian herself and me filling in details as we walked.

Forest taught dramatic art at Yale and had a good musical talent, so I played one of his guitars and sang some songs for them and their two children, Rye and Keele. We stayed the night and left the next day to get to the hotel I had booked near Oyster Bay on Old Orchard Beach, which I hoped would be perfect.

We said our goodbyes and left the following morning to drive up the coast road listening to music along the way; the weather was perfect, hot, dry and sunny and I knew Georgia was making a memory of us both together as father and daughter which would last forever!

We arrived at the beach and found our hotel which was right on the sand as promised. The hotel was a two-story building and faced the ocean, with the beach actually at the doorway of our room. The owner hadn't exaggerated at all and the hotel was perfect.

Old Orchard Beach was a stretch of miles and miles of golden sandy beach that arced around the sea forming a very long wide bay. All Georgia wanted to do was to walk along the sand with me and talk about our past together going over her memories and filling in the missing details, I loved it and I love her very much. At night we drove into Portland to find some restaurants and pubs which were very prevalent there. I told Georgia that I had always wanted to spend some quality time with her, just the two of us, exactly like this.

We stayed at that beach hotel for four days, walking, talking and swimming and I took some beautiful pictures of Georgia by Oyster Bay in the sunset just when the sky was a deep reddish-purple reflecting on the still water of the bay. There were fishing boats in the background and as I took the shot I noticed just behind Georgia a fisherman casting out, perfect. We later took a leisurely drive back to Boston and stopped off at Kennebunk and Kennebunkport an area known for its beautiful homes and the mass of flowers in the town center, where I took a photo of Georgia surrounded by flowers.

Along the way back as we went on to Boston airport, talking and singing to the music, in our convertible Sebring we were completely oblivious of anyone else and just before we reached Boston

International Airport, Georgia asked what Boston was famous for. So I told her that present-day it was lobsters. "Let's get some and take them home to eat," she said on the spur of the moment when we were only ten minutes from the airport. As luck would have it, just at the moment she said that we came across a low white building on the side of the road advertising "Live Lobsters Hundreds to Choose From," and I immediately swung into its small car park. They advertised fresh live lobsters ready to ship to anywhere in the world! (I hoped that Included Indianapolis,) so in we both went and saw six huge tanks teeming with live lobsters of all sizes.

I knew nothing of picking out a lobster and asked the owner if he could pick out two big ones for us which he did. Georgia was fascinated to see the writhing creature as it was picked out of the huge tank and placed carefully into a box of dry ice. The two lobsters should be enough for all of us they were huge. We were both going back to Greenwood before I went back to London with Georgia on business where I could spend time with Amanda.

We arrived home in Greenwood complete with our two huge lobsters sitting outside by our pool in the back garden. The dinner was perfect and Georgia got to spend some quality time with James and Nicky, as she hadn't seen them both for several years. After two days at home, we left for London where I stayed at Amanda's house for a week.

That time was the best time I ever spent with my daughter Georgia; it was meant to be and it was perfect. We had driven up the coast on a warm sunny week in a convertible; we went to restaurants and pubs and we walked along the beach in the hot sun. We both knew that may be the only time we would spend together for a long time.

I learned more about my now grown-up daughter in one week than in a thousand conversations over the phone.

MORE HURDLES

Many companies try to push their customers to buy their sometimes, inferior products, instead of making better products.

I KNEW WITH certainty that if we were going to keep the company going, we had to design something like an American-made competitor to the imported gloves from China and India now coming into the US. market. I didn't believe that customers should "Buy American" simply because something is made here, but only if it is as good or better than what is being imported. Well, that was my decision—to make a better product and to do it in our factory, which would make it an American-made product.

I began to design another new glove from scratch, not just one, but a family of gloves—something that none of my competitors had done yet. I never bothered about my competition or what they were doing, but instead, I focused entirely on what I needed to do and in doing that left them to worry about me and not the other way around.

I got all of the gloves in our market from all of our competitors and placed them on a table in the factory. I then asked my staff to try each pair and compare them with ours. I asked them what the difference was, but they could find little difference between ours and our competition. Every one of them looked the same! No wonder foreign competition was now filtering into the biggest firefighting apparel market in the world.

Following their response I then brought out the new glove from Pakistan and asked them to now compare all of the gloves with this new one, passing it around from person to person.

Factory staff usually only ever saw their own products and seldom, if ever, the competition's. They saw the difference immediately in quality and sewing. I then called the whole factory out and showed them what I was seeing and asked them what they thought. They told me that although the glove seemed better, it couldn't compete with ours as, according to them, we had "such a history in the firefighting market." I explained to them all that it was already here and that it had taken a chunk out of our sales and that if it continued, they would not have jobs anymore.

I told them that we were going to design a new range of gloves to beat the competition and that I would need their help to do this. They unanimously agreed, so I laid out to them all what we had to do. I told them it had to have no seams on the fingertips, no seams between the fingers, had to be very soft with excellent dexterity, yet with exceptional protection and finally, it had to have a thumb positioned so you would feel like you were wearing almost nothing.

Innovation That Worked

I developed the new glove which I was going to call *"Blaze Fighter"* often doing a lot of the work at home on weekends as I was too busy helping run the factory which was getting harder and harder as we tried in vain to keep a more stable staff level.

I finally had the glove design I wanted and it looked very cool and was nothing like any other product on the market. The glove was a totally new concept and no other product on the U.S. market was even close to my radical design.

The back was made of black military-grade Kevlar, with several layers underneath to make the thermal protection to the firefighters as high as possible. There were no seams on the fingertips, no seams between the fingers, a three-dimensional pre-curved design that fitted perfectly to the hand and was the most advanced firefighter glove design on the U.S. market. The dexterity was unbelievable and the whole process had taken me some seven hundred hours, most of which was done at home to get the job done.

I had to get the glove tested and certified and after several additional modifications and another two months of work on the design, we finally had a newly certified firefighting glove. I had laid out a set of design criteria onto a clean piece of paper and had created something that was U.S.-made and so superior to anything else in the market. I hoped that firefighters, would not want to buy gloves made overseas, especially from Pakistan.

I also made a second glove which was even more advanced and was a dual-purpose firefighting and extrication glove to be used with extracting victims from vehicles involved in road accidents. I had two glove designs and got them both certified within three months which was a miracle since the certification process especially for a brand-new product was usually a real problem. I had done it though, to my amazement. I had designed not one but two brand-new products.

Our new *Blaze Fighter* gloves had finally passed the NFPA testing process, so I let everyone know in the factory that we were now ready to go to market with our new gloves.

I took the final version of the gloves around the factory to each of my employees. The final glove was black on the back and palm with bright yellow leather between the fingers and a yellow knuckle patch on the black Kevlar back. It was like nothing else in the market, so I let all my staff try on the new gloves, thanking all those that had been involved in the development, reminding them that while they loved the new gloves now, they would probably hate it later when they were making more than a thousand pairs a day! I always involved my factory staff in both the successes and the failures of our products and our market, letting them know, in early meetings usually at 5:50 a.m. with all the staff present, what the issues facing our company were.

W L Gore had refused to supply us with their breathable barriers and tried very hard to force us out of the firefighting glove market, but they had no idea of the power of 'One' and that was me!

The Launch

I launched the *Blaze Fighter* at the biggest fire equipment trade show in the United States, the FDIC, in Indianapolis in May 2008. I asked the board to let me have some advertising money from our disused line of credit that we had for more than ten years, but they flatly refused, as it would reduce their monthly dividend.

So I made 80 pairs and sent each pair to our top 80 distributors and waited to see what would happen. During the launch at the FDIC in Indianapolis in 2008, the glove was a resounding success, so I had asked Pat and Keith to travel to Indianapolis from Arkansas, to be present at the show to talk about the work that had gone into the development as PR.

I called Sharon and asked her what our sales were like for the two *Blaze Fighter* gloves, although she probably knew, she said she needed to check and call me back. When I got no call back I e-mailed her and asked her for the numbers. She finally told me we had sold $1 million in less than six months. I was elated and made sure that I told all the factory staff of our success.

Before we had launched the new glove the company had been making losses each month as a result of the impact from overseas competition. However, by the end of 2009, only eighteen months after the initial launch, we had turned the significant losses in 2008 into a 'significant' profit and all because of the *Blaze Fighter* glove.

I had designed a total of twelve new products for the company, installed a new and advanced LEAN manufacturing process, developed and built a high-tech adhesive system like nothing that had ever existed in the U.S. glove manufacturing. I had done it all to ensure that each problem we had encountered had been dealt with effectively. If ever I encountered a problem, I would fix it to a better level than it was before the problem existed.

In short, we were now "kicking ass," and before the board meeting in January 2009, I had asked Rob for a raise. I had not had a raise since 2003 and gas prices, food prices, mortgages and everything else had gone up significantly. Rob promised to do something as I had managed to turn the company around.

However, my pay was never brought up in the board meeting, despite an outstanding year-end result and despite a near-fatal prior position in our marketplace. What had passed them by was the fact that we had managed to save the company from imminent closure over and over again and had instead placed ourselves in a position of potentially becoming the biggest glove manufacturing company within the United States, still, read on! Worse was yet to happen! But for me, I had started to, "cross the bridge!"

Pine Bluff Prison

We still had a serious problem in finding staff at the Heber Springs operation and the town of Heber Springs was unwilling to offer any help, or even bother to come to see all of the improvements we had made. So I had to find another solution as our glove sales were increasing and we had an even worse problem with staffing the production lines. That was easier said than done, so I called for help to the one single organization that had helped us in the past. I called the Arkansas Department of Economic Development (ADED) and they came immediately to meet me once again at the factory.

I explained we were not able to keep our staff, despite having great products. I should say here that again we are given all the tools we will ever need to succeed, but it's up to us to make sure we use them. I knew that ADED had a vested interest in seeing our company succeed and would help us find a solution. The town of Heber Springs was uninterested in Glove Corp as too much damage had been done by Frank and the board in keeping the company as a "sweat Shop" long before I had ever taken the company over.

ADED set up a meeting for me to meet the board of the Arkansas Dept. Of Corrections. We met them two weeks later and were invited to go to a correctional facility (prison) in Pine Bluff which was two and a half hours south of Heber Springs. I had never been inside a prison and this was a real experience. All the inmates were dressed in white prison uniforms and walked around the compound to and from their jobs in small groups behind armed guards.

I took Pat with me as Keith had to stay to manage the now very busy factory. We got through the security guards and finally after a lot of information about the prison dos and don'ts and the federal laws of what we could do and couldn't do while we were inside the facility. The room that they had set aside for us was around five thousand square feet and was empty but had air-conditioning, an office, a bathroom and a prison guard who would sit behind a desk every production day. The whole prison facility was a large sprawling operation located in a wooded area with tall trees, sprawling buildings and of course numerous high barbed wire fences everywhere.

The Pine Bluff campus had dusty roads, grassy areas, sprawling buildings and each was area separated by ten feet high razor-wire fence. While working outside, the inmates were always covered by guards with heavy carbines riding on horseback, always watching over the many inmates of which there were upward of over one thousand at Pine Bluff.

Just outside our building was a guard post comprising a tall round, gray-colored concrete tower, some forty feet high, with a windowed office that had 360-degree visibility. The part I thought that was funny was the fact that once they started their daily watch, they were not allowed down under any circumstances. Each tower guard had to pee in a bucket which was hoisted up and down, on a rope at regular intervals, as well as the prison food that they were given during the day. The doorway was locked and was not opened until their watch had finished when they were replaced by another armed guard.

I asked the warden who accompanied us to our potential facility, "What if they have diarrhea, what do they do then?"
He looked at me coolly and said, "They order more buckets." It was funny though, I thought if I wanted to escape I would give them a heavy dose of laxative and watch the fun.

To get to our building, we had to go through the metal screening process, leaving our cell phones and all other objects at the front office. We then waited for each of the five locked gates to be unlocked by a guard in order to get to our factory space.

Our room had several security cameras covering 100 percent of the room with a small army of guards watching us the whole time. We even had our own prison officer to remain with us while we were setting things up.

We began with fifteen inmates to see if it would work. The staff we had here, of course always showed up for work, were never "ill" with a Monday morning sickness that devastated our Heber operation but they would become well again on Tuesday as our Heber Springs staff were often prone to do.

Each inmate was paid State minimum wages of $7.15 per hour of which some of their earnings went to the victim's fund, some went to their upkeep, the remainder was banked for them unless they had a judgment in which they had to pay some reparation or support to their family. They could spend their money in the concessionary store on Thursdays and had to line up early on these days to go over on their weekly visit to buy things using the money they had earned.

We set up some pre-screening criteria in which we would only accept inmates who had been nonviolent while doing time and who had not had any serious infractions while inside. We also insisted that each potential hire had at least a General Education Diploma (GED).

Nicky Joins The Company

We needed more help and I managed to convince Nicky, who had been struggling with drugs, to work with me at the factory for good pay. He needed to be shown some responsibility and to feel that he was needed and was earning his own money. I convinced him to at least come with me to the factory and see if he could do the work. Nicky responded well to Pat's guidance and was given some responsibilities after a few weeks.

We had at that time won a contract for a high dexterity military combat glove which was nothing like anything we had made before. The glove was in camouflage green leather and had a very hard polycarbonate contoured molded knuckle piece on the back.

Nicky helped with the design of an adhesive process for the knuckle which required an infrared heating system. He managed and operated a small production line of workers to attach the hundreds of knuckle pieces every day. He did this with no effort and the staff he was responsible for liked working with him. I took him with me every Sunday night and got home late Thursday or early Friday with Nicky sleeping most of the time along the way.

He responded very well to the responsibility we had given him and began to get off drugs which was a monumental effort for him. I thanked God for the opportunity to turn him around and hoped he would stick with it.

Pat took Nicky to Pine Bluff prison with her where, after he was given his, "prison contractor pass" he worked to design an aptitude test whereby each inmate had to control the operation of a sewing machine to make the sewing foot follow several bold black lines drawn on a piece of cream-colored material, controlling the sewing machine properly.

There were no sewing needles in these test machines, but Nicky explained to each potential hire how to operate the machine and how to lift, turn and sew while following the drawn lines on the fabric as exactly as possible. Nicky would time them for fifteen minutes and see how they followed his instruction and if their speeds increased.

He also observed them during each interview process and gave Pat some insightful observations while watching each interviewee's behavior during the interview.

Pat told me that he was very observant and possessed a good understanding of people, noticing a lot in body language that Pat missed. She relied on his input and if Nicky didn't think an inmate would work out she didn't hire that person. She and Nicky got along very well and Nicky was responding positively to the experience.

The work had given him responsibilities and he had risen to the task. This experience was a key item now on his resume. His brief spell working in my environment taught him what real responsibility was all about.

The Prison Operation

The prison operation at Pine Bluff Arkansas rapidly outgrew that facility as we now had 55 inmates so we had to move our operation to Newport Prison in Arkansas during 2009. We had begun with only fifteen inmates as a trial operation.

It was impressive seeing 55 inmates all dressed in white, sitting at sewing machines and doing well at their work. They had to operate at full production capacity for four ten-hour days with Fridays off.

A Debt Paid In Full

Just after Christmas 2009, one of the inmates spoke to me as he was working sewing palms to backs. "Can I talk to you, Mr. Tony?" he asked, as that was how they all addressed me. "Yes," I replied, "but keep on sewing as we are under constant surveillance." He went on, "I've done some pretty bad things in my life," (he had 3-tear drops on his face) the inmate had been a gang-banger and was doing well in one of my production lines. "But one thing I truly regret," he said, "was that my sister had given me $1,500 for college fifteen years ago, she has never had much money, but I got caught doing some bad things and ended up here," he told me.

"Is this going somewhere?" I asked him and he replied, "Yes, it is," he replied and continued to talk quietly to me so as not to draw attention to his conversation. He went on, while sewing, to tell me that just before Christmas he asked the warden how much money he had in his prison bank account and was told that he had $2,500 accumulated as he never spent any money at the concession shop.

"I have never had that much money ever in my life," he told me. "and I knew what I had to do. I asked the warden if he could find my sister in Alabama and find a way to give it all to her," he said. He went on and told me that just after Christmas he got his first visitor in fifteen years. It was his sister coming to see him.

"I saw her for the first time in fifteen years," he said, she told me that both she and her husband had been laid off at the Tyson chicken processing factory and had no money at all. She told him they were about to lose their house and maybe their children may have to go into care until they could get themselves straightened out. "Then suddenly, she said, $2,500 came to me out of the blue, from you from prison!" she said. "And after all this time it came just when we needed it most. Thank you so much!" she told him. "You saved our family and you did it while you were inside prison."

I could see that the guilt of that debt he had carried had now been paid off in full, though there was still the reason he was inside to deal with. "So that's a good thing then," I said to him adding, "so please just keep doing exactly what you are doing and keep focused on this." "I will," he said, "and I am sending her every penny I make here each month to help her. Thank you, Mr. Tony, for giving me this chance!"

Something good came from our work there while making gloves at the prison. Just as an afterthought though, despite this, whenever

I had to do a "time out" for the fifty-five inmates, I always made sure that the exit door was just behind me and that it was wedged open with an armed guard standing next to me . . . Just in case!

Some risks are worth taking and if the only downside is a little difficult to get it done, then it's still definitely worth it.

NEW YORK NEW YORK!

It was now time to be in the big league!

BLAZE FIGHTER SALES were now climbing in 2009, from the *Blaze Fighter*, samples had been given to FDNY which was the biggest fire department in the world with around eight thousand firefighters. Every equipment company making firefighting products would love to have FDNY as a key account. This was not only the biggest department but also the busiest the most prestigious in the world. FDNY was also the toughest for any company to get their products into.

I presented my glove explaining how the design was different from any other in the market. One strange thing though was that around this time, I noticed that all of my *Blaze Fighter* patterns had been removed from my computer over one weekend. A whole file left on my desktop and Pat's computer had gone. I mentioned it to Pat and Keith but got no response. It didn't matter much though as I had all the knowledge in my head and didn't need hard copies at all. But it was a warning of what was to come.

If I was to have even a slim chance of winning FDNY I had to explain to them how my design was superior to Gore's breathable barrier. Gore's product was in 70% of all US-made gloves. They had threatened my competitor Shelby that if he continued to make gloves with another barrier they would "divorce his company," so he stopped using other barriers. Glove Corp was now the only U.S. glove manufacturer not using the inferior Gore barrier.

5 Super Heroes

I took some samples with me and had a meeting set up with five of the heads of the FDNY's research and development group, through which any and every product that FDNY wanted to use had to go through to be thoroughly tested before a decision was made. The head of the glove project and I worked very closely together.

I made a presentation at FDNY's at their Randall's Island research facility with my local representative, sitting next to me.

That first meeting took me one and a half hours to complete. During this time, I managed to convince them that our manufacturing system was far more advanced than what was being offered by any of the other glove companies who were still using Gore's Crosstech® barrier.

"Why don't you use the Crosstech® barrier?" one of them asked me, so I told them that we were the only glove company in the entire United States that Gore had refused to sell their barrier to, but I didn't know why. I also explained that Gore's senior staff who worked with fire and military markets even sat in the same military glove committee meetings as I had and had told me that "they make fillet mignons, while Glove Corp makes McDonald's." That gave them all in that important meeting a real laugh. I also told them of the design work I was doing for the U.S. Army for several gloves used for combat operations, light-duty utility, and razor wire handling and that did it.

They told me this was a very important part of what we had to offer and that when the time came I had to make sure I mentioned this to the fire chiefs I would meet after they had completed their internal testing of the glove.

The testing went very well and the glove had proven itself to be all that I had said it would be. I was called back to New York again to meet with five of the busiest fire chiefs in the world, located at various fire stations in New York City, to present the glove to them. There would be three other companies who had also become the finalists in the ability to supply a new style of firefighting glove. These were the "on-scene battalion chiefs" that had managed to deal with the terrorist attacks on 9/11 and who had lost many of their firefighters.

I was introduced to the five of them as they entered the room, all were dressed in crisp white shirts and they each shook hands with me, looking me straight in the eye as they did so. I felt in awe of the five of them, as they sat there in front of me in their white uniform shirts with their medals, from 9/11 which was just 8 years prior and with their fire captain's badge on their chests. It was a humbling experience to be discussing the design and concept of my glove with them, for it was their choice as to which glove they would decide to wear. This meeting was a highlight in my present career and naturally, I didn't want my glove to fail.

I said a quiet prayer and hoped that I wouldn't screw this up. "Please, God, don't let me fuck this up," I prayed. The five chiefs sat quietly around the large square table in that research and development headquarters by the entrance to New York City on Randall's Island and let me present the glove.

The room went quiet as I began to present the design, how long it took me to complete why I felt compelled to make this new glove, where it was made, testing the final product samples of which I had brought for them to see at the meeting. I mentioned in passing that imported gloves from Pakistan were probably helping our enemies as everyone knew that Osama bin Laden was hiding in Pakistan.

When I had finished my presentation, they asked many questions but seemed happy with what they had learned during our meeting. I left them with 250 pairs of gloves as requested to be used as a field test of the glove and could do nothing more than wait to see the results.

A week later I was called by one of the R&D chiefs who told me that they unanimously agreed that the presentation I had done was the best of the four. That feedback was great news, but now it was up to the glove to perform well which I hoped it would. Well, so far so good, the rest is now out of my hands.

All the work had been completed so we now had to wait for the goal that we had been working towards.

THE U.S. ARMY

Just when you least expect it everything comes together all at once!

JUST AT THE same time as we were working with FDNY, the army glove I had designed earlier was finally being decided upon by the army. Everything was coming together; all the hard work was finally showing fruition.

In the three years since I had completed the design for the new Light Duty army glove the Glove Corp board, whenever we met, had constantly asked where the army order was and why we had not received it yet.

A representative from army Natick headquarters, called me to let me know that my glove had gone to the Pentagon and had been well accepted as a new "kit bag" item which would lead to hundreds of thousands of pairs per year being bought from whoever won the contract to supply the glove. This was a final part in the acceptance of that glove and it was now ready for purchasing which would now happen very quickly. I was asked by the contracting department to let them have all of my size patterns so that they could be digitally reproduced.

During the next board meeting, I told the board that the army glove was going ahead and I had until January 20 to complete all the documentation. Of course, the board members were only interested in knowing how much we would make on each pair and how many we could sell. I told them that we had not won the contract yet and had to bid for the glove and that if we were awarded the contract we would have to invest in new machines and material to get it ramped up into full production.

I decided that since this Light Duty Utility glove was my design, I would do everything I could to win the contract so I asked Pat and Keith to "imagine" us winning it and making the gloves because if they did that, it was going to happen. This was after all the vision I had for this little company, back in 2002, to make it the biggest glove production company in the United States and we were now finally on that path. I completed the documentation and sent our bid proposal out, along with a perfect sample glove, making sure it got there well before the deadline.

Pat came up to me in the factory a few days later and told me of a dream she had several months before in which she saw me standing in the factory surrounded by hundreds of machines and the factory was full of people making thousands of gloves daily. The way she described it I knew when she told me that we would win the order and that we would have more business than we could manage.

We were next visited by a factory inspector from the army who went through our numbers and agreed that we could make the glove in our facility. We won the army glove bid in May 2009! And we were overjoyed at that accomplishment. The board was, for some reason, getting cold feet now after three years of design and very hard work to make it happen. They had been hounding me as to where the order was for the three years since we started the project, now we had won the bid process they realized that they would have to spend money! When we knew we had won the contract, I called a board meeting to let them know we needed investment capital to buy around forty-nine new machines and staff to make the glove. There was no vote of thanks, no well done, no remotely positive statement about all the work it had taken to do this and to finally win the contract. So much for this ungrateful board!

Where I should have felt great I felt lousy and at the very point in time when I should have been happy with all I had done. We knew it would take around twelve weeks to ramp up and we had prepared a ramp-up plan to show the board. We could only bid for 60 percent of the contract as we were a small business but that would still be ten thousand to fifteen thousand pairs a month. I showed the spreadsheet one Saturday morning, to Rob and Allen, but Allen refused to even see it and chose to walk off from the meeting at a Starbucks on the north side of Indianapolis.

After we had won the contract though, I was told that our work was so well prepared that the army contracting office wanted us to make 100 percent of the contract, which was over twenty thousand pairs a month! This was on top of what we were already doing with the now very successful *Blaze Fighter* glove that I had also designed.

The board agreed to let me use our small line of credit to get the army glove line up to speed. We were hiring staff buying leather in and buying more sewing machines to make the vast quantity of army gloves that we now had orders for. I have never been so busy as I was now, but that was fine I knew this would happen. The board though were becoming aggressive while we were ramping up, demanding to know where the profit was. After owning a failing company for 90 years they still understood nothing!

We were near the end of ramping up for the new army glove and completely on time with all we had planned but in December 2009, we naturally showed a loss since we had been training forty-nine new staff members for three months along with purchasing leather to make the new glove. I was now spending 100% of my time on the new military glove line. The board however got cold feet, just before we were fully up to speed, they pulled the plug on the ramp-up funding just as we were a few weeks from full production! They did this because they did not want to continue spending money and due to our staffing issues, we were, not surprisingly, over on our cost estimates.

Anyway, they had stopped us using the line of credit, just when we were almost at the end of the ramp-up phase and had almost reached the point of profitable operation when we were at our most vulnerable point.

Strange that sometimes when you get what you ask for, you actually do get exactly that, which in this case was the biggest army glove contract in the world. Now that they had the contract and had to invest, they were not prepared to see this through.

My *Blaze Fighter* glove continued to become the single biggest-selling firefighting glove in the United States and was now requiring more staff, more sewing machines and more leather cutting machines (clickers) to make them. The correctional facility operation now had fifty-five staff and was humming along. We had moved all the inmates from Pine Bluff to Newport which was a lot closer and easier to get to.

All that Pat had seen in her dream had come true, as we now had 126 staff all making gloves, a factory completely full of staff, thirteen leather cutters cutting more leather than the company had ever cut in its entire 90-year history.

January 2010, the results of 2009 sales and profits were in and we made a very small loss. The *Blaze Fighter* had sold millions of dollars that year, but we had invested in a large new glove line comprising forty-nine new staff and forty-nine new sewing machines where I was now spending all my time to develop. That plus the new materials and the hiring and training of the new staff had cost the company in investment in the new glove line. However, we had a four-year profitable contract to produce thousands of gloves each week from that point forward and the start-up costs have all been concentrated in a three-month period from July to September and were exactly to plan.

The board though had got cold feet and had pulled the plug just as we were entering the final phase of the start-up, with maximum costs and with profitability just weeks away, in doing so had fatally damaged the company.

As a result of their sudden decision in the fall of 2009 not to let us use more from the line of credit, despite having decided to allow us to do so before we began the production, they had created a situation where we were unable, with insufficient funds, to buy leather right at the final stage of ramp-up.

It made the already difficult job of hiring and training the new staff while making a quota of gloves that we had agreed to for the army, almost impossible now. The board meeting was a fiasco, with Joe shouting down the phone as per usual. and the meeting became intolerable. Allen was vocal, yet he was the one board member who had attended the least number of board meetings and a weird person (according to his mom when she visited the factory). Allen had always wanted to run the company.

This would inevitably lead to the company's demise as I would not put up with this situation and more.

On February 12, I received a phone call from our webmaster who had designed our Web Site and who hosted our e-mail system. He told me my email would be cut off the following Monday and as he saw it I was going to be let go on Monday at 8:00 a.m.!" He told me that he had received a phone call from someone at Glove Corp telling him that he was now running the company and that he had to switch off my e-mails at 8:00 a.m. on Monday. Glove Corp. underestimated the number of friends I had around the business to learn of this in advance.

I was not surprised at all as I knew that this would in all probability happen very soon and I was already looking to my next job as I had been for several months.

A $42 Million Interview

Incidentally, one of the interviews I was invited to do was with David Koch the famous billionaire. I went to Massachusetts for an interview, not knowing who it was with until I got there. I was told to hold a copy of Time magazine in my left arm with his face on the front cover facing outwards. This I thought was a code to David telling him I was the one to hire. I was told not to expect more than 3 minutes of his time for the interview. Well, two and a half hours later I came out of David's office to the amazement of his staff sitting in his outer office. David even made a pot of tea for us both! I calculated that interview cost $42 million of his time. I didn't take the job as it was to run an ultrafiltration company and I was done with separation and filtration when I left Alfa Laval.

Undoing Of Glove Corp

After years of fighting with increased competition, improving the factory, installing LEAN and trying to win over Heber Springs City council, I had succeeded in my vision of making Glove Corp the biggest glove-making operation in the United States with lucrative military contracts as well as creating and marketing the biggest selling firefighting glove in the US. market. I had saved the company from disaster many times over and now had to close that door and move on. I was very happy that I had done, all I said I would do and all I had achieved. I was also happy that I never had to travel to the miserable town of Heber Springs again. Leaving at eleven-thirty each Sunday night and not getting back until late Thursday night or early Friday morning.

I called Pat and told her the news; she appeared to be shocked, but I reminded her that I had been warning her that this would happen because of the dysfunctional board. I suspected that she and Keith had already been told.

For me, to close that door was easy and now I was ready to move on which I was going to do with as much energy as I had put into running Glove Corp.

The following weeks I got calls from just about everyone from competitors, from suppliers, from our many distributors, FDNY and from the army contracting office.

Glove Corp won the FDNY contract in April 2010, after all our hard work, to become the sole supplier of gloves to FDNY the biggest fire department in the world. This would secure new business worth millions of dollars. The company had won the contract based on the glove I had designed and all that I had done. However, After I left, my contacts in the purchasing group asked me if I thought Glove Corp. could handle their military business, I told them no, they were incapable of handling the contract. As a result Glove Corp lost the military contract, for the light Duty glove I had designed because

I was no longer there and in doing so had lost an important part of their manufacturing base that could have guaranteed them survival as a preferred supplier to the U.S. Army.

They didn't know that in not wanting to invest enough funds for the contract, they were preparing their demise. This was the final nail in their coffin. The first was from Heber Springs city council in not wanting to help the company with a small grant; the second was passing the company on to a family member who had no experience in running a business and who had never shown any interest in the family business; the third was in failing to fund the military line then, as a result, losing the military contract, which would have given them a second market in addition to the fire market. The company now had all their eggs in one basket and with no technical or knowledgeable leader, they were now heading for a fall.

As for me? I simply closed the door on the 8 most difficult years in turning a business around and walked away. I took time off and had phone calls from all over the country asking me what the hell had happened and what would I do now. I even had a call from my competitors wanting to know what my plans were. I wasn't surprised at all because I had taken market share from all of them and had severely affected their sales. I was now looking for a new career and had to start the work all over again making a new resume, getting back into a new business.

I was relieved and very happy at not ever having to make the ten-hour drive to Arkansas each week and also, at never having to deal with the dysfunctional, nasty Sturm family members that owned the company. I was sad for the employees, as I knew with certainty that the company would fail before too long.

Where was the Profit?

One final afterthought; I had reduced the product line, introduced LEAN manufacturing, saving 33% of labor costs, reduced the fire glove line to making only the gloves that sold well and finally created a firefighting glove that made five times more profit than any glove they had ever sold and which became 80% percent of all their sales. Yet, despite all of these improvements and cost savings, the company apparently still only broke even! I often thought how was this possible. Why had they not allowed me to close down their miserable head office costing $9,000 per month with just 2 people there and with Sharon who was singularly the most negative person in the company and a person who Pat and Keith hated working with.

Could it be that her management of the finances was the reason we were always running at just above break-even, despite all the cost savings and product profitability improvements that I had implemented? We will never know but for me, I could not care less!

Over the next few weeks, many customers, suppliers and fire departments called me telling me that they were shocked I had been let go, apparently I had made my mark.

They were genuinely concerned and wanted to keep me in the fire business. In March that year, I took my family on a much-needed vacation knowing that I still had no job as yet; but they, like me, needed a break from the hard work of building the company up and the stress of having to deal with the nasty owners.

We were in difficult financial trouble now as we had just recently paid for James's college fees while he went to Columbia College in Chicago. Nevertheless, I had to take a break, after all the hard work I had done, so we went to Boca Raton in Florida—Sue, Nicky, James, two friends from James' dance college, Sue's sister, and her new fiancé, Steve, who came over to join us from England; so the family was all together.

OPPORTUNITIES OPENING-UP

One door closes another opens up!

ONE OF MY suppliers had a holiday home in Boca and had kindly offered it to us for free as I had given him so much business. One of my good friends. Jeff Stull, who sat on the NFPA committee had also called me to see if he could help me find me a job in a bigger company keeping me in the industry, telling me that a friend of his had recently become CEO of a very large competitor, a billion-dollar company called Honeywell. Jeff sent me the contact details of the new CEO suggesting I contact him. I sent him an e-mail telling him who I was and that I was the designer and developer of the *Blaze Fighter* glove adding that it had sold over three million in sales. I congratulated him on being the new CEO and asked how his competing "Superglove" had been selling.

Only twenty minutes later, I received a call from Jeff Morris, CEO of Honeywell First Responder company, and the company Jeff Stull had suggested I contact. He introduced himself to me by saying that he was in New York and was about to get on a flight to Chicago when he received my message.

He told me that he almost fell off his seat when he saw who was e-mailing him. "Did you really sell that much with the *Blaze Fighter* glove?" he asked and I confirmed that we had. He told me that he was about to get on a flight and would call me when he arrived in Chicago. He arranged for me to meet him at an upcoming three-year planning meeting in three weeks in Bolingbrook, a suburb of Chicago. It would be a chance to meet his senior team and to see where we went from there. I agreed on the condition that since I was formerly a strong competitor, he would guarantee my safety and make sure I didn't get lynched!

I drove up to Chicago even though we hardly had enough money for the gas for me to get there. Jeff came out to meet me and to take me into the meeting. We went into a large meeting room, with around twenty vice presidents and other senior staff sitting around a large "U-shaped" table with a projector screen at the front of the room. I was asked to tell them about how I designed my glove and what I saw was wrong with their very expensive glove that I had virtually taken out of the market. I was careful with my words but told them I never considered other gloves as competition, I just focused on what I was doing. I also told them of the strategic plan I created and followed into the success of the company.

At the end of my meeting, Jeff and a consultant took me to a small meeting room to offer me a job. Jeff explained Honeywell's market position adding that within two years they would be over a $2 billion company and focused on the global first responder market. This was very different from the $5million Glove Corp! He told me that he wanted me in his organization. I met Jeff four times over the next three months and we had traded numerous e-mails. The obstacle though was my non-compete agreement with Glove Corp which was binding.

We had a final meeting in April 2010 saying that he had never had so many meetings with his legal team but they could find no possible way that I could be hired without a serious risk of the mean-spirited Glove Corp suing both them and me for "tortious interference" with their business. Funny isn't it that Glove Corp had let me go for no reason given yet could prevent me from gaining another job in the same or even remotely similar businesses.

But after three months of communication back and forth between Jeff and me, the deal could not be done to hire me and he told me over lunch just after the FDIC show in Indianapolis, that he was immersed in a huge acquisition and had to focus on that.

Still, I had to get a job regardless even while I was away on a very much-needed vacation. While I was on the beach I got a phone call from one of my former customers, Ron Myers, who owned a company called "Fire force 1" in Ohio, He was away on spring break with his family when he heard what had happened and had decided to call me. He told me, like many other of my former customers, that he was shocked at the news and wanted to help as he recalled that I had helped him in the past.

Ron asked that I send him my resume saying he would help. I sent him my resume and left it at that as I was still disappointed that the deal with Honeywell had not worked out for me as I knew that I could have done very well for that company.

Moving On

Just one week later, after I had sent my resume to Ron, I got an e-mail from the COO of a company called FireDex which was a company that I had come across many times. They were in the same business making firefighting apparel, but I knew very little about them, I had discounted them as a competitor because they had not ever shown up as a named competitor in any of my glove sales meetings with my distributors.

Although they did make firefighting gloves, I had no relationship with Bill Burke, the owner. However, the one resume I sent to Ron from Fire force 1 had been immediately forwarded to Bill's company, "FireDex."

By now, true to form, I had sent out hundreds of resumes, while we were getting further and further behind in the mortgage payments and other bills. My cell phone had been switched off and that was the worst thing to deal with since all of my contacts knew my cell phone number. I called Verizon and after getting many dead ends, I finally got through to a financial controller that I could talk to. I explained that I was out of work and needed my cell phone otherwise it would be impossible to respond to any calls. Finally, I got through to someone in the accounting department and thankfully he agreed to place me on a payment plan, which many people were on anyway and he switched my phone back on.

Now at least I had a connection to my network of friends and colleagues. Thanks to Sean at Verizon, who understood and let me continue with my cell phone.

Soon after my phone was switched back on, I was contacted by FireDex and asked to go to Medina in Ohio, where the factory was located. I drove up to Medina and met the COO, for the first of a series of interviews.

I was shown into the boardroom where I was to be interviewed over several hours including an aptitude and thinking style test. The whole way through the interview process as well as the written communications between me and FireDex, there was agreement that as soon as my non-compete was finished with Glove Corp, I would help them with a new glove program to compete with Glove Corp. Karma is a bitch!

The interesting fact was that no other glove company, United States or overseas, had yet been able to copy my glove design, at the cost we had managed and as a result, there was no other glove like the *Blaze Fighter* currently in the market.

I got the job and started my new job with FireDex in May 2010, so now I had a job and this company unlike my previous one, everyone in the head office, especially the factory, was positive and had common goals and were happy to be there. I wasn't used to that as in the Glove Corp., the head office staff were extremely negative, making it difficult to keep that company going, let alone having fun doing it.

True to form Glove Corp had contacted FireDex for a copy of my job description which we were happy to send them, much redacted!

NICKY 2010

Drugs are a cancer in our society but even this can be overcome with faith.

IN AUGUST 2010, while I was once again getting on with my new career with FireDex, Nicky, now twenty-one years old, had been on drugs to one degree or another since he was fifteen years old. We knew what started it and we both knew that the lovely boy we used to see as a laughing, happy, sometimes mischievous boy with light, blond hair, had long gone.

The drugs had slowly removed our son and replaced him with a gaunt, pale, thin, angry and a very unhappy person we called our son. I prayed for him, in my car going to someplace or other or in a hotel room or whenever I thought of him, which was all the time.

I knew also that was our way as parents, when faced with a problem of this nature like drugs, is often to hit out in anger and frustration at what we could do nothing about except to see the devastating effects on our sweet boy. Nicky was somewhere in the background now, struggling to come forward, but his dependency on drugs wouldn't let him. One hospital mistake had triggered this.

He lost job after job and I could see that his spirits were getting lower and lower with each rejection. These were of course because of his addiction. He had been showing up late or was too tired or as in one case, he had blacked out while at work, all because of drug addiction. We even had to pay to avoid getting him arrested.

All of his friends who had known him since primary school had gradually stopped seeing him, fading away into his and our past and had been replaced by new friends that we didn't know, like, or recognize. The last we saw of his school friends was when we held a twenty-first birthday party for him and around twenty of his old-school friends came over to see him and us.

Now, however, his lifelong friends were replaced and his new" friends" didn't bother to say hello when they came into our house and ignored us while they were here. Things were getting steadily worse for Nicky. I could see that his new "friends" had no interest in anything else other than keeping themselves in friendships with others who had the same needs so that they could be with others that justified their way of life-based on drug use.

Nicky used to be a happy, funny, always an "up to something" little boy, though now as a young man at twenty-one, he had the little visible will to try to get away from drugs; he became a very different person.

His speech became slow and lethargic as did his demeanor, which was getting worse and worse. I kept trying to talk to him but each time, he got angry and embarrassed, which led to arguments, which I wanted to avoid at all costs, as I didn't want him to turn away from the only two people that loved him and cared for him without condition. I prayed for him every day, on the road traveling, on the way home at night, in the mornings and in bed at night.

I do not believe God is only found in a church. I believe God is with us every day, in the store, sitting in my car with me, in fact everywhere so it didn't matter where I asked for help.

One night, Nicky told me he had stolen a little money from our bank account; in fact, he had been doing this for some time, it wasn't a small amount it had accumulated and had drained our cash over a long period of time.

This alone cost us hundreds of dollars and just when we were already flat broke and trying to get our finances back in order, just as we were trying to recover from my being out of work for four months, while we were trying to make ends meet to pay off our debts incurred through being jobless.

We were angry with him, though Sue had known about this for some time and had decided not to tell me, using this as a threat to Nicky in exchange for "good" behavior while at the same time getting us financially lower and lower.

A Change In The Wind

His theft of our money brought the matter to a head. Nicky promised to try to get off drugs and told us how much he hated who he was now and hated what he had done to us. I wasn't convinced; words are easy to say, but it's actions that count, not words.

I encouraged him by telling him he could have a better life but never while he remained on drugs. I told him to look at all of the movies, how many had ever shown the users winning while using. They never did, adding that he was heading that way right now. He had moved from the age of fifteen when he had started smoking weed, to seventeen being on crack cocaine and now at twenty-one had moved on to heroin. Each was more powerful than the last and each took him deeper and deeper, moving further and further from all who loved him. Nicky had gone and we were talking to his drugs, not to him.

One night, when I was coming back from Springfield Missouri; I got a text from James telling me to get home soon as there was trouble at home with Nicky. Great! What can I do—drive faster, maybe go 150 miles an hour or even teleport myself there?

I arrived home and rushed into the house not knowing what to expect and into the middle of a blazing row with Sue and James both shouting at Nicky, while Nicky looking thoroughly pissed off while shouting back. They were all shouting at one another, but no one was listening.

Nicky was trying to defend himself verbally but not succeeding while they were both so angry with him that he resorted to swearing at them both and the situation was steadily getting worse. I looked at what I was seeing—all the noise, the red faces, the anger—and instead of joining the fray I became very calm inside as I tried to decide the next course of action.

I was extremely worried, on watching Nicky's demeanor that this would lead to something uncontrollable happening very soon. I immediately tried to calm everything down by telling them all to stop shouting. I could see their pain, the same as mine, all three of them, their anger and high emotion, getting louder and angrier.

Nicky shouted at us, telling me that he wanted to end his life and would do it whatever we said as he had no hope at all left for him. This again was the drugs talking. He shouted that we all hated him, everyone hated him and so did he, hate himself, and that this was the only way out. That stopped me, dead cut me like a knife through my heart, as he stomped into the kitchen and grabbed a knife from the kitchen drawer to start cutting his wrist.

I ran and grabbed the knife from him. I found it hard to talk for the grief and sheer desperation that I felt for him right then and there and told him, "If you do that, Nicky, I'll die with you. You are so very precious to us all and no matter what you think about us, you always will be our son who we love no matter what, despite what you think."

I found it hard to speak to him but felt compelled to tell him how much we loved him over and over again. "We love you more than you will ever, despite what you think, we all want you to be happy and be in a better place than where you are right now." I'll never forget that moment maybe because it was a breaking point, or maybe because I felt his pain. After all, it was our pain too. I have an empathic nature and at that moment, I could feel his abject loneliness and desperation; but he had to decide to want to do something for himself as a first step then take action to change his life.

I told Nicky that we were all very angry at not being able to help him as he had continually rejected us again and again and also that when we feel so helpless to help him it makes us even more angry and that in turn makes him angry and when that happens we shout, then he shouts back, so we go off repeatedly round and round, the circle, spiraling around getting nowhere.

I tried to calm him, feeling his utter dejection going right through him and my heart went to him, feeling so completely unable to fend off all of us, his family, as well as the drugs in his system. It had affected his speech and thinking, but that aside it was time for action.

Even as I am writing this, the pain of that moment makes me stop and pray for him and for all of us that together we can get him through this as that's what families are for and was what I had given up my own dreams for, to help take care of my family no matter what. I know that he had to make the first move, but we had to let him know that we were here for him no matter what.

These are the times when I am not sure where God is. We ask, even shout at God to help us help Nicky, but nothing changes. Sometimes it's very hard to see the big picture. He went back into the living room and laid down on the floor, physically and emotionally exhausted and after a while, he asked me to massage his back which I did while trying to soothe my son's pain. At that moment, it didn't matter that this was the result of his addiction only that we had to get him into a better place and fast.

As I stayed there with him, I spoke quietly and told him repeatedly how much he meant to us all and how much we all wanted to help him. I told him that all of us shouting only made it worse, so there was to be no more shouting; we had to deal with this but not with anger and accusation. I told him I would never ever stop loving and helping him, but he had to do his part too and that every step was up to him now. He lay there, gradually calming down after the very high emotional outburst; I saw tears in his eyes at my words of love and support and told him that we would never give up on him ever, that we were his family and we would all be with him to get him through this.

I continued to massage his pain and I noticed that he was so thin and had no muscle tone in his shoulders seeming utterly exhausted and drained as he lay there on the floor "coming down" from the raw emotion of moments before.

The following day I had to leave again but called New Hope Church and left a message for Greg Ponchot who was my pastor there. Greg called me back, later on, that day, so I had to pull over in my car to speak to him. I told him what we were dealing with and how much pain this had caused us all and that Nicky had no health insurance, so he couldn't get help through the medical field.

Greg listened and told me he would call a friend of his who had a facility in Bloomington, some twenty miles south of Greenwood that he would call his friend, Eric, who was the contact and I needed to talk to him. Later that day on my way home from Missouri, I got a call from Eric who went to our church and wanted to know all about Nicky's situation. Sometimes, as I have said, things come into my mind to be said that I can't explain at the time but just say words becoming surprised at what comes out. I think these times are some kind of "divine intervention," and I told Eric right out of the blue, that I always kept with me a picture of Nicky's friend Corky McCormick who had died of an overdose several years before. Corky was only eighteen when this happened on his graduation night from Center Grove School.

Eric stopped dead at my words and said, "Wow, that's a blast from my past. I was with Corky that night, I had supplied him with drugs, as I used to be a dealer." He also said that he, Eric, had gotten down low in his life until God had intervened and saved him from what would have been certain death had he continued doing what he was doing.

Eric told me that after he got clean, he realized that he wanted to help others and had started a facility that had more than fifty people going through his program of hard work and "personal change-based" rehabilitation. He said that he had helped ruin so many lives, so now he wanted to rebuild as many as he could.

He explained that Nicky's problem was one of selfishness, that he had only ever done what suited him and not what pleased others, ever and had never put others' needs before his personal needs.

This was news to me but when I thought about what Eric was telling me, it made sense and I agreed with him totally as I had never thought of this as a part of Nicky's root problem; but now it had been said, I could see the truth in those words like a blindingly obvious truth heard from a total stranger. Eric went on to explain, "He does a good job, but only when he feels like it, then either doesn't show up or can't be bothered. He does things that you as parents tell him to do sometimes but then only when it suits him or not at all, often leaving it to the last minute and only after you have told him repeatedly. He sees his parents as his problem and not himself as his problem and has become so selfish that no one and nothing else is important to him other than what he wants for himself." "That's why he has stolen from you because he sees this as your fault, he feels he deserves the money as it's your fault he is in the position he is in," Eric went on to say.

Eric told me that his facility was a one-year program and that once admitted Nicky could not communicate with anyone for three months at all, no drugs, no alcohol, no tobacco, no internet. He would work during the day at homeless shelters, cooking food for the shelters and soup kitchens and generally earning his keep. He would learn to do things as and when he was told and he would learn to put himself last and that he would keep his room spotless. He would learn to do more than what was asked of him, as and when he was told to do it and would have Bible studies and homework to keep him busy day and night. He would have no TV, no books, no media of any sort for the first three months. After this time, he would be allowed to see us once a month, then once a week.

I told Eric that the only thing that Nicky had ever expressed as possibly wanting to do was to become a counselor helping people in need.

Eric told me that if Nicky really wanted to do this, then they could teach him and help him get a degree in counseling and if successful he could then have a well-paid career and this training would be free of charge for him if he responded to their counseling.

A degree! "but Nicky has to make that call himself, you can't do it for him" were Eric's last words to me.

I couldn't believe it! Here was help
of the best kind available and help that would allow us, Sue, James and myself, to get our own lives back on track and to do something for ourselves while Nicky was in a safe place. I called Sue and she told me that "although it's what he needs right now, Nicky won't go for that and you know it."

We talked some more then Sue had agreed to call our doctor, Dr. Jeff, the following day. She did and he had made arrangements for Nicky to see Dr. Jeff the following day at 5:30 p.m. Things were, at last, starting to move, hopefully, in the right direction. I knew Nicky would learn a lot from Jeff. That night, which was Thursday, we got a call from Dr. Jeff. It was now 9:30 p.m. and Nicky had been with him for over four hours.

I put my phone on speaker on the kitchen table so Sue and James could listen. Jeff told us that he had had a very honest and fruitful talk with Nicky and a lot had come out of it saying that he had heard a lot of promising things that he hadn't heard from Nicky for a long time.

Jeff had done a considerable amount of research into male testosterone and its importance in helping the body to heal properly. Jeff had told us that when people start taking drugs, the side effect is that they significantly reduce the testosterone level in men and in turn begin to become laid-back and unmotivated.

This is a common trait among drug users, especially with weed. Weed is a drug that causes this to happen. It is this that causes us to say, "He's a very laid-back kind of guy, seldom gets upset with anything." Bollocks to that! It's the drugs that have done that resulting in slow speech, a slow thought process, lack of memory, lack of willpower, lack of drive and all because of low testosterone caused by drug use.

Jeff explained to us that in Nicky's case the drugs had probably lowered his testosterone to practically nothing, that in turn, that reduction had prevented his "fight" in trying to overcome his drug use. Also that his back pains were probably caused by inflammation along his spinal muscles which couldn't heal because it was being blocked by lack of sleep, lack of testosterone, by using drugs that were all preventing his body's normal immune system from functioning.

Added to this the drugs were, in turn, preventing his immune system from functioning to heal as they were sending false signals to his brain which was not able to make corrections as the signals were not matching up to his normal functionality and as a result, he wasn't healing properly.

I was so happy to hear this and knew that this could be a real breakthrough for Nicky, who was sitting next to Jeff as he was explaining this to us and we hoped it would help get him back, on form, fighting and ready to stop taking drugs.

I told Jeff that Nicky had told me that he didn't take drugs to get high; he said he took them to get by the pain he always felt all over his body. Jeff confirmed again that that was because of the lack of sleep and lack of testosterone which was making him worse.

Dr. Jeff prescribed a sleeping pill and an anti-inflammatory drug that would reduce the back pain. He also said there would be no charge to us for this, he would do a complete blood workup, the following morning, to see what else was happening with Nicky.

Dr. Jeff had also told us that Nicky had spoken of our love and how much he needed this now to offer hope for his future. Nicky arrived home more hopeful than we had seen him in a long time and I was now cautiously optimistic of his chances for healing.

The following day, I sat with Nicky and we discussed a pact together (he was in a better mood that morning). Our pact was very clear; Nicky had to be honest with us if he "used" again, telling us what he had done and we, in turn, would not shout or get angry if he told us the truth and we would help him all we could to become clean. We would, however, from this point on and after he was physically well again, because of Dr. Jeff's help, make him call Eric to be admitted into rehab if he continued to use after all of our help and assistance.

He agreed! Nicky had the chance to get free of his debilitating drug habit with all of our intervention and will need all the help he can get. Eliminating excuses like "pain management" as a "cause" for his drug use will identify this to him leaving only the actual fact of his drug use would be visible if he should fail.

Nicky must have been draining our accounts for a very long time as his habit continued since we seemed to be broke when we should have had enough money to be financially OK. Every day I found a reason to tell Nicky that I loved him and I didn't care if he ignored it; he's going to understand that we are here for him no matter what and we offered unconditional love and support; we are in his corner as all families are.

It's a long road with many miles to go, but one that we can take and reach the end of, by taking one step in front of another and by helping each other as a very strong family unit. From all of our discussions with doctors, counselors, psychiatrists, the pastor at my church, other families, ex-users and even police along the way was that this drug use depends on an individual's personality and certain people have naturally occurring triggers that enable them to become more easily addicted to drugs, cigarettes, alcohol, gambling and any other forms of more passive kinds of addiction. Eventually, these "triggers" will be identified and will be able to be treated in new and more complete ways, but until then we use all the tools we can to get the job done.

I believe that Nicky's drug use was the result of his Stevens-Johnson disease and the mistake at the hospital. It all started at that time and remembering that his reaction to morphine was immediate. But it made no difference now as to the reason why he began except that he had. His addiction had affected all of us. For now, Nicky was moving in the right direction and with Jeff's help was beginning to put on weight as a result of the testosterone he was now taking. We allowed him to stay at home with us for six weeks in order to fight his drug use, but it was a struggle as he was constantly up one minute and down the next.

Sue wanted him out of the house because she had withstood the worst of all of his mood swings and all of his bad behavior, his anger and shouting because he wanted to stay in bed when she had tried to get him up for work, but he was so far gone, then, he couldn't even get up in the mornings to go to work.

I felt the same in wanting him out of the house and was torn between whether we were enabling him or helping him, but either way, he was our son; we loved him and we had to support him because if we didn't he wouldn't survive. This was what we both thought, but then at a deeper level, maybe that was what he needed to reach his bottom level from which he would finally "get it" and begin to get out of his predicament.

In November that year, Nicky found a clinic in Indianapolis that specialized in alternative treatments for drug abuse that was in addition to simple counseling which had not worked. The clinic was on Forty-Sixth Street and they agreed to take Nicky on for treatment.

The treatment was to substitute the heroin, which he had been using, with methadone which was an alternative drug that would gradually reduce his dependence and more especially his craving for heroin which was now his drug of need. We had been told several years before, while Nicky was in rehab when he was fifteen, that most addicts move on from one drug to another often ending on the really hard stuff like heroin or the cheap meth.

Once they come out of rehab and if they get back onto drugs, when they start up again, they will continue where they left off.

He had to go to the treatment center every day and we paid for each daily treatment, which amounted to over $120 each week plus the fact I drove him there every day. He had begun a hairdressing course at Paul Mitchel school and things seemed to be getting better for him but just one day at a time.

I was ever hopeful but not convinced yet. He got up, with difficulty, at 5:30 a.m. each day and both Sue and I tried to make sure that he attended every day since I was always up at 5:00 a.m. He went to the clinic then went on to school for an 8:30 a.m. start. We had to get him his money each day and only gave him the amount for that day's treatment to avoid any possibility of him "storing" money for more drug use.

Around Christmas that year, we had to change our bank accounts, as Nicky had compromised our accounts and had stolen a lot of money from us. Like all addicts, he was doing things driven by his addiction which he had little to no control over.

Not surprisingly, it caused yet another serious problem for us at home and a quiet Christmas for the family. Nicky's habit had to be stopped, but the only one to stop it was him.

Out of our hands at last

Nicky was fortunate to get into a charity organization called *Harbor Light* which was run by the Salvation Army. He remained there for almost a year and was clean when he left. Their program was excellent and he had to earn his privileges one by one. We visited him every Sunday to see his progress.

Later that year, Nicky got stopped by the police while sitting in his car and they found drug paraphernalia in his possession. He was wheeled away to jail without passing go!

We were relieved because at least he would be clean and when he came out he was remorseful for a full two days, then it was more of the same. The damage Nicky had done to us in stealing money from our accounts, stealing and selling my tools and other things from the had all mounted up, along with the enormous rehab bill, to well over $40,000. But that was nothing compared to the anguish and worry that had been draining us since he was fifteen.

After being stopped again one night by the police, he was finally sent to jail for five months and was now out of our control. But still, he had to take "each day one at a time." Now at least he was trying. We, as every family should, were supporting him to keep clean. If he could continue to stay clean, it will all have been worthwhile, as in the words of Dr. Jeff, "Heroes are made from coming through adversity, never from having a blessed life where everything is normal and uneventful."

After Nicky came out of jail that July he remained clean, got back into the Paul Mitchel School, found a part-time job and began to get his life back on track. He was promoted, in his second job and was now a key holder and an assistant manager.

It was not until 2017 that Nick finally got free of his addiction. He has been clean now ever since and he looks great. He is fit healthy and 'on his game' at last! He now has his act together showing no sign of getting back into his old life and, as ever, we are there for him! But we know we have to take each day.

Way to go Nicky! Keep moving forward. Sue and I met the police officer, who put him in jail, at a local charity event at Sue's bank where she was working and we both thanked him for saving our son's life.

Seeking divine intervention was the right thing and we recognized it when it came to help us.

LESSONS LEARNED SO FAR

When we take a look in the rear-view mirror, we see what we couldn't see beforehand.

WHAT I LEARNED from everything "so far" was first finish what you start and don't ever give up. It was extremely difficult at first, after leaving school, as I had so little money, not even enough to pay my rent or to live on when I left school; but the dividends later were paid in ways I could not ever have imagined.

I finished my apprenticeship and like most teenagers. even though I was not a very serious person at that time I stayed with it, not knowing just how important finishing my apprenticeship would help me my entire life.

When we arrived in America, my green card was easy to obtain because of my five-year apprenticeship, the education I had earned twenty-five years earlier and the marketing work I had done for Alfa Laval. In fact, on my Green Card, I was classed as E16, (a person of extraordinary talent). I never thought at age sixteen that what I was about to do was to take me right through life and to enable doors not only to be opened but also to remain open. I used the skills I learned as a young man and even as a general manager running an entire company applying all I had learned. I found that I could communicate well with the workforce in my factory, I could talk their language and indeed I could communicate to all of the people I met along the way motivating them to do things that needed to be done while showing them how to do what was required.

I asked my managers at Glove Corp., "If you were to describe me to others after I have left here, what would you say?" Pat, said, "I would say that you are the most energetic person I have ever worked with and also that when Tony decides to do something, you better get on board or get out of the way because one thing is absolutely certain. Tony will do what he says he will do and will finish what he started."

That was fine by me and I did make the Glove Corp the biggest glove manufacturing company in the entire USA. That question I asked of my managers is something we all should ask of people we work with as it is through their eyes that we learn who we are which is sometimes not who we think we are.

I won a huge military glove contract and designed the biggest selling firefighting glove in the world. I learned, as I have already said, that I truly believe that each of us is given divine tools — "talents"— to use throughout our life; talents that are there for us and will enable us to do things we were talented to do. If we choose to use these tools, it is a natural thing and when we use them it's as if nothing has happened, a "natural talent" that many of us often take for granted. This is part of who we each are and what we do with each of our lives.

Many of my friends along the way never used their gifts and chose instead to cruise through life reaching a point later on as they got older to think about what they might have been; Dwelling instead on past failures and mishaps instead of the positive lessons they could have learned from these experiences. Many never learn from mistakes that we all make and boy, did I make huge mistakes along the way, as I have shown in my book.

In a recent survey of over 1,500 retirees, they were asked, "What would you change about your life if you could and with your knowledge now?" Most answered quite honestly that they wish they had taken more risks with their lives. How sad it must be to think that thought and at a time when you are now too old to do anything you may have done as a younger person.

Taking a chance sometimes can be something that didn't work out, but that's a risk you take. But if you do take that risk, chances are that it will change something in your life. Then at least you can look back and laugh at yourself for trying and failing or congratulate yourself for succeeding!

I never asked people to do anything that I wouldn't or couldn't do myself. My family has both suffered and gained from all that I managed to accomplish because of my constant traveling. They became strong and despite my traveling, I was nevertheless very, very, close to them all.

I also came to realize that my children, of whom there are four and grandchildren, of whom at this moment in time there are now six, have to have their own experiences and those will be for them to try, maybe fail and try again throughout their lives. My daughters had their own business and I smile when I hear them discussing ideas with me, their energy and positive attitude are a legacy I was happy to give.

Life is a rich experience and it's not where you end up, it's the journey along the way—that is real life so enjoy the ride.

I also believe that there is a divine presence—God—and this has been shown to me with undeniable truth, throughout my life so far, that God can and will help if you ask for his help, but you may have to change as a result. Without this belief, life for me and for everyone else, as I see it, is a meaningless experience that can give you pain and suffering or happiness and success, perhaps in random order; but in the end, if your belief, is that God does not exist, then life leads nowhere at all as we all die.

It is clear to me also that evil does exist and it is present increasingly in our everyday lives, our media, our education system and even our government are moving us gradually away from God. The weaponry that we have developed is ten times more powerful than at any time in our history and is enough to wipe out life on the entire planet. Why have we done this?

John Bleby, Aunties son, once told me and this was while he was head of the Royal Veterinary College, "You know, Tony, we scientists don't believe in God because when you get right down to it on a microbiological level, which is where we are at, you realize that everything is measurable and interrelated, a series of chemicals!" I answered him that I believed he was missing the point, that God in my view is in the spaces between, that stuff that holds everything together and you can't measure that.

So, here I am and who would have thought that in today's world, we would be having religious wars; or that seemingly good people, leaders of men, voted into their office by reasonable people right here, in the USA, in a country that was based on sound Christian values would want to relegate the word of God away from our founding fathers' ideals and to remove him completely from our daily life. If we allow it! This is the evil now prevailing in our world.

The people that propagate this belief have no idea that in their fervor and entirely logical and almost believable explanations of truth and half-truth as they see it, they are helping us to move away from God and the good values that have led us this far.

Everyone I have ever met along the way agrees that there is an evil force moving against us all, so we need to keep our feet firmly on the ground, value our family and treat others as we would like to be treated by them.

I will not allow myself to be swayed away from my faith. I had one more dream that I had experienced back in the mid-nineties, when Sue and I were going through a very rough patch in our relationship and were both drifting apart, possibly to divorce. I had a clear dream in which I was walking toward a long straight path ahead of me, in Hanwell, London, of all places and the sky above me was filled with gray billowing clouds, full of an imminent storm. There were houses on both sides of me that ended at a barrier just a few feet ahead of where I stood.

Ahead of me, the sky was very dark with heavy storm clouds above. There was a path ahead of me that was blocked by a red-and-white barrier pole across the road, where the houses also abruptly ended. An old friend of mine was standing next to the barrier with one hand, ready to lift the bar to let me pass.

It was our friend Ash from the wine bar and as I approached, he said, "Hi, Tony, you have to go that way." As he lifted the barrier, he pointed down the very long dark path ahead. I entered the path as he had shown me and I walked down the path, which I now saw was elevated with a slope on either side of it like a levee.

On either side were dark stormy waters thrashing against the long straight path I was now walking on. On my left was the ocean, with huge waves broiling and black crashing into the levee, while on my right was a huge lake with equally violent waters being blown by a very strong wind. The ocean side on my left was thrashing, with huge waves crashing continuously into my levee; while on the right the black lake water was chopping, forming high peaks and troughs of the storm that it was in and the waters were smashing into the other side of my leveed path. The clouds above grew even more menacing and stormier as I continued onwards.

I knew instinctively that I had to stay on that path and not move in any other direction than straight ahead not looking back. In front of me, miles ahead was a faint glimmering light somewhere where I couldn't see it clearly; but I knew it was there and was directly ahead at the end of the path I was on. I knew that whatever happened and however bad things may get, I had to keep moving forward and not be led off to one side or the other.

It has been the hardest struggle for me to keep my family together throughout was difficult at times, with the normal ups and downs of living. It would have been easier to simply let go and do my own thing leaving all else behind me. What would that say of me and anyone else who allowed that to happen? My own childhood was a little rough at times but certainly, nothing that I couldn't handle, nothing at all, yet in today's life there are more things to make separation at every level a very easy thing to do—from marriage, from work, from beliefs and even from family, all is getting harder for ordinary people to remain on track. My divorce from Jane showed me that divorce is far-reaching for our children, so I made certain that Jane and I remained as close friends and in constant touch so that we were there for each other and for our children.

Most divorces are angry, nasty events with self-centered emotions that tear a family apart. I learned that it doesn't have to be this way and if at all possible, we should spend our energy trying to make our marriage work. If this is not possible then at all costs, try to make it a friendly, or mutually equitable parting so that the children don't have to experience their parents constantly hating each other.

Throughout my life, right at the moment I needed help, I received it through the people I passed along the way; though sometimes at the time I didn't realize that I was being helped along. But I very clearly was being helped The role Auntie played in my early life was profound and I know she was placed into my life just when I needed her help the most.

Shakespeare said, "Give me a child to seven years old and he is mine for life." I get that, Billy boy! What he clearly meant was that those early days are the formative years and are so critically important for each child's development into adulthood.

The question I ask myself is this: "If I could change anything, what would I change?" Probably not much at all, but if there are things that you would change, then go ahead and change them and if it doesn't work out, then so what? Learn from that and try again but never stop trying.

I learned to never give up. Even if the future at that point looks bad, I knew not to worry about the past, but to learn from it and move on and if I got it wrong, I tried again. "I closed the door and moved on."

My hero was Colonel Sanders of the KFC fame; he didn't make it until he was over seventy years old when he made it to his great success! If he can do it, anyone can!

Ian, Adrian and I had all come through difficult times in our childhood and despite this, each of us had made a success of our lives. Ian is now a multimillionaire and if that was his goal then he succeeded.

Adrian became a Vice-Admiral of the Royal Navy, was appointed governor of Gibraltar, was Knighted by The Queen and was also made Second Sea Lord, by Her Majesty, the Queen.

And me? Well, I made my mark in the United States with one of my glove designs now inside every GI's kit bag and a fragrance company that reached number 2 in sales. I have now written 6 books, biographies of well-known celebrities and one political book co-written with Colonel (retired) Andy O'Meara who was General George C. Patton's intelligence officer in the Vietnam war.

Another of my books is as a ghostwriter so my name does not appear which is fine by me. I have 3 books on the way to being released and I co-founded Briton Publishing LLC.

For a short while, I made the biggest-selling firefighting glove in the world, not bad for three Brits coming from very humble backgrounds.

I managed to keep my family together, through thick and thin, with a mom and a dad and I am happy. My next dream is to be living somewhere near the coast and to be able to visit my daughters and grandchildren as many times a year as I want to be closer to them.

Me? I am still "a work in progress, I'm busier now than ever before as a professional writer and loving it!"

I'm wiser now and I will always keep trying to succeed!

MY NEW FAMILY

Never underestimate what life can bring

It's Christmas 2016 and my son James, bought me an Ancestry.com DNA kit as a Christmas Present. I told him thanks but don't expect anything to come from this as I have no other family.

Wow! Was I wrong about that! Later In 2017, I received the results from Ancestry.com that I had a first Cousin with a 99.9% accuracy that this was correct.

On March 22nd I received an email that would explode in my life. I not only had a first cousin in England, who had contacted me, after seeing the DNA results saying we were first cousins, but he also told me I had many additional cousins. It turned out that my beautiful mother Rosina had seven brothers and five sisters!

Francis, one of my "new" first cousins, told me that shortly after my mother married my stepfather, Mr. Charles Willatts, he told the family he would bring me up as his son and they were never to have any further contact with me from that point forward. I assumed there must have been a good reason for this but the past is the past and sometimes, as I thought, it's better to leave it that way.

However, as I was to find out only recently, she did have a favorite sister called Peggy, but none of her family were ever able to find me or to get in touch with me, my stepfather, Charles Willatts, whom she met in the sanitorium and had married a short while before she died, made certain they would have no contact with me. I had no idea about this until my cousin Francis told me.

Then I found out from one of my other cousins, that there was in fact a good reason why my mother left her family to live in London and it was to be devastating for me to find out the reason so many years later.

My mother had to move away with her sister Peggy, from her large family in Northampton, to live in London, as a young single mother leaving them with no way to find ether her or her sister Peggy, with advanced TB and a very young baby. As one of my cousins told me it was because something bad had occurred while Rose was living in

Northampton. Her closest friend at the time was her sister Peggy. Whatever it was, they both left Northampton together. She moved to get away from her large family as she and Peggy decided they could no longer live there in Northampton.

My Step-father, who had been told by my mother what had happened, forbade them from ever reaching out to her or me ever again. My family could never find me until 2017 through a DNA database from Ancestry.com.

It was Auntie who contacted the authorities, after coming to see me, that day in Acton and who forced my stepfather, Charles Willatts, to release me into the care of the London County Council. I was, as you now know, placed into an orphanage and he simply walked away. Both my daughter Georgia and I tried to find out from him if I had any other family, but he told us he knew nothing of any other relatives from my mother's family. Of course, he was lying.

In the end, due to new technology with DNA testing and the internet, my lost family finally found me and what a very large family I now have. Francis, my cousin, told me I had many, 1st cousins In fact I now had 45 of them!

They told me they had tried to find me several times, over the past decades, but once I was under the care of the London County Council, finding me was extremely difficult and in my case, it was impossible since my childhood records were sealed and still are. Only one person, my awful stepfather, knew the truth about me and my mother's family and he refused to tell me anything.

At the end of the day, despite all that happened to me, I now have friends all over the world, whose lives have intertwined with mine.

Despite everything that had happened to me, I became successful across continents however, this is measured and I am happy, I now know I have a huge family that I never knew existed. On my mother's side of my family, I have forty-five First Cousins, I have grandparents and everything a "normal" family has maybe another book is in the works although as I am writing this I have published 5 books with three more coming in 2022! But as for my family, though I gave them copies of my autobiography, none of them bothered to contact me (perhaps they wanted to know if I knew). So I will leave them with their secrets and move on with my life. My mothers wishes, to have no contact with them will be for me too.

Yet Another Family?

In 2018, I found I had yet another family on my father's side who were from Cyprus! My father's name was blank on my birth certificate. Their Ancestry page showing my father's side of the family took 2 years before anyone responded following many emails and messages I sent to the page manager, a Cypriot woman, trying to find out why they had set up a DNA search then did nothing with the results.

I eventually gave up trying but then a Cousin Nik took over the management of their page and reached out to me apologising for his sister, who set herself up to manage their Ancestry page and her lack of interest in following up on the DNA results that led them to me.

I found this out when I was contacted by Nik, who took over their Ancestry page and found my emails. He lived in the US. and after a phone conversation we found we had so much in common, Nik like me, had been through business ups and downs and had come through very well and he, like me, had picked himself up each time and started again.

My father's side of the family originated in Cyprus but because I was getting no response from them, I wrote a letter to the family, to be sent by my cousin Nik, explaining I needed nothing from them except to know who my father was. I did this because there was so much secrecy around the DNA related to them and myself and I got the impression they had a number of business interests and thought they might believe I had some interest there but nothing was further from my mind.

Then I posted a photo, for what was called, "throwback Thursday" in 2019 on my Facebook page. The photo was of four images of my face as I had aged over 40 years from 1972 to 2012. Nik saw it and sent it to his uncle, in Cyprus. His uncle immediately called Nik from Cyprus as soon as he saw the photo. He called Nik in the middle of the night, excitedly telling him, I know who Tony's father is! He said he was 99.9% certain as my photo was a spitting image of who he thought my father was. He told Nik I may have a half-sister and two half-brothers still living! Wow! This was amazing.

As if that wasn't stunning news enough, he told Nik that my father, was still alive, was 92 years old and still living in Ealing, where I had lived nearly all my life and where my daughters Georgia and Amanda and their family still live!

We planned to all meet up in Ealing, with family coming from Cyprus to meet me, to be set up by the family patriarch and what a reunion that would have been. But we unfortunately had to wait until after Covid19 as all travel was banned.

I bought tickets to return to London in February 2020 to meet my father, but because of Covid I couldn't go as planned. Sadly, I was never to meet the man who, after all these years, was my true blood father, who had lived so close to me in Ealing. Did we cross paths? Did we drink at the same pubs? Did they read about my wine bar or read the Ealing Gazette when they posted my autobiography on a 2-page spread revealing details of my mother?

My father Andreas sadly died of complications from dementia before we could meet. My mother had given me a clue in my middle name, Andrew which is Andreas in Greek. The photos Chris sent me of himself and his father showed an uncanny likeness in looks and character and from these photos it was clear Chris was a spitting image of me in my younger days.

I got in contact with my brother Chris but I had to agree to keep the truth secret with him. I agreed to keep my name and relationship secret from Chris's family, although my other half-brother knew of my existence but who would not accept that I could be their sibling and after all I have been through, I had dealt with these attitudes all my life and certainly didn't need it now.

But Chris, told me of our father's passing in February 2022 at age 94 while in hospice care. He sadly died from complications from dementia before the Covid restrictions were lifted.

I now find that I am once again stuck in the middle on my father's side of the family with a sibling not wanting me to reveal the fact we shared the same father, although my mother and their father met long before their first child was born.

I will never meet my father's family because of the secrets and the way my Ealing branch of the family regarded me and the news that I was part of their family. However this was not only the way they treated me. I was in contact with another cousin, Katie, who showed up on Ancestry as a first or second cousin but we couldn't figure out how this could be. It turned out Katie was Chris's daughter!

Chris, my new brother, met his previously unknown daughter Katie in 2020, a father daughter first time reunion. Katie, as we were to discover, was the result of a sperm donor birth from Chris her newly found father and Chris was very happy to meet his daughter Katie.

So things certainly became interesting for me and my new family!

But I decided to move on past my lost family and their hidden secrets. I have my own family and we are all a close and loving family; we are open and have no secrets and had something like this been revealed to us we would have discussed it openly as a family should. We are so different in so many ways and I prefer to keep it that way. I have left out the full names of my other family members, because I think things are better this way.

As for me, following a radio interview with Alexa Servodidio who is a licensed phycologist and has a motivational radio show in New York, I was contacted by Rob Lowe (not the actor) and his wife Brinka who have a talent agency called, *Casting New Lives*. I signed a contract with them as a writer. I then co-founded a publishing company, in 2021 called *"Briton Publishing LLC."* (BRIinka and TONy) with them and I am now a professional writer with 6 books published and several more to be published in 2022. So I, once again reinvented myself proving that we can M*ake Things Happen* at any age and I am proof that no matter how hard things seem to be, we can all *"Make Things Happen"* if we decide to do so.

The Experience Factor In Life and Business

I learned many lessons along the way from my childhood. Most importantly that we can never change the past and also that when fate plays a hand we can only learn to deal with the hand we are given. But we can use these experiences for future decisions and apply what we learned towards the best result in work and at home. I tried this and although it didn't always work out, as I expected or hoped, it didn't deter me from trying, over and over again.

I have shown in my book that life can be such a very rich experience if we allow it to become so. Even the bad times make us wiser and more capable of giving help to others who we pass along the way and we all should do this anytime we can. I do this whenever possible and people tell me I motivate them, which is a compliment.

Losing one's job in today's world is a very serious and sometimes a life-altering event. But climbing back up is not hard once you set your mind on succeeding. Most people are aware beforehand that something is going wrong with their current employment or partner and should be prepared for the outcome. I learned a most valuable lesson; there are none so blind as those that will not see, so when we come across stubbornness it's best to keep focused on what we are doing as we are responsible for our own success or failure. My experiences came from lessons that I learned from four years old and I have never stopped learning.

I hope that in reading about my life so far, that you my readers, are now my unknown friends and can see that what I have experienced from the very earliest age has provided me with a pathway for my own future success as it can for you; Never, never, never, give up!

Changes in life, in business and at home are guaranteed, even as our children change and grow up. In accepting this, I learned to embrace the changes and become part of them.

It is only when we become a willing part of a change, about to occur, that we can most influence how it will affect us.

Finally, if nothing else, I learned that we should never blame past failures or tragedies at home, in our work, or with our friends, as something that prevents us from achieving a brilliant future, as it will with certainty do just that, if we allow it to so!

I found that after each seemingly bad event, even the recent events leading, to me knowing my family, I came out the other side better off! We can all succeed if we have the desire and if we remain positive and I hope my book has shown this to you.

For My Children

I dedicate this book to my children and to my many, many, friends now living all over the world, in the USA, Canada, France, Sweden, South Africa, New Zealand and Australia who upon reading my book may decide to risk failure to risk their success. Success, after all, is whatever we choose to make it and in doing so we measure ourselves by the actions that made us successful.

So, go do it! Live life to the full and each of you make it to your own success regardless of the obstacles you will encounter, then you too will become *one of a kind*.

For my children:
Amanda Jane, living in Ealing, West London
Georgia Mercedes, also living in Ealing, West London
Nicholas Andrew, today living in Greenwood, Indiana
James Alexander, today living in Greenwood, Indiana

And for my grandchildren in London:
Jesse, Eliza Jane, Ruby Rose, Mason, Ziggy and Oscar

To each of you, I hope one day you will read my book and enjoy it as much as I did in living and writing it. In passing it on to each of you, I ask that you write your book too, write about the good and the not-so-good, experiences of your lives, and be truthful. Add your story to mine and when the time is right, pass it on to your children as I have done for you. In this way, we can all learn from our successes and failures and we can all laugh at ourselves along the way! I certainly did!

With love to all of you,
Tony